CROSSFIRE

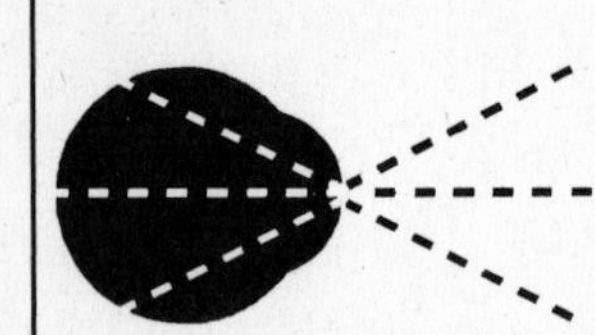

CROSSFIRE

DICK FRANCIS AND FELIX FRANCIS

THORNDIKE PRESS
A part of Gale, Cengage Learning

Detroit • New York • San Francisco • New Haven, Conn • Waterville, Maine • London

This is a work of fiction. Names, characters, places, and incidents either are the product of the author's imagination or are used fictitiously, and any resemblance to actual persons, living or dead, businesses, companies, events, or locales is entirely coincidental.

While the author has made every effort to provide accurate telephone numbers and Internet addresses at the time of publication, neither the publisher nor the author assumes any responsibility for errors, or for changes that occur after publication. Further, the publisher does not have any control over and does not assume any responsibility for author or third-party websites or their content.

Thorndike Press® Large Print Core.
The text of this Large Print edition is unabridged.
Other aspects of the book may vary from the original edition.
Set in 16 pt. Plantin.

LIBRARY OF CONGRESS CATALOGING-IN-PUBLICATION DATA

Francis, Dick.
Crossfire / by Dick Francis and Felix Francis.
p. cm. — (Thorndike Press large print core)
ISBN-13: 978-1-4104-2801-1
ISBN-10: 1-4104-2801-X
1. Soldiers—Great Britain—Fiction. 2. Amputees—Fiction. 3. Homecoming—Fiction. 4. Race horses—Training—Fiction. 5. Extortion—Fiction. 6. Tax evasion—Fiction. 7. Large type books. I. Francis, Felix. II. Title.
PR6056.R27C76 2010b
823'.914—dc22 2010026700

Published in 2010 in arrangement with G. P. Putnam's Sons, a member of Penguin Group (USA) Inc.

Printed in the United States of America
1 2 3 4 5 6 7 14 13 12 11 10

Dedicated to the men and women
of the British forces who have lost
limbs in Afghanistan.
For them the battle is never over.

And to the memory of
DICK FRANCIS
The greatest father and friend a man
could ever have

With loving thanks to
William Francis,
Lieutenant in the Army Air Corps,
graduated from
the Royal Military Academy, Sandhurst,
August 2009,
seconded to the Grenadier Guards
at Nad-e-Ali, Helmand Province,
Afghanistan,
September to December 2009

With loving thanks to
William Harris
Lieutenant in the Army Air Corps
graduated from
the Royal Military Academy, Sandhurst
August 2008
deployed to the [illegible] Guards
at Nad-e-Ali, Helmand Province
Afghanistan
September to December 2009

Prologue

Helmand Province, Afghanistan
October 2009

"Medic! Medic!"

I could see that my platoon sergeant was shouting, but strangely, the sound of his voice seemed muffled, as if I was in a neighboring room rather than out here in the open.

I was lying on the dusty ground with my back up against a low bank so that I was actually half sitting. Sergeant O'Leary was kneeling beside me on my left.

"Medic!" he shouted again urgently, over his shoulder.

He turned his head and looked me in the eyes.

"Are you all right, sir?" he asked.

"What happened?" I said, my own voice sounding loud in my head.

"A bloody IED," he said. He turned away, looked behind him, and shouted again.

"Where's that fucking medic?"

An IED. I knew that I should have known what IED meant, but my brain seemed to be working in slow motion. I finally remembered. IED — improvised explosive device — a roadside bomb.

The sergeant was talking loudly into his personal radio.

"Alpha-four," he said in a rush. "This is Charlie-six-three. IED, IED. One CAT A, several CAT C. Request IRT immediate backup and casevac. Over."

I couldn't hear any response, if there was one. I seemed to have lost my radio headset, along with my helmet.

"CAT A," he'd said. CAT A was army-speak for a seriously injured soldier requiring immediate medical help to prevent loss of life. CAT Cs were walking wounded.

The sergeant turned back to me.

"You still all right, sir?" he asked, the stress apparent on his face.

"Yes," I said, but in truth, I didn't really feel that great. I was cold yet sweaty. "How are the men?" I asked him.

"Don't worry about the men, sir," he said. "I'll look after the men."

"How many are injured?" I asked.

"A few. Minor, mostly," he said. "Just some cuts and a touch of deafness from the blast." I knew what he meant. The sergeant turned away and shouted at the desert-camouflaged figure nearest to him. "Johnson, go and fetch the bloody medic kit from Cummings. Fucking little rat's too shit-scared to move."

He turned back to me once more.

"Won't be long now, sir."

"You said on the radio there's a CAT A. Who is it?"

He looked into my face.

"You, sir," he said.

"Me?"

"The CAT A is you, sir," he said again. "Your fucking foot's been blown off."

ease." I knew what he meant. The sergeant turned away and shouted at the desert-camouflaged figure nearest to him. "Johnson, go and fetch the bloody medic kit from Cummings." [illegible] started to move.

He turned back to the other men.

"Won't be long now, sir."

"You said on the radio there's a CAT A. Who is it?"

He looked into my face.

"You, sir," he said.

"Me?"

"The CAT A is you, sir," he said again. "Your kneecap's been blown off."

1

Four Months Later

I realized as soon as I walked out of the hospital that I had nowhere to go.

I stood holding my bag at the side of the road, watching a line of passengers board a red London bus.

Should I join them, I wondered. But where were they going?

Simply being discharged from National Health Service care had been my overriding aim for weeks, without any thought or reason as to what was to come next. I was like a man released from prison who stands outside the gates gulping down great breaths of fresh, free air without a care for the future. Freedom was what mattered, not the nature of it.

And I had been incarcerated in my own prison, a hospital prison.

I suppose, looking back, I had to admit that it passed quite quickly. But at the time, every hour, even every minute, had dragged interminably. Progress, seen day by day, had been painfully slow, with *painful* being the appropriate word. However, I was now able to walk reasonably well on an artificial foot and, whereas I wouldn't be playing football again for a while, if ever, I could climb up and down stairs unaided and was mostly self-sufficient. I might even have been able to run a few strides to catch that bus, if only I had wanted to go wherever it was bound.

I looked around me. No one had turned up to collect me, nor had I expected them to. None of my family actually knew I was being discharged on that particular Saturday morning and, quite likely, they would not have turned up even if they had.

I had always preferred to do things for myself, and they knew it.

As far as my family was concerned, I was a loner, and happier for it, perhaps the more so after having to rely for months on others for help with my personal, and private, bodily functions.

I wasn't sure who had been the more shocked, my mother or me, when a nurse had asked, during one of her rare visits, if she could help me get dressed. My mother had last seen me naked when I was about seven, and she was more than a little flustered at the prospect of doing so again twenty-five years later. She'd suddenly remembered that she was late for an appointment elsewhere, and had rushed away. The memory of her discomfort had kept me smiling for most of the rest of that day, and I hadn't smiled much recently.

In truth, 25198241 Captain Thomas Vincent Forsyth had not been the most patient of patients.

The army had been my life since the night I had left home after another particularly unpleasant, but not uncommon, argument with my stepfather. I had slept uncomfortably on the steps of the army recruiting office in Oxford and, when the office opened at nine a.m. the following morning, I had walked in and signed on for Queen and Country as a private soldier in the Grenadier Guards.

Guardsman Forsyth had taken to service life like the proverbial duck to water and had risen through the ranks, first to corporal, then to officer cadet, at the Royal Military Academy, Sandhurst, followed by a commission back in my old regiment. The army had been much more to me than just a job. It had been my wife, my friend and my family; it had been all I had known for fifteen years, and I loved it. But now it appeared that my army career might be over, blown apart forever by an Afghan IED.

Consequently, I had not been a happy bunny during the previous four months, and it showed.

In fact, I was an angry young man.

I turned left out of the hospital gates and began walking. Perhaps, I thought, I would see where I had got to by the time I became too tired to continue.

"Tom," shouted a female voice. "Tom."

I stopped and turned around.

Vicki, one of the physiotherapists from the rehabilitation center, was in her car, turning out of the hospital parking lot. She had the passenger window down.

"Do you need a lift?" she asked.

"Where are you going?" I said.

"I was going to Hammersmith," she said. "But I can take you somewhere else if you like."

"Hammersmith would be fine."

I threw my bag onto the backseat and climbed in beside her.

"So they've let you out, then?" she said while turning in to the line of traffic on Roehampton Lane.

"Glad to see the back of me, I expect," I said.

Vicki tactfully didn't say anything. So it was true.

"It's been a very difficult time for you," she said eventually. "It can't have been easy."

I sat in silence. What was she after? An apology? Of course it hadn't been easy.

Losing my foot had, in retrospect, been the most straightforward part. The doctors, first at Camp Bastion in Afghanistan and then at Selly Oak Hospital in Birmingham, had managed to save the rest of my right leg so that it now finished some seven inches below my knee.

My stump, as all the medical staff insisted on calling it, had healed well, and I had quickly become proficient at putting on and taking off my new prosthetic leg, a wonder of steel, leather and plastic that had turned me from a cripple into a normal-looking human being, at least on the outside.

But there had been other physical injuries too. The roadside bomb had burst my eardrums and had driven Afghan desert dust deep into my torn and bruised lungs, to say nothing of the blast damage and lacerations to the rest of my body. Pulmonary infection and then double pneumonia had almost finished off what the explosion failed to do.

The numbing shock that had initially suppressed any feeling of hurt had soon been replaced by a creeping agony in which every part of me seemed to be on fire. It was just as well that I remembered only a smattering of the full casualty-evacuation procedure. Heavy doses of morphine did more than inhibit the pain receptors in the brain — they slowed its very activity down to bare essentials, such as maintaining breathing and the pumping of the heart.

The human body, however, is a wondrous creation and has an amazing ability to mend itself. My ears recovered, the lacerations healed, and my white blood cells slowly won the war against my chest infection, with a little help and reinforcement from some high-powered intravenous antibiotics.

If only the body could grow a new foot.

The mental injuries, however, were proving less easy to spot and far more difficult to repair.

"Where in Hammersmith do you want?" Vicki asked, bringing me back to reality from my daydreaming.

"Anywhere will do," I said.

"But do you live in Hammersmith?"

"No," I said.

"So where do you live?"

Now that was a good question. I suppose that I was technically, and manifestly, homeless.

For the past fifteen years I had lived in army accommodations of one form or another: barracks, Sandhurst, officers' messes, tents and bivouacs, even in the backs of trucks or the cramped insides of Warrior armored cars. I had slept in, under and on top of Land Rovers, and more often than I cared to remember, I had slept where I sat or lay on the ground, half an ear open for the call of a sentry or the sound of an approaching enemy.

However, the army had now sent me "home" for six months.

The major from the Ministry of Defense, the Wounded Personnel Liaison Officer, had been fair but firm during his recent visit. "Six months leave on full pay," he'd said. "To recover. To sort yourself out. Then we'll see."

"I don't need six months," I'd insisted. "I'll be ready to go back in half that time."

" 'Back'?" he'd asked.

"To my regiment."

"We'll see," he had repeated.

"What do you mean 'We'll see'?" I had demanded.

"I'm not sure that going back to your regiment will be possible," he'd said.

"Where, then?" I'd asked, but I'd read the answer in his face before he said it.

"You might be more suited to a civilian job. You wouldn't be passed fit for combat. Not without a foot."

The major and I had been sitting in the reception area of the Douglas Bader Rehabilitation Center in the Queen Mary's Hospital in Roehampton, London.

Part of Headley Court, the military's own state-of-the-art rehab center in Surrey, had been temporarily closed for refurbishment, and the remaining wards had been overwhelmed by the numbers of wounded with missing limbs. Hence I had been sent to Queen Mary's and the National Health Service.

It was testament to the remarkable abilities of the military Incident Response Teams, and to their amazingly well-equipped casevac helicopters, that so many soldiers with battlefield injuries which would in the past have invariably proved fatal were now routinely dealt with and survived. Double and even triple traumatic amputees often lived, when only recently they would have surely bled to death before medical help could arrive.

But not for the first time I'd wondered if it would have been better if I had died. Losing a foot had sometimes seemed to me a worse outcome than losing my life. But I had looked up at the painting on the wall of Douglas Bader, the Second World War pilot, after whom the rehabilitation center was named, and it had given me strength.

"Douglas Bader was passed fit for combat," I'd said.

The major had looked up at me. "Eh?"

"Douglas Bader was passed fit to fight, and he'd lost *both* his feet."

"Things were different then," the major from the MOD had replied somewhat flippantly.

Were they? I wondered.

Bader had been declared fit and had taken to the air in his Spitfire to fight the enemy simply due to his own perseverance. True, the country had been in desperate need of pilots, but he could have easily sat out the war in relative safety if he had wanted to. It had been the weight of his personal determination that had eventually overcome the official reluctance to allow him to fly.

I would take my lead from him.

We'll see, indeed.

I'd show them.

"Will the tube station do?" Vicki said.

"Sorry?" I said.

"The tube station," she repeated. "Is that OK?"

"Fine," I said. "Anywhere."

"Where are you going?" she asked.

"Home, I suppose," I said.

"And where is home?"

"My mother lives in Lambourn," I said.

"Where's that?" she asked.

"Near Newbury, in Berkshire."

"Is that where you're going now?"

Was it? I didn't particularly want to. But where else? I could hardly sleep on the streets of London. Others did, but had I gone down that far?

"Probably," I said. "I'll get the train."

My mind was working on automatic pilot as I negotiated the escalator up from the Underground into Paddington mainline railway station. Only near the top did I realize that I couldn't remember when I had last used an escalator. Stairs had always been my choice, and they had to be taken at a run, never at a walk. And yet here I was, gliding serenely up without moving a muscle.

Fitness had always been a major obsession in a life that was full of obsessions.

Even as a teenager I had been mad about

being fit. I had run every morning on the hills above Lambourn, trying to beat the horses as they chased me along the lush grass, training gallops.

Army life, especially that of the infantry officer at war, was a strange mix of lengthy, boring interludes punctuated by brief but intensely high-adrenaline episodes where the separation between living and dying could be rice-paper thin. With the episode over, if one was still alive and intact, the boredom would recommence until the next "contact" broke the spell once more.

I had always used the boring times to work on my fitness, constantly trying to break my own record for the number of sit-ups, or push-ups, or pull-ups, or anything-else-ups I could think of, all within a five-minute period. What the Taliban had thought of their enemy chinning it up and down in full body armor, plus rifle and helmet, on an improvised bar welded across the back of a Snatch Land Rover is anyone's guess, but I had been shot at twice while trying to break the battalion record, once when I was on track to succeed. The Taliban obviously had no sense of sport, or of timing.

But now look at me: taking the escalator, and placing my bag down on the moving stairway while doing so. Months of sedentary hospital life had left my muscles weak, flabby and lacking any sort of condition. I clearly had much to do before I had any hope of convincing the major from the MOD that I could be "combat-ready" once more.

I stood at the bottom of the steep driveway to my mother's home and experienced the same reluctance to go up that I had so often felt in the past.

I had taken a taxi from Newbury station to Lambourn, purposely asking the driver to drop me some way along the road from my mother's gate so that I could walk the last hundred yards.

It was force of habit, I suppose. I felt happier approaching anywhere on foot. It must have had something to do with being in the infantry. On foot, I could hear the sounds that vehicle engines would drown out, and smell the scents that exhaust fumes would smother. And I could get a proper feel of the lay of the land, essential to anticipate an ambush.

I shook my head and smiled at my folly.

There was unlikely to be a Taliban ambush in a Berkshire village, but I could recall the words of my platoon color sergeant at Sandhurst: "You can never be too careful," he would say. "Never assume anything; always check."

No shots rang out, no IEDs went bang, and no turban-headed Afghan tribesmen sprang out with raised Kalashnikovs as I safely negotiated the climb up from the road to the house, a redbrick-and-flint affair built sometime back between the World Wars.

As usual, in the middle of the day, all was quiet as I wandered around the side of the house towards the back door. A few equine residents put their heads out of their stalls in the nearest stable yard as I crunched across the gravel, inquisitive as ever to see a new arrival.

My mother was out.

I knew she would be. Perhaps that is why I hadn't phoned ahead to say I was coming. Perhaps I needed to be here alone first, to get used to the idea of being back, to have a moment of recollection and renewal before the whirlwind of energy that was my mother swept through and took away any chance I might have of changing my mind.

My mother was a racehorse trainer. But she was much more than just that. She was a phenomenon. In a sport where there were plenty of big egos, my mother had the biggest ego of them all. She did, however, have some justification for her high sense of worth. In just her fifth year in the sport, she had been the first lady to be crowned Champion Jump Trainer, a feat she had repeated for each of the next six seasons.

Her horses had won three Cheltenham Gold Cups and two Grand Nationals, and she was rightly recognized as the "first lady of British racing."

She was also a highly opinionated anti-feminist, a workaholic and no sufferer of fools or knaves. If she had been Prime Minister she would have probably brought back both hanging and the birch, and she was not averse to saying so loudly, and at length, whenever she had the opportunity. Her politics made Genghis Khan seem like an indecisive liberal, but everybody loved her nevertheless. She was a "character."

Everyone, that is, except her ex-husbands and her children.

For about the twentieth time that morning, I asked myself why I had come here. There had to be somewhere else I could go. But I knew there wasn't.

My only friends were in the army, mostly in my regiment, and they were still out in Afghanistan for another five weeks. And anyway, I wasn't ready to see them. Not yet. They would remind me too much of what I was no longer — and I wouldn't be able to stand their pity.

I suppose I could have booked myself into an army officers' mess. No doubt, I would have been made welcome at Wellington Barracks, the Grenadiers' home base in London. But what would I have done there?

What could I do anywhere?

Once again I thought it might have been better if the IED explosion, or the pneumonia, had completed the task: Union Jack–draped coffin, firing of volleys in salute, and I'd be six feet under by now and be done with it all. Instead, I was outside my mother's back door, struggling with a damned artificial foot to get down low enough to find the key that she habitually left under a stone in the flower bed.

And for what?

To get into a house I hated, to stay with a parent I despised. To say nothing of my stepfather, to whom I had hardly spoken a civil word since I had walked out of here, aged seventeen.

I couldn't find the damn key. Perhaps my mother had become more security-minded over the years. There had been a time when she would have left the house unlocked completely. I tried the handle. Not anymore.

I sat down on the doorstep and leaned back against the locked door.

My mother would be home later.

I knew where she was. She was at the races — Cheltenham races, to be precise. I had looked up the runners in the morning paper, as I always did. She had four horses declared, including the favorite in the big race, and my mother would never miss a day at her beloved Cheltenham, the scene of her greatest triumphs. And while today's might be a smaller meeting than the Steeple-chase Festival in March, I could visualize her holding court in the parade ring before the races, and welcoming the winner back after them. I had seen it so often. It had been my childhood.

The sun had long before given up trying to break through the veil of cloud, and it was now beginning to get cold. I sighed. At least the toes on my right foot wouldn't get chilblains. I put my head back against the wood and rested my eyelids.

"Can I help you?" said a voice.

I reopened my eyes. A short man in his mid-thirties wearing faded jeans and a puffy anorak stood on the gravel in front of me. I silently remonstrated with myself. I must have briefly drifted off to sleep, as I hadn't heard him coming. What would my sergeant have said?

"I'm waiting for Mrs. Kauri," I said.

Mrs. Kauri was my mother, Mrs. Josephine Kauri, although Josephine had not been the name with which she had been christened. It was her name of choice. Sometime back, long before I was born, she had obviously decided that Jane, her real name, was not classy enough for her. Kauri was not her proper name, either. It had been the surname of her first husband, and she was now on her third.

"Mrs. Kauri is at the races," replied the man.

"I know," I said. "I'll just wait for her here."

"She won't be back for hours, not until after dark."

"I'll wait," I said. "I'm her son."

"The soldier?" he asked.

"Yes," I said, somewhat surprised that he would know.

But he did know. It was only fleeting, but I didn't miss his glance down at my right foot. He knew only too well.

"I'm Mrs. Kauri's head lad," he said. "Ian Norland."

He held out a hand, and I used it to help me up.

"Tom," I said. "Tom Forsyth. What happened to old Basil?"

"He retired. I've been here three years now."

"It's been a while longer than that since I've been here," I said.

He nodded. "I saw you from the window of my flat," Ian said, pointing to a row of windows above the stables. "Would you like to come in and watch the racing on the telly? It's too bloody cold to wait out here."

"I'd love to."

We climbed the stairs to what I remembered had once been a storage loft over the stables.

"The horses provide great central heating," Ian said over his shoulder as he led the way. "I never have to turn the boiler on until it actually freezes outside."

The narrow stairway opened out into a long open-plan living area with a kitchen at the near end and doors at the far that presumably led to a bedroom and bathroom beyond. There was no sign of any Mrs. Norland, and the place had a "man look" about it, with stacked-up dishes in the sink and newspapers spread over much of the floor.

"Take a pew," Ian said, waving a hand at a brown corduroy–covered sofa placed in front of a huge plasma television. "Fancy a beer?"

"To Cheltenham," he said.

"What for?"

"To keep an eye on the bloody horse, of course," he said angrily. "To make sure no bugger got close enough to nobble him."

"Do you really think the horses are being nobbled?" I asked.

"I don't know," he said. "The bloody dope tests are all negative."

We watched as the horses walked around in circles at the start. Then the starter called them into line, and they were off.

"Come on, Pharm, my old boy," Ian said, his eyes glued to the television image. He was unable to sit down but stood behind the sofa like a little boy watching some scary science-fiction film, ready to dive down at the first approach of the aliens.

Pharmacist appeared to be galloping along with relative ease in about third place of the eight runners as they passed the grandstand on the first circuit. But only when they started down the hill towards the finishing straight for the last time did the race unfold properly, and the pace pick up.

Pharmacist seemed to be still going quite well and even jumped to the front over the second-last. Ian began to breathe a little more easily, but then the horse appeared to fade rapidly, jumping the final fence in a

"Sure," I said. I'd not had a beer in more than five months.

Ian went to a fridge, which appeared to contain nothing but beers. He tossed me a can.

We sat in easy companionship on the brown sofa, watching the racing from Cheltenham on the box. My mother's horse won the second race, and Ian punched the air in delight.

"Good young novice, that," Ian said. "Strong quarters. He'll make a good chaser in time."

He took pleasure in the success of his charges, as I had done in the progress of a guardsman from raw recruit into battle-hardened warrior, a man who could then be trusted with one's life.

"Now for the big one," Ian said. "Pharmacist should win. He's frightened off most of the opposition."

" 'Pharmacist'?" I asked.

"Our Gold Cup hope," he said, in a tone that implied I should have known. "This is his last warm-up for the Festival. He loves Cheltenham."

Ian was referring to the Cheltenham Gold Cup at the Steeplechase Festival in March, the pinnacle of British jump racing.

"What do you mean he's frightened off

the opposition?" I asked.

"Mrs. Kauri's been saying all along that old Pharm will run in this race, and so the other Gold Cup big guns have gone elsewhere. Not good for them to be beat today with only a few weeks left to the Festival."

Ian became more and more nervous, continually getting up and walking around the room for some unnecessary reason or other.

"Fancy another beer?" he asked, standing by the fridge.

"No thanks," I said. He'd given me one only two minutes before.

"God, I hope he wins," he said, sitting down and opening a fresh can with another still half-full on the table.

"I thought you said he would," I said.

"He should do, he's streaks better than the rest, but . . ."

"But what?" I asked.

"Nothing." He paused. "I just hope nothing strange happens, that's all."

"Do you think something strange might happen?"

"Maybe," he said. "Something bloody strange has been happening to our horses recently."

"What sort of things?"

"Bloody strange things," he repeated.

"Like what?"

"Like not winning when they should," he said. "Especially in the big races. Then they come home unwell. You can see it in their eyes. Some have even had diarrhea, and I've never seen racehorses with that before."

We watched as my mother was shown on the screen tossing the jockey up onto Pharmacist's back, the black-and-white-check silks appearing bright against the dull green of the February grass. My stepfather stood nearby, observing events, as he always did.

"God, I hope he's OK," said Ian with a nervous rattle.

The horse looked fine to me, but how would I know? The last horse I'd been clos to had been an Afghan tribesman's nag wit half of one ear shot away, reportedly by i owner as he was trying to shoot and char at the same time. I tactfully hadn't ask him which side he'd been shooting at. A ghani allegiance was variable. It depend on who was paying, and how much.

Ian became more and more nervou the race time approached.

"Calm down," I said. "You'll give you a heart attack."

"I should have gone," he said. "I kr should have gone."

"Gone where?"

very tired manner and almost coming to a halt on landing. He was easily passed by the others on the run-in up the hill, and he crossed the finish line in last place, almost walking.

I didn't know what to say.

"Oh God," said Ian. "He can't run at the Festival, not now."

Pharmacist certainly did not look like a horse that could win a Gold Cup in six weeks' time.

Ian stood rigidly behind the sofa, his white-knuckled hands gripping the corduroy fabric to hold himself upright.

"Bastards," he whimpered. "I'll kill the bastards who did this."

I was not the only angry young man in Lambourn.

2

To say my homecoming was not a happy event would not have been an exaggeration.

No "Hello, darling," no kiss on the cheek, no fatted calf, nothing. But no surprise, either.

My mother walked straight past me as if I had been invisible, her face taut and her lips pursed. I knew that look. She was about to cry but would not do so in public. To my knowledge, my mother had never cried in public.

"Oh, hello," my stepfather said by way of greeting, reluctantly shaking my offered hand.

Lovely to see you too, I thought but decided not to say. No doubt, as usual, we would fight and argue over the coming days but not tonight. It was cold outside and beginning to rain. Tonight I needed a roof over my head.

My stepfather and I had never really got on.

In the mixed-up mind of an unhappy child, I had tried to make my mother feel guilty for driving away my father and had ended up alienating not only her but everyone else.

My father had packed his bags and left when I was just eight, finally fed up with being well behind the horses in my mother's affection. Her horses had always come first, then her dogs, then her stable staff and finally, if there was time, which there invariably wasn't, her family.

How my mother ever had the time to have three children had always been a mystery to me. Both my siblings were older than I, and had been fathered by my mother's first husband, whom she had married when she was seventeen. Richard Kauri had been rich and thirty, a New Zealand playboy who had toyed at being a racehorse trainer. My mother had used his money to further her own ambition in racing, taking over the house and stables as part of their divorce settlement after ten years of turbulent marriage. Their young son and daughter had both sided with their father, a situation I now believed she had encouraged, as it gave her more chance of acquiring the training business if her ex-husband had the children.

Almost immediately she had married again, to my father, a local seed merchant, and had produced me like a present on her twenty-ninth birthday. But I had never been a much-wanted, much-loved child. I think my mother looked upon me as just another of her charges to be fed and watered twice a day, mucked out and exercised as required, and expected to stay quietly in my stable for the rest of the time.

I suppose it had been a lonely childhood, but I hadn't known anything different and, mostly, I'd been happy enough. What I missed in human contact at home I made up for with dogs and horses, both of which had plenty of time for me. I would make up games with them. They were my friends. I could remember thinking the world had ended when Susie, my beloved beagle, had been killed by a car. What had made it much worse was that my mother, far from comforting me, had instead told me to pull myself together, it was only a dog.

When my parents divorced there had been a long and protracted argument over custody of me. It was not until many years later that I realized that they had argued because neither of them had wanted the responsibility of bringing up an eight-year-old misfit.

My mother had lost the argument, so I had lived with her, and my father had disappeared from my life for good. I hadn't thought it a great loss at the time, and I still didn't. He had written to me a few times and had sent an occasional Christmas or birthday card, but he clearly thought he was better off without me, and I was sure I was without him.

"So, darling, how was Afghanistan? You know, to start with, before you were injured?" my mother asked rather tactlessly. "Were you able to enjoy yourself at all?"

My mother had always managed to call me "darling" without any of the emotion the word was designed to imply. In her case there was perhaps even a degree of sarcasm in the way she pronounced it with a long *r* in the middle.

"I wasn't sent there to enjoy myself," I said, slightly irritated. "I was there to fight the Taliban."

"Yes, darling. I know that," she said. "But did you have any good times?"

We were sitting around the kitchen table having dinner, and my mother and stepfather both looked at me expectantly.

It was a bit like asking President Lincoln's wife if she had been enjoying the play before her husband was shot. What should I say?

In truth, I had enjoyed myself immensely before I was blown up, but I wondered if I should actually say so.

Recording my first confirmed "kill" of a Taliban had been exhilarating; and calling in the helicopter gunships to pound an enemy position with body-bursting fifty-millimeter shells had been spine-chillingly exciting. It had sent my adrenaline levels to maximum in preparation for the charge through to finish them off at close quarters.

One wasn't meant to enjoy killing other human beings, but I had.

"I suppose it was OK," I said. "Lots of sitting round doing nothing, really. That, and playing cards."

"Did you see anything of the Taliban?" my stepfather asked.

"A little," I said matter-of-factly. "But mostly at a distance."

A distance of about two feet, impaled on my bayonet.

"But didn't you get to do any shooting?" he asked. He made it sound like a day's sport of driven pheasant.

"Some," I said.

I thought back to the day my platoon had been ambushed and outnumbered by the enemy. I had sat atop an armored car, laying down covering fire with a GPMG, a general-purpose machine gun, known to us all as "the gimpy." I had done so much shooting that day that the gimpy's barrel had glowed red-hot.

I could have told them all of it.

I could have told them of the fear. Not so much the fear of being wounded or killed — more the fear of failing to act. The fear of fear itself.

Throughout history, every soldier has asked themselves the same questions: What will I do when the time comes to fight? How will I perform in the face of the enemy? Shall I kill, or be killed? Shall I be courageous, or will I let down my fellow men?

In the modern British Army, much of the officer training is designed to make young men, and young women, behave in a rational and determined manner in extreme conditions and when under huge stress. Command is what they are taught, the ability to *command* when all hell is breaking loose around them. The *command moment,* it is called, that moment in time when something dramatic occurs, such as an ambush, or a roadside bomb explosion, the moment when all the men turn and look to their officer — that's you — waiting to be told what to do, and how to react. There's no one else to ask. You have to make the decisions, and men's lives will depend on them.

The training also teaches teamwork and, in particular, reliance. Not reliance on others but the belief that others are reliant on you. When push comes to shove, a soldier doesn't stick his head up and shoot back at the enemy for his Queen and Country. Instead, he does it for his mates, his fellow soldiers all around him who will die if he doesn't.

My biological family might have considered me a loner, but I was not. My platoon was my chosen family, and I had regularly placed myself in extreme danger to protect them from harm.

Eventually, my luck had been bound to run out.

Killing the enemy with joy and gusto might lead an onlooker to believe that the soldier places a low worth on human life. But this would be misleading, and untrue. The death of a comrade, a friend, a brother has the most profound effect on the fighting man. Such moments are revisited time and again with the same question always uppermost: Could I have done anything to save him?

Why him and not me? The guilt of the survivor is ever-present and is expunged only by continuation of the job in hand — the killing of the enemy.

"You're not very talkative," my mother said. "I thought that soldiers liked nothing better than to recount stories of past battles."

"There's not much to tell you, really," I said.

Not much to tell, I thought, that wouldn't put her off her dinner.

"I saw you both on the television today," I said, changing the subject, "at Cheltenham. Good win in the novice chase. Shame about Pharmacist, though. At one point I thought he was going to win as well." I knew that it was not a tactful comment, but I was curious to see their reaction.

My mother kept her eyes down as she absentmindedly pushed a potato around and around on her plate.

"Your mother doesn't want to talk about it," my stepfather said in an attempt to terminate conversation on the topic.

He was unsuccessful.

"Your head lad seems to think the horse was nobbled," I said.

My mother's head came up quickly. "Ian doesn't know what he's talking about," she said angrily. "And he shouldn't have been talking to *you.*"

I hoped that I hadn't dropped Ian into too much hot water. But I wasn't finished yet.

"Shouldn't have been talking to me about what?" I asked.

No reply. My mother went back to studying her plate of food, and my stepfather sat stony-faced across the table from her.

"So are the horses being nobbled?" I asked into the silence.

"No, of course not," my mother said. "Pharmacist simply had a bad day. He'll be fine next time out."

I wondered if she was trying to convince me, or herself.

I stoked the fire a little more. "Ian Norland said it wasn't the first time that your horses haven't run as well as expected."

"Ian knows nothing." She was almost shouting. "We've just had some bad luck of late. Perhaps there's a bit of a bug going round the stable. That's all. It'll pass."

She was getting distressed, and I thought it would be better to lay off, just for a bit.

"And Mrs. Kauri doesn't need you spreading any rumors," my stepfather interjected, somewhat clumsily. My mother gave him a look that was close to contempt.

I also looked at my stepfather, and I wondered what he really thought of his wife still using the name of another man.

Only when the other children at my primary school had asked me why I was Thomas Forsyth, and not Thomas Kauri, had I ever questioned the matter. "My father is Mr. Forsyth," I'd told them. "Then why isn't your mother Mrs. Forsyth?" It had been a good question, and one I hadn't been able to answer.

Mrs. Josephine Kauri had been born Miss Jane Brown and was now, by rights, Mrs. Derek Philips, although woe betide anyone who called her that in her hearing. Since first becoming a bride at seventeen, Josephine Kauri had worn the trousers in each of her three marriages, and it was no coincidence that she had retained the marital home in both of her divorces. From the look she had just delivered across the kitchen table, I thought it might not be too long before her divorce lawyer was again picking up his telephone. Mr. Derek Philips may soon be outstaying his welcome at Kauri House Stables.

We ate in silence for a while, finishing off the chicken casserole that my mother's cleaner-cum-housekeeper had prepared that morning and which had been slow-cooking in the Aga all afternoon. Thankfully, there had been more than enough for an uninvited guest.

But I couldn't resist having one more go.

"So will Pharmacist still run in the Gold Cup?"

I thought my stepfather might kick me under the table, such was the fury in his eyes. My mother, however, was more controlled.

"We'll see," she said, echoing the major from the MOD. "It all depends on how he is in the morning. Until then, I can't say another word."

"Is he not back here yet, then?" I asked, not taking the hint to keep quiet.

"Yes," she said without further explanation.

"And have you been out to see him?" I persisted.

"In the morning," my mother replied brusquely. "I said I'd see how he was in the morning." She swallowed noisily. "Now, please, can we drop the subject?"

Even I didn't have the heart to go on. There were limits to the pleasure one could obtain from other people's distress, and distressed she clearly was. It was not a condition I was used to observing in my mother, who had always seemed to be in complete control of any and every situation. It was more usually a state she created in others rather than suffered from herself.

As Ian Norland had said, something very strange was going on.

I went for a walk outside before going to bed. I had done something similar all my life, and the loss of a foot wasn't going to be allowed to change my lifestyle more than I could help it.

I wandered around the garden and along the concrete path to the stables. A few security lights came on as I moved under the sensors, but no one seemed to care and there was no halting shout. There was no one on stag here, no sentries posted.

Not much had changed since I had run away all those years before. The trees had grown up a bit, and the border of bushes down the far side of the house was less of a jungle than I had remembered. Perhaps it was just the effects of the winter months.

I had loved that border as a child and had made no end of "dens" amongst the thick undergrowth, fantasizing great adventures and forever lying in wait for an unseen "enemy," my toy rifle at the ready.

Not much may have changed in the place, but plenty had changed within me.

I stood in the cold and dark and drew

deeply on a cigarette, cupping the glowing end in my hand so that it wasn't visible. Not that anyone would be looking; it was just a force of habit.

I didn't really consider myself a smoker, and I'd never had a cigarette until I first went on ops to Iraq. Then that had changed. Somehow the threat of possibly developing lung cancer in the future was a minor one compared to the risk of having one's head blown off in the morning.

It had seemed that almost everyone smoked in Afghanistan. It had helped to control the fear, to steady the hand, and to relieve the pressure when a cold beer, or any other alcohol, for that matter, was strictly against standing orders. At least I hadn't smoked opium like the locals. That was also against standing orders.

I leaned against the corner of the house and drew a deep breath into my lungs, feeling the familiar rush as the nicotine flooded into my bloodstream and was transported to my brain. Finding the opportunity for a crafty smoke in the hospital had been rare, but here, now, I was my own master again, and I reveled in the freedom.

A light went on in the first-floor room above my head.

"Why the bloody hell did he have to turn

up? That's all we bloody need at the moment."

I could clearly hear my mother in full flow.

"Keep your voice down, he'll hear you."

That was my stepfather.

"No, he won't," she said, again at full volume. "He's gone outside."

"Josephine," my stepfather said angrily, "half the bloody village will hear you if you're not careful."

I was quite surprised that he would talk to her like that. Perhaps there was more to him than I thought. My mother even took notice of him, and they continued their conversation much more quietly. Annoyingly, I couldn't hear anything other than a faint murmur, although I stood there silently for quite a while longer, just in case they reverted to fortissimo.

But sadly, they didn't, and presently, the lights in the room went out.

I lifted the leather flap that covered the face of my watch. The luminous hands showed me it was only ten-thirty. Clearly, racehorse trainers went to bed as early as hospital patients, even on Saturday nights. I was neither, and I enjoyed being outside in the dark, listening and watching.

I had always been completely at home in darkness, and I couldn't understand those who were frightened of it. I suppose it was one thing I should thank my mother for. When I was a child, she had always insisted I sleep with my bedroom lights off and my door firmly closed. Since then the dark had always been my friend.

I stood silently and listened to the night.

In the distance there was music, dance music, the thump, thump, thump of the rhythm clearly audible in the still air. Perhaps someone was having a party. A car drove along the road at the bottom of the driveway, and I watched its red lights as it traveled beyond the village, up the hill and out of sight.

I thought I heard a fox nearby with its high-pitched scream, but I wasn't sure. It might have been a badger. I would have needed a pair of army-issue night-vision goggles to be sure, or better still a U.S. military set, which were far superior.

I lit another cigarette, the flare of the match instantly rendering me blind in the night. Out in Afghanistan I'd had a fancy lighter that could light a cigarette in complete darkness. Needless to say, it hadn't accompanied me on my evacuation. In fact, nothing I had owned in Afghanistan had so far made it back to me.

An infantry soldier's life at war was carried around with him in his backpack, his Bergen. Either that or on his body in the form of helmet, radio, body armor, spare ammunition, boots and camouflage uniform. Then there was his rifle and bayonet to carry in his hands. It all went everywhere with him. Leave a Bergen unattended for even a second and it was gone, spirited away like magic by some innocent-looking Afghan teenager. Leaving a rifle unattended could be a court-martial offense. Everything and anything would "walk" if not tied down or guarded.

The Taliban have described the British soldier as a ferocious fighter but one who moves very slowly. Well, Mr. Taliban, you try running around with seven stone of equipment on your back. It was like carrying your grandmother into battle, but without the benefits.

I wondered where my Bergen had gone. For that matter, I wondered where my uniform had gone, and everything else too. Thanks largely to the dedicated and magnificent volunteers of the CCAST, the Critical Care Air Support Teams, I had arrived back in England not only alive but less than thirty hours after the explosion. But I'd woken up in the Birmingham hospital, naked and without a foot, with not even a toothbrush, just a pair of metal dog tags around my neck, embossed with my name and army service number, an age-old and trusted method of identifying the living, and the dead.

There had been a letter to my mother in the breast pocket of my uniform, to be posted in the event of my death. I wondered where that was too. My mother obviously hadn't received it. But there again, I hadn't died. Not quite.

Eventually, it was the cold that drove me inside.

I went slowly and quietly through the house so as not to disturb those sleeping upstairs. In the past I would have removed my shoes and padded around silently in bare feet, but now, as I could have only one bare foot, I kept my shoes on.

Good as it was, my new right leg had an annoying habit of making a metallic clinking noise every time I put it down, even when I moved slowly. I didn't sound quite like a clanking old truck engine, but an enemy sentry would still have heard me coming from more than a hundred paces on a still night. I would have to do something about that, on top of everything else, if I was ever to convince the MOD major.

I went up the stairs to my old bedroom. My childhood things were long gone, packed up by my mother and either sent to the charity shop or to the council tip just as soon as I had announced I wasn't coming back.

However, the bed looked the same, and the chest of drawers in the corner definitely was, the end now repainted where I had once stuck up bubble-gum cards of army regimental crests.

This wasn't the first night I had been back in this bed. There had been other occasional visits, all started with good intentions but invariably ending in argument and recrimination. To be fair, I was as much, if not more, to blame than my mother and stepfather. There was just something about the three of us together that caused the ire in us to rise inexorably to the point of mutual explosion. And none of us were very good firemen. Rather, we would fan the flames and pour petrol on them in gay abandon. And not one of us was ever prepared to back down or apologize. Nearly always I would end up leaving in anger, vowing never to return.

My most recent visit, five years previously, had been optimistically expected to last five days. I had arrived on Christmas Eve all smiles, with bags of presents and good intent, and I'd left before lunch on Christmas morning, sent on my way by a tirade of abuse. And the silly thing was, I couldn't now remember why we had argued. We didn't seem to need a reason, not a big one anyway.

Perhaps tomorrow would be better. I hoped so, but I doubted it. The lesson of experience over expectation was one I had finally begun to learn.

Maybe I shouldn't have come, but somehow I had needed to. This place was where I'd grown up, and in some odd way it still represented safety and security. And in spite of the shouting, the arguments and the fights, it was the only home I'd ever had.

I lay on the bed and looked up at the familiar ceiling with its decorative molding around the light fixture. It reminded me so much of the hours I had spent lying in exactly the same way as a spotty seventeen-year-old longing to be free, longing to join the army and escape from my adolescent prison. And yet here I was again, back in the same place, imprisoned again, this time by my disability but still longing to be in the army, determined to rejoin my regiment, hungry to be back in command of my troops and eager to be, once more, fighting and killing the enemy.

I sighed, stood up and looked at myself in the mirror on the wardrobe door. I looked normal, but looks could be deceptive.

I sat down on the edge of the bed and removed my prosthesis, rolling down the flesh-colored rubber sleeve that gripped over my real knee, keeping the false lower leg and foot from falling off. I slowly eased my stump out of the tight-fitting cup and removed the foam-plastic liner. It was all very clever. Molded to fit me exactly by the boys at Dorset Orthopedic, they had constructed a limb that I could walk on all day without causing so much as a pressure sore, let alone a blister.

But it still wasn't *me.*

I looked again at the mirror on the wardrobe door. Now my reflection didn't appear so normal.

Over the past few months, I suppose I had become familiar with the sight of my right leg finishing so abruptly some seven inches below my knee. Familiar, it might have been, but I was far from comfortable with the state of affairs, and every time I caught a glimpse of myself in a mirror without my prosthesis, I was still shocked and repulsed by the image.

Why me? I thought for the millionth time.

Why me?

I shook my head.

Feeling sorry for myself wasn't going to help me get back to combat-ready fitness.

3

"Has Josephine Lost Her Magic?"

The front-page headline of Sunday's *Racing Post* couldn't have been more blunt. The paper lay on the kitchen table when I went downstairs at eight o'clock to make myself some coffee after a disturbed night.

I wondered if my mother or stepfather had been down to the kitchen yet, and if so, had they seen the headline? Perhaps I should hide it. I looked around for something to casually place over the paper, as I could hear my mother coming down the stairs, but it was too late anyway.

"That bastard Rambler," she was shouting. "He knows sod all."

She swept into the kitchen in a light-blue quilted dressing gown and white slippers. She snatched up the newspaper from the table and studied the front-page article intently.

"It says here that Pharmacist was distressed after the race." My mother was shouting over her shoulder, obviously for the benefit of my stepfather, who had sensibly stayed upstairs. "That's not bloody true. How would Rambler know anyway? He'd have been propping up a bar somewhere. Everyone knows he's a drunk."

I shifted on my feet, my false leg making its familiar metallic clink.

"Oh, hello," said my mother, apparently seeing me for the first time. "Have you read this rubbish?" she demanded.

"No," I said.

"Well, don't," she said, throwing the paper back down on the table. "It's a load of crap."

She turned on her heel and disappeared back upstairs as quickly as she had arrived, shouting obscenities and telling all the world how she would "have Rambler's head on a platter for this."

I leaned down and turned the paper around so I could read it.

"From our senior correspondent Gordon Rambler at Cheltenham" was printed under the headline. I read on:

> Josephine Kauri was at a loss for words after her eight-year-old Gold Cup prospect, Pharmacist, finished last in the Janes Bank Trophy yesterday at Chelten-

ham. The horse clearly did not stay the three-mile trip, and finished at a walk and in some distress. The Cheltenham stewards ordered that the horse be routine-tested.

This is not the first time in recent weeks that the Kauris' horses have seemingly run out of puff in big races. Her promising novice chaser Scientific suffered the same fate at Kempton in December, and questions were asked about another Kauri horse Oregon at Newbury last week, when it failed to finish in the first half-dozen when a heavily backed favorite.

Is Josephine losing her magic touch that had won her such respect as well as numerous big prizes? With the Cheltenham Festival now only five weeks away, can we expect a repeat of last year's fantastic feats, or have the Kauri horses simply flattered to deceive?

Gordon Rambler had pulled no punches. He went on to speculate that Mrs. Kauri might be overtraining the horses at home, such that they had passed their peak by the time they reached the racetrack. It would not have been the first time a trainer had inadvertently "lost the race on the gallops," as it was known, although I would be surprised if my mother had, not after so many years of experience. Not unless, as the paper said, she had lost her magic touch.

But she hadn't lost her touch for shouting. I could hear her upstairs in full flow, although I couldn't quite make out the words. No doubt my stepfather was suffering the wrath of her tongue. I almost felt sorry for him. But only almost.

I decided it might be prudent for me to get out of the house for a while, so I went for a wander around the stables.

The block nearest the house, the one over which Ian Norland lived, was just one side of three quadrangles of stables, each containing twenty-four stalls, that stretched away from the house.

When my mother had acquired the place from her first husband there had been far fewer stables, laid out in two lines of wooden huts. But by the time my father had packed up and left nine years later, my mother had built the first of the current redbrick rectangles. The second was added when I'd been about fifteen, and the third more recently in what had once been a lunging paddock. And there was still enough of the paddock remaining to add a fourth, if required.

Even on a Sunday morning, the stables were a hive of activity. The horses needed to be fed and watered seven days a week, although my mother, along with most trainers, still resisted the temptation to treat Sunday as just another day to send strings of horses out on the gallops. But that was probably more to do with having to pay staff double time on Sundays rather than any wish to keep the Sabbath special.

"Good morning," Ian Norland called to me as he came out of one of the stalls. "Still here, then?"

"Yes," I said. Surely, I thought, I hadn't implied anything to him the previous afternoon. "Why wouldn't I still be here?"

"No reason," he said, smiling. "Just . . ."

"Just what?" I asked with some determination.

"Just that Mrs. Kauri doesn't seem to like guests staying overnight. Most go home after dinner."

"This is my home," I said.

"Oh," he said. "I suppose it is."

He seemed slightly flustered, as if he had already said too much to the son of his employer. He was right. He had.

"And how is Pharmacist this morning?" I

asked, half hoping for some more indiscretion.

"Fine," he said rather dismissively.

"How fine?" I persisted.

"He's a bit tired after yesterday," he said. "But otherwise, he's OK."

"No diarrhea?" I asked.

He gave me a look that I took to imply that he wished he hadn't mentioned anything about diarrhea to me yesterday.

"No," he said.

"Does he look well in his eyes?" I asked.

"Like I said, he's just tired." He picked up a bucket and began to fill it under a tap. "Sorry, I have to get on." It was my cue that the conversation was over.

"Yes, of course," I said. I started to walk on, but I stopped and turned around. "Which stall is Pharmacist in?"

"Mrs. Kauri wouldn't want anyone seeing him," Ian said. "Not just now."

"Why on earth not?" I said, sounding aggrieved.

"She just wouldn't," he repeated. "Mrs. Kauri doesn't like anyone snooping round the yard. Won't even allow the owners to see their own horses without her there to escort them."

"Nonsense," I said in my best voice-of-command. "I'm not just anyone, you know.

I'm her son."

He wavered, and I thought he was about to tell me when he was saved by the arrival of his employer.

"Morning, Ian," my mother called, striding around the corner towards us. She had swapped the light-blue dressing gown and white slippers for a full-length waxed Barbour coat and green Wellington boots.

"Ah, morning, ma'am," Ian replied with some relief. "I was just talking to your son."

"So I see," she said in a disapproving tone. "Well, don't. You've talked to him too much already."

Ian blushed bright pink, and he stole a glance of displeasure at me.

"Sorry, ma'am," he said.

She nodded firmly at him as if to close the matter. Ian's rebuke may have been short, but I had the distinct impression that his indiscretion would be remembered for much longer. But for now she turned her attention to me. "And what are *you* doing out here, exactly?" she asked accusingly.

"I was just having a look round," I said as innocently as I could.

I was thirty-two years old and still a serving captain in Her Majesty's British Army. Until recently, I had been commanding a platoon of thirty men fighting and killing

Her enemies with zest and gusto, but here I was feeling like a naughty ninth grader caught having a smoke behind the bike sheds by the school principal.

"Well, don't," she said to me in the same tone that she had used towards Ian.

"Why not?" I said belligerently. "Have you something to hide?"

Ian almost choked. It hadn't been the most tactful of comments, and I could see the irritation level rise in my mother's eyes. However, she managed to remain in control of her emotions. There were staff about.

One didn't fight with family in front of staff.

"Of course not," she said with a forced smile. "I just don't want anyone upsetting the horses."

I couldn't actually see how wandering around the stable blocks would upset the horses, but I decided not to say so.

"And how is Pharmacist this morning?" I asked her.

"I was on my way to see him right now," my mother replied, ignoring the implication in my voice. "Come on, Ian," she said, and set off briskly with him in tow.

"Good," I said, walking behind them. "I'll come with you."

My mother said nothing but simply increased her already breakneck pace, with Ian almost running behind her to keep up. Perhaps she thought that with my false foot, I wouldn't be able to. Maybe she was right.

I followed as quickly as I could along the line of stalls and through the corridor into the next stable rectangle. If my mother thought she could go fast enough so that I wouldn't see where she had gone, she was mistaken. I watched as she slid the bolts and went into a stall on the far side, almost pushing Ian through the gap and pulling the door shut behind them. As if that would make them unreachable. Even I knew that stable doors are bolted only from the outside. Perhaps I should lock them in and wait. Now, that would be fun.

Instead, I opened the top half of the door, leaned on the lower portion and looked in.

My mother was bent over, away from me, with her sizeable bottom facing the door. I did not take this as any particular gesture of disapproval, as she was simply running her hands down the backs of Pharmacist's legs, feeling for heat that would imply a soreness of the tendon. Ian was holding the horse's head-collar so that it couldn't move.

"Nothing," my mother said, standing up straight. "Not even a twinge."

"That must be good," I said.

"How would you know?" my mother said caustically.

"Surely it's good if there's no heat in his tendons," I said.

"Not really," she replied. "It means there must be another reason for him finishing so badly yesterday."

That's true, I thought.

"Does he look all right?" I asked.

"No, he's got two heads." My mother's attempts at humor rarely came off. "Of course he looks all right."

"Has he got diarrhea?" I asked.

Ian gave me a pained look.

"And why, pray, would he have diarrhea?" my mother asked haughtily, with strong accusation in her tone.

Ian stood quite still, looking at me. His jaw set as in stone.

"I just wondered," I said, letting him off this particular hook. "I know horses can't vomit, so I just wondered if he had a stomach upset that might show itself as diarrhea."

"Nonsense," my mother said. "Horses only get diarrhea with dirty or moldy feed, and we are very careful to keep our feed clean and fresh. Isn't that right, Ian?"

"Oh yes, ma'am," he said immediately.

I thought, perhaps unfairly, that Ian would

have said "Yes, ma'am" to any request at that precise moment, even if she'd asked him to jump off the stable roof.

The inspection of Pharmacist was over, and my mother came out through the door followed by Ian, who slid home the door bolts.

Personally, if it had been my best horse that had inexplicably run so badly, I would have had a vet out here last night drawing blood and giving him the full once-over, testing his heart, his lungs and everything else, for that matter. Strangely, my mother seemed satisfied with a quick look and a cursory feel of his legs.

"How long before the dope-test results are out?" I said, somewhat unwisely.

"What dope test?" my mother asked sharply.

"The one that was ordered by the stewards."

"And how do you know they ordered a dope test?" she demanded.

"It says so in today's *Racing Post.*"

"I told you not to read that paper," she said crossly.

"I don't always do what I'm told," I said.

"No," my mother said. "That's the problem. You never did."

She turned abruptly and strode away, leaving Ian and me standing alone.

"So what do *you* think?" I asked him.

"Don't involve me," he said. "I'm in enough trouble already."

He turned to walk away.

"But wouldn't you have had a vet in last night?" I said to his retreating back.

"I told you," he said over his shoulder without stopping, "don't involve me. I need this job."

I called after him, "You do realize there won't be a job if someone has been nobbling the horses. There won't be any jobs here. The yard will be closed down."

He stopped and came back.

"Don't you think I know that?" he said through clenched teeth.

"Well, what are you going to do about it?" I asked.

"Nothing," he said.

"Nothing?"

"That's right. Nothing. If I say anything I'll lose my job, and then I'll have no job and no reference. What chance would I have then?"

"Better than having a reputation as a doper," I said.

He stood silently, looking up at me.

"So far the tests have all been negative. Let's hope they stay that way."

"But you think otherwise, don't you?" I said.

"Something strange is going on. That's all I know. Now let me get on with my job, while I still have it."

He strode away purposefully, leaving me alone outside Pharmacist's stall. I opened the top half of the door and took another look at the horse. As yesterday on the television, he looked all right to me.

But, then, I was no vet.

The atmosphere back in the house was frosty, to put it mildly. Positively subzero, and it had nothing to do with Pharmacist or any of the other horses. It had to do with money.

"Josephine, we simply can't afford it."

I could hear my stepfather almost shouting. He and my mother were in the little office off the hallway, while I was sitting very quietly out of sight in the kitchen, eavesdropping. They must have been far too involved in their discussion to have heard me come in from the yard, so I had simply sat down and listened.

Some might have accused me of being somewhat underhanded in secretly listening to their conversation. They would have been right.

"We must be able to afford it," wailed my mother. "I've had the best year ever with the horses."

"Yes, you have, but we've also had other things to contend with, not least the ongoing fallout from your disastrous little scheme." My stepfather's voice was full of incrimination and displeasure.

"Please don't start all that again." Her tone was suddenly more conciliatory and apologetic.

"But it's true," my stepfather went on mercilessly. "Without that, we would've easily been able to buy you a new BMW. As it is . . . well, let's just hope our old Ford doesn't need too much work done on it. Things are tight at present."

I wondered what disastrous little scheme could have resulted in things being so tight financially that one of the top trainers in the country was unable to upgrade her old Ford to a new BMW. But she had never before seemed to care about what sort of car she drove.

I would have loved to listen to them for a while longer.

However, I really didn't want to get caught snooping, so I carefully stood up and silently swiveled back and forth on my good foot from the kitchen table to the back door.

It was a technique I had developed to get around my hospital bed at night once I had removed my prosthesis. I was getting quite good at heel-and-toeing, as the physiotherapists had called it.

I could still hear my mother at high volume. "For God's sake, Derek, there must be something we can do."

"What do you suggest?" my stepfather shouted back at her. "We don't even know who it is."

I opened the back door a few inches, then closed it with a bang.

Their conversation stopped.

I walked through from the kitchen to the hall, my right foot making its familiar clink whenever I put it down. My mother came out of the open office door.

"Hello," I said, as genially as I could.

"Hello, darling," she replied, again placing too much emphasis on the "dar." She took a step towards me, and I thought for a fleeting second she was going to give me a kiss, but she didn't. "Tell me," she said, "how much longer are you planning to stay?"

"I've only just arrived," I said, smiling. "I hadn't thought about leaving just yet."

Oh yes, I had.

"It's just that one has to make plans," my mother said. "It's not that I want you to go, of course, it's just I would like to have some idea of when."

"I haven't even worked out where I would go," I said.

"But you would go back to the army." It was a statement, not a question.

"It's not as simple as that. They want to give me time to get over the injuries. And even then, they're not sure they actually want me anymore. They'll decide when I go back after my leave."

"What?" She sounded genuinely shocked. "But they have to have you. You were injured while working for them, so surely they must have an obligation to go on employing you."

"Mum, it's not like any other job," I said. "I would have to be fit and able to fight. That's what soldiers do."

"But there must be something else you could do," she argued. "They must need people to organize things, people to do the paperwork. Surely those don't have to be fit enough to run round and fight?"

My stepfather came to the office door and leaned on the frame.

"Josephine, my dear. I don't think Tom here would be prepared to be in the army simply to push paper round a desk." He looked me in the eyes and, for the first time in twenty-four years, I thought there might be some flicker of understanding between us.

"Derek is so right," I said.

"So for how long have the army sent you home on leave?" my mother asked. "How long before they decide if they want you back or not?"

"Six months."

"Six months! But you can't possibly stay here six months."

That was clearly true. I had arrived only eighteen hours previously, and I had already been there too long for her liking.

"I'll look for somewhere else to go this week," I said.

"Oh, darling, it's not that I want to throw you out, you understand," she said, "but I think it might be for the best."

Best for her, I thought ungenerously. But perhaps it would be the best for us all. A full-scale shouting match couldn't be very far away.

"I could pay you rent," I said, purposely fishing for a reaction.

"Don't be a silly boy," my mother said. "This is your home. You don't pay rent here."

My home, but I can't stay in it. My mother clearly didn't appreciate the irony of her words.

"A contribution towards your food might be welcome," my stepfather interjected.

Things must have been tight. Very tight, indeed.

I lay on my bed for a while, in the middle of the morning, staring at the molded ceiling and wondering what to do.

Life in the hospital had been so structured: time to wake up, have a cup of tea, read the paper, eat breakfast, have a morning physiotherapy session in the rehab center, return to the ward for lunch in the dayroom, have an afternoon physiotherapy session, return to the ward, watch the evening news, read a book or watch more television, have an evening hot drink, lights out, sleep. Every day the same, except there was no physio on Saturday afternoons or all day Sunday. A strict routine, regular as clockwork, with no decisions having to be made by me.

At first I had hated to have such a straitjacket to my existence, but I'd become used to it. I suppose one gets used to anything.

Abruptly, here in Lambourn, I was on my own, free to make my own choice of activity without a hospital regime to do it for me. And all of a sudden I was lost, unable to make up my mind, mostly because I was at a loss to know *what* to do.

It was a new and alien sensation. Even in the boring times between contacts in Afghanistan I'd had things to do: clean my weapon, fix my kit, train my men, make plans, even write a note home. I had *always* had something to do. In fact, most of the time I had far too much to do, and not enough time.

Yet try as I might, I couldn't think of a single thing I had to do now.

Maybe I could have written a note of thanks to the staff at the rehab clinic, but both they and I would know I didn't mean it.

I had hated feeling that I was being treated like a child, and I hadn't been slow to say so.

Looking back, even after just one day away from it, I could see that my frustration, and my anger, hadn't helped anyone, least of all myself. But it had been the only way I'd known to express my fury at the hand that fate had dealt me. There had been times when, if I'd still had my sidearm with me, I am sure I would have used it to blow my brains out, such had been the depth of my depression.

Even in recent weeks, I had often thought

about suicide. But I could have walked out and thrown myself under the wheels of the London bus right outside the hospital if I'd really wanted to, and I hadn't, so at least I must be on the way up from the nadir.

My life needed targets and objectives.

In the hospital my goal had been simply to be discharged.

Now that I had achieved it, a void had opened up in front of me. A future seemingly devoid of purpose and direction. Only a tentative "we'll see" to give me any hope. Was it enough?

I looked at my watch.

It was twenty to twelve, and I had been lying on my bed doing nothing for nearly three hours, ever since I had walked away from a stormy encounter with my parent out on the driveway.

She had been inspecting her car and I hadn't been able to resist telling her that it was high time she changed her old blue Ford for a new, smarter make.

"Mind your own bloody business," she had hissed at me, thrusting her face towards mine.

"I'm sorry," I'd said, feigning surprise. "I didn't realize the matter touched such a sore nerve."

"It doesn't," she'd replied, back in some

sort of control. “And there’s nothing wrong with this one.”

“But surely a trainer of your standing should have a better car than this. How about a BMW, for example?”

I had really believed she was about to cry again, and quite suddenly, I had been angry with myself. What was I doing? I tried to see myself as she would have, and I didn’t like it. I didn’t like it one bit. So I had turned away and climbed the stairs to my room like a naughty boy.

How long, I wondered, should I remain in my room before I had paid sufficient penance for my misdeeds? An hour? A day? A week? A lifetime?

I sat up on the side of the bed and decided to write to the staff at the rehab center to thank them for their care *and* to apologize for my consistent lack of good humor.

Maybe then they might just believe that I meant it.

4

The remainder of Sunday proved to be a quiet day at Kauri House Stables, with the human residents managing to stay out of arguing distance.

In the afternoon I ventured out into Lambourn, deciding to go for a walk, mostly just to get me out of the house but also because I was curious about how much the place had changed over fifteen years. I didn't intend to go very far. It had been only a week or so since I'd thrown away the crutches, and my leg tended to tire easily.

There were a few more houses than I remembered, a new estate of smart little homes with postage-stamp gardens having sprung up in what once had been a field full of ponies. But overall, the village was as familiar as it had been when I'd delivered the morning papers as a teenager.

And why wouldn't it have been? The previous fifteen years may have changed *me* a great deal, but it was a mere blink of an eye compared to the long history of human habitation in Lambourn.

Modern documented Lambourn dated from the ninth century when the church and village were named in the will of King Alfred, the mighty king of the Saxons, the only monarch of England to have ever been designated "The Great."

But Lambourn had a history that stretched back far further than medieval times. Numerous Bronze Age burial grounds existed on the hills just north of the modern village, together with The Ridgeway, the Stone Age superhighway that had once stretched from the Dorset coast to The Wash.

Nowadays, Lambourn and its surroundings were known as The Valley of the Racehorse, but the racing industry was a relative newcomer. First records show that racehorses were trained here in the late eighteenth century, but it was not until the arrival of the railway a hundred years later that Lambourn became established as a national center for racing, and jump racing in particular, to rival that at Newmarket. Trains enabled the horses to be sent to racetracks farther and farther from home, and hence a national sport was established.

But the major factor that made Lambourn such a wonderful place for horses was simple geology, and had nothing to do with man.

Whereas the rolling Berkshire Downs certainly lent themselves so ideally to the formation of the gallops and the training of the horses, it is what lay beneath the turf that made the real difference. The Downs, together with the Chiltern Hills, were created many millions of years ago, laid down as sediment in some prehistoric organism-rich sea. Billions and billions of primitive sea creatures died, and their skeletons drifted to the bottom, over time being compressed into rock, into the white chalk we see today. It is almost pure calcium carbonate, and the grass that grows on such a base is rich in calcium, ideal for the formation of strong bone in grass-eating racehorses.

I wandered down to the center of the village, past the Norman church that sometime in the twelfth century had replaced the earlier Saxon version. Even though I was not what was known as a "regular" churchgoer, I had been into Lambourn Church many times, mostly along with the other boys and girls from the local primary school. My memory was of somewhere cold, and that was not just because the temperature was always low. It was also due to the realization that people were actually buried beneath my feet, under the stones set in the church floor. I could recall how my overactive childhood imagination had caused me to shiver, as I did so again now.

I stopped and thought it anomalous that the bodies of those buried so long ago could still have such an effect on me, whereas the bodies of the Taliban, those I had so recently sent to their graves, seemingly had none.

I walked on.

The center of the village was mostly unchanged, although some of the shops had different names, and others had different purposes.

I went into the general store to buy a sandwich for lunch and waited for my turn at the checkout.

"Oh, hello," said the woman behind the till, looking at me intently. "It's Tom, isn't it? Tom Kauri?"

I casually looked back at her. She was about my age, with long, fair hair tied back in a ponytail. She wore a loose-fitting dark gray sweatshirt that did a moderate job of camouflaging the fairly substantial body beneath.

"Tom Forsyth," I said, correcting her.

"Oh yes," she said. "That's right. I remember now. But your mum is Mrs. Kauri, isn't she?" I nodded, and she smiled. I handed her my sandwich and can of drink. "You don't remember me, do you?" she said.

I looked at her more closely.

"Sorry," I said. "No."

"I'm Virginia," she said expectantly.

I went on looking at her, obviously with a blank expression.

"Virginia Bayley," she went on. "Ginny." She paused, waiting for a response. "From primary school." Another pause. "Of course, I was Ginny Worthington then."

Ginny Worthington, from primary school? I looked at her once more. I vaguely remembered a Ginny Worthington, but she'd definitely had black hair, and she'd been as thin as a rake.

"Dyed my hair since then." She laughed nervously. "And put on a few pounds, you know, due to having had the kids."

Virginia Bayley, plump and blond, née Ginny Worthington, skinny and brunette. One and the same person.

"How nice to see you again," I said, not really meaning it.

"Staying with your mother, are you?" she asked.

"Yes," I said.

"That's nice." She scanned my sandwich and the can of drink. "Such a lovely woman, your mother. That's three pounds twenty, please." I gave her a five-pound note. "A real star round here." She gave me my change. "Real proud of her, we are, winning that award." She handed me my sandwich and drink in a plastic bag. "Lovely to see you again."

"Thanks," I said, taking the bag. "You too." I started to leave but turned back. "What award?"

"You must know," she said. "The National Woman of the Year Award. Last month. In London. Presented by the Prince of Wales, on the telly."

I looked blank. Had I really been so involved with my own life that I hadn't even noticed my mother receiving such an accolade?

"I can't believe you don't know," Ginny said.

"I've been away," I replied absentmindedly.

I turned away from her again.

She spoke to my back. "You can come and buy me a drink later if you like."

I was about to ask why on earth I would like to buy her a drink when she went on. "My old man has arranged a bit of a get-together in the Wheelwright for my birthday. There'll be others there, too. Some from school. You're welcome to come."

"Thank you," I said. "Where did you say?"

"The Wheelwright," she repeated. "The Wheelwright Arms. At seven o'clock."

"Tonight?"

"Yeah."

"So is it your birthday today?"

"Yeah," she said again, grinning.

"Then happy birthday, Ginny," I said with a flourish.

"Ta," she said, smiling broadly. "Do come tonight if you can. It'll be fun."

I couldn't, offhand, think of a less fun-filled evening than going to the pub birthday party of someone I couldn't really remember, where there would be other people I also wouldn't be able to remember, all of whom had nothing more in common with me than having briefly attended the same school twenty years previously.

But I supposed anything might be preferable to sitting through another excruciating dinner with my mother and stepfather.

"OK," I said. "I will."

"Great," Ginny said.

So I did.

The evening proved to be better than I had

expected, and I so nearly didn't go.

By seven o'clock the rain was falling vertically out of the dark sky, with huge droplets splashing back from the flooded area between the house and the stables.

I looked at my black leather shoes, my only shoes, and wondered if staying at home in front of the television might be the wiser option. Perhaps I could watch the weekly motoring show and use it to bully my mother further over her car.

Well, perhaps not, but it was tempting.

I decided instead to find out if it would be possible to pull a Wellington boot over my false leg. I suppose I could always have worn only one boot while leaving the prosthesis completely bare. I don't think the water would have done it much harm, but the sight of a man walking on such a night with one bare foot might have scared the neighbors, to say nothing of the people in the pub.

I borrowed the largest pair of Wellies I could find in the boot-room and had surprisingly little difficulty in getting both of them on. I also borrowed my mother's long Barbour coat and my step-father's cap. I set off for the Wheelwright Arms relatively well protected but with the rain still running down my neck.

"I thought you wouldn't come," said Ginny, as I stood in the public bar removing my mother's coat, with pools of water forming on the bleached stone floor. "Not with the weather this bad."

"Crazy," I agreed.

"You or me?" she said.

"Both."

She laughed. Ginny was trying very hard to make me feel welcome. Too hard, in fact. She would have been better leaving me alone and enjoying herself with her other guests. Her husband didn't like it either, which I took to be a good sign for their marriage. But he had no worries with me. Ginny was nice enough but not my sort.

What was my sort? I wondered.

I'd slept with plenty of girls, but they had all been casual affairs, sometimes just one-nighters. I'd never had a *real* girlfriend.

Whereas many of my fellow junior officers had enjoyed long-term relationships, even marriages, both at Sandhurst and in the regiment, I was, in truth, married only to the military.

There was no doubt that I had been, as I remained, deeply in love with the army, and I had certainly betrothed myself to *her,* "forsaking all others until death do us part."

But it seemed it wouldn't be death that

would do us part: just the small matter of a missing foot.

"So what do you do for a living?" Ginny's husband asked me.

"I'm between jobs," I said unhelpfully.

"What did you do?" he persisted.

Why, I thought, didn't I simply tell them I was in the army? Was I not proud to be a soldier? I had been before I was injured. Wasn't I still?

"A banker," I said. "In the city."

"Recession got you, did it?" he said, with a slightly mocking laugh in his voice. "Your trouble was too many big bonuses." He nodded. He knew.

"You're probably right," I said.

There were seven of us standing in a circle near the bar. As well as Ginny and her husband, there were two other couples. I didn't recognize any of them, and none of the four looked old enough to have been at school with me.

One of the men stepped forward to buy a round at the bar.

"Should I know any of these?" I said quietly to Ginny, waving a hand at the others.

"No, not these," she said. "I think the weather has put some people off."

I was beginning to wish it had put me off

as well when the door of the pub opened and another couple came in, again dripping water into puddles on the floor.

At least I thought they were a couple until they removed their coats. Both of them were girls — more correctly, they were young women — and one of them I knew the instant she removed her hat and shook out her long blond hair.

"Hello, Isabella," I said.

"My God," she replied. "No one's called me Isabella for years." She looked closely at my face. "Bloody hell. It's Tom Kauri."

"Tom Forsyth," I corrected.

"I know, I know," she said, laughing. "I was just winding you up. As per usual."

It was true. She had teased me mercilessly, ever since I had told her, aged about ten, that I was deeply in love with her, and I had asked her to marry me. She had clearly filled out a bit since then, and in all the right places.

"So what do people call you now?" I asked.

"Bella," she said. "Or Issy. Only my mother calls me Isabella, and then only when I've displeased her."

"And do you displease her often?" I asked flippantly.

She looked me straight in the eyes and

smiled. "As often as possible."

Wow, I thought.

Both Isabella and I rather ignored Ginny's birthday celebration as we renewed our friendship and, in my case anyway, renewed my feelings of longing.

"Are you married?" I asked her almost immediately.

"Why do you want to know?" she replied.

"To know where I stand," I said somewhat clumsily.

"And where exactly do you think you stand?" she said.

I stand on only one leg. Now, what would she say to that?

"You tell me," I said.

But throughout the whole evening, she never did answer my question even though, in a roundabout manner, I asked her three or four times. In the end, I took her silence on the matter to be answer enough, and I wondered who was the lucky man.

At ten o'clock, as people were beginning to drift away, I asked her if I could walk her home.

"How do you know I walked?" she asked.

"When you arrived you were too wet to have simply come in from the parking lot."

"Clever clogs!" She smiled. "OK. But just

a walk home. No bonus."

"I've never heard it called a bonus before." I laughed. "No wonder all those bankers are so keen to keep their bonuses."

She also laughed, and we left the pub in congenial companionship but with her hands firmly planted in her coat pockets so there was no chance of me being able to casually take one of them in mine.

Part of me longed to be with a woman again, just for the sex.

It had been a long time. It was six months or more since I had talked a girl into my bed with stories of heroic encounters with a mysterious enemy, stories of men being men, sweating testosterone through every pore, and satisfying ten maidens each before breakfast. I was good at the game, but recent opportunities had been limited, almost nonexistent.

Six months was a long time, with only the occasional misplaced sponge by a blushing nurse to fulfill the need.

I positively ached to have a "bonus" with Isabella, even here, in the street, in the still pouring rain.

But there was little likelihood of that, and my chances weren't exactly helped when she suddenly stopped.

"What's that noise?" she asked.

"What noise?" I said, stopping next to her and dreading the moment.

"That clicking noise?" She listened. "That's funny. It's stopped now."

She walked on and I followed.

"There it is," she shouted triumphantly. "It's you, when you walk."

"It's nothing," I said quietly. "Just the boots."

I could see she was confused. I was wearing rubber boots. They would make no noise, certainly not a clicking noise.

"No, come on," she said. "That's definitely a sharp metal sound, and you've got Wellies on. So what is it?"

"Leave it," I said sharply, embarrassed and angry. In truth, more angry with myself for not saying than with her for asking.

But she wouldn't leave it.

"Come on," she said again, laughing. "What have you got down there? It's a toy, isn't it? Part of your chat-up technique?" She danced away from me, looking down, searching for the source of the noise and laughing all the while.

I had no choice.

"I've got a false leg," I said quietly.

"What?" She hadn't really heard and was still dancing around, laughing.

"A false leg," I said more loudly. She

stopped dancing.

"I've only got one leg."

She stood still, looking at me.

"Oh, Tom, I'm sorry." I thought for a moment that she was crying, but it might have been the rain on her face. "Oh God, I'm so sorry."

"It's all right," I said.

But it wasn't.

Isabella stood in the street, getting wetter, if that was possible, while I told her everything I could remember about being blown apart by an IED and my subsequent medical history.

She listened, first with horror and then with concern.

She tried to comfort me, and I despised it. I didn't want her pity.

Suddenly I knew why I had come back to Lambourn, to my "home." I must have subconsciously understood that my mother would not have given me the lovey-dovey consoling parental hugs I would have hated. She would not have tried to be reassuring and sympathetic. And she would not have tried to commiserate with me for my loss. I preferred the Kauri "Get on with your own life and let me get on with mine" attitude.

Grief, even the grief for a lost foot or a lost career, was easier to cope with alone.

"Please don't patronize me," I said.

Isabella stopped talking in mid-sentence.

"I wasn't," she said.

"Well, it felt like it," I replied.

"God, you're awkward," she said. "I was only trying to help."

"Well, don't," I said rather cruelly. "I'm fine without it."

"OK," she said, obviously hurt. "If that's the way you feel, then I'll bid you good night."

She turned abruptly and walked away, leaving me standing alone in the rain, confused and bewildered, not knowing whether to be pleased or disappointed, angry or calm.

I felt as though I wanted to run, to run away, but I couldn't even do that, not without a cacophony of metallic clinking.

On Monday morning I went to Aldershot to try to collect my car and my other belongings out of storage.

Isabella came with me.

In fact, to be totally accurate, I went with her.

She drove her VW Golf in a manner akin to a world-championship rally driver.

"Do you always drive like this?" I asked, as we almost collided with an oncoming truck during a somewhat dodgy overtaking maneuver.

"Only when I'm not being patronizing," she said, looking at me for rather longer than I was happy with.

"Watch the road," I said.

She ignored me.

"Please, Isabella," I implored. "I don't want to survive an IED only to be killed on the Bracknell bypass by a lunatic woman."

She had phoned the house early. Too early. I had still been in bed.

"That Warren woman called for you," my mother had said with distaste when I went down to breakfast.

"Warren woman?"

"Married to Jackson Warren."

I'd been none the wiser.

"Who's Jackson Warren?"

"You must know," my mother had said. "Lives in the Hall. Family made pots of money in the colonies." She had sounded very old-fashioned. "Married that young girl when his wife died. She must be thirty years younger than him, at least. That's the one who called. Brazen hussy."

The last two words had been spoken under her breath but had been clearly audible nonetheless.

"Is her name Isabella?" I'd asked.

"That's the one."

So she was married.

"What did she want?" I'd asked.

"I don't know, do I? She wanted to speak to you; that's all I know."

My mother had never liked being in a position where she did not know everything that was going on, and this had been no exception.

"I didn't even know that you knew that woman." She'd said the words with a mixture of disapproval and nosiness.

I hadn't risen to the bait.

Instead, I'd gone out of the kitchen and into the office to return the call to Isabella.

"I'm so sorry about last night," she'd said.

"So am I."

"Please, can we meet again today so that I can apologize in person?"

"I can't," I'd said. "I'm going to Aldershot."

"Can't I take you?" she had replied, rather too eagerly.

"It's all right," I'd said. "I'll get the train from Newbury."

"No." She had almost screamed down the phone. "Please let me take you. It's the least I can do after being so crass last night."

So here we were, dodging trucks on the Bracknell bypass.

Everything I owned, other than my kit for war, had been locked away in a metal cage at an army barracks in Aldershot prior to the regiment's move to Afghanistan. Everything, that is, except my car, which I hoped was still sitting at one end of the huge parking lot set aside for the purpose within the military camp down the road from Aldershot, at Pirbright.

"Let's get my car first," I said. "Then I can load it up with my stuff."

"OK," she said. "But are you sure you'll be able to drive it?"

"No, I'm not at all sure," I said. "But I'll find out soon enough." It was something that had been worrying me. My Jaguar was an automatic, so at least there were only two pedals to cope with, but both of them were designed to be operated by the driver's right foot. I planned to use my false right for the accelerator, and my real left for the brake: two pedals, two feet, just like driving a Formula One racing car.

"But are you insured, you know, to drive with only one leg?"

"To be honest, I'm not really sure about that either, so I'm not asking. I had intended to cancel my insurance and to take the car off the road before I was deployed, but somehow I never found the time. It's been taxed and insured for the past five months without anyone driving it, so they must owe me something. And I haven't told the insurance company about being wounded."

She drove in silence for a while.

"Why didn't you just tell me you were married?" I asked.

"Does it matter?" she replied.

"It might."

"What exactly might matter: the fact that I'm married, or that my husband is more than twice my age?"

"Both."

"I'm actually amazed you didn't know already. Everyone else seems to. Quite the scandal it was, when Jackson and I got married."

"How long ago?" I asked.

"Seven years now," she said. "And before you ask, no, it wasn't for his money. I love the old bugger."

"But the money helped?" I said with some irony.

She glanced at me. It was not a glance of approval.

"You're just like everyone else," she said. "Why does everyone assume that it's all about his money?"

"Isn't it?"

"No," she said defiantly, "it's not. In fact,

I won't get anything when he dies. I said I didn't want it. It all goes to his children."

"Are any of them your children too?" I asked.

"No." I could detect a slight disappointment in her voice. "Sadly not."

"You tried?" I asked.

"At the beginning, but not now. It's too late."

"But you're still young enough."

"I'm all right. It's Jackson that's the problem." She paused, as if wondering whether she should go on. She decided to. "Bloody prostate."

"Cancer?" I asked.

"Yeah." She sighed. "It's a bugger. The doctors say they've caught it early and that it's controllable at his age with drugs. But there are some, shall we say, unfortunate side effects."

She drove on in silence, swerving around a slow-moving truck just in time to avoid an oncoming car.

"Has he tried Viagra?" I asked.

"Tried it?" She laughed. "He's swallowed them like M&M's but still not a flicker. It's the fault of the Zoladex — that's one of the drugs. It seems to switch off his sex drive completely. That's the physical side; mentally he's as rampant as ever."

"I can see that would be a tad frustrating," I said.

"A tad? I'll tell you, it's extremely frustrating. And for both of us." She looked at me as if in embarrassment. "Sorry, I shouldn't have said anything. Far too much information."

"It's fine," I said. "I'm really quite discreet. I'll only tell the Sunday papers if they pay me well."

She laughed.

"From what the Sunday papers said after our wedding, you'd believe that I only married him for the money and that sex between a twenty-three-year-old woman and a man nearing sixty was all in the imagination — his imagination, that is. What rubbish. It was the sex that attracted me to him in the first place."

I sat in silence, just listening. What could I say?

"I was eighteen when I first met him. He was fifty-four, but he didn't look it. He used to play golf with my dad every Sunday morning. Then one Sunday when Mum and Dad were away, he came round to make sure everything was OK. It seems Dad hadn't told Jackson he wouldn't be playing golf that week, at least that's what Jackson told me at the time, but I've since often wondered if it was true." She smiled. "Anyway, to cut a long story short, we ended up in bed together." She laughed. "And the rest is history, or in the papers, at least."

"Was Jackson married at the time?"

"Oh yes," she said. "With two children. They're both older than me. But his wife was already ill by then. She had breast cancer. I helped look after her for nearly three years until she died."

"Were you sleeping with him all the time?" I asked.

She smiled again. "Of course."

"But did you live in their house?"

"Not to start with, but I did for the last six months or so of Barbara's life. His son and daughter treated me as their kid sister."

"But did they know you were sleeping with their father?"

"They didn't exactly say so," she said, "but I think they knew. Their mother certainly did."

"What? Jackson's wife knew that he was sleeping with you?"

"Absolutely. We discussed it. She even gave me advice about what he liked. She used to say it took the pressure off her."

Annoyingly, at this point we arrived at Pirbright Camp, so I heard no more juicy Warren revelations.

Isabella remained in her car while I went into the guardroom to sign in.

"Sorry, sir," said the corporal behind the desk. "I can't let a civilian onto the camp without suitable ID."

"What sort of suitable ID does she need?" I asked him.

"A driver's license or passport," he said.

She had neither with her. I'd already asked.

"Can't I vouch for her?" I asked.

"Not without proper authority."

"Well, get the proper authority," I said in my most commanding officer voice.

"I can't, sir," he said. "You would have to apply to the adjutant, and he's away."

I sighed. "So what do you expect me to do?" I asked him.

"You can go in, sir, but you'll have to walk to get your car."

"But it's miles away." The park was at the other end of the camp.

"Sorry, sir," he said adamantly. "That's the security rules we've been told. No ID, no entrance."

I suppose it was fair. In the army one learned very early on that rules were rules. Security was security, after all.

"Can you please get me some transport, then," I said.

"Sorry, sir," he said again. "There's nothing available."

I stepped back and lifted my right trouser leg up six inches. "How am I going to walk to my car with this damn thing?" I lifted my foot up and down with its familiar metallic clink.

"Afghanistan?" the corporal asked.

I nodded. "IED. In Helmand," I said. "Four months ago."

"No problem, then, sir," he said, suddenly making a decision. "Just get the lady to hand this in when she leaves." He handed me a temporary vehicle pass. "Just don't tell anyone."

"Thanks," I said. "I won't."

False legs clearly brought some small benefit after all.

Funny how rules can be so easily ignored with the application of a modicum of common sense. Security? What security?

I found it was surprisingly easy to drive with a false foot. A few practice circuits of the parking lot and I was ready for the public highway. And I was much more confident about arriving safely at my destination with me driving with only one real leg than I had been in Isabella's VW with her driving with two.

She insisted on following me the nine miles from Pirbright to Aldershot.

"You might need help carrying your things," she'd said. "And you won't get much of it into that."

True, my Jaguar XK coupé was pretty small, but Isabella obviously had no idea how little I had acquired in the way of stuff during fifteen years in the army. I could probably have fitted it into my car twice over. But who was I to turn down the help of a pretty woman even if she was married?

We negotiated the busy Surrey and Hampshire roads without any mishaps and, surprisingly, without my Jag being overtaken by Isabella's dark blue Golf, although I was sure she was going to on a couple of occasions before she obviously remembered she didn't know the way.

"Is that *all?*" Isabella was amazed. "I'd take more than that on a dirty weekend to Paris."

I was standing next to two navy blue holdalls and a four-foot-by-four-inch black heavy-duty cardboard tube. Between them they contained all my meager worldly possessions.

"I've moved a lot," I said, as an explanation.

"At least you don't have to engage Bekins

to shift that lot." She laughed. "What's in the tube?"

"My sword."

"What, a real sword?" She was surprised.

"Absolutely," I said. "Every officer has a sword, but it's for ceremonial use only these days."

"But don't you have any furniture?"

"No."

"Not any?"

"No. I've always used the army stuff. I've lived in barrack blocks all my adult life. I've never even known the luxury of an en suite bathroom, except on holiday."

"I can't believe it," she said. "What century is it?"

"In the army? Twenty-first for weaponry, other than the sword, of course, but still mostly in the nineteenth for home comforts. You have to understand that it's the weapons that matter more than the accommodations. No soldier wants a cheap rifle that won't fire when his life depends on it, or body armor that won't stop a bullet, all because some civil-service jerk spent the available money on a flush toilet."

"You men," Isabella said. "Girls wouldn't put up with it."

"The girls don't fight," I said. "At least, not in the infantry. Not yet."

"Will it happen?" she asked.

"Oh, I expect so," I said.

"Do you mind?"

"Not really, as long as they fight as well as the men. But they will have to be strong to carry all their kit. The Israeli army scrapped their mixed infantry battalions when they suspected the men were carrying the girls' kits in return for sex. They were also worried that the men would stop and look after a wounded female colleague rather than carry on fighting."

"Human nature is human nature," Isabella said.

"Certainly is," I replied. "Any chance of a bonus?"

5

Back at Kauri House Stables there was still tension in the air between my mother and her husband. I suspected that I'd interrupted an argument as I went through the back door into the kitchen with my bags at three o'clock on Monday afternoon.

"Where has all that stuff come from?" my mother asked with a degree of accusation.

"It's just my things that were in storage," I said, "while I was away."

"Well, I don't know why you've brought it all here," she said rather crossly.

"Where else would I take it?"

"Oh, I don't know," she said with almost a sob. "I don't know bloody anything." She stormed out clutching her face. I thought she was crying.

"What's all that about?" I asked my step-father, who had sat silently through the whole exchange.

"Nothing," he said unhelpfully.

"It must be something."

"Nothing for you to worry about," he said.

"Let me be the judge of that," I said. "It's to do with money, isn't it?"

He looked up at me. "I told you, it's nothing."

"Then why can't you afford to buy her a new car?"

He was angry. Bloody furious, in fact. He stood up quickly.

"Who told you that?" he almost shouted at me.

"You did," I said.

"No, I bloody didn't," he said, thrusting his face towards mine and bunching his fists.

"Yes, you did. I overheard you talking to my mother."

I thought for a moment he was going to hit me.

"How dare you listen in to a private conversation."

I thought of saying that I couldn't have helped it, so loud had been their voices, but that wasn't completely accurate. I could have chosen not to stay sitting in the kitchen, listening.

"So why can't you afford a new car?" I asked him bluntly.

"That's none of your business," he replied sharply.

"I think you'll find it is," I said. "Anything to do with my mother is my business."

"No, it bloody isn't!" He now, in turn, stormed out of the kitchen, leaving me alone.

And I thought I was meant to be the angry one.

I could hear my mother and stepfather arguing upstairs, so I casually walked into their office off the hall.

My stepfather had said that they would have been able to afford a new car if it hadn't been for the "ongoing fallout" from my mother's "disastrous little scheme." What sort of scheme? And why was the fallout ongoing?

I looked down at the desk. There were two stacks of papers on each side of a standard keyboard and a computer monitor that had a moving screensaver message "Kauri House Stables" that ran across it, over and over.

I tried to make a mental picture of the desk so that I could ensure that I left it as I found it. I suppose I had made the decision to find out what the hell was going on as soon as I had walked into the office, but that didn't mean I wanted my mother to know I knew.

The stacks of papers had some order to them.

The one on the far left contained bills and receipts having to do with the house: electricity, council tax, etc. All paid by bank direct debit. I scanned through them, but there was nothing out of the ordinary, although I was amazed to see how expensive it was to heat this grand old house with its ill-fitting windows. Of course, I'd never had to pay a heating bill in my life, and I hadn't been concerned by the cost of leaving a window wide open for ventilation, not even if the outside temperature was below freezing. Perhaps the army should start installing meters in every soldier's room and charging them for the energy used. That would teach the soldiers to keep the heat in.

The next stack was bills and receipts for the stables: power, heat, feed, maintenance, together with the salary and tax papers for the stable staff. There were also some training-fee accounts, one or two with checks still attached and waiting to be banked. Nothing appeared out of place, certainly nothing to indicate the existence of any "scheme."

The third pile was simply magazines and other publications, including the blue-printed booklets of the racing calendar.

Nothing unusual there.

But it was in the fourth pile that I found the smoking gun. In fact, there were two smoking guns that, together, gave the story.

The first was in a pile of bank statements. Clearly, my mother had two separate accounts, one for her training business and one for private use. The statements showed that amongst other things, my mother was withdrawing two thousand pounds in cash every week from her private account. This, in itself, would not have been suspicious; many people in racing dealt in cash, especially if they like to gamble in ready money. But it was a second piece of paper that completed the story. It was a simple handwritten note in capital letters scribbled on a sheet torn from a wire-bound notebook. I found it folded inside a plain white envelope addressed to my mother. The message on it was bold and very much to the point.

> THE PAYMENT WAS LATE. IF IT IS LATE ONE MORE TIME, THEN IT WILL INCREASE TO THREE THOUSAND. IF YOU FAIL TO PAY, A CERTAIN PACKAGE WILL BE DELIVERED TO THE AUTHORITIES.

Plain and simple, it was a blackmail note.

The "ongoing fallout" my stepfather had spoken about was having to pay two thousand pounds a week to a blackmailer. That worked out to more than a hundred thousand pounds a year out of their post-tax income. No wonder they couldn't afford a new BMW.

"What the bloody hell do you think you're doing?"

I jumped.

My mother was standing in the office doorway. I hadn't heard her come downstairs. My mind must have been so engaged by what I'd been reading that I hadn't registered that the shouting match above my head had ceased. And there was no way to hide the fact that I was holding the blackmail note.

I looked at her. She looked down at my hand and the paper it held.

"Oh my God!" Her voice was little more than a whisper, and her legs began to buckle.

I stepped quickly towards her, but she went down so fast that I wouldn't have been able to catch her if we had been standing right next to each other.

Fortunately, she went vertically down on her collapsing legs rather than falling straight forward or back, her head making a relatively soft landing on the carpeted floor. But she was still out cold in a dead faint.

I decided to leave her where she had fallen, although I did straighten out her legs a bit. I would have been unable to lift her anyway. As it was, I had to struggle to get down to my knees to place a small pillow under her head.

She started to come around, opening her eyes with a confused expression.

Then she remembered.

"It's all right," I said, trying to give her some comfort.

For the first time that I could remember, my mother looked frightened. In fact, she looked scared out of her wits, with wide staring eyes, and I wasn't sure if the wetness on her brow was the result of fear or of the fainting.

"Stay there," I said to her. "I'll get you something to drink."

I went out into the kitchen to fetch a glass of water. As I did so, I carefully folded the blackmail note back into its envelope and placed it in my pocket along with her private-account bank statement. When I went back, I found my stepfather kneeling down beside his wife, cradling her head in his hands.

"What did you do to her?" he shouted at me in accusation.

"Nothing," I said calmly. "She just fainted."

"Why?" he asked, concerned.

I thought about saying something flippant about lack of blood to the brain but decided against it.

"Derek, he knows," my mother said.

"Knows what?" he demanded, sounding alarmed.

"Everything," she said.

"He can't!"

"I don't know everything," I said to him. "But I do know you're being blackmailed."

It was brandy, not water, that was needed to revive them both, and I had some too.

We were sitting in the drawing room, in deep chintz-covered armchairs with high sides. My mother's face was as pale as the cream-painted walls behind her, and her hands shook as she tried to drink from her glass without it chattering against her teeth.

Derek, my stepfather, sat tight-lipped on the edge of his chair, knocking back Rémy Martin VSOP like it was going out of fashion.

"So tell me," I said for the umpteenth time.

Again there was no reply from either of them.

"If you won't tell me," I said, "then I will have no choice but to report a case of blackmail to the police."

I thought for a moment that my mother was going to faint again.

"No." She did little more than mouth the word. "Please, no."

"Then tell me why not," I said. My voice seemed loud and strong compared to my mother's.

I remembered back to what my platoon color sergeant had said at Sandhurst: "Command needs to be expressed in the correct tone. Half the struggle is won if your men believe you know what you're doing, even if you don't, and a strong, decisive tone will give them that belief."

I was now "in command" of the present situation, whether my mother or stepfather believed it or not.

"Because your mother would go to prison," Derek said slowly.

The brandy must be going to his head, I thought.

"Don't be ridiculous," I said.

"I'm not," he said. "She would. And me too probably, as an accessory."

"An accessory to what?" I said. "Have you

murdered someone?"

"No." He almost smiled. "Not quite that bad."

"Then what is it?"

"Tax," he said. "Evading tax."

I looked at my mother.

The shaking had spread from her hands to much of her body, and she was crying openly as I had never seen her before. She certainly didn't look like the woman that the entire village was proud of. And she was a shadow of the person who must have collected the National Woman of the Year Award on the television just a month before. She suddenly looked much older than her sixty-one years.

"So what are we going to do about it?" I said in my voice-of-command.

"What do you mean?" Derek asked.

"Well, you can't go on paying two thousand pounds a week, now, can you?"

He looked up at me in surprise.

"I saw the bank statements," I said.

He sighed. "It's not just the money. We might cope if it was just the money."

"What else?" I asked him.

His shoulders slumped. "The horses."

"What about the horses?"

"No," my mother said, but it was barely a whisper.

"What about the horses?" I asked again forcefully.

He said nothing.

"Have the horses had to lose to order?" I asked into the silence.

He gulped and looked down, but his head nodded.

"Is that what happened to Pharmacist?" I asked.

He nodded again. My mother meanwhile now had her eyes firmly closed as if no one could see her if she couldn't see them. The shaking had abated, but she rocked gently back and forth in the chair.

"How do you get the orders?" I asked Derek.

"On the telephone," he said.

There were so many questions: how, what, when and, in particular, who?

My mother and stepfather knew the answers to most of them, but sadly, not the last. Of that they were absolutely certain.

I refilled their brandy glasses and started the inquisition.

"How did you get into this mess?" I asked.

Neither of them said anything. My mother had shrunk down into her chair as if trying to make herself even more invisible, while Derek just drank heavily from his glass, hiding behind the cut crystal.

"Look," I said. "If you want me to help you, then you will have to tell me what's been going on."

There was a long pause.

"I don't want your help," my mother said quietly. "I want you to go away and leave us alone."

"But I'm sure we can sort out the problem," I said, in a more comforting manner.

"I can sort it out myself," she said.

"How?" I asked.

There was another long pause.

"I've decided to retire," she said.

My stepfather and I sat there looking at her.

"But you can't retire," he said.

"Why not?" she asked with more determination. She almost sounded like her old self.

"Then how would we pay?" he said in exasperation. I thought that he was now about to cry.

My mother shrank back into her chair.

"The only solution is to find out who is doing this and stop them," I said. "And for that I need you to answer my questions."

"No police," my mother said.

It was my turn to pause.

"But we might need the police to find the blackmailer."

"No," she almost shouted. "No police."

"So tell me about this tax business," I said, trying to make light of it.

"No," she shouted. "No one must know."

She was desperate.

"I can't help you if I don't know," I said with a degree of frustration.

"I don't want your help," my mother said again.

"Josephine, my dear," Derek said. "We do need help from someone."

Another long pause.

"I don't want to go to prison." She was crying again.

I suddenly felt sorry for her.

It wasn't an emotion with which I was very familiar. I had, in fact, spent most of my life wanting to get even with her, getting back for hurts done to me, whether real or imagined, resenting her lack of motherly love and comfort. Perhaps I was now older and more mature. Blood, they say, is always thicker than water. They must be right.

I went over to her chair and sat on the arm, stroking her shoulder and speaking kindly to her for almost the first time in my life.

"Mum," I said. "They won't send you to prison."

"Yes, they will," she said.

"How do you know?" I asked.

"He says so."

"The blackmailer?"

"Yes."

"Well, I wouldn't take his word for it," I said.

"But . . ." she trailed off.

"Why don't you allow me to give you a second opinion?" I said to her calmly.

"Because you'll tell the police."

"No, I won't," I said. But not doing so might make me an accessory as well.

"Do you promise?" she asked.

What could I say? "Of course I promise."

I hoped so much that it was a promise I would be able to keep.

Gradually, with plenty of cajoling and the rest of the bottle of Rémy Martin, I managed to piece together most of the sorry story. And it wasn't good. My mother might indeed go to prison if the police found out. She would almost certainly be convicted of tax evasion. And she would undoubtedly lose her reputation, her home and her business, even if she did manage to retain her liberty.

My mother's "disastrous little scheme" had, it seemed, been the brainchild of a dodgy young accountant she had met at a party about five years previously. He had convinced her that she should register her training business offshore, in particular, in Gibraltar. Then she would enjoy the tax-free status that such a registration would bring.

Value Added Tax, or VAT as it was known, was a tax levied on goods and services in the UK that was collected by the seller of the goods or the provider of the services and then paid over to the government, similar to sales tax except that it applied to services as well as sales, services such as training racehorses. Somehow the dodgy young accountant had managed to assure my mother that even though she could go on adding the VAT amount to the owners' accounts, she was no longer under any obligation to pass on the money to the tax man.

Now, racehorse training fees are not cheap, about the same as sending a teenage child to boarding school, and my mother had seventy-two stables that were always filled to overflowing. She was in demand, and those in demand could charge premium prices. The VAT, somewhere between fifteen and twenty percent of the training fees, must have run into several hundred thousand pounds a year.

"But didn't you think it was a bit suspicious?" I asked her in disbelief.

"Of course not," she said. "Roderick told me it was all aboveboard and legal. He even showed me documents that proved it was all right."

Roderick, it transpired, had been the young accountant.

"Do you still have these documents?"

"No. Roderick kept them."

I bet he did.

"And Roderick said that the owners wouldn't be out of pocket because all racehorse owners can claim back the VAT from the government."

So it was the government that she was stealing from. She wasn't paying the tax as she should, yet at the same time, the owners were claiming it back. What a mess.

"But didn't you think it was too good to be true?" I asked.

"Not really," she said. "Roderick said that everyone would soon be doing it and I would lose out if I didn't get started quickly."

Roderick sounded like quite a smooth operator.

"Which firm does Roderick work for?" I asked.

"He didn't work for a firm, he was self-employed," my mother said. "He'd only recently qualified at university and hadn't joined a firm. We were lucky to find someone who was so cheap."

I could hardly believe my ears.

"What happened to John Milton?" I asked her. John Milton had been my mother's accountant for as long as I could remember.

"He retired," she said. "And I didn't like the young woman who took over at his office. Far too brusque. That's why I was so pleased to have met Roderick."

I could imagine that any accountant who didn't do exactly as my mother demanded would be thought of by her as brusque, at the very least.

"And what is Roderick's surname?"

"His name was Ward," she said.

"Was?"

"He's dead," my mother said with a sigh. "He was in a car accident. About six months ago."

"Are you sure?" I asked.

"What do you mean am I sure?"

"Are you sure that he's dead and hasn't just run away?" I said. "Are you certain he's not the blackmailer?"

"Thomas," she said, "don't be ridiculous. The car crash was reported in the local paper. Of course I'm sure he's dead."

I felt like asking her if she had actually

seen Roderick Ward's lifeless body. In Afghanistan there were no confirmed Taliban "kills" without the corpse, or at least a human head, to prove it.

"So how long did the little scheme of yours run? When did you stop paying the tax man?"

"Nearly four years ago," my mother said in a whimper.

"And when did you start paying again?"

"What do you mean?" she asked.

"Are you paying the VAT to the tax man now?" I asked, dreading the answer.

"No, of course not," she said. "How could I start paying again without them asking questions?"

How, I wondered, had she stopped paying without them asking? Surely it could be only a matter of time before she was investigated. Four years of nonpayment of VAT must add up to nearly a million pounds in unpaid tax. She should indeed be worried about going to prison.

"Who is doing your accounts now?" I asked. "Since this Roderick Ward was killed."

"No one," she said. "I was frightened of getting anyone."

With good reason, I thought.

"Can't you pay the tax now?" I said. "If

you pay everything you owe and explain that you were misled by your accountant, I'm sure that it would prevent you from being sent to prison."

My mother began to cry again.

"We haven't got the money to pay the tax man," Derek said gloomily.

"But what happened to all of the extra you collected?" I asked.

"It's all gone," he said.

"It can't have all gone," I said. "It must be close to a million pounds."

"More," he said.

"So where did it all go?"

"We spent a lot of it," he said. "In the beginning, mostly on holidays. And Roderick had some of it, of course."

Of course.

"And the rest?"

"Some has gone to the blackmailer." He sounded tired and resigned. "I don't honestly know where it went. We've only got about fifty thousand left in the bank."

That was a start.

"So how much are the house and stables worth?" I asked.

My mother looked horrified.

"Mother, dear," I said, trying to be kind but firm. "If I'm going to keep you out of prison, then we have to find a way to pay the tax."

"But you promised me you wouldn't tell the police," she whined.

"I won't," I replied. "But if you really think the tax man won't find out eventually, then you're wrong. The tax office is bound to do a check sometime. And it will be much better for you if we go and tell them before they uncover it for themselves."

"Oh God."

I said nothing, allowing the awful truth to sink in. She must have known, as I did, that the tax inspectors at Her Majesty's Revenue and Customs had little compassion for those they discovered were defrauding the system. The only way to win any friends amongst them was to make a clean breast of things and pay back the money, and before they demanded it.

"Not if I retire," she said suddenly. "The tax man won't ever know if I simply retire."

"But Josephine," my stepfather said, "we've already discussed that. How would we pay *him* if you retired?"

I, meanwhile, wasn't so sure that her retirement wouldn't in fact be the best course of action. At least then she wouldn't be perpetuating the fraud, as she was now, and selling the property might raise the necessary sum. But I certainly didn't share my mother's confidence that her retirement would guarantee that the tax man wouldn't find out. It might even attract the very attention she was trying to avoid.

Overall, it was quite a mess, and I couldn't readily see a way out of it.

My mother and stepfather went off to bed at nine o'clock, tired and emotional from too much brandy and with the awful realization that their secret was out, and their way of life was in for radical change — and probably for the worse.

I too went up to my bedroom, but I didn't go to sleep.

I carefully eased my stump out of the prosthetic leg. It was not a very easy task, as I had been overdoing the walking and my leg was sore, the flesh below my knee swollen by excess fluid. If I wasn't more careful I wouldn't be able to get the damn thing back on again in the morning.

I raised the stump by placing it on a pillow to allow gravity to assist in bringing down the fluid buildup, and then I lay back to think.

There was little doubt that my mother and stepfather were up to their necks in real trouble, and they were sinking deeper into the mire with every day that passed.

The solution for them was simple, at least in theory: raise the money, pay it to the tax man, submit a retrospective tax return, report the blackmail to the police, and then pray for forgiveness.

The blackmailer would no longer have a hold over them, and maybe the police might even find him and recover some of their money, but I wouldn't bet my shirt on it.

So the first thing to be done was to raise more than a million pounds to hand over to the Revenue.

It was easier said than done. Perhaps I could rob a bank.

Reluctantly, my mother and stepfather had agreed that the house and stables, even in the recent depressed property market, could fetch about two and a half million pounds, if they were lucky. But there was a catch. The house was heavily mortgaged, and the stables had been used as collateral for a bank loan to the training business.

I thought back to the brief conversation I'd had with my stepfather after my mother had gone upstairs.

"So how much free capital is there altogether?" I'd asked him.

"About five hundred thousand."

I was surprised that it was so little. "But surely the training business has been earn-ing good money for years."

"It's not as lucrative as you might think, and your mother has always used any profits to build more stables."

"So why is there so little free capital value in the property?"

"Roderick advised us to increase our borrowing," he'd said. "He believed that capital tied up in property wasn't doing anything useful. He told us that as it was, our capital wasn't working properly for us."

"So what did Roderick want you to do with it instead?"

"Buy into an investment fund he was very keen on."

I again hadn't really wanted to believe my ears.

"And did you?" I'd asked him.

"Oh yes," he'd said. "We took out another mortgage and invested it in the fund."

"So that money is still safe?" I had asked with renewed hope.

"Unfortunately, that particular investment fund didn't do too well in the recession."

Why was I not surprised?

"How not too well?" I'd asked him.

"Not well at all, I'm afraid," he said. "In fact, the fund went into bankruptcy last year."

"But surely you were covered by some

kind of government bailout protection insurance?"

"Sadly not," he'd said. "It was some sort of offshore fund."

"A hedge fund?"

"Yes, that's it. I knew it sounded like something to do with gardens."

I simply couldn't believe it. I'd been stunned by his naïveté. And it was of no comfort to know that hedge funds had been so named because they had initially been designed to "hedge" against fluctuations in overall stock prices. The original intention of reducing risks had transformed, over time, into high-risk strategies, capable of returning huge profits when things went well but also huge losses if they didn't. Recent unexpected declines in the world's equity markets, coupled with banks suddenly calling in their loans, had left offshore tax shelters awash with hedge-fund managers in search of new jobs.

"But didn't you take any advice? From an independent financial adviser or something?"

"Roderick said it wasn't necessary."

Roderick would. Mr. Roderick Ward had obviously spotted my complacent mother and her careless husband coming from a long way off.

"But didn't you ever think that Roderick might have been wrong?"

"No," he'd said, almost surprised by the question. "Roderick showed us a brochure about how well the fund had done. It was all very exciting."

"And is there any money left?"

"I had a letter that said they were trying to recover some of the funds and they would let investors know if they succeeded."

I took that to mean no, there was nothing left.

"How much did you invest in this hedge fund?" I'd asked him, dreading his reply.

"There was a minimum amount we had to invest to be able to join." He had sounded almost proud of the fact that they had been allowed into the club. Like being pleased to have won tickets for the maiden voyage of the *Titanic.*

I had stood silently in front of him, blocking his route away, waiting for the answer. He hadn't wanted to tell me, but he could see that I wasn't going to move until he did.

"It was a million U.S. dollars."

More than six hundred thousand pounds at the prevailing rate. I suppose it could have been worse, but not much. At least there was some capital left in the real estate, although not enough.

"What about other investments?"

"I've got a few ISAs," he'd said.

Ironically, an ISA, an individual savings account, was designed for tax-free saving, but there was a limit on investment, and each ISA could amount to only a few thousand pounds per year. They would help, but alone they were not the solution.

I wondered if the training business itself had any value. It would have if my mother was still the trainer, but I doubted that anyone buying the stables would pay much for the business. I had spent my childhood, at my mother's knee, being amazed how contrary racehorse owners could be.

Some of them behaved just like the owners of football clubs, firing the team manager because their team of no-hopers wasn't winning, when the solution would have been to buy better, and more expensive, players in the first place. A cheap, slow horse is just like a cheap two-left-footed footballer — neither will be any good, however well they're trained.

There is no telling if the owners would stay or take their horses elsewhere. The latter would be the more likely, unless the person who took over the training was of the same standing as Josephine Kauri, and who could that be who didn't already have a stable full of their own charges?

I had to assume that the business had no intrinsic value other than the real estate in which it operated, plus a bit extra for the tack and the rest of the stable kit.

I lay on my bed and did some mental adding up: The house and stables might raise half a million, the business might just fetch fifty thousand, and there was another fifty thousand in the bank. Add the ISAs and a few pieces of antique furniture and we were probably still short by more than four hundred thousand.

And my mother and Derek had to live somewhere. Where would they go and what could they earn if Kauri House Stables was sold? My mother was hardly going to find work as a cleaner, especially in Lambourn. She would have rather gone to prison.

But going to prison wasn't an either/or solution anyway. If she was sent down she would still have to pay the tax, and the penalties.

Over the years I had saved regularly from my army pay and had accumulated quite a reasonable nest egg that I had planned to use sometime as a down payment on a house. And I had invested it in a far more secure manner than my parent, so I could be pretty sure of still having about sixty thousand pounds to my name.

I wondered if the Revenue would take installments on the never-never.

The only other solution I came up with was to approach the circumstances as if I had been in command of my platoon in the middle of Afghanistan planning a combat estimate for an operation against the Taliban.

PROBLEM: enemy in control of objective (tax papers and money)

MISSION: neutralize enemy and retake objective

SITUATION: enemy forces — number, identity and location all unknown
friendly forces — self only, no reinforcements available

WEAPONS: as required and/or as available

EXECUTION: Initially find and interrogate Roderick Ward or, if in fact really dead, his known associates. Follow up on blackmail notes and telephone messages to determine source.

TACTICS: absolute stealth, no local authorities to be alerted, enemy to be kept unaware of operation until final strike

TIMINGS: task to be completed asap, and

before exposure by local authorities — their timescale unknown

H HOUR: operation start time: **right now**

6

All I could see of him were his eyes, his cold, black eyes that stared at me from beneath his turban. He showed no emotion but simply raised a rusty Kalashnikov to his shoulder. I fired at him, but he continued to lift the gun. I fired at him again, over and over, but without any visible effects. I was desperate. I emptied my complete magazine into him, but still he swung the barrel of the AK-47 around towards me, lining up the sights with my head. A smile showed in his eyes, and I began to scream.

I woke with a start, my heart pumping madly and with sweat all over my body.

"Thomas! Thomas!" someone was shouting, and there was banging on my bedroom door.

"Yes," I called back into the darkness. "I'm fine."

"You were screaming." It was my mother. She was outside my room on the landing.

"I'm sorry," I said. "It was just a bad dream."

"Good night, then," she called suddenly, and I could hear her footfalls as she moved away.

"Good night," I called back, too quietly and too late.

I suppose it was too much to expect my mother to change the habits of a lifetime, but it would have been nice if she had asked me how I was, or if I needed anything, or at least if she could come into my room to cool my sweating brow, or anything.

I laid my head back onto the pillow.

I could still remember the dream so clearly. In the last couple of months, I had started to have them fairly regularly about the war. They were always a jumble of memories of real incidents coupled with the imagination of my subconscious brain, unalike insofar as they were of different events but all with a common thread — they all ended with me in panic and utter terror. I was always more terrified by the dreams than I remember ever having been in reality.

Except, of course, at the roadside after the IED.

I could remember all too vividly the terrible fear and the awful dread of dying I had experienced as Sergeant O'Leary and I had waited for the medevac helicopter. If I closed my eyes and concentrated I could, even now, see the faces of my platoon as we had passed those ten or fifteen minutes — minutes that had felt like endless hours. I could still remember the look of shock in the face of the platoon's newest arrival, a young eighteen-year-old replacement for a previously wounded comrade. It had been his first sight of real war, and the horror it can do to the frail human body. And I could also recall the mixture of anxiety and relief in the faces of those with more experience: their anxiety for me, and their almost overwhelming relief that it wasn't them lying there with no right foot, their lifeblood draining away into the sand.

I reached over and turned on the light. My bedside clock showed me that it was two-thirty in the morning.

I must have been making quite a lot of noise for it to have woken my mother from the other end of the house. That was assuming that she had actually been sleeping and not lying awake, contemplating her own troubles.

I sat up on the side of the bed. I needed to go to the bathroom for a pee, but it was not as simple as it sounded. The bathroom was three doors away, and that was too far to heel-and-toe or to hop.

I now wished I'd accepted the hospital's offer of crutches.

Instead, I went through the whole wretched rigmarole of attaching my false foot and ankle just in order to go to the loo. How I longed for the days of springing out of bed ready and able to complete a five-mile run before breakfast, or to fight off a Taliban early-morning attack.

Once or twice I had done just that, half asleep and forgetting that I was sans foot. But I had soon been reminded when I'd crashed to the floor. On one occasion I'd done myself a real mischief, opening up the surgical wound on my stump as well as splitting the back of my head on a hospital bedside locker. My surgeon had not been amused.

I made it without upset to the bathroom along the landing and gratefully relieved myself. I caught a glimpse of my face in the shaving mirror as I clumsily turned around in the enclosed space.

"What do you want from life?" I asked my image.

"I don't know," it answered.

What I really wanted I knew, in my heart, I couldn't have. Flying an airplane with tin legs, even a Spitfire, was a totally different ball game to commanding an infantry platoon. The very word *infantry* implied a foot soldier. I suppose I could ask for a transfer to a tank regiment, but even then, the "tankies" became foot soldiers if and when their carriage lost a track. I could hardly say, "Sorry, chaps, you'll have to carry on fighting without me," as I sat there with my false leg waiting for a lift, now, could I?

So what were the reasons I had so enjoyed being an infantry platoon commander? And could I find the same things elsewhere?

I went back to my room and back to bed, leaving my prosthesis standing alone by the bedroom wall as if on sentry duty.

But sleep didn't come easily.

For the first time since my injury I had faced the true reality of my future, and I didn't like it.

Why me? I asked, yet again. Why had it been me who'd been injured?

Yes, I was angry with the Taliban, and also with life in general and the destiny it had dealt me, but almost more so, I was frustrated and fed up with myself.

Why had I allowed this to happen? Why? Why?

And what could I do now?

Why me?

I lay awake for a long while, trying to find solutions to the unanswerable puzzles of my mind.

In the morning, I set to the more immediate task at hand: identifying the blackmailer, recovering the papers and my mother's money, and making things good with the tax man. It sounded deceptively simple. But where did I start?

With Roderick Ward, the con man accountant. He had been the architect of this misery, so discovering his whereabouts, alive or dead, must be the first goal. Where had he come from? Was he actually qualified, or was that a lie too? Were there co-conspirators, or did he work alone? There were so many questions. Now it was time for answers.

I called Isabella Warren from the phone in the drawing room.

"Oh, hello," she said. "We're still speaking, then?"

"Why shouldn't we be?" I asked.

"No reason," she said. "Just thought you were disappointed."

I had been, but if I didn't speak to people who disappointed me, then I'd hardly speak to anyone.

"What are you up to today?" I asked her.

"Nothing," she said, "as usual."

Did I detect a touch of irritation?

"Do you fancy helping me with something?"

"No bonus payments involved?"

"No," I said. "I promise. And none will even be requested."

"I don't mind you asking," she said with a laugh. "As long as you don't mind being refused."

I wouldn't ask, though, I thought, because I *did* mind being refused.

"Can you pick me up at ten?" I asked.

"I thought you said you'd never let me drive you again." She was still laughing.

"I'll chance it," I said. "I need to go into Newbury, and the parking is dreadful."

"Can't you park anywhere," she said, "with that leg?"

"I haven't applied for a disabled permit," I said. "And I don't intend being qualified to."

"What do you mean?"

"I want to be able to walk as well as the next man," I said. "I don't want to be identified as 'disabled.' "

"But parking is so much easier with a blue badge. You can park almost anywhere."

"No matter," I said. "I don't have one

today, and I need a driver. Are you on?"

"Definitely," she said. "I'll be there at ten."

I went out into the kitchen to find my mother coming in from the stables.

"Good morning," I said to her, still employing my friendlier tone from the previous evening.

"What's good about it?" she said.

"We're both alive," I said.

She gave me a look that made me wonder if she had thought about not being alive this morning. Was suicide really on her mind?

"We will sort out this problem," I said in reassurance. "You've done the hard bit by admitting it to me."

"I didn't have any choice, did I?" she said angrily. "You snooped through my office."

"Please don't be annoyed with me," I said in my most calming way. "I'm here to help you."

Her shoulders drooped and she slumped onto a chair at the kitchen table.

"I'm tired," she said. "I don't feel I can carry on."

"What, with the training?"

"With life," she said.

"Now, don't be ridiculous."

"I'm not," she said. "I've spent most of the night thinking about it. If I died it would solve all the problems."

"That's crazy," I said. "What would Derek do, for a start?"

She placed her arms on the table and rested her head on them. "It would clear all the problems for him."

"No, it wouldn't," I said with certainty. "It would just create more. The training business would still have to pay the tax it owes. The house and stables would then definitely have to be sold. You dying would leave Derek homeless and alone as well as broke. Is that what you want?"

She looked up at me. "I don't know what I want."

How strange, I thought. I had said the same thing to myself in the night. Neither of us was happy with the futures we saw staring us in the face.

"Don't you want to go on training?" I asked.

She didn't reply but placed her head back down on her arms.

"Assuming the tax problems were solved and the blackmailer was stopped, would you still want to go on training?"

"I suppose so," she said without looking up. "It's all I know."

"And you are so good at it," I said, trying my best to raise her spirits. "But tell me, how did you stop Pharmacist winning on

Saturday?"

She sat back in the chair and almost smiled. "I gave him a tummy ache."

"But how?" I asked.

"I fed him some rotten food."

"Moldy oats?" I asked.

"No," she said. "Green sprouting potatoes."

"Green potatoes! How on earth did you think of green potatoes?"

"It had worked before," she said. "When *he* called the first time and said that Scientific had to lose, I was at my wit's end of what to do. If I'd over-galloped him everyone in the stable would know." She gulped. "I had to do something. I was desperate. But what could I give him? I had some old potatoes that had gone green, and they were moldy and sprouting. I remembered one of my dogs being ill after eating a green-skinned potato, so I peeled them all and then liquidized the peel. I simply poured it down Scientific's throat and hoped it would make him ill."

"How on earth did you get him to swallow it? It must be so bitter."

"I simply tied his head up high using the hay-net hook and used a tube to pour it down into his stomach."

"And it worked?" I asked.

"Seemed to, although the poor old boy was really very ill afterwards. Horses can't vomit, so the stuff had to go right through him. I was really scared that he'd die. So I reduced the amount the next time."

"And it still worked?"

"Yes. But I was so frightened about Pharmacist that I used more again that time. I was worried the potatoes weren't green and rotten enough. I'd had to buy some more."

"Do you have any of them left?" I asked her.

"They're in the boiler room, with the light on," she said. "I read somewhere that high temperatures and bright light make potatoes go green quicker."

"And how many times have you done this altogether?" I asked her.

"Only six times," she said, almost apologetically. "But Perfidio won even though I'd given him the potato peel. It didn't seem to affect him one bit."

"Did you give it to Oregon at Newbury last week?" Oregon had been one of the horses that Gordon Rambler had written about in the *Racing Post.*

She nodded.

I walked through and opened the boiler room by the back door. The light was indeed on, and there were six neat rows of potatoes sitting on top of the boiler, all of them turning nicely green, some with sprouting eyes.

Would the British Horseracing Authority ever have thought of dope-testing for liquidized green, sprouting, rotten potato peel?

I somehow doubted it.

Isabella took me first to the Newbury Public Library. I wanted to look at past editions of the local newspapers to see what they had to say about the supposed death of one Roderick Ward.

My mother was right. The story of his car crash had been prominently covered on page three of the *Newbury Weekly News* for Thursday, July 16.

Another Fatal Accident at Local Black Spot

Police are investigating after yet another death at one of the most dangerous spots on Oxfordshire's roads. Roderick Ward, 33, of Oxford, was discovered dead in his car around eight a.m. on Monday morning. It is assumed by police that Mr. Ward's dark blue Renault Mégane left the road in the early hours of Monday after failing to negotiate the S-bends on the A415 near Standlake. The vehicle is thought to have collided with a bridge wall before toppling into the River Windrush near where it joins the Thames at Newbridge. Mr. Ward's car was found almost totally immersed in the water, and he is thought to have died of drowning rather than as a result of any trauma caused by the accident. An inquest was opened and adjourned on Tuesday at Oxford Coroner's Court.

The piece discussed at length the relative merits of placing a safety barrier and/or altering the speed limits at that point in the road. It then went on to report on two other fatal accidents in the same week elsewhere within the newspaper's region. I searched the following Thursday's paper for any follow-up report on Roderick Ward but with no success.

I used the library's computerized index to check for any other references to Roderick Ward in the *Newbury Weekly News.* There was nothing else about his accident or death, but there was a brief mention from three months before it. The paper reported that a Mr. Roderick Ward of Oxford had pleaded guilty in Newbury Magistrates' Court to a charge of causing criminal damage to a private home in Hungerford. It stated that he had been observed by a police officer throwing a brick through a window of a house in Willow Close. He was bound over to keep the peace by the magistrates and warned as to his future conduct. In addition, he was ordered to pay two hundred and fifty pounds to the home owner in compensation for the broken glass and for the distress caused.

Unfortunately, the report gave no further details, for example, the name of the house owner or the identity of the policeman who witnessed the event.

I searched through the index again, but there was no report of any inquest into Roderick Ward's untimely death. For that, I suspected, I would have to go to Oxford, to the archive of the *Oxford Mail* or *The Oxford Times.*

Isabella had been waiting patiently, exploring the fiction shelves of the library as I had been scanning the newspapers using the microfiche machines.

"Finished?" she asked, as I reappeared from the darkened room where the machines were kept.

"Yes," I said. "For the time being."

"Where to now?" she said, as we climbed back into her Golf.

"Oxford," I said. I thought for a moment. "Or Hungerford."

"Which?"

"Hungerford. I think I can probably find what I want from Oxford on the Internet." If I could get onto it, I thought. My mother had to have broadband. Surely it was needed for her to do the race entries.

"So where in Hungerford?"

"Willow Close."

"Where's that?"

"I've no idea," I said. "But it's in Hungerford somewhere."

Isabella looked at me quizzically but resisted the temptation to actually ask why I wanted to go to Willow Close in Hungerford. Instead, she started the car and turned out of the library parking lot.

In truth, I could have easily parked my Jaguar at the library, and I was pretty sure from its name that parking in Willow Close wouldn't be a problem, either. I probably hadn't needed to ask Isabella to drive me, but it felt more like an adventure with someone else to share it.

Willow Close, when we finally found it, was deep in a housing estate off the Salisbury Road in the southwestern corner of the town. There were twenty or so houses in the close, all little detached boxes with neat open-plan front gardens, each one indistinguishable from those recently built in Lambourn. I feared for the individual character of villages and towns with so many identical little homes springing up all over the countryside.

"Which number?" Isabella said.

"I've no idea," I said again.

"What are we looking for?" she asked patiently.

"I've no idea of that either."

"Useful." She was smiling. "Then you start at one end and I'll start at the other."

"Doing what?" I asked.

"Asking if anyone has any idea why we're here."

"Someone threw a brick through the window of one of these houses, and I would like to know why."

"Any particular brick?" she asked sarcastically.

"OK, OK," I said. "I know it sounds odd, but that's why we're here. I'd like to talk to the person whose window was smashed."

"Why?" she asked, unable to contain her curiosity any longer. "What is this all about?"

It was a good question. Coming to Hungerford had probably been a wild-goose chase anyway. I didn't particularly want to tell Isabella about Roderick Ward, mostly because I had absolutely no intention of explaining anything to her about my mother's tax situation.

"The young man who's been accused of throwing the brick is a soldier in my platoon," I lied. "It's an officer's job to look after his troops, and I promised him I would investigate. That's all."

She seemed satisfied, if a little uninterested. "And do you have a name for the person whose window was broken?"

"No."

"And no address," she said.

"No," I agreed, "but it was reported in the local newspaper as having happened in Willow Close, Hungerford."

"Right, then," she said decisively. "Let's go and ask someone."

We climbed out of the car.

"Let's start at number sixteen," I said, pointing to one of the houses. "I saw the net curtains in the front room twitch when we arrived. Perhaps they keep an eye on everything that goes on here."

"I'm not buying," an elderly woman shouted through the door of number sixteen. "I never buy from door-to-door salesmen."

"We're not selling," I shouted back through the wood. "We'd just like to ask you some questions."

"I don't want any religion, either," the woman shouted again. "Go away."

"Do you remember someone throwing a brick through one of your neighbors' windows?" I asked her.

"What?" she said.

I repeated the question with more volume.

"That wasn't one of my neighbors," she said with certainty. "That was down the end of the close."

"Which house?" I asked her, still through the closed door.

"Down the end," she repeated.

"I know," I said, "but which house?"

"George Sutton's house."

"Which number?" I asked.

"I don't know numbers," she said. "Now go away."

I noted that there was a Neighborhood Watch sticker on the frosted glass next to the door, and I didn't really want her calling the police.

"Come on, let's go," I said to Isabella. "Thank you," I called loudly through the door at the woman. "Have a nice day."

We went back to the Golf, and I could see the net curtains twitching again. I waved as we climbed back into Isabella's car and she drove away down towards the end of the close and out of the woman's sight.

"Which house do you fancy?" I asked, as we stopped at the end.

"Let's try the one with the car in the drive," Isabella said.

We walked up the driveway past a bright yellow Honda Jazz and rang the doorbell. A smart young woman answered, carrying a baby on her hip.

"Yes?" she said. "Can I help you?"

"Hello," said Isabella, jumping in and taking the lead. "Hello, little one," she said to the child, tickling its chin. "We're trying to find Mr. Sutton."

"Old Man Sutton or his son?" the young woman asked helpfully.

"Either," Isabella said, still fussing over the child.

"Old Man Sutton has gone into an old-folks nursing home," the woman said. "His son comes round sometimes to collect his mail."

"How long has Mr. Sutton been in a nursing home?" I asked.

"Since just before Christmas. He'd been going downhill for quite a while. Such a shame. He seemed a nice old chap."

"Do you know which home he's in?" I

asked her.

"Sorry," she said, shaking her head.

"And which house is his?"

"Number eight," she said, pointing across the road.

"Do you remember an incident when someone threw a brick through his window?" I asked.

"I heard about it, but it happened before we moved in," she said. "We've only been here eight months or so. Since Jimbo here was born." She smiled down at the baby.

"Do you know how I can contact Mr. Sutton's son?" I asked her.

"Hold on," she said. "I've got his telephone number somewhere."

She disappeared into the house but was soon back with a business card but without little Jimbo.

"Here it is," she said. "Fred Sutton." She read out his number, and Isabella wrote it down.

"Thank you," I said. "I'll give him a call."

"He might be at work right now," the woman said. "He works shifts."

"I'll try him anyway," I said. "What does he do?"

She consulted the business card that was still in her hand.

"He's a policeman," she said. "A detective

sergeant."

"So why, all of a sudden, don't you want to call this Fred Sutton?" Isabella demanded. We were again sitting in her car, having driven out of Willow Close and into the center of Hungerford.

"I will. But I'll call him later."

"But I thought you wanted to know about this brick through the window," she said.

"I do." I dearly wanted to know why the brick was thrown, but did I now dare ask?

"Well, call him, then."

I was beginning to be sorry that I had asked Isabella to drive me. How could I explain to her that I didn't want to discuss anything to do with Willow Close with any member of the police, let alone a detective sergeant? If he was any good at his job, his detective antennae would be throbbing wildly as soon as I mentioned anything to do with a Roderick Ward, especially if, as I suspected, DS Fred Sutton had been the policeman who had witnessed young Mr. Ward throwing the brick through his father's window in the first place.

"I can't," I said. "I can't involve the police."

"Why on earth not?" she asked, rather self-righteously.

"I just can't," I said. "I promised my young soldier I wouldn't talk to the police."

"But why not?" she asked again, imploring me to answer.

I looked at her. "I'm really sorry," I said. "But I can't tell you why." Even to my ears, I sounded melodramatic.

"Don't be so bloody ridiculous." She was clearly annoyed. "I think I'd better take you home now."

"Maybe that would be best," I said.

My chances of any future bonuses had obviously diminished somewhat.

I passed the afternoon using my mother's computer in her office and its Internet connection. She probably wouldn't have liked it, but, as she was out when Isabella had dropped me back, I hadn't asked.

I did have my own computer, a laptop. It had been in one of the blue holdalls I'd retrieved from Aldershot, but my mother hadn't moved into the wireless age yet, so it was easier to use her old desktop model with its Internet cable plugged straight into the telephone point in the wall.

I looked up reports of inquests using the online service of the *Oxford Mail*. There were masses of them, hundreds and hundreds, even thousands.

I searched for an inquest with the name Roderick Ward, and there it was, reported briefly by the paper on Wednesday, July 15. But it had been only the opening and adjournment of the inquest immediately after the accident.

It would appear that the full inquest was yet to be heard. However, the short report did contain one interesting piece of information that the *Newbury Weekly News* had omitted. According to the *Oxford Mail* website, Roderick Ward's body had been formally identified at the short hearing by his sister, a Mrs. Stella Beecher, also from Oxford.

Perhaps Mr. Roderick Ward really was dead, after all.

7

At nine o'clock sharp on Tuesday evening my mother received another demand from the blackmailer.

The three residents of Kauri House were suffering through another unhappy dinner around the kitchen table when the telephone rang. Both my mother and stepfather jumped, and then they looked at each other.

"Nine o'clock," my stepfather said. "*He* always calls at exactly nine o'clock."

The phone continued to ring. Neither of them seemed very keen to answer it, so I stood up and started to move over towards it.

"No," my mother screamed, leaping to her feet. "I'll get it."

She pushed past me and grabbed the receiver.

"Hello," she said tentatively into the phone. "Yes, this is Mrs. Kauri."

I was standing right next to her, and I

tried to hear what the person at the other end was saying, but he or she was speaking too softly.

My mother listened for less than a minute.

"Yes. I understand," my mother said finally. She placed the phone back in its cradle. "Scientific at Newbury, on Saturday."

"To lose?" I asked.

She nodded. "In the Game Spirit Steeplechase."

She walked like a zombie back to her chair and sat down heavily.

I picked up the phone and dialed 1471, the code to find the number of the last caller.

"Sorry," said a computerized female voice, "the caller withheld their number."

I hadn't expected anything else, but it had been worth a try. I wondered if the phone company might be able to give me the number, but that, I was sure, would involve explaining why I needed it. I also thought it highly unlikely that the blackmailer had been using his own phone or a number that was traceable back to him.

"What chance would you expect Scientific to have anyway?" I asked.

"Fairly good," she said. "He's really only a novice, and this race is a considerable step up in class, but I think he's ready for it." Her shoulders slumped. "But it's not bloody fair on the horse. If I make him ill again, it may ruin him forever. He'll always associate racing with being ill."

"Would he really remember?" I asked.

"Oh yes," she said. "Lots of my good chasers over the years have been hopeless at home only to run like the wind on a racetrack because they liked it there. One I had years ago, a chestnut called Butterfield, he only ran well at Sandown." She smiled, remembering. "Old boy loved Sandown. I thought it was to do with right-handed tracks, but he wouldn't go at Kempton. It had to be Sandown. He definitely remembered."

I could see a glimpse of why my mother was such a good trainer. She adored her horses, and she spoke of Butterfield as an individual, and with real affection.

"But Scientific is not the odds-on sure thing that Pharmacist was meant to be at Cheltenham last week?"

"No," she said. "There's another very good chaser in the race, Sovereign Owner. He'll probably start favorite, although I really think we could beat him, especially if it rains a bit more before Saturday. And Newark Hall may run in the race as well.

He's one of Ewen's, and he should have a reasonable chance."

"Ewen?" I asked.

"Ewen Yorke," she said. "Trains in the village. Has some really good horses this year. The up-and-coming young opposition."

From her tone, I concluded that Ewen Yorke was more of a threat to her position as top dog in Lambourn than she was happy with.

"So Scientific is far from a dead cert?" I said.

"He should win," she stressed again. "Unless he crossfires."

" 'Crossfires'?" I asked. "What's that?"

"It's when a horse canters and leads with a different leg in front than he does at the rear," she explained.

"OK," I said slowly, none the wiser. "And does Scientific do that?"

"Sometimes. Unusually he tends to canter between his walk and gallop," she said. "And if he crossfires, he can cut into himself, hitting his front leg with his hind hoof. But he hasn't done it recently. Not for ages."

"OK," I said again. "So even supposing that Scientific doesn't crossfire, no one would be vastly surprised if he didn't win."

"No," she agreed. "It would be disappointing but no surprise."

"So," I said, "after that call from our friend just now, all we have to do is ensure he doesn't win on Saturday without making him so ill he gives up on the idea of racing altogether."

She stared at me. "But how?"

"I can think of a number of ways," I said. "How about if he doesn't run in the first place? You could simply not declare him and tell everyone he was lame or something."

"*He* said the horse had to run," she replied gloomily.

Time to move on to plan B.

"Well, how about a bit of overtraining on Thursday or Friday? Give him too much of a gallop so he's worn out on Saturday."

"But everyone would know," she said.

"Would they really?" I thought she was being overly worried.

"Oh yes, they would," she said. "There are always people watching the horses work. Some of them are from the media, but most are spotters for the bookmaking firms. They know every horse in Lambourn by sight, and they would see all too easily if I gave Scientific anything more than a gentle pipe-opener on Thursday or Friday."

Was there a plan C?

"Can't you make his saddle slip or something?" I asked.

"The girths will be tightened by the assistant starter just before the race starts."

"But can't you go down to the start and do it yourself and just leave them loose?" Was I clutching at straws?

"But the jockey would fall off," she said.

"At least that would stop him from winning," I said with a smile.

"But he might be injured." She shook her head. "I can't do that."

Plan D?

"How about if you cut through the reins just enough so that they break during the race? If the jockey can't steer, then he surely can't win."

"Tell that to Fred Winter," she said.

"What?"

"Fred Winter," she repeated. "He won the Grand Steeple-Chase de Paris on Mandarin with no steering, way back in the early sixties. The bit broke, which meant he had no brakes, either. He used his legs, pressing on the sides of the horse to keep it on the figure-eight course. It was an absolutely amazing piece of riding."

"And will this Fred Winter be the jockey on Scientific on Saturday?" I asked.

"No, of course not," she said. "He died years ago."

"Well, in that case, don't you think it's a

good idea?"

"What?"

"To make the reins break." God, this was hard work.

"But . . ."

"But what?" I asked.

"I'd be the laughingstock," she said miserably. "Horses from Kauri House Stables don't go to the races with substandard tack."

"Would you rather be laughed at or arrested for tax evasion?"

It was a cruel thing to say, but it did bring the problems she faced into relative order.

"Thomas is right, dear," my stepfather said, somewhat belatedly entering the conversation.

"So it's agreed, then," I said. "We won't subject Scientific to the green-potato-peel treatment, but we will try and arrange for his reins to break during the race. And we take our chances."

"I suppose so," my mother said reluctantly.

"Right," I said positively. "That's the first decision made."

My mother looked up at me. "And what other decisions do you have in mind?"

"Nothing specific as yet," I said. "But I do have some questions."

She looked back at me with doleful eyes.

Why did I think she knew the questions wouldn't be welcome?

"First," I said, "when is your next Value Added Tax return due?"

"I told you I don't pay VAT," my mother said.

"But the stables must have a VAT registration for the other bills, like the horses' feed, the purchase of tack, and all sorts of other stuff. Don't the race entries attract VAT?"

"Roderick canceled our registration," she said.

If Roderick hadn't already been dead, I'd have wrung his bloody neck.

"How about the other tax returns?" I said. "Your personal one and the training-business return. When are they due?"

"Roderick dealt with all that."

"But who has been doing it since Roderick died?" I asked in desperation.

"No one," she said. "But I did manage to do the PAYE return last month on my own."

At least that was something. PAYE, or Pay-As-You-Earn, was the way most UK workers paid their income tax. The tax amount was deducted by their employer out of their paychecks, and paid directly to the Treasury. The non-arrival of the PAYE money was usually the first indication to the tax man that a company was in deep financial trouble. It would have rung serious alarm bells at the tax office, and representatives of Her Majesty's Revenue and Customs would have been hammering on the kitchen door long before now.

"Where do you keep your tax papers?" I asked.

"Roderick had them."

"But you must have copies of your tax returns," I implored.

"I expect so," she said. "They might be in one of the filing cabinets in the office."

I was amazed that anyone who was so brilliant at the organization and training of seventy-two racehorses, with all the decisions and red tape that must be involved to satisfy the Rules of Racing, could be so completely hopeless when it came to anything financial.

"Don't you have a secretary?" I asked.

"No," she said. "Derek and I do all the paperwork between us."

Or not, I thought, as the case may be.

I was pretty certain that my mother's individual self-assessment tax return, as for every other self-employed person in the United Kingdom, should have been filed with the tax office by midnight on January 31 at the very latest, along with the payment of any income tax due. Unlike in the United States, where the filing date is April 15 and one is able to file for an extension, in the UK January 31 is the deadline, period.

I looked up at the calendar on the wall above her desk. It was already February 9. There were no exceptions to the deadline, so she would have already incurred a penalty for late filing, to say nothing of the interest for late payment.

I'd checked the tax office website on the Internet. It confirmed that she would have notched up an automatic one-hundred-pound late-filing penalty plus interest on the overdue tax. It also said that she had until the end of February before a five percent surcharge of the tax due was added, on top of the interest.

Very soon now, the Revenue was probably going to start asking difficult questions about my mother's accounts. The time left to sort out the mess was unknown, but it had to be short. Maybe it was already too late and the Revenue would be at her door in the morning.

I wondered about my own tax affairs.

As an employee, I paid my tax as I earned through the PAYE system, which meant I didn't need to complete an annual tax return. The army deducted my tax and National Insurance before it paid the remainder of my salary into my bank account. Mostly they took off my board and lodging costs too, but there hadn't been any of those for a while. Even the army couldn't charge me to stay in a National Health Service hospital.

Sometime soon I should be receiving a tax-free lump sum of nearly a hundred thousand pounds from the Armed Forces Compensation Scheme, although how they could put a value on the loss of a lower leg and foot is anyone's guess. The major from the MOD had taken away my completed AFCS form with a promise that it would be dealt with promptly. That had been nearly three weeks ago now, but I had long learned that anything less than six months was "promptly" as far as army finances were concerned.

Perhaps it might help to keep the tax man's handcuffs from my mother's wrists. But would it be enough? And would it arrive in time?

I searched through my mother's filing cabinets, and eventually I found her previous year's tax return filed under *R* for Roderick. Where else?

The tax return was a piece of art. It clearly showed that my mother had only minimal personal income, well below that which would have incurred any tax to be paid. It stated that her monthly income was just two hundred pounds from her business, mere pocket money.

Perhaps the Revenue might not be knocking at her door in the morning after all, even if they could find it.

Possibly designed to confuse them, the return was not in the name of Mrs. Josephine Kauri, and her address was not recorded as Kauri House Stables. It wasn't even in Lambourn but at 26 Banbury Drive, Oxford. However, I did recognize the signature as being that of my mother, in her familiar curly handwriting.

Only the name was unfamiliar. She had signed the form Jane Philips, her real, legal, married name.

In the same filing cabinet, I also found a Kauri House Stables Ltd corporate tax return for the previous year. It was dated May and they were annual so at least we had some breathing space before the next one was due.

I looked through it. Roderick had worked his magic here as well.

How, I wondered, did my mother afford

to pay two thousand pounds a week in blackmail demands if, as according to the tax returns, her personal income was less than two and a half thousand a year, and her business made such a small profit that it paid tax only in three figures, in spite of all the extras paid by the horse owners in nonexistent VAT.

But, of course, I could find no records of the profits made by the company called Kauri House Stables (Gibraltar) Ltd. In fact, there was no reference to any such entity anywhere in the *R* for Roderick drawer of the filing cabinet, or anywhere else, for that matter. However, I did find one interesting sheet of paper nestling amongst the tax returns. It was a letter from an investment fund manager welcoming my mother and stepfather into the select group of individuals invited to invest in his fund. The letter was dated three years previously and had been signed by a Mr. Anthony Cigar of Rock Bank (Gibraltar) Ltd.

Mr. Cigar hadn't actually used the term "hedge fund," but it was quite clear from his letter, and from the attached fee schedule, that a hedge fund was what he'd managed.

I sat at my mother's desk and looked up

Rock Bank (Gibraltar) Ltd on the Internet. I typed the name into Google and then clicked on the bank's own Web address. The computer came back with the answer that the website was under construction and was unavailable to be displayed.

I went back to the Google page and clicked on the site for the *Gibraltar Chronicle,* one of the references that had mentioned the Rock Bank. It reported that back in September, Parkin & Cleeve Ltd, a UK-based firm of liquidators, had unsuccessfully filed a suit in the High Court in London against the individual directors of Rock Bank (Gibraltar) Ltd in an attempt to recover money on behalf of several of their clients. The directors were not named by the report, and the *Chronicle* had been unable to obtain a response from any representative of the bank.

It didn't bode well for the recovery of my mother's million dollars.

I yawned and looked at my watch. It was ten to midnight, and my mother and Derek had long before gone up to bed, and it was also well past my bedtime.

I flicked off the light in the office and went up the stairs.

My first day as sleuth-in-residence at Kauri House Stables hadn't gone all my own way. I hoped for better news in the morning.

When I came down to breakfast at eight o'clock I found my stepfather sitting silently, staring at a single brown envelope lying on the bleached-pine kitchen table, with "On Her Majesty's Service" printed in bold type along the top.

"Have you opened it?" I asked him.

"Of course not," he said. "It's addressed to your mother."

"Where is she?" I asked.

"Still out with the first lot," he said.

I picked up the envelope and looked at the back. "In case of non-delivery, please return to HMRC" was printed across the flap, so there was no mistake — it was definitely from the tax man.

I slid my finger under the flap and ripped open the envelope.

"You can't do that," my stepfather said indignantly.

"I just did," I said, taking out the contents. I unfolded the letter. It was simply a reminder for her Pay-As–You-Earn payments for the stable staff.

"It's OK," I said. "This is just a routine monthly reminder notice. It was generated by a computer. No one is going to come here. Not yet anyway."

"Are you sure?" he asked, still looking worried.

"Yes," I said. "But they will come in the end if we don't do something about this mess."

"But what can we do?" he said.

It was a good question.

"I don't know yet," I said, "but I do know that we will be in even more trouble if we do nothing and then the tax man comes calling. We simply have to go to them with answers before they come to us with questions."

My mother swept into the kitchen and placed her hands on the Aga.

"God, it's cold out there," she said. Neither my stepfather nor I said anything. She turned around. "What's wrong with you two? Quiet all of a sudden?"

"A letter has arrived from the tax office," my stepfather said.

In spite of her cold-induced rosy cheeks, my mother went a shade paler.

"It's all right," I said in a more reassuring tone than her husband's had been. "It's just an automatic PAYE reminder. Nothing to worry about." I tossed the letter onto the kitchen table.

"Are you certain?" she asked, moving

forward and picking it up.

"Yes," I said. "But I was saying to Derek here, we will have to tell the tax man soon about what's happened, and before he starts asking us difficult questions we can't answer."

"Why would he?"

"Because you should have sent them a tax return by January thirty-first."

"Oh," she said. "But why does that mean we have to tell them everything? Why can't I just send them a tax return now?"

Why not indeed? I thought. As things stood, I could just about argue that I was not an accessory to tax evasion, but I certainly wouldn't be able to if I helped her send in a fraudulent tax return.

Junior officers have to learn, from cover to cover, the contents of a booklet titled *Values and Standards of the British Army.* Paragraph twenty-seven states:

> Those entrusted with public and non-public funds must adhere unswervingly to the appropriate financial regulations. Dishonesty and deception in the control and management of these funds is not a *"victimless crime"* but shows a lack of integrity and moral courage, which has a corrosive effect on operational ef-

fectiveness through the breakdown in trust.

"Let's leave it for a few days," I said. "The tax website says you won't get any more penalties until the end of the month." Other than the interest, of course.

I left my mother and Derek to reflect on things in the kitchen while I went out to the stable yard in search of Ian Norland.

"You're still here, then?" he said as I found him in the feed store.

"Seems so," I said.

I stood in silence and watched him measure out some oats from a hopper into some metal bowls.

"I'm not going to talk to you," he said. "It nearly cost me my job last time."

"We've moved on since then."

"Who has?"

"My mother and me," I said. "We're now on the same side."

"I'll wait for her to tell me that, if you don't mind."

"She's in the kitchen right now," I said. "Go and ask her."

"I think I'll wait for her to come out."

"No," I insisted. "Please go and ask her now. I need to talk to you."

He went off reluctantly in the direction of the house, looking back once or twice as if I might call him back and say it was all a joke. I hoped my mother wouldn't actually bite his head off.

In his absence I went from the feed store into the tack room next door. It was all very neat and smelled strongly of leather, like those handbag counters in Oxford Street department stores. On the left-hand wall there were about twenty metal saddle racks, about half of which were occupied by saddles with their girths wrapped around them. On the opposite wall there were rows of coat hooks holdings bridles, and at the end between the saddles and bridles, there were shelves of folded horse rugs and other paraphernalia, including a box of assorted bits and a couple of riding helmets.

It was the bridles I was most interested in.

As I looked at them one of the stable staff came in and collected a saddle from one of the racks and a bridle from a hook.

"Are these bridles specific to each horse?" I asked him.

"No, mate," he said. "Not usually. The lads have one each, and there are a few spare. This is mine." He held up the one he had just removed from a hook. "My saddle too."

"Did you have to buy it?" I asked him.

"Naah, of course not," he said with a grin. "This is the one the guv'nor gives me to use, while I'm 'ere, like."

"And are these saddles also used in the races?"

"Naah," he said again. "The jocks have their own saddles."

"And their own bridles?"

"Naah," he said once more. "But we 'ave special racing ones of those. Jack keeps them in the racing tack room with the other stuff."

"Who's Jack?" I said.

"Traveling 'ead lad." He paused. "Who are you anyway?"

"I'm Mrs. Kauri's son," I said.

"Oh, yeah," he said, glancing down at my right leg. " 'Eard you were 'ere."

"Where is the racing tack room?" I asked him.

"Round the other side," he said, pointing through the far wall, the one with the shelves.

"Thank you, Declan," my mother said domineeringly, coming into the tack room. "Now, get on."

Declan went bright pink and scurried away with his saddle and bridle under his arm.

"I'll thank you not to interrogate my staff," she said.

I walked around her and pulled the tack-room door shut.

"Mother," I said formally. "If you want me to go now, I will." I paused briefly. "I'll also try to visit you in Holloway Prison." She opened her mouth to speak, but I cut her off. "Or you can let me help you, and I might just keep you out of jail."

Actually, secretly, I was beginning to think that the chances of managing that were very slight.

She stood tight-lipped in front of me. I thought she might cry again, but at that moment Ian Norland opened the tack-room door behind her and joined us.

"Ian," my mother said without turning around, her voice full of emotion. "You may say what you like to my son. Please answer any questions he might ask you. Show him whatever he wants to see. Give him whatever help he needs."

With that, she turned abruptly and marched out of the tack room, closing the door behind her.

"I told you last week that something bloody strange was going on round here," Ian said. "And it sure is." He paused. "I'll answer your questions and I'll show you what you want to see, but don't ask me to help you if it's illegal."

"I won't," I said.

"Or against the Rules of Racing," he said.

"I won't do that either," I said. "I promise."

I hoped it was another promise I'd be able to keep.

To my eye, the racing bridles looked identical to those in the general tack room. However, Ian assured me they were newer and of better quality.

"The reins are all double-stitched to the bit rings," he said, showing me, "so that there's less chance of them breaking during the race."

Both the bridles and the reins were predominantly made of leather, although there was a fair amount of metal and rubber as well.

"Does each horse have its own bridle?" I asked.

"They do on any given race day," Ian said. "But we have fifteen racing bridles in here, and they do for all our runners."

We were in the racing tack room. Apart from the bridles hanging on hooks, there was a mountain of other equipment, the most colorful being the mass of jockeys' silks hanging on a rail. There were also two boxes of special bits, and others of blinkers, visors, cheek pieces and sheepskin nose-bands. Up against the far wall, on top of a sort of sideboard, there were neat stacks of horse blankets, weight cloths and under-saddle pads, and there was even a collection of padded jackets for the stable staff to wear in the parade ring.

"So, say on Saturday, when Scientific runs at Newbury," I said. "Can you tell which bridle he'll use?"

Ian looked at me strangely. "No," he said. "Jack will take any one of these." He waved a hand at the fifteen bridles on their hooks.

To be honest, that wasn't the most helpful of answers.

"Don't any of the horses have their own bridle?" I asked, trying not to sound desperate.

"One or two," he said. "Old Perfidio has his own. That's because he has a special bit to try and stop him from biting his tongue during the race."

"But doesn't sharing tack result in cross-contamination?" I said.

"Not that we've noticed. We always dip bridles in disinfectant after every use, even the regular exercise ones."

I could see that making Scientific's bridle

or reins break on Saturday in the Game Spirit Steeplechase was not going to be as easy as I had imagined, at least not without Ian or Jack knowing about it.

"How about special nosebands?" I asked. "Why, for example, do some horses run in sheepskin nosebands?"

"Some trainers run all their horses in sheepskin nosebands," Ian said. "It helps them to see which horse is theirs. The colors aren't very easy to see when the horses are coming straight at you, especially if it's muddy."

"Do my mother's horses all wear them?"

"No," he said. "Not as a general rule. But we do use them occasionally if a horse tends to run with his head held up."

"Why's that?"

"If a horse runs with his head too high he isn't looking at the bottom of the fences, and also when the jockey pulls the reins the horse will lift it higher, not put it down like he should. So we put a nice thick sheepskin on him and he has to lower his head a little to see where he's going."

"Amazing," I said. "Does it really work?"

"Of course it works," he said, almost affronted. "We wouldn't do it if it didn't work. We also sometimes put cross nosebands on them to keep their mouths shut, especially if they're a puller. Keeping their mouths closed often stops them from pulling too hard. Or an Australian noseband will lift the bit higher in the mouth to stop a horse from putting his tongue over it."

"Is that important?" I asked.

"It can be," Ian said. "If a horse puts his tongue over the bit it can push on the back of the mouth and put pressure on the airway so the horse can't breathe properly."

There was clearly so much I didn't know about racehorse training.

"I think you might have to revert to the liquidized green potato peel," I said to my mother when I went back into the kitchen.

"Why?" she said.

"Because I can't see how we are going to arrange for Scientific's reins to break during the race on Saturday if we can't even be sure which bridle he'll be wearing."

"I'll ask Jack," she said.

"That might be a bit suspicious," I said. "Especially after the race. Much better if we can be sure ahead of time which bridle he'll be wearing. Can't you run him in a sheepskin noseband?"

"That won't help," she said. "We simply fit the sheepskin to a regular bridle using Velcro."

"Can't you think of anything?" I asked, not quite in desperation. "How about a cross or an Australian noseband?"

"He could run in an Australian, I suppose. That would mean he would have to have the one bridle we have fitted with it."

"Good," I said. "But you'll have to show me."

"What, now?"

"No, later, when Ian and Jack have gone," I said. "And make sure Scientific is the only horse this week that runs in it."

The phone rang. My mother walked across the kitchen and picked it up.

"Hello," she said. "Kauri House."

She listened for a moment.

"It's for you," she said, holding the telephone out towards me. I thought I detected a touch of irritation in her voice.

"Hello," I said.

"Hi, Tom. Would you like to come to supper tomorrow night?" It was Isabella.

"I thought you were cross with me," I said.

"I am," she replied bluntly. "But I always invite people I'm cross with to supper. Have you tasted my cooking?"

I laughed. "OK, I'll chance it. Thanks."

"Great. Seven-thirty or thereabouts, at the Hall."

"Black tie?" I asked.

"Absolutely," she said, laughing. "No, of course not. Very casual. I'll be in jeans. It's just a kitchen supper with friends."

"I'll bring a bottle."

"That would be great," she said. "See you tomorrow."

She disconnected, and I handed the phone back to my mother, smiling.

"I don't know why you want to associate with that woman," she said in her most haughty voice. She made it sound as though I was fraternizing with the enemy.

I wasn't in the mood to have yet another argument with her over whom I should and should not be friends with. We had done enough of that throughout my teenage years, and she had usually won by refusing entry to the house for my friends of whom she hadn't approved, which, if I remembered correctly, had been most of them.

"Are you going to the races today?" I asked her instead.

"No," she replied. "I've no runners today."

"Do you only go to the races if you have a runner?" I asked.

She looked at me as if I was a fool. "Of course."

"I thought you might go just for the enjoyment of it," I said.

"Going to the races is my job," she said.

"Would you do your job on days you didn't have to, just for the enjoyment?"

Actually, I would have, but there again, I enjoyed doing the things others might have been squeamish about.

"I might," I said.

"Not to Ludlow or Carlisle on a cold winter Wednesday, you wouldn't." She had a point. "It's not like Royal Ascot in June."

"No," I agreed. "So you can show me which bridle Scientific will use after lunch when the stable staff are off."

"Do you really think you can make the reins break during the race?" she asked.

"I had a good look at them," I said. "I think it might be possible."

"But how?"

"The reins are made of leather, but they have a nonslip rubber covering sewn round them, like the rubber on a table-tennis bat but with smaller pimples." She nodded. "The rubber is thin and not very strong. If I was able to break the leather inside the rubber, then it wouldn't be visible, and the reins would part during the race when the jockey pulls on them."

"It seems very risky," she said.

"Would you rather use your green-potato-peel soup?" I asked.

"No," she said adamantly. "That would

ruin the horse forever."

"OK," I said. "You show me which bridle Scientific will wear, and I'll do the rest."

Was I getting myself in too deep here?

Was I about to become an accessory to a fraud on the betting public as well as to tax evasion?

Yes. Guilty on both counts.

8

I spent much of Thursday morning on a reasonably fruitful journey to Oxford.

Banbury Drive was in Summertown, a northern suburb of the city, and number twenty-six was one of a row of 1950s-built semidetached houses with bay windows and pebble-dash walls. Twenty-six Banbury Drive was the supposed address of Mrs. Jane Philips, my mother, which Roderick Ward had included on her tax return.

I parked my Jaguar a little way down the road, so it wouldn't be so visible, and walked to the front door of number twenty-six. I rang the bell.

I didn't really know what to expect, but nevertheless I was a little surprised when the door was opened a fraction by an elderly white-haired gentleman wearing maroon carpet slippers, no socks and brown trousers that had been pulled up a good six inches too far.

"What do you want?" he snapped at me through the narrow gap.

"Does someone called Mr. Roderick Ward live here?" I asked.

"Who?" he said, cupping a hand to his ear.

"Roderick Ward," I repeated.

"Never heard of him," said the man. "Now go away."

The door began to close.

"He was killed in a car crash last July," I said quickly, but the door continued to close. I placed my false foot into the diminishing space between the door and the frame. At least it wouldn't hurt if he tried to slam the door shut.

"He had a sister called Stella," I said loudly. "Stella Beecher."

The door stopped moving and reopened just a fraction. I removed my foot.

"Do you know Stella?" I asked him.

"Someone called Stella brings my Meals-on-Wheels," the man said.

"Every day?" I asked.

"Yes," he said.

"What time?" I asked. It was already nearly twelve o'clock.

"Around one," he said.

"Thank you, sir," I said formally. "And what is your name, please?"

“Are you from the council?” he asked.
“Of course,” I said.
“Then you should know my bloody name,” he said, and he slammed the door shut.

Damn it, I thought. That was stupid.

I stood on the pavement for a while, but it was cold and my real toes became chilled inside my inappropriate indoor footwear.

Of course, I had no toes on my right side, but that didn’t mean I had no feeling there. The nerves that had once stretched all the way to my toes now ended seven inches below my knee. However, they often sent signals as if they had come from my foot.

In particular, when my real left foot was cold, the nerves in my right leg tended to confuse the situation by sometimes sending cold signals to my brain or, worse, as now, hot ones. It felt as though I had one foot inside a block of ice while the other was resting on a red-hot griddle plate. The sensation from the truncated nerves may have been from only a phantom limb, but they were real enough in my head, and they hurt.

I took shelter from the cold in my car. I started the engine and switched on the heater.

Consequently, I almost missed the arrival

of the old man's meal.

A dark blue Nissan came towards me and pulled up in front of the house, and a middle-aged woman leapt out and almost ran to the old man's door carrying a foil-covered tray. She had a key and let herself in. Only a few seconds later she emerged again, slammed the door shut and was back in her car almost before I had a chance to get out of mine.

I walked in the road so she couldn't leave without reversing or running me over. She sounded the horn and waved me out of the way. I put up a hand in a police-style stop signal.

"I'm in a hurry," she shouted.

"I just need to ask you a question," I shouted back.

The driver's window slid down a few inches.

"Are you Stella Beecher?" I asked, coming alongside the car.

"No," she said.

"The old man said Stella delivered his meals."

She smiled. "He calls all of us Stella," she said. "Someone called Stella used to do it for him, but she hasn't been here for months."

"Is her name Stella Beecher?" I asked.

"I don't really know," the woman said. "We're volunteers. I'd only just started when she stopped coming." She looked at her watch. "Sorry, I've got to go. The old people don't like me being late with their food."

"How can I contact Stella?" I asked.

"Sorry," she said. "I've no idea where she is now."

"What's his name?" I asked, nodding at the house.

"Mr. Horner," she said. "He's a cantankerous old git. And he never even bothered to wash up his plate from yesterday." I could see his dirty plate lying on the front seat beside her. "Must dash."

She revved the engine and was gone.

I stood there, wishing I'd asked her name or for her contact details, or at least for the name of the organization for whom she acted as a volunteer. Perhaps the council would know, I thought. I'd ask them.

I walked back up the driveway of number twenty-six and rang the bell.

There was no reply.

I leaned down and called through the letter box. "Mr. Horner," I shouted. "I need to ask you some questions."

"Go away." I could hear him in the distance. "I'm having my lunch."

"I only want a minute," I shouted, again through the letter box. "I need to ask you about your post."

"What about my post?" he said from much closer.

I stood up straight, and he opened the door a crack on a security chain.

"Do you ever receive post for other people?" I asked him.

"How do you mean?" he said.

"Do letters arrive here for other people with your house address on them?"

"Sometimes," he said.

"What do you do with them?" I asked.

"Stella takes them," he said.

"And did Stella take them today?" I asked, knowing that the lady he called Stella hadn't taken anything away from here except the dirty plate.

"No," he said.

"Have you got any post for other people at the moment?" I asked.

"Lots of it," he said.

"Shall I take it away for you?" I asked him.

He closed the door and I thought I had missed my chance, but he was only undoing the security chain. The door opened wide.

"It's in there," he said, pointing to a rectangular cardboard box standing next to his feet.

I looked down. There must have been at least thirty items of various shapes and sizes lying in a heap in the box.

"I've been wondering about it," he said. "Most of it's been there for months. Stella doesn't seem to take it anymore."

Without asking again, I reached down, picked up the box and walked off with it towards my car.

"Hey," old Mr. Horner shouted after me. "You can't do that. I need that box to put the next lot into."

I poured the contents out onto the front seat of the Jaguar and took the empty box back to him.

"That's better," he said, dropping the box back onto the floor and kicking it into position next to the door.

"Don't forget your lunch," I said, turning back towards my car. "Don't let it get cold."

"Oh," he said. "Right. 'Bye." He closed the door, and I was back in my car and speeding off before he had time to rethink the last few minutes.

I spent the afternoon in my bedroom, first impersonating a government official and then knowingly opening other people's mail. I was pretty sure that both actions were dishonest, and, even if they weren't against the letter of the law, they would certainly be in breach of *Values and Standards of the British Army.*

First, using the local Yellow Pages directory, I started calling nursing homes, claiming to be an official from the Pensions Office inquiring after the well-being of a Mr. George Sutton. I told them that I was checking that Mr. Sutton was still alive and entitled to his state pension.

I had never before realized there were so many nursing homes. After about fifty fruitless calls, I was at the point of giving up when someone at the Silver Pines Nursing Home in Newbury Road, Andover, informed me in no uncertain terms that Mr. George Sutton was indeed very much alive and kicking, and that his pension was an essential part of the payment for his care and I'd better leave it alone, or else.

I had to assure them profusely that I would take no action to stop it.

Next, I turned to the mail sent to 26 Banbury Drive, Oxford.

In all, there had been forty-two different items in Mr. Horner's cardboard box, but most of them were junk circulars and free papers with no name or address. Six of them, however, were of particular interest to me. Three were addressed to Mr. R.

Ward, a fourth to Mrs. Jane Philips, my mother, and the two others to a Mrs. Stella Beecher, all three persons supposedly resident at 26 Banbury Drive, Oxford.

Two of the letters to Roderick Ward had not been that informative, simply being tax circulars giving general notes of new tax bands. The third, however, was from Mr. Anthony Cigar of Rock Bank (Gibraltar) Ltd, formally confirming the immediate closure of the bank's investment fund and the imminent proceedings in the Gibraltar bankruptcy court. The letter was, in fact, a copy of one addressed to my mother and stepfather at Kauri House. It was dated July 7, 2009, and almost certainly did not arrive in Banbury Drive until after Roderick's fatal car accident of the night of July 12.

On the other hand, the letter to Mrs. Jane Philips, my mother, was much more recent. It was a computer-generated notice of an automatic penalty of one hundred pounds for the late filing of her tax return which had been due just ten days ago.

But it was the two letters to Mrs. Stella Beecher that were the real find.

One was from the Oxford Coroner's Office, informing her that the adjourned inquest into the death of her brother, Roderick Ward, was due to be reconvened on February 15 — next Monday.

And the other was a handwritten note on lined paper that simply read, in capital letters:

> I DON'T KNOW WHETHER THIS WILL GET THERE IN TIME, BUT TELL HIM I HAVE THE STUFF HE WANTS.

I picked up the envelope in which it had arrived. It was a standard white envelope available from any high-street store. The address had also been handwritten in the same manner as the note. The postmark was slightly blurred, and it was difficult to tell where it had actually been posted. However, the date was clear to see. The letter had been mailed on Monday, July 13, the day after Roderick Ward supposedly died, the very day his body had been discovered.

I sat on my bed for quite a while, looking at the note and wondering if "in time" meant before the "accident" occurred and if "the stuff" had anything to do with my mother's tax papers.

I looked carefully at it once again. Now, I was no handwriting expert, but this message to Stella Beecher looked, to my eyes, to have been written in the same style, and to be on the same type of paper, as the blackmail note that I had found on my mother's desk.

On Thursday evening, at seven forty-five, I carried a bottle of fairly reasonable red wine around from Kauri House to the Hall in Lambourn for a kitchen supper with Isabella and her guests. I was looking forward to a change in both venue and company.

As I had expected, the supper was not quite as casual as Isabella had made out. Far from being in jeans, she herself was wearing a tight black dress that showed off her alluring curves to their best advantage. I was pleased with myself that I had decided to put on a jacket and tie, but there again, I'd worn a jacket and tie for dinner in officers' messes for years, especially on a weekday. Dressing for dinner, even for a kitchen supper, was like a comfort blanket. For all its preoccupation with killing the enemy, the British Army was still very formal in its manners.

"Tom," she squealed, opening the front door wide and taking my offered bottle. "How lovely. Come and meet the others."

I followed her from the hallway towards the kitchen, and the noise. The room was already pretty full of guests. Isabella grabbed my arm and pulled me into the throng, where everyone seemed to be talking at once.

"Ewen," she shouted to a fair-haired man about forty years old. "Ewen," she shouted again, grabbing hold of his sleeve. "I want you to meet Tom. Tom, this is Ewen Yorke. Ewen, Tom."

We shook hands.

"Tom Forsyth," I said.

"Ah," he said in a dramatic manner, throwing an arm wide and nearly knocking over someone's glass behind him. "Jackson, we have a spy in our midst."

"A spy?" Isabella said.

"Yes," Ewen said. "A damn spy from Kauri Stables. Come to steal our secrets about Saturday."

"Ah," I said. "You must mean about Newark Hall in the Game Spirit." His mouth opened. "You've got no chance with Scientific running."

"There you are," he boomed. "What did I tell you? He's a bloody spy. Fetch the firing squad." He laughed heartily at his own joke, and we all joined in. Little did he know.

"Where is this spy?" said a tall man, pushing his way past people towards me.

"Tom," said Isabella. "This is my husband, Jackson Warren."

"Good to meet you," I said, shaking his

offered hand and hoping he couldn't see the envy in my eyes, envy that he had managed to snare my beautiful Isabella.

Jackson Warren certainly didn't give the impression of someone suffering from prostate cancer. I knew that he was sixty-one years old because I'd looked him up on the Internet, but his lack of any gray hair seemed to belie the fact. Rather unkindly, I wondered if he dyed it, or perhaps just being married to a much younger woman had helped keep him youthful.

"So, are you spying on us, or on Ewen?" he asked jovially, with an infectious booming laugh.

"Both," I said jokily, but I had partially misjudged the moment.

"Not for the Sunday papers, I hope," he said, changing his mood instantly from amusement to disdain. "Though, I suppose, one more bastard won't make any difference." He laughed once more, but this time, the amusement didn't reach his eyes and there was an unsettling seriousness about his face.

"Come on, darling," said Isabella, sensing his unease. "Relax. Tom's not a spy. In fact, he's a hero."

I gave her a stern look as if to say, "No, please don't," but the message didn't get through.

"A hero?" said Ewen.

Isabella was about to reply when I cut her off sharply.

"Isabella exaggerates," I said quickly. "I'm in the army, that's all. And I've been in Afghanistan."

"Really," said an attractive woman in a low-cut dress who was standing next to Ewen. "Was it very hot?"

"No, not really," I said. "It's very hot in the summer, but it's damn cold in the winter, especially at night." Trust a Brit, I thought, to talk about the weather.

"Did you see any action?" Ewen asked.

"A fair bit," I said. "But I was only there for a couple of months this last time."

"So you've been before?" Ewen said.

"I've been in the army since I was seventeen," I said. "I've been most places."

"Were you in Iraq?" the woman asked with intensity.

"Yes. In Basra. And also in Bosnia and Kosovo. The modern army keeps you busy." I laughed.

"How exciting," she said.

"It can be," I agreed. "But only in short bursts. Mostly it's very boring." Time, I thought, to change the subject. "So, Ewen," I said, "how many horses do you train?"

"There you are," he said expansively. "I told you he was a spy."

We all laughed.

The attractive woman next to Ewen turned out to be his wife, Julie, and I found myself sitting next to her at supper at one of two large round tables set up in the extensive Lambourn Hall kitchen.

On the other side, on my left, was a Mrs. Toleron, a rather dull gray-haired woman who didn't stop telling me about how successful her "wonderful" husband had been in business. She had even introduced herself as Mrs. Martin Toleron, as if I would recognize her spouse's name.

"You must have heard of him," she exclaimed, amazed that I hadn't. "He was head of Toleron Plastics until we sold out a few months ago. It was all in the papers at the time, and on the television."

I didn't tell her that a few months ago I had been fighting for my life in a Birmingham hospital and, at the time, the business news hadn't been very high on my agenda.

"We were the biggest plastic-drainpipe manufacturer in Europe."

"Really," I said, trying to keep myself from yawning.

"Yes," she said, incorrectly sensing some interest on my part. "We made white, gray or black drainpipe in continuous lengths. Mile after mile of it."

"Thank goodness for rain," I said, but she didn't get the joke.

As soon as I was able, and without appearing too rude, I managed to stem the tide of plastic drainpipe from my left, turning more eagerly towards Julie on my right.

"So, how many horses does Ewen train?" I asked her, as we tucked in to lasagna and garlic bread. "He never did tell me."

"About sixty," she said. "But it's getting more all the time. We're no longer really big enough at home, so we are looking to buy the Webster place."

"Webster place?" I asked.

"You must know, on the hill off the Wantage Road. Old Larry Webster used to train there, but he dropped down dead a couple of years ago now. It's been on the market for months and months. Price is too high, I reckon, and it needs a lot doing to it. Ewen's dead keen to open another yard, but I'd rather stay the size we are." She sighed. "Ewen says we're too small, but the truth is, he's not very good at saying no to new owners." She smiled wearily.

"He's lucky in the current economic climate to have the option," I said.

"I know," she agreed. "Lots of trainers are

having troubles. I hear it all the time from their wives at the races."

"Do you go racing a lot?" I asked.

"Not as much as I once did," she said. "Ewen is always so busy these days that I never see him like I used to, either at the races or at home."

She sighed again. Clearly, success had not brought happiness, at least not for Mrs. Yorke.

"But enough about me. Tell me about you." She turned in her chair to give me her full attention, and a much better view of her ample cleavage. Ewen should spend more time with her, I thought, both at home and at the races, or he might soon find her straying.

"Not much to tell," I said.

"Now, come on. You must have lots of stories."

"None that I'd be happy to repeat," I said.

"Go on," she said, putting her hand on my arm. "You can tell me." She fluttered her eyelashes at me. It made me think that it was probably already too late for Ewen, far too late.

Isabella insisted that everyone move around after the lasagna and so, in spite of Julie Yorke's best efforts, I escaped her advances before they became too obvious, but not before she'd had the shock of her life trying to play footsie under the table with my prosthesis.

"My God! What's that?" she had exclaimed, but quietly, almost under her breath.

And so I'd been forced to explain about the IED and all the other things I would have preferred to keep confidential.

Far from turning her off, the idea of a man with only one leg had seemed to excite her yet further. She had become even more determined to invade my privacy with intimate questions that I was seriously not prepared to answer.

As soon as Isabella suggested it, I was quick and happy to move seats, opting to sit between Jackson Warren and another man at the second table.

I'd had my fill of the female of the species for one night.

"So how long have you been back?" Jackson asked me as I sat down.

"In Lambourn?" I asked.

"From Afghanistan."

"Four months," I said.

"In hospital?" he asked.

I nodded. Isabella must have told him.

"In hospital?" the man on my other side asked.

"Yes," I said. "I was wounded."

He looked at me and was clearly waiting for me to expand on my answer. As far as I was concerned, he was waiting in vain.

"Tom, here, lost a foot," Jackson said, filling the silence.

It felt as though I'd jumped out of one frying pan and into another.

"Really," said the man with astonishment. "Which one?"

"Does it matter?" I asked with obvious displeasure.

"Er . . . er . . ." He was suddenly uncomfortable, and I sat silently, doing nothing to relieve his embarrassment. "No," he said finally, "I suppose not."

It mattered to me.

"I'm sorry," he said, looking down and intently studying his dessert plate of chocolate mousse with brandy snaps and cream.

I nearly asked him if he was sorry for my losing a foot or sorry for asking me which one I'd lost, but it was Jackson I should have been really cross with, for mentioning it in the first place.

"Thank you," I said. I paused. "It was my right foot."

"It's amazing," he said, looking up at my

face. “I watched you walk over here just now and I had no idea.”

“Prosthetic limbs have come a long way since the days of Long John Silver,” I said. “There were some at the rehab center who could run up stairs two at a time.”

“Amazing,” he said again.

“I’m Tom Forsyth,” I said.

“Oh, I’m sorry,” he replied. “Alex Reece. Good to meet you.”

We shook hands in the awkward manner of people sitting alongside each other. He was a small man in his thirties, with thinning ginger hair and horn-rimmed spectacles of the same color. He was wearing a navy cardigan over a white shirt, and brown flannel trousers.

“Are you a trainer too?” I asked.

“Oh no,” he said with a nervous laugh. “I haven’t a clue about horses. In fact, to tell you the truth, I’m rather frightened of them. I’m an accountant.”

“Alex, here,” Jackson interjected, “keeps my hard-earned income out of the grasping hands of the tax man.”

“I try,” Alex said with a smile.

“Legally?” I asked, smiling back.

“Of course legally,” said Jackson, feigning annoyance.

“The line between avoidance, which is

legal, and evasion, which isn't, can sometimes be somewhat blurred," Alex said, ignoring him.

"And what exactly is that meant to mean?" demanded Jackson, the simulated irritation having been replaced by the real thing.

"Nothing," Alex said, backpedaling furiously, and again embarrassed. "Just that sometimes what we believe is avoidance may be seen as evasion by the Revenue." Alex Reece was digging himself deeper into the hole.

"And who is right?" I asked, enjoying his discomfort.

"We are," Jackson stated firmly. "Aren't we, Alex?" he insisted.

"It is the courts who ultimately decide who's right," Alex said, clearly oblivious to the thinness of the thread by which his employment was dangling.

"In what way?" I asked.

"We put in a return based on our understanding of the tax law," he said, seemingly unaware of Jackson's staring eyes to my left. "If the Revenue challenge that understanding, they might demand that we pay more tax. If we then challenge their challenge and refuse to pay, they have to take us to court, and then a jury will decide whose interpretation of the law is correct."

"Sounds simple," I said.

"But it can be very expensive," Alex said. "If you lose in court, you will end up paying far more than the tax you should have paid in the first place, because they will fine you on top. And, of course, the court has the power to do more than just take away your money. They can also send you to prison if they think you were trying to evade paying tax on purpose. To say nothing of what else the Revenue might turn up with their digging. It's a risk we shouldn't take."

"Are you trying to tell me something, Alex?" Jackson asked angrily, leaning over me and pointing his right forefinger at his accountant's face. "Because I'm warning you, if I end up in court I will tell them it was all my accountant's idea."

"What was his idea?" I asked tactlessly.

"Nothing," said Jackson, suddenly realizing he'd said too much.

There was an uncomfortable few moments of silence. The others at the table, who had been listening to the exchange, suddenly decided it was best to start talking amongst themselves again, and turned away.

Jackson stood up, scraping his chair on the stone floor, and stomped out of the room.

"So how long have you been Jackson's accountant?" I asked Alex.

He didn't answer but simply watched the door through which Jackson had disappeared.

"Sorry. What did you say?" he said eventually.

"I asked you how long you'd been Jackson's accountant."

He stared at me. "Too long," he said.

The kitchen supper soon broke up and most of the guests departed, Alex Reece being the first out of the door, almost at a run. Eventually, there were only a handful remaining, and I found myself amongst them. I had tried, politely, to depart, but Isabella had insisted on my staying for a nightcap, and I had been easily persuaded. I had nothing much to get up early for in the morning.

In all, five of us moved through from the kitchen into the equally spacious drawing room, including a couple I had seen only at a distance across the room earlier. He was wearing a dark suit and blue-striped tie while she was in a long charcoal-colored jersey over a brown skirt. I placed them both in their early sixties.

"Hello," I said to them. "I'm Tom Forsyth." I held out my hand.

"Yes," said the man rather sneeringly, not shaking it. "We know. Bella spoke of little else over dinner."

"Oh, really," I said with a laugh. "All good, I hope. And you are?"

The man said nothing.

"Peter and Rebecca Garraway," the woman said softly. "Please excuse my husband. He's just jealous because Bella doesn't speak about him all the time."

I wasn't sure if she was joking or not. Peter Garraway certainly wasn't laughing. Instead, he turned away, sat down on a sofa and patted the seat beside him. His wife obediently went over and joined him. What a bundle of fun, I thought, not. Why didn't they just go home?

Isabella handed around drinks while her husband remained conspicuous by his continued absence. But no one mentioned it, not even me.

"I thought all you trainers went to bed early," I said to Ewen Yorke as he sank into the armchair next to me and buried his nose into a brandy snifter.

"You must be joking," he said. "And turn down our Bella's best VSOP? Not bloody likely." He tilted his head right back and poured the golden-brown liquid down his throat. I couldn't help but think of my mother pouring her green-potato-peel concoction down her horses' throats in the same manner.

Ewen's wife, Julie, had departed with the other guests, saying she was tired and was going home to bed. Her husband seemed to be in no hurry to join her. Isabella refilled his glass.

"So, Tom," he said, taking another sizable mouthful. "Where does the army send you next? Back to Afghanistan? Back to the fight?"

Isabella was looking at me intently.

"I think my fighting days are over," I said. "I'm getting too old for that."

"Nonsense," Isabella said. "You're the same age as me."

"But front-line fighting is for younger men. More than half of those in the army that have been killed in Afghanistan were under twenty-four, and more of them were teenagers than were older than me. In the modern infantry, you're past it by the age of thirty."

"I can't believe that," Ewen said. "I was still wet behind the ears until I was at least thirty."

"But it's true," I said. "In a ten-year period, Alexander the Great, the Greek King of Macedonia, conquered Turkey and

Egypt, much of the rest of the Middle East, as well as all of Persia and parts of India as far away as the Himalayas, and he managed it all by the time he was thirty. He is still revered by soldiers the world over as one of the greatest military commanders of all time, yet he was only thirty-two when he died. Sadly, the truth of the matter is that I'm over the hill already."

Was I trying to convince them, or myself?

"So what will you do instead?" Ewen asked.

"I'm not really sure," I said. "Perhaps I'll take up racehorse training."

"It's not always as exciting as it appears," he said. "Particularly not at seven-thirty on cold, wet winter mornings."

"Especially after a late night out drinking," said Isabella with a laugh.

"Oh God," said Ewen, looking at his watch. "Quick. Give me another brandy."

Isabella and I laughed. Peter Garraway sat stony-faced on the sofa.

"At least it would be a bit safer than you're used to," Rebecca Garraway said.

"I don't really think I'll be joining the ranks of racehorse trainers," I said with a smile. "It was only a joke."

However, neither Rebecca nor her husband seemed amused by it.

"I think it's time I was off," I said, standing up. "Isabella, thank you for a lovely evening. Good night, all."

"Good night," Ewen and Rebecca called back as Isabella showed me out into the hallway. Peter Garraway said nothing.

"Thank you for tonight," I said, as Isabella opened the front door. "It's been great fun."

"I'm sorry about the Garraways," she said, lowering her voice. "They can be a bit strange at times, especially him. I think he fancies me." She laughed. "But I think he's creepy."

"And rather rude," I whispered back, pulling a face. "Who are they?"

"Old friends of Jackson's." She rolled her eyes. "Unfortunately, they're our houseguests. The Garraways always come over for the end of the pheasant-shooting season — Peter is a great shot — and they're staying on for the races on Saturday."

"At Newbury?"

She nodded. "Are you going?"

"Probably," I said.

"Great. Maybe see you there." She laughed. "Unless, of course, you see the Garraways first."

"What exactly does Peter Garraway do?" I asked.

"He makes pots and pots of money," she said. "And he owns racehorses. Ewen trains some of them."

I thought that explained a lot.

"I don't think Mr. Garraway is overimpressed by his trainer drinking your brandy until all hours of the night."

"Oh, that's not the problem," she said. "I think it's because Peter and Jackson had a bit of a stand-up row earlier. Over some business project they're working on together. I didn't really listen."

"What sort of business?" I asked.

"Financial services or something," she said. "I don't really know. Business is not my thing." She laughed. "But Peter must do very well out of it. We go and stay with them occasionally, and their house makes this place look like a weekend cottage. It's absolutely huge."

"Where is it?" I asked.

"In Gibraltar."

9

The Silver Pines Nursing Home was a modern redbrick monstrosity built onto the side of what had once been an attractive Victorian residence on the northern edge of the town of Andover, in Hampshire.

"Certainly, sir," said one of the pink-uniformed lady carers when I asked if I might visit Mr. Sutton. "Are you a relative?"

"No," I said. "I live in the same road as Mr. Sutton. In Hungerford."

"I see," said the carer. She wasn't really interested. "I think he's in the dayroom. He sits there most mornings after breakfast."

I followed her along the corridor into what had once been the old house. The dayroom was the large bay-windowed front parlor, and there were about fifteen high-backed upright armchairs arranged around by the walls. About half of the chairs were occupied, and most of the occupants were asleep.

"Mr. Sutton," called the pink lady walking towards one elderly gentleman. "Wake up, Mr. Sutton. You've got a visitor." She shook the old boy, and he slowly raised his head and opened his eyes. "That's better." She spoke to him as if he were a child, then she leaned forward and wiped a drop of dribble from the corner of his mouth. I began to think that I shouldn't have come.

"Hello, Mr. Sutton." I spoke in the same loud manner that the lady had used. "Do you remember me?" I asked. "It's John, John from Willow Close." Unsurprisingly, he stared at me without recognition. "Jimbo and his mum send their love. Has your son, Fred, been in yet today?"

The pink lady seemed satisfied. "Can I leave you two together, then?" she asked. "The tea trolley will be round soon if you want anything."

"Thank you," I said.

She walked away, back towards the entrance, and I sat down on an empty chair next to Old Man Sutton. All the while, he went on staring at me.

"I don't know you," he said.

I watched with distaste as he used his right hand to remove a set of false teeth from his mouth. He studied them closely, took a wooden toothpick from his shirt pocket and used it to remove a piece of his breakfast that had become stuck in a crevice. Satisfied, he returned the denture to his mouth with an audible snap.

"I don't know you," he said again, the teeth now safely back in position.

I looked around me. There were six other residents in the room, and all but one had now drifted off to sleep. The one whose eyes were open was staring out through the window at the garden and ignoring us.

"Mr. Sutton," I said, straight to his face. "I want to ask you about a man called Roderick Ward."

I hadn't been sure what reaction to expect. I'd thought that maybe Old Man Sutton wouldn't be able to remember what he'd had for dinner last night, let alone something that happened nearly a year previously.

I was wrong.

He remembered, all right. I could see it in his eyes.

"Roderick Ward is a thieving little bastard." He said it softly but very clearly. "I'd like to wring his bloody neck." He held out his hands towards me as if he might wring my neck instead.

"Roderick Ward is already dead," I said.

Old Man Sutton dropped his hands into

his lap. "Good," he said. "Who killed him?"

"He died in a road accident," I said.

"That was too good for him," the old man said with venom. "I'd have killed him slowly."

I was slightly taken aback. "What did he do to you?" I asked. It had to be more than throwing a brick through his window.

"He stole my life savings," he said.

"How?" I asked.

"Some harebrained scheme of his that went bust," he said. He shook his head. "I should never have listened to him."

"So he didn't exactly steal your savings?"

"As good as," Mr. Sutton replied. "My son was furious with me. Kept saying I'd gambled away his inheritance."

I didn't think it had been the most tactful of comments.

"And what exactly was Roderick Ward's harebrained scheme?" I asked.

He sat silently for a while, looking at me, as if deciding what to tell. Or perhaps he was trying to remember.

He again removed his false teeth and studied them closely. I wasn't at all sure that he had understood my question, but after a while he replaced his teeth in his mouth and began. "I borrowed some money against my house to invest in some fancy investment fund that Roderick Bastard Ward guaranteed would make me rich." He sighed. "All that happened was the fund went bust and I now have a bloody great mortgage, and I can't afford the interest."

I could understand why Detective Sergeant Fred had been so furious.

"What sort of investment fund was it?" I asked.

"I don't remember," he said. Perhaps he just didn't want to.

"So how come Ward threw a brick through your window?" I asked.

He smiled. "I poured tea in his lap."

"What?" I said, astonished. "How?"

"He came to tell me that I'd lost all my money. I said to him that there must be something we could do, but he just sat there, arrogantly telling me that I should have realized that investments could go down as well as up." He smiled again. "So I simply poured the hot tea from the teapot I was holding straight into his lap." He laughed, and his false teeth almost popped out of his mouth. He pushed them back in with his thumb. "You should have seen him jump. Almost ripped his trousers off. Accused me of scalding his wedding tackle. Wish now I'd cut them off completely."

"So he went out and threw the brick

through your window?"

"Yeah, as he was leaving, but my son saw him do it and arrested him." He stopped laughing. "But then I had to tell Fred the whole story about losing the money."

So he had lost his money about a year ago. Before the same fate had befallen my mother.

"Mr. Sutton," I said. "Can you remember anything at all about the investment fund that went bust?"

He shook his head.

"Was it an offshore fund?" I asked.

He looked quizzically at me. The term *offshore* clearly hadn't rung any bells in his memory.

"I don't know about that," he said. "I don't think so."

"Did it have anything to do with Gibraltar?" I asked.

He shook his head once more. "I can't remember." He began to dribble again from the corner of his mouth, and there were tears in his eyes.

It was time for me to go.

Saturday morning dawned crisp and bright, with the winter sun doing its best to thaw the frosty ground. The radio in the kitchen reported that there was to be a second inspection of the course at Newbury at nine o'clock to decide whether racing could go ahead. Apparently, the takeoff and landing areas of every jump had been covered overnight, and the stewards were hopeful the meeting could take place.

I, meanwhile, was crossing my fingers that it would be abandoned.

I had spent more than an hour in the racing tack room on Friday afternoon doing my best to try to ensure that Scientific's reins would part during his race. My mother had shown me which one of the bridles had the Australian noseband fitted, and I had been dismayed to see its pristine condition. As my mother had said, horses from Kauri House Stables didn't go to the races with substandard tack.

I had thought that it would be an easy task to bend the leather back and forth a few times inside the nonslip rubber sleeve until it broke, leaving only the rubber holding the reins together. The rubber should then part in the hustle and bustle of the race when the jockey pulled on the reins.

Sadly, I found that it was not as simple as I had thought. The leather was far too new.

I'd looked at where the reins were attached to the metal rings on either side of the bit. The leather was sewn back on itself with multiple stitches of strong thread. I had tested it with all my strength without even an iota of separation. How about if I cut through most of the stitches? But with what? And wouldn't it show? Wouldn't Jack be sure to see it when he gathered the tack together?

There were four green first-aid boxes stacked on a shelf in the racing tack room, and I'd opened one, looking for a pair of scissors. I'd found something better. Carefully protected by a transparent plastic sheath had been a surgical scalpel.

With great care I had started to cut through the stitches on the right side of the bridle, the side that would be farthest from the stable lad when he led the horse around the parade ring. I'd been careful to cut only the stitches in the middle, leaving both ends intact so the sabotage was less obvious. In the end I had severed all but a very few stitches at either end. I had no idea if it was enough, but it would have to do.

I hovered nervously around the racing tack-room door as Jack gathered together all the equipment for the day, loading it into a huge wicker basket. I saw as he lifted the bridle with the Australian noseband and placed it in the basket.

There was no shout of discovery, no tut-

tutting over the state of the reins.

So far, so good. But the real test would come when he placed the bridle on to Scientific later in the afternoon in the racetrack stables.

I had done my best to disguise the effects of the scalpel. The stiffness of the leather had helped to keep the sides together, and I had been careful not to leave any frayed ends of thread visible. It had been a matter of trying to make the reins appear to be normal and intact while, at the same time, ensuring they were sufficiently weakened to separate during the race. And I had absolutely no idea if I had managed to get the balance right.

Unfortunately, the covers had done their job in saving the meeting from the frost, and so my mother drove the three of us to Newbury in her battered old blue Ford, my stepfather sitting next to her in the front while I was in the back behind her, as I had been so often before on the way to and from the races.

Going racing had been such a huge part of my young life that at one time, my knowledge of British geography had been based solely on the locations of the racetracks. By the time I learned to drive when

I was seventeen, I had no idea where the big cities might be, but I could unerringly find my way to such places as Market Rasen, Plumpton or Fakenham, and I also knew the best shortcuts to beat the race-day traffic.

Newbury is the most local course to Lambourn, being just fifteen miles away, and is thought of as "home" for most of the village's trainers, who all have as many runners here as possible, not least because of the low transport costs.

By the time my mother pulled into the trainers' parking lot it was nearly full, and I noticed with dismay how far I was going to have to walk to get into the racetrack. I was still suffering from excess fluid in the tissues of my leg, and I had promised myself to take things a little easier for a while. So much for my good intentions.

"Hello, Josephine," called a voice as we stepped out of the car. Ewen Yorke was standing just in front of us, struggling into his sheepskin overcoat.

"Oh, hello, Ewen," replied my mother without warmth.

"Hiya, Tom," Julie Yorke called as she climbed out of their top-of-the-range, brand-new white BMW, a fact not lost on my mother, who positively fumed. Now I realized why she had suddenly become so keen on upgrading her old Ford.

For once, Julie was accompanying Ewen to the races, and she was dressed in a thin figure-hugging silk dress with a matching, but equally thin, print-patterned topcoat. Rather inappropriate, I thought, for a cold and dank February afternoon, but it clearly warmed the hearts of several male admirers who walked by with smiles on their faces and sparkles in their eyes.

"Hi, Julie," I replied with a small wave that brought the same response of recognition from Ewen.

My mother looked across the car at me disapprovingly. I was sure that she would be desperate to discover how it was that I knew them, and be eager for me to enlighten her. But I decided not to. I'd not mentioned to her where I had gone to dinner on Thursday night. I had simply let her assume, incorrectly, that I had gone down to one of the village pubs. She obviously hadn't suffered under my Sandhurst color sergeant, or she would have known never to assume anything but always to check.

We hung back, putting on our own coats and hats, as the Yorkes made their way across the grass to the entrance. We watched them go.

"If Scientific is not able to win today," my mother said icily, "I just hope it's not bloody Newark Hall. I can't stand that man."

I looked around quickly to see if anyone had heard her comment.

"If I were you," I said, forcefully but quietly, "I'd keep my voice down. This parking lot is also used by the stewards."

We made it unchallenged into the racetrack, my mother obtaining a member's club ticket for me at the gate, just as she always had. But now I was no longer the little boy in a cap that the gateman had let through with a smile, although I felt the same excitement.

However, my excitement today was combined with acute nervousness.

Had I done enough to make Scientific's reins part? Would the horse and rider be all right? Would I be found out by Jack?

The Game Spirit Steeplechase was the second race on the card, and so anxious was I that I didn't take the slightest notice of the first. Instead, I stood nervously at the entrance to the pre-parade ring, waiting for the horses to be led in by the stable lads.

To say that I was relieved when Scientific came into the ring was an understatement. I started breathing again. As the horse was walked around and around, I looked closely at his bridle, and it certainly appeared to be the same one that I had tampered with on the previous afternoon.

So far, so good.

I wandered over to the saddling stalls and leaned on a white wooden rail, waiting for Scientific to be brought over by the stable lad, who, I noticed, was Declan, the same young man that I had spoken to in the Kauri Stables tack room.

Presently my mother and stepfather arrived, then Jack appeared, trotting into the saddling stall with the jockey's minuscule saddle under his arm.

Declan stood in front of the horse, restraining its head using the reins on both sides of the bit. I was again holding my breath. Would he notice the sabotage?

My mother and Jack busied themselves, one on each side of the animal, applying under-saddle pad, weight cloth, number cloth and then the saddle to its back, pulling the girths tight around its belly. Next, Jack threw a heavy red, black and gold horse rug over the whole lot to keep the horse warm against the February chill. With a slap on his neck from Jack, Scientific was sent to the parade ring for inspection by the betting public.

Why, I wondered, did the blackmailer

want Scientific to lose?

Was it because he wanted another specific horse to win?

Probably not, I thought.

Before the onset of Internet gambling, the only people who could really gain financially from knowing a horse would definitely lose a race were the bookmakers, who could then offer much better odds on it and rake in the bets, safe in the knowledge that they wouldn't have to pay out. However, nowadays anyone could act as a bookmaker by "laying" the horse on the Internet, effectively betting that it would lose. It didn't matter which other horse won, as long as it wasn't the surefire loser.

So anyone could gain by knowing that Scientific would not win this race. If only I had access to see who was "laying" the horse on the Net. But there would be no chance of that, even if I had been prepared to tell the authorities why I needed it.

I watched absentmindedly as the twelve horses in the race were walked around and around. I had never been a gambler myself and had never really understood the passion and concentration with which some punters would study the runners in the parade ring before making their bets. I had been told over and over again by my mother that how well a horse looks in the paddock can be such a good indicator of how fast it will run on the course, but I personally couldn't see it.

A racetrack official rang a handbell, and I watched with interest as Declan turned Scientific inwards, waiting for my mother and stepfather to walk over with the horse's owner and jockey. My mother made great play in removing the rug and checking the girths but without going near the bridle or the reins. Declan stood impassively, holding the horse's head as my mother tossed the lightweight rider up onto his equally slight saddle.

The jockey placed his feet in the stirrup irons and then gathered the reins, making a knot with the ends to ensure that they didn't separate. After another brief circuit of the ring, the horses moved down the horse walk towards the racetrack, and the crowd moved as if one, towards the grandstand, in search of a good viewing position. I was amongst them.

"Hello, Tom," said a voice from behind my shoulder.

I turned around. "Oh, hello." I kissed Isabella on the cheek. Jackson was with her, and they had the Garraways in tow.

"Fancy a drink?" Jackson said, clapping

me on the shoulder.

A drink sounded just the thing to calm my nerves.

"Later," I said. "I want to watch this race."

"So do we," said Jackson with his booming laugh. "Come on up to our box and we can do both."

I had been trying to spot my mother in the throng of people so I could watch the race with her. I had one last look around, but I couldn't see her or my stepfather anywhere. It was probably just as well, I thought, as together we would have been a pair of nervous wrecks.

"Thank you, I'd love to," I said to Jackson, smiling at Isabella.

"Good," she said, smiling back.

"And thank you both for such a lovely evening on Thursday," I said. "I meant to bring you round a note."

"That's all right, don't bother," said Jackson. "It was a pleasure to have you. We all really enjoyed it." Unsurprisingly, he made no mention of his early departure from supper, nor his untimely row with Alex Reece.

"How's Alex?" I asked, perhaps unwisely.

"Alex?" he said, looking at me.

"Alex Reece," I said. "Your accountant."

"Oh, him," Jackson said, with a forced smile. "Bloody little weasel needs a good kick up the arse." He guffawed loudly.

"Really?" I said with mock sincerity. "I'll be needing an accountant soon myself. I thought I might go and see him. Are you saying I shouldn't?"

I was playing with him, and he suddenly didn't like it. The amusement evaporated from his eyes.

"Ask whoever you bloody like," he said dismissively.

As we climbed the few steps to the entrance to the Berkshire Stand we were joined by the Yorkes.

"Ah, the spy again," said Ewen, smiling.

I smiled back at him.

I found myself crammed into the lift with my back against the wall and with Julie Yorke standing far too close in front. Ewen would almost certainly have had a fit if he had realized that without any discernible sign to the others, she managed to slide her silk-sheathed firm and rounded buttocks back and forth across my groin in a manner guaranteed to excite.

By the time we arrived at the fourth floor I was glad to be able to pull my overcoat tight around me to save myself from major embarrassment. Julie smiled as I held the door of the box open for her, a seductive inviting smile with an open mouth and her tongue visible between her teeth.

"Come and see me sometime," she whispered in my ear as she went past.

I reckoned she must be crazy if she thought it was an invitation I was going to accept. Avoidance and evasion were definitely the names of the game here too. Jackson offered me a glass of champagne, and I took it out onto the balcony to watch the horses, and to escape from Julie Yorke.

"Do you think he'll win?" It was a moment before I realized that Rebecca Garraway was talking to me.

"Sorry?" I said.

"Do you think he'll win?" she repeated.

"Who?" I asked.

"Newark Hall, of course," she said. "Our horse."

I hadn't realized that the Garraways were Newark Hall's owners. I looked down at my race card, but it stated that the horse was owned by a company called Budsam Ltd.

"He has a good chance," I said back to her.

In truth, he had a better chance than she appreciated.

Ewen Yorke was standing to my left, looking through his large racing binoculars towards the two-and-a-half-mile start.

"Oh, hello," he said without lowering his

binoculars. "Seems we have a problem."

"What problem?" Rebecca Garraway demanded with concern in her voice.

"It's OK," Ewen said, while still looking. "It's not Newark Hall, it's Scientific. Seems his reins have snapped. He's running away."

I looked down the course in horror, but without the benefit of Ewen's multi-magnification, I was unable to see exactly what was going on. I took a large gulp of my champagne. I should have asked Jackson for a whisky.

"Good. They've caught him," Ewen said, putting down his glasses. "No real harm done."

"So what will happen now?" I asked, trying hard to keep my voice as normal as possible. "Will Scientific be withdrawn?"

"Oh no, he'll run, all right, no problem. They'll just fit a new bridle on him down at the start," Ewen said. "The starter always has a spare, just in case something breaks. Indeed, just for situations like this. Most unlike your mother to have a tack malfunction." He almost laughed.

I felt sick. All that hard work with the scalpel, to say nothing about the expenditure of so much nervous energy since, and for what? Nothing. The horse would now run with perfect, uncut, unbreakable reins.

"That's good," I said, not actually thinking it was good for a second.

What, I wondered, would the blackmailer do if Scientific won?

I was doubly glad that I wasn't standing next to my mother on the owners' and trainers' stand. By now she would have become more of a head case than was usual. I just hoped she wasn't planning an Emily Davison suffragette-style dash out in front of her horse during the race to prevent it from winning. But in her present state of mind, I'd not put anything past her.

"They're off!" announced the public-address system, and all twelve runners moved away slowly, not one of the jockeys eager to set the early pace. They jumped the first fence without even breaking into a proper gallop, and only then did the horses gather pace and the race was on.

Even though I wanted to, I couldn't take my eyes off Scientific.

I suppose I was hoping he might have crossfired and cut into himself, but the horse appeared to gallop along easily, without any problems. Perhaps he would make an error, I thought, peck badly on landing, and unseat his rider.

But he didn't.

My mother had said that Scientific was a

good novice but that the Game Spirit Steeplechase was a considerable step up in class. It didn't show. The horse jumped all the way around without putting a hoof wrong, and he was well placed in the leading trio as they turned into the finishing straight for the second and final time. The other two contenders were, as my mother had predicted they would be, Newark Hall and Sovereign Owner.

The three horses jumped the last fence abreast and battled together all the way to the finish line with the crowd cheering them on. Even the quiet, reserved Rebecca Garraway was jumping up and down, screaming encouragement, urging Newark Hall to summon up one last ounce of energy.

"Photograph, photograph!" announced the judge as the horses flashed past the winning post, each of them striving to get his nose in front.

No one in the box was sure which of the three had won.

Ewen Yorke and the Garraways rushed out to get to the winner's enclosure, confident that their horse had done enough, and Jackson went with them, leaving me in the box alone with Isabella and Julie.

"Do you think we won?" Julie asked, without much enthusiasm.

I was about to say that I had no idea when the public address announced, "Here is the result of the photograph. First number ten, second number six, third number eleven."

Number ten, the winner, was *Scientific.* He'd won by a short head from Newark Hall. Sovereign Owner had been third, another nose behind.

Oh shit, I thought.

"Oh, well," said Julie, shrugging her shoulders. "There's always next time. But Ewen will be like a caged tiger tonight, he hates so much to lose." She smiled at me again and raised her eyebrows in a seductive and questioning manner.

It wasn't Ewen, I thought, who was the caged tiger, it was his wife. And I had no desire to release her.

I watched on the television in the corner of the box as my mother greeted her winner, a genuine smile of triumph on her face. In the euphoria of victory, in the moment of ecstasy of beating Ewen Yorke, she had clearly forgotten that she had disobeyed the instructions of the man who might hold the keys to her prison cell.

It was too late to change anything now, I thought, so she might as well enjoy it while she could. Perhaps the stewards would find that Scientific had bumped into or somehow impeded one of the other horses.

But, of course, they didn't. And there were no objections, other than mine, and that wouldn't carry much authority with the stewards.

Scientific had won against the orders.

Only time would tell what the blackmailer thought.

10

"What the bloody hell is going on?" Ian Norland stood full square in the middle of the Kauri House kitchen, shouting at my mother and me. He had thrown the bridle with the broken reins onto the bleached pine table.

"Ian, please don't shout at me," my mother said. "And what's the problem anyway? Scientific won, didn't he?"

"More by luck than judgment," Ian almost shouted at her. "It was just fortunate that the reins parted on the way to the start rather than in the race itself."

Or unfortunate, I thought.

"Why?" Ian said in exasperation. "Just tell me why."

"Why what?" I asked.

"Why did you made the reins break?"

"Are you accusing us of deliberately sabotaging the reins?" my mother asked in her most pompous manner.

"Yes," he said flatly. "I am. There's no other explanation. This bridle was brand-new. I put the Australian noseband on it myself just a few days ago."

"Perhaps there was a fault in its manufacture," I said.

He looked at me with contempt. "Do you take me for an idiot or something?"

I assumed it was a rhetorical question, and so I kept quiet.

"If I don't get some answers," he said, "then I'm leaving here tonight for good, and I will take this to the racing authorities on Monday morning." He picked up the bridle in his hand.

I wondered if it was worth pointing out to him that the bridle was not actually his to take away.

"But why?" my mother said. "Nothing happened. Scientific won the race."

"But you tried to make him lose it," Ian said, his voice again rising in volume towards a shout.

"What on earth makes you think we had anything to do with the reins breaking?" I asked him, all innocently.

He again gave me his contemptuous look. "Because you've been so bloody interested in the racing tack all week, asking questions and all. What else am I going to think?"

"Don't be ridiculous," said my mother.

"And how about the others?" he said.

"What others?" my mother asked rather carelessly.

"Pharmacist last week and Oregon the week before. Did you stop them from winning too?"

"No, of course not." My mother sounded affronted.

"Why should I believe you?" Ian said.

"Because, Ian," I said, in my best voice-of-command, "you must." He turned to look at me with fire in his eyes. I ignored him. "Of course you can go to the authorities if that is what you want. But what would you tell them? That you suspect your employer of stopping her horses. But why? And how? By cutting the reins? But it would not have been the first time that reins have broken on a racetrack, now, would it?"

"But —" Ian started.

"But nothing," I replied, cutting him off. "If you choose to leave here now, then I will have to insist that you do not take any of my mother's property with you, and that includes that bridle." I held out my hand towards him with the palm uppermost and curled my fingers back and forth. Reluctantly, he passed the bridle over to me.

"Good," I said. "Now let us understand

each other. My mother's horses are always doing their best to win, and the stable is committed to winning on every occasion the horses run. My mother will not tolerate any of her employees who might suggest otherwise. She expects complete loyalty from her staff, and if you are not able to guarantee such loyalty, then indeed, you had better leave here this evening. Do I make myself clear?"

He looked at me in mild surprise.

"I suppose so," he said. "But you have to promise me that the horses will always be doing their best to win, and that there will be no more of this." He pointed to the bridle.

"I do promise," I said. There was no way I would be trying this cutting-the-reins malarkey again, I thought, and the horses would be doing their best even if they might be somewhat hampered by feeling ill. "Does that mean you're staying?"

"Maybe," he said slowly. "I'll decide in the morning."

"OK," I said. "We'll see you in the morning, then." I said it by way of dismissal, and he reluctantly turned away.

"I'll put the bridle back in the tack room for repair," he said, turning back and reaching out for it.

"No," I said, keeping a tight hold of the leather. "Leave it here."

He looked at me with displeasure, but there was absolutely no way I was going to let Ian leave the kitchen with the sabotaged bridle. Without it, he had nothing to show the authorities, even though, to my eyes, the ends of the stitches that I had cut with the scalpel looked identical to the few I had left intact, and which had then broken on the way to the start.

Ian must have seen the determination with which I was holding on to the bridle, and short of fighting me for it, he had to realize he wasn't going anywhere with it. But still he didn't leave.

"Thank you, Ian," my mother said firmly. "That will be all."

"Right, then," he said. "I'll see you both in the morning."

He slammed the door in frustration on his way out. I went over to the kitchen window and watched as he crunched across the gravel in the direction of his flat.

"How good a head lad is he?" I asked, without turning around.

"What do you mean?" my mother said.

"Can you afford to lose him?"

"No one is indispensable," she said, rather arrogantly.

I turned to face her. "Not even you?"
"Don't be ridiculous," she said again.
"I'm not," I said.

Dinner on Saturday night was a grim affair. Had it really been only one week since my arrival at Kauri House? It felt more like a month.

As before, the three of us sat at the kitchen table, eating a casserole that had been slow-cooking in the Aga while we had been at the races. I think on this occasion it was beef, but I didn't really care, and the conversation was equally unappetizing.

"So what do we do now?" I asked into the silence.

"What do you mean?" my stepfather said.

"Do we just sit and wait for the blackmailer to come a-calling?"

"What else do you suggest?" my mother asked.

"Oh, I don't know," I said in frustration. "I just feel it's time for us to start controlling him, not the other way round."

We sat there in silence for a while.

"Have you paid him this week?" I asked.

"Yes, of course," my stepfather replied.

"So how did you pay?"

"In cash," he said.

"Yes, but how did you give him the cash?"

"The same way as always."

"And that is?" I asked. Why was extracting answers from him always such hard work?

"By post."

"But to what address?" I asked patiently.

"Somewhere in Newbury," he said.

"And how did you get the address in the first place?"

"It was included with the first blackmail note."

"And when did that arrive?"

"In July last year."

When Roderick Ward had his accident.

"And the address has been the same since the beginning?" I asked him.

"Yes," he said. "I have to place two thousand pounds in fifty-pound notes in a padded envelope and post it by first-class mail each Thursday."

I thought back to the blackmail note that I had found on my mother's desk. "What happened that time to make you late with the payment?"

"I got stuck in traffic, and I didn't get to the bank in time to draw out the money before they shut."

"Couldn't you use a debit card in a cash machine?"

"It would only give me two hundred and fifty."

"Can you get me the address?" I asked.

As he stood up to fetch it, the telephone rang. As one, we all looked at the kitchen clock. It was exactly nine o'clock.

"Oh God," my mother said.

"Let me answer it," I said, standing up and striding across the kitchen.

"No," my mother shouted, jumping up. But I ignored her.

"Hello," I said into the phone.

There was silence from the other end.

"Hello," I said again. "Who is this?"

Again nothing.

"Who is this?" I repeated.

There was a click on the line and then a single tone. The person at the other end had hung up.

I replaced the receiver back on its cradle.

"Talkative, isn't he?" I said, smiling at my mother.

She was cross. "Why did you do that?" she demanded.

"Because he has to learn that we aren't going to just roll over and do everything he says."

"But it's not you that would go to prison," my stepfather said angrily.

"No," I said. "But I thought we'd agreed

that we can't go on paying the blackmailer forever. Something has to be done to resolve the VAT situation, and the first thing I need to know is who the blackmailer is. I need to force him into a mistake. I want him to put his head up above the parapet, just for a second, so I can see him."

Or better still, I thought, so I can shoot him.

The phone rang again.

My mother stepped forward, but I beat her to it.

"Hello," I said. "Kauri House Stables."

There was silence again.

"Kauri House Stables," I repeated. "Can I help you?"

"Mrs. Kauri, please," said a whispered voice.

"Sorry?" I said. "Can you please speak up? I can't hear you."

"Mrs. Kauri," the voice repeated, still in the same quiet whisper.

"I'm sorry," I said extra-loudly. "She can't speak to you just now. Can I give her a message?"

"Give me Mrs. Kauri," the person whispered again.

"No," I said. "You will have to talk to me."

The line went click again as he hung up.

My mother was crosser than ever.

"Thomas," she said, "please do not do that again." She was almost crying. "We must do as he says."

"Why?" I asked.

"Why!" she almost screamed. "Because he'll send the stuff to the tax man if we don't."

"No, he won't," I said confidently.

"How can you know?" she shouted. "He might."

"I think it most unlikely that he'll do anything," I said.

"I hope you're right," my stepfather said gloomily.

"What has he to gain?" I said. "In fact, he has everything to lose."

"I'm the one with everything to lose," my mother said.

"Yes," I agreed. "But you are paying the blackmailer two thousand a week, and he won't get that if he tips off the tax man. He's not going to give up that lucrative arrangement just because I won't let him speak to you on the telephone."

"But why are you antagonizing him?" my stepfather said.

More than two thousand years ago Sun Tzu, a mysterious Chinese soldier and philosopher, wrote what has since become the textbook of war, a volume that is still studied in military academies today. In *The Art of War* he stated that one should "beat the grass to startle the snake." What he meant was to do something unexpected to make the enemy give away their position.

"Because I need to see who it is," I said. "If I knew the identity of the enemy, I could then start to fight him."

"I don't want you to fight him," my mother said forlornly.

"Well, we have to do something. Tax returns are overdue, and it is only a matter of time before the VAT fraud is discovered. I need to identify the enemy, neutralize him, recover your money and tax papers and then pay the tax. And we need to do it all quickly."

The phone rang again. I picked it up.

"Kauri House Stables," I said.

Silence.

"Now, listen here you little creep," I said, beating the grass still further. "You can't speak to Mrs. Kauri. You'll have to speak to me. I'm her son, Thomas Forsyth."

More silence.

"And another thing," I said, "all the horses from these stables will, in the future, be trying their best to win. And if you don't like it, hard bloody luck. You can come and speak to me about it anytime you like, face-to-face. Do you understand?"

I listened. There was another few seconds of silence, followed by the now familiar click as he disconnected.

I had just committed a huge tactical gamble. I had put *my* head way up over the parapet, exposing myself to the enemy, beating the grass in the hope that this particular snake would be startled enough to give away his position, so I could shoot him.

But would he shoot me first?

Sunday had been an uneventful day, with apparently no further telephone calls from the whispering blackmailer. However, I couldn't be certain that he hadn't called during the time I'd been out in the middle of the day.

My mother had responded to my initiative of Saturday evening by withdrawing into her shell and not appearing at all from her bedroom until six in the evening, and only then briefly to raid the drinks cabinet before returning upstairs to bed. Derek had been dispatched downstairs later to make her a sandwich for her dinner.

I was certain that if the whisperer had called while I was out, my mother wouldn't have told me. Perhaps she felt like most of the civilians I had encountered in Afghanistan. Even though we firmly believed that we were fighting the Taliban on behalf of the Afghan people, they didn't seem to share the same view. The old adage "my enemy's enemy is therefore my friend" simply didn't apply. It was true that most of the population loathed the Taliban, but deep down they also hated the foreigners in their midst who were fighting them.

In the same way, I wondered if my mother considered me to be as much her enemy as her blackmailer.

Ian Norland had not made another appearance in the house on Sunday morning, and I had watched through the kitchen window as he had directed the stable staff in the mucking out, feeding and watering of the horses. I had taken it to mean that he had decided to stay, at least for the time being. Meanwhile, the broken reins in question were sitting safely in the locked trunk of my car.

At noon on Sunday I had driven into Newbury, using the Jaguar's satellite navigation system to find the address that Derek had finally given me, the address to which he sent the weekly cash payments.

"But it's so close," I'd said to my stepfather. "Surely you've been to see where it is you send all this money."

"He said not to," he'd replied.

"And you obeyed him?" I'd asked incredulously. "Didn't you just drive past to see? Even in the middle of the night?"

"We mustn't. We have to do exactly what he says." He had been close to tears. "We're so frightened."

I could see. "And how specifically did he tell you not to go and see where the money was going?"

"In a note."

"And where's the note now?" I'd asked him.

"I threw it away," he'd said. "I know I shouldn't have, but they made me feel sick. I threw all the notes away."

All of them except the one I'd found on my mother's desk.

"So when did the telephone calls start?"

"When he started telling us the horses must lose."

"And when was that?" I'd asked.

"Just before Christmas." Two months ago.

I hadn't really expected the address to provide any great revelation into the identity of the blackmailer, and I'd been right.

Forty-six Cheap Street in Newbury turned out to be a shop with rentable mailboxes, a whole wall of them, and suite 116 was not a suite of offices as one might have thought, but a single, six-by-four-inch gray mailbox at shoulder level. The shop had been closed on Sunday, but I had no great expectation that, had the staff been there, they would have told me who had rented box number 116. In due course, when I was ready, the police might be able to find out.

I had returned to Kauri House from Newbury via the Wheelwright Arms in the village for a leisurely lunch of roast beef with all the trimmings. I'd been in no particular hurry to get back to the depressing atmosphere at home. I decided it was time to start looking for more agreeable accommodation — past time, in fact.

Early the next morning, I drove to Oxford and parked in the multistory parking lot near the Westgate shopping center. The city center was quiet, even for a Monday in February. The persistent cold snap had deepened with a bitter wind from the north that cut through my overcoat as effortlessly as a well-honed bayonet through a Taliban's kurta. Most sensible people had obviously decided to stay at home, in the warm.

Oxford Coroner's Court was housed next door to the Oxfordshire County Council building in New Road, near the old prison. According to the court proceedings notice, the case in which I was interested was the second on the coroner's list for the day, the case of Roderick Ward, deceased.

It was too cold to hang around outside, so I sat in the public gallery for the first case of the day, the suicide of a troubled young man in his early twenties who had hanged himself in a house he'd shared with other students. His two female housemates cried almost continuously throughout the short proceedings. They had discovered the swinging body when they had returned from a nightclub at two o'clock in the morning, having literally stumbled into it in the dark.

A pathologist described the mechanics of death by strangulation due to hanging, and a policeman reported the existence of a suicide note found in the house.

Then the young man's father spoke briefly about his son and his expectations for the future that would now not be fulfilled. It was a moving eulogy, delivered with great dignity but with huge sadness.

The coroner, having listened to the evidence, thanked the witnesses for attending, then officially recorded that the young man had taken his own life.

We all stood up, the coroner bowed to us, we bowed back, and he departed through a door behind his chair. In all, the formal proceedings had taken just twenty minutes. It seemed to me to be a very swift finale to a life that had lasted some twenty-two years.

Next up was the inquest into the death of Roderick Ward.

There was an exchange of personnel in the courtroom. The young suicide's father and his weeping ex-housemates trooped out, along with the policeman and the pathologist who had given evidence. In came different men in suits, plus one in a navy blue sweater and jeans who joined me in the public gallery.

I glanced at him, and just for a moment, I thought he looked familiar, but when he turned full-face towards me, I didn't know him, and he showed no sign of having recognized me.

There was no young woman in the court who might have been Stella Beecher. But there again, she had never received the letter sent to her at 26 Banbury Drive by the Coroner's Office, to inform her that the inquest was going to reconvene today. I was absolutely sure of that, because the said letter was currently in my pocket.

The inquest began with the coroner giving the details of the deceased, Mr. Roderick Ward. His address was given as 26 Banbury Drive, Oxford, but even I knew that was false. So why didn't the court? I wanted to stand up and tell them they were wrong, but how could I do it without explaining how I knew? Once I started there would be no stopping, and the whole sorry saga of the tax evasion would be laid bare for all to see, and especially for the Revenue to see. My mother would be up on a charge quicker than a guardsman found sleeping on sentry duty.

The coroner went on to say that the body of the deceased had been identified by his sister, Mrs. Stella Beecher, of the same address. Another lie. Had the whole identification been a lie? Was the body found in the car actually that of Roderick Ward, or of someone else? And where was Stella Beecher now? Why wasn't she here? The whole business seemed fishy to me, but only because I knew that Roderick Ward himself had been busily working outside the law. To everyone else it was a simple but tragic road accident.

The first witness was a policeman from the Thames Valley Road Traffic Accident Investigation Team, who described the circumstances, as he had determined them, surrounding the death of Roderick Ward on the night of Sunday, July 12.

"Mr. Ward's dark blue Renault Mégane

had been proceeding along the A415 in a southerly direction," he said formally. "The tire marks on the grass verge indicate that the driver failed to negotiate the bend, veered over to the wrong side of the road and struck the concrete parapet of the bridge where the A415 crosses over the River Windrush. The vehicle appeared to have then gone into the river, where it was found by a fisherman at eight a.m. on the morning of Monday, July thirteenth. The vehicle was lying on its side with just six inches or so of it visible above the water level."

The coroner stopped him there as he made some handwritten notes. "Go on," he said eventually, looking up at the policeman.

"The vehicle was removed from the river by crane later that morning, at approximately ten-thirty. The deceased's body was discovered inside the vehicle when it was lifted. He was still strapped into the driver's seat by his seat belt. The Coroner's Office was immediately informed, and a pathologist attended the scene, arriving at" — he consulted his notebook — "eleven twenty-eight, by which time I had also arrived at the scene to begin my investigation."

The policeman paused again as the coroner wrote furiously in his own notebook. When the writing paused, the policeman went on.

"I examined the vehicle both at the scene and also at our vehicle-testing facility in Kidlington. It had been slightly damaged by the collision with the bridge but, other than that, was found to be in full working order with no deficiencies observed in either the braking or the steering. The seat belts were also noted to be in perfect condition, locking and unlocking with ease. At the scene I examined the concrete parapet of the bridge and the tire skid marks on the grass verge. There were no marks visible on the road surface. It appeared to me from my examinations that while the vehicle had struck the bridge wall, this collision in itself was unlikely to have been of sufficient force to prove fatal. While it was noted that the airbag in the vehicle had deployed, the damage to both vehicle and bridge indicated that the collision was minor and had occurred at a relatively low speed."

He paused and drank some water from a glass.

"From the position and directions of the marks on the grass and the lack of skid marks on the road, I conclude that the driver might have fallen asleep at the wheel, been awakened when the vehicle rose up onto the grass verge, had then braked hard, slowing the vehicle to between ten and fifteen miles per hour, before it struck the bridge parapet. The force of the collision, although fairly minor, had been sufficient to bounce the vehicle sideways into the river, the damage to the car and the bridge being consistent with that conclusion."

The policeman stopped and waited while the coroner continued to make notes.

"Has anyone any questions for this officer," said the coroner, raising his head from his notebook.

"Yes, sir," said a tall gentleman in a pin-striped suit, standing up.

The coroner nodded at him, clearly in recognition.

"Officer," the tall man said, turning to the policeman in the witness box. "In your opinion, would this life have been saved if a crash barrier had been fitted at the point where the car went off the road into the water?"

"Most probably, yes," said the policeman.

"And would you agree with me," the pin-striped suit went on, "in your capacity as a senior police accident investigator, that the failure of the Oxfordshire County Council to erect a crash barrier at that known accident black spot was tantamount to negligence on their behalf, negligence that resulted in the death of Roderick Ward?"

"Objection," said another suit, also standing up. "Counsel is leading the witness."

"Thank you, Mr. Sims," said the coroner. "I know the procedures of this court." He turned towards the first suit. "Now, Mr. Hoogland, I agreed that you could ask questions of the witnesses in this case, but you know as well as I do that the purpose of this court is to determine the circumstances of death and not to apportion blame."

"Yes, sir," replied Mr. Hoogland, "but it can be within the remit of this court to determine if there has been some failure in the system. It is my client's position that a systematic failure by the county council to address the safety of the public at this point on the highway network has contributed to the death of Mr. Ward."

"Thank you, Mr. Hoogland. I am also well aware of the remits and responsibilities of this court." The coroner was clearly not amused at being lectured in his own courtroom. "However, your question of the officer was whether, in his opinion, there had been negligence in the matter of this death. This question is not answerable by this court, and would be better asked in any civil case that may be brought in a county court." He turned to the witness. "I uphold Mr. Sims's objection. Officer, you need not answer Mr. Hoogland's question."

The policeman looked relieved.

"Are there any further questions of this witness?"

There was no fresh movement from Mr. Hoogland other than to sit down. He had made his point.

However, I now wanted to stand up and ask the officer if, in his opinion as a senior police accident investigator, the circumstances of this death could have been staged such that it only appeared that the deceased had fallen asleep, hit the bridge and ended up in the river, when, in fact, he had been murdered?

But of course I didn't. Instead, I sat quietly in the public gallery in frustration, wondering why I was suddenly becoming obsessed with the idea that Roderick Ward had been murdered. What evidence did I have? None. And indeed, was the deceased actually Roderick Ward in the first place?

"Thank you, officer," said the coroner. "You may step down, but please remain within the vicinity of the court in case you are needed again."

The policeman left the witness box and

was replaced by a balding, white-haired man with half-moon spectacles and wearing a tweed suit. He stated his name as Dr. Geoffrey Vegas, resident pathologist at the John Radcliffe Hospital in Oxford.

"Now, Dr. Vegas," said the coroner, "can you please tell the court what knowledge you have concerning the deceased, Mr. Roderick Ward?"

"Certainly," replied the doctor, removing some papers from the inside pocket of his jacket. "On the morning of July thirteenth I was asked to attend the scene of an RTA — a road traffic accident — near Newbridge, where a body had been discovered in a submerged vehicle. When I arrived at the scene the body was still in the car, but the car had been lifted from the river and was on the road. I examined the body in situ and confirmed that it was of a male adult and that life was extinct. I gave instructions that the body be removed to my laboratory at the John Radcliffe."

"Did you notice any external injuries?" asked the coroner.

"Not at that time," replied the doctor. "The surface of the skin had suffered from immersion in the water, and the extremities and the face were somewhat bloated. The cramped conditions in the car did not lend themselves to more than a limited examination."

And I bet they weren't very pleasant conditions, either. I'd once had to deal with some dead Taliban whose bodies had been submerged in water, and it was not a task I chose to dwell on.

"And did you perform a postmortem examination at the hospital?"

"Yes," replied Dr. Vegas. "I completed a standard autopsy examination of the deceased that afternoon in my laboratory. My full report has been laid before the court. I concluded that death was due to asphyxia, that's suffocation, resulting in cerebral hypoxia and then cardiac arrest. The asphyxia appeared to be due to prolonged immersion in water. Put simply, he drowned."

"Are you certain of that?" the coroner asked.

"As certain as any pathologist could be. There was water present in the lungs, and in the stomach, both of which indicate that the deceased was alive when he entered the water."

"Are there any other findings that you would like to bring specifically to the court's attention?" asked the coroner, who, I thought, must have surely read the pathologist's full report prior to the hearing.

"A blood test indicated that the deceased had been more than three times over the legal alcohol limit for driving a vehicle on the public highway." He said it in a manner that clearly indicated that the accident, and the death, had been the deceased's own fault, and nothing else mattered.

"Thank you, doctor," said the coroner. "Does anyone else have any questions for this witness?"

I wanted to jump up and ask him if he had carried out a DNA test to be certain that the body was actually that of Roderick Ward. The police must have had his DNA on record after his arrest for throwing the brick in Hungerford. And I also wanted to ask the doctor why he was so certain that the deceased had died in the way he had described. Had he done a test to confirm that the water in the lungs had actually come from the river? Could the man not have been forced to drink heavily, then been drowned elsewhere and just tipped into the river in his car when he was already dead? Could the pathologist be certain it wasn't murder? Had he, in fact, even considered murder as an option?

But of course, again I didn't. Once more I remained sitting silently in the public gallery, wondering if I was looking for something sinister in this death that didn't actually exist. Something that might begin to lead me to a resolution of my mother's problems.

Mr. Hoogland, however, did stand up again to ask some questions of the doctor, but even he would have had to admit that in the light of the blood-alcohol evidence, he was on a hiding to nothing.

"Dr. Vegas," he began anyway, "can you tell the court if, in your opinion, Mr. Ward would be alive today if a crash barrier had been installed at that location, preventing his vehicle from entering the water? Were there, for example, any injuries you found that he had sustained in the accident that would, by themselves, have proved fatal without his drowning?"

"I can state that there were no injuries that Mr. Ward had suffered in the collision which would normally have resulted in loss of life," the doctor replied. "In fact, there were almost no injuries of note, just a minor contusion to the right side of the head that would be consistent with it banging against the driver's-door window during the collision with the bridge." He turned to the coroner. "This may have been sufficient to render the deceased briefly unconscious or unaware, especially in his inebriated condition, but it would have been insufficient, on its own, to cause death. On examination of the deceased's brain, I found no evidence of injury as a result of the collision."

It was obviously not the specific unequivocal answer that Mr. Hoogland had been hoping for. He tried again. "So let me get this clear, Dr. Vegas. Are you saying that Mr. Ward would now be alive if a safety barrier had been present at the spot?"

"That I cannot say," replied the doctor. He pulled himself up to his full height and delivered the killer blow to Mr. Hoogland's argument. "In the state that Mr. Ward must have been in that night from drink, there is no saying that if he had been able to drive on from that point, he wouldn't have killed himself, and possibly others, in another road traffic accident somewhere else."

The coroner, using his notes, summed up the evidence and then recorded a verdict of accidental death, with Mr. Ward's excessive alcohol consumption as a contributory factor.

No one objected, no one cried foul, no one believed that a whitewash had occurred. No one other than me, that was. And maybe I was just being paranoid.

I stood up and followed the man in the navy blue sweater and jeans out of the courtroom.

"Are you family?" I asked his back.

He turned towards me, and I thought again that I recognized him.

"No," he said. "Are you?"

"No," I said.

He smiled and turned away. In profile, I was struck once more by his familiarity. I was about to say something more to him when I realized who he must be.

It was true that I'd never met the man before, but I was certain I'd spoken to his father only the previous Friday. They had exactly the same shape of head.

The other man in the public gallery had been Fred Sutton, the detective sergeant son of Old Man Sutton, he of the broken window and the false teeth.

I hung back as Fred Sutton made his way out of the court building. I didn't really want to talk to him, but I did want to speak to the unfortunate Mr. Hoogland.

I caught up with him in the lobby. Close up he was even taller than he had appeared in court. I was almost six foot, but he towered over me.

"Excuse me, Mr. Hoogland," I said, touching him on the arm. "I was in the court just now, and I wondered who you were acting for."

He turned and looked down at me. "And who are you?" he demanded.

"Just a friend of Roderick Ward's," I said. "I wondered if you were acting for his family. None of them seem to be here."

He looked at me for a second or two, as if deciding whether to tell me or not. "I am acting for a life insurance company," he said.

"Really," I said. "So was Roderick's life insured?"

"I couldn't say," said the lawyer, but it was pretty obvious it had been; otherwise, why was he here asking questions and trying to imply negligence by the county council? Insurance companies would try anything to save themselves from having to pay out.

And who, I wondered, was the potential beneficiary of the insurance?

"So were you satisfied with the verdict?" I asked.

"It's what we expected," Mr. Hoogland said dismissively, looking past my right shoulder.

Time to dive in, I thought. "Are you absolutely sure that the dead man in the car was Roderick Ward?"

"What?" he said, suddenly giving me his full attention.

"Are you sure that it was Roderick Ward in that car?" I asked again.

"Yes, of course. The body was identified by his sister."

"Yes, but where is the sister today?" I said. "And is she the beneficiary of your client's insurance policy?"

He stared at me. "What are you implying?"

"Nothing," I lied. "I'm just curious. If my brother had died, and I'd been the one to identify him, then I'd be at the inquest." Mr. Hoogland wasn't to know that the coroner's letter to Stella Beecher was in my pocket.

"Why didn't you say this in court?" he asked.

"I'm not what they call an 'officially interested party,' " I said. "So why would I be allowed to speak? And it's not compulsory for members of the deceased's family to be present at an inquest. Anyway, I don't have access to the full pathologist's report. For all I know, he might have already done a DNA test and double-checked it against the national DNA database."

"Why would Roderick Ward's DNA be in the database?" he asked.

"Because he was arrested two years ago for breaking windows," I replied. "It should be there."

Mr. Hoogland opened a notebook and made some notes.

"And what is your name?" he asked.

"Is that important?" I said.

"You can't go round making accusations anonymously."

"I'm not accusing anyone," I said. "I just asked you if you were sure it was Roderick Ward in that car."

"That in itself is an accusation of fraud."

"Or murder," I said.

He stared at me again. "Are you serious?"

"Very," I said.

"But why?"

"It just seems too easy," I said. "Late at night on a country road with little or no traffic, low-speed collision, contusion on the side of the head, alcohol, car tips into convenient deep stretch of river, no attempt to get out of the car, life insurance. Need I go on?"

"So what are you going to do about your theory?"

"Nothing," I said. "It's not me that has the client who's about to pay out a large sum in life insurance."

I could see in his face that he was having doubts. He must be asking himself if I was a complete nutter.

"You've nothing to lose," I said. "At least find out for sure if the deceased really was Roderick Ward by getting a DNA test done. Maybe the pathologist already has. Look in his report."

He said nothing but stared at a point somewhere over the top of my head.

"And ask the pathologist if he tested to determine if the water in the lungs actually came from the river."

"You *do* have a suspicious mind," he said, again looking down at my face.

"Did Little Bo Peep actually lose her sheep, or were they stolen?"

He laughed. "Did Humpty Dumpty fall, or was he pushed?"

"Exactly," I said. "Do you have a card?"

He fished one out of his jacket pocket and gave it to me.

"I'll call you," I said, turning away.

"Right," he shouted to my departing back. "You do that."

11

I woke in agony. And in the dark, pitch-black dark.

Where was I?

My arms hurt badly, and my head was spinning, and there was some sort of cloth on my face, rough cloth, like a sack.

What had happened?

It felt as if I was hanging by my arms and my shoulders didn't like it, not one bit. My whole back ached, and my head pounded as if there were jackhammers trying to break out of my skull behind my eyes. I felt sick, very sick, and I could smell the rancid odor of vomit on the cloth over my face.

How had I got here?

I tried to remember, but the pain in my arms clouded every thought. Being blown up by an IED had nothing on this. My upper body screamed in agony, and I could hear myself screaming with it. Whoever thought too much pain brought on unconsciousness was an idiot. My brain, now awake, clearly had no intention of switching off again. How much pain does it take to kill, I wondered. Surely it was time for me to die?

Was this just another bad dream?

No, I decided, this was no dream. This agony, sadly, was reality.

I wondered if my arms were actually being pulled from their sockets. I couldn't feel my hands, and I was suddenly very afraid.

Had I been captured by the Taliban? The very thought struck terror into my heart. I could feel myself coming close to panic, so I put such thoughts back in their box and tried to concentrate solely on the locations of my pain and its causes.

Apart from the ongoing fire in my back and arms, my left leg also hurt — in particular, my heel. "Concentrate," I shouted out loud at myself. "Concentrate." Why does my heel hurt? Because it's pressing on the floor. Now I realized for the first time that I wasn't hanging straight down. My left foot was stretched out in front of me. I bent my knee, pulled my foot back, and stood up. The searing agony in my shoulders instantly abated. The change was dramatic. I no longer wanted to die. Instead, I became determined to live.

Where was I? What happened? Why was I here? And how did I get here?

The same questions kept rotating over and over in my head.

I knew that I couldn't have been captured by the Taliban. I remembered that I was in England, not in Afghanistan. At least, I assumed I was still in England. But could I assume anything? The world had suddenly gone mad.

I felt dizzy. Why couldn't I stand up properly?

Then I remembered that too.

I reached down to the floor with my right leg. Nothing. My prosthesis was missing. I could feel the empty right trouser leg flapping against my left calf as I moved my leg back and forth.

Standing up, even on one leg, had vastly improved the pain in my back and shoulders, and feeling was beginning to return to my hands with the onset of horrendous pins and needles. But that was a pain I could bear. It was a good sign. In fact, it was the only good sign I could think of at the moment.

My head went on throbbing, and I continued to feel sick.

I turned my head from side to side, which did nothing to improve my nausea. Not a chink of light was visible at any point through the hood. I heel-and-toed myself through half a revolution and looked again. Still nothing.

I was at home in darkness, but even so, I closed my eyes tight. I had discovered many years ago that with my eyes firmly held shut I could somehow switch off that part of my brain that dealt with visual images and increase the concentration on my other senses.

I listened but could hear nothing, save for my own breathing inside the hood.

I smelled the air, but the overpowering stench of vomit clouded out almost everything. There was, however, a faint sweet smell alongside it. Glue, perhaps, I thought, or something like an alcoholic solvent.

With my now recovered and responsive fingers, I searched the space above my head. My wrists were tightly bound together by some sort of thin plastic, which was in turn attached to a chain. I followed the chain along its short length until I came to a ring fixed into the solid wall. The ring was set just over my head height, six-feet-six or so from the floor, and was about two inches across. I could feel that the chain was secured to it by a padlock.

I leaned forward against the wall. There

was something running horizontally that was sticking into my elbows. I couldn't quite get my hands low enough to feel it, so I used my face through the cloth. The horizontal bar ran in both directions as far as I could feel, with a small ledge above it. I banged on the wall with my arms, and suddenly I knew where I was.

I was in a stable. The horizontal bar and ledge that I could feel was the top of the wooden boarding that runs around a stall to protect a horse from kicking out at the unforgiving brick or stone. And the ring in the wall was there to tie up the horse, or to hang a hay net.

But which stable was I in? Was it in my mother's stable yard? Was Ian Norland asleep upstairs?

I shouted. "Can anyone hear me? Help! Help!"

I went on shouting for ages, but no one came running. I don't think the hood helped. My voice sounded very loud to me inside it, but I wondered if the noise had even penetrated beyond the stable.

I was pretty sure I wasn't at Kauri House Stables. When I stopped shouting to listen, it was too quiet. Even if there had been an empty stall in my mother's yard, there would be horses nearby, and horses make noises, even at night, and especially if someone is shouting their head off next door.

I was beginning to be particularly irritated by the hood, not least by having to breathe vomit fumes, even if it was my own vomit. I tried to hold the material and pull it off, but it was tied too tightly around my neck and I couldn't reach down with my hands far enough to untie it. I would just have to stand the irritation. It was nothing compared to the previous pain in my shoulders.

I stood on my one leg for a long time. Occasionally I would lean back against the wall, but mostly I just stood.

I wondered how long I had been here before I woke, and how much longer I was to remain. But that decision wasn't mine.

Night turned into day. I found that I could tell because a very small amount of light did penetrate the dark cloth of the hood, and if I turned my head, I could just tell that there was a window to my left as I stood with the wall behind me.

The day brought nothing new.

I went on standing for hours.

I was hungry and thirsty, and my leg began to ache. And to make matters worse, I desperately needed to pee.

I tried to remember how I had come to be

here. I could recall the inquest and speaking to Mr. Hoogland. What had happened after that?

I had walked back to my car in the multistory parking lot. I could remember being annoyed that someone had parked so close to my Jaguar on the driver's side. I had purposely parked it on a high level, well away from any other cars, and it was not just because I didn't want to get my paintwork scratched. The attaching system for my prosthetic leg meant I couldn't bend my right knee through more than about seventy degrees, so getting into my low sports car was not as easy now as it had once been.

My annoyance had stemmed from the fact that the particular level of the parking lot was still almost empty, but nevertheless, someone had parked within a foot of the off side of my car. I remembered wondering how on earth I was going to open the driver's door wide enough to get my arm in, let alone my whole body.

But I had never reached the door to try.

Something had knocked me down, and I remembered having a towel wrapped around my face. The towel had been soaked in ether. I had known immediately what it was. The boys from the transport pool had used ether in Norway when the battalion had been there on winter exercise. They'd injected it straight into the engine cylinders to get the army trucks started when the diesel fuel was too cold to ignite. All the troops, including me, had tried to sniff the stuff to get high. But ether was also an anesthetic.

And the next thing I'd known had been waking up in this predicament.

Who could have done such a thing?

And why had I been so careless as to let it happen? I'd been off my guard, thinking about the inquest and my conversation with the lawyer, Mr. Hoogland. I had stuck my head up over the parapet, but I hadn't been shot, I'd been kidnapped.

I wasn't sure which was worse.

As time passed, I became hungrier and the pain in my bladder grew to the extent that in the end, I had to let go, the urine briefly warming my leg as it ran down to the floor.

But it was the thirst and the fatigue that were becoming my greatest problems.

In the army, soldiers were used to standing for long periods, especially in the Guards regiments. Lengthy stints of ceremonial duty outside the royal palaces in London taught all guardsmen to stand completely still for hours, unmoved and unamused by the antics of camera-wielding tourists or little boys with water pistols.

I had done my time there as a young guardsman, but nothing had prepared me for the hours of standing on only one leg, unable to go for a march up and down to alleviate the pain, and especially the cramp that started to appear in my calf. I tried rocking back and forth from heel to toe, but my heel was still sore and it didn't do much good. I tried resting my elbows on the ledge at the top of the wooden paneling to relieve the pressure. But nothing helped for long.

I bent my knee and allowed some of my weight to hang once more from my hands, but soon the pain in my shoulders returned and my hands started to go numb once more.

I spent some more time shouting, but no one came, and it just made me even thirstier.

What did the people who did this want from me?

I would gladly give them everything I owned just to sit down with a glass of water.

Values and Standards of the British Army stated that prisoners must be treated with respect and in accordance with both British and international laws. International Law is based on the four Geneva Convention treaties and the three additional protocols that set the standards for the humanitarian treatment of victims of war.

I knew; I'd been taught it at Sandhurst.

In particular, the conventions prohibit the use of torture. Hooding, sleep deprivation and continuous standing had all been designated as torture by case law in the European Court of Human Rights. To say nothing of the withholding of food and water.

Surely someone had to come soon.

But they didn't, and the light from the window went away as day turned into my second night in the stable.

I passed some of the time counting seconds.

Mississippi one, Mississippi two, Mississippi three, and so on . . . and on . . . and on. Mississippi sixty to one minute, Mississippi sixty times sixty to one hour. Anything to keep my mind off the pain in my leg.

Eventually, sometime that I reckoned, from my counting, must be after midnight, it dawned on me that my kidnapper simply wasn't going to arrive with food and water for his hostage. If he had been going to, he'd have come during the daylight hours or in the early evening.

I faced the shocking reality that I wasn't

here to be ransomed, I was here to die.

In spite of the pain in my leg, I went to sleep standing up.

I only realized when I lost my balance and was woken by the jerk of the chain attached to my wrists. I twisted around so I was facing the wall and stood up again.

I was cold.

I could tell that I was only in my shirtsleeves. I'd been wearing an overcoat when I walked back to the car from the Coroner's Court, but it had obviously been removed.

I shivered, but the cold was the least of my worries.

I was desperately thirsty, and I knew that my body must be getting dehydrated. My kidneys had gone on making urine, and I had peed three times during the day, losing liquid down my leg that I could ill afford. I knew from my training that in these cool conditions, human beings could live for several weeks without food but only a matter of a few days without water.

The knowledge was not hugely comforting.

I thought back to the survival-skills instructor at Sandhurst who had told me that. The whole platoon had sat up and taken special notice of the attractive female captain from the Royal Army Medical Corps who had taught us about the physiological effects of the various situations in which we might find ourselves.

Sadly, there hadn't been a lecture on how to stand forever on one leg.

But the captain had turned out to be more than just an army medico who knew the theory, she was a get-up-and-go girl who had put it into practice. She was the female equivalent of Bear Grylls, spending all her army leave on expeditions to remote parts, and she could count both poles as well as the top of Everest in her résumé.

"If you're in a bit of a spot," she had said, grossly understating some of the "spots" she had described from her own experiences, "never just sit and wait to be rescued. Your best bet for survival is always to evacuate under your own steam if that is humanly possible. There are well-documented occasions when people with broken legs, or worse, left for dead high up on Everest, have subsequently turned up alive at Base Camp. They crawled off the mountain. No one else was going to save them, so they saved themselves."

I was definitely in a bit of a spot.

Time, I thought, to save myself.

■ ■ ■ ■

First things first. I had to get myself disconnected from the ring in the wall. It sounded deceptively easy.

I reached up with my hands to where the chain was attached by the padlock. The ring stuck straight out from the wall as if it had been screwed in as a single piece. I grabbed hold of it with my right hand and tried to twist it anticlockwise. It didn't budge an iota.

I went on trying for a long time. I wrapped the chain around the ring and put all my weight on it. I then tried to twist the chain, rotating my body around and around, back and forth, hoping that I would find a weak link to snap. Nothing.

Next, I tried turning the ring clockwise in case it had a left-hand screw thread. Still nothing, other than sore fingers.

I jerked it with the chain, on one occasion throwing myself off balance and back into the hanging-by-shoulders position. But still the damn ring didn't shift. If I couldn't detach myself from the ring, then I would simply hang here until I died of dehydration, and the exertions of trying to escape would reduce the time that would take.

"Always to evacuate under your own steam if that is humanly possible." That's what the lady captain had said. Maybe freeing myself from the ring wasn't humanly possible.

I felt like crying, but I knew that would be another loss of precious fluid.

And I desperately needed an evacuation of a different kind.

How degrading bodily functions could be when they occurred in the wrong place at the wrong time. At least in the hospital, when I'd been bedridden and incapable, there had been bedpans and nurses close by to assist. Here I was, standing on my one very sore leg, imprisoned in a stable, unable even to remove my trousers, let alone to squat or sit on a toilet.

Who was the bastard who would force me to shit in my pants?

I was angry. Bloody angry.

I tried to channel my anger into a resurgence of energy and strength as I once more gripped the ring and tried to turn it. Again it resisted.

"Come on, you bugger, move!" I shouted at the ring. But it didn't.

I rested my head in frustration on the ledge at the top of the wooden paneling. So fed up was I that I bit through the cloth of the hood into the wood.

It moved.

I thought I must be imagining it, so I bit the wood again. It definitely moved.

I felt around with my face. The ledge on the top of the paneling was about an inch and a half wide, with its front edge curved, and it was the curved edge that had moved. It was obviously a facing strip that had been glued or nailed to the front of the ledge.

I bit into the wood again. Even through the hood, I found I could get my front teeth behind the curved beading. I bit hard and pulled backwards, using my arms to press on the wall. The curved beading strip came away from the ledge far enough for me to get my mouth around it properly. I pulled back again and it came away some more.

I was pulling so hard with my mouth that when one end of the strip came completely free, I again lost my balance and ended up hanging from the chain.

But I didn't care.

I pulled my knee back under me and stood up. The beading was flapping, with one end free and the other not. There had obviously been a join in the wood just a little way to my left.

I held the wood in my mouth and twisted my neck to the right, making the free end bend upwards. I could feel the free end on my arms, and finally, after nearly twisting myself again off my foot, I was able to grasp the strip in my hands.

I now bent myself to the right, folding the strip back on itself.

It snapped with a splintering crack, leaving me holding a free length of the beading. I couldn't see how long it was, but I carefully fed it through my fingers until I reached the end. This I put through the ring, and then I used it like a crowbar.

Still the ring resisted, and I again lost my balance and ended hanging by the chain as the end of the wood broke off. But I didn't let go of the rest of it.

I stood up once more and passed the broken end back through the ring.

This time I turned the wood through ninety degrees so that it was edge on, and hoped it would be more difficult to break. Then I leaned on it with as much weight as I dared.

The ring moved. I felt it. I leaned again. It moved some more.

I was so excited that I was laughing.

The ring had almost moved half a revolution. I put the wooden strip into my mouth to hold it, almost gagging on the vomit-tasting cloth. I then reached up and tried to turn the ring with my fingers. It was stiff, but it turned, slowly at first, then over and over until I could feel it part company with the wall.

I could lower my arms. I was free of my shackle. What bliss!

I quickly hauled down my pants and underwear, and then crouched against the wall to defecate. I could remember from my boyhood that my father had often described his morning constitutional on the lavatory as his golden moment of the day. Now, at long last, I knew what he meant. The relief was incredible. So much so that I hardly cared that disengaging myself from the wall was only the first step in my escape.

I pulled my pants up and then heel-and-toed my way along the wall until I found a corner. With difficulty, I sat down on the floor. I still had my wrists tied and I was still wearing the hood, but the joy of not having to stand up any longer was immense.

Stage one was complete. Now I had to remove the hood and free my wrists. No problem, I thought. If I could get away from that wall, everything else must be a piece of cake.

I lifted my hands to my neck and found the drawstring of the hood. With my hands still bound together at the wrists, it was not easy to untie the knot, and I'd probably tightened it with all my earlier tugging. However, I finally managed to get the string free, and I gratefully pulled the oppressive, fetid cloth over my head. I breathed deeply. The atmosphere in the stable may not have been that fresh, for obvious reasons, but it was a whole lot better than the rancid, vomit-smelling air I'd been breathing for the past thirty-six hours.

I shook my head and pushed my fingers through my hair.

Stage two complete. Now for my hands.

It was too dark to really see how they were tied, but by feeling with my tongue, I worked out that my kidnapper had used the sort of ties that gardeners use to secure bags of garden waste, or saplings to poles. The loose end went through a collar on the other end, and was then pulled tight, very tight, one tie on each wrist interlooped both with each other and with the chain.

I tried biting my way through the plastic, but it was too tough and my efforts ended with me still tied up, but now with a sore mouth where the free ends of the ties kept sticking into my gums.

I looked around. It may have been dark, but there was just enough light entering for me to see the position of the window. I thought that if I could get outside, I might be able to find something to cut the plastic. But how was I going to get outside with only one leg, and with my wrists tied up?

How about the glass in the window? Could I use that to cut the plastic?

If getting down to the floor had been difficult, it was nothing compared to getting up again. Finally, I was upright, but a cramp in my calf had me hopping around to try to ease it. I leaned on the wall and stretched forward, and the cramp thankfully subsided.

I hopped along the wall to the window.

It wasn't glass, it was Plexiglas. It would be. I suppose the horses would break glass. The window was actually made of two panes of Plexiglas in wooden frames, one above the other, like a sash window. I slid the bottom pane up. The real outdoor fresh air tasted so sweet.

But now I discovered there was another problem.

The window was covered on the outside by metal bars set about four inches apart. I'd had no food for two days, but even I wasn't yet slim enough to fit through that gap. I rested my head on my arms. I could feel the panic beginning to rise in me again. I was so thirsty, yet I could hear the rain. I held my arms out through the window as far as they would go, but they didn't reach the falling water. There was just enough light for me to see that the roof had an overhang. I would have needed arms six feet long to reach the rain. And to add insult to injury, it began to fall more heavily, beating like a drum against the stable roof.

"Water, water everywhere, Nor any drop to drink."

More in hope than expectation, I hopped farther along the wall to the stable doors. As expected, they were bolted. I pushed at them, but unsurprisingly, they didn't shift. I would have stood and kicked them down if only I'd had a second leg to stand on while I did so.

Instead, I slithered down in the corner by the door until I was again sitting on the floor. Wiggling myself into position on my back, I tried to use my left leg to kick the lower section of the door. I kicked as hard as I could, but the door didn't budge. All I managed to do was to slide myself in the other direction across the stone floor.

I gave up and went to sleep.

It was light when I woke, and I could see my prison cell properly for the first time. It was nothing extraordinary, just a regular stable stall with black-painted wooden boarding around the walls, and timber roof beams visible above.

I worked myself back into the corner by the door and sat up, leaning against the wall, to inspect the bindings on my wrists that were beginning to really annoy me.

The black plastic ties looked so thin and flimsy, but try as I might, I couldn't break them. I twisted my wrists first one way then the other, but all that happened was that the plastic dug painfully into my flesh, causing it to bleed. The damned plastic ties seemed totally unaffected.

The length of chain was still attached to the ties. It was gray and looked to me like galvanized steel. There were fifteen links in all, I counted them, each link a little under one inch long with a shiny brass padlock still attaching the end link to the now-unscrewed ring. The chain looked brand-new. No wonder I hadn't been able to break it.

I tried to use the point of the ring to cut through one of the ties, but I couldn't get a proper grip on it and only managed instead to cut through the skin at the base of my thumb as the point slipped off the surface of the plastic.

I looked around the stable for something

sharp, or for a rough brick corner, anything I could use to saw my way through my bonds. Up on the wall opposite the window was a salt-lick housing, a metal slot about four inches wide, seven high and one inch deep, into which a block of salt or minerals could be dropped so that, as the name suggested, the horse could lick it. The housing was empty, old and rusting.

I struggled up from the floor and hopped over to it. As I had hoped, the top of the metal slot had been roughened by the rust. I hooked the plastic ties over one of the edges, with a wrist on either side, and sawed back and forth. The plastic was no match for the metal edge, and the tie on my left wrist parted quite easily. Wonderful!

I massaged the flesh, then set about ridding myself completely of the remaining tie around my right wrist and the chain that still hung from it. That task proved a little more difficult, but after a few minutes, I was finally free of the damn things.

Stage three was complete. Now to get out of this stable.

Stable doors are always locked from the outside, whether or not the horse has bolted first, and this one was no exception.

I could just see the locks from the window.

The metal bars were bowed away slightly from the frame, and by turning sideways I could use my left eye to see the bolts, top and bottom in the lower door and a single bolt in the upper. All three had been slid fully away from me, and then folded flat.

I took the window bars in my hands and tried to shake them. Not even a quiver. It was as if they were set in concrete.

So there was no easy way out, but I'd hardly expected there to be. No one was going to go to the trouble of shackling me to the wall with a chain and padlock only then to leave the door wide open.

The way out, as I saw it, was to go up.

I could see from the window that the stable where I was imprisoned was just one in a whole line of them that stretched away in both directions. The walls between the individual stalls did not go all the way to the pitched roof; they were the same height as the walls at the front and rear of the building, about nine feet high. So there was a triangular space between the top of the wall and the roof. A wooden roof truss sat on top of the wall, but there was still plenty of room for someone to get through the gap from one stall to the next. All I had to do was climb the wall.

Easy, I thought. There had been walls

much higher than this on the assault course at Sandhurst, walls I had been forced to cross time and time again. However, there were some big differences. Either there had been a rope hanging from the top of the wall or there'd been a team of us working together. And I had been much fitter and stronger when at Sandhurst, and, of course, I'd had two feet to work with.

I looked at either side of the stable. Which way should I go?

In the end, the decision was simple. In the corner opposite the door was a metal manger set across the angle. It was about four feet from the floor. I may have had only one foot, but I had two knees, and I was soon using them to kneel on the edge of the manger while reaching up with my fingers for the top of the wall.

All those hours of trying to break the battalion record for pull-ups finally paid off. Fueled by a massive determination to free myself, together with the all-consuming craving for a drink, I pulled myself up onto the top of the wall and swung my legs through the gap in the truss and into the next stall.

Dropping down was less easy, and I ended up sprawled on my back. But I didn't care; I was laughing again. I turned over and crawled on my hands and knees to the door.

It was locked.

My cries of joy turned to tears of frustration.

OK, I thought, getting a grip on things, how about the window?

More bars. Squeezing myself up against them, I could see that there were bars on all the stable windows.

OK, I just have to keep going. One of these damn stables must have a door that's open.

Having done it once, it was easier the second time. I even managed not to end up horizontal on the floor. But the next door was also locked.

What if they were all locked? Was I wasting my energy and, worse still, breathing out precious water vapor in a fruitless attempt?

I clambered onto the manger in the corner and went over the next wall. The door to that stall was also locked. I sat in the corner and wept. I realized that I must be dehydrated, as I wept without tears.

What would happen, I wondered, when the lack of water became critical? I'd been thirsty now for so long that every part of my mouth and throat was sore, but I didn't feel that I was dying yet. How would my body react over the next day or so? What would be the first sign that it was shutting down? Would I even realize?

I thrust such thoughts out of my mind. Come on, I told myself. Maybe the door will be open in the next stall.

It wasn't.

My fingers hurt from pulling myself up, and on that occasion, I had twisted my ankle when I dropped down. Thankfully, it wasn't a bad injury, but it was enough to send me into another bout of despair. Was this how it would happen? Would I become an emotional gibbering wreck? Would I eventually just curl up in a ball in a corner and die?

"No!" I shouted out loud. "I will not die here."

Willpower alone pulled me up over the next wall. Beyond it I found not another stable but an empty and disused tack room at the end of the row. I used the saddle racks to ease my way to the floor and save my ankle from further punishment.

The tack-room door was locked. It would be.

And I could see there was nowhere else to go. The far wall of the tack room went all the way to the roof. It was the end of the building, the end of the line.

The door had a mortise deadlock, I could see through the keyhole. Why, I wondered, had someone bothered to lock an empty room?

I leaned against the locked door in renewed frustration. For the very first time I really began to believe that I would die in this stable block.

My stomach hurt from lack of food, and my throat felt as though it was on fire from lack of water. I had expended so much of my reserves just getting to the tack room that the thought of going all the way back to where I'd started, and then beyond, filled me with horror. And there was no saying that I would be able to. The mangers would now all be on the wrong side of the walls.

I looked through the small window alongside the door. The light was beginning to fade as fresh, delicious, glorious rain fell again into puddles that were tantalizingly out of my reach. It would soon be dark. This would be my third night of captivity. Without water to drink, would I still be alive for a fourth?

Suddenly, as I looked through at the gloom and rain, I realized there were no bars on this window. The bars had been placed over the stable windows to keep the horses' heads in, not to keep burglars out.

There were no horses in the tack room, so no bars.

And the single pane of this window was glass, not plastic like the others.

I looked around for something with which I could break it. There was absolutely nothing, so I sat on one of the saddle racks and removed my shoe.

The glass was no match for a thirsty man in a frenzy. I used the shoe to knock all the glass from the frame, careful to leave no jagged shards behind.

The window was small, but it was big enough. I clambered through headfirst, using the end of my stump to stand on the frame while I pulled my complete leg through to stand up on the outside of the building.

What a magnificent feeling. Stage four was complete.

I hopped out from under the overhanging roof to stand in the rain with my head held back and my mouth wide open.

Never had anything tasted so sweet.

12

Escaping from the stable building was only the first of the hurdles.

I didn't know where I was, and I could hardly hop very far, I was hungry with no food and, perhaps most important of all, I had no idea who had tried to kill me.

Would they try again when they discovered that I was still alive?

And would they come back here to check? To dispose of the body?

Why had they not made sure by bashing my head in rather than leaving me alive to die slowly?

I knew from my own experience that killing another person wasn't easy. It was fine if you could do it at a distance. Firing a rocket-propelled grenade into an enemy position was easy. Taking out an enemy commander from half a mile away using a sniper rifle and a telescopic sight was a piece of cake. But sticking a bayonet into the chest of a squirming, screaming human being at arm's length was quite another matter.

Whoever had done this had left me alive in the stable for their own benefit, not for mine. They had intended to kill me but had wanted time and dehydration to do their dirty work for them.

In that respect, I had an advantage over them. If, and when, we met again, they might hesitate before killing me outright, and that hesitation would be enough for me, and an end for them. Another Sandhurst instructor floated into my memory. "Never hesitate," he'd said. "Hesitate, and you're dead."

The falling rain did not give me anywhere near enough water to quench my roaring thirst, so I tried one of the taps that were positioned outside each stable. I turned the handle, but no water came out. Not surprisingly, the water was off.

In the end, I lay down on the concrete and lapped water from a puddle like a dog. It was easier and more fulfilling than using my cupped hands to try to lift it to my mouth.

Hunger and mobility were now my highest priorities.

What I needed was a crutch, something like a broom, to put under my arm. I crawled on hands and knees back along the line of stables until I came to the one I had been held in. I pulled myself upright, slid the bolts on both parts of the door, and opened them wide. I had become used to the fresh outside air, and the rank, disgusting smell in the stable caught me unawares. I retched, but there was nothing in my stomach to throw up. Had I really lived in there for two days? How bad would the smell have been if I'd died there?

There was no broom in the stable, I knew that, but I had decided to take the ring, the chain and the padlock away with me. If I did go to the police, I would have them as evidence. I also collected the bits of the plastic ties. One never knew, perhaps they were distinctive enough to point to whoever had bought them.

I looked around my prison cell one last time before closing the door. I slid home the bolts, as if wanting to lock the place out of my memory.

I hopped along the line and opened the next stable, looking for a broom, but I discovered something a whole lot better.

Suddenly things were looking up. Lying on the floor was my artificial leg, together with my overcoat.

Hanging me up to die had been a calculated evil. But removing my leg had been nothing more than pure malice. I resolved, there and then, that I would make the person who did this to me pay a heavy price.

I leaned against the door frame and put the leg on, rolling the securing rubber sleeve up over my knee.

I had always rather hated it, this *thing* that wasn't a real part of me. But now I gladly accepted it back as more than a necessary evil — it was a chum, an ally and a brother. If nothing else, the last two days had taught me that without my metal-and-plastic companion, I would be a helpless and incapable warrior in battle. But together, my prosthesis and I would be a force to be reckoned with.

The joy of walking again on two legs was immense. The familiar clink-clink was like music to my soul.

I picked up my coat and put it on against the cold. My shirt was still wet from standing in the rain, and I was grateful for the coat's thick, warm, fleecy lining. I put my hands into the pockets and found, to my surprise, my cell phone, my wallet, my car keys and the business card from Mr. Hoogland.

The phone was off. I'd switched it off for the inquest. So I turned it on and the familiar screen appeared. I wondered who I should call.

Who did I trust?

I explored the stable block to try to find out where I was.

I could have probably used my cell to call the police and they would have been able to trace where the signal came from, but I really wanted to find out for myself.

I had visions of lying in wait for my would-be murderer to come back to check that I was dead. What chance would I have of getting my payback if the boys in blue arrived with flashing lights and sirens, clomping around the place in their size-ten boots, letting the world know I'd been found and frightening away my quarry?

But before all that, I desperately needed some food. And a shower.

There were no horses in any of the stalls. And there were no people in the big house alongside them. The place was like a ghost town. And all the doors were locked. So I walked across the gravel turning area, past the house and down the driveway.

For the umpteenth time I went to look at my watch, but it wasn't on my wrist. It was the one thing I'd had with me in Oxford that was still missing, other than my Jaguar. My would-be murderer must have removed it to tie me up. I had looked all around to try to find it, without success.

However, I judged from the light that it must be after five o'clock. There was just enough brightness for me to see where I was going, but full darkness would not be far away.

The driveway was long but downhill, which helped, and at the end there were some imposing seven-feet-high wrought-iron gates between equally impressive stone pillars. The gates were closed and firmly locked together by a length of chain and a padlock that both looked suspiciously similar to those in my coat pocket.

I looked up at the top of the gates. Did I really have to start climbing again?

No, I didn't. A quick excursion ten yards to the left allowed me to step through a post-and-rail fence. The imposing gates were more for show than for security. But the chain and padlock would have been enough to prevent some passing Nosey Parker from driving up to the house to have a look around, someone who might then have found me in the stables.

There was a plastic sign attached to the

outside of one of the gateposts.

"FOR SALE," it said in bold capital letters, then gave the telephone number of a realtor. I recognized the dialing code: 01635 was Newbury.

The realtor's sign was nailed over another wooden notice. I pulled the for-sale sign away to reveal the notice beneath, and I could just see the painted words in the gathering gloom. "Greystone Stables," it read. And in smaller letters underneath, "Larry Webster — Racehorse Trainer."

I could remember someone had told me about this place. "The Webster place," they'd said. "On the hill off the Wantage Road." So I was back in Lambourn, or just outside. And I could see the village lights about half a mile or so away, down the road.

What do I do now, I thought.

Do I phone my mother and ask her to collect me, or do I call the police and report a kidnapping and an attempted murder? I knew I should. It was the right and the sensible thing to do. I should have done it as soon as I found my phone. And then my mother would simply have to take her chances with the tax man, and the courts.

Something was stopping me from calling the police, and it wasn't only the belief that my mother would then end up losing everything: her house, her stables, her business, her freedom and, perhaps worst of all for her to bear, her reputation.

It was something more than that. Maybe it was the need to fight my own battles, to prove to myself that I still could. Possibly it was to show the major from the MOD that I wasn't ready for retirement and the military scrap heap.

But above all, I think it was the desire to inflict personal revenge on the person who had done this to me.

Perhaps it was some sort of madness, but I put the phone in my pocket and called no one. I simply started walking towards the lights, and home.

I was alive and free, and for as long as someone believed that I was tied up and dead, I had the element of surprise on my side. In strategic terms, surprise was everything. The air attack on Pearl Harbor just before eight o'clock on a sleepy Sunday morning in December 1941 was testament to that. Eleven ships had been either sunk or seriously damaged and nearly two hundred aircraft destroyed on the ground for fewer than thirty of the attackers shot down. More than three and a half thousand Americans had been killed or wounded for the loss of just sixty-five Japanese casualties. I knew because at Sandhurst, each officer cadet had to give a presentation to their fellow trainees about a Second World War engagement, and I had been allocated Pearl Harbor.

Surprise had been crucial.

I had already shown myself to the enemy once, and I had barely survived the consequences. Now I would remain hidden, and better still, my enemy must surely believe that I'd already been neutralized and was no longer a threat. Just when he thought I was dead I would rise up and bite him. I wanted my Glenn-Close-in-the-bath moment from *Fatal Attraction,* but I wasn't going to then get shot and killed, as her character had been.

I walked through the village, keeping to the shadows and avoiding the busy center, where someone might have spotted me near the brightly lit shop windows. Only the damn clink-clink of my right leg could have given me away. I resolved to find a way to make my walking silent once more.

When I arrived at the driveway of Kauri House I paused.

Did I really want my mother and stepfather to know what had happened to me? How could I explain my dirty and disheveled condition to them without explaining how I came to be in such a state? And could I then trust them not to pass on the knowledge to others, even accidentally? Absolute secrecy might be vital. "Loose talk costs lives" had been a wartime slogan. I certainly didn't want it costing mine.

But I urgently needed to eat, and I also wanted to wash and put on some clean clothes.

As I approached I could see that the lights were on in the stables and the staff were busily mucking out and feeding their charges.

I skirted around the house and approached down the outside of the nearest stable rectangle, trying to keep my leg as quiet as possible. Only at the very last instant did I briefly step into the light, and only then when I was sure no one was looking.

I went quickly up the stairs and let myself in to Ian Norland's unlocked flat above the stables.

I'd taken a chance that Ian would not have locked the door while he was downstairs with the horses, and I'd been right. Now I had to decide what to tell him. It had to be enough to engage his help, but amongst other things, I thought it best not to inform him that his employer was effectively trading while insolvent, something that was strictly against the law. And I didn't want to scare him into instantly calling the police. I decided that I wouldn't tell him the whole truth, but I would try not to tell him any outright lies.

While I waited for him to finish with the horses, I raided his refrigerator. Amongst the cans of beer there were precious few food items, so I helped myself to a two-liter plastic bottle of milk. It had been as much as I could do not to go into The Rice Bowl Chinese takeaway in the village on my way through. But I had every intention of convincing Ian that he needed to go there for me the minute he came up from the stables.

I'd completely finished his two liters of milk by the time I heard him climbing the stairs.

I stood tight behind the door as he came in, but he saw me as soon as he closed it. After the cut-bridle altercation of the previous Saturday, I wasn't exactly expecting a warm welcome, and I didn't get it.

"What the fuck are you doing here?" he demanded loudly.

"Ian, I need your help," I said quickly.

He looked at me closely, at my filthy and

torn clothes and the stubble on my chin. "Why are you in such a mess?" he asked accusingly. "What have you been up to?"

"Nothing," I said. "I'm just a bit dirty and hungry, that's all."

"Why?" he said.

"Why what?" I said.

"Why everything?" he said. "Why are you lurking in my flat like a burglar? Why didn't you go to the house? And why are you hungry and dirty?"

"I'll explain everything," I said. "But I need your help, and I don't really want my mother to know I'm here."

"Why not?" he demanded. "Are you in trouble with the law?"

"No, of course not," I said, trying to sound affronted.

"Then why don't you want your mother to know you're here?"

What could I say that would convince him?

"My mother and I have had an argument," I said. I'd clearly failed dismally in my aim of not telling him any lies.

"What over?" he said.

"Does it matter?" I said. "You know my mother. She can argue over the smallest of things."

"Yeah, I know," he said. "But what was

this particular argument about?"

I could see that he was going to be persistent. He needed an answer.

"Over the running of the horses," I said.

Now he was interested.

"Tell me."

"Can I use your bathroom first?" I asked. "I'm desperate for a shower. I don't suppose you have any spare clothes my size?"

"Where are yours?"

"In the house."

"Do you want me to fetch them?" he asked.

"How could you?" I said. "My mother would surely see."

"She's out," he said. "She and Mr. Philips have gone to some big event in London. Saw them go myself round five o'clock. All dressed up to the nines, they were. She told me she'd be back for first lot in the morning."

"But there are lights on in the house."

"For the dogs," he said. "I'll go over and let them out before I go to bed. I'll turn off the lights and lock up, then."

So I could have probably gone into the house all along and never bothered Ian. I remonstrated with myself for insufficient reconnaissance of the place before I'd come up to Ian's flat. I'd assumed my mother was at home, but I should have checked.

"But my mother's car is in the driveway," I said. I remembered having seen it as I rounded the house.

"They were collected by a big flashy car with a driver," he said. "Seems like Mrs. Kauri was the guest of honor or something."

"Will they be back tonight?"

"I don't know," he said. "All she said was she'd see me at seven-thirty in the morning."

Maybe I hadn't needed to involve Ian at all, but now that I had, could he still help me?

"Right, then," I said decisively, using my voice-of-command. "I'll go over to the house to have a shower and change while you go to the Chinese takeaway and get us both dinner. I'll have beef in black bean sauce with fried rice." I held out some money from my wallet. "And buy some milk as well. I'm afraid I've drunk yours."

He stood silently, looking at me, but he took the money.

I glanced at the clock on his wall. "I'll be back here in forty-five minutes to eat and talk."

It was nearer to fifty minutes by the time I climbed back up the stairs to Ian's flat, having enjoyed a long soak in a hot bath to ease my still-aching shoulders. And I'd brought some of my stuff with me.

"What's in the tube?" Ian asked.

"My sword," I said. "I thought it might be useful."

"For what?" he said in alarm. "I'm not doing anything illegal."

"It's OK," I said. "Calm down. I promise I won't ask you to do anything illegal."

"How about you?" he asked, still disturbed.

"I won't do anything illegal either," I assured him. "I promise."

Another of those promises that I wondered if I could keep. In this case, I was rather hopeful that I wouldn't be able to, but I decided not to tell that to Ian.

He relaxed somewhat.

"So can I stay here?" I asked, placing my bag and the tube on the floor.

"What? Sleep here?" he said.

"Yes."

"But I've only got the one bed." From his tone I gathered that he had no desire to share.

"That's OK," I said. "I only want the floor."

"You can have the sofa."

"Even better," I said. "Now, how about

that food? I'm starving."

He served it out onto two fairly clean plates on his tiny kitchen table, and I tucked in to mine with gusto. I suspect a doctor would have told me that a bellyful of Chinese was not really the best medicine for a starved stomach, but I didn't care. It tasted pretty good to me.

Finally, I sat back and pushed the plate away with a sigh. I was full.

"Blimey," said Ian, who had only just started his sweet-and-sour pork. "Anyone would think you hadn't eaten for a week."

"What day is it?" I asked.

He looked at me strangely. "Wednesday."

Had it really only been on Monday that I'd gone to Oxford for the inquest? Just two and a half days ago? It seemed like longer. In fact, it felt like half a lifetime.

Did I want to tell Ian why I was so hungry? Did he need to know why I hadn't eaten since Monday morning? Perhaps not. It would take too much explaining, and he might not be very happy that I hadn't called the cops.

"Not too many restaurants about when you're living rough," I said.

" 'Living rough'?"

"Yeah," I said. "I've been up on the

Downs for a couple of nights in a shelter I made."

"But it's so cold, and it's done nothing but rain all week."

"Yeah, and don't I know it. I couldn't light my fire," I said. "But it's all good training. Nothing like a bit of discomfort to harden you up."

"You army blokes are barmy," Ian said. "You wouldn't catch me outside all night in this weather." He poured more bright pink sweet-and-sour sauce over his dinner.

So much for not telling him outright lies; I'd hardly uttered a word that was true.

"So tell me," he said. "What was it about the running of the horses that you argued with your mother about?"

"Oh, nothing really," I said, backpedaling madly. "And I am sure she wouldn't want me talking to you about it."

"You might be right there," he said, smiling. "But tell me anyway."

"I told you, it was nothing," I said. "I just told her that in my opinion, and based on his last run at Cheltenham, Pharmacist wasn't ready for the Gold Cup."

"And what did she say?" Ian asked, pointing his fork at me.

"She told me to stick my opinion up my you-know-where."

He laughed. "For once, I agree with her."

"You do?" I said, sounding surprised. "When I was here, you know, when we watched the race on the television, you said that he couldn't now run at the Festival."

"Well," he said defensively, "I may have done at the time, in the heat of the moment, like, but I didn't really mean it. One bad performance doesn't make him a bad horse, now, does it?"

"But I only said it to my mother because I thought that's what you thought."

"You should have bloody asked me, then." He speared a pork ball on his fork and popped it into his mouth.

"Looks like I'll have to beg forgiveness and ask to be allowed home."

"Did she throw you out just for saying that?" He spoke with his mouth full, giving me a fine view of his sweet-and-sour pork ball rotating around like the contents of a cement mixer.

"Well, there were a few other things too," I said. "You know, personal family things."

He nodded knowingly. "In a good row, one thing just leads to another and then another, don't it." He sounded experienced in the matter, and I wondered whether there had once been a Mrs. Norland.

"You are so right."

"So, do you still want to stay here?" he asked.

"Absolutely," I said. "I'm not going home to my mother with my tail between my legs, I can tell you. I'd never hear the end of it."

He laughed again and took another mouthful of his pork. "Fine by me, but I warn you, I get up early."

"I want to be gone before first light."

"The sun comes up at seven these days," he said. "It's light for a good half an hour or so before then."

"Then I'll be well gone by six," I said.

"To avoid your mother?"

"Perhaps," I said. "But you can ask her where she thinks I am. I'd love to know what she says, but don't tell her I've been here."

"OK, I'll ask her, and I won't tell her you're here, or what we talked about," he said, "but where are you going?"

"Back to where I've been for these past few days," I said. "I've some unfinished business there."

I took my sword, still safely stowed in its tube, when I slipped out of Ian's flat at just after five-thirty on Thursday morning. I also took the uneaten remains of the Chinese takeaway, and half the milk that Ian had bought the night before.

In addition, I took my freshly charged cell phone and the card from Mr. Hoogland. I might need something to pass the time.

I retraced my path from Kauri House, through the still sleeping village, and down the Wantage Road to Greystone Stables. One of the major successes of the night was that I had managed to stop my leg from clinking every time I put it down. The problem, I discovered, had been where the leg post met the ankle. The joint was tight enough, but the clink was made by two metal parts coming together when I put my weight on it. I'd eventually silenced it using an adjustable wrench and a square of rubber that Ian had cut from an old leaking Wellington boot. Now I relished being able to move silently once more.

The gates at the bottom of the driveway were still locked together with the chain and padlock, and they didn't appear to have been touched since I'd left them the previous evening. However, I wasn't going to assume that no one had been up to the stables in the intervening twelve hours; I would check.

I stepped back through the post-and-rail fence and climbed carefully and clink-free up the hill, keeping off the tarmac surface to reduce noise, listening and watching for anything unusual. Halfway up the drive, I checked the spot where the previous evening I had placed a stick leaning on a small stone. A car's tire would have had to disturb it to pass by, but the stick was still in place. No one had driven up this hill overnight, not unless they had come by motorbike.

I wasn't sure whether I should be pleased or disappointed.

Even so, I was still watchful as I approached the house, keeping within the line of vegetation to one side of a small overgrown front lawn. The sky was lightening in the east with a lovely display of blues, purples and reds. In spite of being completely at home in the dark, I had always loved the coming of the dawn, the start of a new day.

The arrival of the sun, bringing light and warmth and driving away the cold and darkness of the night, was like a piece of daily magic, revered and worshipped by man and beast alike. How does it happen? And why? Let us just be thankful that it did. If the sun went out, we would all be in the poop, and no mistake.

The rim of the fiery ball popped up over the horizon and flooded the hillside with an orange glow, banishing the gloom from beneath the bushes.

I silently tried the doors of the house. They were still locked.

I went right around the house, across the gravel turning area and back into the familiar stable yard beyond. In the bright morning light it looked very different from the rain-soaked space of the evening before. The stables had been built as a rectangular quadrangle with stalls along three sides, with the fourth open end facing the house.

First I went down to the far end of the left-hand block, knelt down, and carefully picked up all the shards of glass that still lay on the concrete below the window I'd broken. I placed them all carefully back through the window and out of sight. I had no way of replacing the glass pane, but one had to look closely to see that it was missing.

I walked down the row of stalls to my prison cell and opened both leaves of the stable door, hooking them open so that no one could quickly shut me in again before I could react.

I searched around the stall once more, mostly for my watch, but also in case I had missed anything else in the murk of the previous evening. I found nothing other than the small pile of my own excrement nicely drying next to the wall beneath where the ring had been secured. I knew that Special Forces teams such as the British SAS or the American Delta Force, when dropped in behind enemy lines, were trained not to leave any trace of their presence, and that included collecting their own feces in sealable plastic bags and keeping them in their packs.

In the absence of a suitable plastic bag, I decided to leave mine exactly where they were.

I quickly searched the stall next door, the one where I had found my prosthetic leg and my coat. My watch wasn't there, either. Damn it, I thought. I really liked that watch.

I closed and rebolted the stable doors and spent a moment or two checking that the positions of the bolts were precisely as I had found them. Now all I needed was a place to hide and wait.

I thought of using one of the other stables farther along, but I quickly rejected the idea. For one thing, I would have had no obvious route of retreat if things started going badly. And second, I really did not want my enemy to spot that the bolts were not properly shut and simply to lock me in as they passed, maybe even unaware that I was waiting inside. I'd had my fill of being locked in stables for this week.

In the end I found the perfect location.

Across the concrete stable yard, opposite the block of stalls in which I'd been imprisoned, there was a second row of stables facing them. In the middle of the row, there was a passageway that ran right through the building from front to rear. The passage had a door in it, on the stable-yard end, but the latch was a simple lever, not a bolt. The door was made from slats of wood screwed to a simple frame, with inch-wide gaps between the slats to allow the wind to blow through. The door had a spring near the hinge to keep it closed, but that would have not been there as a security measure, merely to keep the door shut so as to prevent any loose horses from getting through and escaping.

I lifted the latch, pulled open the door and went through the passageway. Behind the stables was a muck heap, the pile of soiled straw and wood-chip bedding where the stable staff would dump the horse dung ready for the manure man to collect periodically and sell to eager gardeners. Except that this muck heap hadn't been cleared for a long while, and there were clumps of bright green grass growing through the straw on its surface.

The passageway had obviously been placed there to provide the access to the muck heap from the stable yard. And it made an ideal hiding place.

Out the back, I found an empty blue plastic drum that would do well as a seat, and I was soon sitting behind the door in the passageway, watching and waiting for my enemy to arrive.

I longed to have my trusty SA80 assault rifle beside me, with fixed bayonet. Or better still, a gimpy with a full belt of ammunition.

Instead, all I had was my sword, but it was drawn from its scabbard and ready for action.

13

I waited a long time.

I couldn't see the sun from my hiding place, but I could tell from the movement of the shadows that many hours had passed, a fact borne out by the clock readout on the screen of my cell phone when I turned it on briefly to check.

I drank some of the milk, and went on waiting.

No one came.

Every so often I would stand up and walk back and forth a few times along the short passageway to get the blood moving in my legs. But I didn't want to go out into the stable yard in case my quarry arrived whilst I was there.

I began to wish that I had chosen a spot where I could see the gate at the bottom of the drive. From my hiding place in the passageway, I wouldn't have any warning of an arrival before they were upon me.

I went over and over the scenario, rehearsing it in my mind.

I fully expected that my would-be murderer would arrive up the driveway by car, drive across the gravel turning area, through the open gateway into the stable yard, and park close to the stall where he would expect me still to be. My plan was to leave my hiding place just as he entered the stable, to move silently and quickly across the yard, and simply to lock him into my erstwhile prison cell almost before he had a chance to realize that I wasn't still hanging there, dead.

What would happen next remained a little hazy in my mind. Much might depend on who it was. A young fit man would be able to escape over the walls and through the tack room, as I had done. An elderly or overweight adversary would prove less of a problem. I would simply be able to leave them in the stable for a bit of their own medicine. But would I leave them there to die?

And what would I do if my enemy turned out to be more than one person?

It was a question I had pondered all morning. An unconscious man, even a one-legged unconscious man, was heavy and cumbersome to move. Could one person have had enough strength to carry me into the stable and also to hold me up while padlocking me to the ring? If so, he must be a very strong individual, and escape through the tack-room window would be a real possibility.

The more I thought about it, the more convinced I became that there must have been at least two of them. And that put a completely different slant on things. Would I consider taking on an enemy that outnumbered me by two to one, or even more?

Sun Tzu, the ancient Chinese philosopher, the father of battle tactics, stated that "If you are in equal number to your enemy, then fight if you are able to surprise; if you are fewer, then keep away."

I decided that if two or more turned up, then I would just watch from my hiding place, and I'd keep away.

At three in the afternoon, while still maintaining a close watch of the stable yard, I called Mr. Hoogland. I was careful to withhold my phone number, as I didn't want him inadvertently passing it on to the wrong person.

"Ah, hello," he said. "I've been waiting for you to call."

"Why?" I asked.

"I got some answers to your questions."

"And?" I prompted.

"The deceased definitely was Roderick Ward," he said.

"Oh."

"You sound disappointed."

"No, not really," I said. "Just a bit surprised. I'd convinced myself that Roderick Ward had staged his own apparent death, while he was actually still alive."

"So who did you think was found in the car?" he asked.

"I don't know. I was just doubtful that it was Ward. How come you're so sure it was him?"

"I asked the pathologist."

"So he had done the DNA test, then?"

"Well, no, he hadn't. Not until after I asked him." He laughed. "I think I gave the poor man a bit of a fright. He went pale and rushed off to his lab. But he called me this morning to confirm that he has now tested some of the samples he kept, and the profile matches the one for Ward in the database. There's absolutely no doubt that the body in the river was who we thought it was."

Well, at least that ruled out Roderick as the blackmailer.

"Did the pathologist confirm if the water

in Ward's lungs matched that from the river?"

"Oh, sorry. I forgot to ask him."

"And how about Ward's sister?" I asked. "Did you find out anything about her?"

"Yes, as a matter of fact, I did. It seems her car broke down on the morning of the inquest, and she couldn't get to the court in time. The Coroner's Office told her they would have to proceed without her, and she agreed."

"But she only lives in Oxford," I said. "Couldn't she had taken a bus? Or walked?"

"Apparently, she's moved," he said. "They did give me her address, but I can't remember it exactly. But it was in Andover."

"Oh," I said. "Well, thanks for asking. Seems I may have been barking up the wrong tree."

"Yeah," he said wistfully. "Shame. It would have made for a good story."

"Yeah," I echoed.

"Who are you anyway?" he said.

"Never you mind," I replied.

"A journalist, maybe?" he said, fishing.

"I'm just a born skeptic," I said with a laugh. " 'Bye, now."

I hung up, smiling, and turned off my phone.

And still no one came.

■ ■ ■ ■

I ate the cold remains of the previous evening's Chinese food, and drank some more of the milk.

Why would anyone want me dead? And there was now no doubt that my death was what they had intended. I couldn't imagine what state I would have been in if I'd had to stand on one leg for four whole days and three nights. I would surely have been close to death by then, if not already gone.

So who wanted me dead? And why?

It seemed a massive overreaction to being told on the telephone that Mrs. Kauri's horses would, henceforth, be running on their merits and not to the order of a blackmailer.

Deliberate cold-blooded murder was a pretty drastic course of action, and there was no doubt that my abduction and imprisonment had been premeditated as well as cold-blooded. No one carries an ether-soaked towel around on the off chance that it might be useful to render someone unconscious, or have some plastic ties, a handy length of galvanized chain and a padlock lying about just in case someone needs to be hung on a wall. My kidnap had been well planned and executed, and I didn't expect there would be much forensic evidence available that would point to the perpetrators, if any.

So would they even bother to come back and check on their handiwork? Returning here would greatly increase their chances of leaving something incriminating, or of being seen. Wouldn't they just assume that I was dead?

But didn't they know? Never assume anything; always check.

The sun went down soon after five o'clock, and the temperature went down with it.

Still I waited, and still no one came.

Was I wasting my time?

Probably, I thought, but what else did I have to do with it? At least being out in the fresh air was better for me than lying on my bed, staring at the molded ceiling of my room.

I stamped around a bit to get some warmth into my left toes. Meanwhile, my phantom right toes were baking hot. It was all very boring.

When my telephone told me it was nine o'clock in the evening, I decided that enough was enough, and it was time to go back to Ian's flat before he went to bed and locked me out. I had never intended to stay at Greystone Stables all night. Twenty-four-hour stag duty was too much for one person. I had already found myself nodding off during the evening, and a sleeping sentry was worse than no sentry at all.

I put my sword back in its scabbard, and then I put that back in the cardboard tube, which I swung over my shoulder.

Halfway down the driveway I checked that the stick was still resting on the stone. It was. I set up another on the other side of the drive a few yards farther down, just in case the strengthening breeze blew one of them over.

Apart from the slight chill of the wind, it was a beautiful evening with a full canopy of bright stars in the jet-black sky. But it was going to be a cold night. The warm blanket of cloud of the previous few days had been blown away, and there was already a frost in the air that caused my breath to form a white mist in front of my face as I walked down towards the gates.

I was climbing through the post-and-rail fence when I saw the headlights of a car coming along the Wantage Road from the direction of Lambourn village. I thought nothing of it. The road could hardly be described as busy, but three or four cars had passed by the gates in the time it had taken for me to walk down the driveway.

I decided, however, that it would not be such a clever idea to be spotted actually climbing through the fence, so I lay down in the long grass and waited for the car to pass by.

But it didn't pass by.

It pulled off the road and stopped close to the gates. The headlights went out, and I heard rather than saw the driver get out of the car and close the door.

I lay silently, facedown in the grass, about ten yards away. I had the tube with my sword in it close to my side, but there would be no chance of extracting it here without giving away my position.

I lifted my head just a fraction, but I couldn't see anything. The glare of the headlights had destroyed my night vision, and in any case, the person would have been out of my sight behind the stone gatepost.

I closed my eyes tight shut and listened.

I could hear the chain jingling as it was pulled through the metal posts of the gates. Whoever had just arrived in the car had brought with them the key to the padlock. This was indeed my enemy.

I heard the gates squeak a little as they were opened wide.

I again lifted my head a fraction and stole a look as the driver returned to the car, but my view was obstructed by the open car door. I was lying in a shallow ditch beneath the post-and-rail fence, and my eye line was consequently below the level of the driveway. From that angle it had been impossible to see who it was.

I heard the engine start, and the headlights came back on.

I was sure the car would go up the driveway, but I was wrong.

It reversed out onto the road and drove away, back towards the village. I rose quickly to my knees. If I'd only had my SA80 at hand I could easily have put a few rounds through the back window and taken out the driver, as I had once done when a Toyota truck had crashed through a vehicle checkpoint in Helmand. As it was, I simply knelt in the grass with my heart thumping loudly in my chest.

I hadn't identified my enemy, but even in the dark, I thought I'd recognized the make of the car, even if I couldn't see the color.

"So what did my mother say?" I asked Ian when I returned to his flat at Kauri House Stables.

"About what?" he said.

"About where I was."

"Oh, that. She was rather vague. Just said you'd gone away."

"So what did you say?" I pressed.

"Well, like you told me to, I asked her where you'd gone." He paused.

"And?"

"She told me it was none of my business."

I laughed. "So what did you say to that?"

"I told her, like you said, that you'd left a pen here when you watched the races and I wanted to give it back." He infuriatingly paused once more.

"And?"

"She said to give the pen to her and she'd get it returned to you. She said that you had unexpectedly been called to London by the army and she didn't know when you would be back. Your note hadn't said that."

"My note?" I said in surprise.

"Yeah. Mrs. Kauri said you sent her a note."

"From London?" I asked.

"Oh, I don't know that," Ian said. "She didn't say, but there was no note, right?"

"No," I said truthfully. "I definitely didn't send her any note."

But someone else may have.

I woke at five after another restless night on

Ian's couch. My mind was too full of questions to relax, and I lay awake in the dark, thinking.

Why had my enemy not gone up to the stables to make sure I was dead? Was it because they were convinced that by now I would be? Perhaps they didn't want to chance leaving any new evidence, like fresh tire tracks in the stable yard. Maybe it was because it didn't matter anymore. Or was it just because they didn't want to have to see the gruesome results of their handiwork? I didn't blame them on that count. Human bodies — dead ones that is — are mostly the stuff of nightmares, especially those that die from unnatural or violent causes. I knew, because I'd seen too many of them over the years.

If my enemy hadn't bothered to go up to the hill the previous evening after unlocking the gates, I didn't expect them ever to go back there again. So I decided not to spend any more of my time waiting for them in the Greystone Stables passageway. Anyway, I had different plans for today.

"Andover," the lawyer Hoogland had said.

Now, why did that ring a bell?

Old Man Sutton, I thought. He now lived in a care home in Andover. I'd been to see him. And Old Man Sutton's son, Detective

Sergeant Fred, had been at Roderick Ward's inquest. And Roderick Ward's sister had moved to live in Andover. Was that just a coincidence?

I heard Ian get up and have a shower at six.

I sat on the sofa and attached my leg. Funny how quickly one's love for something can sway back and forth like a sail in the wind. On Wednesday afternoon I had embraced my prosthesis like a dear long-lost brother. It had given me back my mobility. Now, just thirty-six hours later, I was reverting to viewing it as an alien being, almost a foe rather than a friend, a necessary evil.

Perhaps the major from the MOD had been right. Maybe it really was time to look for a different direction in my life. If I survived my present difficulties, that was.

"Can I borrow your car?" I asked Ian over breakfast.

"How long for?" he said.

"I don't know," I said. "I've got to go to an ATM to get some money for a start. And I might be out all morning, or even all day."

"I need to go to the supermarket," he said. "I've run out of food."

"I'll buy you some," I said. "After all, I'm the one who's eaten all your cereal."

"All right, then," he said, smiling. "I'd

much rather stay here and watch the racing from Sandown on the telly."

"Do we have any runners?" I asked, surprising myself by the use of the word *we.*

"Three," Ian said. "Including one in the Artillery Gold Cup."

"Who's riding it?" I asked. The Royal Artillery Gold Cup was restricted to amateur riders who were serving, or who had served, in the armed forces of the United Kingdom.

"Some chap with a peculiar name," he said, somewhat unhelpfully.

"Which peculiar name in particular?"

"Hold on," he said. He dug into a pile of papers on a table by the television. "I know it's here somewhere." He went on looking. "Here." He triumphantly held up a sheet of paper. "Everton."

"Everton who?" I asked.

"Major Jeremy Everton."

"Never heard of him," I said. It was not that surprising. There were more than fourteen thousand serving officers in the regular army, and more still in the Territorials, to say nothing of those who had already left the service.

Ian laughed. "And he's never heard of you either."

"How do you know?" I asked.

He laughed again. "I don't."

I laughed back. "So can I borrow your car?"

"Where's yours?"

"In Oxford," I said truthfully. "The head gasket has blown," I lied. "It's in a garage."

I thought that my Jaguar was probably still in the multistory parking lot in Oxford city center, and I had decided to leave it there. To move it would be to advertise, to those who might care, that I wasn't hung up dead in a deserted stable.

"OK. You can borrow it," he said, "provided you're insured."

I should be, I thought, through the policy on my own car, provided they didn't object to my driving with an artificial foot.

"I am," I said confidently. "And I'll fill it with fuel for you."

"That would be great," Ian said. He tossed me the keys. "The handbrake doesn't work too well. Leave it in gear if you park on a hill."

I caught the keys. "Thanks."

"Will you be back here tonight?" he asked.

"If you'll have me," I said. "Do you fancy Indian?"

"Yeah," he said. "Good idea. Get me a chicken balti and a couple of onion bhajis. And some naan." He spoke with the assurance of a man who dined often from the village takeaway menus. "And I'll have some raita on the side."

It was only fair, I thought, that I bought the dinner.

"OK," I said. "About seven-thirty?"

"Make it seven," he said. "I go down to the Wheelwright on a Friday."

"Seven it is, then. See you later."

I slipped out of Ian's flat while it was still dark, and as quietly as possible, I drove his wreck of a Vauxhall Corsa down the drive and out into the village.

Newbury was quiet at seven o'clock on a Friday morning, although Sainsbury's parking lot was already bustling with early-morning shoppers eager to beat the weekend rush for groceries.

I parked in a free space between two other cars, but I didn't go into the supermarket. Instead, I walked in the opposite direction, out of the parking lot, across the A339 divided highway and into the town center.

Forty-six Cheap Street was just one amongst the long rows of shops that lined both sides of the road, most of them with flats or offices above. The mailbox shop that occupied the address opened at eight-thirty and closed at six, Monday to Friday, and from nine until one on Saturdays. It said so on the door.

If, as usual, my stepfather had mailed the weekly package to the blackmailer, the one containing the two thousand pounds, on Thursday afternoon, then the package he sent yesterday should arrive at 46 Cheap Street sometime today and be placed in mailbox 116, ready for collection.

Mailbox 116 was visible through the front window of the shop, and I intended to watch it all day to see if anyone arrived to make a collection. However, I could hardly stand outside on the pavement, scrutinizing every customer who came along. For a start, they would then be able to see me, and I certainly didn't want that to happen.

That was why I had come into Newbury so early, so that I could make a full reconnaissance of the area and determine my tactics to fit in with the local conditions and pattern of life.

At first glance there seemed to be two promising locations from which to observe the comings and goings at number forty-six without revealing my presence. The first was an American-style coffee shop about thirty yards away, and the second was the Taj Mahal Indian restaurant that was directly opposite.

I decided that the restaurant was the better of the two, not only because it was in such a good position but because there was a curtain hanging from a brass bar halfway down the window, behind which I could easily hide while keeping watch through the gap in the middle. All I needed was to secure the correct table. A notice hanging on the restaurant door told me that it opened for lunch at noon. Until then I would have to make do with the coffee shop, which began serving in half an hour, at eight o'clock.

I wanted to be well in place before the mailbox shop opened. I had no idea at what time the post was delivered, but if I'd been the blackmailer, I wouldn't have left the package lying about for long, not with that much money in it.

I went around the corner and onto Market Street and found a bank with an ATM. I drew out two hundred pounds and used some of it to buy a newspaper at the newsagent's on the corner. It wasn't that I needed something to read — doing that might cause me to miss seeing the collector — but I did need something to hide behind while sitting in the large windows of the coffee shop.

■ ■ ■ ■

At eight-thirty sharp, I watched from behind my newspaper as a man and a woman arrived, unlocked the front door of the mailbox shop and went in. From my vantage point I could just about see box number 116, but the reflection from the window didn't make it very easy. As far as I could tell, neither of the two arrivals opened that box, or any other, for that matter, but as they were the shop staff, they wouldn't have had to. They would have had access to all the boxes from behind.

I drank cups of coffee and glasses of orange juice and hoped that I looked to all the world like a man idling away the morning, reading his newspaper. On two occasions one of the coffee-shop staff came over and asked me if I needed refills, and both times I accepted. I didn't want them asking me to move on, but I was becoming worried about my level of liquid intake, and the inevitable consequences. I could hardly ask one of the staff to watch the mailbox for me while I nipped to the loo.

By ten o'clock, I had drunk nearly three large cups of coffee, as well as three orange juices, and I was becoming desperate. It reminded me of the agony I'd suffered in the stable, but on this occasion I wasn't chained to a wall. I left my newspaper and coffee cup on the table by the window to save my place, and rushed to the gents.

Nothing outside appeared to have changed in the short time I was away. The street had become gradually busier as the morning wore on, but so far, I'd not recognized anyone. I quickly rescanned the faces in front of me so as not to miss a familiar one, but there were none.

At ten to eleven I did spot someone coming slowly down the street that I recognized. I didn't know the man himself, but I did know his business. It was the postman. He was pushing a small four-wheeled bright red trolley, and he was stopping at each shop and doorway to make his deliveries. He went into the mailbox shop with a huge armful of mail held together by rubber bands. From the distance I was away, I couldn't tell whether my stepfather's package had been amongst it or not, but I suspected it had. And the blackmailer would surely assume so.

"Are you staying all day?" A young female staff member from the coffee shop was standing at my elbow.

"Sorry?" I asked.

"Are you staying all day?" she asked again.

"Is there a law against it?" I asked. "I've ordered lots of coffee, three orange juices and a Danish pastry."

"But my friend and I think you're up to something," she said. I turned in my chair and looked at her friend, who was watching me from behind the relative safety of the chest-high counter. I turned back and checked the street outside.

"Now, why is that?" I asked.

"You're not reading that newspaper," she said accusingly.

"And why do you think that?"

"You've been on the same page for at least the past hour," she said. "We've been watching. No one reads a paper that slowly."

"So what do you think I'm doing?" I asked her, still keeping my eyes on the mailbox shop.

"We think you're keeping watch for bank robbers." She smiled. "You're a cop, aren't you?"

I put a finger to my lips. "Shhh," I said, with a wink.

The girl scuttled back to her friend, and when I looked at them a minute or two later, they both put fingers to their lips and collapsed in fits of giggles.

I had half an hour to go before the Taj

Mahal opened, but I reckoned I couldn't stay here any longer. I wasn't keen on the attention I was now receiving from just about all the coffee-shop staff, as well as from some of the customers.

I beckoned the girl back over to me.

"I've got to go now," I said quietly, paying my bill. "My shift is over. But remember" — I put my finger to my lips again — "shhh. No telling."

"No, of course not," she said, all seriously.

I stood up, collected my unread newspaper and walked out. I thought that by lunchtime she would have told all her friends of the encounter, and half of their friends' friends would probably know by this evening.

I walked away down the street, certain that my every move was being watched by the girl, her friend and most of the other coffee-shop staff. I couldn't just hang around outside, so I went into the shop right next door to the Indian restaurant. It sold computers and all things electronic.

"Can I help you, sir?" asked a young man, approaching me.

"No thanks," I said. "I'm just looking."

Looking through the window.

"Just call if you want anything," he said, and he returned to where he was fiddling with the insides of a stripped-down computer.

"I will," I assured him.

I stood by a display case at the window and went on watching the shop across the road through the glass. I glanced at the display case. It was full of cameras.

"I'd like to buy a camera," I said, without turning around.

"Certainly, sir," said the young man. "Any particular one?"

"I want one I can use straightaway," I said. "And one with a good zoom."

"How about the new Panasonic?" he said. "That has an eighteen-times optical zoom and a Leica lens."

"Is that good?" I asked, still not turning around to him.

"The best," he said.

"OK, I'll have one," I said. "But it will work straightaway?"

"It should do," he said. "You'll have to charge the battery pretty soon, but they usually come with a little bit of charge in them."

"Can you make sure?" I asked.

"Of course."

"And can you set it up so it's ready to shoot immediately?"

"Certainly, sir," said the young man. "This one records direct to a memory card. Would you like me to include one?"

"Yes please," I said, keeping my eyes on the mailbox shop.

"Two-gigabyte?" he asked.

"Fine."

I went on watching the street as the young man fiddled with the camera, checking the battery and installing the memory card.

"Shall I put it back in the box?" he asked.

"No," I said. "Leave it out."

I handed him my credit card and looked down briefly to enter my PIN, and also to check that I wasn't spending a fortune.

"And please leave the camera switched on."

"The battery won't last if I do that," he said. "But it's dead easy to turn on when you need it. You just push this here." He pointed. "Then you just aim and shoot with this." He pointed to another button. "The camera does the rest."

"And the zoom?"

"Here," he said. He showed me how to zoom in and out.

"Great. Thanks."

He held out a plastic bag. "The charger, the instructions and the warranty are in the box."

"Thanks," I said again, taking the bag.

I went swiftly out of the camera shop and

into the adjacent Taj Mahal Indian restaurant just as a waiter turned the CLOSED sign to OPEN on the door.

"I'd like that table there, please," I said, pointing.

"But, sir," said the waiter, "that is for four people."

"I'm expecting three others," I said, moving over to the table and sitting down before he had a chance to stop me.

I ordered a sparkling mineral water, and when the waiter departed to fetch it, I opened the curtains in the window a few inches so I could clearly see mailbox 116.

The package was collected at twenty past one, by which time the Indian waiter no longer really believed that another three people were coming to join me for lunch.

I had almost eaten the restaurant out of poppadoms and mango chutney, and I was again getting desperate to have a pee, when I suddenly recognized a face across the road. And I would have surely missed the person completely if I'd gone to the loo.

It took only a few seconds for the collector to go into the mailbox shop, open box 116 with a key, remove the contents, close the box again and leave.

But not before I had snapped away vigorously with my new purchase.

I sat at the table and looked through the photos that I'd taken.

Quite a few were of the back of the person's head, and a few more had missed the mark altogether, but there were three perfect shots, in full-zoom close-up. Two of them showed the collector in profile as the package was being removed from the box, and one was full face as the person left through the shop door.

In truth, I hadn't really known who to expect, but the person who looked out at me from the camera screen hadn't even been on my list of possible candidates.

The face in the photograph, the face of my mother's blackmailer, was that of Julie Yorke, the caged tigress.

14

On Saturday morning at nine o'clock, I was sitting in Ian's car parked in a gateway halfway up the Baydon Road. I had chosen the position so I could easily see the traffic that came up the hill towards me out of Lambourn village. I was waiting for one particular vehicle, and I'd been here for half an hour already.

I had woken early again after another troubled night's sleep.

The same questions had been revolving around and around in my head since the early hours. How could Julie Yorke be the blackmailer? How had she obtained my mother's tax papers or, at least, the information in them?

And in particular, who was she working with?

There had to be someone else involved. My mother had always referred to the blackmailer as "him," and I had heard the whisperer myself on the telephone, and was pretty certain that it had been a man.

A motorized horse van came up the hill towards me. I sank down in the seat so that the driver wouldn't see me. I was not waiting for a horse van.

I yawned. I was tired due to lack of sleep, but I knew that I could exist indefinitely on just a few hours a night. Sometimes I'd survived for weeks on far less than that. And my overriding memory of my time at Sandhurst was that I was always completely exhausted, sometimes to the point of collapse, but I somehow kept going, as had all my fellow officer cadets.

I had again left Kauri House in Ian's car well before dawn, and before the lights had gone on in my mother's bedroom. I'd driven out of the village along the Wantage Road and had chanced driving in through the open gates of Greystone Stables, and up the tarmac driveway. I'd crept forward slowly, scanning the surface in front of me in the glow of the headlights. My two sticks remained exactly where I'd left them, leaning on the small stones. Still no cars had been driven up here since the gates had been unlocked.

It had been a calculated risk to drive up to the sticks, but no more so than leaving the car down by the gate and walking. As it was, I'd been there no more than a minute in total.

I had then driven on into Wantage and parked in the market square under the imposing statue of King Alfred the Great with his battle-ax in one hand and roll of parchment in the other, designed to depict the Saxon warrior who became the lawgiver.

I'd bought the *Racing Post* from a newsagent in the town, not having wanted to buy one at the shop in Lambourn village in case I was spotted by someone who thought I was dead, or dying.

According to the paper, Ewen Yorke had seven horses running that afternoon at two different racetracks: three at Haydock Park and four at Ascot, including two in their big race of the day, the Group 1 Make-a-Wager Gold Cup.

Haydock was about midway between Manchester and Liverpool, and a good three hours' drive away. Ascot, meanwhile, was much closer, in the same county as Lambourn, and just a fifty-minute trip down the M4 motorway, with maybe a bit extra to allow for race-day traffic.

Ewen had a runner in the first race at both courses, and if he was going to be at Haydock Park in time for the first, he would be expected to drive his distinctive top-of-the-range white BMW up the hill on the Baydon Road sometime around ten o'clock, and by ten-thirty at the very latest.

So I sat and waited some more.

I turned on the car radio, but like the handbrake, it didn't work too well. In fact, it made an annoying buzzing noise even when the engine wasn't running. It was worse than having no radio at all, so I turned it off again.

I looked at the new watch I'd bought in Newbury the previous afternoon. It told me it was nine-thirty.

At nine forty-five I recognized a car coming up the hill towards me. It wasn't a white BMW but an aging and battered blue Ford — my mother's car.

I sank down as far as I could in the seat as she drove by, hoping that she wouldn't identify the vehicle in the gateway as that of her head lad. Even if she'd done so, I knew she wouldn't have stopped to enquire after "staff," and I gratefully watched as her car disappeared around the next corner. As I had expected, my mother was off to the Haydock Park races, where she had Oregon running in the novice hurdle, his last outing before the Triumph Hurdle at the Cheltenham Festival. Ian had told me that he was looking forward to watching the race on Channel 4.

I went back to watching and waiting, but there was no sign of a white BMW.

At ten to eleven I decided it was time to move. I hadn't seen Ewen's car go past, but that didn't mean he hadn't gone to Haydock, it just meant he hadn't gone there via the Baydon Road. It was the most likely route from the Yorkes' house but certainly not the only one.

I moved Ian's car from the gateway on Baydon Road to another similarly positioned on Hungerford Hill, another of the roads out of Lambourn. If Ewen Yorke was going to Ascot this afternoon he would almost certainly pass this way, and would do so by twelve-thirty at the absolute latest if he was going to be in time to saddle his runner in the first race.

The distinctive white top-of-the-range BMW swept up the hill at five minutes to twelve, and I pulled out of the gateway behind it.

I had planned to follow him at a safe distance to avoid detection, and to make sure that he actually did drive to the motorway and join it going east towards Ascot. As it was, I had no need to worry about keeping far enough back so that the driver couldn't see that it was me behind him. Ian Norland's little Corsa struggled up Hungerford Hill as fast as it could, but Ewen Yorke's powerful BMW was already long gone, and was well out of sight by the time I reached the top road by The Hare pub.

I didn't like doing it, but I'd have to assume that he had, in fact, gone to Ascot and that he wouldn't be back in Lambourn for at least the next five hours. Once upon a time I would have been able to check by watching the racing from Ascot on BBC television. That was sadly no longer the case, as, except for the Grand National, the BBC had cut back its jump-race coverage to almost nothing. Someone in that organization seemed to believe that if a sport didn't involve wheels, balls or skis, it was hardly worth reporting.

Instead, I pulled into the parking lot of The Hare and waited, watching the road to see if the white BMW came back. Maybe he had forgotten something and would return to get it.

He didn't.

I waited a full thirty minutes before I was sure enough that Ewen and his BMW were away for the afternoon. He wouldn't now have had enough time to return home and then make it to Ascot for the first race.

I drove the Corsa out of the pub's parking lot, down the hill to Lambourn village, and pulled up on the gravel driveway next to the Yorkes' front door.

Julie seemed surprised to see me, but maybe not so surprised as if she had believed me dead.

"What are you doing here?" she asked from behind the door through a six-inch gap.

"I thought you said at Newbury races to come and see you sometime," I said. "So here I am."

She blushed slightly across her neck.

"What's in the bag?" she asked, looking at the plastic bag I was holding.

"Champagne," I said.

She blushed again, and this time, it reached her cheeks.

"You had better come in, then," she said, opening the door wide for me to pass. She looked out beyond me, as if concerned that someone had seen my arrival. It was not just her who hoped they hadn't.

"How lovely," I said, admiring the white curved staircase in the hallway. "Which way's the bedroom?"

"My," she said with a giggle. "You are an

eager boy."

"No time like the present," I said. "Is your husband in?"

"No," she said, giggling again. "He's gone to the races."

"I know," I said. "I watched him go."

"You are such a naughty boy," she said, wagging a finger at me.

"So what are you going to do about it, then?" I asked her.

She breathed deeply with excitement, her breasts rising and falling under her flimsy sweater.

"Get some glasses," I said, starting to climb the stairs. "Go on," I said, seeing her still standing in the hallway.

She skipped away while I continued up.

"In the guest room," she shouted. "On the left."

I went into the guest room on the left, and pulled back the duvet on the king-size bed.

A couple of life's little questions crossed my mind.

Was I really going to have sex with this woman?

I suppose it depended if she wanted it, and so far, the signs had been pretty positive. But did I want it too?

And there was one other pressing question.

Did I leave my leg on, or did I take it off?

On this occasion I decided that leaving it on was definitely better, especially as a quick getaway would be a likely necessity.

I went into the en suite bathroom. I thought briefly about having a shower, but it would mean taking off my leg and then putting it on again. The foot may have been waterproof, but the join between the real me and the false was not.

I stripped off, left my clothes on the bathroom floor and climbed into the bed, pulling the duvet up to my waist.

I had never paid for sex, although I'd bought quite a few expensive dinners in my time, which was tantamount to the same thing. On this occasion, however, my mother had been paying two thousand pounds a week for the past seven months. I hoped it was going to be worth it.

Julie appeared in the doorway carrying two champagne flutes in her left hand and wearing a flimsy housecoat that she allowed to fall open, revealing her nakedness beneath.

"Now, just how naughty have you been?" she asked, swinging a leather riding whip into view.

"Very," I said, opening the champagne with a loud pop.

"Oh, goodie," she replied.

It wasn't quite what I had in mind, but I went along with her little game for a while as she became more and more excited.

"Just a minute," I said, getting off the bed.

"What?" she gasped. "Get back here now!"

"Just a minute," I repeated. "I need the bathroom."

She was lying on her back, half sitting up, resting on her elbows with the whip in her right hand, her knees drawn up, and her legs spread wide apart. She threw her head back. "I just don't believe it," she cried. "You get back here right now or you'll really be in trouble."

I ignored her, went into the bathroom and put on my boxer shorts. I then took my new camera from the cupboard under the sink where I had placed it when I arrived, and checked that it was switched on. The champagne hadn't been the only thing in the plastic bag.

"Hurry up, you naughty boy," she shouted.

"Coming," I shouted back.

I came out of the bathroom taking shot after shot of her naked body as she lay on the bed, still in the same compromising position. She'd had her eyes closed, and it was a few seconds before she realized what I was doing.

"What the fuck's going on?" she screamed, throwing the whip at me and grabbing the duvet to cover herself.

"Just taking some photos," I said calmly.

"What the fuck for?" she shouted angrily.

"Blackmail," I replied.

"Blackmail!" she shrieked.

"Yes," I said. "Do you want to see?"

I held the camera towards her so she could see the screen on the back of it. But the photograph I showed her wasn't one of those I'd just taken; it was the one with her face in profile from yesterday, the one with her hand reaching into mailbox number 116 to collect the package of money.

She cried a lot.

We were still in her guest bedroom. I had thrown her the housecoat when I'd gone into the bathroom to put on my shirt and trousers, and when I'd reemerged, she had been sitting up in bed, wearing the coat, with the duvet pulled right up. Somehow she didn't look like someone up to their neck in a criminal conspiracy. She had even straightened her hair.

"It was only a game," she said.

"Murder is never a game," I said, standing at the end of the bed.

"Murder?" She went very pale. "What murder?"

My murder, I thought. Hanging on a wall in Greystone Stables.

"Who was murdered?" she demanded.

"Someone called Roderick Ward," I said, even though I had no evidence that it was true.

"No," she wailed. "Roderick wasn't murdered; he died in a car crash."

So she knew of Roderick Ward.

"That's what it was meant to look like," I said. "Who killed him?"

"I didn't kill anybody," she shouted.

"Someone did," I said. "Was it Ewen?"

"Ewen?" She almost laughed. "The only thing Ewen is interested in is bloody horses. That and whisky. Horses all day and whisky all night."

Perhaps that explained her sexually flirtatious nature — she couldn't get any satisfaction in the marital bed, so she had looked elsewhere.

"So who killed Roderick Ward?" I asked her again.

"No one," she said. "I told you. He died in a car crash."

"Who says so?" I asked. She didn't respond. I looked down at her. "Do you know what the sentence is for being an accessory to murder?" There was still no response. "Life in prison," I said. "That's a very long time for someone as young as you."

"I told you, I didn't murder anyone." She was now crying again.

"But do you think a jury will believe you once they've convicted you for blackmail?" She went on crying, the tears smudging her mascara and dripping black marks onto the white bed linens. "So tell me, who did kill Roderick Ward?" I asked.

She didn't say anything; she just buried her face in a pillow and sobbed.

"You will tell me," I said. "Eventually. Are you aware that the maximum sentence for blackmail is fourteen years?"

That brought her head back up. "No." It was almost a plea.

"Oh yes," I said. "And the same for conspiracy to blackmail."

I knew. I'd looked it up on the Internet.

"Where's the money?" I asked, changing direction.

"What money?" she said.

"The money you collected yesterday from Newbury."

"In my handbag," she whimpered.

"And how about the rest of it?"

"The rest?" she said.

"Yes, all the packages you've been collecting each week for the past seven months. Where's all that money?"

"I don't have it," she said.

"So who has?"

She still didn't want to tell me.

"Julie," I said. "You are leaving me no alternative but to give the picture of you in Newbury yesterday to the police."

"No," she wailed again.

"But I can only help you if you will help me," I said softly. "Otherwise, I will also have to send the other photos to Ewen." Both of us knew what the other photos showed. *Set a thief to catch a thief,* or, as in this case, set a blackmailer to catch a blackmailer.

"No, please." She was begging.

"Then tell me who has the money."

"Can't I pay you back in a different way?" she asked, pulling down the duvet and opening her housecoat to reveal her left breast.

"No," I said emphatically. "You cannot."

She covered herself up again.

"Julie," I said in my voice-of-command, "this is your last chance. Either you tell me now who's got the money or I will call the police." She wasn't to know that I had absolutely no intention of doing that.

"I can't tell you," she said forlornly.

"What are you frightened of?" I asked.

"Nothing."

"But you claimed it was only a game," I said. "Was it him who told you that?" I paused. She gave no answer. "Did he just ask you to collect something for him from a mailbox each week?" I paused again. Again there was no answer, but she began to cry once more. "Did he tell you that you wouldn't get caught?" She nodded slightly. "Only now you have been." She nodded again, tears flowing freely down her cheeks. "And you're not going to tell me who it was. That's not very clever, you know. You'll end up taking all the blame."

"I don't want to go to prison," she sobbed, echoing my mother.

"You don't have to," I said. "If you tell me who you give the money to, I am sure the courts won't send you to prison." Not for long anyway, I thought. Certainly not for the maximum fourteen years.

I could see that she still didn't want to say. Was it fear, I wondered, or some misguided sense of loyalty.

"Do you love him?" I asked her.

She looked up at me, still sobbing. But

she nodded.

"Then why are you doing *this?*" I waved my arm at her, at the bed, and at the riding whip that still lay on the floor where she had thrown it. She had hardly acted as if she was deeply in love with someone.

"Habit, I suppose," she said quietly.

Some habit, I thought.

"Does he love you?" I asked.

"He says so," she said, but I detected some hesitancy in her voice.

"But you're not so sure?" I asked.

"No."

"Then why on earth are you protecting him?" She gave me no answer. "OK," I said at length. "Don't say that I haven't warned you." I took my cell phone from my pocket. "And I'm sure Ewen is going to find the photographs of you most interesting. Does he know about your secret blackmailing lover? Because he will soon."

I unfolded my phone and showed her as I pushed the number nine key three times in a row, the emergency number. The phone obligingly emitted a beep each time I pressed it. I then held the phone to my ear. She wasn't to know that I hadn't also pressed the connect button.

"Hello," I said into the dead phone. "Police, please." I smiled down at Julie.

"This is your last chance," I said.

"All right," she shouted. "All right. I'll tell you."

"Sorry," I said again into the dead phone. "There's been a mistake. All is well now. Thank you." I folded my phone together.

"So who is it?" I asked.

She said nothing.

"Come on," I said, unfolding the phone again. "Tell me. Who do you give the blackmail money to?"

"Alex Reece," she said slowly.

"What?" I said, astounded. "The weasel accountant?"

"Alex is not a weasel," she said defensively. "He's lovely."

I thought back to the hours I had spent chained to a wall, and I couldn't agree with her. "So was it you and Alex Reece who chained me to a wall to die?" I was suddenly very angry, and it showed.

"No," she said. "Of course not. What are you talking about?"

"I'm talking about you leaving me to die of dehydration."

She was shocked. "I have absolutely no idea what you're talking about."

"Told you that he'd come back and let me go, did he?" I asked, my anger still very close to the surface.

"He didn't tell me anything of the sort," she said.

"But you did help him to kidnap me?" I shouted at her.

"Tom, stop it," she pleaded. "You're frightening me. And I really don't know what you are talking about. I have never kidnapped anyone in my life, and I've certainly never chained anyone to anything. I promise."

"Why should I believe you?" I asked. But I had seen the fear in her eyes, and I did believe her. But if she hadn't helped kidnap and chain me to a wall, who had?

Or could Alex Reece, my mother's blackmailer, really not be the same person as my would-be murderer?

There was very little else that Julie had to tell me. She collected the package from the mailbox shop in Newbury only when Alex Reece was unable to do so, and she didn't even know how much money was in it. When we finally went downstairs to her kitchen and she took the package from her handbag, she could hardly believe her eyes when I removed the two thousand pounds.

"It's no game," I told her. "Two thousand every week is no game."

"But she can afford it," Julie said, defiantly.

"No, she can't. And why would that make any difference, even if she could?"

"Alex says it's just redistributing the wealth," she said.

"And that makes it all right, does it?" She said nothing. "Suppose I just steal your brand-new BMW to 'redistribute the wealth.' Is that then OK with you? Or do you call the cops?"

"Alex says —" she started.

"I don't care what Alex says," I shouted, cutting her off. "Alex is nothing more than a common thief, and he clearly saw you coming. And the sooner you realize it, the better it will be for you. Or else you'll be in the dock with him, and then in prison."

And now, I thought, it was time for me to meet again with Mr. Alex Reece, and I had absolutely no intention of letting him see *me* coming.

"When and where are you meant to give this package to Reece?" I asked.

"He gets back tomorrow."

"From where?" I asked.

"Gibraltar," she said. "He went there with the Garraways on Tuesday."

So it couldn't have been him who unlocked the gates of Greystone Stables on Thursday evening.

"So when are you meant to give him the

package?" I demanded.

She clearly didn't want to tell me, but I stood next to her, drumming my fingers noisily on the kitchen worktop. "He said to bring it to Newbury on Monday," she said eventually.

"Where in Newbury?"

"There's a coffee shop in Cheap Street," she said. "That's where we always meet on Friday mornings. Except this week, of course, when he was away."

Thank goodness for that, I thought.

"So are you meeting him at the coffee shop on Monday?" I asked.

"Yes," she replied. "At ten-thirty."

It was far too public a place for what I wanted to do to him.

"Change it," I said. "Get him to collect it from here."

"Oh no. He won't ever come here. He refuses to."

"So where else do you two get together?" I didn't think a cup of coffee or two in Newbury would be quite sufficient to satisfy her other cravings.

"At his place," she said, blushing slightly.

"Which is where?" I asked impatiently.

"Greenham," she said.

Greenham was a village that had almost been consumed by the ever-expanding sprawl of Newbury town. It was most famous for its common, and the U.S. cruise missiles that had been based there at the height of the Cold War. Everyone in these parts knew of Greenham Common, and remembered the peace camps erected by antinuclear protesters.

"Where in Greenham?" I demanded.

"What are you going to do to him?"

"Nothing," I said. "As long as he cooperates."

"Cooperates how?" she asked.

"If he gives me my mother's money back, then I'll let him go."

I'd also take her tax papers.

"And if he doesn't?" she asked.

"Then I'll persuade him," I said, smiling.

"How?" she said. "Will you take photos of him naked too?"

"I doubt that," I said. "But I'll think of something."

Blitzkrieg is a German word that means "lightning war." It was used to describe the attacks on Poland, France and the Low Countries by the Nazis. Unlike the war of attrition that had existed for mile after hundred-mile of trenches in Flanders during World War I, blitzkrieg was the surprise and overwhelming attack on just a few points in the enemy's line. An attack that drove straight through to the heart of political power almost before any of the defenders had had a chance to react.

The blitzkrieg unleashed by the German forces on Poland had started on the first day of September 1939, and within a week, Wehrmacht tanks and troops were in the suburbs of Warsaw, nearly two hundred miles from their starting point. The whole of Poland had capitulated within five weeks at a cost of only ten thousand Germans killed. Compare that to the advance of only six miles gained in four and a half months by British and French troops at the Battle of the Somme, and at a cost of more than six hundred thousand dead and wounded on each side.

So if the past had taught the modern soldier anything, then it was that blitzkrieg-like "shock and awe" was the key to victory in battle, and I had every intention of creating some shock and awe in the life of one Alex Reece.

15

Bush Close in Greenham was full of those ubiquitous modern little box houses, and number sixteen, Alex Reece's home, was one at the far end of the cul-de-sac.

It was late Saturday afternoon, and I had left Julie Yorke in a state of near collapse. I had merely suggested to her that to have any contact whatsoever with Alex Reece in the next thirty-six hours, in person, by e-mail or by phone, would be reason enough for me to send the explicit photographs to her husband, in addition to posting them on my new Facebook page on the Internet.

She had begged me to delete the pictures from my camera, but as I had pointed out, it was she and Alex who had started this blackmail business, and they really couldn't now complain if they were receiving a bit of their own medicine.

I had parked Ian Norland's car out on Water Lane in Greenham and had walked around the corner into Bush Close. I was carrying a pile of free newspapers that I had picked up at a petrol station, and I walked down the road, pushing one of them through every letter box. The houses were not identical, but they were similar, and number sixteen had the same style of plastic-framed front door as all the others.

"What time does Alex get back?" I had asked Julie.

"His plane lands at Heathrow at six-twenty tomorrow evening."

"And how does he get home to Greenham?"

"I've no idea."

I lingered for a moment outside the front door of number sixteen and adjusted the pile of remaining newspapers. I glanced around, looking for suitable hiding places, but the short driveway was bordered by nothing but grass. I looked to see which of the other houses had a direct line of sight to the front door of number sixteen, set back as it was beside the single garage.

Only number fifteen, opposite, had an unobstructed view.

I walked away from number sixteen and pushed newspapers through the front doors of a few more houses, including the one opposite, before moving off down the road, back towards Ian's car. However, instead of immediately driving away, I walked through a gateway and into the adjacent field. Alex Reece's house, together with all the other even-numbered houses in Bush Close, backed onto farmland, and I spent some time carefully reconnoitering the whole area.

I looked at my watch. It was just after five-thirty, and the light was beginning to fade rapidly.

Alex Reece couldn't possibly be back here the following evening until eight o'clock at the earliest, and it would probably be nearer to nine if he had to collect luggage at the airport. And that was assuming his flight landed on time. By eight o'clock, of course, it would have been fully dark for hours.

Keeping in the shadows of some trees, I skirted around the backs of the gardens in Bush Close until I arrived at number sixteen. There were lights on in the kitchen of number fourteen next door, and I could see a man and a woman in there talking. That was good, I thought. No one can see outside at dusk when they have the lights on inside, due to the reflection in the window glass, and especially when they are busy talking. There was little or no chance that they could see me watching them.

I quickly rolled my body over the low back fence and into Alex Reece's garden. It was mostly simply laid to grass, with no tangly flower beds or thorny rosebushes to worry about.

I moved silently to the back of the garage and looked in. Even in the fast disappearing light I could see the shiny shape of a car in there. So Mr. Reece would probably arrive home by taxi, either direct from the airport or from the railway station in Newbury.

And I'd be waiting for him.

"Did we win?" I asked Ian, as I walked in through his door at seven o'clock.

"Win what?" he said, without taking his eyes off the television screen.

"Oregon," I said, "in the race at Haydock."

"Trotted up," he said, still not turning around. "Won by six lengths. Reckon he'll be hard to beat in the Triumph."

"Good," I said to the back of his head. "What are you watching?"

"Just some TV talent show."

"Have you eaten?" I asked.

"Had a pizza for lunch," he said. "From the freezer. One of them you bought yesterday. But I didn't have that until after the race. I was too nervous to eat before."

"So are you hungry?"

"Not really. Not yet. Maybe I'll have Chinese later."

"Great idea," I said. "I'll buy."

He turned around and smiled, and I guessed that was what he was hoping I'd say.

"How long are you staying?" he asked, turning back to the screen.

"I'll find somewhere else if you want," I said. "You know the houseguests and the three-day-smell rule, and my time is up tonight."

"Stay as long as you like," he said. "I'm enjoying the company."

And the free food, I thought, perhaps ungraciously.

"I'll stay another day or two, if that's all right."

"As I said, stay as long as you want, if you don't mind the couch."

I didn't. It was a lot more comfortable than some of the places I'd slept, and warmer too.

"Can I borrow your car again tomorrow?" I asked.

"Sorry, mate. I need it," he said. "I'm going to Sunday lunch with my folks."

"Where do they live?"

"Near Banbury," he said.

"So what time will you be back?" I asked.

"It'll be before five," he said. "Evening stables are at five on Sundays."

"Can I borrow the car after that?"

"Sure," he said. "But it might need more petrol by then."

"OK," I said. "I'll fill it up."

I could tell he was smiling, even though he didn't turn around. Why didn't he just ask me to pay for the use of his car? I suppose it was a little game.

I could have gone to fetch my Jaguar, but it was a very distinctive car, and I wasn't particularly keen to advertise my whereabouts to anyone. Ian's little Corsa was far more anonymous. I just hoped my Jaguar was still sitting in the parking lot in Oxford, awaiting my return.

I spent Sunday morning making my plans and sorting my kit. I had been back into Kauri House on Saturday afternoon after leaving Julie Yorke, and before my excursion to Greenham.

The house had been empty, save for the dogs, who had watched me idly and unconcerned as I'd passed through the kitchen, stepping over their beds in front of the Aga. My mother and stepfather had been safely away at Haydock races, but nevertheless, I had remained in the house for only fifteen or twenty minutes, just time enough to have a quick shower and collect a few things from my room.

I did not really want my mother coming back unexpectedly and finding me there. It was not because I didn't trust her not to give away my presence, even unwittingly, it was more that I didn't want to have to explain to her what I was going to do. She probably wouldn't have approved, so it was much better that she didn't know beforehand, if ever.

Ian left for his Sunday lunch trip at eleven, promising that he would be back in time to start work at five.

After I was sure Ian wasn't going to come back, I sorted the equipment I would need for my mission. Bits of it I had owned previously, but some things I'd driven into Newbury to buy specifically the previous afternoon on my way to Greenham.

I laid out my black roll-necked pullover, a pair of old, dark navy blue jeans, some dark socks, a black knitted ski hat and some matching gloves that I'd bought from the sports shop in Market Street, where I'd also obtained a pair of all-black Converse basketball boots.

Next to the clothes I placed the rest of my

kit: a small dark blue rucksack, some black heavy-duty garden ties similar to those that had been used to bind my wrists in the stables, a small red first-aid kit, three six-by-four-inch prints of the mailbox-shop photos, a certain metal ring with a piece of galvanized steel chain attached to it by a padlock, my camera and, finally, a roll of gray duct tape.

There is a saying in every organization of the world, either military or civilian, that if something doesn't move when it should, use WD-40, and if it moves when it shouldn't, use duct tape. Originally designed during the Second World War to keep gun magazines and ammunition boxes watertight in jungle conditions, duct tape has since become the must-have item for each and every mission. It was even used to fix a fender on the *Apollo 17* Lunar Rover when it was broken on the moon, as well as making the circular CO_2 scrubbers "fit" square holes to save the lives of the crew of the stricken *Apollo 13*.

I had decided against taking my sword. I would have loved to have had a weapon of some kind, if only for the shock value, but the sword was impractical and cumbersome. A regulation-issue Browning nine-millimeter sidearm would have been my weapon of choice, but I could hardly run around the English countryside brandishing an illegal firearm, even if I'd had one. In the end, I also elected not to borrow one of Ian's kitchen knives.

It was not as if I intended to kill anyone. Not yet anyway.

At ten minutes to eight I was in position alongside Alex Reece's house, on the dark side, away from the glow from the solitary streetlamp outside number twelve, two houses down.

I had already made a thorough reconnaissance of the area, including a special look at number fifteen, the house opposite, the one with a direct view of Alex Reece's front door. As far as I could tell, the house was unoccupied, but that might be temporary. Maybe the residents were just out for the afternoon.

Most of the other houses, including number fourteen next door, had people going about their usual Sunday-evening activities. I was actually amazed at how few of the residents of Bush Close pulled their curtains, especially at the back. Not that they would usually expect anyone to be lurking in a field, spying on them as they watched their televisions or read their books.

Eight o'clock came and went, and I continued to wait. A fine drizzle began to fall, but that didn't worry me. Rain was likely to keep the other residents inside. I had been unable to tell if any of them had a dog to walk.

At eight-eighteen a car pulled into Bush Close and drove down to the end. I was all ready for action with the adrenaline rushing through my system, but the car pulled into the driveway of number fifteen, opposite, and a couple and two young children climbed out. I breathed heavily, calming myself down, and put the surprise "jack" back in his box.

I stood silently in the shadows. I was pretty sure that no one would be able to see *me,* although I could see *them* clearly, the more so when the man turned on an outside light next to their front door. I was close to the wall, and I remained completely still.

It was movement more than anything that gave people away, caught in peripheral vision and attracting immediate attention. My dark clothes would blend into the blackness of the background; only my face might be visible, and that was streaked with homemade mud-based camouflage cream to break up the familiar shape.

There were no shouts of discovery, and

presently, the family gathered their things from the car and went inside. The outside light went out again, plunging me back into darkness. I eased myself back and forth, relieving the tension in my muscles, and went on waiting.

Alex Reece arrived home just before nine o'clock, but he didn't come by taxi.

Isabella's dark blue Volkswagen Golf pulled into the driveway at high speed and stopped abruptly with a slight squeal of its brakes. I couldn't exactly see who was at the wheel, but from past experience of her driving on the Bracknell bypass, I was pretty sure it was Isabella herself.

I pressed myself close to the wall and peeked around the corner so I could see.

Alex Reece opened the rear door and stood up next to the car with a flight bag in his hand.

"Thanks for the lift," he called, before closing the door and removing a small suitcase from the car trunk.

He stood and waved as the Golf was backed out onto the road and then driven away again at high speed. I thought the fact that Alex had been sitting in the back of the car implied that there was at least one other person in there, in addition to Isabella. Maybe it was Jackson.

I watched as Alex fumbled in his flight bag for the key to his front door. In those few seconds, I also scanned the road and the windows of the house opposite. No one was about.

It was time for action.

In the instant after he successfully opened the front door, and before he had time to reach down for his suitcase, I struck him hard midway between his shoulder blades, forcing him through the open doorway and onto the floor in the still-dark hallway. I crashed down on top of him, his flight bag sliding across the polished wood and into the kitchen.

"Scream and I'll kill you," I said loudly into his ear.

He didn't scream, but it wasn't only because he was frightened of being killed. I had purposely chosen that type of blow because it would have driven the air from his chest, and without air, he couldn't scream. In fact, he didn't react in any way. Just as I had hoped, my blitzkrieg attack had rendered him shocked and awestruck.

I pulled both his arms around to the small of his back and used the garden ties from my pocket to secure his wrists. Next, I used another pair of the ties to bind his ankles together.

The whole process had taken no more than a few seconds.

I stood up and went outside. I picked up Alex's suitcase from the step, glanced casually all around to check that nothing had stirred, then stepped back inside again, closing the front door. Alex hadn't moved a muscle.

Albert Pierrepoint, the renowned English hangman of the nineteen-forties and -fifties, always maintained that a successful execution was one when the prisoner hardly had time to realize what was happening to him before he was dangling dead at the end of the rope. He had once famously dispatched a man named James Inglis within just seven and a half seconds of his leaving the condemned cell.

Pierrepoint would have been proud of me tonight. Alex wasn't actually dead, but he had been trussed up like a chicken ready for the oven in not much longer than Albert had taken to hang a man.

And now Mr. Reece was ready for a spot of roasting.

"I have no idea what you're talking about." It was only to be expected that he would deny any knowledge of blackmail.

He was still lying on the hall floor, but I

had rolled him over onto his back so he could see me. I'd patted down his pockets, removed his cell telephone and turned it off. All the while, he had stared at me with wide eyes, the whites showing all around the irises. But he had known immediately who I was, in spite of my dark clothes, hat and mud-streaked face.

"So you deny you have been blackmailing my mother?" I asked him.

"I do," he said emphatically. "I've never heard such nonsense. Now let me go or I'll call the police."

"You are in no position to call anyone," I said. "And if anyone will be calling the police, it will be me."

"Go on, then," he said. "It's not me who would be in the most trouble."

"And what is that meant to imply?"

"Work it out," he said, becoming more sure of himself.

"Are you aware of what the maximum sentence is for blackmail?" I asked.

He said nothing.

"Fourteen years."

His eyes didn't even flicker. He clearly thought he was onto a good thing. He was assuming that I would just threaten him a bit, then let him go and do nothing more.

But one should never assume anything.

I had told Ian that I would be out all night. No one was expecting me back for hours and hours. So I was in no hurry.

I left him lying on the hard hall floor and went into the kitchen to see if I could find myself a drink. Waiting all that time outside had made me thirsty.

"Let me go," he shouted from the hallway.

"No," I shouted back, putting his phone down on the worktop.

"Help," he shouted, this time much louder.

I went quickly through into the hall.

"I wouldn't do that if I were you."

"Why not?" he said belligerently.

I shrugged myself free of the small rucksack on my back and removed the roll of duct tape. I held it towards him and pulled the end of the tape free. "Because I would be forced to wrap your head in this. Is that what you want?"

He didn't shout again as I went back into the kitchen and fetched a can of Heineken from his fridge. I took a drink, allowing a little of the beer to pour out of the corner of my mouth and drip onto the floor near his legs.

"Do you have any idea how long a human being can go on living without taking in any fluid?" He went on staring at me. "How long it would be before chronic dehydration causes irreversible kidney failure, and death?"

He obviously didn't like the question, but he still wasn't particularly worried.

I bent down to my rucksack and dug around for the short piece of chain attached to the ring by the padlock. I held it up for him to see, but it was clear from his lack of expression that he didn't know where it had come from, or its significance. He probably wasn't fully aware that his lack of reaction may have saved his life. Maybe I didn't now want to kill the little weasel, but that didn't mean I didn't want to use him.

"Are you a diabetic?" I asked.

"No," he said.

"Lucky you."

I removed the red-colored first-aid kit from my rucksack. It was what was known in the expedition business as an "anti-AIDS kit." It was a small zipped-up pouch containing two each of sterile syringes, hypodermic needles, intravenous drip cannulas, ready-threaded suture needles and scalpels, plus three small sterile pouches of saline solution for emergency rehydration. I had bought it some years previously to take on a regimental jolly, a trip to climb Mount Kilimanjaro. It was designed to allow access to sterile equipment in the event of one of the team having to have an emergency medical procedure, something that was not always readily available, especially in some of the more remote hospitals of HIV-ridden sub-Saharan Africa.

Thankfully, no one on the expedition had needed it, and the kit had returned with me to the UK intact. But now it might just prove to have been a worthwhile purchase.

I removed one of the syringes and attached it to one of the hypodermic needles. Alex watched me.

"What are you doing?" He sounded worried for the first time.

"Time for my insulin," I said. "You wouldn't want me collapsing in a diabetic coma, now, would you? Not with you in that state."

Alex watched carefully as I unpacked one of the pouches of saline solution from its sterile packaging and hung it up on the stair banister. The packaging had an official-looking label stuck on the side with "insulin" printed on it in large bold capital letters that he couldn't have failed to see. I had asked him if he was a diabetic, and he'd said no. I hoped that he wouldn't know that insulin is nearly always provided either in ready-loaded injecting devices or in little glass bottles. I had produced the official-looking insulin label that afternoon using Ian Norland's printer.

I drew a very little amount of the clear liquid into the smaller of the two syringes, pulled up the front of my black roll-necked sweater, pinched the flesh of my abdomen together and inserted the needle. I depressed the plunger and injected the fluid under my skin. I smiled down at Alex.

"How often do you have to do that?" he asked.

"Two or three times a day," I said.

"And what exactly is insulin?"

"It's a hormone," I said, "that allows the muscles to use the energy from glucose carried in the blood. In most people it is created naturally in the pancreas."

"So what happens if you don't take it?"

"The glucose level in my blood would have become so high that my organs would stop working properly, and I would eventually go into a coma, and then die."

I smiled down at him again. "We wouldn't want that, now, would we?"

He didn't answer. Perhaps me in a coma or dead was exactly what he wanted. But it wasn't going to happen. I wasn't really diabetic, but my best friend at secondary school had been, and I'd watched him inject himself with insulin hundreds of times, although he'd always used a special syringe with a finer and less painful needle. Injecting small amounts of sterile saline solution under my skin might be slightly uncomfortable, but it was harmless.

I went back into the kitchen and picked up his flight bag from where it had come to rest. It was heavy. Inside, amongst other things, were a laptop computer and a large bottle of duty-free vodka that had somehow survived the impact with the hall floor. I put the bag down on the kitchen table, removed the computer and turned it on. While it booted up I took an upright chair out into the hallway, placed it near Alex's feet and sat down.

"Now," I said, leaning forward. "I have some questions I need you to answer."

"I'm not answering anything unless you let me go."

"Oh, I think you will," I said. "It's a long night."

I stood up and went back into the kitchen. I pulled down the blind over the window, turned on a television set and sat down at the kitchen table with Alex's computer.

"Hey," he called after about five minutes.

"Yes," I shouted back. "What do you want?"

"Are you just going to leave me here?"

"Yes," I said, turning up the volume on the television.

"How long for?" he shouted louder.

"How long do you need?"

"Need?" he shouted. "What do mean 'need'?"

"How long do you need before you will answer my questions?"

"What questions?"

I went back into the hall and sat down on the chair by his feet.

"How long have you been having an affair with Julie Yorke?" I said.

It wasn't a question he had been expecting, but he recovered quickly.

"I've no idea what you're talking about."

It seemed we hadn't come too far in the past half-hour.

"Please yourself," I said, standing up and walking back to the kitchen table, and his computer.

There was a soccer-highlights program on the television, and I turned the volume up even higher so that Alex wouldn't hear me tapping away on his laptop keyboard.

The computer automatically connected to his wireless Internet router, so I clicked on his e-mail, and opened the inbox. Careless of him, I thought, not to have it password-protected. I highlighted all his messages received during the past two weeks and forwarded them, en masse, to my own e-mail account. Next, I did the same to his sent-items folder. One never knew how useful the information might prove to be, and it was no coincidence that the first thing the police searched when arresting someone was their computer hard drive.

I glanced up at the soccer on the television and ignored the whining from the hallway.

"Let me go," Alex bleated. "My hands hurt."

I went back to studying the computer screen.

"I need to sit up," he whined. "My back aches."

I continued to ignore him.

I opened a computer folder called Rock Accounts. There were twenty or so files in the folder, and I highlighted them all, attached them to an e-mail and again sent them to my computer.

The soccer-highlights program finished, and the evening news had started. Fortunately, there were no reports about an ongoing case of forced imprisonment in the village of Greenham.

I clicked on the search button on the computer's start menu and asked it to search itself for files containing the terms *password* or *user name.* Obligingly, it came up with eight references, so I attached those files to another e-mail, and off they went as well.

"OK, OK!" he shouted finally. "I'll answer your question."

The messages from one further e-mail folder, one simply named Gibraltar, were also dispatched through cyberspace. I then checked that everything had gone before erasing the sent records for my forwarded files so Alex would have no knowledge that I had copied them. I closed the lid of the laptop and returned it to the flight bag, which I placed back on the floor.

I then went out into the hall, sat down once again on the upright chair and leaned forward over him menacingly.

But I didn't ask him the same question as before. Using my best voice-of-command, I asked him something completely different.

"Why did you murder Roderick Ward?"

He was shocked.

"I — I didn't," he stammered.

"So who did?" I asked.

"I don't know."

"So he *was* murdered?" I said.

"No," he whined. "It was an accident."

"No, it wasn't. That car crash was far too

contrived. It had to be a setup."

"The car crash wasn't the accident," he said flatly. "It was the fact that he died that was the accident. I tried to warn them, but I was too late."

" 'Them'?" I asked, intrigued.

He clammed up.

I removed a folded piece of paper from my pocket and held it out to him.

He looked at it in disbelief.

I knew the words written there by heart, so often had I looked at them during the past few days. It was the handwritten note that had been addressed to Mrs. Stella Beecher at 26 Banbury Drive in Oxford, the note I had found in the pile of mail I had taken from the cardboard box that Meals-on-Wheels Mr. Horner kept by his front door.

I DON'T KNOW WHETHER THIS WILL GET THERE IN TIME, BUT TELL HIM I HAVE THE STUFF HE WANTS.

"What stuff?" I demanded.

He said nothing.

"And tell who?"

Again there was no response.

"And in time for what?"

He just stared at me.

"You will have to answer my questions, or you will leave me with no alternative but . . ." I trailed off.

"No alternative but what?" he asked in a panic.

"To kill you," I said calmly.

I quickly grabbed his bound feet and swiftly removed his left shoe and sock. I used the duct tape to bind his left foot upright against one of the spindles on the stairway so that it was completely immobile.

"What are you doing?" he screamed.

"Preparations," I said. "I always have to make the right preparations before I kill someone."

"Help," he yelled. But I had left the television on with the volume turned up, and his shout was drowned out by some advertisement music.

However, to be sure that he wouldn't be heard, I took a piece of the duct tape and fixed it firmly over his mouth to stop him from yelling again. Instead, he began breathing heavily through his nose, hyperventilating, his nostrils alternatively flaring and contracting below a pair of big frightened eyes.

"Now then, Alex," I said, in as calm a manner as I could manage. "You seem not to fully appreciate the rather dangerous predicament in which you have found yourself." He stared at me unblinkingly. "So let me explain it to you. You have been blackmailing my mother to the tune of two thousand pounds per week for the past seven months, to say nothing about the demands on her to fix races. Some weeks you collect the money yourself from the mailbox in Cheap Street, and sometimes you get Julie Yorke to collect it for you."

I removed the three prints of the photos I had taken of Julie through the window of the Taj Mahal Indian restaurant and held them up to him. With the tape on his mouth, it was difficult to fully gauge his reaction, but he went pale and looked from the photos to my face with doleful, pleading eyes.

"And," I went on, "you are blackmailing my mother over the knowledge you have that she has not been paying the tax that she should have been. Which means you either have her tax papers in your possession or have had access to them."

I reached down into my rucksack and again brought out the red "anti-AIDS" kit. If anything, Alex went paler.

"Now, my problem is this," I said. "If I let you go, you will still have my mother's tax papers. And even if you give me back the papers, you would still have the knowledge."

I took the large syringe out of the kit, attached a new needle, and then drew up a large quantity of the saline solution from the bag that was still hanging on the stair banister, the bag with the insulin label.

"So you see," I said, "if you won't help me, then I will have no alternative but to prevent you from speaking to the tax authorities."

I held the syringe up to the light and squirted a little of the fluid out in a fine jet.

"Did you know that insulin is essential for proper body functions?" I asked. "But that too much of it causes the glucose level in the blood to drop far too low, which in turn triggers a condition called hypoglycemia? That usually results in a seizure, followed by coma and death. Do you remember the case of that nurse, Beverley Allitt, who killed those children in Grantham hospital? Dubbed the Angel of Death by the media, she murdered some of them by injecting large overdoses of insulin."

I knew because I'd looked that up on the Internet as well.

I touched his foot.

"And do you know, Alex, if you inject insulin between someone's toes it is very difficult, if not impossible, to find the puncture mark on the skin, and the insulin would be undetectable, because you create it naturally in your body? It would appear you died of a seizure followed by a heart attack."

The statement wasn't entirely accurate. The insulin used nowadays to treat diabetics is almost exclusively synthetic insulin, and it can be detected as being different from the natural human product.

But Alex wasn't to know that.

"Now, then," I said, smiling and holding up the syringe to him again. "Between which two toes would you like it?"

16

I was worried that he was going to pass out. His eyes started to roll back in their sockets, and his breathing suddenly became shallower. I didn't want him to have a heart attack simply from fear. That might take some explaining.

"Alex," I shouted at him, bringing his eyes back into focus on my face. "You can prevent this, you know. All you have to do is cooperate and answer all my questions. But you have to be completely candid and tell me everything. Do you understand?"

He nodded eagerly.

"And do you agree to answer everything?"

He nodded again.

"Nothing held back?"

He shook his head from side to side, so I stepped forward and tore off the tape from across his mouth.

"Now, for a start," I said, "who killed Roderick Ward?"

He still wouldn't answer.

"I won't give you another chance," I said seriously.

"How do I know you won't kill me anyway, after I've told you?"

"You don't," I said. "But do you have any choice? And if I gather enough incriminating information about you, so that you would also be in big trouble if you told the tax man about my mother, then we would both have a weapon of mass destruction, as it were. Either of us telling the authorities would result in the very thing we were trying so hard to prevent. We would both have the safety of mutually assured annihilation, a bit like nuclear deterrence. Neither of us would use the information for fear of the retaliation."

"But you could still kill me," he said.

"Yes," I agreed, "I suppose I could, but why would I? There would be no need, and even I don't kill people without a reason."

He didn't look terribly reassured, so I untaped his foot from the spindle and then pulled him across the floor so he was sitting up with his back against the wall by the kitchen door.

"Now," I said, sitting down once more on the upright chair. "If you didn't kill Roderick Ward, who did?"

I still wasn't sure he would tell me, so seemingly absentmindedly, I picked up the syringe and made another fine spray of fluid shoot from the needle.

"His sister," Alex said.

I looked at him. "Stella Beecher?"

He seemed surprised I knew her name, but I'd already shown him the note he had sent to her. He nodded.

"Now, why would she kill her own brother?"

"She didn't mean to," he said. "It was an accident."

"You mean the car crash?"

"No," he said. "He was already dead when he went into the river. He drowned in a bath."

"What on earth was Stella Beecher doing giving him a bath?"

"She wasn't exactly giving him a bath. They were trying to get him to tell them where the money had gone."

"What money?" I asked.

"Fred's father's money."

I was confused. "Fred?"

"Fred Sutton," he said.

Old Man Sutton's son. The man I had seen in the public gallery at Roderick Ward's inquest.

"So Fred Sutton and Stella Beecher know

each other?" I asked.

"Know each other!" He laughed. "They live together. They're almost married."

In Andover, I thought, close to Old Man Sutton and his nursing home. So it had been no coincidence at all that Stella Beecher had moved to Andover.

It took more than an hour, but in the end, Alex told me how, and why, Roderick Ward was found dead in his car, submerged in the River Windrush.

Ward had been introduced to Old Man Sutton by Stella Beecher, who had been in a relationship with Detective Sergeant Fred for some time. Unbeknownst to either Fred or Stella, Roderick had somehow conned the old man into borrowing against his house and investing the cash in a non-existent hedge fund in Gibraltar. Fred found out about it only after he'd seen the brick being thrown through his father's window. It was like a soap opera.

"How do you know all this?" I asked Alex. "What's your connection?"

"I worked with Roderick Ward."

"So you are implicated in this sham hedge-fund business?"

He didn't really want to admit it. He must have known that my mother had been conned in the same way. He looked away from my face, but he nodded.

"So who's the brains behind it?" I asked.

He turned his eyes back to mine. "Do you think I'm stupid or something?" he said. "If I told you who it was then *you* wouldn't need to kill me because they'd do it for you."

Actually, I did think him stupid. But not as stupid as Roderick Ward. Fancy stealing from the father of your sister's boyfriend, especially when the boyfriend just happened to be a police detective — now, that was really stupid!

"Let's go back to Roderick Ward," I said. "Why did you send a note to Stella Beecher saying you had the stuff? What stuff? And how did you know Stella anyway?"

"I didn't," he said. "But I knew her address, because Roderick had said it was the same address he used, the one in Oxford."

"So what was all this about having the stuff? And hoping it was in time?"

"Fred Sutton had been harassing Roderick and me at an office we'd rented in Wantage, threatening us and so on."

I didn't blame him, I thought.

"He told me that he'd get a warrant for my arrest, and he'd use his police contacts to fit me up good and proper. He said I'd get ten years unless I gave him some papers he wanted about where his dad's money had gone."

"So why the note?" I asked.

"I made the copies of the papers, but he didn't come to collect them on the Monday morning as he'd said he would. He told me he'd definitely be at the office by eight, and I was waiting. But he didn't come all day, and Roderick didn't show up, either. I thought the two of them must have done a deal, and I would end up carrying the can. I was shit scared, I can tell you. And I had no other way of contacting him, so I sent the note."

So I had been wrong about "the stuff" being something to do with my mother's tax papers, and also "in time" had not been about before Roderick Ward's "accident," but about before getting an arrest warrant issued.

Never assume anything, I reminded myself.

But I'd been right about one thing: Alex Reece was indeed stupid.

"So how do you know that Fred Sutton and Stella killed Roderick Ward?" I asked him.

"Fred pitches up first thing the next day and demands the papers, but I told him to get stuffed. If he thought I was going to take the blame for what Roderick had been doing, he had another think coming. But he says Roderick's dead and I'll go the same way if I didn't give him the papers."

He paused only to draw breath.

"So I says to him that I didn't believe him that Roderick was dead. I told him he was only saying it to frighten me. He tells me that I should be frightened because they murdered him in the bath, but then he thinks better of it and claims it was an accident, that they'd only meant to scare him into telling them where the money had gone. But Fred says that Stella pulled his feet and his head went under and he just . . . died. Killed her own brother, just like that, Fred said. One minute they were asking him questions, the next he was dead."

"So did you give Fred the papers he wanted?" I asked.

"Yeah," he said. "But they wouldn't have done him much good. It's been ages since his money went, and they change the numbers and stuff all the time."

" 'They'?" I asked.

He clammed up tight, pursing his lips and shaking his head at me.

But I'd been doing a lot of thinking while I'd sat waiting in Greystone Stables and in the Newbury coffee shop, and the more I had thought about it, the more convinced I had become.

"You mean Jackson Warren and Peter Garraway," I said. It was a statement rather than a question.

He stared at me with his mouth hanging open. So I was right.

But it had to be them.

"And who is Mr. Cigar?" I asked him.

He laughed. "No one," he said. "That was Roderick's idea. They all thought it a great joke as they puffed on their own great big Havanas."

"And Rock Bank Ltd?" I said. "Is that a myth too?"

"Oh no, that exists, all right," he said. "But it's not really a bank. It's just a Gibraltar holding company. When money comes in, it sits there for a while, and then leaves again."

"How much money?" I asked.

"Depends on how much people invest."

"And where does it go when it leaves Rock Bank?"

"I arrange a transfer into another Gibraltar account, but it doesn't stay long there either," he said. "I don't know where it goes then. I'm pretty sure it ends up in a secret numbered Swiss account."

"How long does it stay in Rock Bank?"

"About a week," he said. "Just long enough to allow for clearance of the transfer and for any problems to get sorted."

So Rock Bank (Gibraltar) Ltd had no assets of its own. No wonder the London-based liquidation firm was attempting to pursue the individual directors.

"And where does it come from?" I asked him.

"The mugs," he said, with a laugh.

"You're the mug," I said. "Look at you. You don't look quite so clever at the moment. And I bet you don't get to keep much of the money."

"I get my cut," he boasted.

"And how long in prison will your cut be worth when this all falls apart, as it surely must? Or when will Warren and Garraway decide you are no longer worth your cut? Then you might end up drowned in a bath, just like Roderick."

"They need me," he boasted again. "I'm the CPA. They need me to square the audit. You're just jealous of a successful business."

"But it's not a business," I said. "You are simply stealing from people."

"They can afford it," he said, sneering.

I wasn't going to argue with him, because there was no point. He probably agreed with the philosophy of Pol Pot and the Khmer Rouge.

"So how do Jackson Warren and Peter Garraway know each other?"

"I don't know," he said. "But they've done so for years. Long before I met them."

"And how long have you known them?" I asked.

"Too long," he said, echoing what he'd said to me at Isabella's kitchen supper.

"And how long is that?" I persisted.

"About four years."

"Was that when the fake-hedge-fund scheme started?"

"Yeah, about then."

"Is that what you were referring to when you had that little spat with Jackson Warren, you know, that night when I first I met you?"

"No," he said. "That was over his and Peter's other little fiddle."

"And what's that?" I asked.

"No way," he said, shaking his head. "I've already said too much as it is."

At least he was right on that count.

"You think the Revenue will investigate their other little fiddle?" I asked him, thinking back to the supper exchange between him and Jackson. What was it he had said then? Something about that there was no telling what else the Revenue might dig up.

"And you're worried about that investigation finding out about everything else?"

It was a guess but not a bad one.

"Bloody stupid, if you ask me," he said.

I *was* asking him.

"Why take the risk?" I said.

"Exactly."

"So their other little fiddle is about tax?"

"Look," he said, changing the subject and completely ignoring my question, "I had a few beers on the flight, and now I desperately need to take a piss."

I thought back to my time in the stable. Should I make him wet himself just as I had been forced to do?

"Come on," he shouted at me. "I'm bloody bursting."

Reluctantly, I took a pair of scissors from my rucksack, leaned down and cut the ties holding Alex's hands behind his back.

"I might run away," he said, sitting up and rubbing his wrists.

"Not like that you won't." I pointed to the plastic ties that still bound his ankles together.

"Come on," he said. "Cut them too."

"No," I said. "You can hop."

Grudgingly, he pulled himself upright and hopped into the bathroom beneath the stairs.

I thought it unlikely that there would be a phone in the bathroom, but nevertheless, I took the precaution of removing the house telephone from its cradle in the kitchen. You can't dial out on one extension if another is off the hook, and his cell was still lying, switched off, on the kitchen counter where I'd left it.

Alex was taking his time, and I was beginning to think he might be trying to escape out of the bathroom window, when I heard the flush. Presently, he reappeared, hobbling out into the hall.

"Cut these bloody things off," he demanded angrily. He had obviously been using the time to try to break the plastic ties around his ankles, but I knew from experience that they were tougher than they looked. Much tougher indeed than his skin, which was chafed and reddening.

"No," I said.

"What the bloody hell more do you want?" he asked angrily.

"My WMD," I said.

"Eh?"

"My weapon of mass destruction," I said. "My nuclear deterrent. I need some hard evidence."

"What sort of evidence?"

"Evidence of conspiracy to defraud my

mother of one million U.S. dollars."

"Dream on," he said, smiling.

"Maybe I should just ring up Jackson Warren and ask him about my mother's money, telling him that it was you who suggested I did so."

"You wouldn't do that," he said, looking a little worried.

"Don't tempt me," I said.

"He'd bloody kill me just for talking to you."

Good, I thought. It was much to my advantage that Alex remained more frightened of Jackson Warren than he was of me. That alone would prevent him from telling Jackson anything about this nocturnal encounter. Maybe that in itself was my nuclear deterrence.

"Or perhaps I should call Jackson and ask for the number of the Swiss bank account into which he and Garraway put all the money they steal."

"You'd better bloody not," Alex said. "Or I'll be onto the tax man about your mother."

I strode into the kitchen, and he hobbled in behind me. I walked straight past his flight bag, and I glimpsed out of the corner of my eye as he pushed it farther out of sight beneath the table. I didn't mind one bit that

Alex believed I hadn't accessed his computer.

"Sit down," I said sharply, pointing to one of the kitchen chairs.

I don't think he really knew how to react. He didn't move.

"Sit down," I said again, in my best voice-of-command.

He wavered, but after a few seconds, he pulled the chair out from under the table and sat down while I sat on the chair opposite him.

"So whose idea was it to get my mother's horses to lose?" I asked.

"Julie's," he said.

"So she could bet against them on the Internet?"

"No, nothing like that," he said. "She just wanted to give her old man's horses a better chance of winning. He gives her such a hard time when they lose. It was me who bets against the horses on the Internet. Not too much, like, not enough to attract attention. But it's been a nice little earner."

Amateurs, I thought. These people were amateurs.

The doorbell rang, making both of us jump. It was followed by a persistent gentle knocking at the door. I glanced at my watch. It was ten to one in the morning.

"Stay there," I ordered. "And keep quiet. Neither of us wants the police involved in this, do we?"

Alex shook his head, but I thought it most improbable that the police would knock so softly. They were far more likely to break the door down.

I walked through into the dark front room and looked out through the window. Julie Yorke was standing outside the door, rapping her knuckles gently against the glass. I went back into the hall and opened the door.

"What have you done to him?" Julie asked in a breathless voice.

"Nothing," I said.

"Where is he, then?" she demanded.

"In the kitchen," I said, standing aside to let her pass. I glanced out at the dark and silent road and closed the door.

When I went back into the kitchen Julie was standing behind Alex, stroking his fine ginger hair. In other circumstances, it might have been a touching scene.

I could see that she was still wearing a nightdress under her raincoat.

"Couldn't sleep?" I asked sarcastically.

"I had to wait for my bloody husband to drop off," she said. "I've taken a bloody big chance coming here, I can tell you. I tried to call, but it was permanently engaged and

Alex's cell went straight to voice mail."

I looked across the kitchen at the house phone still lying off the hook on the countertop, and at the switched-off cell alongside it.

"I thought I told you not to contact Alex," I said sharply, pointing to her.

"You said not in the next thirty-six hours," she replied in a pained tone. "That ran out at ten forty-five this evening."

I hadn't been counting, but she obviously had.

"So what happens now?" Alex asked into the silence.

"Well," I said, "for a start, you return all the blackmail money to my mother. I reckon that's about sixty thousand pounds."

"I can't," he said. "We've spent it. And anyway, why would I?"

"Because you obtained it illegally," I pointed out.

"But your mother should have paid it to the tax man."

"And so she will when you give it back."

"Dream on," he said again, with a laugh.

"OK," I said. "If that's your attitude, I will have to go to Jackson Warren and Peter Garraway and ask them for it."

"You'll be lucky," he said, still laughing. "They're the most tight-fisted pair of bastards I've ever met."

"I'll tell them you said that."

The laughter died in his throat.

"Now, don't you go telling them anything of the sort, or I'll be straight on the blower to the Revenue."

Mutually assured destruction — it was what nuclear deterrence was all about.

"And what about my pictures?" Julie demanded, gaining some confidence from Alex.

"They prove nothing," Alex said. "All they show is that you were in the mailbox shop. That doesn't mean you were blackmailing anyone."

"Not those pictures," Julie said, irritated. "The other pictures he took of me yesterday."

"What other pictures?" Alex demanded, turning to me.

Oh dear, I thought. This could get really nasty. How might Alex react to my taking explicit images of his naked girlfriend? I sensed that Julie had also worked it out that if Alex hadn't already seen them, it might be much better for her if he didn't do so now.

"Er," she said, backtracking fast. "They're not that important."

"But pictures of what?" Alex persisted,

still looking at me.

Should I tell him? Should I show him just the sort of girl she was? Or could the pictures still be useful to me as a lever to apply to Julie?

"Just some photos I took outside the Yorkes' house yesterday afternoon."

"Show me," he said belligerently.

I thought of my camera, still safely out of sight in my little rucksack.

"I can't," I said. "I don't have the camera with me."

"But why were you taking photos of Julie outside her house?" he demanded.

I thought quickly. "To record her reaction when I showed her the prints of her in the mailbox shop. That's when I told her not to contact you for thirty-six hours."

Julie seemed relieved, and Alex appeared satisfied by the answer, even if he was a tad confused.

"So what happens now?" he asked again.

It was a good question.

I thought about asking Julie if she knew anything of Warren and Garraway's other little fiddle, the tax one, but I decided I might get more from her without Alex being there, especially if I were to use my photo lever on her.

"Well, I don't know about you two," I

said, standing up, "but I'm going home to bed." And, I thought, to read Alex's e-mails.

I collected my "insulin" bag from the stairs, slung my rucksack onto my back and left the two lovebirds in the kitchen as I left the house by the front door. But I didn't walk off down the road. I removed the camera from my rucksack and went quickly down the side of the house to the rear garden and the kitchen window.

I had purposely left a small space at the bottom when I'd closed the blind, and I now put my eyes up close to the glass and looked in.

Alex and Julie really weren't very discreet. Making sure the flash was switched off, I took twenty or more photos through the window of them kissing, him sliding his hands inside her coat and pulling up her nightdress. Even though Julie's back was mostly towards the window, there was little doubt where Alex was placing his fingers, and my eighteen-times optical zoom Leica lens captured everything.

Presently, Julie cut the plastic ties from around Alex's ankles and they went, hand-in-hand, out of the kitchen and, I presumed, up the stairs to bed. Short of shinning up a drainpipe, I would see nothing more, and in spite of being called Tom, my artificial leg didn't lend itself readily to climbing up to peep through bedroom windows.

Even then I didn't return to Ian's car and go home. Instead, I went back down the side of the house and out into Bush Close, to where Julie had parked the white BMW. It was some way down the road, well beyond the glow from the streetlight outside number twelve. I tried the doors, but she had locked them, so I sat down on the pavement, leaned up against the passenger door and waited.

I was getting quite used to waiting, and thinking.

Alex Reece clearly received more than an average bonus after being away for five days in Gibraltar, and I was just beginning to think that Julie was staying for the whole night when, about an hour after I left, I saw her coming towards me through the pool of light produced by the solitary streetlamp.

I pulled myself to my feet using the car's door handle but I remained crouched down below the window level so Julie couldn't see me as she walked along the road. When she was about ten yards away, she pushed the remote unlock button on her key and the indicator lights flashed once in response. As she opened the driver's door to get in, I opened the passenger one to do likewise, so we ended up sitting down side by side with both doors slamming shut in unison.

Startled, she immediately tried to open the door again, but I grabbed her arm on the steering wheel.

"Don't," I said in my voice-of-command. "Just drive."

"Where to?" she said.

"Anywhere," I said with authority. "Now. Drive out of this road."

Julie started the car and reversed it into one of the driveways to turn around. In truth, it was not the best-performed driving-test maneuver, and there would probably be BMW tire marks on the front lawn of number eight in the morning, but at least she didn't hit anything, and I wasn't an examiner.

She pulled out into Water Lane and turned right towards Newbury, towards home. We went a few hundred yards in silence.

"OK," I said. "Pull over here."

She stopped the car at the side of the road.

"What do you want?" she said, rather forlornly.

"Just a little more help," I said.

"Can't you just leave us alone?"

"But why should I?" I exclaimed. "My mother has paid you more than sixty thousand pounds over the past seven months, and I think that entitles me to demand something from you."

"But Alex told you," she said. "You can't have it back. We've spent it."

"On what?" I asked.

She looked across at me. "What do you mean 'on what'?"

"What have you spent my mother's money on?"

"You mean you don't know?"

"No. How could I?"

She laughed. "Coke, of course. Lots of lovely coke."

I didn't think she meant Coca-Cola.

"And bottles of bubbly. Only the best, you know. Cases and cases of lovely Dom." She laughed again.

I realized that she must have been sampling one or the other during the past hour with Alex. It was not only fear that had caused her to drive on the grass. I couldn't smell alcohol on her breath, so it had to have been the coke.

"Does Ewen know you take cocaine?" I asked.

"Don't be fucking stupid," she said. "Ewen wouldn't know a line of coke if it ran up his nose. If it hasn't got four legs and a mane, Ewen couldn't care less. I think he'd much rather screw the bloody horses than me."

"So what is Jackson Warren and Peter Garraway's little tax fiddle?"

"Eh?"

"What is Jackson and Peter's tax fiddle?" I asked again.

"You mean their VAT fiddle?" she asked.

"Yes," I said excitedly. I waited in silence.

She paused for a bit, but eventually she started. "Did you know that racehorse owners can recover the VAT on training fees?"

"My mother said something about it," I said.

"And on their other costs as well, those they attribute to their racing business, like transport and telephone charges and vet's fees. They can even recover the VAT they have to pay when they buy the horses in the first place."

The VAT rate was at nearly twenty percent. That was a lot of tax to recover on expensive horseflesh.

"So what's the fiddle?" I asked.

"What makes you think I'd ever tell you?" she said, turning in the car towards me.

"So you do know, then?" I asked.

"I might," she said arrogantly.

"I'll delete the pictures if you tell me."

Even in her cocaine-induced state, she

knew that the pictures were the key.

"How can I trust you?"

"I'm an officer in the British Army," I said, rather pompously. "My word is my bond."

"Do you promise?" she said.

"I promise," I said formally, holding up my right hand. Yet another of those promises I might keep.

She paused a while longer before starting again.

"Garraway lives in Gibraltar, and he's not registered for VAT in the UK. He actually could be, but he's obsessive about not having anything to do with the tax people here because he's a tax exile. He only lives in Gibraltar to avoid paying tax. Hates the place, really." She paused.

"So?" I said, prompting her to continue.

"So all Peter Garraway's horses are officially owned by Jackson Warren. Jackson pays the training fees and all the other bills, and then he claims back the VAT. He even buys the horses for Garraway in the first place and gets the VAT back on that too. He uses a company called Budsam Ltd."

"So why is that a fiddle?" I asked. "If Jackson buys them and pays the fees, then *he* is the owner, not Garraway."

"Yes," she said, "but Peter Garraway pays

Jackson back for all the costs."

"Doesn't that show up in Jackson's accounts or those of the company?"

"No." She smiled. "That's the clever bit. Peter pays Jackson into an offshore account in Gibraltar that Jackson doesn't declare to the Revenue. Alex says it's very clever because Jackson gets his money offshore without ever having to transfer anything from a UK bank, which would be required by law to tell the tax people about it."

"How many horses does Peter Garraway own in this way?" I asked.

"Masses. He has ten or twelve with us and loads more with other trainers."

"But don't they pay for themselves with the prize money?"

"No, of course not," she said. "Most horses don't make in prize money anything like what they cost to keep, especially not jumpers. Far from it. Not unless you count the betting winnings, and Garraway gets to keep those himself."

"So why doesn't Peter Garraway register himself as an owner in the UK for the VAT scheme?"

"I told you," she said. "He's paranoid about the British tax people. They've been trying forever to get him for tax evasion. He's obsessive about the number of days he stays here, and he and his wife even travel on separate planes so they won't both be killed in a crash and his family get done here for inheritance tax. There's no way he'll register. Alex thinks it's stupid. He told them it would solve the problem of the VAT without any risk, but Garraway won't listen."

I listened, all right.

Wasn't it Archimedes who claimed that if you gave him a lever long enough, he could lift the world?

I listened to Julie with mounting glee. Perhaps now I had a lever long enough to pry my mother's money back from under the Rock of Gibraltar.

All I had to do was work out on whom to apply it, and when.

17

I spent much of the night downloading Alex's files and e-mails onto my laptop using the Internet connection in my mother's office.

I had let myself into the kitchen silently using Ian's key. The dogs had been unperturbed by their nocturnal visitor, sniffing my hand as I'd passed them and then going back to sleep, happy that I was friend, not foe.

I worked solely by the light of the computer screen and left everything exactly as I'd found it. I didn't know why I still thought it was necessary for my presence to be a secret from my mother, but I wasn't yet ready to try to explain to her what had been going on.

It might also have been safer for me if she didn't know where I was.

After I had left Julie to drive herself home in the white BMW, I'd taken Ian's car slowly up the driveway of Greystone Stables. My two telltale sticks on their stones were broken. Someone had been up to the stable yard, someone who would now know I wasn't dead, someone who might try to kill me again. But they would have to find me first.

I slept fitfully on Ian's sofa, and he left me there snoozing when he went out to morning stables at half past six on Monday morning.

By the time he returned at about noon, I had read through all of Alex's downloaded information on my laptop. Most of it was boring, but amongst the dross, there were some real gems, and three standout sparkling diamonds.

Maybe I wouldn't need to use my lever after all.

One of the diamonds was that Alex, it transpired, was not only the accountant for Rock Bank (Gibraltar) Ltd but also one of the signatories of the company's bank account, and best of all, I had downloaded all the passwords and user names that he needed to access the account online.

I would try to log in to the account tonight, I thought, when I had access to the Internet from my mother's office.

The other diamonds were the e-mails sent by Jackson Warren to Alex Reece concerning me, the first a message sent on the night of Isabella's kitchen supper, and the second after the races at Newbury on the day Scientific had won. The first had been sent in a fit of anger, and the second as a warning, but nevertheless, it amazed me how lax people could be with e-mail security.

In the army, all messages were encrypted before sending so that they were not readable by the enemy. Even cell phones were not permitted to be used in Afghanistan in case the Taliban were listening to the transmissions and gaining information that could be useful either in a tactical way or simply to undermine the morale of the troops.

No parents, having been called by their soldier offspring one evening from a cell telephone in Helmand province, would welcome then receiving a second call, this time from an English-speaking member of the Taliban, who would inform them that their son was going to be targeted in the morning, and that he would be returning home to them in a wooden box.

It had happened.

Yet here was a supposedly sensible person, Jackson Warren, sending clear text messages by e-mail for all to read. Well, for me to read anyway.

"What the bloody hell do you think you were doing talking so openly in front of Thomas Forsyth?" Jackson had written soon after storming out of the supper. "His mother was one of those who invested heavily in our little scheme. KEEP YOUR BLOODY LIPS SEALED — DO YOU HEAR?"

Capital letters in an e-mail were equivalent to shouting, and I could vividly recall the way Jackson had stormed out of the room that night. He would certainly have been shouting.

The second e-mail was calmer but no less direct, and had been sent by Jackson to Alex at five o'clock on the afternoon of the races. He must have written it as soon as he arrived home from Newbury.

"Thomas Forsyth told me this afternoon that he wants to contact you. I am making arrangements to ensure that he cannot. However, if he manages to be in contact with you before my arrangements are in position, you are hereby warned NOT to speak with him or communicate with him in any way. This is extremely important, especially in the light of the company business this coming week."

I knew only too well what arrangements

Jackson had subsequently taken to stop me from speaking with Alex — my shoulders still ached from them. But what, I wondered, had been the company business? Perhaps all would be revealed by access to the company bank account later.

"So how are the horses?" I asked Ian, as he slumped down onto the brown sofa and switched on the television.

"They're all right," he said with a mighty sigh.

"What's wrong, then?" I asked. "Would you like me to leave?"

"As you like," he said, seemingly uninterested in the conversation as he flicked through the channels with the remote control.

"Bad day at the office?" I asked.

"Yeah," he said. "You could say that."

I said nothing. He'd tell me if he wanted to.

He did.

"When I took this job I thought it would be more as an assistant trainer rather than just as 'head lad.' That's what Mrs. Kauri implied. She told me she doesn't have an assistant, as such, so I thought the role of head lad would be more important to her than to other trainers."

He paused, perhaps remembering that I was Mrs. Kauri's son.

"And?" I prompted.

"And nothing," he said. He turned off the TV and swiveled around on the sofa to face me. "I was wrong, that's all. It turns out she doesn't have an assistant because she can't delegate anything to anybody. She even treats me the same as one of the young boys straight out from school. She tells the staff to do things that I should be telling them to do, and often it is directly opposite to what I've already said. I feel worthless and undermined."

Story of my life, I thought.

At least, it had been the story of my life until I'd left home to join the army. It seemed to me that Ian was already on the road to somewhere else. It was a shame. I'd seen him working with the horses, and even I could see that he was good, calming the younger ones and standing no nonsense from the old hands. He also had a passion for them, and he longed for them to win. Losing Ian Norland would be a sad day for Kauri House Stables.

"Have you been looking?" I asked.

"There's a possibility of a new stable opening that's quite exciting," he said, suddenly more alive. "It's some way off yet, but

I'm going to keep my options open. But don't you go telling your mother. She'd be furious."

He was right, she would be furious. She demanded absolute loyalty from everyone around her, but sadly, she repaid it in short measure, and she wasn't about to change now.

"Which stables?" I asked.

"Rumor has it that one of the trainers in the village is going to open up a second yard, and he'll be needing a new assistant to run it. I thought I might apply."

"Which trainer?" I asked.

"Ewen Yorke," he said. "Apparently, he's buying Greystone Stables."

He'd have to fix the broken pane in the tack-room window.

The statements of the bank account of Rock Bank (Gibraltar) Ltd were most revealing.

I had spent the afternoon rereading all the e-mails that I had downloaded from Alex Reece's computer inbox and sent-items folder, as well as the Gibraltar folder. Quite a few of the e-mails were communications back and forth with someone named Sigurd Bellido, the senior cashier at the real Gibraltar bank that held the Rock Bank Ltd account, discussing the transfer of funds in and out. Unfortunately, there were no references to account names and numbers from which, and to which, the transfers were made, although strangely they all discussed the ongoing health of Mr. Bellido's mother-in-law.

When, at two in the morning, I logged on to the online banking system in my mother's office, I could see that the recent transfers discussed with Mr. Bellido were reflected in the various changes to the account balance.

As Alex had said, money periodically came into the account, presumably from the "investors" in the UK, and then left again about a week later. If Alex was right, it disappeared eventually into some secret Swiss account belonging to Garraway or Warren.

I looked particularly at the transactions for the past week to see if they showed any evidence of the "company business" that Jackson had referred to in his e-mail.

There had been two large deposits. Both were in American dollars, one for one million and the other for two million. A couple more mugs, I thought, duped into investing in a nonexistent hedge fund.

One of the deposits, the two million dollars, had a name attached to it — Toleron. I knew I'd heard that name before, but I couldn't place where, so I typed "Toleron" into the Google search on my computer, and it instantly gave me the answer.

"Toleron Plastics" appeared across my screen in large red letters, with "the largest drainpipe manufacturer in Europe" running underneath in slightly smaller ones. Mrs. Martin Toleron had been the rather boring lady I'd sat next to at Isabella's kitchen supper, who would, it appeared, very soon be finding out that her "wonderful" husband wasn't quite as good at business as she had claimed. I almost felt sorry for her.

Had that really been only eleven days ago? So much had happened in the interim.

I searched further for Mr. Martin Toleron. Nearly every reference was connected with the sale of his company the previous November to a Russian conglomerate, reputedly adding more than a hundred million dollars to his personal fortune.

Suddenly I didn't feel quite so sorry for his wife over the loss of a mere two million.

As Alex would have said, they could afford it.

Early on Tuesday morning, while my mother was away on the gallops watching her horses exercise, I borrowed Ian Norland's car once more, and went to see Mr. Martin Toleron.

According to the Internet, he lived in the

village of Hermitage, a few miles to the north of Newbury, and I found the exact address easily enough by asking directions in the village shop.

"Oh yes," said the plump middle-aged woman behind the counter. "We all know the Tolerons round here, especially Mrs. Toleron." Her tone implied that Mrs. Toleron wasn't necessarily the most welcome of customers in the shop. I thought it might have had something to do with the never-ending praise of her "wonderful" husband or, more likely, was just straightforward envy of the rich.

Martin Toleron's house, near the edge of the village on the Yattenden Road, was a grand affair, in keeping with his "captain of industry" billing. I pulled up in front of the firmly closed six-foot-high iron gates and pushed the button on the intercom box fixed to the gatepost, but I wasn't quite sure what I was going to say if someone answered.

"Hello," said a man's voice through the box.

"Mr. Toleron?" I asked.

"Yes," the man said.

"Mr. Martin Toleron?"

"Yes." He sounded a little impatient.

"My name is Thomas Forsyth," I said. "I'd

like to —"

"Look, I'm sorry," he replied, cutting me off. "I don't take cold calls at my gate. Good-bye." There was a click, and the box went dead.

I pushed the button again. No reply, so I pushed it once more, and for much longer.

Eventually, he came back on the line. "What do you want?" he asked, with increased impatience.

"Does Rock Bank Ltd of Gibraltar mean anything to you?" I asked.

There was a pause before he replied, "Who did you say you are?"

"Open the gates and you'll find out," I said.

"Stay there," he said. "I'm coming out."

I waited, and soon a small, portly man emerged, walking down the driveway towards me. I vaguely remembered him from Isabella's supper even though we hadn't spoken. Looks, I thought, could be deceiving. Martin Toleron didn't give the appearance of being a multimillionaire captain of industry, but then again, Alexander the Great had hardly been an Adonis, having reputedly been very short, with a twisted neck and different-colored eyes, one blue and the other brown.

Martin Toleron stopped some ten feet

from the gates.

"What do you want?" he demanded.

"Just to talk," I said.

"Are you from the tax authorities?" he asked.

I thought it a strange question, but perhaps he was afraid I was going to hand him a summons.

"No," I said. "I was at the same dinner party as you, at Jackson and Isabella Warren's place last week. I sat next to your wife."

He took a couple of paces towards the gates and squinted at me.

"But what do you want?" he said again.

"I want to talk to you about Rock Bank Ltd and the investment you have just made with them in Gibraltar."

"That's none of your business," he said.

I didn't reply but stood silently, waiting for curiosity to get the better of him.

"And how do *you* know about it?" he asked, as I knew he would.

"I think it might be better for us to go inside to discuss this rather than to shout a conversation through these gates where anyone could overhear us. Don't you agree?"

He obviously did agree, because he removed a small black box from his pocket and pushed a button. The gates swung open as I returned to Ian's car.

I parked on the gravel drive in front of the mock-Georgian front door and pillared portico of his modern redbrick mansion.

"Come into my office," Martin Toleron said, leading the way past the grand front door to a smaller one set between the main house and an extensive garage block. I followed him into a large oak-paneled room with a built-in matching oak desk and bookcases behind it.

"Sit down," he said decisively, pointing to one of two armchairs, and I glimpsed for the first time the confidence and resolution that would have served him well in his business. I resolved to ensure that Martin Toleron became a valuable friend rather than a challenging enemy.

"What is this about?" he said, sitting in the other chair and turning towards me, jutting out his jaw.

"I believe that you have recently sent a large sum of money to Rock Bank Ltd of Gibraltar as an investment in a hedge fund."

I paused, but he didn't respond. He just continued to stare at me with unfriendly eyes. It was slightly unnerving, and I began to question if coming here had been a mistake. I suddenly wondered whether Toleron was, in fact, part of the conspiracy. Had I just walked into the lion's den like a naïve lamb to the slaughter?

"And I have reason to believe," I went on, "that the investment fund in question does not actually exist, and you are being defrauded of your money."

He continued to sit and look at me.

"Why are you telling me this?" he demanded, suddenly standing up. "What do you want from me?"

"Nothing," I said.

"You must want something." He was almost shouting. "Otherwise, why are you here? You didn't come here to give me bad news so you could simply gloat. Is it money you're after?"

"No, of course not," I said defensively. "I came here to warn you."

"But why?" he said aggressively. "If, as you say, I have already invested money in a fraud, your warning would then be too late. And why is it you believe I'm being defrauded anyway? Are you the one who's doing it?"

Things were not going well.

"I just thought that you would like to know so that you didn't send any more," I said, again on the defensive. "I am not involved in the fraud other than being the son of another victim. I had hoped that you might have some information that would be helpful to me in trying to recover her money. That's all."

He sat down again and remained silent for a few seconds.

"What sort of information?" he asked eventually, and more calmly.

"Well," I said, "with respect, my mother is no financial wizard, far from it, and I can see how she was duped, but you . . ." I left the implication hanging in the air.

He stood up from the chair again and went to the desk. He picked up a large white envelope and tossed it into my lap. It contained the glossy offering document for what it called the "opportunity-of-a-lifetime investment." I skimmed through the brochure. It was very convincing, and certainly gave the impression of being from a legitimate organization, with photos of supposed business offices in Gibraltar and graphs of past and predicted investment performance, all of which moved in the right direction, and with wonderful glowing testimonials from other satisfied investors.

"Why do you think it a fraud?" he asked.

"I know of two separate cases when people, including my mother and stepfather, after investing through Rock Bank Ltd, have lost all their money. They were both told that the hedge fund in which their money had been placed had subsequently gone bankrupt, leaving no assets. I have reason to believe that the funds never actually existed in the first place and the money was simply stolen."

I flicked through the glossy brochure once more.

"It's a very professional job," he said. "It gives all the right information and assurances."

If they were after "investments" in million-dollar chunks, it would have to be a professional job.

"But did you check up on any of it?" I asked.

He didn't answer, but I could tell from his face that he hadn't.

"Why didn't your mother complain to the police?" he said. "Then there might have been a warning issued."

"She couldn't," I said, without further clarification.

I thought back to his strange question at the gate about me being from the tax authorities, and his rather belligerent attitude towards me since. "Mr. Toleron," I said. "Excuse my asking, but are you being blackmailed?"

■ ■ ■ ■

As in my mother's case, it wasn't the loss of his money that worried Martin Toleron the most; it was the potential loss of face because he'd been conned.

If I thought he would thank me for pointing out that his investment was a fake, then I was mistaken. Indirectly, he even offered to pay me not to make that knowledge public.

"Of course I won't make it public," I said, horrified by his insinuation.

"Everyone else I know would have," he said, with something of a sigh. "They would gleefully sell it to the highest bidder from the gutter press." He may have been a highly successful businessman, and he had clearly made pots of money, but he'd obviously been accompanied by precious few real friends on the journey.

He was not being blackmailed, at least he denied he was to me, but he did admit that someone had recently tried to extort money from him, accusing him of falsifying a tax return that stated he was not a tax resident in the UK, when in fact he was.

"I told him to bugger off," he said. "But it took me a lot of time and money to get things straightened out. The last bloody thing I want is an audit by the Revenue."

"So you are fiddling something, then?" I asked.

"No, of course not," he said. "I'm just sailing close to the wind, you know, trying it on with a few things."

"VAT?" I asked.

"As a matter of fact, yes," he said. "Is that why your mother didn't go to the authorities and complain?"

"Is what why?" I asked.

"She was being blackmailed."

I simply nodded, echoing my mother's belief that in not saying anything out loud, it somehow diminished the admission.

"Did you know someone called Roderick Ward?"

"Don't you mention that name here," he said explosively. "Called himself an accountant, but he was nothing more than a damn bookkeeper. It was thanks to him that I nearly copped it with the Revenue."

I wondered how on earth a captain of industry had become tangled up with such a dodgy accountant.

"How did you come to know him?" I asked.

"He was my elder daughter's boyfriend for a while. Kept coming round here and telling me how I could save more tax. I should've never listened to the little bastard."

Oh! What a tangled web he weaved, when first he practiced to deceive!

"Do you know what happened to him?" I asked.

"I heard somewhere that he died in a car crash."

"Actually, he was murdered," I said.

He was surprised but not shocked. "Not by me, he wasn't. Although I would've happily done it. Good riddance, I say!"

"He was murdered by someone else he stole money from."

"Well done, them." He smiled for the first time since I'd been there. But then the smile vanished as quickly as it had arrived. "Hold on a minute," he said. "Didn't Ward die last summer?"

"Yes," I said. "In July."

"So who is robbing me now?"

"Who gave you the offering document? Who was it who recommended the investment to you?"

"How do you know someone did?" he asked.

"No one invests in something from a cold call, or from a brochure that just drops through their letter box. Certainly not to the tune of two million dollars. You had to be told about it by someone."

He seemed slightly surprised I knew the exact size of his investment.

"Did Jackson tell you the amount?" he asked.

"So it *was* Jackson Warren who recommended it," I said. "You asked me who was robbing you, and that's your answer — Jackson Warren, together with Peter Garraway."

He didn't believe it. I could read the doubt in his face.

"Surely not?" he said. "Why would he? Jackson Warren's got lots of money of his own."

"Maybe that's because he steals it from other people."

"Don't be ridiculous," he said.

"I'm not. I'll show you. Do you have an Internet connection?"

"But how did you get access?" Martin Toleron was astounded as I brought up the recent transactions of Rock Bank (Gibraltar) Ltd on my laptop computer screen. "You must be involved somehow."

"I'm not," I said.

"Then how did you get the passwords?"

"Don't ask," I said. "You don't want to know."

He looked at me strangely, but he didn't ask, simply turning his attention back to the screen.

"Whose is the other investment?" he asked.

"I was hoping you could tell me," I said.

"I've no idea. I've only spoken about the fund with Jackson Warren."

"Did he raise it, or did you?"

"He did. He told me at that supper that he had a great investment tip for me."

"Did he indicate that he was going to invest in the fund himself?"

"He told me he had made his investment sometime in the past, and he claimed that it had performed very well since, very well indeed. That's why he was so keen on it." He paused. "I believed him, and to be fair, you haven't shown me anything substantive to contradict that belief."

I opened one of the e-mails from Alex Reece's inbox from the previous week.

"Alex," it said. "We should expect a two-unit sum into the account this coming week from our drainpipe friend. Please ensure it takes the usual route, and issue the usual note of acceptance. Your commission will be transferred in due course. JW."

"That doesn't prove it's a fraud," Toleron said.

"Maybe not directly," I said. "But did Jackson Warren tell you that he was actually running the fund that he was so keen to promote?"

"No. He did not."

"But he clearly must be running it if he's ordering the issuing of acceptance notes to investors." I paused to allow that to sink in. "Is that enough proof for you? If not, there's plenty more."

"Show me," Toleron said.

I pulled up another of Alex Reece's e-mails to the screen, this time one he had sent to Sigurd Bellido, the chief cashier in Gibraltar, about a transfer.

"Sigurd. Please transfer the million dollars, received into the Rock Bank Ltd account last week from the UK, into the usual other account at your bank. I trust your mother-in-law's health problems are improving. AR."

Martin Toleron read it over my shoulder. "That doesn't prove anything."

"No," I said. "But read this."

I pulled up another e-mail from Alex's Gibraltar folder, this one to Jackson Warren, sent on the same day as the previous one.

"Jackson. I have issued the instruction to SB (and his mother-in-law), and the funds should be available in your usual account later today for further transfer. AR."

"What's all that mother-in-law business about?" he asked.

"I don't know," I said. "But it appears in all the e-mails sent to SB, that's Sigurd Bellido, the chief cashier who makes the transfers in Gibraltar. Funny thing is, he doesn't ever mention her in his replies."

Toleron thought for a moment. "Perhaps it's a code to prove that the transfer request really is from this AR person."

"Alex Reece," I said.

"Didn't I meet him at that dinner party? Ginger-haired fellow?"

"That's him," I said. "Slightly odd sort of person. He's Jackson Warren's accountant, but he's up to his neck in the fraud."

"But Warren must surely know that I would suspect him if the fund went bust and I lost all my money."

"But he would simply apologize for the bad investment advice and say that he'd also lost a packet and, if the newspaper reports of your company sale are to be believed, you would have been able to afford the loss more than he would. In fact, I bet you would have ended up feeling sorry for him, rather than accusing him of stealing from you."

"Don't ever believe what you read in the

papers," he said. "But I get your point. The very fact that it was a relatively small investment is why I did it in the first place. I can afford to lose it. Not, of course, that I want to."

How lovely it must be for him, I thought, to be so rich that two million dollars was a relatively small investment, and one that he could afford to lose.

"So all we need to do now is to get this Alex Reece chappy to e-mail SB in Gibraltar and get him to return the money whence it came." Martin Toleron smiled at me. "Then I'll have my money back. Shouldn't be too difficult to arrange, surely?"

He certainly made it sound easy, but I'm not sure that Alex Reece would play ball. He might be more afraid of Jackson Warren and Peter Garraway than he was of Martin Toleron, or even of me and my syringes.

"I have a better idea," I said. "We could send an e-mail to SB, pretending to be Alex Reece."

"But that's not as easy as you think," Martin said. "Not without his e-mail account password."

Now it was my turn to smile at him. "And what makes you think I don't already have it?"

18

The e-mail to Sigurd Bellido was ready to go by half past eleven.

Sigurd. There has been a mix-up at our end, and I need to transfer back to the UK the last two payments that were made into the Rock Bank Ltd account on Thursday and Friday of last week. Please transfer, as soon as possible, from the Rock Bank Ltd account (number 01201030866) at your bank:

(1) U.S. $2,000,000 (two million U.S. dollars) to Barclays Bank plc, SWIFT code BARCGB2LBGA, Belgravia branch, for further credit to Mr. Martin Toleron, sort code 20-62-18, account number 81634587

(2) U.S. $1,000,000 (one million U.S. dollars) to HSBC bank plc, SWIFT code HSBCGB6174A, Hungerford Branch, for further credit to Mrs. Josephine Kauri, sort code 40-28-73, account number 15638409

Please carry out these transfers as soon as possible, preferably immediately. I trust your mother-in-law continues to make a sound recovery. Many thanks. AR.

Martin Toleron and I had looked through all the transfer requests in Alex Reece's Gibraltar folder, and we had studied closely the language and layout he had used in the past.

"Are you happy with it?" Martin asked.

"As happy as I can be," I said.

"Do you think it will work?"

"Maybe," I said. "But we have nothing to lose by trying."

"I have," he said. "I stand to lose two million dollars."

I decided against saying that he'd told me he could afford it. "You've already lost it, but this might just get it back. It's worth a try, but it's a hell of a lot of money for a bank to transfer without making any other checks."

"They'll e-mail him back, though," Martin said.

"Oh, for sure."

By looking at all the e-mails to and from SB and AR we had discovered a pattern. Alex would e-mail the request always at about midday or five minutes either side,

UK time. Sigurd would then e-mail straight back, acknowledging receipt and requesting confirmation. Alex would then instantly respond to that with a note that contained some comment, not now about Sigurd's mother-in-law but about the weather in the UK.

The Taliban would have had a field day with this pathetic level of security. I only hoped that Alex hadn't realized that I had copied his messages and compromised his defenses.

"Are you ready to intercept SB's reply?" Martin asked.

"As ready as I can be," I said. "I'm logged on to Alex Reece's e-mail account via the *mail2web* webmail service, but it will all go wrong if Alex downloads the reply straight to his computer from the server. We'll just have to take the chance that he doesn't click on send/receive at that precise moment."

"Do you have the reply ready?" He was hopping from foot to foot with his nervousness as he stood behind me at his desk.

"Calm down, Martin," I said. "Let's just hope that the real Alex Reece isn't sending his own transfer e-mail to SB today."

"Oh my God," said Martin. "That would really confuse things."

"The shortest time that money has spent

in the account before being moved on is six days. It is now five days since the first one arrived and four since the second. So I don't expect a real transfer request from Alex today."

"How about if SB knows that it has to be a minimum of six days or it's a fake request?"

"We'll know that soon enough," I said. "It's two minutes to twelve."

I pushed the send button, and the message disappeared from the screen. It was on its way, and we were left holding our breaths.

We both waited in silence as I continually refreshed the webmail page. The clock on the computer moved past twelve o'clock to twelve oh-one. I refreshed the page once more. Nothing. I forced myself to be calm and wait for a count of ten before I clicked on the refresh button again. Still nothing. I counted again, slowly, this time to fifteen, but still nothing came.

The reply arrived at nine minutes past twelve, by which time I had all but given up hope.

Alex. I acknowledge receipt of your instructions.

To which party do I charge the transfer

costs? SB.

I had the reply ready to send, but I quickly pulled it up to make the changes. I typed in the new information.

Sigurd, I confirm receipt of your acknowledgment and I endorse the instructions. Please charge the transfer costs to the recipients. Thank goodness spring is nearly here in the UK and the temperature has begun to rise. AR.

I pushed the send button, and again the message disappeared from the screen. Next, I used the *mail2web* tools to delete SB's reply from the server so that it would not appear on Alex's computer when he downloaded his mail.

"Now we wait and see," I said. But I went on monitoring the webmail page for another forty minutes before I was happy that SB wasn't going to ask another question.

"Do you think it will work?" he said.

"Do you?" I asked in reply.

"Not really," he said. "It was much too easy."

"Yes," I said. "Almost as easy as getting you to part with the two million dollars in the first place!"

■ ■ ■ ■

Martin called his bank and asked them to inform him by telephone immediately if a large deposit arrived. My mother, meanwhile, might simply have to wait to see if it appeared on her bank statement.

"Call me if you hear anything," I said, shaking his hand in the driveway.

"Don't worry, I will," he said with a smile. "Quite an entertaining morning, I'd say. Much more exciting than the boring existence I have now found for myself."

"You miss running your company, then?" I asked.

"Miss it!" he said. "I grieve for my loss."

"But you have all that money."

"Yes," he said rather forlornly. "But what can I do every day? Count it? I started in business when I was straight out of school, aged sixteen. It wasn't plastics in those days, it was cardboard. Cardboard boxes for home-moving companies. They were all still using old tea chests then, and I reckoned that cardboard would be better. I started by collecting old cardboard boxes from shops and passing them on to the moving men. Then I started importing boxes, both cardboard and plastic."

He sighed.

"Where did the drainpipes come from?" I asked.

"The man who made the plastic boxes in Germany also made drainpipe, and I bought the UK rights from him. And it just took off. That was years ago."

"Why did you sell?"

"I'm sixty-eight, and neither of my children are interested in running any business, let alone a drainpipe business. Far too boring for them. But I loved it. I used to get to the factory in Swindon at seven in the morning, and often I'd not leave before ten at night. It was such fun."

"Didn't your wife object?" I asked.

"Oh, I expect so," he said, laughing. "But she does so enjoy shopping in Harrods."

"So what will you do in the future? Will you start something else?"

"No," he said, with another sigh. "I don't think so. I suppose I'll have to go to Harrods more often with my wife. We need to do something with all that money."

The prospect of more shopping with his wife clearly didn't make him happy. I obviously wasn't the only person viewing his future life with anxiety and trepidation.

"Shop for some racehorses," I said. "I hear that's a great way to spend loads of money, and it can be lots of fun too."

"What a great idea," he said. "I'll do just that."

"And," I said, "I know a way to save you all the VAT."

We both laughed out loud.

As I had hoped, Martin Toleron and I parted as friends, not foes.

Martin called my cell phone at a quarter past three as I was dozing on Ian's sofa, half watching the racing from Huntingdon on the television.

"Have you heard from the bank?" I asked, instantly wide awake.

"No, nothing from them," he said. "But I've just had a call from Jackson Warren."

"Wow," I said, clapping my hands together. "And what did he say?"

"He tried to tell me that the bank in Gibraltar had made an error and had inexplicably returned my two million dollars to my account. He asked if I would mind instructing my bank to send it again."

"And what did you say?" I asked.

"I expressed surprise that Jackson was calling me, as I had no idea that he was involved with the organization of the fund. I told him that I thought he was just another satisfied investor."

"And what did he say then?"

"He tried to tell me that he had only been called by the fund manager because he, the manager, knew that Jackson was a friend of mine."

He paused. "Yes?" I said. "Go on."

"I lost my rag a bit. I told him to get stuffed. I said that I would not be investing in anything to do with him, as he had purposely misled me. I also told him I'd be reporting the incident to the Financial Services Authority."

"I bet he didn't take kindly to that."

"No, he didn't," Martin said. "In fact, he threatened me."

"He what?"

"He told me straight-out that if I went to the FSA I'd regret it. I asked him what exactly he meant by that, but all he said was 'Work it out.' "

That was the same phrase that Alex had said to me.

"And," Martin went on, "he doesn't seem to be too pleased with you either."

"How so?" I asked.

"He point-blank accused me of conspiring with you to defraud him. I told him that was rich coming from him, and he could go and boil his brains, or words to that effect."

I wasn't altogether sure that insulting

Jackson Warren was a sensible policy. Insults sometimes provoked extreme reactions, and some historians now believed that Saddam Hussein's cruel invasion of Kuwait in 1990 was the direct result of a personal insult to the Iraqi people from the Emir.

"Did he ask if you knew where I was?" I asked.

"Ask me?" He laughed. "He demanded that I tell him. I simply said that I had no idea where you were, and also that I wouldn't have told him if I did."

"How secure are your gates?" I asked.

"Why?" He sounded slightly worried for the first time.

"I think that Jackson Warren is a very dangerous man," I said seriously. "Martin, this is not a game. He has already tried to kill me once, and I am sure he would do it again without hesitation. So keep your gates locked and watch your back."

"I will," he said, and hung up, no doubt, to go outside rapidly and make sure his gates were closed and bolted.

Was it now time, I wondered, to involve the police and be damned about the tax consequences? But what could I say to them? "Well, officer, Mr. Jackson Warren tried to kill me by hanging me up to starve to death in a disused stable when I had to stand on only one leg for days, but I escaped by unscrewing the hay-net ring, climbing over the stable walls and breaking a window in the tack room, but I've only now decided to tell you about it, a week later, after I've been sneaking around Berkshire in camouflage cream, attacking and torturing one of Mr. Warren's associates using fake insulin and a hypodermic needle, and using the information I illegally obtained from him to transfer one million American dollars from Mr. Warren's company in Gibraltar into my mother's personal bank account in Hungerford."

Somehow, I didn't think it would bring the Thames Valley Constabulary rushing to Jackson's front door to make an immediate arrest. They would be far more likely to send me to a psychiatrist, and then Jackson would know exactly where I was.

It was much safer, I thought, to lie low for a while and let things blow over.

How mistaken could I be? The answer was badly.

The first sign that things had gone dangerously wrong was a hammering on the door of Ian's flat that woke me from a deep sleep.

It was pitch-black, and I struggled to find my way to the light switch. The hammering continued unabated. I turned on the light and looked at the clock. It was one-thirty in the morning. Who could be knocking at this ungodly hour?

I grabbed my shirt and went over to the door. I was about to unlock it when I suddenly stepped back. Could it be Jackson Warren outside? Or Alex Reece? Or Peter Garraway?

"Who is it?" I shouted.

"Derek Philips," came the reply. My stepfather.

Ian appeared from his bedroom, bleary-eyed and wearing blue-striped boxer shorts.

"What the hell's going on?" he said, squinting against the brightness.

"It's my stepfather," I said to him.

"Well, open the door, then."

But I wasn't sure enough. "Are you alone?" I shouted.

"What bloody difference does that make?" Ian said, striding towards me. "Open the bloody door. Here." He pushed past and unlocked it himself.

Derek almost fell into the room as the door opened, and he was alone.

"Thank God," he said. Then he saw me. "What the bloody hell are *you* doing here?"

I ignored his question. "Derek, what's wrong?" I asked.

"It's your mother," he said, clearly distressed.

Oh no, I thought. She must have decided to kill herself after all.

"What about her?" I asked, dreading the answer.

"She's been kidnapped."

"What?" I said in disbelief.

"She's been kidnapped," he repeated.

It sounded so unlikely.

"Who by?" I asked.

"Two men," he said. "They came looking for you."

Derek and Ian both looked at me accusingly.

"Who were they?" Ian asked him.

"I don't know," Derek said. "They were wearing those ski masks, like balaclavas, but I don't think either of them was very young."

"Why not?"

"Something about the way they moved," Derek said.

I, meanwhile, believed I knew exactly who they were, and Derek was right, neither of them was young. Two desperate men in their sixties, trying to recover the money they thought they had successfully stolen, but which I had then stolen back. But where was Alex Reece?

"Are you sure there were just two of them?" I asked. "Not three?"

"I only saw two," Derek said. "Why? Do you know who they are?" He and Ian looked accusingly at me once more.

"What exactly did they say?" I asked, trying to ignore their stares.

"I don't really remember. It all happened so fast," he said. "They had somehow got into the house and were in our bedroom. One of them poked me with the barrels of a shotgun to wake me up." He was almost in tears, and I could understand how frightened he and my mother must have been. "They said they wanted you, but we told them we didn't know where you were. We said we thought you were in London."

So not telling my mother where I was had saved me a visit from the ski-masked duo. But at what cost to her?

"But why did they take her with them?" I asked, but I already knew the answer. They knew that I'd come to them if they had my mother. "Did they tell you where they were taking her?"

"No," Derek said. "But they did tell me that you would know where she would be."

"Have you called the police?" Ian asked.

"No police," Derek said urgently. "They told me that I mustn't call the police. Call

the police and Josephine dies, that's what they said. They told me to think about it for a while and then to call you." He nodded at me. "But I didn't know where you were, and I don't even have your phone number." He was crying now. "All I could think of was asking Ian."

I would know where she would be. That's what the kidnappers had told Derek.

I would know where she would be.

And I did.

I approached Greystone Stables, not from the road and up the driveway as my enemy might have expected but from the opposite direction over the undulating farmland, and through the woods on the hill above.

In war, tactical surprise is essential, as it had been during the recapture of the Falkland Islands. The Argentine forces, far superior in number, had believed that it was impossible for the British to approach Stanley, the island capital, across the swampy, uncharted interior, and had dug in their defenses for an attack from the sea. How wrong they were. The Royal Marines and Parachute Regiment's "yomp" across the island, carrying eighty-pound Bergens over more than fifty-six miles in three days, has since become the stuff of folklore in the army. It had been one of the major factors in that victory.

In my case, I was just glad not to have an eighty-pound Bergen on my back.

I stopped a few feet short of the limit of the trees and knelt down on my left knee. I looked again at my watch with its luminous face. More than two hours had passed since Derek had arrived so distressed at the door of Ian's flat. It was now three forty-two a.m. The windless night was beautifully clear, with a wonderful canopy of twinkling stars. The moon's phase was just past first quarter, and it was sinking rapidly towards the western horizon to my left. In forty minutes or so, the moon would be down completely, and the blackness of the night would deepen for a couple of hours before the arrival of the sun, and the dawning of another day.

I liked the darkness. It was my friend.

In the last of the moonlight I studied the layout of the deserted house and stables spread out below me. I could see no lights, and no movement, but I was sure this was where the two men had meant when they'd told Derek I would know where my mother would be.

But would she actually be here, or had it been a ruse to bring me to this place on a wild-goose chase, to fall willingly into their waiting hands while my mother was actually incarcerated somewhere else?

It had taken all my limited powers of persuasion to convince Ian not to call the police immediately. Derek too had begged him not to.

"But we must call the police," Ian had said with certainty.

"We will," I'd replied. "But give me a chance to free my mother first."

Did I really think that Jackson Warren and Peter Garraway would harm her, or even kill her? I thought it unlikely, but I couldn't know for sure. Desperate people do desperate things, and I remembered only too well how they had left me to die horribly from starvation and dehydration.

I had left Derek and Ian in the latter's flat, Derek cuddling a bottle of brandy he had returned briefly to Kauri House to collect, and Ian with a list of detailed instructions, including one to telephone the police immediately if he hadn't heard from me by six-thirty in the morning.

They had both watched with rising interest and astonishment as I had made my mission preparations. First I'd changed into my dark clothes, together with the all-black Converse basketball boots, the right one requiring me to remove my false leg to force the canvas shoe over the plastic foot. Next, I had gathered the equipment into my little rucksack: black garden ties, scissors, duct tape, the red-colored first-aid kit, the length of chain with the padlock still attached, a torch and a box of matches, all of them wrapped up in a large navy blue towel to prevent any noise when I moved. This time I did borrow one of Ian's kitchen knives, a large, sharp carving knife, and I'd placed it on top of everything else in the rucksack, ready for easy access. I had then borrowed a pair of racing binoculars from my mother's office, and finally, I'd removed my sword from its protective cardboard tube and scabbard.

"Surely you're not going to use *that,*" Derek had said, with his large brandy-filling eyes staring at the three-foot-long blade.

"Not unless I have to," I had replied casually, as I'd rubbed black boot polish onto the blade to reduce its shine. But I would use it, I thought, and without hesitation, if the need arose.

Killing the enemy had been my raison d'être for the past fifteen years, and I'd been good at it. *Values and Standards of the British Army* demanded it. Paragraph ten states that "All soldiers must be prepared to use lethal force to fight: to take the lives of others, and knowingly to risk their own."

But was I still a soldier? Was this a war? And was I knowingly risking my own life or that of my mother?

I wasn't sure about the answers to any of those questions, but I knew one thing for certain. I felt alive again, whole and intact, and eager for the fray.

I scanned the buildings below me once more, using my mother's binoculars, searching for a light or a movement, any sign that would give away the enemy's position, but there was still nothing.

Was I wrong? Was this not the place they had meant?

I had skirted around the walls of Lambourn Hall on my way to this point, but it had been dark, locked and seemingly deserted.

They had to be here.

The moonlight was disappearing fast, and I would soon need to be on the move down across the open ground between my current location and the rear of the stables. I took one last look through the binoculars, and there it was, a movement, maybe only a stretching of a cramped leg or a warming rub of a freezing foot but a telltale movement nevertheless. Someone was waiting for me in the line of trees just to the right of the house as I looked. From that position he would have commanded a fine view of the driveway and the road below.

But if he was looking down there, he was looking the wrong way.

I was behind him.

But where was his accomplice?

The moon finally dipped out of sight, and the light rushed away with it. But I didn't move immediately, not for a minute or two, not until I was sure my eyes had fully adjusted to the change. In truth, the night had not become totally black, as there was still a slight glow from the stars, but it was no longer possible for me to see Greystone Stables from this position. Likewise, it would now be impossible for anyone down there to see *me.*

I checked once more that my cell phone was switched off, stood up and started forward across the grass.

19

I approached the stables in such a way as to take me past the muck heap near the back end of the passageway in which I had hidden the previous week.

I was ultracareful not to trip over any unseen debris as I eased myself silently through the fence that separated the stable buildings from the paddock behind. How I longed to have a set of night-vision goggles, the magic piece of kit that enabled soldiers to see in the dark, albeit with a green hue. My only consolation was that it was most unlikely that my enemy had them either — we would be as blind as one another.

I stood up close against the stable wall at the back of the short passageway, closed my eyes tight and listened. Nothing. No breath, no scraping of a foot, no cough. I went on listening for well over a minute, keeping my own breathing shallow and silent. Still nothing.

Confident that there was no one hiding in the passageway, I stepped forward. Here, under the roof, it was truly pitch-black. I tried to recall an image in my head of the inside of the passageway from my time here last week. I remembered that I had used an empty blue plastic drum as a seat. That would be here somewhere in the darkness. I could also recall that there were some wooden staves leaning up against one of the walls.

I moved along the passage very slowly, feeling ahead into the darkness with my hands and my real foot. The canvas basketball boots were thin — in truth, rather too thin for such a cold night — but they allowed me to sense the underfoot conditions so much better than I could have in regulation-issue thick-soled army boots.

My foot touched the plastic drum, and I eased around it to the door. I pressed my face to it, looking through the gaps between the widely spaced wooden slats.

Compared to the total blackness of the passageway, the stable yard beyond seemed quite bright, but there was still not enough light to see into the shadows of the overhanging roof. I couldn't see if any of the stable doors were open but, equally, that would mean that no one would be able to see me as I eased open the slatted door from the passageway and stepped out into the yard.

I slowly closed the spring-loaded door and then stood very still, listening again for anyone's breathing, but there was no sound, not even the slight rustling of a breeze.

Provided he hadn't changed his position, the man I had seen from the woods on the hillside, the man who had made a movement, would have been out of sight from where I was, even in bright sunshine, but I knew there had to be at least one other person around here somewhere. And if Alex Reece had joined Warren and Garraway, there would be three of them to deal with. The quote from Sun Tzu in *The Art of War* about relative army sizes floated into my head once more.

> If you are in equal number to your enemy, then fight if you are able to surprise; if you are fewer, then keep away.

I was one and they were two, maybe even three. Should I not just keep away?

Another of Sun Tzu's pearls of wisdom drifted into my consciousness.

> All warfare is based on deception . . . When we are near, we must make the enemy believe we are far away; when far away, we must make him believe we are near . . . Hold out baits to entice the enemy. Feign disorder, and crush him.

I folded back the sleeve of my black roll-necked sweater and looked at the watch beneath. It was four forty-seven.

In eighteen minutes, at five minutes past five precisely, a car would drive through the gates at the bottom of the Greystone Stables driveway and stop. The driver would sound the car horn once, and the car would remain there with the headlights blazing and the engine running for exactly five minutes. Then it would reverse out again onto the road and drive away. At least, it would do all of those things if Ian Norland obeyed to the letter the instructions I had left him.

He hadn't been very keen on the plan, and that was putting it mildly, but I'd promised him that he was in no danger, provided he kept the car doors locked. It was yet another one of those dodgy promises of mine. But I didn't actually believe that Jackson Warren and Peter Garraway would kill me there and then. Not before I'd returned the million dollars.

"Warfare is based on deception . . . When we are near, we must make the enemy believe we are far away." When I was in the stable yard searching for my mother, I'd make Warren and Garraway believe I was down near the gates.

"Hold out baits to entice the enemy." Make the car wait with its lights on to draw them down the hill away from the stables, and away from me.

"Feign disorder, and crush him." Only time would tell on that one.

I moved slowly and silently to my right, around the closed end of the quadrangle of stables, keeping in the darkest corners under the overhanging roof. Where would my mother be? I felt for all the bolts on the stable doors. They were all firmly closed. I decided, at this stage, not to try to open any, as it would surely make some noise.

Unsurprisingly, no one had mended the pane of glass in the tack-room window that I'd broken to get out. I leaned right in through the opening, closed my eyes tight and listened.

I could hear someone whimpering. My mother was indeed here. The sound was slight but unmistakable, and it came from my left. She was in one of the stalls on the same side of the stables as I had been.

I listened some more. Once or twice I heard her move, but the sound was not close, and other than an occasional muffled cry, I could not hear her breathing. There were ten stalls down each of the long sides of the quadrangle, and I reckoned she must be at least three away from the tack room, probably more. Maybe she was in the same stall in which I had been imprisoned.

I looked again at my watch. Four fifty-nine.

Six minutes until the car arrived — I hoped.

I withdrew my head and shoulders from through the broken window and moved very slowly along the line of stables, counting the doors. I could remember clearly having to climb over five dividing walls to get to the tack room. I counted four stable doors, then I stopped. The stall I had been in was the next one along.

Would there be a sentry? Would anyone be on guard?

I stood very still and made my breathing as silent as I could. I dared not look again at my watch in case the luminosity of the face gave me away.

I waited in the dark, listening and counting the seconds — Mississippi one, Mississippi two, Mississippi three and so on. Just as I had done here before.

I waited and waited, and I began to doubt that Ian was coming. I was well past Mississippi twenty in the third minute when I heard the car horn, a long two-second blast. Good boy.

There was immediate movement from the end of the row of stables not twenty yards from where I was standing. Someone had been sitting there in silence, but now I clearly heard the person walk away, back towards the house, crunching across the gravel turning area. I heard him call out to someone else, asking what the noise was, and there was a murmured reply from farther away that I couldn't catch.

I went swiftly to the door of the stall and eased back the bolts. They made a slight scrape but nothing that would be heard from around near the house. The door swung open outwards.

"Mum," I whispered into the darkness.

There was no reply.

I stood and listened, trying hard to control the thump-thump of the heart in my chest.

I heard her whimper again, but it still came from some way to my left. She wasn't in this stall but in one a bit farther along.

I recognized the need to be as fast as possible, but equally, I had to make my search undetected. I moved as quickly as I dared along the row of stables, carefully sliding back the bolt on the upper half of each door and calling into the space with a whisper.

She was in the second stall from the end, close to where the man had been sitting on guard, and by the time I found her, I was becoming desperate about the time it was taking.

I thought that Ian must surely be about to reverse the car to the road and depart. Five minutes would seem a very long time to someone simply sitting there afraid that something would happen, and hoping that it wouldn't. Ian must have been so nervous in the car, willing the hands of his watch to move around faster. I wouldn't have blamed him if he'd decided to leave early.

When I'd opened the stable door and whispered, my mother had been unable to answer me properly, but she had managed to murmur loudly.

"Shhh," I said, going towards the sound and down onto my left knee. It was absolutely pitch-black in the stable. I removed one of my black woolen gloves and "saw" by feel, moving my left hand around until I found her.

She had tape stuck over her mouth and had been bound hand and foot with the same plastic garden ties as had been used to secure me. Thankfully, she hadn't been left hanging from a ring in the wall but was sitting on the hard floor close to the door with her back up against the wooden paneling.

I laid my sword down carefully so it didn't clatter on the concrete, then I swung the rucksack off my back and opened the flap. Ian's carving knife sliced easily through the plastic ties holding my mother's ankles and wrists together.

"Be very, very quiet," I whispered in her ear, leaning down. "Leave the tape on your mouth. Come on, let's go."

I helped her up to her feet and was about to bend down for the rucksack and the sword when she turned and hugged me. She held me so tightly that I could hardly breathe. And she was crying. I couldn't tell if it was from pain, from fear or in joy, but I could feel her tears on my face.

"Mum, let me go," I managed to whisper in her ear. "We have to get out of here."

She eased the pressure but didn't let go completely, hanging on to my left arm. I prized her away from me and swung the rucksack over my right shoulder. As I reached down again for my sword, she leaned heavily against me and I stumbled slightly, kicking the sword with my unfeeling right foot. It scraped across the floor with a metallic rattle that sounded dreadfully loud in the confines of the stall but probably wouldn't have been audible at more than ten paces outside.

But had there been anyone outside within ten paces to hear it?

I reached down, grabbed the sword and led my mother to the door.

Ian must have completed his five-minute linger by now, and I hoped he had safely departed back to his flat to sit by the telephone, waiting for my call and ready to summon the cavalry if things went wrong. But where, I wondered, were my enemies? Were they still around at the driveway? Or had they come back?

My mother and I stepped through the stable door and out into the yard, with her hanging on to my left arm as though she would never let it go again.

There were no shouts of discovery, no running feet, just the darkness and the stillness of the night. But my enemies were out there somewhere, watching and waiting, and they outnumbered me. It was time to leave.

"He who fights and runs away, lives to fight another day."

But I never did get to run away.

My mother and I were halfway across the stable yard, taking the shortest route to the muck-heap passageway, when the headlights of a car parked close to the house suddenly came on, catching us full in their beams.

Whoever was in the car couldn't help but see us.

"Run," I shouted in my mother's ear, but running wasn't really in her exercise repertoire, even when in mortal danger. It was only ten yards or so to the passageway door, but I wasn't at all sure we would make it. I dragged her along as all hell broke loose behind me.

There were shouts and running footsteps on the gravel near the house.

Then there was a shot, and another.

Shotgun pellets peppered my back, stinging my neck and shoulders, but the rucksack took most of them. The shooter was too far away for the shot to inflict much damage, but he would get closer, especially as my dear mother was so slow.

We reached the passageway door, and I swung it open, pushing her through it ahead of me, both of us nearly falling over the blue plastic drum.

"Mum, please," I said loudly to her. "Go through the passage and out the back. Then hide."

But she wouldn't let go of my arm. She was simply too frightened to move. Conditioning young men not to freeze under fire was a common problem in the army, and one that wasn't always solved, so I could hardly blame my mother for doing so now.

Another shot rang out, and some of the wood of the door splintered behind us. That was a bit closer, I thought — far too close, in fact. The shooter had now closed to within killing range. Maybe I'd been wrong about them wanting the million dollars returned before they'd kill me. Another shot tore into the wooden roof above our heads.

"Come on," I said to my mother as calmly as I could. "Let's get out of here."

I firmly removed her hand from my arm and then held it in mine as I almost dragged her down the passageway and out into the space behind. I could hear shouts from the stable yard as someone was directing his troops around the end of the building to find us. However, the man who was doing the shouting stayed where he was, in the yard. He obviously didn't fancy walking into the dark passageway, in case I was in there waiting for him.

I pulled my mother around behind the muck heap. There was a tall, narrow space between the rear retaining wall of the heap and a hay barn beyond.

"Get in there," I said quietly, in my best voice-of-command. "And lie facedown."

She didn't like it, I could tell by the way she kicked at the wet ground, but she couldn't protest, as the tape was still over her mouth. She hesitated.

"Mum," I said. "Please. Otherwise, we will die."

There was just enough light from the stars for me to see the fear in her eyes. Still she clung to me, so I eased up the corner of the tape over her mouth and peeled it away.

"Mum," I said again. "Please do it now." I kissed her softly on the forehead, but then I firmly pushed her away from me and into the gap.

"Oh God," she whispered in despair. "Help me."

"It's all right," I said, trying to reassure her. "Just lie down here for a while and it will all be fine."

She obviously didn't want to, but she didn't say so. She knelt down in the gap and then lay flat on to her tummy, as I'd asked. I pulled some of the old straw down off the muck heap and covered her as best I could. It probably didn't smell too good, but so what? Fear didn't smell great, either.

I left her there and went back to the end

of the passageway. Whoever had been shooting had still not come through, but I could see that the car was being driven around the end of the stable buildings so that its lights were about to shine down the back, straight towards where I was standing.

I stepped again into the passageway.

The car's headlights were both a help and a hindrance. They helped in showing me the position of at least one of my enemies, but at the same time, their brightness destroyed my night vision.

Consequently, the passageway appeared darker than ever, but from my previous visits, I could visualize the location of every obstruction on the floor, and I easily stepped silently around them. I pressed my eyes up against the gaps between the door slats and looked out once more into the stable yard beyond.

There was plenty of light from the still-maneuvering car for me to see clearly. Jackson Warren was standing in the center of the yard, talking with Peter Garraway. They were each holding a shotgun in a manner that suggested that they both knew how to use them. What was it that Isabella had said? "The Garraways always come over for the end of the pheasant-shooting season — Peter is a great shot."

I think I'd have rather not known that, not right now.

As I could see Warren and Garraway in the stable yard, it must be Alex Reece who was driving the car.

"You go round the back," Jackson was saying to Garraway. "Flush him out. I'll stay here in case he comes through."

I could tell from his body language that Peter Garraway really didn't like taking orders. I also suspected that he didn't much fancy "going round the back" either, good shot or not. "Why don't I wait here and you go round the back?" he replied.

"Oh, for God's sake," said Jackson, clearly annoyed. "All right. But keep your eyes fixed on that door and, if he appears, shoot him. But try to hit him in the legs."

That was slightly encouraging, I thought, but the notion of being captured alive was not. I had already experienced their brand of hospitality in these stables, and I had no desire to do so again.

Jackson Warren walked off towards the car, leaving a nervous-looking Peter Garraway standing alone in the stable yard.

Yet another Sun Tzu quote floated into my head. "In war, the way is to avoid what is strong and to strike at what is weak."

Peter Garraway was weak. I could tell by

the way he kept looking towards the car and in the direction that Jackson had gone in the hope of being relieved, rather than towards the door to the passageway, as he'd been told. He obviously didn't like being left there alone. And shooting pheasants was one thing, but shooting a person would be quite another matter.

Reece had finally managed to get the car around behind the stables, and I could see the glow of its lights at the back end of the passageway. That was not good, I thought, as my position was becoming outflanked and I would soon find myself liable to attack from opposite directions.

I looked at my watch. It was only five-seventeen. Just twelve minutes had elapsed since Ian had sounded the car horn, but it felt like so much longer, and there would still be another hour of darkness.

I took another quick glimpse through the slats at Peter Garraway in the stable yard. He was resting his double-barreled shotgun in the crook of his right arm, as someone might do while waiting for the beaters to drive pheasants into the air from a game crop. It was not the way a soldier would hold a weapon — and it was not ready for immediate action.

I threw open the passageway door and ran

right at him with my sword held straight out in front of me, the point aimed directly at his face, like a cavalry officer but without the horse.

He was quite quick in raising his gun but nowhere near quick enough. I was on him so fast, and as he swung the barrels up, I struck his right arm, the point of my sword tearing through both his coat and the flesh beneath. In the same motion, I hit him full on the nose with the sword's nickel-plated hand guard. He immediately went sprawling straight down onto the concrete floor, dropping the gun and clutching at his bleeding face with both hands.

I stood over him with my sword raised high, like a matador about to deliver the coup de grâce. Garraway, meanwhile, curled himself into a ball with his arms up around his head, whimpering and shaking like a scolded puppy.

I aimed at his heart, and my arm began to fall.

"What are you doing?" I suddenly asked myself out loud, stopping the rapidly descending blade when it was just inches from his chest.

Values and Standards of the British Army, paragraph sixteen, states that soldiers must treat all human beings with respect, especially the victims of conflict, such as the dead, the wounded, prisoners and civilians. All soldiers must act within the law. "Soldiering," it says, "is about duty: so soldiers should be ready to uphold the rights of others before claiming their own."

Killing Peter Garraway like this would certainly not be within the law, and would definitely be a breach of his rights as my unarmed and wounded prisoner. I would simply be taking revenge for the pain and suffering that he had inflicted on me.

I noticed that he had peed himself, just as I had done the previous week in the stable, although, in my case, it hadn't been from fear. Maybe that would have to be revenge enough. I leaned down, picked up his shotgun and left him where he was, holding his face and arm, and quivering like a jelly.

I went quickly across the yard and out towards the house with the gun in one hand and my sword in the other. But the sword had now outlived its usefulness. I tossed it into the shadows at the end of the stable building and put both my hands on the gun — that was better.

I had no real plan in mind, but I knew that somehow I had to draw Jackson Warren towards me and away from my mother.

I broke open the shotgun. There was a live

cartridge in each of the two chambers, but I cursed myself for not having looked for more in Peter Garraway's pockets. I could hear him behind me, calling out pitifully for Jackson, so I reckoned it was too late to go back and find them now.

So I had only two shots. I would need to make both of them count. I closed the gun once more and pushed the safety catch to off.

If I wanted to draw Jackson and Alex away from my mother, I would have to reveal my position, something that was utterly alien to any infantryman.

The headlights were still shining brightly down the back of the stables towards the muck heap, but I wasn't there anymore. I was about forty yards away, where the driveway met the turning circle near the house. I could see the car clearly from where I stood; at least I could see the headlights but from side-on.

How could I attract attention to myself?

I lifted the shotgun to my shoulder and fired one of my precious cartridges at the car. At this range the shot wouldn't penetrate the vehicle's skin, although it might just break a window. However, one thing was for sure, Alex Reece in the car would certainly know all about it.

I could hear Jackson shouting. Perhaps he had been too close to the shot for comfort. But did I care? Now they would know exactly where I was, and the car was already turning my way.

I purposely lingered a moment too long, just long enough, in fact, for the headlight beams to fall on my departing back. I weaved in the light for a split second before diving once more into the darkness down the side of the house. A shot rang out, but I was already safely protected around the corner.

I moved swiftly, grateful that I had made an extensive reconnaissance here the previous Thursday. I knew that the concrete path alongside the exterior walls ran completely around the rectangular building, the only obstacle being a small gate at one of the back corners.

In no time, I had completed the circuit and approached the front of the house again, but now I was behind the car, its headlamps still blazing towards where I had been just seconds before. In the glow I could see Jackson creeping forward towards the corner, his gun raised to his shoulder, ready to fire.

The driver's door of the car suddenly

opened, and Alex stood up next to the vehicle, facing away from me, watching Jackson intently.

I moved slowly forward, being very careful to be as silent as possible in my basketball boots on the loose gravel. Alex would have certainly heard me if the engine of the car hadn't been left running. As it was, I was able to approach him completely undetected.

He was wearing a baggy sweatshirt and a large woolen cap.

I lifted the shotgun and placed the ends of the barrels firmly onto the bare skin visible just beneath his left ear.

"Move an inch and you will die," I said to him in my best voice-of-command. But he immediately disobeyed me and turned around. But when I saw his face I realized I'd been so wrong, the car driver wasn't Alex Reece, as I'd thought.

"Hello, Tom," said Isabella.

I was stunned. I lowered the barrels.

"But why?" I asked.

"I'm so sorry," she said in answer.

"Was it you who unlocked the gates?" I asked her.

She seemed surprised that I knew, but she nodded. "Jackson was in Gibraltar."

It had been a VW Golf that I had seen

that night. Perhaps I had been subconsciously convincing myself ever since that it hadn't been Isabella's car, but it had.

"Why didn't you come and help me?"

All the misery of those three days in the stable floated into my mind.

She looked down at her feet. "Because I didn't know that you were there, not last week. I only found out tonight when I heard Peter talking about it, and how he couldn't believe you'd managed to escape." She gulped. "Jackson just phoned home on Thursday and asked me to unlock the gates."

I wanted to believe her, but then why was she driving the car here tonight? She couldn't claim now that she didn't know what was going on, not with Warren and Garraway running around with guns.

"Why are you here?" I asked. "Why are you doing this?"

She looked back up at my face and then towards Jackson. "Because I love him," she said. It was almost an apology.

I too looked at Jackson, who was still inching carefully away from me towards the corner of the house, oblivious to the fact that I was standing behind him next to the car. I suddenly wanted nothing more than to shoot him, to kill him in revenge for what his greed had done to us all. And he was not a prisoner but an armed enemy combatant. There were no *Value and Standards* concerns here. I lifted the gun and aimed.

"No," Isabella screamed, grabbing the barrels.

Jackson turned towards the noise, but he would have been unable to see anything, as he would be looking straight into the headlights. But he started to move back towards the car.

I threw Isabella to the ground and again raised the shotgun towards Jackson, but I hadn't bargained on Isabella's panic-driven determination. She grabbed my knees like a rugby player and pushed against the car, forcing me backwards over onto the gravel.

One of the huge disadvantages of having an artificial leg is that it seriously hampers recovery from a horizontal position, as it's impossible to bend the knee sufficiently. I rolled over on the gravel to be facedown and drew my good leg under me, but Isabella had been quicker.

She was already on her feet, and she wrenched the shotgun from my hand, stamping on my wrist for good measure.

How embarrassing, I thought, to be disarmed by a woman. Perhaps the major from the ministry had been right all along.

But Isabella didn't turn the gun on me, she simply ran away with it while I struggled to my feet, using the car door handle to pull me up.

A shot rang out. It was very close.

I turned quickly to see Jackson running towards a figure lying very still on the ground in the light from the headlights, a figure whose hat had come off, revealing long blond hair, hair that was already soaking up an ever-increasing pool of bright red blood.

In another incident of what the military euphemistically call "friendly fire," Jackson Warren had killed Isabella.

He sank down onto his knees beside her, dropping his gun onto the gravel alongside the one that Isabella had been carrying. I walked the few yards from the car and picked up both weapons. I unloaded their second barrels, placing the unfired cartridges in my pocket. There had been enough shooting for one night. In fact, there had been far too much.

Jackson turned his head slightly to see me.

"I thought it was you," he said. He made it sound like an excuse, as if shooting me would have been acceptable. He turned back and cradled his wife's lifeless head on his lap. "I'd told her to stay in the car. I saw someone running with a gun." He looked up at me again, now with tears in his eyes. "I just assumed it was you."

He should have checked.

Epilogue

Three weeks later, Pharmacist, this time with no green potato peel–induced tummy ache, romped up the finishing hill to win the Cheltenham Gold Cup by a neck. It was the second Kauri House Stables success of the afternoon, after Oregon had justified his favoritism to win the Triumph Hurdle. My mother positively glowed.

In the post–Gold Cup press conference, she stunned the massed ranks of reporters, as well as the wider public watching on television, by announcing her retirement from the sport with immediate effect.

"I'm going out on a huge high," she told them, beaming from ear to ear. "I'm handing over the reins to the next generation."

I stood at the back of the room, watching her answer all the journalists' questions with ease, making them laugh with her. Here was the Josephine Kauri that everyone knew and expected: confident and in control of the situation, in keeping with her status as National Woman of the Year.

I believed that she was as happy that day as I had ever seen her. It had been a somewhat different matter when I had returned to her hiding place that night at Greystone Stables to find her frightened, exhausted, bedraggled and to the point of complete mental and physical collapse.

But much had changed since that dreadful night, not least the removal of the imminent threat of public disgrace, and the prospect of being arrested for tax evasion. Not that the senior inspector from Her Majesty's Revenue and Customs hadn't been pretty cross. He had. But nowhere near as cross as he would surely have been if we hadn't arrived to see him with a check for all the back tax.

Martin Toleron had worked some magic, producing a team of accountants to sift through the shambles and to bring some order and transparency to my mother's business accounts. It had been quite an undertaking.

"It's the least I can do," Martin had said, happily agreeing also to pay the accountant's bill.

So the previous Monday, my mother, Derek and I had arrived by appointment at the tax office in Newbury, not only with a check made out for well over a million pounds of back tax, but with a set of up-to-date business accounts and a series of signed and sworn affidavits as to how and why the tax had not been paid at the correct time.

We had sat in the senior inspector's office for more than an hour as he had silently scrutinized our documents, never once putting down the check, which he held between the index finger and thumb of his left hand.

"Most unusual," he'd said at some length. "Most unusual, indeed."

Then he had returned to his reading for another hour, still clutching the check.

I didn't really think the inspector knew what to say. The accountants had calculated not only the tax that was overdue but also the amount of interest that should have been levied for its late arrival.

The amount on the check had taken all of the million dollars that had been returned from Gibraltar, together with every penny that the three of us had been able to muster, including Derek's ISAs, another mortgage on the house and the proceeds from some sales of my mother's favorite antique furniture, as well as all my savings, including the injury-compensation payout that had arrived from the Ministry of Defense.

"Are you sure that's wise?" Martin Toleron had asked me when I'd offered it.

"No," I had said. "In fact, I'm damned sure that it's not wise. But what else can I do?"

"You can come and help buy me some racehorses," he'd replied.

"Now, are *you* sure that's wise?"

We had laughed, but he'd been entirely serious, and he had already engaged the services of a bloodstock agent to find him a top young steeplechaser.

"I have to spend the money on something," Martin had said. "I don't want to leave it all to my bone-idle children. So I might as well enjoy spending it, and trips to the races will sure as hell beat going to Harrods every week with my wife."

My mother, Derek and I had sat in the tax inspector's office for nearly three hours in total while he had read through everything twice, and then while he had gone to consult someone at tax HQ, wherever that might be.

"Now I have to tell you, Mrs. Kauri," he'd said to my mother on his return from the consultation, "we at the Revenue take a very dim view of people who don't pay their taxes on time." I thought that he'd been about to wag his finger at her. "In the light of these affidavits and the payment of the back tax due, we have decided to take no action against you at this point. However, we will be carrying out our own audit of your tax affairs to ensure that you have given us a full and frank disclosure of the situation before we can close the matter entirely."

"Of course," my mother had replied, stony-faced.

"And finally," the inspector had said, standing up and now with a smile, "it is such an honor to meet you. I'm a great admirer, and over the years, I've backed lots of your winners."

So it was official, some tax men could be human after all.

The post-race press conference was still in full swing, and my mother appeared to be absolutely loving it.

"No, of course I'm not ill," she said, putting Gordon Rambler from the *Racing Post* in his place with a stare. "I'm retiring, not dying." She laughed, and the throng laughed with her.

No, I thought, my mother wasn't dying, but Isabella had, snuffed out in the prime of her life. The paramedics had tried to revive her, but she had lost far too much blood, to say nothing of the gaping hole that Jackson had made in her side. There had never been any hope with a shot from such close range.

Strangely, in spite of everything, I grieved for Isabella. I hadn't been wrong when I'd told her, aged ten, that I loved her. I still did. But now there would be no bonus, nor even the prospect of one. Isabella, my sweetheart, who had unknowingly helped in her own downfall by acting as my driver the day we had been to Old Man Sutton's house in Hungerford.

Needless to say, the Thames Valley Constabulary had not been greatly impressed by all the nocturnal activity that had been going on at Greystone Stables. I had called them using my cell phone as soon as Isabella had been hit, and they had subsequently arrived in convoy with an ambulance, and had promptly arrested everyone.

"You should have called us immediately if someone had been kidnapped," they said later at Newbury police station, their ill-disguised anger clearly directed at me for having taken things into my own hands.

"But we couldn't," my stepfather had said with conviction, coming to my defense.

"The kidnappers told me that they would kill Josephine if the police were involved."

The police, of course, thought that was an insufficient reason for not involving them, especially, as they had pointed out, I appeared to know exactly where the kidnappers had taken their hostage.

Alex Reece had apparently wanted nothing to do with Warren and Garraway's plan to recover the money, and had decided that flight would be a much better policy. He had consequently boarded a British Airways jumbo from Heathrow to New York just a few hours before the shootout at the Greystone Stables corral began.

Somewhat carelessly, however, he had failed to clean out his suitcase properly and had been apprehended by a sniffer dog from the U.S. customs on his arrival at Kennedy Airport. He had subsequently been charged with importing cocaine into the United States, and was presently languishing in jail on Rikers Island in New York, waiting to be served with extradition papers by the government of Gibraltar on fraud charges.

Garraway, meanwhile, had been singing like a canary and blaming everything on Jackson Warren, so much so that his lawyers had successfully persuaded a judge to grant him bail on the kidnapping and false-imprisonment charges. However, the judge had ordered that Garraway's passport be confiscated, and as I heard unofficially from the tax inspector, the Revenue were greatly looking forward to the day, very soon, when Peter Garraway's enforced extended stay in the United Kingdom would automatically make him resident here for tax purposes. The inspector had smiled broadly and rubbed his hands together. "We've been trying to get him for years," he'd said. "And now we will."

"So who is taking over the training license?" It was Gordon Rambler who asked my mother the inevitable question. "And what will happen to the horses?"

"The horses will all be staying at Kauri House Stables," she said. "I spoke with all my owners yesterday, and they are all supportive."

That wasn't entirely true, and some of her owners were decidedly unsupportive, but they had all been convinced, out of loyalty to her, to stay on board, at least for the immediate future. And Martin Toleron had helped here too, vocally pledging his support, and his future horses, to the new training regime.

"So who is it?" Rambler was becoming

impatient. "Who's taking over?"

They were all expecting one of the sport's up-and-coming young trainers to be moving into the big league.

"My son," she said with a flourish. "My son, Thomas Forsyth, will henceforth be training the horses at Kauri Stables."

I think it would be fair to say that there was a slight intake of breath, even amongst the most hardened of the racing journalists.

"And," my mother went on, into the silence, "he will be assisted by Ian Norland, my previous head lad, who has been promoted to assistant trainer."

"Can we all assume," Gordon Rambler said, recovering his composure, "that you will still be round to guide and advise them when necessary?"

"Of course," she said, smiling broadly.

But one should never assume anything.

ABOUT THE AUTHORS

Dick Francis is the author of forty-six books, including twenty-five top-ten *New York Times* bestsellers. A three-time Edgar Award best-novel winner, he also received the prestigious Cartier Diamond Dagger award from the British Crime Writers' Association. He was named Grand Master by the Mystery Writers of America, and was awarded a CBE by the Queen of England in her Birthday Honours List of June 2000. He died in February 2010, at age eighty-nine, and remains among the greatest thriller writers of all time.

Felix Francis, a graduate of London University, spent seventeen years teaching A-level physics before taking on an active role in his father's career. He has assisted with the research of many of the Dick Francis novels, including *Shattered, Under Orders,* and *Twice Shy,* which drew on Felix's experiences as a physics teacher and as an international marksman. He is coauthor with his father of the *New York Times* best-sellers *Even Money, Silks,* and *Dead Heat.* He lives in England.

For more information please go to www.dickfrancis.com.

The employees of Thorndike Press hope you have enjoyed this Large Print book. All our Thorndike, Wheeler, and Kennebec Large Print titles are designed for easy reading, and all our books are made to last. Other Thorndike Press Large Print books are available at your library, through selected bookstores, or directly from us.

For information about titles, please call:

(800) 223-1244

or visit our Web site at:

http://gale.cengage.com/thorndike

To share your comments, please write:

Publisher
Thorndike Press
295 Kennedy Memorial Drive
Waterville, ME 04901

BALDWIN PUBLIC LIBRARY
3 1115 00590 0468

WOMEN IN MEDIEVAL HISTORY AND HISTORIOGRAPHY

University of Pennsylvania Press

Middle Ages Series

Edited by EDWARD PETERS

Henry Charles Lea Professor
of Medieval History
University of Pennsylvania

A complete listing of the books in this series appears at the back of this volume

WOMEN IN MEDIEVAL HISTORY & HISTORIOGRAPHY

Edited by
SUSAN MOSHER STUARD

upp UNIVERSITY OF PENNSYLVANIA PRESS
Philadelphia • 1987

Library of Congress Cataloging-in-Publication Data

Women in medieval history and historiography.

(The Middle Ages)
Bibliography: p.
Includes index.
1. Women—History—Middle Ages, 500–1500.
2. Women historians. I. Stuard, Susan Mosher.
II. Series.
HQ1143.W635 1987 305.4'09'02 86-30917
ISBN 0-88122-8048-2 (alk. paper)

Designed by Adrianne Onderdonk Dudden

CONTENTS

INTRODUCTION

The past dozen years have witnessed a developing interest in the history of medieval women. In Western European countries and in North America, an audience waits to learn of new findings in the field and women scholars choose medieval studies as their profession. It would be valuable to learn why medieval women have aroused so much interest: have they always been a focus for research by scholars and chosen reading for an educated public? Have the results of recent research on medieval women won recognition and been incorporated into the general histories of the era? What interpretive constructs have been applied to surviving evidence about medieval women?

Two related observations prompt these questions. First, acquaintance with the source material from the European centuries before 1500 suggests that women may have had a prominence then which they have since lost. Documented roles played then ask today's historian to reconcile forceful, powerful, and effective women—women who were as capable of historical agency as men—with interpretive frameworks that frequently afford men that opportunity but seldom extend it to women.

Second, the possibility arises that women, and by implication men, exhibited far different "natures" in medieval centuries than they do now, or to state the issue in different terms, their behavior supports a current feminist argument that gender, the system of relations between women and men, is socially constructed and has altered so substantially over the centuries in the West that we no longer recognize antecedents to present roles.

Transferring any constant—and surely women's and men's "natures" have often served as constants in interpretive constructs of history—into the category of dynamic elements that change over time, requires effort. It demands a critical re-examination of assumptions about the past and attention to the constructs we have been employing to organize historical knowledge. That effort may force us to reappraise our conclusions about earlier ages.

In the interest of that reappraisal the authors in this anthology have investigated the national traditions of historical writing of four European nations: England, France, Germany, and Italy, as well as medieval history composed in North America, for answers to questions about medieval women and the status that they earned or that was ascribed to them. First, the essayists ask if women have been incorporated into the national histories of the Middle Ages. As the extensive bibliographies gathered at the end of the book reveal, much has been written about the women of Europe's medieval centuries. But, as we have also learned, that is no guarantee that researched, written, and published history will be heeded and its conclusions reconciled with and incorporated into general interpretive studies. To the feminist concern voiced in the 1970s, that no history of women exists, we must answer that a history has in truth been written, but it has been, for the most part, ignored. It has languished on the shelves of libraries or been allowed to go out of print. These essays seriously investigate why that neglect has occurred. Medieval women's presence in the general histories represents a variable, not a constant, of historiography since the Renaissance. From country to country women's history has followed sharply distinct courses in rhythm with other concerns in national historical writing.

Our history has passed beyond national historiographical concerns just far enough to allow us to estimate the national tradition's consequence for past interpretation of earlier ages. Products themselves of a particular and regional experience, national historiographies may identify fairly accurately some variants that affected medieval women's lives. National histories reveal where a "Roman" or politically imposed law came to define women's place and where women's status remained tied to many customary laws. National history is a highly reliable source for establishing the urban and commercial tenor of long-term change, or, by contrast, the more agrarian and aristocratic evolution of a society, either of which profoundly affect women. Historians raised the woman question outside the context of national history first in the Low Countries and Germany where small nation states or an often fragmented nation turned some historians' attention to questions about Europe's general evolution as a society. Was the woman question among those concerns that originally challenged historiography to provide a more encompassing and comparative vision, first European in scope, but now more global in dimension? If so, it suggests women's history need not remain imbedded within the framework of national history. Nevertheless, lacking national histories, medieval women might well have been deprived of a documented presence. Surfeited with national histories, we possess a record of their lives often colored by national history's parochial concerns.

Some currents that have affected women's presence in the historical record have crossed national frontiers. "Scientific" history, for example, which entered European historiography in two waves, has given us much of what we know about medieval women. From Italy, Vico's ideas first influenced the French historian Jules Michelet and through him other traditions of historical writing. Like nascent eighteenth-century anthropology and political economy, Vico's cultural investigations may have opened opportunities to study women in a complex social milieu. Later, the research techniques and methodology taught by Leopold von Ranke had major ramifications not only in Germany but in all Western nations. And if this wave of German "scientific" history both revealed and suppressed women's history, according to the national traditions it influenced, it was not the new scientific methods that were responsible, but the ways the new methods were applied to entrenched concerns and current debates in the discipline.

In the hands of Third Republic French historians, Ranke's ideas combined with Comtean positivism became a means for removing reference to women from the historical record. August Comte advocated applying the scientific method to the social sciences in order to reveal the laws governing society. His fundamental assumptions placed "positive" or scientific truth at the highest stage of human knowledge and identified history as an essential preliminary phase in constructing a progressive social order. That history should trace the milestones of human progress, typically understood as the growth of social order and scientific discoveries. If women's experience did not conform to that agenda, it found no place in positivist history.

Medievalists led the reform to positivism in France and were also the leaders in the movement to remove mention of women from general histories. By contrast, in North America and in Germany and the Low Countries, where an interest in the woman question had developed, Ranke's seminar-taught method, with its emphasis on close and extensive document reading, served occasionally to uncover vital information about medieval women. The English, who also admired Ranke's method, developed an ancillary but surprisingly robust tradition of carefully documented historical writing about medieval women, their contributions to national development, and their legal rights.

When traveling across frontiers the critical textual analysis advocated by Ranke adapted to new causes, frequently abandoning Ranke's own providential theory of history, which located the historical process in the political realm, specifically in the Prussian state. In France scientific history migrated toward the social sciences and lodged comfortably under the Comtean umbrella of secular history and positivism. In fact, the union grew so successful that among European historians in general Ranke's scientific method and positivism were often conflated so that neither kept its original theoretical or ideological content but both were reduced to method alone. Theoretically at least, method so easily uncoupled from its original ideological purpose could be marshalled in the cause of women's history. Yet that development seldom occurred, because neither Ranke's original theory nor positivism identified women as appropriate for historical investigation nor gender as a salient category of analysis.

More recently historians have directed their attention beyond close reading of historical documents which raise essentially philological questions about texts, and towards the various constructions favored by contemporary social science. The initiative has had varying results for women's history. Structures borrowed from anthropology provide both a way to avoid considering women directly and a method for affording women a place within a general interpretive framework. Similarly, the robust tradition of Marxist history divides on the woman question. In England Marxist historians have often regarded women as an important focus for study. In Italy Marxist historians have largely ignored the woman question as too redolent of the elitist concerns they seek to avoid. Demographic history can by turns identify women as the essential reproductive population, hence worthy of study, or the family as the critical demographic unit, paying scant attention to women's choices and their lives. These examples confirm again that historical methods and historical constructs supply scholars with pliant instruments for uncovering the past when they are consciously employed, but they may mask as well as reveal. In a discipline held to the ideal of the most complete history sources allow, the woman question often tests the adequacy of our devices.

If sequential trends in historiography have affected the treatment of medieval women in different ways, the long-standing interdisciplinary organization of medieval studies has consistently promoted attention to their condition. Medievalists who have written about the past in response to questions posed by modern generations have also educated their modern readers by examining a broad spectrum of surviving evidence. Medievalists strive to examine all the preserved literary, legal, political, economic, and social records at their disposal. On the simple grounds that women appear in surviving medieval records, they warrant consideration in at least some avenue of historical investigation. Medieval history has spawned some recognized subfields or specialities, and women generally receive attention in certain of these. The study of law, particularly the early German law codes, has yielded significant information on women. Analysis of the sagas and epics with their casts of women characters has led inquiry into women's condition in the early Middle Ages. A large literature on medieval marriage and family has introduced medieval women into the historical literature.

The extent of information about medieval women uncovered is substantial, but that provides no guarantee that it will in turn affect general understandings of the age. If, as has been true in the past, questions related to women's social and legal rights receive attention only under the rubric of private law, then generalists who have used distinctions between public and private spheres to organize their scholarly investigations feel justified in excluding information about women. They defend their choice on the grounds that their history is public history, not the history of private life. Whenever this has occurred, an anachronistic imposition of the modern barriers separating public and private spheres has been imposed on a more remote past. This inhibits historical understanding because it interferes with the perception of that earlier age when those distinctions of public and private were neither drawn in so definite a fashion nor along the exact lines as we draw them today.

Attention to the moment when historians began to write histories of women as distinct from men confirms the gulf that separates us from our medieval forebears. When historians have generalized about an age, its people, its values, and its accomplishments, were both the men and women of the age intended, or do the generalities apply primarily to men's experience? By the seventeenth century at least, a tradition that addressed women as distinct personages requiring their own separate history had developed in Western Europe. This suggests an early recognition that the generalizations that were routinely applied to society as a whole did not necessarily apply to the women of the age. From that time onward historians have composed separate histories of women. Sometimes they have featured women's voices. This has been the case in collected writings of medieval women authors. Sometimes they have taken the form of biographies of women worthies. These frequently featured the lives of royal women, although they might also examine women whose accomplishments lay in learning or whose religious, cultural, or social roles brought them notice. Saints and queens dominate the biographical literature of the Middle Ages.

More recently, economic and social historians note women's contributions to production and exchange within their communities and occasionally a woman in an ordinary walk of life will receive an historian's attention. Sometimes the literature on a prominent woman is large: in the case of Joan of Arc possibly more has been written about her life than about that of any other medieval personage. This late medieval peasant woman has been readdressed and reinterpreted in every phase of France's political and social evolution from the fifteenth century to the present. Elizabeth of England has inspired equal enthusiasm and has a formidable historical literature to her credit.

Histories of ideas, or what is sometimes known as intellectual history, seldom mention medieval women and their contribution to letters, despite the fact that Anna Comnena numbers among Europe's earliest historians and the first autobiography composed in English was written by Margery Kempe. Still, the exceptional intellectual history like the longitudinal study of Arthur Lovejoy, *History of the Idea of Primitivism,* does include women.[1] In Lovejoy's work, which sweeps from antiquity to the present, the line of male authorities on the idea of primitivism parts to include a series of medieval women authorities, all of whom were in orders and all of whom figured as leading thinkers of their day. Why, when women were not authorities in ancient or more modern times, were these medieval women part of the learned tradition? Such questions point up the importance of understanding women in the context of their own society and the opportunities that their times afforded. Women's contributions to intellectual life in one age, which did not recur in subsequent centuries, challenge the presumption that women and men share equal opportunities. But noting women's learned voices from the Middle Ages does not in any useful fashion explain why women could achieve the status of scholars and authorities in that age and yet have often failed to do so since. For answers to questions of this complexity, highly focused studies on the organization of knowledge and gender presumptions about women's intellectual capacities are necessary. We look to present-day scholars for answers to these questions.

Women as historians have a tradition of comparable length to the history of women, although learned women have often found fields other than history more accessible. In Italy, where women participated in learned circles, where a university degree was first awarded to a woman in the seventeenth century, and where the women of Bologna became learned authorities in the eighteenth century, women seldom participated in the interpretation of the past. Yet in France feminism dates from the immigrant Christian de Pizan (c. 1363–1431), and by the seventeenth century feminist scholars possessed a tradition of writing about women as historical characters. In the Germanies select bodies of scholars controlled access to publication until the nineteenth century. Since women historians were seldom included in these learned organizations, they possessed no vehicle to publish history even if they were disposed to.

By the nineteenth century women were active in writing history throughout Europe and America, even if they were seldom active in the academy. Lina Eckenstein's study of women in early monasticism provides an example of a serious study by a woman working outside recognized institutions of higher learning. Most of Lina Eckenstein's historical writing addressed an audience of women who were similarly excluded from the community of scholars within academia. While her work, and that of a host of women who like her wrote history for the general public, seldom earned the attention and praise of medieval scholars, it represented an original contribution to the field and to women's history. In the twentieth century women have become recognized authorities with training at the

Ph.D. level and positions in academia. The interests women historians bring to the Middle Ages, their contributions to historiography, and their methods and approaches, form an important theme in these essays. If in some countries women historians have clustered in the field of medieval studies, it should prompt us to ask why: are medieval times compelling for women scholars, and do perceived differences between medieval times and the present influence women historians to devote their careers and scholarship to the era?

Successive waves of feminism in the twentieth century have affected the writing of women's history, and it is appropriate to inquire about the interests feminists have brought to the study of medieval women in Western society. Early twentieth-century feminists in Europe and America often pursued active careers in academia and expressed their feminist concerns through their scholarly writing. They tended to concern themselves with exceptional women, and their histories derived from a conviction that women were capable of playing authoritative roles and affecting the course of history if their age afforded them that chance. Medieval women provided these feminists exemplary lives they could document in support of their position. More recent feminists have looked back to the Middle Ages to test the hypothesis that gender is a socially constructed category that has followed its own distinct course through history. For these more recent feminists, the Middle Ages yield evidence that gender assumptions about women in the modern age emerged relatively recently in the Western tradition and that European society's presumptions about women's and men's ordained roles developed in correspondence with other changes in early modern culture and society. For feminists and for many other women scholars, reading about medieval women provides the sheer delight of encountering lives where perimeters were drawn capaciously, allowing a wide range for women's energies and talents.

In the last analysis, the study of medieval women attracts contemporary readers because the surviving records of women's acts surprise us. The deeds of men in Europe's heroic age surprise as well, but even when those acts seem larger than life, men's deeds seldom require us to make a thoroughgoing re-examination of our assumptions about human nature, about history, and the course of Western civilization itself. Medieval women's acts and deeds often place that necessity upon us. Ten years ago, in a valuable essay on the history of European women, Natalie Zemon Davis suggested that women's history began as a study of prominent women and progressed to a study of women in the social and economic context of their day. She then noted in recent decades historians have employed quantification and methods borrowed from the social sciences to measure the perimeters of women's roles with precision.[2] Trusting to this course, we might hope that medieval women will receive ever better treatment from historians. But historiography itself serves as a caution against easy optimism. Because medieval women surprise, they test the assumptions of the composers of history, and the last three centuries of historiography provide no easy guarantee that the primary concerns of historical writing necessarily channel attention towards women.

With these challenges in mind, the authors of the essays in this volume have explored some national traditions of historical writing. The essays are not arranged in the order of their importance. Cross references allow the reader to trace influences among the essays, but order in the volume is not intended to signify either chronological development or the relative importance of one tradition of historical writing over another. Ideally essays on Slavic, Iberian, and Scandinavian historiography would flesh out the study, but scholars investigating women in these traditions note that much needs to be done before a study of this nature is attempted. General works as well as more narrowly focused studies fill the bibliographies on Italy, France, Germany, and England grouped at the end of the volume. The bibliographies gather together studies representative of particular strains in national historiography and in some cases include general titles which, nevertheless, mask a more specialized study. For example, Edith Ennen's recent *Die Frau im Mittelalter*[3] concerns primarily German women, although it makes some observations about medieval women in general. The authors believe these bibliographies can serve as points of departure for future investigation of medieval women.

In the debate within our discipline—whether it is more important to examine what has been said about women or what women did and said—these essays take the middle ground and differ even among themselves in emphasis. Yet surely the deeds and acts of medieval women reach us filtered through the words of historians. So understanding historians, where they account well, where they neglect evidence, and where they reify into construct their own contemporary notions, aids in the recovery of knowledge about the past. These essays also identify what valuable knowledge historians provide us about medieval women. This may be the first collection of historiographical essays in women's history; if so, it reflects a new stage of maturity in our field and the need to pause and reflect on what has been written in the past to aid us in our reappraisals and to point towards a new history of the Middle Ages in which women will receive adequate recognition.

Notes

1. Arthur Lovejoy, *History of the Idea of Primitivism* (Baltimore, 1950).
2. Natalie Zemon Davis, "Women's History in Transition: The European Case," *Feminist Studies* 3 (1976), 83–103.
3. Edith Ennen, *Die Frau im Mittelalter* (Munich, 1984).

1

Golden Ages for the History of Medieval English Women

BARBARA A. HANAWALT

> It was disappointing not to have brought back in the evening some important statement, some authentic fact. Women are poorer than men because—this or that. Perhaps now it would be better to give up seeking for the truth, and receiving on one's head an avalanche of opinion hot as lava, discoloured as dish-water. It would be better to draw the curtains; to shut out distractions; to light the lamp; to narrow the inquiry and to ask the historian, who records not opinions but facts, to describe under what conditions women lived, not throughout the ages, but in England, say in the time of Elizabeth.[1]

One can imagine Virginia Woolf's frustration at the end of a day searching in the British Museum for some viable facts about women; some hint of the origins of misogyny or at least a description of how women lived. When she wrote *A Room of One's Own* in the 1920s, interest in the history of women was on the wane in England and political history, the arena of men, was once again ascendant. Women disappeared from the pages of history books, even many of those on social history and everyday life. Twenty years before, however, the condition of women in history, particularly in the Middle Ages, had been of great interest to historians who wished to explore the origins of women's legal position. Fifty years after Woolf so forcefully expressed her exasperation with the lack of information on women in past times, the study of women's history was once again popular.

The many schools of historiography that formed the way British scholars wrote history had, as we shall see, little influence on the inclusion of medieval women in history or the way they were perceived until the late nineteenth century. One necessary condition, of course, was that medieval history be considered a fit matter for investigation. The Renaissance and Enlightenment historians had little interest in the period and less in the women who lived during it. But the real fascination with women as historical subject matter emerged in England only when political concern for women's rights coincided with historiographical traditions that encouraged investigations of social classes and conditions of everyday life. Thus in the last half of the nineteenth century and the last quarter of the twentieth century, the convergence of political and historical interest in women has produced a flurry of scholarship.

The medieval chroniclers, who sought to keep a running account of notable events, kept a good tally of royal marriages and queens. English history produced some notable and strong characters among its queens and, because women were not legally barred from inheriting titles and land, it was always possible for England to have a female monarch. Chroniclers did not dwell at length on the queens of England, but when they did comment on them, they tended to be equitable and often favorable.[2] The courtly love literature of the twelfth century influenced some chroniclers to dwell on female monarchs. In general chroniclers resorted to gender descriptions of women's actions. Women either exhibited the virtue of being "manly" or the deviousness of acting "womanly."[3]

Polydore Vergil, the first writer to apply to Renaissance rigor of historical analysis to English history, treated women as historical subjects much as he treated men. When he told a racy tale about William the Conqueror's mother he said that he included it "because there is no lawe limited to an historie that it should kepe enie deed secret." Commenting on Joan of Arc's male attire he compared her favorably with a heroine of the ancient world. In his high praise of Margaret, wife of Henry VI, he spoke of her having "all manly qualities . . . great witt, great diligence, greate heede, and carefulness."[4] Absent from the early English chroniclers and historians were both the rampant misogyny and the romanticization of female rulers that appeared on the continent.

David Hume, in his entertaining *History of England,* interspersed his narrative with his own insights into the behavior of his actors. His judgments of women often took on a traditional garb, but he never neglected to give their historical roles full coverage. For instance, he analyzed Matilda's maneuvers in the civil war against Stephen but concluded that they failed partly because "the princess, besides the disadvantages of her sex, which weakened her influence over a turbulent and martial people, was of a passionate, imperious spirit, and knew not how to temper with affability the harshness of a refusal." Of Eleanor of Aquitaine he commented: "Queen Eleanor, who had disgusted her first husband by her gallantries, was no less offensive to her second by her jealousy; and after this manner carried to extremity, in different periods of her life, every circumstance of female weakness."[5] True to the historical traditions of the enlightenment historians, Hume was judgmental of political and human behavior in the Middle Ages in general. Women received stereotypical criticisms just as the church and religion did.

The historiographical tradition of the Romantic period took a firm hold on England. Sir Walter Scott[6] is, perhaps, the best known of the antiquarians who delved into the Middle Ages and made the period popular with a broad public. He is, however, only one of a number of early nineteenth-century antiquarians who sought to preserve in writing the literature and customs of a dying traditional culture. Memorable women appeared in Scott's novels of the Middle Ages and in the ballads and snatches of poetry that antiquarians so avidly sought out, but they were not the centerpieces of either the novels or the collections. Nevertheless, the Romantic movement did stimulate interest in the Middle Ages, if not specifically in the women living then.

The collecting, preserving, and dissemination of historical materials became a serious and scientific pursuit with the positivists. The passion for establishing the sources for historical study led to the publication of medieval government documents, chronicles, and ecclesiastical materials. The Record Commission, the Royal Commission on Historical Manuscripts, the British Academy, British Record Society, Harleian Society, Rolls Series, and so on all entered into the publication of manuscripts with enthusiasm, but women only incidentally appeared in these male-dominated documents and chronicles. The only societies that did publish materials relating to women were the Early English Text Society and the Camden Society. A threatening woman first appeared in the Camden Society series: *A Contemporary Narrative of the Proceedings against Dame Alice Kyteler, Prosecuted for Sorcery in 1324,* but in 1853 they published *The Ancren Riwle* and in 1863 *Letters of Queen Margaret of Anjou.*[7] These volumes, however, were only three out of over one hundred in the Old Series of the Society.

Nineteenth-century historians, however, witnessed the conjunction of two forceful political and intellectual movements that would eventually encourage both the study of the Middle Ages and of women. In the late eighteenth century Catherine Macaulay wrote a history of England that Mary Wollstonecraft praised as being free from the usual sexual biases. She also wrote a measured account of the subordination of women. Mary Wollstonecraft, consciously taking Macaulay as a model, published a more passionate treatise on the same subject, *A Vindication of the Rights of Women*.[8] Both women were influenced by the revolutions at the end of the eighteenth century, and Macaulay even traveled to America to see the new revolutionary society. Women of outstanding achievement, such as the scientist Mary Somerville, continued to press for reforms in the treatment of women.

By the 1860s the women's rights movement had gained momentum. John Stuart Mill published *The Subjection of Women* in 1869 and gave his support to women's demands for educational opportunity, divorce laws, and the vote.[9] Gradually, concern over the position of women led to the passage of major acts protecting women and, finally, in the early twentieth century, instituting women suffrage. Women's colleges were established, and some women entered professions for the first time. In fighting for access to education and for political and legal rights, some women became interested in the history of women and turned their newly acquired education toward writing their own history.

Concurrently with the increased interest in the position of women, English intellectuals grew skeptical of Renaissance and Enlightenment views of the Middle Ages, and became fascinated with medieval art, literature, crafts, and history. Ruskin's writing, of course, spurred the new enthusiasm for medieval aesthetics. He soon had a devoted following, and medieval culture acquired admirers and imitators. Artists such as Burne-Jones and Rossetti sought out women as models and wives who seemed to them to embody the medieval ideal of feminine beauty. William Morris wrote poems about medieval heroines. They all encouraged their women to participate in artistic production as well.

Morris had a further interest in the Middle Ages. He respected and imitated the handicrafts of the period and offered as an explanation for medieval craft's superiority the close identity of the craftsman with the finished product. Along with Marx and many others in the middle of the nineteenth century, he was appalled by the working conditions in the factories. Factory aesthetics also repulsed him. The heightened social concern about workers led him and others to explore the social history of the Middle Ages—a period viewed with perhaps undeserved nostalgia as far as the lives of peasants and craftsmen were concerned. Whatever the motivation of the inquiries into the past, Morris's movement stimulated research into medieval social and economic history. Both professional and amateur historians produced books on their medieval forebears.

The historiography of the late nineteenth century also encouraged an interest in social history. Although Marx and scholars adopting his historical interpretation had no particular interest in the oppression of women per se, some of the women who attached themselves to the Fabian Socialist movement united their interest in social injustice with their interest in history.[10] Alice Clark, for instance, wrote *Working Life of Women in the Seventeenth Century* with these motivations.[11] Like the Marxist historians, those embracing von Ranke's ideas on the practice of historians were not particularly interested in women in medieval history, but their approach to historical materials were adopted by those who did write serious histories of women.

One can trace the increased interest in the Middle Ages and women who lived during that period in the works of a leading antiquarian, Thomas Wright, who devoted an entire book to the social study of women. In dedicating *Womankind in Western Europe from the Earliest Times to the Seventeenth Century* to Lord Lytton in 1869, he said that he was not going to write on the character of women or on women's claims or women's rights; indeed, he expressed a rather dim view of the scholarship on those subjects to date.[12] Instead, he wanted to give a true historical picture and avoid presenting speculative views. His approach was unique as he himself said: "I am not aware that any writer has previously attempted otherwise than very briefly to give a picture of women's life in a feudal castle, yet it is that which has contributed probably more than anything else to the formation of her character in modern society." He noted that the sources—literary, chronicles, and artistic—were remarkably rich and relatively untapped. His book is devoted to the feudal lady with only one slim chapter on bourgeois and peasant women.

Wright's interest in the history of women shows that he had undergone a considerable change in outlook since his earlier *Domestic Manners and Sentiments*.[13] In his dedication to Lady Londesborough he told her that he wanted to portray the history of the English home, for he was more interested in the people than their rulers. In a book on early English homelife it is curious that only 24 out of 500 pages are devoted to the role of women in domesticity.

The social history of "merry old England" was a popular topic for books in the nineteenth and early twentieth centuries, but most of the authors were more interested in male institutions and their yeoman forebears.[14] If the authors of these histories are to be believed, men in the Middle Ages must have been lonely, for there is little mention of women in their lives. J. Frederick Hodgetts in *The English in the Middle Ages* discussed weaponry.[15] George M. Trevelyan in *England in the Age of Wycliffe* wrote of Lollards and peasant revolt but not of women.[16] Women receive attention in one section out of fifteen in G. G. Coulton's *Social Life in Britain from the Conquest to the Reformation.*[17] Women do not even appear in the section on birth and nurture, although there is a section about fatherhood. F. J. Snell in *The Customs of Old England* included an essay on vowesses,[18] and L. F. Salzman, *English Life in the Middle Ages,* discussed medieval women's vanity, inability to keep secrets, and education.[19] The exclusion of women from medieval society continued in almost all social histories of England, including a volume Geoffrey Barraclough edited in 1960, *Social Life in Early England.*[20]

The absence of women in history was noted. In her search for information on the ordinary lives of women, Virginia Woolf took down Trevelyan's history of England from the shelf, looked up "women, position of" and found only that "wife-beating was a recognized right of man," betrothals took place against the will of daughters, and children were married in their cradles in Trevelyan's England of 1470.[21]

One curious aspect of these general social histories is that they were all lavishly illustrated with drawings from manuscripts, sketches of sculpture, and miniatures. The artistic representations contained numerous pictures of women actively involved in field work, court life, dance, banking, craft shops, and so on. They are the same pictures that teachers now use to illustrate lectures. And yet the authors after Wright, from whose book most of the illustrations were pirated, did not discuss the women illustrating their books.

The exceptions to the rule came largely from women authors. For instance, Annie Abram, publishing *English Life and Manners in the Later*

Middle Ages in 1913, devoted a full chapter to the position of women and also integrated women into discussions of recreation, business, agriculture, public life, and family.[22] She was one of the few writers on general social history to give women a routine place in society and in the index of her book. Abram's ideology was neither feminist nor socialist. Although she noted the decline of women's independence and importance in the economy since the Middle Ages, her upper class biases were more important to her. She dwelt on the legal handicaps and other disabilities of feudal ladies and concluded that, with the enlightened passage of the Married Women's Property Act, the evils of the Middle Ages could not return for ladies. Her focus on property rights made her exceptional among female scholars writing general surveys of the history of women, for it led her to conclude that women's position got better in the nineteenth century.

By the end of the nineteenth century, British historians had for the most part adopted a theory of progress in history. They saw an inevitable march of events toward the better world in which they lived. Among the women writing about women in history, Abram was alone in seeing an improved position for women. The attack on the inevitable progress of history toward a better life for "mankind" came from women who surveyed the social and economic status of women. Their research showed that the position of women deteriorated rather than improved over the centuries. These historians were the first to portray a "golden age" for women in the Middle Ages.[23] Georgiana Hill in *Women in English Life from Medieval to Modern Times,* published in 1896, was an eloquent exponent for this view. Her two-volume book reads like a passionate polemic, but her standards of research were excellent for her time. In many respects, the study tells us as much about the frustrations of feminists of the nineteenth century as it does about medieval women. She discovered women's participation in trades, work, religion, and so on and used these discoveries to argue against the cultural limitations imposed on Victorian women: "It does not appear that in the past such views were entertained, that women were considered to be going out of their 'sphere' when they entered the world of trade, or that it was an attempt to deny them any of the privileges which might attach to commercial pursuits."[24] Hill not only provided the first comprehensive history of women written by a female historian but also established the idea, still at the base of much current research, that women suffered a falling away of rights since the Middle Ages.

Clark's *Working Life of Women in the Seventeenth Century* (1919) brought a sophisticated theoretical framework to bear on the shrinkage of women's "sphere" in the new industrial age. A George Bernard Shaw scholar at the London School of Economics, Clark's Fabian ideology influenced her theory. She identified three economic environments for women's work. The traditional one was the domestic industry in which the woman's economic contribution included childrearing and generally providing for the immediate needs of the family. The second was family industry in which women, along with other members of the family including apprentices, produced goods for sale. The family was the unit of production controlling both labor and capital and producing goods in the home. The third economy, capitalist industry or industrialism, undermined women's value in the economy by diminishing her productive capacity, placing a lower value on motherhood and domestic industry, and reversing the importance of married women relative to single women. Single women in the capitalist industry could sell their labor, whereas married women were tied to the now nonproductive home economy. Clark's theories apply equally well to medieval women as seventeenth-century ones. Her approach is still worthy of discussion and argument, and the book has been recently republished.

Doris Mary Stenton in *The English Woman in History,* written in the 1950s, also addressed the issue of women's decline in status since the Middle Ages.[25] Dame Stenton is known primarily for her work on the Pipe Rolls and other administrative aspects of early English history. She had already written a very successful social history volume for the Penguin series on English history when she embarked on the project. Her inspiration for writing the book did not come from feminist leanings. She played a devoted second fiddle to her husband, Sir Frank, and the political climate of the 1950s was hardly one to encourage feminist historiography. Indeed, in her preface she pointedly remarked, "I have no desire to set out an orderly catalogue of female excellence." Rather, she was struck by the difference in legal rights and social roles of the early English women compared to women after the Norman Conquest. She also noted that while noble women lost much freedom with the Conquest, peasant women continued to enjoy the more liberal provisions of customary law. She carried her theme down through the nineteenth century, and her passion for her subject matter increased as she approached the modern period.

Strikingly absent from most English surveys of women in history was a catalogue of either female vices or virtues. The women historians were more interested in observing the position of women and the progress of women's rights than listing female virtues. Those men who did treat the subject of women were interested in their daily life. While many historians ignored women, they did not use their histories as misogynist tracts.

In addition to the general surveys of women in the Middle Ages, books and essays on the queens and princesses of England enjoyed an early prominence.[26] No doubt the presence of a female monarch on the throne encouraged historians to think of other queens in England's history. Indeed, it is an interesting coincidence that both periods in which women's history has flourished in England have been periods of female rule, those of Victoria and Elizabeth II. Agnes Strickland wrote *Lives of the Queens of England from the Norman Conquest* in 1843. In 1850 Mary Green published *Lives of the Princesses of England from the Norman Conquest,* basing her work on careful study of original manuscripts and documents.[27] For the most part, however, the English queens have not inspired prolific biography. Margaret of Anjou was the subject of a biography by John Bagley, and Eleanor of Aquitaine is a favorite with many, although none have handled her as well as the American scholar, Amy Kelly, in *Eleanor of Aquitaine and the Four Kings*.[28] Kelly's biography is a model for accomplishing the difficult task of weaving the bits of chronicle, official documents, and literature into a vivid tapestry of medieval life.

Short biographies were far easier to write and were useful in forming a picture of the daily lives of women in historical times. Emily Putnam in *The Lady: Studies of Certain Significant Phases of her History* used this approach.[29] Eileen Power's imaginative biographies of a prioress and a bourgeois Parisian in *Medieval People* stand the test of time and are as accurate and fresh today as when they were first published.[30] In general, medieval biography is difficult because of the paucity of personal records; the dearth of documentation is more severe for women than men.

In the search for women who could carve out a niche in society independent of marriage and males, nuns and religious women were soon chosen as a subject for women to study. One of the few early publications of a work pertaining exclusively to women in medieval history was, as we have observed, the *Ancren Riwle*. This instruction manual for women who wished to make a religious retreat from the world showed that some medieval women led rigorously pious lives independent of male control. Rotha

Mary Clay, an indefatigable researcher who had already written *The Medieval Hospitals of England,* published *The Hermits and the Anchorites of England* in 1914.[31] The most famous of the anchorites, Julian of Norwich, inspired study not only because of her life but because of the literary merit of the vernacular rendition of her visions.[32] The individual, mystical experiences of English women in the centuries following the Norman Conquest did not gain them the recognition of sainthood, although many of the early Christian saints, such as Saint Katherine, were popular in the Middle Ages.[33]

Nineteenth-century women historians consciously turned to women in nunneries for examples of independent women. Lina Eckenstein in her preface to *Women under Monasticism,* which appeared in 1896, observed that "the right to self-development and social responsibility which the woman of today so persistently asks for, is in many ways analogous to the right which the convent secured for womankind a thousand years ago."[34] Her pioneering work set high standards for the study of nunneries. Eileen Power's dissertation and first major book was *Medieval English Nunneries,* an extraordinarily fine study both as a piece of research and as historical writing.[35] Her interest in the subject continued, and M. M. Postan published one of her public addresses on the topic in *Medieval Women.*[36]

Closely allied with religious life in the Middle Ages was education. With women increasingly demanding professional training in the nineteenth century, interest in educational opportunities for women in the past became a topic of research. Dorothy Kempe Gardiner traced the educational experiences of women in *English Girlhood at School: A Study of Women's Education Through Twelve Centuries.* Again, an insightful paper on the subject by Eileen Power is included in *Medieval Women.* Another theme that has been a perennial favorite since the late nineteenth century is the role of women in medicine, particularly midwifery.[37]

Nineteenth-century historians were fascinated with public institutions and studied the development of medieval monarchy and Parliament. One of England's proudest achievements in the medieval period was the development of law. Virginia Woolf's uncle, J. F. Stephen, wrote a famous *History of the Criminal Law in England* and found that some discussion of women in the criminal courts had to be included.[38] L. O. Pike had written a two-volume *History of Crime in England* in 1873 that presented a confused picture of medieval women in crime.[39] On the one hand, he felt that they could not exercise their true criminal potential because of their physical weakness and that only the gun could overcome this handicap. On the other hand, he cites a virago who murdered her husband and attempted to hide the crime by burning him in her oven. But it was the serious issues of the Married Women's Property Act and other legislation concerning women's rights that significantly stimulated historical inquiry. Arthur Rackham Cleveland published *Women under the English Law* in 1896 as a polemical piece.[40] He argued that it was impossible to conceive of "any state of society composed of men and women whose system of jurisprudence could be such that the same laws would apply equally to both sexes." He conceded that the nineteenth-century English legislation was removing some of the medieval disabilities.

The work that all those interested in women's history have turned to has been *The History of English Law Before the Time of Edward I* by Frederick Pollock and Frederic Maitland, first published in 1895 and still indispensable as an introduction to the complex problems of women in medieval law. Many researchers in the area have memorized their famous summary:

> As regards private rights women are on the same level as men, though postponed in the canons of inheritance; but public functions they have none. In the camp, at the council board, on the bench, in the jury box there is no place for them.[41]

Following the disillusionments of World War I and the rise of totalitarian governments in the period before World War II, attention turned from social history, and romanticization of the medieval aesthetics died out.[42] Increasingly, historians shifted their focus to the origins of democratic institutions such as the justices of the peace, Parliament, the constitution, and limitations on absolute monarchy. In general, historians of the Middle Ages were concerned with how democracy had developed in England and was exported to its Empire and why Germany, Italy, and France were being so pigheaded about evolving into this obviously superior form of government. As Maitland had said, women were not at camp or council in the Middle Ages, and, consequently, there was very little written about women in the 1930s through the 1950s. Furthermore, the success of the women's suffrage movement in the 1920s led to a decreased interest in women's rights and women's history—women had gotten what they wanted politically and were no longer in the public consciousness or on the historian's research agenda. Furthermore, women who chose careers as academic historians found it increasingly difficult to find positions or even graduate training outside women's colleges. Institutions that had given women opportunity for higher education became a means for segregating women.

Eileen Power did not give up her interest in women's history and continued to address the matter in public lectures. Likewise, women did not completely disappear from works of economic and social history, and historians such as H. S. Bennett and George Homans included women in their broader studies.[43] Women with important political connections continued to appear in historical surveys and record societies, and the Early English Text society published more materials relating to the history of women. But the topic of women in the Middle Ages, as an independent field of research, shrank into obscurity.

Before leaving the early flowering of interest in women's history a word or two about professional women historians is in order,[44] although strictly outside the scope of an essay dealing with the portrayal of women by British historians. With the establishment of women's colleges at Oxford, Cambridge, and London and the generally liberalized trend in educating women, some fine female historians were trained. Some of these wrote as private authors, but others such as Eileen Power and Mary Bateson took academic appointments. Most of these first professional women medievalists, both British and American, did not follow Eileen Power's interest in the history of women. The great works of Nellie Nielson, Bertha Haven Putnam, Helen Cam, and Margaret Hastings were in legal and administrative history. Sylvia Thrupp and E. M. Carus-Wilson, both students of Power, turned their attention to economic history. In entering the male world of academic history, they wrote on the subjects on which men wrote.

Rather like the 1860s, the 1960s again coupled political activism for women's rights with a new enthusiasm for social history. The result was a renewed study of women's history. Historians became increasingly interested in social history, as they once again wanted to know what the Bishop of Bristol, in his forword to Rotha Clay's book on the hospitals, called "real history, the history of ordinary human beings rather than of generals and of kings." But rather than being fascinated with the origins in the English gentry and yeomanry, modern historians wanted to know about the working class, the slaves, and the third world populations—oppressed people who had little voice of their own. The new interest in social history was described as "history from the bottom up" or the "underside of history," metaphors that lead one to imagine this was the proctological approach to historical analysis. Because sources for studying people who left few letters or memoirs were scattered among official government records, new methodologies were needed to write about these people. Quantitative methods and computers made the study of lengthy, repetitive government sources, such as census returns and court records, possible.

Although the methodologies for studying the new social history, as it has been called, were novel, much of the historiography reverted to the late nineteenth century. Marxist historiography was once again enjoying some vogue and, although it stimulated sharp counterattacks among many historians, under its influence class, economic influences, and man's inhumanity to man (and woman) were to become central issues for study.

Interest in the history of the common man and oppressed men were partly inspired by the civil rights movement in United States, the increased concern on both sides of the Atlantic with the conditions of peoples in third world economies, and the usual ancestor worship. Unlike the bourgeois historians of nineteenth-century England, who glorified their landed-gentry ancestors, modern historians explored the experiences of their working class forebears. This interest in the lower class ancestry partly reflected the increased democratization of higher education following World War II; a different class of men and women were entering the academic world.

Concern with social injustices to underprivileged social groups began to awaken in female historians a questioning about their own position both currently and historically. As women fought for equal rights, they once again became curious about the role of women in times past. A new era of women's history began.

As in the late nineteenth century, women began to seek greater political and social freedom and to pursue higher degrees in preparation for writing history and taking academic positions. Research on the history of women was slower to develop than studies of workers and minorities, but by the mid 1970s there was a growing body of literature on women, including medieval English women. There were also academic positions specifically advertised for historians of women's history. As in the earlier flourishing of interest in medieval women, not all of the women who became professional historians studied women's history, and not all of the studies published have been written by women. Women and men both became interested in researching women's experience in the Middle Ages.

Sampling some of the standard bibliographical references in history reveals the chronology of the growing literature. There are two companion bibliographical references in history for American and British dissertations in the twentieth century: Warren F. Kuel, *Dissertations in History, 1873–1960 in United States and Canada* (Lexington KY, 1965) and P. M. Jacobs, *History Theses* (London, 1976). There were no dissertations in America on medieval women up to 1960 and only one or two on medieval women in Great Britain. In two more recent bibliographical series—*American Doctoral Dissertations* and *Indexes to Theses in Great Britain and Ireland*—women had almost no importance as subjects of theses until the late seventies. Beginning in 1975, however, theses devoted to the subject of medieval English women began to appear in the American dissertations, and in the 1981 volume there were a number of theses on women. In Great Britain noblemen, gentry men, Parliament, and womenless economic history continue almost undisturbed. Thus there are the beginnings of work at the dissertation level that can be identified in graduate schools in United States and Canada.

Some general characteristics of the new study of medieval English women will help to put the more specific areas of research into perspective. The new women's history has not produced any of the grand summaries of women in England through the ages. Doris M. Stenton's history, reissued in 1977, must still serve as a survey. Eileen Power did not live to complete her projected history of medieval women, but her various public addresses were collected and published in 1975. Historical scholarship tends these days to emphasize careful research rather than broad synthesis. Much of the literature, therefore, is in article or monograph form or in collections of essays such as *Women in Medieval Society,* edited by Susan Mosher Stuard, and the festshrift for Rosalind M. T. Hill, *Medieval Women.*[45] Furthermore, a characteristic of the new social history is that women are now always included. Thus a history of the family would no longer be written, as Wright's was, largely excluding women. Since the new social history tends to look at groups in the aggregate rather than as individuals, biography of medieval women has not been a flourishing area. In spite of these departures from the earlier scholarship on women, some continuities are striking. Historians are still struggling with the question raised by Hill, Clark, Power, and Stenton—was women's position significantly better in the Middle Ages?

The new research on the history of women has been both in areas involving new methodologies and in the more traditional areas of research.[46] Demographers have been leaders in quantitative methods and, of course, had to include women in their studies both because they constitute approximately half of the populations they are looking at and because such cultural matters involving women as age of marriage, contraception, and infanticide can influence demographic patterns. J. C. Russell pioneered medieval demography with his *British Medieval Population* and others have followed his lead, accepting or modifying his results.[47] Demographic sources usually list male heads of household, so that fitting in female members has been a matter involving considerable ingenuity in determining the size and structure of households.

An outgrowth of demographic history has been family history. Here inheritance practices, age of majority, family economic strategies, and family affection have been major concerns.[48]

Some of the best historical writing has been on the contract and fact of marriage in the Middle Ages. Relying both on canon law and church court records, M. M. Sheehan was one of the first to work with the canonical theory of marriage and its actual practice. His work, published in articles in *Medieval Studies* and elsewhere, has laid the groundwork for serious consideration of medieval marriage.[49] Richard Helmholz in *Marriage Litigation in Medieval England* pushed even further with the diocesan records on marriage.[50] Although cautious in their conclusions, these historians suggest that the consensual theory of marriage developed during the Middle Ages may have given women some freedom in the choice of marriage partner. Using secular court records rather than ecclesiastical records, Sue Sheridan Walker has addressed the problem from the viewpoint of common and feudal law applying to noble women in medieval England. Her studies of cases of kidnapping of feudal heiresses are balanced by accounts of the heiresses who paid to remain single. Joel Rosenthal has looked at the powerful noble dowagers of the fifteenth century and the ways they benefited from inheritances.[51] The experience of peasant women is being treated with thoroughness by Eleanor Searle, Jean Schammell, and Judith Bennett.[52]

In general, legal sources have proved to be rich in information on medieval women. Studies of criminal court records have taken our knowledge of female participation in crime far beyond the speculations of L. O. Pike.[53] Medieval women were as uncriminous as modern ones, comprising only ten percent of the indictments and even fewer of the convictions. This continuity in women's low rate of participation in crime is one of the interesting insights that historical study has given to an understanding of women's social roles and raises questions of the relative importance of nature versus nurture in explaining women's infrequent participation in crime. Manorial court rolls have also proved to be valuable sources of information on peasant women, and the fine village studies that have been done recently routinely include women as they appear as landholders, widows, entrepreneurs, mothers, and wives. The new methodology of reconstituting village families from court rolls, introduced by J. Ambrose Raftis, has made women's roles more apparent.[54] So important have village women become in balancing the picture of peasant society that R. H. Hilton included a lecture on them in his Ford Lectures on the peasantry of late medieval England.[55]

One of the most sophisticated areas of research on medieval women to come out of the late nineteenth- and early twentieth-century enthusiasm for women's history was economic history. Alice Clark and Eileen Power, a professor at the London School of Economics, both contributed stimulating background for further research. And yet this area is only beginning to become a major field of research.[56]

Anglo-Saxon women have received more attention from historians than women in other historical periods. One reason that Doris Stenton was able to write so expertly on the decline of women's position from the Anglo-Saxon period to the Norman one was that the research in the early period was somewhat more advanced than other areas of women's history. Her husband, for instance, working from charters, had written on women's property holdings, and women's wills had been published. Recently, a rich variety of essays and books have brought together archaeological, literary, and historical materials on Anglo-Saxon women.[57]

As Lena Eckenstein so clearly perceived, women in monastic orders and religion drew researchers because these women were the closest to independent women of today. Of special interest have been the religious women of the late Middle Ages. Ann K. Warren's monograph, *Anchorites and Their Patrons in Medieval England* is a thorough study replacing the earlier one by Rotha Clay. Margery Kempe's autobiography was found and published only in the late thirties, so it was a new and unique piece of historical evidence. Only in the last few years have historians looked closely at this remarkably independent woman who traveled extensively on pilgrimages and who was regarded by many as an eccentric and even a heretic, but who won the respect of a number of the leading churchmen of her day. The sources of her visions and the unusual aspects of her life have drawn both scholarly and popular attention.[58]

A striking alteration in the writing of political history is the inclusion of women. As political history has broadened from a narrative of battles and an analysis of constitutional and administrative changes, women have come into a greater prominence. A major aspect of political history, particularly in the fifteenth century, was the marriage alliances that brought factions together or drove them apart. J. R. Lander in *Crown and Nobility, 1450–1509* has an essay on marriage and politics, and the book edited by Charles Ross, *Patronage, Pedigree, and Power in Later Medieval England* also printed an essay dealing with women and family.[59]

The recent pursuit of women's historical role, like the late nineteenth-century one, quickly produced ideological identifications similar to those of Georgiana Hill and Alice Clark. When these two historians looked at the medieval and early modern records, women appeared to be more independent and valued in business, in the work force, in contributions to the home economy, and in disposal of their wealth and property than they were in the nineteenth century. Eileen Power shared some of the same commitment to the idea that the Middle Ages was something of a golden age for women. In the scramble in the 1970s to find anything on the history of women, their texts were avidly read once again.

Although modern historians are trained to hide their biases and not use history for polemical purposes, the underlying message of many historical essays has been apparent. Some historians have tried to document a decline in rights since the Middle Ages and place blame on various institutions such as the church, capitalism, or common law for the loss of a golden age. Others have seen the whole history of women as one of continual oppression from the beginning. Further research, however, has diminished enthusiastic searches for a medieval El Dorado. Many of the examples of female miners or members of male craft gilds turned out to be exceptions to the rule, nuggets and not gold ore. The search for such an El Dorado has ceased. Likewise, the gloomy approach of documenting oppression is fading, and historians are beginning to ask who among women were better off or able to wield power. Were widows legally privileged over married women? Did fifteenth-century women wage earners fare better than those in the sixteenth century? Was it only the individual, forceful women who were able to manipulate disadvantageous situations to their own profit? The topic of medieval women and their lives has proved far more interesting and important than it is when used merely for polemic.

The thesis of this discussion of medieval women in the English historiographical tradition has been that the inclusion of women in histories has depended upon the complementary developments of research in social history and political activity in support of women's rights. In the nineteenth and early twentieth centuries the combination of the revival of interest in the Middle Ages and medieval social life with the struggle of women for legal rights and the vote led to publications about medieval women. England's struggle against totalitarianism in the first half of the twentieth century thrust women into the background, and political and historical interests turned toward the development of Parliament and other magisterial roles—areas from which women were barred in the Middle Ages. In the late 1960s the new fascination with social history, histories of the oppressed, and new methodologies borrowed from sociology and anthropology once again stirred historians to look at society as a whole rather than only the political elites. The renewed feminist pressure for equal rights meant that the new social history would be applied to women. If the Middle Ages was not a golden age for women, at least the history of medieval women has had two golden ages. In 1929 Virginia Woolf declared that "what one wants—and why does not some brilliant student at Newnham or Girton supply it?—is a mass of information; at what age did she [the medieval woman] marry; how did many children had she as a rule; what was her house like, had she a room to herself; did she do the cooking; would she be likely to have a servant?"[60] Fifty years later she would have found some of the answers to her questions and have the expectation that future research would produce more.

Notes

1. Virginia Woolf, *A Room of One's Own* (London, 1929), p. 43.

2. Unlike French and Italian chroniclers, English chroniclers and early historians were not preoccupied with applying the labels of virtue or vice to their queens.

3. Betty Bandel, "The English Chronicler's Attitude toward Women," *Journal of the History of Ideas,* 16 (1955), 113–18.

4. *Polydore Vergil's English History from an Early Translation,* ed. Henry Ellis, Camden Society, 36 (London, 1846), p. 284. *Three Books of Polydore Vergil's English History, Henry VI, Edward IV, and Richard III,* ed. Henry Ellis, Camden Society, 29 (London, 1844), pp. 38, 71.

5. David Hume, *The History of England* (London, 1840), pp. 72–73, 80.

6. Sir Walter Scott was translated into French and Italian and provided impetus for the study of the Middle Ages in both countries. His novelistic form of history encouraged the development of historical personalities in writing histories.

7. 24 (London, 1843) and 57 (London, 1853).

8. Catherine Macaulay, *The History of England from the Accession of James I to that of the Brunswick Line* (London, 1763) and *Letters on Education* (London, 1790). Mary Wollstonecraft, *A Vindication of the Rights of Women,* 3rd ed. (London, 1796).

9. John Stuart Mill, *The Subjection of Women* (London, 1869).

10. The popularity of Marxist historiography in Italy following the Second World War did not produce a similar interest in the history of women.

11. Alice Clark, *Working Life of Women in the Seventeenth Century* (London, 1919).

12. Thomas Wright, *Womenkind in Western Europe: From the Earliest Times to the Seventeenth Century* (London, 1869).

13. Thomas Wright, *A History of Domestic Manners and Sentiments in England During the Middle Ages* (London, 1862).

14. Interest in medieval social history flourished in universities in the United States as well as in England. One wonders if Henry Adams was influenced by this Anglo-Saxon interest in forming his own conceptions of history.

15. J. Frederick Hodgetts. *The English in the Middle Ages* (London, 1885).

16. George M. Trevelyan. *England in the Age of Wycliffe* (London, 1899).

17. G. G. Coulton, *Social Life in Britain from the Conquest to the Reformation* (New York, 1968).

18. F. J. Snell, *The Customs of Old England* (London, 1911).

19. L. F. Salzman, *English Life in the Middle Ages* (London, 1927).

20. Geoffrey Barraclough, ed. *Social Life in Early England* (London, 1960).

21. Woolf, *A Room of One's Own,* pp. 72–73.

22. Annie Abram, *English Life and Manners in the Later Middle Ages* (London,

1913) and *Social Life in England in the Fifteenth Century* (London, 1909). See also "Women Traders in Medieval London," *Economic Journal,* 26 (1916), 276–85.

23. In United States, Florence Griswold Buckstaff showed interests parallel to those in England at the time and also documented the loss of women's legal rights. Because of the long duration of the customary laws in England, women enjoyed legal rights that were effectively removed by the reintroduction of the Corpus Juris Civilis in Italy. English women's access to property and to courts was freer, although they too were barred from magisterial roles.

24. Georgiana Hill, *Women in English Life from Medieval to Modern Times,* 2 vols. (London, 1896).

25. Doris M. Stenton, *The English Woman in History* (London, 1957). Eileen Power, "The Position of Women," in *Legacy of the Middle Ages,* ed. G. C. Crump and E. F. Jacob (Oxford, 1926), pp. 401–33 also accepted the idea of a better social and economic role for women in the Middle Ages.

26. Queens tended to be something of a bellwether for historiography of women. In France Marie Antoinette represented cruel queens and inspired a history of crimes of queens. England's experiences were more positive. Elizabeth I, Victoria, and Elizabeth II inspired positive histories of queenship. In Italy such rulers as Margaret of Tuscany and Joann of Naples were made to serve the political needs of the times; positive if unification were in the air and negative if republican virtues were popular.

27. Agnes Strickland, *Lives of the Queens of England from the Norman Conquest,* 5 vols. (New York, 1843). Mary Green, *Lives of the Princesses of England from the Norman Conquest* (London, 1850). Elsie Thornton-Cook, *Her Majesty; The Romance of the Queens of England, 1066–1910* (New York, 1926) dedicated her book to Queen Mary. She commented that one historian omitted Elizabeth from a history of England because "she was a woman" and for that reason she wrote her study. With the accession of Elizabeth II the topic was again popular, and Geoffrey Tease published *The Seven Queens of England* (London, 1953).

28. John J. Bagley, *Margaret of Anjou, Queen of England* (London, 1948). Amy Kelly, *Eleanor of Aquitaine and the Four Kings* (Cambridge, 1950). E. Jacob Abbott, *History of Margaret of Anjou, Queen of Henry VI of England* (New York, 1861). Mary Ann Hookham, *The Life and Times of Margaret of Anjou, Queen of England and France* (London, 1872). Blanche Christable Hardy, *Philippa of Hainault and Her Times* (London, 1910). A modern, popular biography of Eleanor of Aquitaine may be found in M. Meade, *Eleanor of Aquitaine: A Biography* (London, 1978).

29. Emily J. Putnam, *The Lady: Studies of Certain Significant Phases of her History* (New York, 1910).

30. Eileen Power, *Medieval People* (New York, 1966). See also H. S. Bennett, *Six Medieval Men and Women* (New York, 1962) and A. Kemp-Welch, *Of Six Medieval Women* (London, 1913).

31. Rotha M. Clay, *The Medieval Hospitals of England* (London, 1909); *The Hermits and the Anchorites of England* (London, 1914).

32. Percy Franklin, ed., *Julian of Norwich: An Introductory Appreciation and an Interpretative Anthology* (New York, 1955); P. Molinari, *Julian of Norwich, the Teachings of a Fourteenth-Century Mystic* (London, 1958).

33. Saints had less of a pull on the English both in the Middle Ages and later when they were writing about the religious experiences of women than they did in Italy. The flamboyant Margery Kempe and the mystic Julian of Norwich have attracted more attention then female saints. Nunneries and communities of women have also attracted English historians.

34. Lina Eckenstein, *Women under Monasticism* (Cambridge, 1896). See also Mary Byrne, *The Tradition of the Nun in Medieval England* (Washington, DC, 1932). Rose Graham, *St. Gilbert of Sempringham and the Gilbertines: A History of the Only English Monastic Order* (London, 1901). Mary Bateson, "The Origins and Early History of Double Monasteries," *Transactions of the Royal Historical Society,* new ser. 12 (1899), 137–98.

35. Eileen Power, *Medieval English Nunneries, 1275–1535* (Cambridge, 1922).

36. Eileen Power, *Medieval Women,* ed. M. M. Postan (New York, 1975).

37. Dorothy Kempe Gardiner, *English Girlhood at School: A Study of Women's Education Through Twelve Centuries* (London, 1929). Arthur F. Leach, "The Medieval Education of Women in England," *Journal of Education,* 42 (1910), 838–41. James Aveling, *English Midwives; Their History and Prospects* (London, 1872).

38. J. B. Stephen, *A History of Criminal Law in England,* 3 vols. (London, 1883).

39. L. O. Pike, *History of Crime in England,* 2 vols. (London, 1873).

40. Arthur Rackham Cleveland, *Women under the English Law* (London, 1896).

41. Frederick Pollock and F. W. Maitland, *History of English Law Before the Time of Edward I,* vol. 1 (London, 1923), p. 485.

42. In France as well the preoccupation with administrative history effectively removed any research into the history of women.

43. H. S. Bennett, *Life on the English Manor; A Study of Peasant Conditions, 1150–1400* (New York, 1937); *The Pastons and Their England; Studies in an Age of Transition* (Cambridge, 1922). George Homans, *English Villagers of the Thirteenth Century* (Cambridge, MA, 1941).

44. See Stuard's essay on the education of university women in the United States.

45. Susan Mosher Stuard, ed., *Women in Medieval Society* (Philadelphia, 1976) has two essays on English women. Derek Baker, ed., *Medieval Women, Dedicated and Presented to Professor Rosalind M. T. Hill on the Occasion of her Seventieth Birthday* (Oxford, 1978) contains a number of essays on English women. A popular survey, F. and J. Gies, *Women in the Middle Ages* (New York, 1978) has very little original to contribute. See also B. Kanner, ed., *The Women of England from Anglo-Saxon Times to the Present: Interpretative Bibliographical Essays* (London, 1980). Rosmarie Thee Morewedge, ed., *The Role of Women in the Middle Ages* (Binghampton, NY, 1975).

46. The new interest in social history quickly led to research on women in the

United States. England tended to lag behind and is only beginning to make substantial contributions. In both France and Italy the study of women in the Middle Ages has been slow to get underway.

47. J. C. Russell, *British Medieval Population* (Albuquerque, NM, 1948). P. E. H. Hair, "Bridal Pregnancy in Rural England in Earlier Centuries," *Population Studies*, 20(1966–67), 233–43. J. Hajnal, "European Marriage Patterns in Perspective," in *Population in History: Essays in Historical Demography*, ed. D. V. Glass and D. E. C. Eversley (Chicago, 1965), pp. 101–43. H. E. Hallam, "Population Density in the Medieval Fenland," *Economic History Review*, 2nd ser. 14 (1961), pp. 71–81 and "Some Thirteenth-Century Censuses," *Economic History Review*, 2nd ser. 10 (1958), 340–61. John Hatcher, *Plague, Population, and the English Economy, 1348–1530* (London, 1977). J. Krause, "The Medieval Household: Large or Small?" *Economic History Review*, 2nd ser. 9 (1957), 402–32. Zvi Razi, *Life, Marriage, and Death in the Medieval Parish: Economy, Society, and Demography in Halesowen, 1270–1400* (Cambridge, 1980). Richard M. Smith, "Hypotheses sur la nuptialité en Angleterre au XIIe–XIVe siècles," *Annales, Economies, Sociétes, Civilisations*, 38 (1983), 107–36. B. Rowland, ed. and trans., *Medieval Woman's Guide to Health: The First English Gynaecological Handbook* (London, 1981). The publication of N. David, ed., *The Pastons Letters and Papers of the Fifteenth Century*, 3 vols. (Oxford, 1976) has made the family life of the Paston women much more accessible.

48. Richard Helmholz, "Infanticide in the Province of Canterbury during the Fifteenth Century," *History of Childhood Quarterly*, 2 (1974–75), 282–390. Cecily Howell, "Peasant Inheritance Customs in the Midlands, 1280–1700." In *Family and Inheritance: Rural Society in Western Europe*, ed. J. Goody, J. Thirsk, and E. P. Thompson (Cambridge, 1976), pp. 112–55. Barbara Hanawalt, "Childrearing Among the Lower Classes of Late Medieval England," *Journal of Interdisciplinary History* 8 (1977), 1–22 and *The Ties That Bound: Medieval English Peasant Families* (New York, 1986).

49. Michael M. Sheehan, "The Formation and Stability of Marriage in Fourteenth-Century England: Evidence of an Ely Register," *Mediaeval Studies*, 33 (1971), 228–63 and "The Influence of Canon Law on the Property Rights of Married Women in England," *Medieval Studies*, 25 (1963), 109–24.

50. Richard Helmholz, *Marriage Litigation in Medieval England* (Cambridge, 1974) and "Bastardy Litigation in Medieval England," *American Journal of Legal History*, 13 (1969), 360–83.

51. Sue Sheridan Walker, "Violence and the Exercise of Feudal Guardianship: The Action of '*Ejectio Custodia*,'" *American Journal of Legal History*, 16 (1972), 320–33. Joel Rosenthal, *Nobles and the Noble Life, 1295–1500* (London, 1976).

52. Jean Schamell, "Freedom and Marriage in Medieval England," *Economic History Review*, 2nd ser. 27 (1974), 523–37 and "Wife-Rents and Merchet," *Economic History Review*, 2nd ser. 28 (1976), 487–90. Eleanor Searle, "Freedom and Marriage in Medieval England: An Alternative Hypothesis," *Economic History Review*, 2nd ser. 29 (1976), 482–86, and "Seigneurial Control of Women's Mar-

riages: The Antecedents and Function of Merchet in England," *Past and Present,* 82 (1979), 4–43. Judith Bennett, "Medieval Peasant Marriage: An Examination of Marriage Licence Fines in the *Liber Gersumarum.* In *Pathways to Medieval Peasants,* ed. J. Ambrose Raftis (Toronto, 1981), pp. 193–246 and "The Tie that Binds: Peasant Marriages and Peasant Families in Late Medieval England," *Journal of Interdisciplinary History,* 15 (1984), 111–29.

53. James B. Given, *Society and Homicide in Thirteenth-Century England* (Palo Alto, CA, 1977). Barbara A. Hanawalt, *Crime and Conflict in English Communities, 1300–1348* (Cambridge, MA, 1979).

54. J. Ambrose Raftis, *Tenure and Mobility: Studies in the Social History of the Medieval English Village* (Toronto, 1964) and *Warboys: Two Hundred Years of an English Medieval Village* (Toronto, 1974). Edwin DeWindt, *Land and People in Holywell-Cum-Needingworth* (Toronto, 1974). Edward Britton, *The Community of the Vill: A Study in the History of the Family and Village Life in Fourteenth-Century England* (Toronto, 1977). Elaine Clark, "Debt Litigation in a Late Medieval English Vill," in *Pathways to Medieval Peasants,* ed. J. Ambrose Raftis (Toronto, 1981), pp. 307–20 and "Some Aspects of Social Security in Medieval England," *Journal of Family History,* 7 (1982), 307–20.

55. R. H. Hilton, *The English Peasantry in the Later Middle Ages: The Ford Lectures for 1973 and Related Studies* (Oxford, 1975).

56. Lindsey Charlesan, Lorna Duffin, eds., *Women and Work in Pre-Industrial England* (London, 1985). Barbara A. Hanawalt, ed., *Women and Work in Preindustrial Europe* (Bloomington, IN, 1986).

57. Christine Fell, *Women in Anglo-Saxon England and the Impact of 1066* (Bloomington, IN, 1984) has both a chapter on the historiography of the study of Anglo-Saxon women and a bibliography of relevant books and articles. The tradition of studying Anglo-Saxon women is more venerable than more general studies of medieval women. F. M. Stenton, for instance, wrote "The Historical Bearing of Place-Name Studies: The Place of Women in Anglo-Saxon Society," *Transactions of the Royal Historical Society,* 4th ser. 25, pp. 1–13 in 1943. Since then there have been a number of articles on the legal position of Anglo-Saxon women and the role of women in religious life.

58. Ann K. Warren, *Anchorites and Their Patrons in Medieval England* (Berkeley, CA, 1985). *The Book of Margery Kempe* was discovered only in the twentieth century and first appeared in print edited by Sanford B. Meech and Hope Emily Allen (London, 1944). It took awhile for scholars to classify Margery and assimilate her eccentric autobiography. The first book length study was meant for a popular audience, Louise Collis, *The Apprentice Saint* (London, 1964). More recently, however, Clarissa W. Atkinson, *Mystic and Pilgrim: The Book and the World of Margery Kempe* (Ithaca, 1983) has offered a scholarly study of Margery and her particular religious visions. Meanwhile, Julian of Norwich has lost none of her appeal and is still the topic of study. See for instance, B. A. Windeatt, "Julian of Norwich and Her Audience," *Review of English Studies,* new ser. 28 (1977), pp. 1–17. A. Zet-

tersten, ed., *English Text of the Ancrene Riwle* (Oxford, 1976) indicates the continued interest in that document as does A. Barratt, "Anchorite Aspects of *Ancrene Wisse*," *Medium Aevuum*, 49 (1980), 32–56. Women under monasticism is far from a dead issue in general. See for instance, J. E. Burton, *The Yorkshire Nunneries in the Twelfth and Thirteenth Centuries* (York, 1979) and M. A. Meyer, "Women and the Tenth Century English Monastic Reform," *Revue benedictine*, 87 (1977), 34–61. M. Aston, "Lollard Women Priests?" *Journal of Ecclesiastical History*, 31 (1980), 441–61. Women in witchcraft has also been investigated for England: Jeffrey Burton Russell, *Witchcraft in the Middle Ages* (Ithaca, NY, 1972) has looked into the case of Kyeler.

59. J. R. Lander, "Marriage and Politics in Fifteenth-Century England: The Nevilles and the Wydevilles," in *Crown and Nobility, 1450–1509* (London, 1976), pp. 94–126. R. A. Griffiths, "Queen Katherine of Valois and a Missing Statute of the Realm," *Law Quarterly Review*, 93 (1977), 248–58. Charles Ross, ed., *Patronage, Pedigree, and Power in Later Medieval England* (Gloucester, 1979).

60. Woolf, *A Room of One's Own*, pp. 77–78.

2

Invisible Madonnas? The Italian Historiographical Tradition and the Women of Medieval Italy

DIANE OWEN HUGHES

Excluded by law and tradition from a public voice in the medieval commune, women of the Italian peninsula were consequently deprived of a place in Italy's precocious historical consciousness, which had been inspired by urban renewal and which was nourished by civic pride.[1] Although Lombard insistence on a woman's permanent minority gradually gave way in the Italy of the communes to principles of Roman law that recognized her legal personality,[2] she was not awarded an equivalent civil *persona*. Indeed Roman law itself served to sanction her overwhelmingly private nature. As a frequently quoted commonplace from the *Digest* put it,

> Women are excluded from all civil and public offices; and thus they may not be judges, nor magistrates, nor advocates; nor may they intervene on another's behalf, nor act as agents.[3]

Such women were necessarily invisible to an historical tradition increasingly structured by political models and wedded to a narrative mode. Those historians from the Renaissance onward who chronicled the state as a work of art, to use Burckhardt's phrase, would not only have found few women among its medieval designers, they would also have had some difficulty in seeing and describing them in the active voice that narrative demands.

The aristocratic women of the Renaissance, learned, articulate, and politically astute, may have threatened but they never destroyed a widespread acceptance in Italy of woman's natural political incapacity and historical invisibility. As late as 1562, Tasso was still trying to reconcile women's natural incapacity with the fact of capable women rulers. In his *Discorso della virtù feminile e donnesca,* he allows that in certain cases status might take precedence over gender. Hence a noble woman called by that status to leadership would be required to deny her feminine nature to fulfill her social and political duties.[4] And hence, if we may extend Tasso's arguments to our purposes, the exceptional woman of aristocratic birth might also find an individual place in history. Yet in practice, historians would always find it hard to write women into their narrative histories "as if they were men," for when they thought of women at all, they thought of them in iconic rather than narrative terms.

Nicolosa Sanuti, the learned and beautiful lover of Sante Bentivoglio, who stepped briefly into the history of her city when she composed in 1453 an eloquent appeal for the abolition of the sumptuary restrictions that an ecclesiastical government had placed on the women of Bologna, exploits to her own purposes this essentially iconic nature of woman's identity. Taking the *Digest* as her source, she focuses her argument on the female sex's forced withdrawal from history:

> Magistracies are not conceded to women; nor do they strive for priesthoods, triumphs, or the spoils of war because these are considered the honors of men. Ornament and apparel, because they are our insignia of worth, we cannot suffer to be taken from us.[5]

Sanuti is understandably less inclined than her male contemporaries to attribute this reduced condition (*deterior conditio,* as the commonplace ran) of women in law—their removal from succession, office, and privilege—to those qualities of *levitas, fragilitas, imbecillitas,* and *infermitas* that were held to characterize the female nature.[6] For, as she relates at some length, where women had been awarded a full public role, they had ably fulfilled it. The ancient gods and goddesses shared a joint responsibility for the world and its creatures. Once Prometheus had fired his clay creatures into men, it was the goddesses who, by imparting the skills of agriculture, weaving, and letters, let them not only survive but rise above the beasts. And as an age of gods gave way to an age of heroes, women showed themselves capable of leaving hoe and loom to adapt to an age of iron, leading their peoples to military victory with the strength, valor, and liberality generally called manly traits. Only when these mythic ages of gods and heroes gave way in their turn to an historic age of men, to anticipate Vico's threefold scheme, were women denied an active public *persona* and hence excluded from history's narrative as they had never been excluded from the poetry of myth and epic. In the historic age of men, these static women, frozen out of the flow of history, were best described and understood not by narrative devices but rather by iconic means. So, according to Sanuti, they deserved—even needed—their clothes and their finery without which their status and their worth were inexpressible.

At the level of history, it was not clothes that made the woman, but virtues—or vices. The heroines who might people a *cité des dames,* as Christine de Pisan entitled the handbook of illustrious women that she wrote from Paris in 1404, served the purposes not of narrative history but of iconography.[7] Her book, written for a French audience, had the larger purpose of challenging the popular misogyny of Jean de Meung's *Romance of the Rose,* but it drew on the traditions of her native land where such books, modeled on Boccaccio's *De claris mulieribus,* had been providing reasons for unearthing and a means of popularizing the histories of women who had left an individual mark on their age. That history, real or imagined, was the work's enticement. Its purpose was the moral lesson to be learned from these women's lives. Take, for example, the *Gynevera delle clare donne,* composed in 1483 by Giovanni Sabadino degli Arienti, a writer who, though neither elegant nor original, may have been surprisingly subtle.[8] Illustrating the lives of thirty or so notable women, his work has the merit of including alongside the more predictable heroines of the past, numerous women who had more recently made their mark on Italian and even on Bolognese history. Yet in the end, each is distinguished not by the events that shaped her career or by the effect that she had on her age, but rather by those moral qualities that made her a part (or in rare cases separated her from) womankind. It is the iconic quality of the book that lets its author put virgin saints on the same footing as political figures and encourages him finally to present as the last member of this group of *clare donne* his wife, whose works are otherwise uncelebrated and whose beauty would always be unsung: "While thanking God for the gift of such a woman, I confess that her looks were only ordinary." Her only outstanding trait was an excessive and pious generosity, which, to the author's considerable regret, encouraged the poor and hungry to beat a nightly path to their door.

Liberality is nevertheless the one distinctively male trait that Giovanni freely allowed his historical heroines. In other respects, whatever their historical accomplishments, they were forced to exemplify the feminine virtues of modesty, chastity, and submission. Did Caterina Visconte, widow of Gian Galeazzo, valiantly lead Milan through the military storm that gathered at his death? No matter. It is her piety, chastity, liberality, and justice that characterize "that prudent duchess," whom at death the heavens "recalled with glory from a most honorable widowhood." As in a saint's tale, action only elaborates and exemplifies moral character. Likewise Theodelinda, the Bavarian princess who became by her marriage to King Aufari a queen of the Lombards so esteemed that at his death she was allowed to choose (and marry) the next king, whom she eventually guided toward an accommodation with the Church, becomes in our author's hands not just the faithful and generous daughter of the Church that she seems indeed to have been, but a passive saint whose static example, rather than dynamic action, moved her subjects to obedience. Her final widowhood was lived "with such honesty, chastity,and regal splendor of justice" that she reigned by word and example where former kings had required the action of arms. Strength and valor had always to be compensated for by the womanly virtues of submission (in Theodelinda's case to the Church), modesty, and chastity. Indeed all of Joanne's heroines, whether virgin, married, or widowed, had to be chaste, like the learned Isotta Nogarola, who, having given herself to God and to learning, put on widow's weeds.

> She wore her head covered. She did not play the virgin's role as do you who have no shame. . . . oh widows, who do not cover your heads as pious honor would demand and as today in our city we have the example of the perpetual widowhood of Magdalena, daughter of that most pure count Gian Antonio II di Lambertini, who although young and beautiful is always seen enveloped in black. But you go forth with necks bared and with your hair well dressed and parted, and in place of an honest black mantle you wear rich, transparent veils skillfully arranged to hide your imperfections so that young men will be drawn to you.

Does our author forget that when, in her first widowhood, the noble Theodelinda choose Aigulf, Duke of Turin, as her second husband, she traveled to Turin to make him her own? Meeting him at Lumello, she invited him to drink from her own wine cup, after which *cum rubore subridens* she allowed him to kiss her lips and thus declared her purpose.[9]

Or is this whole work a subtle condemnation of a woman ruler, whose methods were, according to Tasso's distinction, more regal than womanly? The book is dedicated to Ginevra di Bentivoglio, whom on the one hand Giovanni sought as his patron, but who on the other imperfectly displayed those feminine virtues that he held so dear.[10] Considered a virago in many quarters, famous for her vengeance, she had maintained her power by throwing a chaste modesty to the winds. A mere seven months after the death of her first husband, Sante Bentivoglio, who had left her a childless widow at the age of twenty-one, Ginevra tore off her widow's weeds—*impia conjunx,* as a contemporary could not resist commenting[11]—and rushed into marriage with her probable lover, Giovanni II Bentivoglio, whose name restored to her that place of privilege that Sante's death had threatened to remove. With a marital career so reminiscent of Theodelinda's, could she fail to read the message contained in that life? Of course the history of men and nations, like the history of heroes, might also serve moral ends, but narrative helped it and them to escape those confines. The consistent impulse to see women in iconic rather than in narrative terms inevitably reduced their historical presence, perhaps almost as much as those legal barriers that had kept them from a public life.

This is a legacy that has burdened and limited until the present day the Italian historiographical treatment of women. Although a similar bias in the sources accounts for some of its force, that alone cannot explain the subordination of narrative to static moral statement in the treatment of the women of medieval Italy. In a popular history written by Pasquale Villari in the first decade of this century, for example, the intriguing tenth-century female triumvirate of Theodora and her daughters Marozia and Theodora II become the sign of a Rome without authority, an Italy without unity:

> The three women, as famous for their beauty as they were notorious for their licentiousness and gift of intrigue met with no hindrance to their tyranny. This political ascendancy of dissolute women is frequently found existing in very corrupt societies, but it is rare to meet with a spectacle of such scandal and disorder.[12]

Since Villari's book celebrated the fullness of Italy's past as a prelude to the newly created nation of his day, it seems important that Rome could only begin its political revival when Marozia's son Alberic, "whose proud spirit could ill brook his mother's rapid succession of husbands," drove her latest,

Hugh of Provence, out of the city, bidding the citizens to "rise against the insupportable rule of a women and of barbarians who, in ancient times, had been the slaves of Rome." Pope John XI, a child who was generally supposed to be Marozia's son by the former pope Sergius III, fell with her, allowing Alberic to unite the city under his benevolent and manly rule. The barbarians were driven out, the papacy contained, a strong leader governed the city as *Princeps atque omnium Romanorum Senator.* Could his readers have missed the parallel with Risorgimento slogans? Marozia thus came to symbolize the vices that had for so long kept Italy from unity; but, as Villari assured his readers, "With the disappearance of Marozia, female rule had come to an end in Rome."

Women's banishment from public office—and hence from those public histories that, beginning with the earliest communal chronicles, were written at the behest of governments, often by their public servants[13]—was not simply a result of a crippling legal tradition that denied their political capacity or even of a general philosophical position that accepted their natural political inferiority. Their political exile is also the product of a communal policy that consciously sought to crush a social and political world over many of whose territories noble women in fact held sway. As cities of the twelfth and thirteenth centuries forced into political submission the noble feudatories that challenged their new and still fragile authority, they confronted women who through inheritance or marriage exercised control over lands and men in the Italian countryside and even in the city itself.[14] Gregorian reform, one of whose major platforms advocated clerical celibacy and whose most dramatic early battles were waged in the streets of Milan, had clearly demonstrated to a wide urban audience the danger such women posed to institutional independence. Their marriages to ecclesiastics not only polluted Christ's ministers, they threatened the sovereignty of their office and ultimately that of the Church itself as husband priests and bishops dipped into ecclesiastical benefices to provide marriage portions for their noble brides.[15] Urban offices and urban rulers were no less vulnerable. Caught in a similar web of marital and familial concerns, urban governments also sought to free themselves from private interests that were increasingly perceived as threatening.

Women's centrality in that private world of family and patronage, which the communes strove to weaken by insisting on the public institutions of law and contract, made them seem dangerous. Rooted in that older, private world, they could not respond to the individual and civilizing impulses that drew men out of a blood-based network of corporate obligation. Women could not rise to the cultural demands of the city, which required its citizens—much as Gregorian reformers had required priests—to abandon those obligations and to create new ties and loyalties based on common belief and shared enterprise. Such an attitude toward women was implicit in the ordering of the commune, an exclusively male corporation whose earliest laws not only excluded women from membership but also sought to limit their dominance in the private sphere, restricting those marriage festivities, mourning ceremonies, and birth celebrations that had accorded women a central role. Cities thus hoped to reduce the claims of patronage and kinship that women's rituals served to strengthen and to curb the disorder produced by vengeance, which, they felt, women's passions constantly fueled.[16]

The Florentine chronicler Dino Compagni assigned the initiative for the factional strife that rent Florence in the thirteenth century—that struggle between the Blacks and Whites whose origins are still badly understood—to a woman, Gualdrada, the wife of Fortiguerra dei Donati. One day in 1215 she tempted with one of her two daughters Buondalmonte dei Buondalmonti, who had the misfortune to be contracted to another.

> Beholding him pass by, she called him in and showed him one of these daughters and said to him, "Whom have you taken for your wife? I was keeping this one for you."[17]

Falling under their power, Buondalmonte abandoned his contracted marriage and his fiancée, whose father's vengeance initiated a feud that ripped apart the delicate fabric of civil association and concord on which urban institutions depended. The essential truth of this story was accepted by later historians like Isidoro Del Lungo, whose *La donna fiorentina del buon tempo antico,* first published in 1906, had the admirable ambition of recalling the women of medieval Florence from their historical limbo. If the book partially succeeded in putting these women in the active voice, it nevertheless served to demonstrate how often that voice was destructive of the civic values on which Florence's historiographic reputation rested.[18] Like the wicked female triumvirate of tenth-century Rome, Gualdrada and her daughters used their sexual powers to corrupt civil society. Their self-interested machinations tangled the warp of the social fabric and destroyed an intricately woven pattern of civic relationships. However, the historiography of the event deserves our consideration.

Although most chroniclers agree that Buondalmonte's broken marriage contract produced the extravagant revenge that launched the famous feud, the earliest account locates its origins not in the sexual machinations of women but in the violent play of men.[19] According to the pseudo-Brunetto Latini, the feud between the Blacks and the Whites actually began at a feast given to celebrate the knighting of a Florentine aristocrat. During the meal, one of the guests, Uberto dell' Infangatti, strenuously objected when a buffoon snatched away the full plate he was sharing with Buondalmonte dei Buondalmonti. When another of the guests, Oddo Arrighi, rebuked Uberto for his anger and the latter retorted with an insult, Oddo responded by throwing a plate full of meat in Uberto's face. Buondalmonte supported his tablemate, and in the ensuing brawl he wounded Oddo Arrighi with a knife. Oddo's niece, whom Buondalmonte agreed to marry to escape the consequences of a vendetta, was extended as a peaceweaver, sacrificed by her family to bind the social fabric that men's intemperance had torn apart.

These events make Gualdrada's actions part of a more complex pattern. The pseudo-Latini has her mock Buondalmonte as a *chavaliere vitiperato,* a "knight dishonored" by a marriage induced by fear and social force. As she offers to that knight an escape from dishonor into a free marriage with her daughter, she also offers to women an alternative to their position as pawns in the game of civilization.

Although most public histories ignore the essential role of wives in the initial stages of the creation of a civic peace, domestic chronicles remind us, as they reminded the families whose memory they were written to preserve, of the historically creative and potentially threatening centrality of women in the social and civilizing process. In Florence, where the form seems to have attained a rare popularity and where a remarkable number of *ricordanze* have been preserved,[20] very early examples acknowledge women's vital peacemaking role. What may be a fragment of a thirteenth-century domestic chronicle from that city has as its central figure the daughter of Rinieri Zingani dei Buondalmonti, whose marriage in 1239 to Neri Piccolini degli Uberti was designed to seal a peace between the two feuding families.[21] Its failure to achieve that end was dramatically demonstrated in a

Buondalmonti massacre of the Uberti, and although her husband was spared, the young alien bride lost him. For Neri sent his Buondalmonti bride home to her father: he was unwilling to father the sons of a race of traitors." Married for a second time, the woman could not bring herself to consummate the marriage:

> "I cannot be your wife," she told her husband as he claimed his marital debt, "for I am the wife of the wisest and best knight in all Italy, messer Neri Piccolino degli Uberti of Florence."

Whereupon her gentle second husband let her retire to a nunnery. If this is indeed a fragment of a domestic chronicle (imbedded in a more public work), it was clearly written by an Uberti. Its function may well have been to inscribe the vendetta in the memory of future generations. Yet it was impossible to erase the connection with a woman whose character had seemed to transcend, as her marital role was designed to bridge, the lineal boundaries that defined the vendetta.

Ricordanze passed from father to son and had as their purpose the preservation of the memory of the male line, but few of their authors could ignore the women who belonged to the lineage or who through marriage had served it. Donato Velluti might not always recall the names of his female ancestors and relatives, but his chronicle of their dignity and strength kept their memory bright for future generations within the family.[22] Nor was the role of women gauged chiefly by their private, domestic qualities. It turned rather on the public honor—or dishonor—they conferred on the family. The ricordanze of Paolo Sassetti, for example, do not ignore the death in 1383 of

> the ill-famed Letta, daughter of Federigo di Pierozzo Sassetti in the house of Giovanni Noldo Porcellini, in Borgo Ogni Santi. She was buried by the friars of the church of Ogni Santi at the hour of vespers. May the devil take her soul, for she has brought shame and dishonor to our family. May it please God to pay whoever was blameworthy. And this is sufficient to describe this evil memory, which has dishonored us all. But man cannot change that which God, for our sins, has willed. But we are contemplating a vendetta which will bring some balm to our feelings.[23]

At no time was a family's honor more exposed than at a marriage. This was the moment when, through dowries given or received, the wealth and standing of a house might be known or estimated and community status measured. Urban chroniclers sensed, as we have seen, the potential for civic disruption in marriage and those other family rites in which women fully participated; but for the domestic chronicler they often provided the work's structure, for they were in reality landmarks on the family map. The ricordanze of the Corsini family are not unusual in recording as vital family statistics the dowries that they gave to the daughters who left their house, as well as those they received from the wives and daughters-in-law who entered it.[24] This was partly a matter of bookkeeping, for dowries had, of course, to be restored. But it also recognized the extent to which the internal economy and the public reputation of a family depended on those women whom the commune had confined to a domestic space.

For public historians, however, the banishment of women from the public life that developed on city streets seemed to arrest their historical development: women existed in the generational time of the family rather than the historical time of the commune; they celebrated the endlessly repetitive rites of an age of blood rather than sharing in the limited and changing encounters of an age of contract. Champions of the institutions of the commune, these historians were suspicious of that earlier precommunal world. The communal bias of most historical writing in northern Italy thus began, as early as the fourteenth century, to deprive women of a creative role in history, just as surely as a bar to office had begun to deprive them of a public role in the commune itself.

Although muted in the early modern period when independent urban republics were absorbed into larger territorial states whose dynastic concerns gave women greater visibility, that communal bias revived in the nineteenth century to give historical justification to the cause of Italian unification. Memories of the republican commune (and its underlying hostility to the forces of blood and patronage that women seemed to incarnate) had a profound influence on Risorgimento activists who, like Villari, saw the writing of an Italian history as a first intellectual step toward political unification and found in the communal period of the Middle Ages ethical and political traditions on which unification might be based.

Those northern traditions were not native to Villari. Born in Naples in 1826, he had been forced to flee his native South after implication in the Neapolitan rising of 1848.[25] From Florence, whose archives he systematically exploited in the first decades of his exile, he discovered that his fervent belief in political freedom and sacrifice of self for the public good, his hatred of political patronage and repression, were the natural themes of medieval communal history. It is not surprising that he turned his attention to Savonarola, the Dominican reformer of the city in the fifteenth century. In calling on Florence to reject the familial politics of their Medici leaders, who ruled through a network of patronage and prostituted Florentine independence for foreign alliances, Savonarola tried to restore to the city those civic ideals that had kept it free. Villari championed Savonarola's boys, young Florentines who often provided the focus of those religious processions on which the reformer lavished great attention during his brief but memorable ascendancy.[26] Those young boys not only challenged the spiritual efficacy of traditional female piety within the city, they also castigated less pious women on the streets and stripped them of their finery. Women's wigs and baubles, consigned to those bonfires of the vanities that had become familiar civic spectacles in the fifteenth century, symbolized the selfish concerns that were consuming civic energy and destroying urban bonds. For Villari, Savonarola's boys were the guardians of republican virtue, and he tacitly accepted the Dominican's argument that women were insensitive to that self-sacrifice needed to restore the republic.[27]

The Risorgimento concerns that lie barely disguised in such histories did not allow space to aristocratic women who had made a mark on the history of their age; for their power was based in familial privilege and their virtue—when they possessed it—had been shaped more by ecclesiastical than by civic ideals. Matilda of Tuscany, one of the most effective rulers in post-Carolingian Europe, had been a difficult heroine for the towns, which, even if they had received concessions from her, took advantage of the power vacuum created by her death to assert their sovereignty. She was rarely accorded a significant place in their histories, and her life attracted little independent attention. As that urban sovereignty came to be stifled by Renaissance states that were governed by dynastic rather than republican principles, however, Matilda's life assumed a new importance and acceptability. For Scipione Ammirato writing his *Istorie fiorentine,* the unified rule that Matilda had given Tuscany in the eleventh century prefigured the creation of the grand duchy by Florence's Medici leaders, who had commissioned his work.[28] Matilda's untiring support of the reformed papacy under Gregory VII also made her an important figure for the historiographers and hagiographers of the post-Tridentine church for whom she was "a resplendent star, the friend of all virtues and the enemy of every vice."[29] It is not surprising that the contemporary biography of the countess written by her chaplain Donizio would find an editor in the eighteenth century in Lodovico Antonio Muratori in his great *Rerum Italicarum Scriptores*. An ecclesiastic who wrote under the patronage of the Estensi, he had no trouble appreciating the central role played by that aristocratic stateswoman, military leader, and ruler of lands and cities in the imperial-papal struggles of the Gregorian Age.[30] But just as the communal growth of the twelfth century had deprived Matilda of political descendants, so the development of an antiaristocratic, anticlerical, national ideology in the nineteenth century diminished her place in the history of a new nation. Unlike the Maid of Orleans, a female leader whom republicans could accept as a genuine savior of the nation even after France had cut its ties with a royal and Christian past, Matilda of Tuscany was for nineteenth-century Italian reformers the embodiment of that past from which they sought to extricate their new nation. Joan of Arc, free of family and abandoned by the church, could be molded into a secular saint by the fiercely republican Jules Michelet.[31] Matilda, loyal daughter of the pope and upholder of the interests of her house, necessarily found no equivalent Risorgimento hagiographer.

Although secular women of action were not accorded sainthood, there were women of the peninsula who acquired national prominence through their saintly lives. Yet they have hardly fared better at the hands of historians. In *Saints and Society,* Weinstein and Bell have noticed a dramatic rise in the number of female saints throughout urban Europe in the later Middle Ages, an increase that might seem to cast suspicion on

> the argument that the position of women deteriorated in the transition from a feudal to an urban commercial society. . . . Among saints, at least, the reverse was true. Beginning in the thirteenth century, possibly as early as the twelfth, there were not only more female saints but more women pioneering new forms of piety. The rise of the mendicant orders . . . appealed to women as well as to men. Less often were young girls dumped into a convent by fathers who were not able to marry them off and more often did inspired girls . . . struggle against their families to fulfill visionary aspiration.[32]

There is another way of assessing their rise and the intensity of their visionary life. As cities came more strictly to divide private life from public activity and as urban women were excluded from institutional life and barred from the public space, they lost the voice that had been theirs in an earlier age of family politics. Holiness might be seen as a response to that loss. The fasts and visions of Italy's holy women were not only signs of their spiritual withdrawal, they became a means by which they might renounce the family ties and domestic concerns that trapped them in a private space; just as their visions let them find a public voice in a world whose institutions were becoming at once more public and more masculine. The rejection of family ties and loyalties and the abandonment of domestic duties are hagiographical refrains, but they are particularly frequent and forceful in the lives of women saints. St. Francis of Assisi broke once with his father to stand naked and alone before God.[33] For his near contemporary Umiliana dei Cerchi of Florence, life was a constant battle against family claims and domestic obligations. Having recoiled from her husband's embrace and renounced her father's designs to place her in a second marriage, Umiliana had constantly to resist a devil who used family bonds to tempt her from holy solitude: he sent her daughter to entice Umiliana from a vow of silence; he paraded the dead bodies of her relatives before her to redirect her mourning from sin to her loved ones. The holy woman's strength in refusing these private calls legitimated her public role as a repository of spiritual power and as a figure of charity on city streets.[34]

By resisting the cloistering impulses of family and church, many urban holy women succeeded in opening their visionary world to public scrutiny and in achieving through their visions access to the public world of event. None was more visible than Caterina Benincasa—St. Catherine of Siena—who participated not only in the public life of her native city but also in the high politics of her age. Catherine's local reputation as a peacemaker in faction-ridden Siena secured her a place in local historiography as it propelled her to a wider prominence. Her role in restoring the pope to Rome and her later missions in his name made her a part of ecclesiastical history as she never became part of the national story,[35] for her papal peacemaking sought to bend republican knees to papal authority. Although the saint's mystic marriage to Christ, her stigmata, and her constructive support of public peace over the feud clearly placed her outside the private world of house, lineage, and patronage that Risorgimento historians abhorred, her actions were based on extraterritorial loyalties unacceptable to that newly national peninsula. Yet the public appeal of St. Catherine and her lesser sisters cannot be denied. Their mystical voice described an alternate road to the civic peace paved by the institutional law of the commune, and that voice spoke, in a way the text did not, to women as well as to men.

To judge from their canonization investigations, contemporaries acknowledged the power and civic importance of medieval holy women more readily than public historians, who have generally been content to abandon these women to the hagiographers, who preferred on the whole to use them as static *exampla* rather than cast them as actors in a larger social drama. Thus although the congregation of female saints who seem to belie the invisibility of women in communal Italy did often escape the domestic constraints that barred others of their sex from public event and public history, they were less successful in animating the iconic tradition that froze women out of narrative's stream. Perhaps women were a particularly suitable subject for purveyors of sacred history, a field that emerged in the Renaissance as a result of humanistic historiography's abandonment of the sacred for the profane in much the same way as it rejected the domestic to create a public history. Humanist historians wrote of a public world of profane event whose agents were men; sacred historians of a world in which public and private, spiritual and profane, were intertwined, and whose agent was God. If the heroes of such history "were merely passive instruments in the hand of the sole cause, immediate as well as ultimate, of all historical events,"[36] how much better would be *female* saints, whose sex traditionally excluded them from historical agency.

Saintly women became, in a sense, antidotes to history, their power able to protect those bruised by historical event. As Franco Cardini reminded the readers of *Bullettino senese di storia patria* in 1981,

> Catherine is thus with us. Still today. Catherine the woman, Catherine the daughter, wife, mother, as occasion demands. Catherine who consoles and who heals the sick, Catherine who remains beside the defamed and persecuted, Catherine who does not retreat before danger, Catherine who joins in prayer with the falsely condemned. Catherine here, Catherine now. Catherine forever.[37]

For his local readers Catherine was also the saint of their city, a city whose power was in decline as her legend was being created on its streets. As Siena lost its own historical voice, subsumed in a larger Tuscan history that Florence dominated, Catherine became the ahistorical guardian of a civic spirit that history could no longer record or preserve. She became the saint of a city in retreat from historical event, one which would look more and more to ritual and legend for self-definition, as it would turn to the Virgin for protection.

Venice, secure in its island fastness from the factional pressures of a feudal hinterland and committed, in spite of its republican form, to the rule of a doge, offers a partial contrast to the implacable hostility toward public women expressed by most northern cities. Although the doge was elected, he ruled for life in a manner reminiscent of aristocratic houses, and his wife played an acknowledged role within the city. The firm grip, after the Serrata of 1297–8, of a defined number of patrician families on the major offices of government further encouraged a preoccupation with family ties at the expense, perhaps, of that neighborhood patronage necessarily cultivated in communes where office was more openly and widely competitive.[38] In such an aristocratic setting, women were valued as the means by which alliances might be built and influence peddled within the governing class. Not only did Venetian women individually mark their children with their status, they also placed a collective mark on the history of the republic. In his famous Renaissance *Diaries,* Marin Sanudo intermingles the strictly political events of government with the more social, but to him clearly still political, high gossip of marriage, feasts, and balls, a recognition of the significance of female activity that carried over into his history. In the course of his historical account of the invasion of Charles VIII, for example, Sanudo interrupts the narrative to inform his readers that the "king of the Romans had for a wife *madona* Bianca, sister of the former duke of Milan."[39] For Venetians, marriage alliance always remained a central fact of political life. And Venetian historiography is notable for its insistent extension of the domestic into the political realm. Although his great study, *La storia di Venezia nella vita privata,* in which women and their customs play so large a role, explicitly focuses on private life, Pompeo Molmenti set it firmly within a larger civic frame whose boundaries are constantly altered by the private events and attitudes he describes. In its profound awareness of the interplay between public and private, men and women, the political and the domestic, Molmenti's work stands apart from many other, more narrowly domestic investigations of *la vita privata* that were produced throughout the nineteenth century in Italy. The importance of the family as a constituent and controlling element in Venetian political life may thus help to explain the particular visibility of the city's women in its historiography.

The chief exception to the communal North was, however, the feudal South, whose political life had been dominated by dynastic concerns throughout the Middle Ages and which therefore found it harder to banish women from its history.

The great historians of Naples, lacking the republican formation of their northern colleagues, were more inclined to recognize women's political role. The female ruler who exercised the greatest claim on their historical imagination was Joanna I, daughter of King Robert of Anjou and queen of Naples in her own right, who found a place of honor in Boccaccio's *De claris mulieribus* as the ornament and pride of Italy.[40] Historians were not always so complimentary. Her contemporary, the notary-historian Domenico de Gravina, began a chronicle of his native Puglia by lamenting Joanna's accession to the Neapolitan throne, supporting his view of her unworthiness with a vivid description of her assassination of her husband, Andrew of Hungary. For Domenico, Puglia's decline in the mid-fourteenth century had been brought about not just by Joanna's rule but more generally by the rule of a woman: "Oh how unhappy that kingdom that has been reduced to the rule of women and children."[41] Yet even he was forced to take the queen and the dynastic concerns of her house seriously; and later historians of a Naples whose annexation to the Spanish crown marked the beginning of a long decline began to look back with nostalgia on Joanna's golden reign. As Eric Cochrane has recently shown, Neapolitan historians advocated as a solution to Naples's problems, "the reestablishment of a strong baronage under the control, or better under the leadership, of a strong and righteous monarch."[42] Joanna became a righteous model, an icon in her turn. Tristano Caracciolo, searching in the sixteenth century for lives that might inspire the young, was able to find in her a model of humane learning and administrative brilliance, a queen who filled her courts with letters and her kingdom with wealth and commerce.[43] And the meticulous Angelo di Costanzo in his remarkable *Istoria del Regno di Napoli* of 1572–81 praised her extravagantly as the wisest queen who had ever filled a throne from the days of the Queen of Sheba to his own times.[44] Joanna remained a heroine to the influential Enlightenment historian Pietro Giannone, who, borrowing Costanzo's account, championed her from his Swiss exile as a model of majesty, learning, justice, and propriety—a support of the state against the powers of the Church, which had eventually gained control of the South, taking it out of the dynamic of history and repressing its citizens through a malevolent and obscurantist bureaucracy, in whose prisons Giannone would lose his life.[45]

In spite of their attempts to redeem Joanna's character by absolving her of any responsibility for the murder of her first husband, Andrew of Hungary, a crime in which Muratori felt she had a share, both her character and the nature of her reign remained ambiguous. But this ambiguity, rather than intriguing the historians of the Romantic Age, repelled them. A heroine of the Enlightenment, Joanna could not live up to the virtuous demands of the Risorgimento. Part of the acknowledged purpose of Villari's popular history of medieval Italy was to present to a newly unified peninsula a sympathetic case for his native South:

> During the national revival we have frequently been forced to observe that the social and political conditions in the South of Italy are very inferior in comparison with those of the Centre and North. And instead of seeking in the past the original cause and historical explanation of this fact, we have a priori believed it to be the fatal consequence of some natural law, almost as though Italy were people by two different races.[46]

For Villari, the life of Joanna and the dissoluteness of her court—reminiscent perhaps of Theodora and her daughters in Rome—might have seemed a case study of the political conditions that had kept the South enslaved. Hers was not a life to be celebrated in a national history. It is, therefore, hardly surprising that a Frenchman, not an Italian, determined in the twentieth century to lay bare the facts of the life of Joanna of Sicily, Queen of Naples and Countess of Provence.[47]

Dynastic intrigue formed the dark center of Joanna's reign and eventually brought her to death at the hands of a strangler. Her reign cannot be fully comprehended through public chronicles of patriotism, bureaucratic development, and affairs of state, but must be seen through a more personal lens that reveals ties of patronage and kinship, emotions of love and hatred. It must also be centered on a domestic space, one that attained a new legitimacy even in northern Italy during the Renaissance as historiographic attention turned from urban streets to urban courts. As the republican commune of the Middle Ages gave way to Renaissance lordships and dynastic ambitions played out in the closeness of a court rather than on city streets encouraged rulers to flout legal restrictions that barred women from active public life, woman's private domestic role became more public. What Sante Bentivoglio's wife Ginevra and his lover Nicolosa Sanuti, the first through her life, the second in her oration on behalf of her sex, have constantly before them is the reality of dynastic ties, which not only determined the aristocratic woman's status but also made available to her a public and hence a historic persona. The public woman became a fact of Renaissance life as membership in a successful dynasty freed women, according to Tasso, to adopt the virtues of men and step into history as rulers (or, one might add, the consorts of rulers); and court chronicles recorded their deeds and assessed their historical significance. But even without assuming specifically political roles, Renaissance women were becoming more visible. For the institutional failure of the democratic commune renewed the validity of those ancient institutions of family and lordship, whose bonding devices of kinship and friendship would always play an important role in Italian political life. Women, more notably in the Middle Ages and Renaissance than in our own day, were instrumental in forging and maintaining those bonds, which on the Italian peninsula held together a society that came so late to substitute for them the ties and allegiances of the bureaucratic state.

At their center lay marriage, which, according to Sanuti, in an opinion with which Vico would concur three centuries later, was a fundamental political act, one that allowed women a collective way back into history. If Sanuti could not resist reminding her plague-conscious contemporaries that women had within them the power of the Sabines to recall a society from demographic ruin, she also saw in the marriage tie a means of securing lasting alliances that might convert warring states into peaceful and civilized societies. Within a system of virilocal marriage, women were binding gifts, the civilizing, peace-giving links on which social and political union depended. A domestic theme enshrined in the *ricordanze* thus rose in the Renaissance to the stature of a public concern, the subject of historical notice and enquiry.

But it was in the eighteenth century that familial rites and ceremonies—themes that were being relegated to a private, ahistorical world elsewhere in Europe as bureaucratic states began to shape the nature of historical enquiry—received in Italy their fullest legitimation: in Giambattista Vico's *Scienza nuova,* first published in 1725 and enlarged and emended in two subsequent editions of 1730 and 1744.[48] A professor of rhetoric at the University of Naples who aspired unsuccessfully throughout his life to the chair of civil law for which he had been trained, Vico turned his enormous legal and classical learning to history, elevating it above the natural sciences by arguing that the social world, having been made by man could be fully comprehended only by him, an effort lost on the natural world, which being God's creation was also ultimately his domain. In so arguing he made of the study of human society not just a "new science" but the most fundamental of sciences, and he ennobled the historian, who through a mastery of its rules and properties—that is, its languages, customs, and beliefs—might come not only to reveal the past but also to discover the nature of his own society. By locating the generation of civil society in the thunderclap that produced Zeus, or Jupiter, he betrays a strong identity with the humanistic writers of the Renaissance—not the historians who, like Bruni or Guicciardini, saw their works as an extension of their political lives, but rather those *literati* for whom human bonds and emotions seemed more important and enduring than the divisive and ephemeral political events of their age. If the birth of a hierarchy of gods is, for Vico, the intellectual sign of the birth of a civilized life, its social sign is the institution of marriage. For that same thunderbolt that produced the gods and gave man fire, frightened him sufficiently that he fled into a cave, where he learned to content himself with one sexual partner over whose offspring he began to exert his authority.[49] The orderly lines of descent and inheritance that monogamy made possible were the basis on which political, social, and economic organization rested; and it was one in which women shared. Vico's three principles of civil society, namely, religion, marriage, and burial of the dead, are not the privileges of men but the rites of all civilized peoples.

Those rites had already received inventive attention at the beginning of the sixteenth century in work of another genre, Marco Antonio Altieri's *Li nuptiali,* a symposium on the institution of marriage composed between 1506 and 1509.[50] As a way of justifying his subject, he shows how the Romans celebrated as their most precious rites (which he calls mysteries) these three events: birth (when legitimate descent is acknowledged or rejected), burial (when ancestral ties are remembered and commemorated), and marriage (when social links are forged). Like Nicolosa Sanuti's oration, Altieri's much longer and more original work opposed restrictions on the amount of energy and money that citizens would expend on the ceremony, costume, and conviviality that these rites traditionally demanded.[51] Civil governments had seen a threat to political stability in the expression of these ancient rites, which served to strengthen ties of family and friendship and in whose ceremonies and celebrations women recovered their voice. For Altieri, as for Vico, it was these social rites that marked a civilization. To reduce their nature, or to ignore the importance of their traditions, was to reduce one's social existence and to lose touch with one's history.

Vico gave this argument historical legitimacy by making these rites the principles of a civil society for whose history he offered a philosophical base. The wealth of legal and rhetorical learning in his treatise assured its popularity within a university curriculum in which law and rhetoric continued to flourish. Faculties of law, in whose lecture halls many future historians learned the rudiments of their trade, propagated Vico's methods and beliefs, drawing on their first expression in his *Diritto universale* of 1720.[52] Both that work and his later *Scienza nuova,* which tried to construct from particular legal and linguistic forms a general philosophy of civilization, seemed to reinforce and elevate even the work of local historians. Grand narrative had seldom served their purposes, and they usually abandoned its design to linger over those human rites that Vico's scheme moved to center stage; for in societies whose political development may have been insignificant and that were not ruled or rent by great ideological principles, it was Vico's human rites that had generally provoked the social tension (and provided a means to its resolution) that such historians like to explore. The Vichean tradition gave larger meaning to, even legitimated, the countless studies of marital and funerary traditions, of wedding gifts and wedding clothes, that fill the local journals that often had to be invented to contain the enthusiasm for local history that arose in the nineteenth century.[53]

Moreover, the celebration of human rites over political institutions came as a relief in a land that had lost control of its political destiny. Vico's scheme let Italians share in human history when they could not yet write a national one. It is therefore not surprising that the poet Ugo Foscolo remembered even in his English exile enough of the Vicheanism he had imbibed during his university days in Padua to date the civil (and historical) state

> from the day when nuptials, law-courts, and altars caused the wild, bestial men of primeval times to feel compassion for themselves and their kin."[54]

His interesting substitution of law courts for Vico's burial is a sign of the direction that historical study was taking in his age, as a legal approach and methodology rose to dominate this kind of historical enquiry.

In their encyclopedic histories as well as in their detailed studies, a school of Italian legal historians used the laws and legal practices of medieval Italy as a vital, unifying tradition that had given social coherence to the peninsula, even in the long centuries when it had lacked political unity. Roman law, to which Italy laid claim and which reemerged in its urban schools, had triumphed over local custom to provide a legal standard validated not by memory but by a text, governed not by tradition but by principle. Yet although its early association with commercial and communal development enhanced its reputation and historical appeal, Italian historians never let the public use of Roman law limit their own inquiry. Vichean principles underlay their legal histories, turning the pursuit of legal texts and the writing of a history of law into an excavation of the foundation of human institutions. They were quick to realize the importance of women's legal status to that study; for in an age that used law as a means of promoting the public over the private while at the same time denying women a public role, women's legal status provided a touchstone to institutional change. Thus the conflict between Germanic (Lombard and Frankish) legal traditions and the principles of Roman law might often best be expressed in Italy in terms of the legal position of women. The freeing of communal institutions from feudal authority might be traced in Genoa, for example, to that early imperial concession in the tenth century to all Genoese women, whether or not they lived under its sway, of the legal personality allowed by Roman law.[55] Both in that Ligurian city and throughout Tuscany, the victory of Roman law and the public and commercial policies it supported might be described in the substitution of a Roman counterdower for the Germanic marriage gifts husbands had traditionally awarded their brides.[56] The wealth throughout Italy of written sources susceptible to such analysis spawned schools of historians whose methodologies were legal, but whose interests were largely local. Yet such legal tools and methodologies gave local historical enquiry the scientific rigor that a nineteenth-century professionalism was coming to demand, while Vico's historical philosophy kept it from antiquarianism by supplying the broadly human interests that gave history a general audience.

Nineteenth-century historians had not yet tailored their histories to the specialized requirements and abilities of their craft and might still direct their narratives to a general audience of literate adults. Yet the hunger of that ever larger reading public for historical fictions had already begun to threaten the historian, purveyor of historical truths. In France the success of Walter Scott's novels tormented the historian Michelet, who proposed Vico's *New Science* as an antidote.[57] He saw that the historical romance's appeal was less the freedom that fictionality offered to the author of its plot than the human scale and sexual interest that shaped its scenes. Vico's human rites let the historian explore the institutions of a society without losing sight of the human actors that had created them and whom they served. Unlike the French, who came to the *New Science* through Michelet's exposition of it, Italians had always known it. And Italian historians seem consequently to have found Scott and his followers much less of a threat. Michele Amari, chronicler of his native Sicily, translated many of Scott's poems and novels; some of the novelist's narrative techniques may be discerned in his dramatic retelling of the Sicilian Vespers. Yet he reached out to Vichean principles as his historical purposes grew stronger, and he could expect his audience to respond to them in his monumental, yet popular study of the Moslems in Sicily.[58]

Those Vichean principles also survived the pressures of nationalism that the Risorgimento and unification inevitably introduced. For the distinguished legal historian Nino Tamassia, it was only through a fuller understanding of the human rites that Italy had brought to refinement, most fully in the Renaissance, that Italians and Europeans might come to know and respect her greatness. Hence in a preface to *La famiglia italiana nei secoli decimoquinto e decimosesto,* published in 1910, he offers a book on the family, its history and ceremonies, in nationalistic terms:

> I will be content if my notes call many to those studies from which Italy rightly awaits the revelation of its glories and of its griefs, the one

> and the other gained through long centuries of material and moral servitude. And to this sweet end we should return with noble national pride to the sources of our greatness and, we can loudly proclaim, those of European civilization. The history of our house, that is for us to write.[59]

The captivating notions of statehood, coming to full flower under Fascism, did eventually pervert the history of the "house" into that of a more institutional and corporate state, one from which women, given the traditional denial of their public role, would be necessarily excluded. But not before Matilda of Tuscany was resurrected as a secular saint. Perhaps her devoted support of the church suggested to a budding religious historian like Leone Tondelli the kind of union of secular and spiritual leadership that he hoped Fascism could provide through accommodation with the papacy. When issuing a new edition of his popular life of the countess in 1925, he certainly presented her as a model and inspiration to those women gathering under the Fascist banner who would create in Italy of the twentieth century, as Matilda had in the eleventh, a new moral order:

> Since the time of the first edition, the figure of Matilda has returned under flags of battle. Our young women especially those of Emilia and Tuscany, in their passionate struggles, have been seized with admiration for this legendary heroine, whose character was both generous and martial.[60]

In general, however, the historians who supported Fascism, in embracing the mysticism of the state, turned away from those local and social histories that had accorded women a collective role in the work of building social institutions.[61]

We cannot look to the economic historians (either Marxist or non-Marxist) who dominated postwar Italian scholarship for a restoration of woman's voice. Their emphasis on the world of great business and commerce, an interest undoubtedly stimulated by the direction and scale of economic recovery in northern Italy, left women little place in their histories. For, of course, women did not participate in the great medieval banking or trading companies, nor in Italy did they rise to prominence in urban gilds. It was as workers and investors that medieval women were, if not visible, then at least more significant. Before the War, Robert Lopez had noticed the unusually conjugal basis of the wool industry in thirteenth-century Genoa.[62] And, in a series of later articles, the American Hilmar Krueger drew attention to the importance of women as investors in Genoese trade.[63] Their economic presence was in both cases recorded in the notarial records that fill Italy's urban archives, which historians had exhaustively exploited to investigate the nature of business contracts, discover the directions of trade, assess the products traded, and weigh the value of monies exchanged. Women are everywhere present in these documents, not only as woolworkers or investors of modest sums in the trading ventures of male merchants. Young girls are given in apprenticeship, often to women skilled in a craft. Lactating women are engaged as nurses. Exotic women are bought and sold as domestic slaves. Without the nurses the bourgeois family might not have been so large nor the bourgeoisie so stable. Without its domestic slaves the domestic extravagance characteristic of urban Italy in the later Middle Ages and Renaissance might have been harder to achieve in the decades after the Black Death; and we might have lost those feasts and ceremonies that are a focus of the age and were a stimulus to the luxury production that sustained it. Without female labor always supplementing a family's budget might domestic poverty and urban unrest have been greater, or without female labor to exploit might industry have proved more responsive to labor's demands? Few of the historians who sifted through thousands of those precious records of the intimate transactions of public life posed such questions.[64] Perhaps the contemporary Italian situation in which women were economically impotent encouraged postwar historians to overlook even the monetary power of women of an earlier age, whose dowries often served to underwrite the ventures of that great commercial world ruled by men.

Less excusably, they chose to ignore women as consumers, something medieval and Renaissance contemporaries could never do. Preachers, lawmakers, and chroniclers had condemned the seemingly unquenchable consumerism of the female sex, which was not appreciated as a stimulus to industry but viewed rather as a threat to the solvency of households and of the state itself.[65] As symbols of status in an increasingly status-conscious society, women of the later Middle Ages displayed in their jewels and clothes the family's position and ambitions. Nicolosa Sanuti does not notice or mention it, but the ornaments of apparel that were their insignia of worth served male as well as female desires. The sumptuary laws written to contain women's appetites and men's social ambitions, became in the century or so after their demise the subject of considerable local study; and many of the laws were edited and published.[66] The history of demand that they record, a demand that came to focus on women, seems not to have appealed to modern economic historians, who are more interested in questions of supply. Yet insofar as late medieval and Renaissance taste can be measured in terms of refinement and variation, the period is better understood through the demand and consumption that women seemed to epitomize than through the supply and production that men chiefly organized.[67] A serious study of consumption would necessarily restore to women not only an economic role but also a public dimension. For at the intersection between the private house and public square, between the isolated lineage and socializing kindred, between private fortune and public credit, stands the private woman dressed for public eyes.

A greater sensitivity to women's pivotal position at the border between the public world of history and the private world of domestic chronicle might help historians to use recent approaches and methodologies without being trapped in their assumptions. Most tempting of these is probably the Annalistes' mapping of the silent world of those ruled by structure rather than event—that world of Braudel's *longue durée,* controlled by biological rather than historical time, ruled by private rhythms rather than a public calendar.[68] Italian historians have followed the French pioneers of this approach deep into the households of medieval and Renaissance Italy; and there, with the help of remarkably detailed demographic records, they have encountered as a newly legitimate subject for historical study, the Italian madonna and her daughters. New attention to household relations and rituals and a new freedom from narrative have allowed historians to focus on these women's central role within the enclosed domestic space. In the process they have uncovered a reservoir of information about women's daily lives lived, as are most lives, in the endless repetitions and ahistorical rhythms of the longue durée.[69] It would be easy to equate the structural world of nonevent with the world of women; for if privileged men moved easily into the civic and evenemental world created by their actions, the rejection of women's public role by the Italian city might seem to have imprisoned all women in the private time and domestic attitudes that the cities rejected. We might indeed return with Dino Compagni to see her as a willful promoter of the traditional relationships of that domestic world against the artificial structures imposed by public institutions. On the basis of the demographic information contained in the Florentine *catasto* of 1427, Herlihy has insisted that the late medieval and Renaissance household in Tuscany beame increasingly a woman's world, as delayed marriage for men increased the chances that either Florentine children would normally live in homes ruled not by men but by their widowed mothers.[70] Should we then see in that Renaissance embellishment of the domestic space, in its proliferation of private genealogies and memorials, and in the intensification of the rituals surrounding family events a form of female revenge on a public world that had excluded women?

It would seem better to question the historian's attempt to divide premodern societies into an elite of actors who participate in public historical events and a majority, which includes almost all women, who, sharing the slower cycles of a more natural and more private existence, are tightly enclosed in Baudel's "long-term prisons." First, such an attempt uncritically accepts the myths created by civic historians to strengthen and dignify the fragile institutions of their new urban society. Public life always overran the public piazze and even the bounds of the city itself. Political bonds were strengthened during summer festivities at a villa, just as alliances were made (and unmade) through marriage. The conduct of wives and daughters was not a private matter. Men supervised it closely precisely because a woman's private shame, which might make her a public woman, could destroy a man's public honor, forcing him to retire to the private sphere.

There is a further reason to reject an easy dichotomy between public and private, historical and natural, evenemental and cyclic: it is a means of denying agency to those whom historians have forgotten. This denial of individual intention to the historically mute, who are assigned a collective mentality that is fashioned by nature but never fashions it, deserves to be questioned.[71] Their language waits to be uncoded and their actions interpreted. It is perhaps time for the historians of medieval Italy to listen again to some original voices of their past: to Vico, who through myth and fable sought to give voice to the mute makers of human history; to Altieri, who read in the steps of a dance the patterns of his culture; even to Sanuti, who by defending fashion, which gave costume a dimension of historicity, fought those legislators who would strip women of their role as flamboyant agents and chroniclers of change.

Notes

1. On the awakening of historical consciousness, see Craig B. Fischer, "The Pisan Clergy and an Awakening of Historical Interest in a Medieval Commune," *Studies in Medieval and Renaissance History,* 3 (1966), 143–219. A close association between historiographical views and political perceptions is argued by Nicolai Rubinstein, "Some Ideas on Municipal Progress and Decline in the Italy of the Communes," in *Fritz Saxl Memorial Essays,* ed. D. J. Gordon (London, 1957), pp. 165–83.

2. Carlo Calisse, *A History of Italian Law,* trans. Layton B. Register (Boston, 1928), Title II, ch. 2. As early as 1056, the city of Genoa secured the concession from its overlord that Lombard women living within the city might sell or alienate their goods freely as if they were Roman, *Codice diplomatico della Repubblica di Genova,* ed. Cesare Imperiale di Sant'Angelo, 3 vols., Fonti per la storia d'Italia, 77, 79, 89 (Rome, 1936–42), 1:7.

3. *Digest* 50.17.2. On the use of this commonplace in the Renaissance, see Ian Maclean, *The Renaissance Notion of Women* (Cambridge, 1980), pp. 77–78.

4. *Discorso della virtù feminile e donnesca,* in *Le prose diverse, di Torquato Tasso* ed. Cesare Guasti (Florence, 1875), 2:203–12. Lucrezia Marinella objected to Tasso's exemption of only "heroic" women from such "natural" incapacity: *La nobilità e l'eccellenza co'diffetti e mancamenti de gli huomini* (Venice, 1621), 171–74.

5. The oration is edited by L. Frati, *La vita privata a Bologna dal secolo XIII al XVII,* 2nd ed. (Bologna, 1928), pp. 251–62. On the reaction it provoked, see ibid., pp. 33–35.

6. See Maclean, *The Renaissance Notion of Women,* pp. 72–75.

7. Christine de Pizan, *The Book of the City of Ladies,* trans. E. J. Richards (New York, 1982). However, her championing of some active women, such as the Amazons, may have served as an underhand encouragement to her female readers and followers, as Natalie Zemon Davis argues in "Women on Top: Symbolic Inversion and Political Disorder in Early Modern Europe," in *The Reversible World,* ed. Barbara Babcock (Ithaca and London, 1976), pp. 173–74.

8. Ed. Corrado Ricci and A. Bacchi della Lega, Scelta di curiosità letterarie inedite or rare, 223 (Bologna, 1888).

9. See Pasquale Villari, *The Barbarian Invasions of Italy,* trans. Linda Villari, 3 vols. (New York, 1902), 2:315.

10. Cecilia M. Ady, *The Bentivoglio of Bologna* (London, 1937), pp. 136–37, gives a characteristically shrewd assessment of her character. For a more thoroughly approving one, see Albano Sorbelli, *I Bentivoglio,* ed. Marsilio Bacci (n. p., 1969), pp. 175–79.

11. See *Gynevera delle clare donne,* p. xviii.

12. Pasquale Villari, *Medieval Italy from Charlemagne to Henry VII,* trans. Constance Hufton (London, 1910), p. 55.

13. This was clearly true in Genoa, where Caffaro's chronicle, begun in about 1118 by a man who occupied the city's highest magistracies, was continued for over two centuries by governmental appointees, and in Venice, where an official chronicle, kept from the thirteenth century, was at least once composed by the doge himself. See Giovanni Petti Balbi, "La storiografia genovese fino al secolo XV." In *Studi sul medioevo cristiano offerti a Raffaelo Morghen,* 2 vols., Istituto storico italiano per il medio evo, Studi storici, 83–92 (Rome, 1974), 2:763–850; Antonio Carile, "Aspetti della cronachista veneziana nei secoli XIII e XIV." In *La storiografia veneziana fino al secolo XVI,* ed. Agostino Pertusi (Florence, 1970), pp. 75–126; and Girolamo Arnaldi, "Andrea Dandolo Doge-cronista," in ibid. pp. 127–268.

14. See generally David Herlihy, "Land, Family, and Women in Continental Europe, 701–1200," *Traditio,* 18 (1962), 89–120.

15. It may not be insignificant that Lombard cities, whose struggle for independence so often coincided with the struggle for Gregorian reform, were among the most hostile to Germanic marriage portions, Manlio Bellomo, *Ricerche sui rapporti patrimoniali tra coniugi* (Milan, 1961), ch. 1.

16. On these early "sumptuary" controls, see Diane Owen Hughes, "Sumptuary Law and Social Relations in Renaissance Italy," in *Disputes and Settlements: Law and Human Relations in the West,* ed. John Bossy (Cambridge, 1983), pp. 69–99.

17. Dino Compagni, *Cronica,* ed. Gino Luzzatto (Turin, 1968), p. 8, now translated as *Dino Compagni's "Chronicle of Florence,"* Daniel E. Bornstein (Philadelphia, 1986), p. 6.

18. Judicial records tell a somewhat different story, letting us see women of all social groups particularly vulnerable to the threat of patrician violence and hence in need of the civic institutions that the patriciate often disdained. See Guido Ruggiero, *Violence in Early Renaissance Venice* (New Brunswick, 1980).

19. In the *Chronica fiorentina,* ed. Pasquale Villari, in *I primi due secoli della storia de Firenze,* 2 vols. (Florence, 1893), 2:233–34. Although Villari recognized the diverging chronicle traditions and specifically cited Compagni's account (whose dating has always been problematic) as shorter than and inferior to that of the pseudo-Brunetto Latini, he nevertheless failed in his work to detail the "dissension . . . already lurking among certain of the nobles," which had been quieted but hardly silenced by a forced marriage that ultimately let Gualdrada pursue her course. I am indebted in this comparison of the chronicle tradition to the thesis of Carol Lansing, "Nobility in a Medieval Commune: The Florentine Magnates, 1260–1300," University of Michigan, 1984, pp. 192–94.

20. A sketch of the nature and possibilities appears in Philip J. Jones, "Florentine Families and Florentine Diaries in the Fourteenth Century," *Papers of the British School at Rome,* 24 (1956), 183–205.

21. It is imbedded in the *Annales florentini,* ed. by Otto Hartwig, *Quellen und Forschungen zur Altesten Geschichte der Stadt Florenz,* 2 vols. (Marburg, 1875–80), 2:225. The suggestion that the account is a remnant of a domestic chronicle comes

from R. Renier, ed., *Liriche edite ed inedite di Fazio degli Uberti* (Florence, 1883), p. xxxv.

22. Donato Velluti, *La cronica domestica scritta fra il 1367 e il 1370, con le addizioni di Paolo Velluti scritte fra il 1555 e il 1560,* ed. I. Del Lungo and G. Volpe (Florence, 1914).

23. (Trans. by Gene Brucker), *The Society of Renaissance Florence* (New York, 1971), p. 42.

24. *Il libro di ricordanze dei Corsini (1362–1457),* ed. Armando Petrucci, Fonti per la storia d'Italia, 100 (Rome, 1965), pp. 5, and passim.

25. For a brief account of his life, see the *Enciclopedia italiana,* 35: 368–69.

26. See now the new, full interpretation of Savonarola's manipulation of public pageantry by Richard C. Trexler, *Public Life in Renaissance Florence* (New York, 1980), p. 359.

27. Pasquale Villari, *Life and Times of Girolamo Savonarola,* trans. Linda Villari, 2 vols. (New York, 1969), 2:44–46, 133–39. This is a reprint of the translation made by his wife in 1888. The first Italian edition appeared in 1863.

28. *Istorie fiorentine,* ed. F. Ranalli (Florence, 1846).

29. So P. D. Benedetto Lucchino Da Mantova, *Cronica della vera origine et attioni della . . . contessa Matilda et de'suoi antecessori et discendenti . . .* (Mantua, 1592), cited by Eric Cochrane, *Historians and Historiography in the Italian Renaissance* (Chicago, 1981), p. 419.

30. For the relation between this first Italian edition and two earlier German ones, see Lino Lionello Ghirardini, "L'edizione muratoriana della *Vita* Mathildis di Donizone," in *L. A. Muratori storiografo,* Atti del Convegno internazionale di studi muratoriani, Modena, 1972 (Florence, 1975), pp. 107–16. In 1756, twenty-two years after Muratori's edition, the great editor of ecclesiastical texts, Gian Domenico Mansi, reissued a biography of the countess written in 1645 by Francesco Maria Fiorentini of Lucca, appending a series of original documents, *Memorie della Gran Contessa Matilda restituita alla patria lucchese da Francesco Maria Fiorentina . . .* (Lucca, 1756).

31. His study of Joan first appeared in 1841 as three chapters in the fifth volume of his *Histoire de France.* It was republished separately with some changes in 1853. A critical review of Michelet's use and abuse of his sources in constructing his enormously popular account of Joan can be found in Gustave Rudler, *Michelet, historien de Jeanne d'Arc,* 2 vols. (Paris, 1925–26). On Michelet's Joan, see the essay in this collection by Susan Mosher Stuard, "Fashion's Captives: Medieval Women in French Historiography."

32. Donald Weinstein and Rudolph Bell, *Saints and Society* (Chicago, 1982), p. 224.

33. *The First Life of St. Francis* by Thomas of Celano, in *St. Francis of Assisi, Writings and Early Biographies,* ed. Marion A. Habig (Chicago, 1972), par. 14–15, pp. 240–41.

34. Vito of Cortona, "Vita de B. Aemiliana seu Umiliana," *Acta Sanctorum* 17, ed. G. Henschenio and D. Papebrochio (Paris and Rome, 1966), 19 May, pp. 385–402.

35. See A. Capelcelatro, *Storia di Santa Caterina da Siena e del papato del suo tempo* (Siena, 1876). The fullest narrative remains E. G. Gardner, *Saint Catherine of Siena* (London and New York, 1907). Her role in the events of 1376–78 that restored the pope to Rome were minimized in the important study by Robert Fawtier, *Sainte Catherine de Sienne. Essai de critique de sources: sources hagiographiques*. Bibliothèque de l'Ecole Française de Rome, 121 (Paris, 1921).

36. Cochrane, *Historians and Historiography in the Italian Renaissance,* p. 468.

37. Franco Cardino, "Santa Caterina da Siena nella vita del Trecento," *Bullettino senese di storia patria,* 88 (1981), 20.

38. According to Samuel Cohn, only in the Renaissance did the Florentine patriciate abandon neighborhood for class solidarity, choosing in the fifteenth century to reject marriage partners from the district in favor of fellow patricians who might be scattered throughout the city: *The Laboring Classes in Renaissance Florence* (New York, 1980).

39. Cited by Cochrane, *Historians and Historiography,* p. 167.

40. Boccaccio admitted that "She is magnificent not in a womanly but in a regal way," but he did not fail to note that she acted so modestly and discreetly that her subjects might say that she was "not their queen but rather their friend," *Opere,* ed. Pier Giorgio Ricci (Milan and Naples, n.d.), pp. 778–80.

41. *Chronicon de Rebus in Apulia Gestis,* ed. Albano Sorbelli, Rerum Italicarum Scriptores, new ed., vol. XIII[3] (Citta di Castello, 1903), p. 19.

42. *Historians and Historiography in Renaissance Italy,* p. 275.

43. *Vita Joannae Primae,* ed. Giuseppe Paladino, Rerum Italicarum Scriptores, new ed., vol. XXII[1] (Bologna, 1934); and see B. Carlo De Frede, "L'umanista Tristano Caracciola e la sua 'Vita di Giovanna I,'" *Archivio storico italiano,* 105 (1947), 50–64, who, with Muratori (in his preface to the first edition of the work [Naples, 1769], p. 4), recognizes the hagiographical nature of Caracciola's work.

44. 3rd ed. (Turin, 1886).

45. Pietro Giannone, *Istoria civile del regno di Napoli,* 2 vols. (Lugano, 1839), 2:101–29. On Giannone see Giuseppe Ricuperti, *L'esperienza civile e religiosa di Pietro Giannone* (Milan and Naples, 1970).

46. Villari, *Medieval Italy from Charlemagne to Henry VII,* p. viii.

47. Emile G. Léonard, *Histoire de Jeanne Ire, reine de Naples, comtesse de Provence (1343–1382),* 3 vols. (Monaco and Paris, 1932–37). See also his incomplete studies of the woman and her reign collected in *Les Angevins de Naples* (Paris, 1954). In Italy Giovanna's life was more frequently left to the purveyors of historical fictions. Giacinto Battaglia, a minor Milanese playwright managed to carve out a reputation with a series of historical dramas, one of which was *Giovanna I di Napoli* (1838). Two years later he published her life as an historical romance, *Giovanna Prima regina di Napoli* (Naples, 1840). Now, however, Italian readers can turn to

something more substantial, a popular but historical account of her life written by Italo De Feo, *Giovanna d'Angio regina di Napoli* (Naples, 1968). De Feo sees her faults as a queen inextricably bound to the nature of female incapacity. He closes his book with the judgment of the poet Fazio degli Uberti, who, speaking of the Kingdom of Naples, wrote "You do not have a king but a queen / Young and beautiful ruling the kingdom. / She is very courtly, but she cannot wield a sword."

48. Ed. Fausto Nicolini, 2 vols. (Bari, 1942) and trans. Thomas Goddard Bergin and Max Harold Fisch as *The New Science of Giambattista Vico,* 2nd ed. (Ithaca, 1968).

49. *Scienza nuova,* par. 13.

50. Ed. E. Narducci (Rome, 1873). For a sensitive account of the author and his work, see Christiane Klapisch-Zuber, "Une ethnologie du mariage au temps de l'humanisme," *Annales E. S. C.,* 36 (1981), 1016–27, now translated in her *Women, Family, and Ritual in Renaissance Italy,* trans. Lydia Cochrane (Chicago, 1985), pp. 207–46.

51. Yet he was not opposed to the sumptuary laws, which, by keeping social groups in their places, reduced the need for the aristocracy to exhaust its fortunes in a war of social competition.

52. Elio Gianturco, "Vico's Significance in the History of Legal Thought," in *Giambattista Vico, an International Symposium,* ed. Giorgio Tagliacozzo and Hayden V. White (Baltimore, 1969), pp. 338–42.

53. The seriousness with which Italian historians viewed events and institutions that were coming to be called private (and risked banishment from history) is apparent in numerous studies of "la vita privata" that appeared at the end of the nineteenth century. Many remain the fullest and most serious accounts of medieval Italian women. See, for example, *La storia di Venezia nella vita privata dalle origini alla caduta della Repubblica* written by Pompeo G. Molmenti in 1880 and expanded and emended through seven editions (7th ed., 3 vols. [Bergamo, 1927–29]).

54. *I sepolcri* (1807), 11. 91–93, in Ugo Foscolo, *Opere,* ed. Guido Bezzola, 2 vols. (Milan, 1956), 1:87; and see Enrico De Mas, "Vico and Italian Thought," In *Giambattista Vico, an International Symposium,* pp. 147–64.

55. G. Salvioli, "La condizione giuridica delle donne a Genova nel secolo XI," *Rivista di storia e filosofia del diritto,* 1 (1897), 198–206.

56. Ludovico Zdekauer. "Le doti in Firenze nel Dugento," in *Miscellanea fiorentina di erudizione e storia* I (1886).

57. Jules Michelet, *Journal,* ed. Paul Viallaneix and Paul Digeon, 4 vols. (Paris, 1959–76), 1:415. In 1828 Michelet published an adapted translation of Vico's *New Science.* For evidence that Michelet was not overestimating Scott's hold on the reading public see Martyn Lyons, "The Audience for Romanticism: Walter Scott in France, 1815–51," *European History Quarterly,* 14 (1984), 21–43.

58. Amari came to history from a literary rather than a legal background, and claimed that Scott has inspired him to return in 1827 to his recently abandoned studies. In 1832 his translation of Scott's *Flodden Field* appeared. The novelist

clearly remained an inspiration as Amari struggled with the narrative of *La guerra del Vespro siciliano o un periodo delle istorie siciliane del secolo XIII,* published in 1843, before he had seriously confronted Vico. By the time he wrote the first volume of his *Storia dei musulmani di Sicilia,* however, Amari had encountered the Neapolitan thinker, with whose philosophy of history he favorably compared that of Ibn Kaldun (p. 181). Although Amari firmly rejected philosophies of history in favor of a documented history of human events, his work was obviously influenced by Vichean considerations. A useful study of Amari's life and work is Illuminato Peri, *Michele Amari* (Naples, 1976). See the discussion of Scott in Barbara Hanawalt's "Golden Ages for the History of Medieval English Women."

59. P. ix.

60. *Matilda di Canossa,* 2nd ed. (Reggio-Emilia, 1925), pp. vi–vii; the first edition appeared in 1915. On Tondelli, whose work did point out that Matilda was neither a saint nor a virgin but which saw her nevertheless as a protector of the catholic youth he supported, see Alcide Spaggiari, "Mons. Leone Tondalli, l'uomo e la storia," *Atti e memorie della Deputazione di Storia Patria per le Antiche Provincie Modonesi,* 9th ser. 1 (1979), 269–85.

Three years later in 1928, Natale Grimaldi, placing Matilda in the context of the great feudal family, dedicated his *La contessa Matilda e la sua stirpe feudale* (Florence, 1928) to the minister of education Pietro Fedele, who claimed her life would show "the instrinsic values of our civilization and culture and the traditions and aspirations that operate through history to make the national conscience a living and working force" (p. 6). Such an attitude would have become more unusual as the Fascists developed programs to bind women to the household and domestic economy; see Victoria de Grazia, *The Culture of Consent. Mass Organization of Leisure in Fascist Italy* (Cambridge, 1981), pp. 42–43.

61. Some approaches to a new Fascist history are sketched in Gabriele Turi's account of writing of the *Enciclopedia italiana,* an important Fascist enterprise that engaged the talents of the prominent medievalist Giacomo Volpe, *Il fascismo e il consenso degli intellettuali* (Bologna, 1980), pp. 110–30.

62. Roberto Lopez, "Le origini dell'arte della lana," in his *Studi sull' economia genovese nel medio evo* (Milan, 1936), pp. 114–15.

63. Hilmar C. Krueger, "Genoese Merchants, Their Partnerships and Investments, 1155 to 1164," in *Studi in onore di Armando Sapori,* 2 vols. (Milan, 1957), 1:257–72, and "Genoese Merchants, Their Associations and Investments, 1150 to 1230," in *Studi in onore di Amintore Fanfani,* 6 vols. (Milan, 1962), 1:413–26.

64. Some exceptions deserve to be noted here: Iris Origo, "The Domestic Enemy: Eastern Slaves in Tuscany in the Fourteenth and Fifteen Centuries," *Speculum* 30 (1955), 321–66; Domenico Gioffrè, *Il mercato degli schiavi a Genova nel secolo XV* (Genoa, 1971); Christiane Klapisch-Zuber, "Genitori naturali e genitori di latte nella Firenze del Quattrocento," *Quaderni storici,* 44 (1980), 543–63.

65. See Diane Owen Hughes, "Distinguishing Signs: Earrings, Jews, and Franciscan Rhetoric in the Italian Renaissance City," *Past and Present,* 112 (1985), 3–59.

66. Significant contributions are Ariodante Fabretti, *Statuti e ordinamenti suntuarii intorno al vestire degli uomini e delle donne in Perugia all'anno 1266 al 1536,* Memorie della R. Accademia delle Scienze di Torino, 2nd. ser., 38 (Turin, 1886); Umberto Dallari and Luigi Alberto Gandini, "Lo statuto suntuario bolognese del 1401 e il registro delle vesti bollate," *Atti e memorie della R. Deputazione di Storia Patria per le Provincie de Romagna,* 3rd ser., 7 (1889), 8–22; Antonio Bonardi, *Il lusso di altri tempi in Padova* (Venice, 1910); G. Bistort, *Il magistrato alle pompe nella Repubblica di Venezia* (Venice, 1912).

67. An exception (though it deals with buildings) is the study by Richard A. Goldthwaite, *The Building of Renaissance Florence* (Baltimore and London, 1980).

68. F. Braudel, "Histoire et sciences sociales: la longue durée," *Annales E.S.C.,* 13 (1958); on the Annales School, see Susan Mosher Stuard, "Fashion's Captives: Medieval Women in French Historiography."

69. See, for example, a recent issue of *Quaderni storici,* 44 (1980), which concentrates on the domestic woman: *Parto e maternità. Momenti della autobiografia femminile.* Not all of the articles, however, conform strictly to this theme.

70. David Herlihy, "The Tuscan Town in the Quattrocento, a Demographic Profile," *Medievalia et Humanistica,* new ser. 1 (1970), 68–81; "Mapping Families in Medieval Italy," *Catholic Historical Review,* 58 (1972), 1–24; "Veillir au Quattrocento," *Annales E.S.C.,* 24 (1972), 1338–52. On the myths constructed to protect men of the lineage from the fact of this demographic situation, which might deprive them of their mother's dowry if she remarried or put them under the authority of a woman if she did not, see Christiane Klapisch-Zuber, "La 'mère cruelle.' Maternité, veuvage et dot dans la Florence des XIVe–XVe siècles," *Annales E.S.C.,* 38 (1983), 1097–1109, now translated in *Women, Family, and Ritual,* pp. 117–31.

71. For a critical view of some assumptions of the Annalistes, see Stuart Clark, "French Historians and Early Modern Popular Culture," *Past and Present,* 100 (1983), 62–99.

3

Fashion's Captives: Medieval Women in French Historiography

SUSAN MOSHER STUARD

Secular and religious women of France's formative age have gone in and out of historiographical fashion with a speed matching the more outré Parisian fashions. A few endure: Saint Joan, Clothilde, Eloise, and Blanche of Castile inhabit a special category of stock figures whom even style in historical writing cannot dislodge. One once numbered among them, St. Geneviève, lost her shrine and relics to the Pantheon honoring republican men in 1793, and even exacting nineteenth-century scholarship could not return her to the honor she had enjoyed. Montaillou's Beatrice de Planisolles and her gossips have entered the circle noted by historians, if not for themselves then for the structure of household in which they were made to move. But little has been said of Elizabeth de Jaligny, whose feudal values prompted her to defend the family's castle, and Agnes of Burgundy, whose ambition led her to fight battles. As faceless masses, rather than as glassmakers and silk workers who were active participants in change, some working women have now entered the ranks of those counted by historians. The woman who bore issue in or out of wedlock regardless of class or wealth has a chance to be numbered as well. Subduing aggressive, vigorous women who were active agents of change to a patriotic narrative of emerging nationhood cast some powerful medieval women into oblivion. As yet others have not been elevated to active roles, now that history has passed on to new questions.

Medieval chronicles and histories mentioned women, often imposing on later historians the continuing task of reconciling powerful and public women actors to successive styles of historical writing, none of which easily countenanced them. Gregory of Tours, despite his Gallo-Roman antecedents, revealed the new age in his narrative through just such devices as women's presence.[1] From the Blessed Clothilde to Brunhild, Fredegund, and Radegund of his own generation, Gregory extolled women's virtues and condemned their faults. They were powerful forces within Frankish society; he understood that and dutifully recorded their histories. The *topos* of classical literary tradition, in which decorum demanded that important or superior women be mentioned as little as possible, best, not at all, had been eclipsed.[2] In the new world of Frankish society women were not closeted away. On the contrary they competed for power with men; they might be notorious in Gregory's eyes, but they are visible in his text. After Gregory the chroniclers of the great noble houses and the monarchy acknowledged women's importance by recording their histories.[3] Joan the Maid was immortalized in both history and legend.[4] Edigna, daughter of Henry I, Princess Isabelle of France, and Jeanne de Valois have had their hagiographers. Women were present in the French annals, chronicles, and histories from the days of Gregory of Tours until the great burst of nineteenth-century scholarship under the Romantics.

Enlightenment history, of course, proved to be the exception. Women's erasure from the learned treatises of the eighteenth century represented not a slight to medieval women but to their age and the intellectual tradition that assigned women the didactic, timeless roles of moral exemplars. This rationalist fastidiousness was sometimes met with resistance from a literate audience desiring the return of their favorite stories from history, so the nineteenth-century Romantic historians exhibited fewer scruples over reassigning women the didactic moral roles of the inherited French tradition. Furthermore, the Romantics could concede medieval women space in their narratives on the grounds that women's social power and prominence were the exotic, flamboyant excess of a primitive stage of Western development.

Still, how could forceful and effective women be accommodated into an interpretive framework that assumed that men were the active agents of historical change? Until the idea came under review in the twentieth century, it was a premise of French historical writing that individuals controlled events, and individualism, a man's province, demanded male agency. If women were to share the capacity to control events, hence history, what limits remained for isolating historical personages out of the countless numbers from the past? Nineteenth-century Romantic historians were as unprepared to deal with such a question as writers of earlier generations, with the added impediment that powerful women were only tolerable at a distance. Closer to the present, the association of *lex salica's* supposed disinheritance of daughters and the emergence of the French state had eliminated women from privileged offices and thus from consideration in the histories that celebrated the growth of a public sphere and the public offices essential to state formation.[5]

An ingenious accommodation was at hand for historians in the nineteenth century who paid careful heed to medieval texts and the use of the feminine made there. The seven industrial arts had been represented as female both in literary works and in stone; those within the north portal at Chartres still solemnly work their crafts. These were joined by the seven female liberal arts, or the seven sciences, the four cardinal virtues or beatitudes, who were sometimes augmented to seven virtues. Of course, the latter were balanced by the corresponding four or seven vices, who were also female. A fund of various characterizations had been devised by medieval authorities embellishing Latinate constructions that expressed abstract qualities in the feminine voice. In some of the medieval glossing of classical texts, complementary female models were portrayed to balance male exemplars. Thus there were seven wise women to balance the seven male sages; nine women worthies were aligned opposite their nine, sometimes ten, male counterparts.[6] Boccaccio in *De claris mulieribus* created an illustrious compendium of women's lives to inspire emulation.[7] Both the literature of *courtesie* and defenders of women in the *querelle des femmes* took up the scheme. Illustrations from the lives of exemplary women became a major literary form aimed at the instruction of the small literate audience and, numerically more significant, their listeners. The virtues, particularly in the instances in which they were presented as virgins, appeared helmeted and armed, doing vigorous battle with the unchaste vices, who were often led by *Libido* and *Luxuria*. Allegory was explicit, not merely suggestive, and it displayed a preference for virtues piling full tilt into battle rather than immobilely displaying their iconography. In 1502 in *La Vie de femmes célèbres,* Antoine Dufour provided Diana, Saint Helena, Minerva, and Joan the Maid freely invented, episodic lives in which generosity of spirit vied with athletic feats for attention.[8] Thus adventure could discharge moral purpose, and the construct was commodious indeed. It offered an explanatory framework for women in numerous roles, enough roles, in sum, to provide a richly textured, if not particularly true or accurate, explanation for forceful women's presence in the historical record.

Feminists from Christine de Pisan to savants in the pay of Anne of Burgundy had praised women. The illustrious in their hands were not necessarily historical personages within recall or within the native historical tradition, however. They were purely imagined in Christine's *Citie des Femmes,* and in the hands of others they increasingly became women recalled from times and places remote from medieval France. In time Zenobia, the queen of Palmyra, came to represent a woman's authority as ruler for an audience that now understood that their Frankish law forbade women that opportunity at home.

This inherited tradition offered Jules Michelet and the Romantic historians of his generation historical figures as alluring as the heroines in popular novels by Madame Cottin, Sir Walter Scott and, by the 1840s, Victor Hugo. Since much popular interest in novels lay in the historical tableaux through which fictional characters moved, historians who desired to be read, and read aloud, lured an audience away from the novelists by filling their histories with authentic people from the past. Relying on inherited characterizations, Romantic historians displayed a certain consistency in their representation of medieval women. Women embodied, if they were historical personages, abstract qualities of an instructive nature; both exemplary, that is, to be imitated, and admonitory, that is, to be understood as cautionary tales. In their pages Temperantia and Justitia became women who had once lived, and Superbia bore many faces. And these women were consistently paired with male figures.

Historians were, then, appropriating rather indiscriminately the literary devices that they encountered in their medieval sources and that had served as instructive devices in their own educations. By linking women who were historical actors to men who possessed equal if not greater claims to making history, the Romantics avoided coming to grips with why medieval women were capable of playing their active roles.[9] Moreover, the complementary male figure allowed the historian, and his reader, to gaze in awe and wonder at viragoes, scholars, queens, and saints, with no implied threat to shared assumptions about propriety and patriarchy. Each powerful woman figure played out her role in correspondence to a man.

The historiographical dilemma posed by women as historical personages and agents of change never surfaced, because the Romantic historian never found it necessary to treat medieval women as autonomous persons who controlled events.

This pairing had a profound impact upon French historiography and upon the public's imagination. Eleanor of Aquitaine was paired with Louis VII or Henry II, and Eloise was coupled so frequently with Abelard that it has been difficult to arouse any interest in her later years as abbess and successful administrator of the Paraclete. Joan the Maid, possibly the most independent of all medieval French women, was similarly paired with her Dauphin. Blanche of Castile was coupled with her son, Louis IX. Who can even think of Clothilde without Clovis? The association has become automatic with the mention of her name. Other European national histories perpetuated similar pairings of female and male saints and of kings and queens; in fact, the tendency is universal, if Claude Levi-Strauss and the structuralist anthropologists who espouse his views are to be believed. Yet the Romantic's use differed substantially from other systems because a complementary alignment was employed more frequently than apposition. A Scholastic or Aristotelian polarizing of men's and women's natures was little valued in nineteenth-century French reconstructions of the past. Pairs became teams in which the male partner occupied historical space achieved by both his own efforts and those of his woman partner.

The French Romantics held to this convention with such consistency that it is difficult to identify an unpaired, historically significant, female figure. Michelet viewed Joan the Maid as a national heroine because he found her energies directed at furthering the Dauphin's cause.[10] Historians of the monarchy rigidly disciplined their depiction of Carolingian and Capetian queenship into the complementary mold. Possibly that widely read and thinly disguised fiction masquerading as history, the *Récits des temps mérovingiens* of Augustin Thierry, most perfectly illustrated this tendency in nineteenth-century historical writing.[11] Women were so completely cast in the complementary mold that in scene after scene they were paired with men. The most powerful male figures juxtaposed to Merovingian women were churchmen. Each scene became a dramatic encounter of virtue and vice interpreted through gender, or of virtue in its various guises, again differentiated and elucidated by gender. Thierry defined character: "Brunhild possessed in the highest degree that vindictive and relentless character whose archetype is personified by the old Germanic poets in a women bearing the same name."[12] He placed words in women's mouths: "Most holy priest, I want to leave this world and take the veil! I entreat you, most holy priest, consecrate me to the lord!"[13] And he attributed motives to women: "Meanwhile, Fredegund—a more determined hater and in any case more energetic than her husband. . . ."[14] The narrative was as gripping as a Romantic novel. Perhaps it was more compelling for readers because it had the ring of historical truth.

Jules Michelet transcended this formula with the same ease with which he moved beyond other conventions in the historical discourse of his own generation. Although efforts to document Ste. Geneviève's historicity had failed to restore her popularity among the French, Michelet succeeded in recasting Joan as a republican and secular saint and, if anything, raised her fortunes as a historical personage for modern generations. Quicherat's scrupulous five-volume documentation of the events surrounding Joan's trial, published in 1841–49, might verify her existence, but Michelet's appeal to a republican audience in 1853 could do much more than that. It could divert attention from the divisive issue of church and state by affirming Joan's secular influence on the growth of the nation.[15]

Joan's history or the tales of Thierry were considered seemly and instructive works, far superior to novels, and so they might be read aloud in schools and even in convents during meals or in periods set aside for recreation.[16] Better still, they could be employed in the bourgeois household for a winter evening's entertainment. The children of the family who had mastered the language sufficiently might take turns reading the works out loud. It fell to history to both affirm new scientific principles for evidence and appeal to a popular audience. Michelet's *The People,* in which vivid portraits of women and men of diverse classes appeared in a boldly sketched historical drama, rich in contexts as well as typologies, produced some of the most brilliant historical writing of the day. But where formula dominated and history was not completely distinguished from fiction, as in Thierry's tales, history only confirmed inherited stereotypes.

France's royal queens fell victim to this stereotyping on more than one occasion. Louise Keralio Robert, a much read and prolific historian, had offered *Les crimes des reines de France* (Paris, 1791) to a reading public ready to believe that queens even prior to Marie Antoinette had exerted a malign influence on the kingdom. Any queen pursuing a forceful role against royal father, husband, or son (and French medieval history offered a whole cast of such women) became in her history a perpetrator of heinous crimes against the French people. If illiterate daughters had fairy tales to acquaint them with the danger of wicked queens, and the pernicious influence of women wielding independent authority, literate daughters had history books in which the lives of royal women instilled the same lesson. The evil queen, acting out her own designs, became a powerful figure in popular imagination.[17]

Just as Romantic historians found it essential to make a reference to the Revolution in their histories, so they found it equally compelling to comment upon French men and women of Gaulic times and the Frankish settlement. But while historians might differ in their interpretation of the Revolution according to their political persuasions, in presenting a historical cast of medieval women they displayed a remarkable concurrence. Even Michelet did not entirely escape the penchant for moralizing. In his early years he had served as tutor to the royal daughters of Louis XVIII, and he did not entirely resist the temptation to instill lessons about the abuses of intimacy and personal access to the monarch by reference to France's increasingly notorious medieval queens. Setting specific educational tasks to a national history that had become a popular literary genre forced a division far deeper than contemporary politics upon the writing of medieval history: men's roles often bore the weight of the new historicity, whereas women's roles still provided moral lessons and appealed to the popular audience.

Lest the Romantics be made to appear less sophisticated than they were, they did not view women's complementary roles as inevitable or imbedded in the natural order of things. They saw those roles as the result of acculturation, a willed accommodation so that modern French society might emerge; historians conceded that they might be purchased at some cost to the individual. When complementary role-playing failed, as it has in more modern times, society had suffered, according to common wisdom. Antoine Léonard Thomas argued that by 1750 the two sexes behaved as if they had "changed characters; the men set too high a value upon personal charms, the women on independence."[18] Such reversals in role-playing were conceded to be within the realm of possibility. They were also widely believed to be detrimental to society, and nineteenth-century Frenchmen were reassured about the vigor of their medieval antecedents in learning that no such reversals had occurred then.

No sooner had these extraordinary characterizations become favorites with the literate public than history itself was reinterpreted. In the last decades of the nineteenth century Leopold von Ranke's influence on French historians triumphed. With the advent of the Third Republic and "scientific" history, women were dropped from the historical texts with bewildering speed. It was not medieval women in themselves whom the new positivists despised, apparently, but the excesses of imaginative reconstruction that they had inspired among the Romantics. As medieval women had gone out of style for a time in the Enlightenment, they again disappeared from the histories written after 1870. The positivists separated their history from the popular Romantic tradition through just such devices as omission of reference to women. The "lively garrulous chronicles," as Fernand Braudel has called them, grew no less narrative in the hands of the triumphant positivists, but new criteria for inclusion were established, and these excised women for the most part.[19] Where characterizations of medieval women had rested much more securely on the medieval literary tradition than upon specific trustworthy sources for a particular woman's life and acts, much could be cut from the history texts. Abstract qualities that had been assigned women could seldom be verified, and the richly textured if suspect characterizations fell away. Charles Morel seldom mentioned women; they did not belong in his record of public, verifiable history.[20] Albert Monot bemoaned the public's indifference to the reformed history; some of its lack of popularity lay in the loss of what he and his fellow positivists had deleted from their accounts. The old characterizations of women had thrilled and dazzled. The new history was dull and pedantic by contrast.[21]

Achille Luchaire, who was less willing to discard the old interests, was among the last historians of the monarchy to consider seriously the question of medieval women and political power. He offered the imaginative, even daring, hypothesis that Capetian rule was institutionally a trinity of king, queen, and dauphin acting in concert.[22] His claims involved cultural and institutional questions not easily investigated applying Rankean criteria construed in a narrow sense, yet it was that narrow construction which Third Republic historians increasingly applied to purge their history of embellishment and grandiloquent claims. The next generation's historian of the monarchy, Charles Petit-Dutaillis of the University of Caen, dealt with queenship and women as little as possible. His institutional history concerned instead the evolution of administrative agency and the course of public history.[23] Life at court, plots, intrigues involving queens and their kin, and like matters were outside the sober concerns of his history, to be sternly remanded to their place. Reform, then, characterized history practiced in the provinces as well as in Parisian centers of learning. With the great multivolume Lavisse series editorial policy decreed standards for inclusion. By the criteria established, many anecdotes and scenes involving women were banished as the gossipmongering of a chronicler or the product of a naive medieval mind.[24] Other evidence from the same source, if it related information on formulation of law or administrative agency, was treated as credible. This canonizing of the historical texts did not banish cherished lore about women altogether, but it did label much of it apocryphal. If women appeared at all they were likely to be in the illustrated Lavisse, in which pictures told a story about historical roles for women no longer confirmed by the text itself. Positivism afforded medieval women a presence only inadvertently: in editing and publishing medieval texts, particularly those related to economic and social history, careful scholarship recorded women's names and their acts, but that historical presence would have to wait for later generations to be interpreted.

Charles Seignobos, duly acknowledged as an eminent medievalist, took his painstaking investigation into areas of research where the problem of women seldom arose. He simply did not encounter women in the sources he chose to investigate.[25] Jules Quicherat had been sufficiently scientific in his approach to Joan the Maid's trial (in his five-volume work published between 1841 and 1849) to escape the condemnations of the positivists, but most other accounts of historically prominent women survived only in popular literature.[26] Ranke, who had inspired the new thinking, fastidiously avoided legend and popular embellishment in his history. The French of the Third Republic would do likewise, even at the cost of leaving prized stories out of their works of history.

After passage of the *loi Camille Sée* providing higher education for women in 1880, young women in the lycées and collèges were introduced to the general histories composed by Charles Seignobos on civilization, and on the Middle Ages, the Renaissance, and the contemporary age. In contrast to daughters of an earlier generation, these young women learned about the past free from references to women's role in history. History lessons about exemplary women were now content for primary schools.[27] Advanced history texts reinforced Sée's purpose that women participate in the regeneration of France by serving as educated, companionate wives and mothers to public men. History texts did so by omission; young women saw in their authoritative texts that the great nation of France had emerged without French women playing any consequential public roles whatsoever.[28]

Thus twentieth-century French historians inherited a dubious tradition on the position of medieval women. The Romantic historian's use of pairing and complementarity, implying as it did that women lived their lives through men and thereby derived their status, distorted and masked much of importance, but it had allowed women to appear in the historical record, to be noted, and to be considered.[29] The positivists had dismissed much of the accumulated wisdom and lore on women as unsubstantiated. Bertrada de Montfort and Constance d'Arles, to mention but two, raised problems of interpretation that historians of the twentieth century no longer felt they could resolve with the freewheeling imaginative flair of former generations. Positivists recognized that in confronting these strong actors at court they would be precipitated headlong into a discussion of family and sexuality and the problematic sources on each. These issues, they believed, more than any others, had proved stumbling blocks for the Romantics who had preceded them. Better to leave the question alone than blunder into imaginative reconstructions of women's thoughts and their personal motivations. Historians resolutely turned their backs on women and composed public history. Women were discredited because the history written about them had been discredited. In such an intellectual environment the barrier between the public and the private spheres, which characterized fin de siècle French society, became an organizing criterion for historical scholarship. Men's deeds surfaced above the barrier, at least those deeds that were verifiably public acts, yet even men's acts were distorted by this selectivity because medieval society had recognized no clear division between a public and a private sphere. Women's deeds were omitted by the same criterion: if acts were identifiably public, on the grounds that it was open to question that women would behave so, and if they were judged to be private acts, in the interests of drawing a curtain of respectability before them. Medieval women came close to disappearing from history altogether, not as a result of their own words and deeds but because the modern world made a distinction that aroused doubts about their acts, and a new sensibility removed them from the scrutiny of history.

These vagaries in medieval women's popularity affected in turn a remarkable revolution in historical writing that occurred in the third and fourth decades of the twentieth century. French social and economic historians, in particular Lucien Febvre and Marc Bloch, repudiated the narrative history of the positivists who had come before them because they found it inadequate, or, to credit their vehemence, irrelevant. Societies, mentalities, sensibilities, the composition of the family, economic trends and conjunctures were to be examined instead. By the fifth decade of the century Fernand Braudel had become a leading figure among these historians. He proposed to write a trailblazing history of the masses.[30] And these voiceless figures who, however unconsciously, created history numbered among them women. In fact, if the positivist history of the preceding generation was to be condemned for what it had failed to examine, certainly the role of women stood out as a glaring example of the overlooked.

Under these circumstances should we expect to find that Fernand Braudel and associated members of the Annales School restored women to the historical record? It appears that there are a number of reasons why it was difficult for them to do so. Certainly some have tried. Andrée and Georges Duby composed a critical historiographical study of St. Joan's biographers.[31] Lucien Febvre, the first and most active proponent of a new method and a new social history, resorted to biography (which in other instances he had condemned as inappropriate for the study of history) because he harbored a fascination with Marguerite de Navarre.[32] In the few instances where the new radical historians did consider women, they dressed their reconstructions in highly traditional garb.[33] Thus we have a history of "man" or mankind that is innovative, even radical, in its approach, accompanied by a brief Annales School history of prominent women that is the very essence of event-oriented, positivist history.

Historians in this new and daring discipline appear to have been oblivious to the fact that they had inherited a positivist tradition for prominent men, which, for all its shortcomings, described roles and social expectations, that is, contributed a step toward delineating gender roles for men, but provided no comparable underpinning for a new social history of women. Even if their debt was often unacknowledged, the new social and economic historians built upon the history of the past, and in the case of the inherited positivist history of medieval men they built upon a sound foundation of carefully researched lives set in the context of the times. This may be one reason why these intellectually venturesome historians fell so easily into writing two histories; their inheritance, unless they turned back to the gifted Michelet, left them little other choice.

In *La Société Féodale* Marc Bloch attempted, in his own words, to analyze and explain the social structure of feudalism and its unifying principles.[34] He saw feudalism's relation to all of medieval life and particularly to family, but when he came to describe this he found it necessary to do so without reference to women for the most part. Women's right of inheritance in feudal law warranted only two paragraphs in his discussion, and many of his related questions outran the capacity of inherited evidence to supply answers. For matronyms, which he regarded with great interest, he made a fleeting reference to St. Joan's testimony at her trial (had he no other example at hand?).[35] For the claims of matriliny he turned to the example of Queen Edith of Wessex.[36] These two, St. Joan and Queen Edith, became the two medieval women among many hundreds of men noted in his magisterial study. The social structures of feudalism and family appear in all their complexity and consequence where the lives of men are employed to elucidate them. As soon as a dimension of the question shifts attention to women's lives or descent through women the discussion shades off into allusions, generalities, and speculation. Marc Bloch simply did not have at his disposal the reconstructed lives of feudal women to use as a basis for his great synthesis.

In lieu of a reconstruction of evolving gender expectations for women, comparable to received knowledge about the roles of medieval men, the new social historians divided in their response, and some substituted current ideas borrowed from related disciplines to apply when the woman question arose. For example, with only a very small historiographical tradition on which to rely for information about women, Rétif de la Bretonne, Emmanuel LeRoy Ladurie's naive anthropologist, was brought forward to serve instead. This commentator employed conventional wisdom to interpret French women for all time within the *topos* of domesticity. Marriage defined women; their relationships to their husbands and families gave purpose and meaning to their existence on earth. The household was their sphere of influence. "When she marries a woman gives up everything to immerse herself in the sorrows and hardships of the household: her only music is the crying of little children, her only dancing when she dandles them; her conversation is to chatter with them as she carries them in her arms wherever she goes."[37] This domestic context may have only become an essential notion for organizing the lives of French women in the eighteenth century but Rétif de la Bretonne had no way to know that.[38] What is somewhat more remarkable is that his admirers among the medieval historians in the Annales school, LeRoy Ladurie in particular, did not realize it either. LeRoy Ladurie appears to be unaware that gender is a socially constructed category, like so many of the others which he has described for us, and that it may change over the long term in significant ways for women as well as for men.

By such formulations gender for women, if not for men, was assumed to be a historical constant, not a dynamic category that had changed in Europe's formative centuries and changed again with the transition into modern times. In similar fashion, the structuralism of Claude Levi-Strauss supplied Fernand Braudel with a device: a simplified and universal formula based again upon the primacy of the household but adding to it a socially necessary exchange of women among households. "Societies have three languages," Claude Levi-Strauss had suggested to Fernand Braudel, "messages, goods and services, and women, who may be exchanged between households."[39] Once adopted, the formula obtained a powerful hold on historical interpretation. In fact, among the Annales School historians, structuralism may have had a more robust life and a longer tenure than within the discipline of anthropology itself. The domestic ideal coupled with a structuralist device simplified the task of interpretation because it reduced complex questions related to understanding women within the contexts of their societies to a mere process of exchange. Thus women in Braudel's pioneering study of the masses, *Capitalism and the Material Life,* need not occasion discussion, and in LeRoy Ladurie's *Montaillou,* Béatrice de Planissoles and her friends may be constrained entirely by the households in which they live. The price paid by overreliance on a structuralist framework has been the careful historicism that differentiated the history of the Annales School from the less time-sensitive social sciences. The interpretation of women here proved an exception. In failing to respect the rigorous historicism advocated by the Annales School, answers to the woman question challenge high ideals through reference to the interpretive mechanisms that are used to account for women.

This also means that certain traditional questions in French historiography remain uninvestigated. If with men's lives Annales School history was constructed on the strong foundation of positivist history, even while it repudiated the concerns of that history, in the case of women no adequate positivist history of even prominent women had been inherited, with the exception of a few saints and a few other notable women. Therefore there has been no history to reform or reinterpret; there has been a vacuum to fill.

Even some general questions about political history and state formation suffer from inadequate attention on this account. There appears to have been one significant office created out of the Carolingian royal household that has eluded analysis by French historians, and that was the office of queen consort. If the English historian Pauline Stafford is correct on the Anglo-Saxon adoption of queenship from current Frankish practice (to replace "king's wife" in Wessex), then the Carolingian court needs investigating so we can understand the creation of the office and its responsibilities and authority.[40] Suzanne Wemple gave the question serious attention in her book *Women in Frankish Society,* although the issue has been largely ignored by French historians.[41] Next the fate of that office under the rule of the Capetians should be examined. The French have published the histories of their queens but as private lives to be studied and wondered at. The office they held has not been a concern of French scholars since Achille Luchaire originally asserted that early Capetian rule was not a monarchy but a trinity involving the participation of king, queen consort, and dauphin.[42] The relationship of king and dauphin has dominated studies of the monarchy without attention being paid to the third party of the queen. Since the development and then the dismantling of the offices of queen followed a separate course, distinct from the evolution of the offices of monarch and dauphin, the history of queenship needs to be reconstructed apart from the others and then integrated with them in order to reach a general understanding of the formation of royal authority and the growth of the state.[43]

At the moment when Henry II held Eleanor of Aquitaine in jail for revolt in supporting her younger son's claims to inherit her lands, the third wife of Louis VII, Adele de Champagne, led a revolt with her brothers against her son, Philip II. Both responded to an older, less centralized notion of royal office than that advocated by the king, and both held very different assumptions about women's proper roles from those now held by historians who look back upon their behavior. Because both lost to the centralizing power of an increasingly powerful monarchy, the office of queen changed and with it the nature of monarchical institutions themselves.[44] This is the necessary background for understanding the issue of Salic law that dominated French politics in the later Middle Ages. Based upon a greatly altered office of queen, the lawyer's claim that an ancient Frankish prohibition blocked inheritance of the throne through the female line, as well as women's accession to the throne, could gain currency.[45]

Among medieval historians writing today, few write on the importance of social history and the institution of marriage as sensitively and wisely as Georges Duby. He says of marriage in France's formative age,

> It is through the institution of marriage, through the rules governing marriage and the way those rules are applied, that human societies control the future. . . . Through marriage, societies try to maintain and perpetuate their own structures, seen in terms of a set of symbols and of the image they have of their own ideal perfection. The rites of marriage are instituted to ensure an orderly distribution of the women among the men; to regulate competition between males for females; to 'officialize' and socialize procreation. . . . [Marriage] distinguishes lawful unions from others and gives their progeny the status of heirs—i.e., it gives the offspring ancestors, a name, and rights. Marriage establishes relations of kinship. It underlies the whole society and is the keystone of the social edifice.[46]

And he commits himself to understanding the role of women within this system. "Such was the role assigned to women in the great parade of this chivalric male society. A woman was an object, a valuable object carefully guarded because of all the advantages that could be obtained through her."[47] In the course of the eleventh and twelfth centuries he sees marriage evolve in significant ways at the highest social levels, and he gives a thorough report of how this affected men or, by his own definition, society. There was no corresponding change in social expectations for women in his discussion, but then women are pawns within his construct rather than participants in the chivalric world. He attempts to explain that women lost rights over these two centuries, but his oddly ahistorical women remain largely out of focus, so the relation of that loss is not entirely persuasive. Georges Duby returns often to the task of reconciling feudal women to his definition of society. If Elizabeth de Jaligny comported herself bravely in defending the castle of which she was in charge it is not because of herself, rather, "Her honor came from men. . . . She owed it to these reflected merits to be active; the text explicitly says that it was this 'manly boldness' which made her free of feminine weaknesses."[48] Assigning Elizabeth masculine traits to assure her the 'female' agency of which he searches seems to leave Duby dissatisfied with an inherited framework that defines men as society and women as their reflected shadows or articles of exchange. Despite a lack of women's clear voices in chronicles devoted to men's houses, he senses some historical agency in the chronicler's traditional opinions. Projected public and private spheres do not contain Duby's medieval world, and that places him today close to where Jules Michelet stood over a century ago, contemplating the anomalous elements of the medieval world, where women's acts surprise. The anomalous or surprising may serve as an entry point for understanding an age. In moving beyond structures of the household Duby may return historical agency to women and make them as essential as men are within French historical discourse, ending that caprice of fashion that has determined medieval women's fortunes.

The lack of interpretive framework to apply to women lives in the general histories is remediable because of the existence of an excellent corpus of scholarly literature on questions that can help delineate medieval women's roles. Word for word, page for page, perhaps more has been written about medieval French women in scholarly journals and monographs than about women in any other national historical tradition. The biographies of French women have not always been filled with romantic exaggeration; some were serious works of scholarship.[49] Régine Pernoud, writing for a popular and a scholarly audience, has synthesized contemporary scholarship to highlight the roles medieval women have played (see bibliography). Under the rubric of private law, women and women's rights in marriage have been investigated in a scholarly fashion for over a century. Until now all subsumed under *loi privé* may have stood outside the concerns of general history, but to a generation which acknowledges that historical achievements may be constructed in the private sphere and that the Middle Ages recognized no such division, the distinction no longer pertains.

Women's rights in canon and civil law, as unmarried, married, or widowed women, their families, their dowries, their inheritance rights and authority over offspring, their educations, religious practices, and their pasttimes have received substantial attention from French scholars. As objects of Provencal courtly love tributes, yet seldom as writers themselves, they have been studied.[50] Women of France have a history. It is a scholarly history in which historians of varying political persuasions have participated, but it is a history that has not often influenced general interpretations and has not yet modified opinion about the movement of history to any great degree. This want could be remedied. If the historical literature on French women were employed to restore women from being exchange tokens to full members of society, to understand that women's lives are subject to change over time, and to come to terms with women as historical agents, women's history could serve, as men's has, as a foundation for evermore encompassing, synthetic studies of social institutions.

Women as historians, if not as a subject of history, have been less constrained by the whim of fashion in French intellectual life. That has been particularly true in the twentieth century among social and economic historians. Elizabeth Carpentier became an early member of the reforming Annales School, uncovering rhythms of family and household as they pertained to women, within her epidemiological studies. Currently Christine Klapisch-Zuber brings to the Centre de recherches historiques a perspective on the households of Renaissance Italy that attaches great importance to women who have been long overlooked. Young Marxist women have joined together to edit the journal *Penelope,* which has as its stated aim the restoration of French women to history.[51] With women participating in historical interpretation perhaps a new revolution is in the making and the women of France's formative age will no longer confound by their forceful presence and will at last win a place in the history books that style cannot dismiss.

From the Enlightenment to the present, French historical writing has been enriched, assuredly, by foreign influence, but, more critically, by resort to its own great intellectual tradition and by the stimulant of embarking upon sudden and brilliant departures in interpretive ventures. Inspired always by the desire for elegance in the formulation of ideas, true to the quest for Cartesian clarity in any construct that they place upon history,

French historians, perhaps more than others, are capable of distinguishing between their own discourse on history and the reality of the past they hope to recover. Now when historiography is moving beyond the Annaliste structures that have opened a new world to us, where change in *la longue durée* overwhelms the acts of privileged men in determining the future, medieval women may find their interpreters.

Notes

1. *History of the Franks, by Gregory, Bishop of Tours, Selections,* trans. Ernest Brehaut (New York, 1965). French works will be cited in translation in the notes wherever possible. French editions may be noted in the bibliography. Names of women have been given according to common American usage. St. Joan, Eleanor of Aquitaine, and Eloise are given in the English version of their names, Christine de Pisan in French as she is commonly known, and so forth.

2. David Schaps, "The Women Least Mentioned, Etiquette and Women's Names," *Classical Quarterly,* 27:2 (1977), 323–30, is useful to acquaint the reader with the idea in classical literature.

3. Georges Duby's extensive works on northern France are a good introduction; see in particular *The Chivalrous Society,* trans. Cynthia Poston (Berkeley, 1977); the original French, *La société aux XIe et XIIe siècles dans la région mâconnaise* (Paris, 1963). On the chroniclers of St. Denis, Gabrielle Spiegel provides an excellent introduction in *The Chronicle Tradition of Saint Denis* (Brookline, MA, 1978).

4. See, for example, Alphonse Equiros, *Les Vierges martyres* (Paris, 1842). Marina Warner, *Joan of Arc: The Image of Female Heroism* (New York, 1981), is an excellent introduction to the Joan literature over the centuries.

5. Alexander C. Murray, *Germanic Kinship Structures* (Toronto, 1983) pp. 115–34 provides a recent review of the debate over editing the *lex salica* and how it was colored by the late medieval controversy over inheritance of the French crown through the female line. We may, of course, speculate on childhood influences on all France's historians in regard to women's disinheritance. In their scholarly interpretations French historians acknowledge that "no woman nor her son can succeed to the monarchy" was a fourteenth-century understanding of the ancient Frankish law, but nevertheless the "Salic law," as it was known to every schoolboy, could have worked at some deeper level to undermine confidence in women's capacity to assume authoritative roles in the medieval era.

6. Geoffrey Chaucer, *Canterbury Tales,* ed. A. C. Cawley (London, 1975), uses the list of the nine wise women in the Wife of Bath's Tale.

7. Giovanni Boccaccio, *Concerning Famous Women,* trans. Guido A. Guavino (New Brunswick, NJ, 1963). For comment on Boccaccio's attitude toward women, see Marshall Brown, "In the Valley of Ladies," *Italian Quarterly,* 18 (1975), 33–52.

Christine de Pisan, *The Book of the City of Ladies,* trans. E. J. Richards (New York, 1982), adds a feminist voice to the debate. See Joan Kelly, "Early Feminist Theory and the Querelle des Femmes, 1400–1789," *Signs,* 8 (1982), 4–28 and Ian Maclean, *The Renaissance Notion of Woman* (Cambridge, MA, 1982) for a discussion of both male and female feminists on women embodying the abstract qualities.

8. Antoine Dufour, *La Vie des femmes célèbres,* published with an introduction by G. Jeanneau (Geneva, 1970).

9. This is one reason why Joan may have survived as a historical figure when Geneviève did not. Ste. Geneviève as savior of Paris continues to be viewed as a single figure, although she was reburied beside Clovis, giving her something of the status of consort. On modern reconstructions of her historical role, see Charles Kohler, *Etude critique . . . sur Geneviève* (Paris, 1881); A. D. Sertillanges, *Sainte Geneviève* (Paris, 1917); and Henri Lesêstre, *Sainte Geneviève* (Paris, 1900).

10. Jules Michelet, *Joan of Arc,* trans. Albert Guerard (Ann Arbor, MI, 1957). First published as *Jeanne d'Arc* (Paris, 1853). It is important to remember that Jules Michelet, skilled literary craftsman as well as historian, could often satisfy two audiences at once, with men's history fulfilling the criteria of the new historicism and women's histories appealing to the literate public that would buy history books. In that gender division Joan inhabited medium ground, drawing upon both the historicism characterizing Michelet's treatment of men and the drama he employed to characterize historical women.

11. Augustin Thierry, *Tales of the Early Franks, Episodes from Merovingian History,* trans. M. F. O. Jenkins (University City, AL, 1977). Originally *Récits des temps mérovingiens précédés de considérations sur l'histoire de France* (Paris, 1840).

12. Ibid., p. 411.

13. Speech attributed to Radegund, ibid., p. 115.

14. Ibid., p. 60.

15. For the influence of Vico and the "New Science" on Jules Michelet, see the essay in this collection by Diane Owen Hughes, "Invisible Madonnas? The Italian Historiographical Tradition and the Women of Medieval Italy."

16. Jules Michelet, *Joan of Arc;* Jules Quicherat, *Procès de condamnation et de réhabilitation de Jeanne d'Arc dite la Pucelle* (Paris, 1841–9). On Ste. Geneviève as a historical figure, see note 9.

17. See Bonnie Smith, *Ladies of the Leisure Class* (Princeton, 1981). The habit of reading out loud was common in affluent bourgeois households and in convents. Jules Michelet, *The People,* trans. Joan P. McKey (Urbana, IL, 1973), first French edition; *Le peuple* (Paris, 1846); see also his *Woman,* trans. J. Palmer (New York, 1873), first French edition, *La femme* (Paris, 1860); and *Le prêtre, la femme et la famille* (Paris, 1845). On the treatment of women by the Romantics see the special issue of *Romantisme* (Paris, Revue de la Société des Etudes romantiques, p. 13, 1976).

18. Antoine Léonard Thomas, *Essays on the Character, Manners, and Genius of Women in Different Ages,* enlarged from the French of M. Thomas by Mr. Russell,

2 vols. (Philadelphia, 1774). On this subject Traian Stoianovich has made some comments in "Gender and Family," *History Teacher,* 15:1 (1981), 77.

19. Fernand Braudel, *Capitalism and Material Life* (New York, 1976), p. xv; original French title, *Civilisation matérielle et capitalisme* (Paris, 1967).

20. From his position as editor of *Revue critique d'histoire et de litterature,* Charles Morel set standards for verification and critical examination of sources. See his *Genève et la colonie de Vienne* (Geneva, 1888) and with Jules Nicole, *Archives militaires du 1er siècles* (Geneva, 1900).

21. Richard Keylor, *Academy and Community* (Cambridge, MA, 1975), p. 2. Keylor asserts that medievalists of the Third Republic led the reform of history to positivism in the era after the Franco-Prussian War. For Albert Monot, see *La plus ancienne ville de la France, Vienne (Isère), la Rome des Gaules* (Lyons, 1904).

22. Achille Luchaire, *Histoire des institutions monarchiques de la France sous le premiers Capetiens,* 2nd ed. (Paris, 1891), p. 133. See also Marion Facinger, "A Study of Medieval Queenship: Capetian France," *Studies in Medieval and Renaissance History,* 5 (1968), 3–48.

23. Keylor, *Academy and Community,* p. 137; he also rejected the "excessive emphasis" on a number of theories and systems in the work of former generations. As such he represents the extreme in historical empiricism. Charles Petit-Dutaillis, *Histoire de France depuis les origines jusqu'à la revolution* (Paris, 1900) and *La monarchie féodale en France et en Angleterre* (Paris, 1933).

24. Ernest Lavisse and Alfred Rambaud, eds., *Histoire général de IVe siècle à nos jours,* 12 vols. (Paris, 1892–1901).

25. Charles Seignobos, *Histoire politique de l'Europe* (Paris, 1924) and *La Méthode historique appliquée aux sciences sociales* (Paris, 1901). Besides his scholarly general works, Seignobos composed a two-volume*Histoire de la civilisation* to be used in the lycées for women, which opened in 1880. See *Histoire de la civilisation dans l'antiquité jusqu'au temps de Charlemagne* (Paris, 1885) and *Histoire de la civilisation au Moyen Age et dans les temps moderns* (Paris, 1887). His lack of reference to women seems all the more striking since he wrote for the instruction of women. Besides Keylor see Claude Digeon, *La crise allemande de la pensée française* (Paris, 1959); Robert Smith, *Ecole Normale Supérieure and the Third Republic* (Albany, 1982); and for a list of normaliens including historians influenced by the curriculum, see *Association amicale des anciens élèves de l'Ecole Normale Supérieure* (Paris, 1969).

26. Jules Quicherat, *Procès de condamnation et de réhabilitation de Jeanne d'Arc dite la Pucelle.*

27. On the education of French women in both primary and advanced education, see Linda Clark, *Schooling the Daughters of Marianne* (Albany, 1983) and Laura Struminger, *What Were Little Girls Made Of?* (Albany, 1982).

28. Karen Offen, "The Second Sex and the Baccalaureat in Republican France, 1880–1924," *French Historical Studies,* 13 (1983), 252–86; Françoise Mayeur, *L'Enseignement secondaire des jeunes filles sous la Troisième République* (Paris, 1977).

29. On the role of complementarity and apposition in the European intellectual tradition, see Ian MacLain, *The Renaissance Notion of Woman* (Cambridge, 1980). On classical thought see G. E. R. Lloyd, *Analogy and Polarity* (Cambridge, 1966).

30. Fernand Braudel, *Capitalism and the Material Life,* p. xv. For the Annales School approach to women, see Susan Mosher Stuard, "The Annales School and Feminist History," *Signs: Journal of Women in Culture and Society,* 7 (1981) 135–43.

31. Andrée and Georges Duby, *Les Procès de Jeanne d'Arc* (Paris, 1962).

32. Lucien Febvre, "Autour de l'Heptaméron—amour sacre, amour profane," *Nouvelle Revue Française* (1944).

33. Natalie Zemon Davis, "'Women's History' in Transition: The European Case," *Feminist Studies* 8 (1976), 83–103. For further historiographical studies, see note 49.

34. Marc Bloch, *Feudal Society,* trans. L. A. Manyon, 2 vols. (Chicago, 1964), see Introduction, p. xix.

35. Ibid., p. 138.

36. Ibid., p. 432.

37. Emmanuel LeRoy Ladurie, "Rétif de la Bretonne as a Social Anthropologist," *The Mind and Method of the Historian,* trans. Siân Reynolds and Ben Reynolds (Chicago, 1981), 264.

38. Charles-Jean-Marie Le Tourneau, *La condition de la femme dans les diverses civilisations,* Bibliothèque sociologique internationale, 26 (Paris, 1903), encapsulates much of this thinking. For antecedents see Adolphe Thiers, "De la famille," *Almanach du cultivateur dauphinois pour l'année 1850,* pp. 60–62; see also Madame Guizot, *Lettres de familles sur l'education* (Paris, 1954). There are other works too numerous to cite, for example, Madame de Remusat on the education of women (1824) and Josef-Alexandre de Ségur on women (1803).

39. Fernand Braudel, "History and the Social Sciences," in *Economy and Society in Early Modern Europe,* ed. Peter Burke (New York, 1972), pp. 11–42.

40. Pauline Stafford, "The King's Wife in Wessex," *Past and Present,* 91 (1981), 3–27.

41. Suzanne Wemple, *Women in Frankish Society* (Philadelphia, 1981).

42. Luchaire, *Histoire des institutions monarchiques,* p. 133.

43. Beyond early work by Marion Facinger, the work of Spiegel and Wemple cited in the preceding notes, and that of Elizabeth Brown, see Harriet L. Lightman, *Sons and Mothers, Queens and Minor Kings in French Constitutional Law,* (Ph.D. diss., Bryn Mawr College, 1981) and Françoise Barry, *La reine de France* (Paris, 1964).

44. For example, Elizabeth Brown has turned her attention toward the question of the feudal rights of Capetian queens in "Queens, Regencies and Royal Power in Thirteenth and Fourteenth Century France," paper delivered at the American Historical Association, Washington, DC, December 27–30, 1982. See also "Royal Marriage, Royal Property, and the Patrimony of the Crown: In-

alienability and the Prerogative in Fourteenth Century France," *Humanities Working Paper 70* (Division of the Humanities and Social Sciences, California Institute of Technology, Pasadena, January, 1982).

45. A grounding in comparative study of family and role expectations for women in the barbarian law codes is essential here as well. See Alexander C. Murray, *Germanic Kinship Structures*. The direction followed by Murray may be traced back to Bertha Phillpotts, *Kindred and Clan in the Middle Ages and After* (Cambridge, 1913).

46. Georges Duby, *Le chevalier, la femme, et le prêtre* (Paris, 1981), translated as *The Knight, The Lady, and the Priest* by Barbara Bray (New York, 1983), pp. 17–18.

47. Ibid., p. 234.

48. Ibid., p. 232.

49. There has been an attempt to use biography to uncover the lives of medieval women in a manner as scholarly as that applied to men's biographies. Maurice Bardeche,*L'histoire des femmes.* 2 vols(Paris, 1968), remains a standard work. André Lehmann, *La rôle de la femme dans l'histoire de France au moyen âge* (Paris, 1952) represents another widely cited text. Evelyne Sullerot has shown interest in the antecedents to modern women's roles in *Le fait feminin* (Paris, 1978), but she allowed herself to be guided almost entirely by Annales School historians for the medieval and early modern centuries. The Jean Bodin Society has encouraged the study of women in medieval French society; see its 1962 volume on women.

50. See Bibliography under France, Culture, for a full list of titles.

51. See Christine Fauré, "L'Absente," *Temps modernes* 410 (September, 1980), 502–513. (For a translation see *Signs: Journal of Women in Culture and Society,* 7 (1981), 125–35. On contemporary French feminism see *French Feminist Criticism,* ed. Elissa D. Gelfand and Virginia Hules (New York, 1984) and *New French Feminisms: An Anthology,* ed. Elaine Marks and Isabelle de Courtivron (New York, 1981); Olwen Hufton, "Women in History: The Early Modern Period," *Past and Present,* 101 (1983), 125–41.

4

A New Dimension? North American Scholars Contribute Their Perspective

SUSAN MOSHER STUARD

In North America, over three generations and by an indirect route, a new perspective on the role of women in medieval society has appeared. It now exerts some influence on general understandings of European history, and it constitutes a perspective in which the historical profession may take some pride and which feminists may value and respect. At first glance it may seem more a matter of chance than an intentional challenge to Old World interpretations that this new direction in scholarship has been advanced, but that appearance may be deceptive. It may mask distinctive features in the organization of higher learning in the United States and Canada and important differences in the structuring of historical studies this side of the Atlantic. But surely it would be difficult to make a case for conscious intent. The accomplishment seems to consist in roughly equal parts of the brashness of young nations encountering the high tradition of European learning, incomplete assimilation of the interests governing positivist history (although Americans wrote positivist history perfectly well), and a genuine impulse to rethink the medieval past and apply its lessons in the New World. If, for this development in North American scholarship, it is impossible to make a case for conscious intent, surely disclaimers are not in order either.

New world feminism began early enough in Boston to influence historical scholarship and early in its own course recognized the importance of medieval women. Paulina Wright Davis writing in *The Una* before the Civil War argued that paradoxically women's journey back to the Middle

Ages was a journey of progress. Then women had been physicians and notaries and held positions of authority, whereas in the nineteenth century their only job opportunities were the classroom and the factory at slave wages.[1] But this hard-headed approach to an age best known to the American reading public through the Romantic novels of Sir Walter Scott had no direct influence on the fledgling profession of medieval historical studies that began soon after the Civil War. Feminist influence, if felt at all, was indirect. In championing higher education for women, feminism inspired the founding of women's colleges, in which young women could study the history of all ages.

In America's new colleges women pursued the same curriculum as men and studied under historians who were likely to be men trained abroad in the German methods of historical analysis proudly touted as positivism, the "new scientific history." One such medievalist, Herbert Baxter Adams, divided his teaching year between Johns Hopkins University and Smith College after the latter was founded in the 1870s. Adams believed history was the study of documents and saw to it that his Smith women and his Johns Hopkins men pursued careful research projects. He also believed the medieval past should be made relevant through investigations into the underlying political and social institutions that the New World had inherited from the Old. Setting his students to investigate and report on these, and writing on them himself in "The German Origins of New England Villages," Herbert Baxter Adams used the curriculum to heighten interest in a European cultural heritage. Women students were made aware of the relevance of studying the Middle Ages because in the hands of this skilled teacher of history they were put in touch with the past. Not all historical personages women students encountered in the study of history were men, and some medieval institutions presented by Adams permitted women's participation. In his four years of teaching at Smith College, Adams encouraged women to pursue medieval history and recommended two women to continue for the Ph.D. degree.[2]

His more famous contemporary Henry Adams was also led to medieval scholarship through the challenge of pedagogy, but the Harvard College curriculum to which he turned his efforts placed distinctly different demands upon him. Unlike Herbert Baxter Adams, who had been thoroughly trained in Rankean methods and medieval history at the University of Leipzig, Henry Adams had pursued only two years of advanced historical training in Germany and studied only modern history. In 1870 when President Elliot of Harvard drafted him to present a bridge of medieval lectures between Professor Gourney's classical course and Professor Torrey's modern one, Henry Adams demurred on the grounds that he knew no medieval history, but Elliot prevailed and Henry Adams began to read documents as his brief training at Leipzig had prescribed. The result was History One, or the prototype of the American survey source.[3] By his own admission Henry Adams possessed no text and could discern no great truth with which to edify his students, yet by 1876 he had created his own interpretive framework, which anticipated contemporary understanding of mentalities in uncanny ways. With all the brashness of youth he entered the field of cultural and social history and turned to the condition of women as a way of monitoring the state of health of Western society. In 1876 he was ready to challenge European authorities and, more significantly, prevailing Victorian notions on the evolution of primitive societies by reference to Europe's Barbaric Age. His Lowell lecture that year on "The Primitive Rights of Women" was presumptuous: he attacked John F. MacLennan's respected and popular *Primitive Marriage* by implication, and Henry Maine's authoritative study of *Ancient Law* directly. He offered an unsentimental review of the law, chronicles, and sagas that anticipated our contemporary formulations on gender in important ways.[4]

Adams had come to the conclusion that a "social balance" had existed between men and women in Germanic society: a parity qualified solely by a woman's subjection to guardianship. "A woman could not go to war" he asserted, that is, she risked her property and legal rights if she did so. He challenged established authority on the role of the Church: "Historians . . . have . . . assumed the elevation of women from what was supposed to have been their previous condition of degradation and servitude was due to the humanitarian influence of the Church. In truth the share of the Church in the elevation of women was for the most part restricted." He goes on to be far more critical by asserting that the Church abhorred most strong women and over time actually forced a diminution of women's rights. This was unorthodox enough, but he asserted next that the "social balance" between the sexes, particularly in the family, explains Europe's dynamic pattern of growth, yet, paradoxically, the balance was thrown out of equilibrium by the "exigencies of a pressing immediate necessity," that is, state building. He concluded with a dire warning: we must revitalize the family by restoring the social balance between the sexes. Not to do so will carry us down the road to ruin as Rome was ruined; to do so will hasten the dawn of the bright new age.[5]

His morally uplifting conclusion might shock, but it could also appeal to a Boston audience that relished a call to reform. It turned on its head the European nations' argument that their treatment of women was a proof of the west's superiority over decadent or primitive peoples and an imperative to enlighten and reform others. But Adams's view also constituted an original contribution to medieval scholarship, I would argue, because Adams saw gender as a historical product, and subject to change over time, and he viewed its shifts as integral to other changes in society over the long term. Interest in the long term was, in some degree, a response to the challenge of the survey course he presented, and in that sense his pedagogy inspired his scholarship. But his insight did not in its turn inform his teaching of history. In his attempt to echo the categories introduced by Gourney in his classical lectures and carried forward by Torrey on the modern era, Adams suppressed his own ideas about causation and presented a chronology of reigns, wars, and administrative milestones. He did not teach about women, culture, and society; he taught public history, a failure by his own admission.

Adams met failure in his private life in the same years and the weight of it led him to abandon his autobiography; he did not return to the task of examining his successes and failures for twenty years.[6] By that time he had achieved an accommodation with the values of his age and found another formulation on the woman question. In *Mont St. Michel and Chartres* and later with his famous metaphor of the Virgin and the Dynamo, Henry Adams stressed medieval women's elevation in step with society's increased refinement. This conformed much more closely to the values of his Victorian audience and consequently these were the ideas for which he became known. Adams's original interpretations, that is, that parity between the sexes had once existed in the West and that considering women's position in society had the capacity to force reinterpretation of the age, were lost to all but a few.

Instead, most North American medievalists in the young discipline espoused current ideas about causality in history and accepted the lead of European authorities. For women, if they were considered at all, civilization brought progress understood as refinement, the Church served to elevate women's status in European society, and patriarchy, often synonymous in Victorian circles with advanced moral order, brought substantial benefits to women as well as to men. But if this represented the view of the majority, Henry Adams's radical early position did not disappear altogether. One scholar in particular kept his original idea alive, and thus she mounted a challenge to common assumptions about women's past and to generally held views within the historical profession. Florence Griswold Buckstaff, first woman regent of the University of Wisconsin and an organizer of social welfare services in that state, had prepared in medieval history.[7] After graduation from the University of Wisconsin in 1883 she pursued graduate study in history in Cambridge, Massachusetts (her obituary coyly refused to note the institution of higher learning). She published "Married Women's Property Rights in Anglo-Saxon and Anglo-Norman Law" in the *Annals of the American Academy* in 1886.[8] This work emphasized early rights of women and a loss of positive legal rights for them in England after the Norman conquest. Florence Griswold Buckstaff left the field of medieval studies, but it is clear that her scholarship on early Europe informed her social activism. Her published study added some scholarly references to Adams's innovative but less than fully substantiated thesis on medieval women presented in the Lowell lecture of 1876.

Adams's and Buckstaff's ideas in turn played into the interests of a Stanford University historian, George E. Howard. His extensive researches during the last decade of the nineteenth century resulted in a three-volume history of matrimonial institutions that he published in 1904.[9] He became the United States's leading authority on the history of marriage as a result, and his strong advocacy of divorce as a right for women was based upon his understanding of women's former right to divorce in the common law tradition. His longitudinal approach associated the loss of such rights with other social evils, and his careful scholarship was deemed sufficient authority to promote his stand on divorce in a number of states. Reform followed, providing a striking example of the practical application of historical scholarship to American life.[10] Howard was a major influence on Mary Roberts Smith Coolidge, whose *Why Women Are So* helped launch modern research into the acculturation of women. Coolidge adopted a position that prevailed among some pioneering social scientists of the day: that human nature is highly plastic and influenced by social conditions in different times and places.[11] The long term of change in women's condition in the West presented in Howard's study affected Griswold's thinking.

In America, where faculties were gathered into collegial disciplines, a historical argument that carried little weight within its own established profession might find a responsive audience elsewhere. In such a manner the original idea suggested by Adams and researched by Buckstaff was taken up and developed by fledgling departments of the social sciences. Within a few years it was buttressed further by the painstaking scholarship of the British historian, Bertha Phillpotts, whose *Kindred and Clan in the Middle Ages* (1913) thoroughly characterized the early world in which women had played their consequential roles.[12] This work came recommended by its own air of authoritative English scholarship (endorsed by publication at Cambridge University Press), so it did not matter that it languished on the shelves of European libraries and was allowed to go out of print. In the quest for the legitimizing function American scholars sought from serious European scholarship, the imprimateur was sufficient. Fortunately, Bertha Phillpotts's scholarship was formidable and her arguments could stand on their own. American scholars had conclusive historical evidence that women had once held positive legal rights that they had long since lost.

This scholarly pursuit at the junction of the high tradition of historical writing and the new concerns of the social sciences continued through the first wave of twentieth-century American feminism. In new departments at respected women's colleges like Barnard, and in major universities where women were accepted in graduate programs, scholars ventured the idea that gender roles were socially constructed and had their roots in specific historical conditions. For the most part this work was pursued in the new scholarly disciplines, not within departments of history. Elsie Clews Parsons had originally looked to history but she found the discipline of anthropology more accommodating for the sorts of questions she wished to raise about societies. Ruth Benedict had attempted to write the history of prominent women such as Mary Wollstonecraft, but she grew frustrated at the inability of biography to produce the answers that she sought and she trained in anthropology.[13] The new social sciences were pursued by thinkers who had made a conscious decision that interpretive framework was more critical to their investigations than the field of study. For this reason the case for gender as a socially constructed category was more likely to be argued in reference to remote stateless societies rather than by reference to Europe's formative age.

This highly pragmatic approach was not chosen by all aspiring scholars, however. Herbert Baxter Adams, the inspiring teacher who had recommended two of his original Smith College women for the history Ph.D., had his successors. Professors encouraged women to pursue the high tradition of historical study of the Middle Ages, and in one fashion or another convinced women that their questions would find answers in the documents of history. This essentially philological approach to history was presented to students as neutral in regard to gender and all similar cultural artifacts, and, through applying the strict rules of Rankean positivism, capable of revealing whatever reality lay embedded in the early records of the European past. One might argue that this was a naively idealistic view of the purposes to which positivist history was to be directed and that the historical profession in general had no particular desire for reappraisals of history from young and untried American scholars who had the further disadvantage of being female. Such considerations, however, did not prevent women from entering the historical profession. Women expected to be accepted on the strength of their scholarship and of their careful reconstructions of the past. And women were, to a surprising degree, capable of finding their way as medieval historians and respected scholars in the North American university system.

Within the profession, women historians took up important posts in institutions of higher learning, and many of these successful scholars had been trained as medievalists. Helen Cam at Harvard University and Sylvia Thrupp at the University of Michigan were sole women in departments of history and they were both medievalists.[14] Later Marie Boroff occupied the same sole position in medieval studies and comparative literature at Yale University. Catherine Boyd published her dissertation on Cistercian nuns and taught at Carleton College. Katherine Fisher Drew edited the Lombard laws and chaired her history department at Rice University. Emily Hope Allen never completed her degree but provided the notes for the first published edition of Margery Kempe's autobiography.[15] Mt. Holyoke provided her institutional identification regardless of an uncompleted degree. It also provided a professorship for Nelly Neilson, who pioneered studies in medieval agriculture and served as the first woman president of the American Historical Association.[16] Emily Putnam produced her important study, *The Lady,* and then became dean, next president, of Barnard College.[17]

If North America could not train sufficient women medievalists it could count on England to supply a few. Eleanor Shipley Duckett, a Cambridge-trained medievalist, transferred her scholarly interests to women in the Middle Ages and her home to the United States. Her own estimates of her chances of being taken seriously were not optimistic, yet she continued to study early medieval culture and to write about women who, for the variety of roles they played and the latitude permitted them, were exotic and exceptional by twentieth-century standards.[18]

Before World War II, when women were not well represented in the American Historical Association, the Mediaeval Academy of America enrolled women at roughly twenty to forty percent of membership.[19] The determined interdisciplinary stance of the Academy made this possible; women were generally better represented in the literary disciplines than in history, but women historians clustering in the medieval field became members as well. Helen Wieruszowski, a historian, served as president of the Academy for a term. Women served on the editorial and advisory boards of *Speculum,* and their works were published as contributions to the monograph series of the Academy from the very beginning.[20]

These women did not necessarily enter the historical profession with the same interests as women who brought their feminist researches to other fields of social science, of course. If Helen Cam found anything interesting to investigate about women it is not clear from her published works on the history of the law, the state, and bureaucracy, except possibly in the title she chose for her textbook, *England before Elizabeth.* But other women in medieval history studied social and economic history, the early sagas and epics with their casts of women characters, the early law codes with their positive legal rights for women, and early European institutions like double monasteries that were dominated by women. Their scholarly products were, for the most, securely in the mainstream of positivist history: the thoroughly researched monograph and the well-edited text were women's contributions to medieval scholarship. It could be argued that this was a thin positivism in some cases because it was accompanied by no effort to force a reinterpretation of the general course of medieval times based upon the cumulative evidence. But, since this scholarly literature was very respectable and, in fact, respected by the profession, it could not be entirely ignored.

Positivism's neutrality, directed toward uncovering all the documented evidence from the early European centuries, was a two-edged sword. If its concerns had been "public" history, it could just as well have suppressed information about medieval women, but in this instance it was directed in precisely the opposite direction. Without a question much of the history written in North America, like positivist history written elsewhere, directed attention away from women. Yet the history written by some well-established historians in the field uncovered information about women's roles, their lives, and their positive legal rights. Added to the scholarship on women produced in England, it could provide in some instances almost as substantive a cumulative history of women as the cumulative history of medieval men.

Some women scholars, then, chose this path, pursued the discipline of history, and trusted to the positivism that had been presented to them in their student years as a scholarly weapon with the capacity to set the historical record straight. These women believed in the force of history, and perhaps in the isolation of the New World they were free to do so. The scholarship that Americans produced pleased European historians, not because of its findings necessarily but because it confirmed Europeans' own belief in the consequence of their medieval past. But if English historians could ignore works written by Bertha Phillpotts, Georgiana Hill, and Alice Clark on medieval women, they would not have trouble ignoring what American scholars had to say on the same subject.[21] Continental historians were less than eager to bridge the language barrier to read monographs produced by American scholars, particularly when they did not see the consequence of learning about medieval women in the first place. Americans were welcome to participate in European medieval studies through visiting Europe, studying, and doing research there, but Old World scholars did not necessarily believe they needed Americans to interpret the medieval past to them.

With conscious intent or less fully articulated motives, American medievalists who prided themselves on the full general picture of the Middle Ages that they presented in the classroom continued to raise the subject of medieval women for their students. Barbara Kreutz, former graduate dean at Bryn Mawr College, noted of her training at University of Wisconsin with Robert Reynolds and Gaines Post that both men encouraged her to explore the lives of medieval women. "Both of them when writing history, followed the scholarly mode of their day . . . but as teachers they were unabashedly romantic, loving anecdotes and color—and thereby delighting generations of undergraduates. Gaines Post, as I recall, always had various women or women-related topics on the list of 'suggested topics for papers.' . . . Of course it would be foolish to claim that either Post or Reynolds were feminist historians, yet I am firmly convinced that both of them would have been 'open' to feminist history, for they were open to any ideas, any approaches, which could expand history."[22] So women students continued to be drawn to the study of the Middle Ages. Medieval women might be subjects of scholarly papers if they were not a prominent part of the course lecture. For these students medieval women were authenticated and highly compelling figures, the product of an exotic age, far removed from the world of twentieth-century study of history and, quite possibly, not well understood in the context of their own time, but no less interesting to inquiring students on that account.

After World War II, when American historical study was enriched by the example and teaching of Europe's refugee intellectuals, and its own tradition of scholarship had achieved a higher degree of maturity, original formulations began to appear in print in greater numbers. The editors of one of the more controversial scholarly journals of the day, *The Journal of the History of Ideas,* had the presence of mind to recognize in a brief communication from a medievalist at the University of Vermont, Betty Bandel, a comment on gender roles that confirmed their editorial stance on the historical consequence of ideas. In an article entitled "The English Chronicler's Attitude Towards Women,"[23] Betty Bandel focused upon English chroniclers' relation of active deeds in the histories of certain women rulers, particularly well-documented Saxon queens, and later, the Empress Matilda. She noted that before the Norman Conquest chroniclers expressed no wonder at women wielding political power; it was taken as a matter of course. After the conquest such acts were singled out by the chroniclers as "manly" and remarkable. By the late Middle Ages chroniclers doubted the authenticity of the early histories, disclaiming such recorded acts on grounds that women could not have behaved in such a fashion. In the most extreme case, that of the Empress Matilda, recorded deeds were reascribed to her brother on the assumption that a woman could not have fought as actively as the chronicle sources insisted she had for the right of her son to sit upon the throne.

Bandel's contribution to the history of ideas lay in tracing the growing specificity of the concept of gender from the eleventh to the fourteenth century. What was manly or womanly had little significance in the earlier chronicles; by the time of Matthew Paris and other late medieval writers, it was important and sufficiently entrenched in the minds of the chroniclers and, presumably, their audience, to number among the essential organizing ideas in their recorded histories. Bandel had seen what few scholars before her had taken the trouble to notice. By distinguishing between the perception of women and women's acts, and charting this over a sufficient time interval so the dynamic quality of change in perceptions could be communicated, she had turned positivist analysis to the literary texts in such a way that it could be used to uncover gender roles. The implication of her work was that gender as an organizing idea was a relatively late accretion in the Western tradition, and that women's roles would become more circumscribed as restricted gender expectations came to figure in European life. She made it clear in her brief essay that women's history did move on an upward course, in fact it was evident that notions of gender contributed to an erosion of status and opportunity for women.

This is the inheritance of medieval historiography before the great interest in economic and social history of the Middle Ages which began to flourish in the 1960s in North America. At the University of Toronto Ambrose Raftis investigated the lives of English peasants, giving a greater role to women in the process and Michael Sheehan began investigations of marriage, the family, and the role marriage partners' consent came to play in validating marriage.[24] Jill Ker Conway and Natalie Zemon Davis offered the first survey course on women in European history at the University of Toronto. David Herlihy, a young medieval scholar teaching at Bryn Mawr College in that decade, began to apply the insights of social and economic history to understanding women's roles. He says of his early interest that in viewing the documents of the early Middle Ages, women's importance was obvious and certainly worthy of investigation. Was their greater presence then than at later stages in Western development mysterious? It seemed to be a significant question. He is uncertain about any influence a woman's college such as Bryn Mawr may have had upon his thought. Certainly his first scholarly attempt, "Land, Women and Family in Continental Europe, 700–1200," had not been written for assignment in the classroom.[25] Still, Herlihy speculated that it was possible that Bryn Mawr's stated intent, that is, to prepare women to follow productive roles in society, operated to create a climate in which investigation of women's roles was an appropriate area for historical research. The result was an article that substantiated through reference to the charters the fact that women's rights of possession had been strongest in the eleventh century and declined thereafter. Herlihy speculated on the reasons for this and continued to address the question of the change in women's status in his research because he found it a sensitive indicator of social and economic change in the medieval and Renaissance centuries.[26]

The emergence of a new interest in medieval women and a method for analyzing literary texts to reveal assumptions about gender or sex roles corresponded with other important changes in the American world of letters. By the 1960s Europeans had ceased to view American contributions to medieval scholarship as unnecessary offerings. In the train of that scholarship came ideas about medieval women and their roles which, if they had earlier aroused the interest of German historians (the celebrated *frauenfrage*), and had always been a peripheral interest in English historiography, had nonetheless remained largely outside the interests of the national schools of historical writing.[27] Since so much of the Americans' contribution to scholarship ignored the boundaries laid down by the national traditions in any event, this was hardly surprising. The selection of medieval women as a proper subject for historical research received some encouragement from the fact that some American scholars used women's condition as a means to measure other changes in society. In emphasizing the social and economic structures that had promoted Europe's development, and casting the question over a long term, Americans offered women's roles as a bell wether of substantive change. Their work even suggested a new chronology: the emergence of institutions in the centuries after the break up of the Carolingian empire when women played consequential roles, and a later stage, beginning in the late eleventh and the twelfth centuries, when women were separated from the institutions and positions that had permitted them to play forceful roles. Finally in the thirteenth century increasingly powerful institutions deprived women of positive legal rights, and relegated them more and more to the domestic household. Perspectives that disturbed the old categories and chronologies were in vogue in the intellectual world by the late sixties and seventies, and ideas about medieval women received a hearing on that account, one which would have been unlikely at any earlier date.

This spate of scholarship on women corresponded with the second wave of American feminism of the 1960s. If late twentieth-century feminism was less tied to scholarship and institutions of learning than early twentieth-century feminism, there were still numerous questions that feminists wished to ask of history, their own history as women viewed over the long term. Medieval history as it had developed could offer two specific and complementary perspectives to feminists. First, it could, in the tradition of positivist history, point to accomplishments in the era before the constraints of a division of the private from the public sphere inhibited women from playing effective public roles. There was proof available from the medieval record that women were capable of assuming authoritative roles: they could write learned treatises, administer institutions, serve as physicians, what the early nineteenth-century feminist, Paulina Wright Davis, had noted long before. The findings suggested that women's history was written on a separate trajectory from men's. History became a subject worth investigating for those feminists who wanted an explanation for why this had occurred and wished to understand the points of divergence in the course of men's and women's distinct histories.

Along with this uncovered past, feminists could also find an additional tradition of scholarship that had begun to look at the notion of gender itself as a socially constructed product. Women's behavior and perceptions of women's behavior could be compared, as Bandel had done in 1955. Investigations of sex roles were frequently undertaken in the disciplines of cultural anthropology and sociology, but medieval history could provide comparable opportunities for investigation because of a wealth of documentation and a major tradition of scholarship that had uncovered essential evidence. Since European history, particularly the history of the Enlightenment, the Renaissance, and the Middle Ages, was understood to be our heritage, and a proud tradition to own, investigating gender in this context might hold more consequence than raising the same question about more geographically remote societies.

The conjunction of the two strains in the work of gifted historians could produce innovative history that had the capacity to affect general understanding of the European past. Ruth Kelso in *Doctrine of the Lady in the Renaissance* questioned whether women were full participants in an era commonly understood to mark a major transition for men in Western society. Joan Kelly asked directly whether women had a Renaissance at all.[28] The findings of both inquiries identified in the medieval past a major transition for women that preceded the transition and watersheds claimed for men. David Herlihy noted of the Mediaeval Academy of America, "In 1982 the sex ratio of entering members, 92, dropped to its historic low [92 men to 100 women]. There are no indications that this fall in sex ratios is abating."[29] With the conviction that critical answers lie in the medieval past many women hope to uncover the historical roots of the condition of women before and during modern times.

Since World War II, contemporary scholarship on medieval women has added some impressive accomplishments to its name, and three at least deserve mention. First, the contribution of medieval women, particularly women in monastic orders, to the creation of European society and culture, has been uncovered. The extent and variety of the influence exerted by monastic women began to be investigated in England in the nineteenth century with Lina Eckenstein's still valuable study, and it was later joined by Eileen Power's important work on monastic houses and women in orders.[30] A major literature on the religious institutions that women created and staffed now exists. American women have added to it, revealing not only how critical women were to the development of institutions in the West, but also how long they remained important in the power equation of medieval society. Second, scholars now recognize that charting dynamic change within the family provides some of the earliest indications of Europe's transition to the modern age. It now appears evident that roles women played within the family underwent earlier change than men's in reaction to the increase in complexity and the shift to a cash economy that marked the earliest phases of modern development. Last, a careful monitoring of medieval women's history allows the investigator to identify by region and locale those moments when the public and the private spheres grew separate and distinct from each other. With the divergence came those gender expectations that clearly circumscribed future expectations and roles for women and for men in modern Western societies. Women's history from the Middle Ages to the present is no longer construed as progress, and its separate course stands as a caution against constructing any general interpretive framework in the progressive idiom. Adams's dire warning that a society's treatment of women determines its ultimate fate may have gone the way of most other Victorian moral dictums, but his early formulation on women led to observations of a critical nature on how societies define gender, and how mentalities change and new gender associations emerge. If the youthful Adams's ideas about medieval women were unthinkable in America's Gilded Age of institution building, they are not unthinkable in our age with its re-evaluation of our Western heritage.

In the present generation scholars in the tradition of those women noted in this essay continue to investigate medieval society, but today the edited text and the narrowly defined monograph composed in the positivist tradition are only two of the means available for investigating the past. History has borrowed from sociology, economics, and cultural anthropology. Quantitative studies have confirmed what could only be suggested before: the extent of medieval women's landholding, the number of convents in Europe, the growth of women's dowries. Sensibilities and the mental equipment of the age are standard subjects for research, and gender formulations figure among those topics. The validity of the transitions associated with the Renaissance and the Reformation have been questioned by reference to women's experience. Woman's experience takes on the same consequence as men's for interpreting change.

Today scholarship on medieval women is frequently conducted in collaborative efforts in which a wealth of documentation produced by numerous scholars drawing from different bodies of evidence confirms a shared interpretive approach and purpose. James Bruce Ross and Mary Martin McLaughlin began their collaboration with *The Portable Medieval Reader* in 1949, giving "The Body Social" and some commentary on women first place in their collection. They have continued their collaboration in paired articles. Jo-Ann McNamara and Suzanne Wemple collaborated on pathfinding studies of the early Middle Ages.[31] Anthologies often carry the burden of the interpretation of medieval women in contemporary scholarship.[32] These collaborative studies, produced largely but by no means exclusively by women, bear the particular stamp of American scholarship, and the work is no longer overlooked on that account, but rather known and considered for what this dimension affords our general understanding of the past.

The peculiarly American combination of brashness, an idiosyncratic reading of the purposes that positivist history might serve, and a genuine impulse to understand the Old World and apply its lessons in the New, have brought medieval studies to this unexpected pass. As we enter into an era of historiography that transcends the limits of national schools of history, this new dimension American scholarship has brought to medieval studies provides a valuable point of departure for the investigations that lie ahead.

Notes

1. Pauline Wright Davis, "Remarks at the Convention," *The Una* (September, 1853), 136–37. See Susan Conrad, *Perish the Thought* (Metuchen, NJ, 1978), chapter 4, for comment on these Boston feminists. I am grateful to Ann Hibner Koblitz for pointing out this early American feminist reference to medieval women.

2. Herbert Baxter Adams, "Special Methods of Historical Study as pursued at the Johns Hopkins University and at Smith College," *Johns Hopkins University Studies in Historical and Political Science*, 2 (1884), 5–23; see also his "German Origins of New England Towns" ibid., Ser. 1, pt. 2. A New Englander, Adams spent his spring semesters at Smith looking into the origins of his native region, eastern New England. John Higham, "Herbert Baxter Adams and the Study of Local History," *American Historical Review,* 89 (1984), 1125–39. On Herbert Baxter Adams's impact on his Smith College students, see Natalie Zemon Davis, "Women's History as Women's Education," a lecture delivered at Smith College on April 17, 1985, published *Women's History as Women's Education* (Northampton, 1985). On the "scientific" history of Herbert Baxter Adams and Henry Adams, see Dorothy Ross, "Historical Consciousness in Nineteenth Century America," *American Historical Review,* 89 (1984), 909–28.

3. *The Education of Henry Adams* (Boston, 1918). William Courtney, "The Virgin and the Dynamo," in *Medieval Studies in North America, Past, Present and Future,* ed. Francis G. Gentry and Christopher Kleinhenz (New York, 1982), p. 1–16.

4. Henry Maine, *Ancient Law,* 1st ed. (London, 1861); by 1876, and Adams's Lowell lecture, this work had undergone six editions. John F. MacLennan, *Primitive Marriage* (Edinburgh, 1867). MacLennan's work was also very popular, but his posthumous *Patriarchal Theory* published under the editorship of Donald MacLennan (1885) was an even more influential work and marked the ascendancy of Maine's and MacLennan's views on primitive phases of European development.

5. Henry Adams, "The Primitive Rights of Women," in *Historical Essays* (New York, 1891), pp. 36–41. Adams biographers have not emphasized this early interpretation of medieval women and the change in his opinion over the decades. On this topic T. J. Jackson Lears, *No Place of Grace* (New York, 1981), pp. 261–96 is interesting.

6. Henry Adams's wife committed suicide, precipitating a severe personal crisis, a change in career and in residence.

7. Obituary of Florence Griswold Buckstaff, Oshkosh, Wisconsin *Daily Northwestern* February 11, 1948, p. 4.

8. Florence Griswold Buckstaff, "Married Women's Property Rights in Anglo-Saxon and Anglo-Norman Law," *Annals of the American Academy* (1886), 233–64.

9. George E. Howard, *A History of Matrimonial Institutions,* 3 vols. (Chicago, 1904).

10. William O'Neill, *Divorce in the Progressive Era* (New Haven, 1967).

11. Mary Roberts Smith (Coolidge), *Why Women Are So* (New York, 1912). Her earlier study in sociology, which established her reputation, was *Chinese Immigration* (New York, 1909). She had studied with George E. Howard in the 1890s. Later with Clelia Mosher she launched modern sex research. See Rosalind Rosenberg, *Beyond Separate Spheres* (New Haven, 1982), pp. 178–80.

12. Bertha Phillpotts, *Kindred and Clan in the Middle Ages* (Cambridge, 1913). On this seminal work going out of print, see Sylvia Thrupp, *Early Medieval Society,* (New York, 1967), p. ix.

13. Ruth Benedict, after graduating from Vassar College in 1909, tried writing about important women in history but found it difficult to work in complete isolation. She returned to school in 1919 at the New School for Social Research and soon began her productive years under the influence of the anthropologist Franz Boas. See Rosalind Rosenberg, *Beyond Separate Spheres,* p. 223.

14. Helen Cam, *The Hundred and the Hundred Roles* (London, 1930) marked her entry into the field of scholarship on administrative, legal, and state history. She served a term as chair of the Department of History at Harvard University; she also produced a textbook for college students, *England before Elizabeth* (London and New York, 1950). Sylvia Thrupp, *A Short History of the Worshipful Company of Bakers of London* (Croydon, England, 1933) wrote social history. See also her *Merchant Class of Medieval London* (Chicago, 1948) and numerous articles.

15. Marie Boroff, *Sir Gawain and the Green Knight, A Stylistic and Metrical Study* (New Haven, 1962) among other works. She has been on the Yale faculty since 1971. Hope Emily Allen, *The Book of Margery Kempe* (Oxford, 1940); idem, ed., *The English Writings of Richard Rolle* (Oxford, 1931); idem, *The Manuel des Pechiez and the Scholastic Prologue* (New York, 1918). Katherine Fisher Drew, *The Burgundian Code* (Philadelphia, 1949; rev. ed. 1972); idem, "Note on Lombard Institutions," *Rice University Institute* (1956). Catherine Boyd, *A Cistercian Nunnery in Italy in the Thirteenth Century* (Cambridge, Mass. 1943); idem, *Tithes and Parishes in Medieval Italy* (Ithaca, 1952). This list is far from exhaustive but provides a sample of women in the medieval field and their scholarly contributions.

16. Nellie Neilson, *Economic Conditions on the Manors of Ramsey Abbey* (Philadelphia, 1898); idem, *Customary Rents* (Oxford, 1910); idem, *Fleet* (Oxford, 1920); idem, *Medieval Agrarian Economy* (New York, 1936). Emily Pocock, "Presi-

dents of the American Historical Association," *American Historical Review,* 89 (1984), 1240–58.

17. Emily Putnam, *The Lady* (New York, 1910; repr. Chicago, 1975). Mary Beard, *Women as a Force in History* (New York, 1945) also featured prominent medieval women in her longitudinal study, although the framework she employed did not direct her to the question of gender and changes in roles and status for women.

18. Eleanor Shipley Duckett, "Women and their Letters in the Early Middle Ages" (Northampton, 1964); idem, *Anglo-Saxon Saints and Scholars* (New York, 1947); idem, *Gateway to the Middle Ages* (New York, 1938). Duckett produced works for a scholarly audience and a popular audience as well. See forthcoming article on historiography of women by Elizabeth Fox-Genovese in *Signs: Journal of Women in Culture and Society.* See also Bonnie Smith, "The Contribution of Women to Modern Historiography," *American Historical Review,* 89 (1983), 709–32. Helen Cam was also English.

19. David Herlihy, "The American Medievalist," *Speculum,* 58 (1983), 881–88. Natalie Zemon Davis estimated women as 1% of the membership of the American Historical Association in 1885, and 4½% in 1984. "Discovery and Renewal in the History of Women," American Historical Association Centennial Session, Chicago, December 30, 1984.

20. Cornelia Catlin Coulter served on the first Advisory Board of *Speculum* in the 1930s; Margaret Schlauch served on its editorial board, while Nellie Neilson served on the Advisory Board. Women returned to this responsibility in the 1970s with Margaret Hastings and Joan Ferrante both serving on the Advisory Board. Alice Beardwood, *Alien Merchants in England* (Cambridge, MA, 1931) was the eighth publication in the monographic series of the Mediaeval Academy of America. Florence Edler (de Roover), *Glossary of Mediaeval Terms of Business* (Cambridge, MA, 1934) was the eighteenth. Pearl Kibre's *Scholarly Privileges in the Middle Ages* (Cambridge, MA, 1962) was one of two monographs composed by Kibre that the Academy published.

21. On English historiography see the article in this volume by Barbara Hanawalt.

22. Personal correspondence with Barbara Kreutz, Dean of the Graduate School, Bryn Mawr College, July 5, 1982.

23. Betty Bandel, "The English Chroniclers' Attitude Toward Women," *Journal of the History of Ideas,* 16 (1955), 113–18.

24. Ambrose Raftis, *The Estates of Ramsey Abbey* (Toronto, 1957); idem, *Tenure and Mobility: Studies in the Social History of the Mediaeval English Village* (Toronto, 1964); idem, ed., *Pathways to Medieval Peasants* (Toronto, 1981). Michael Sheehan, "Marriage and Family in English Conciliar and Synodal Legislation," *Essays in Honor of Anton Charles Pegis,* ed. J. R. O'Donnell (Toronto, 1974) pp. 205–14; idem, "The Formation and Stability of Marriage in Fourteenth-Century England: Evidence of an Ely Register," *Mediaeval Studies,* 33 (1971), 228–63.

More recently see *Sources of Social History: Private Acts of the Late Middle Ages,* ed. Paolo Brezzi and Egmont Lee (Toronto, 1984).

25. David Herlihy, "Land, Family and Women in Continental Europe, 700–1200," first published in the 1962 volume of *Journal of Social History,* reprinted in *Women in Medieval Society,* ed. Susan Mosher Stuard (Philadelphia, 1976), pp. 13–47. For a list of Herlihy's studies that feature women's condition as an indicator of change, see the bibliography in David Herlihy and Christiane Klapisch-Zuber, *Les Toscans et leurs familles* (Paris, 1978).

26. Personal interview with David Herlihy, San Francisco, California, December 29, 1982. For men who are eminent American medievalists and have devoted some of their research interest to medieval women see Giles Constable, "Aelred of Rievaulx and the nun of Watton: an episode in the early history of the Gilbertine order," in Derek Baker, *Medieval Women,* Oxford, 1978, pp. 205–66; Werner L. Gundersheimer, "Women, Learning and Power: Eleanora of Aragon and the Court of Ferrara" and Paul Oskar Kristeller, "Learned Women of Early Modern Italy: Humanists and University Scholars" in Patricia LaBalme, *Beyond Their Sex,* New York, 1980, pp. 43–65 and 91–116. The tendency to write about women in the course of general study has become more pronounced in the past few years. Many names could be added to this list.

27. See essays in this volume on German historiography by Martha Howell and on English historiography by Barbara Hanawalt.

28. Joan Kelly-Gadol, "The Social Relation of the Sexes," *Signs: Journal of Women in Culture and Society,* 1 (1976) 809–23. Ruth Kelso, *Doctrine for a Lady of the Renaissance,* (Urbana, IL, 1956).

29. David Herlihy, "The American Medievalist," pp. 886–88.

30. Eileen Power, *Medieval English Nunneries* (Cambridge, 1972). Lina Eckenstein, *Women under Monasticism* (Cambridge, 1896).

31. *The Portable Medieval Reader* (New York, 1949), went through fourteen printings in its first dozen years; Ross and McLaughlin produced paired articles in Lloyd DeMause, *The History of Childhood* (New York, 1977). James Bruce Ross is a woman. See articles by Jo-Ann McNamara and Suzanne Wemple in Berenice Carroll, *Clio's Consciousness Raised* (Urbana, IL, 1979) and *Becoming Visible* (Boston, 1976).

32. See, for example, the ten contributors in Susan Mosher Stuard, *Women in Medieval Society* (Philadelphia, 1976) and, recently, Barbara Hanawalt, *Women and Work in Pre-industrial Europe* (Bloomington, IN, 1985).

5

A Documented Presence: Medieval Women in Germanic Historiography

MARTHA HOWELL *with the collaboration of*
SUZANNE WEMPLE *and*
DENISE KAISER

Women's history has never been a central concern of the academic historians who have long dominated history writing in Germany.[1] Nevertheless, the traditions of historical scholarship established there in the nineteenth century have been indirectly responsible for some of the earliest and still among the best investigations into the lives of medieval women, both in the Low Countries, where the links with certain aspects of German historical scholarship have at times been very close, and in Germany itself.

The renewed interest in women's history during the last twenty years in much of Europe and in the United States has not, however, been as widely shared in the German academy, and until very recently medievalists in Germany by and large pursued the same questions and methodologies that engaged their predecessors several generations ago. While producing a few welcome and predictably sound monographs since the 1960s, they have tended to concentrate on painstaking analysis of primary sources, casting hardly a glance at the larger questions of gender, sexuality, socio-economic structure, ideology, and historical change that inform feminist historical scholarship elsewhere.

In the Low Countries, women's history has generated greater enthusiasm, but it is in Belgium rather than The Netherlands that the Middle Ages have been a focus of women's historians. While scholars in the North are, to be sure, energetically following the course set by American, British, and French practitioners of the new scholarship on women, the historians among them, in keeping with Dutch traditions of historical scholarship, have concentrated on the period after the establishment of their state rather than the Middle Ages. In Belgium, in contrast, medieval social and economic history retains the preeminence Henri Pirenne gave it in the early twentieth century. Admittedly, the concerns that motivate research on women elsewhere have not yet been fully assimilated in Belgium, but medievalists there, already cautiously adopting investigative frameworks borrowed from the Annales school and from western Marxist historians, are now deploying their impressive forces in search of family and women's history.

The Methodological Route to a Germanic History of Medieval Women

Before the nineteenth century, history writing in Germany followed paths much like those elsewhere in Europe, and none of them led to investigations of the lives of medieval women. During the Renaissance, the aims and methods of historians in Germany changed in now familiar ways: no longer the tableau of God's unfolding plan, history became a means for uncovering and defining a cultural past.[3] While humanist scholars occasionally unearthed manuscripts written by women, such as that of Hroswitha published by Konrad Celtis in 1501, they took little interest in the study of women as such. With the Protestant Reformation came a number of partisan histories extolling the Empire and attacking the bishop of Rome, but their writers made no place for women, who were not, they assumed, actors in the political and ecclesiastical narratives they published. Historians of the late seventeenth and early eighteenth centuries, who initiated the concern with sources that was to distinguish German historical scholarship, shared their predecessor's assumption that women were not part of the historical record.[4]

The methodological and historical concerns that led to studies of medieval women were born, along with modern German historical scholarship itself, in the nineteenth century. This new history originated as part of a reaction to the abstract rationalism of the Enlightenment and to the Napoleonic regime. Underlying Enlightenment thought was a natural law theory, which postulated a universal, eternal moral law accessible by human reason and which reduced history to "philosophy teaching by examples."[5] Historians were to relate the successes and failures of past generations in adhering to the eternal, immutable standards of natural law, thus producing moral instruction for the present generation. Neither the Middle Ages nor women were of real interest to the philosophes. The former subject found occasional chroniclers only because these centuries offered so many instructive examples of errors and superstitions that the eighteenth century had superseded, but the latter was almost entirely ignored because women played little part in the philosophes's story of mankind's progressive civilization under the leadership of wise and great men.

This approach to history writing found opponents even in eighteenth-century France, but it was in nineteenth-century Germany under the leadership of Leopold von Ranke (1795–1886) that a fundamentally different vision of history and of the historical enterprise was institutionalized. German Romanticism, in its literary and theological origins, was one important source of Ranke's vision. Inaugurated by Johann Gottfied Herder (1744–1803), this cultural Romanticism made the *Volk* a central unit of history, a Volk conceived of as an organic, collective whole that united diverse individuals through a common language, shared institutions, the arts, and literature. For Herder, if not for the historians after him, the Volk was a cultural entity that had much to fear from the state, an institution based on coercion and power and the potential destroyer of arts and literature.

Because the Volk was like an organism that grew, developed, and died, it could only be understood historically. Herder's notions were thus compatible in some respects with contemporary ideas about historical development borrowed from biology, Vico's among them. But Herder had no satisfactory explanation for historical change. While rejecting the French notion that history had progressed towards the rational eighteenth century and promised future advancement, Herder simply asserted that the self-contained Volk knew "progression" (*Fortgänge*) by which one Volk was replaced by another in a process leading to no apparent goal. Late in his life, Herder did suggest that Divine Providence might be directing human history towards greater *Humanität,* but this was not like the philosophes' steady improvement towards greater happiness and reason.

While Herder's ideas were an important source of the synthesis achieved by Ranke, the work of a group of historians originally centered in Göttingen played as key a role. Combining the traditions of textual criticism developed in classical philology and the work of previous legal historians, they also believed that a nation was a unique blend of spiritual forces that could only be understood historically. These scholars deliberately turned away from the study of universal natural law towards an investigation of positive law, which grew with the Volk. Their ideas were institutionalized, in a way entirely compatible with the Rankean tradition, in the "historische Rechtsschule" under the leadership of Friedrich Karl von Savigny (1779–1861). The mutability of law and legal institutions were emphasized both in Savigny's own research on the transformation of Roman law during the early Middle Ages and in the work of his associates and successors, which more often focused on the Middle Ages as the time when both the German Volk and its distinctive legal system were thought to have taken shape.

These two versions of history, while differing in important ways, had in common both an opposition to the kind of history deriving from French rationalism as well as an agreement that the *Volksseele* rather than rational progress constituted the proper object of historical inquiry. Ranke's vision of the past and the methods he instituted to study it owed much to both traditions. But Ranke's history ought also be seen as a reaction to the Hegelian notion that history was simply the field on which the world spirit achieved its dialectical, inexorable progress. Like most historians, Ranke resisted Hegelian theory because it discounted the individual event and explored the past only as it led to future.

The alternative Ranke offered was historicist: he insisted upon the individuality of each age and saw each culture as unique because it was the product of its particular past, its particular leaders, and its particular consciousness. For Ranke, the historian's job was to understand the past on its own terms; to perform his task, the historian had to bury himself (the feminine reflexive would not have occurred to Ranke) in the documents surviving from the age. He was charged with examining, not just the document's content, but both the conditions under which it was created and its creator. Rather than shaping the material, embellishing the story, or judging the actors according to the values of his own age, the historian was allowed only to render an objective narrative of events that revealed the *Zeitgeist* of the past era.

Ranke's fame, especially outside Germany, rests today principally on his success in institutionalizing his method of "scientific history." At Berlin, Ranke established the historical seminar, the first of its kind, where he trained students in textual criticism and imparted the wide range of technical skills that were to make Germany's historians the most sophisticated in the West and were later to transform methodology outside of Germany. As influential as Ranke's method was, however, his notion of historical development affected the historical consciousness in Germany as deeply. Building upon the idea that a Volk grew uniquely and historically, Ranke was convinced that the development occurred according to the plan of a Divine Providence. Each age gained its coherence through its particular spirit (its Zeitgeist), and the historian grasped this spirit, after total immersion in the sources, by an intuitive process Ranke called *Ahnen*. Accompanying his idea that a divine plan directed historical change was his belief that the civic realm was the highest embodiment of a Volk, not, as Herder believed, its possible enemy. This aspect of Ranke's history firmly locates him in nineteenth-century Europe where his own Prussian state and Metternichean politics flourished, but it also betrays links with the Hegelian theory that Ranke otherwise rejected. Ranke's civic realm was not, however, the German state alone, but a system of national states, each of which represented a unique configuration of law, politics, and customs.

Given his emphasis on the political and his insistence that historical writing be based on the document itself, it is no wonder that Rankean history came to mean the political narrative. Even Ranke himself, whose genius transcended the narrow, sometimes polemical, concerns of historians after him, published most extensively on statesmanship, diplomacy, and war. The route from this vision of history to a history of medieval women was, to be sure, indirect. It did not emerge out of the political narrative itself, but developed out of Rankean method and its requirement that any past era be investigated as thoroughly and as fully as the documents allowed.

Along the way, however, some uniquely Germanic turns were taken. In the hands of Ranke's successors, who dominated late nineteenth-century history writing in Germany, political history—in this period, history *par excellence*—became distinctly nationalist in tone. Heinrich von Treitschke (1834–96), who followed Ranke at Berlin, not only jettisoned Ranke's belief in the ethical purposes of the state and in Divine Providence, but he abandoned as well his mentor's exacting methods of research. Others belonging to this "Prussian school" remained truer to Rankean method and less enamoured of power politics; while they produced nationalist histories, they are better remembered for their contributions of a methodological kind: Theodor Mommsen's (1817–1903) *Corpus Inscriptionum Latinarum;* Friedrich Dahlmann's (1785–1860) bibliographic handbook, later continued by Georg Waitz (1813–86), now simply referred to as "Dahlmann-Waitz"; and Heinrich von Sybel's (1817–95) German Historical Institute in Rome as well as his *Historische Zeitschrift* (1859), which was explicitly intended to broadcast Ranke's scientific method to the world.

Ranke and his students put German history writing far ahead of other national traditions in terms of methodological sophistication, and it was not until after 1860 that German methods would be transferred to France, England, America, Belgium, and the Netherlands. In each of these nations, Rankean method took root in different ways but was everywhere by and large divorced from the metaphysical and historicist position that marked it in Germany. Eventually Rankean method outside Germany came to mean little more than scientific fact gathering, and was even equated with the methods of positivist research, which also emphasized careful fact gathering and critical analysis of primary sources.

In Germany, however, positivism long retained its original theoretical meaning as formulated by August Comte (1798–1857), which posited that societies, past and present, obey universal laws analogous to those of the physical sciences and discoverable by the same methods of research. Few historians in Germany could accept this concept, because they could not bring themselves to abandon the historicist idea that events and people, as part of an organic developmental process, were products of a distinct culture rooted in political, legal, and cultural institutions, themselves the formal structures of that organic whole. Positivism in Germany, in the pure Comtean form advanced by its leading German proponent, Karl Lamprecht (1886–1915), consequently met eager and articulate opponents such as Johann G. Droysen (1838–1908), Friedrich Meinicke (1862–1954), Georg von Below (1858–1927), and Georg Waitz. Only among scholars doing economic and social history such as Werner Sombart (1863–1941) and Gustav Schmoller (1838–1917), along with Henri Pirenne (1862–1935), who was to transform medieval history writing in Belgium, did Lamprecht receive a cautious hearing.

German historians accorded Marxism an even less cordial reception, but they could not entirely ignore either positivism or Marxism, because their own historicist position, when shed of Ranke's belief in Divine Providence and the ethical capacity of the state, led to little more than source analysis and the narrative it yielded. The effort to rescue German historiography from the relativism this manner of history writing encouraged, while not entirely successful, in the end provided a stronger justification for social and economic history and expanded the field of inquiry permitted political history. Both tendencies fostered investigations that yielded information about women.

Wilhelm Dilthey and Max Weber (significantly, neither was an historian) are principally responsible for this reassessment. While they did not return to a grand theory of historical change or purpose, they did insist that the past, like the present, could be analyzed as a system of interlocking structures. They agreed with the positivists that events had to be understood in the structural context in which they occurred, that pure narration was insufficient, and that the "story" had to be supplemented by analysis. Politics, moreover, was no longer viewed as the keystone to history; not only was it necessary to understand the interaction of political with social and economic factors, but it was possible to write a history that devoted itself to nonpolitical spheres of society. This vision was enriched by Weber's productive dialogue with Marxism regarding the nature and logic of social hierarchies and of the causes of historical change.

While this vision was to have little effect on mainstream historiography in Germany until after the Second World War, it did influence the social and economic history then being written by members of the "school of national economy." This literature was the product of an historiographical tradition specific to Germany, which, as we have seen, had developed independently of positivist influence. Its practitioners, led by Sombart and Schmoller, directly opposed the positivist implications of neoclassical economics, for they emphasized economic institutions and development rather than timeless market forces, the distant past rather than the immediate past, and the historically concrete rather than the abstract. Being profoundly influenced by the nationalist biases of their traditions, moreover, these historians could not have imagined economic development except as part of the development of legal and political institutions, which were, by definition, national. Hence, these scholars conceived of their project as a study of *national* economy, by which they meant the economic institutions and practices that characterized a national culture.

Concern with questions of economic change marked their work (the transition from *Naturwirtschaft* to *Geldwirtschaft* was a favorite subject; another was the shift from the ancient to the medieval economy and then from the medieval to the modern economy), but so did a concentration on urban history in which they explored some of the same questions as constitutional and political historians—urban origins and development, sociopolitical structures, constitutional crises and change. Henri Pirenne of Belgium perhaps best exemplifies these interests. Although not a German, he consciously adopted German critical method and modeled his own historical seminar at Ghent (which remains today a noted center for medieval social and economic history) on the German example. His work on European economic development, urban origins, medieval capitalism, and constitutional change in cities—to name just a few of the subjects on which he set the terms of debate—makes him perhaps the best-known representative of this kind of history.

The histories of medieval social and economic development that these students of national economy produced, institutional in character and constructed with the critical tools of Rankean method, command the serious attention both of medievalists and of historians of medieval women today. It was not from social and economic historians alone, however, that historical data about medieval women emerged within the Rankean tradition. In fact, two other impulses within that tradition are even more directly responsible for the medieval women's history we have.

A major impulse was simply the interest in medieval history itself. From its earliest days, the Rankean tradition fueled the Romantic interest in the medieval past, when the German spirit was thought to have manifested itself in a brilliant age. Magnificent text editions and source collections followed, including the *Monumenta Germaniae Historiae;* the *Regesta,* covering the acts of various emperors from 928 through 1399; and the *Fontes Rerum Germanicarum,* which also focused on the Middle Ages. The *Monumenta Germaniae Historia* (MGH) is indisputably one of the major landmarks in the development of scientific history. Founded by Freiherr von Stein in 1819 (even before Ranke had established himself), the MGH was to be a collection of critical and objective renderings of medieval texts, published in chronological order according to topic. The series itself remains a major institution of historical scholarship in Germany.

The bulk of the studies German medievalists published were, of course, political in nature, and few of those included women in their narratives. The strong interest in legal history contained within that tradition meant, however, that careful and detailed histories of both public and private law were written. The latter subject, necessary because the family was recognized as the basic political unit in medieval Europe, naturally included studies of marriage and inheritance. This is the second major impulse accounting for the contributions Germanic scholars have made to medieval women's history. More than any genre of modern Germanic historiography, these legal studies have yielded extensive and technically proficient studies of the roles and status of certain classes of women in medieval Europe.

Hence, partly as a by-product of their principal research interests, Germanic historians from the nineteenth century on have documented women's roles in certain social, economic, cultural, and legal institutions. To be sure, it should not be assumed that the Rankean ideal of "objective" and value-free history was actually achieved or that politics did not affect what was written and how it was written. German historiography was in fact profoundly affected by political forces outside the academy.

Periods of feminist action have been one important influence on the academic production of medieval women's history. The women's movement of the nineteenth and early twentieth century, in particular, prompted a great many historians to search their documents for evidence about women. Among these scholars were a few women who had managed to join the academic community and who had generally written, as they do today, history just like that of their male colleagues. Much of the literature on women's past, especially the past of women in the Middle Ages when Germanic culture was born, dates from this period. Not all of the female authors were academics—and those that were not could seldom meet the high technical standards of German scholarship—but a few studies such as Marianne Weber's *Ehefrau und Mutter in der Rechtsentwicklung* (Tübingen, 1907) or Lily Braun's *Die Frauenfrage, ihre geschichtliche Entwicklung und ihre wirtschaftliche Seite* (Leipzig, 1901) earned a place in Germanic scholarly literature. Significantly, the first is a legal history and the second an economic history. The last twenty years have again encouraged women medievalists to consider their own history. Edith Ennen, one of Germany's senior historians of urban economies and institutions, has lately published several articles and a book on medieval women, and her student Margret Wensky has contributed a monograph on working women in Cologne.[6] Similarly, in Belgium and Holland, women scholars are increasingly turning to women's history; there, more than in Germany itself, women's history as it is written in America and Britain has met an enthusiastic welcome.

The Nazi period, in contrast, produced a change for the worse. Then, as is well known, Nazi rule fostered a resurrection and intensification of latent polemical, nationalist tendencies among German historians. While the Nazis were not long enough in control entirely to overturn the stubborn routine of academic history, with its text criticism, objectivity, *Verstehen,* and seminars, the Nazi idealization of a national past rooted in a vision of free, strong Germans did find sympathies within the academy. Over the long term even these scholars would almost certainly have found their critical methodology an obstacle to acceptance of the groundless Nazi theories about racial superiority and the Aryan past. They would not, however, have succeeded in opposing the state; as it was, the Nazis ousted a number of Jewish history professors, and in 1935 achieved control over several scholarly publishing bastions, including the steering committee of the MGH. As we shall see, Nazi ideology had ramifications for women's history as well.

After the defeat of the Nazis, the profession as a whole timidly returned to old methods and concerns. When change did come, it understandably did not first arrive in the tradition-ridden medieval academy, but among historians of modern Germany trying to explain the Nazis. Innovative efforts outside of Germany to expand the scope of medieval history and give it theoretical rigor, the most important led by scholars associated with the Annales School or with western Marxism, met with little enthusiasm. In recent years, however, new theoretical and methodological issues, originating in Germany but influenced by developments elsewhere, have begun to enliven medieval history writing in Germany. They may portend new investigations into the lives of medieval women that productively use, but are not limited by, the traditional strengths of nineteenth-century Germany historiography. In the narrative that follows, we will return to these stirrings.

The Substantive Contributions of Germanic Historiography to the History of Medieval Women

Despite its inherent conservatism, the Rankean tradition can be credited with several important contributions to medieval women's history. The first, undoubtedly the most important, originated in the legal history principally associated with Savigny's historische Rechtsschule. Using the powerful tools of textual and historical analysis attributed to Ranke and much influenced by the well-established interest in medieval history, Germany's legal historians have produced a rich body of literature tracing medieval public and private law. To these continuing studies, we owe much of our knowledge of "family" and inheritance law, which together constitute the basis of our understanding of women's legal status in the age.

Jacob Grimm produced an early example of the genre; his 1828 investigation of marriage customs among the early Germans raised a question that continues to engage legal historians today. According to him, women were so valued in Germanic society that they were treated as commodities and sold into marriage under a system dubbed *Kaufehe.*[7] Later scholars, such as Lothar Dargun, who was influenced by the anthropological theories of Morgan and Bachofen (which informed Engels' almost contemporaneous *The Origin of the Family, Private Property and the State* as well), argued for the existence, indeed the primacy, of two additional forms of marriage.[8] One was a marriage between equals, a *Friedelehe;* in this contract he saw evidence that Germans had once lived in a matrilineal society. While Germans and Aryans did capture women as well, his sources demonstrated, they took such women from the outside and never acquired women from their own people in this way. Other contemporary experts on law, however, entirely discounted the importance of these more egalitarian marriages called Friedelehe, stressing that, in contrast, *Raubehe* and Kaufehe were the prevailing forms of marriage.[9]

Under the Nazis, the question of marriage gained new currency, for it was central to their ideas about the status and roles of German women in medieval Europe. The general framework was established by works such as Elsbet Kaiser's *Frauendienst im mittelhochdeutschen Volksepos* (Breslau, 1921), contrasting the resilient women of the heroic epic with the idolized women of the courtly literature, and Lulu von Strauss und Torney's book, which praised the women of the tenth through thirteenth centuries as "immer zum Opfer fähig und bereit" and, as the truly feminine beings they were, eager to bear children and keep house.[10] The question of the original German marriage was obviously key to this historiography. As Nazi-inspired historians saw it, the debate turned on whether German women had married freely and by choice (as befitted a free people) or were "sold" into marriage by guardians or, worse, taken by rape. Gerda von Merschberger

(1937) argued that the only form possible among Germans was free marriage (Freidelehe) and called the other forms "rassfeindlich." The same argument occurred in a work by R. Köstler (1943), who rejected Raub- and Kaufehe as marriage arrangements too barbaric for the Germans ever to have practiced.[11] In Friedelehe, after all, a woman retained her freedom; she received a gift (*Morgengabe*) from the male and became the mistress of his household. Women were captured or given as gifts, according to Köstler, only to assert the power of the male; even so, the practice was not truly Germanic and must be attributed to foreign influences.

Postwar scholars, freed from the myths of Nazi history writing, have profitably returned to the question of marriage customs among the early Germans. In 1946 a French scholar, Noel Senn, reopened the debate with an argument that the Freidelehe contained remnants of the old purchase price, a conclusion reached after careful analysis of the codes themselves. In 1967 August Eckhardt attacked the unlikely notion that the Friedelehe was the result of a romantic attachment; Friedelehe was simply an endogamous marriage, while Kaufehe und Raubehe were exogamous unions.[12] Although some scholars have continued to refer to Friedelehe without embarrassment, others have questioned whether it existed as a distinct form of marriage, or simply as a variant form of marriage through capture.[13]

Building on the work of predecessors as well as the literature regarding the social and political structure of Frankish and Carolingian society, Suzanne Wemple has returned to the codes and brought order to the confusion.[14] Through an analysis of Merovingian and Carolingian sexual unions, she has demonstrated that among the early Germans, marriage was not a legal relationship created through the discharge of prescribed procedures, but an arrangement, accepted as a social fact, whereby a man cohabitated with a woman for the sake of sexual union, begetting children, and sharing subsistence responsibilities.

The actual property arrangements made reflected the fact that women had distinct functions in economic production and that when a woman married, rights to her production passed from her father to her husband. While social ranks existed, the division of labor was determined not by class but by sex. Men were the warriors, whereas women worked in the fields, looked after the home, and bore and cared for the children. Because most marriages were patrilocal, with the groom bringing the bride home and depleting the bride's household of a worker, the groom had to recompense the family for the loss of a daughter's labor. He, in return, received arms as a wedding gift from her kin. If, however, the bridegroom was well enough placed, wives were offered to him without compensation, since the kinship ties issuing from such a union were more important than economic considerations. In exceptional cases, marriages were matrilocal. A king or a chieftain might recompense one of his men who fought valiantly for him with the hand of a daughter who, with any children she might have, remained under her father's protection.

In marrying his daughter, the father (or the guardian) conveyed his right of protection over to her husband, and the husband could then claim compensation for any injury she or the future children might suffer. But to gain this right, he had to present a marriage gift (*dos*) to the bride. Although it was expressed in monetary values in the codes, the gift was usually in the form of land. Thus, the dos, together with the Morgengabe gave the bride considerable power in marriage.

While Raubehe continued to exist (towards the end of the sixth century, Childebert II decreed that a man who abducted a woman against her will would be killed or exiled), it was the Kaufehe, whereby the husband gained formal rights or protection over his wife and their children, which was most favored by the Germans and their codes. The Freidelehe, which left some property and maternal rights with women, was recognized in some codes; the Bavarian Code was exceptionally liberal for the woman who had the courage to risk either living with man or having sexual relations without formal contract of betrothal. In other codes, voluntary sexual unions were held to be adultery, usually punished at the expense of the woman.

Wemple also analyzed the extent of the Carolingians' influence on early Germanic marriages. Merovingian marriages had remained surprisingly innocent of Christian teachings. Polygamy, concubinage, and divorce were common. The early Carolingians, however, brought about a social revolution by insisting upon the binding nature of marriage; not even adultery could dissolve the union. While there was some relaxation during the second half of the ninth century and while the new marriage regulations were not always observed, by the end of the Carolingian era the Christian ideal of marriage, a union binding for life, was institutionalized in secular and ecclesiastical legislation.

German historians have equally well chronicled the history of marital property arrangements among the nobility after Charlemagne's time. R. Schröder's study of 1863–74 traced the transformation of the dos, under Charlemagne a gift to the father of the bride, into the dos and *sponsalia,* the latter a present to the bride after the wedding night, and finally in the thirteenth century into the *dotalitium* or dos, given to the bride either by her husband or father.[15]

The work German historians have done on women rulers, especially among the Ottonians and Saxons, even more directly reflects the traditional interests and methods of German medieval historiography. Max Kirschner's 1910 study traced marriage practices among the Ottonians and the conventions according to which, from the time of Edith, the first wife of Otto I, women were independently crowned.[16] In a more recent study, T. Vogelsang has investigated the meaning of shared rule, arguing that the term *consors imperii nostri,* first used in 866, described a real coruler who could act as regent, advisor to her husband, and corecipient of the religious authority then due rulers following the late antique conception institutionalized under Christianity.[17] The rulers of post-Carolingian Europe personally embodied public power and earned their legitimacy in part through the religious authority they bore. Their wives, as property owners in their own right and controllers of land held in fief, shared this authority. The formula and the reality of the consors imperii nostri, Vogelsang argues, held until the twelfth century in much of Europe, when changes in the nature of the state and in the idea of rule undermined the power of the woman consort.

A good part of Hans Thieme's "Die Rechtsstellung der Frau in Deutschland," which appeared in the volume *La Femme,* published by the Société Jean Bodin in 1962, is drawn from legal and political histories such as Vogelsang's, which are themselves based on the careful textual analysis typical of German medieval scholarship. Thieme's coauthors Gilissen and Bosch, on the southern and northern Netherlands, respectively, had equally rich fields of monographs and published source collections to mine, thanks again to the influence of German legal historians on the historiography of their own countries.

The authors of the essays in this volume were not, however, limited to legal and political histories drawn from law codes and diplomatic documents, which could at best reveal practices among the elite in the early and high Middle Ages. Beginning around 1100, European society became increasingly complex as cities emerged, and legal historians concerned with this period of German medieval history could not assume, as specialists of earlier periods appear to have done, that the history of the German nation was written in its law codes. While urban law was influenced by traditional custom, both codified and uncodified, it had evolved in response to the circumstances of the day, and it varied from place to place and period to period. It was systematized, and subjected to the learned commentary that would have helped systematize it, only with the sixteenth-century reception of Roman law.

To trace the evolution of law and public institutions in late medieval Germany, legal and constitutional scholars turned to the abundant documents left by medieval urban institutions recording inheritances, marriages, guardianship practices, and property relations. The abstracts and typologies of local systems they constructed have served as the basis for most of what we know about the "legal status" of medieval urban women today. The essays prepared for the Société de Jean Bodin volumes rely heavily on this literature. Even more illustrative of the wealth of data available about these subjects is the essay by Gerhard Köbler in the recent *Haus und Familie*.[18] The author's charge was to relate the "family law" of late medieval cities; as he pointed out, there was no notion of "family law" in the period, and it is only by using different parts of the entire legislative and judicial records of a locality that we can construct what we today consider "family law." For Köbler, it consisted of marriage customs, guardianship practices, and property relations between husband and wife. His essay, a systematic review of the conclusions to be drawn from the existing literature on each of these topics, demonstrates how much we can learn about medieval women from published information alone.

Among the hundreds of monographs cited in Köbler's article, two exemplify the strengths of German legal scholarship on medieval women. One is R. Schröder's *Geschichte des ehelichen Güterrechts in Deutschland* (1863–74), a two-part, four-volume review of the history of property relations within marriage from the beginnings of European society through the Middle Ages. The other is Gustav Schmelzeisen's *Die Rechtsstellung der Frau in den deutschen Stadtwirtschaft im Spätmittelalter* (Stuttgart, 1935); in part a compendium of women's legal rights, based on a careful survey of monograph literature and published sources relating to his theme, Schmelzeisen's book offers a great deal more. Schooled as he evidently was in urban constitutional and legal theory, Schmelzeisen was able to move beyond cataloging women's legal rights, and he tried to make sense of the patterns he traced using theory about the place of the family in the urban community and the hierarchal structure of the medieval household. Although by no means fully worked out, his hypotheses are nevertheless thought-provoking aids to future research. It is regrettable, but perhaps characteristic, that his suggestions have found no appreciable response in the German academy.

Social and economic historians have produced almost as important a body of literature on medieval women. An eminent contributor to this literature was Karl Bücher, best known and appreciated for his pathbreaking demographic study of Frankfurt am Main and his theory of economic development set forth in his *Die Entstehung der Volkswirtschaft*.[19] His importance for medieval women's history, as German historians have written it, lies, however, in other works, principally in his *Die Frauenfrage im Mittelalter*. First published as an essay in 1882, the book was enlarged and reissued in 1910 with a small scholarly apparatus; it proposed a thesis that has occupied generations of German economic and social historians since and has influenced almost every study thereafter undertaken on late medieval women.

Bücher argued that because women in late medieval cities outnumbered men by a significant percentage (owing to men's greater vulnerability to disease, their greater exposure to the hazards of medieval travel, and their participation in warfare), medieval cities were typically short of men and, conversely, faced with an overabundance of women. Women alone in the world had to fend for themselves. The unlucky became camp followers, prostitutes, vagabonds, and beggars. Luckier ones found piecework in textiles, entered domestic service, took up street peddling, or found sanctuary in the convent. The luckiest worked in crafts and trade, filling the empty spots in the most prestigious sectors of medieval urban market production. This last route was so common, Bücher claimed, that women "were excluded from no trade for which their strength was adequate. They had the right, as a matter of course, to learn all crafts [and] to practice them, as apprentices, even as mistresses."

By the early modern period, in Bücher's view, the situation had been "righted." Women no longer outnumbered men and, thanks to the renewed consciousness of the importance of family life during the Reformation era, the household had been restored to its rightful place at the center of women's lives. Then, according to Bücher, "a new ideal of womanhood" had emerged, one "which laid heavy emphasis on the purity of soul and the unique morality of the German housewife and mother."

Bücher's book was written during the days of the late nineteenth-century feminist movement, which was as strong in Germany as anywhere in the West. While not entirely unsympathetic with certain of the movement's goals, Bücher was obviously threatened by the revolution in gender relations that it portended, and he intended his book, one suspects, as much to educate his contemporaries about the causes, risks, and possible resolution of the "women problem" in his own era as to enlighten his academic colleagues about the importance of women's work in the medieval past. In one passage, for example, he urged the women of his day to retreat from market production and reassert the primacy of the household. In doing so, women would resist the capitalist market economy which, according to Bücher, rendered all labor a commodity, pitted women against men in the competition for jobs, and destroyed centuries of social and ethical development, all leading to a "retreat into barbarity, a disruption of family order which had taken shape since the Reformation, a destruction of the household, in which the woman ruled, and the entry of women into the world of economic production in which they could find places only as the servile members." "Shouldn't we work with all our strength so that all classes of the population are assured the peace and the comfort of the domestic hearth, which strengthens family consciousness and which provides a woman the single sphere where she feels the happiest and in which she creates the value more precious to the nation than whatever increase in production she might achieve with her 'cheap labor' ['billige Hände']."[20]

Neither Bücher's contemporary medievalists nor his successors showed such willingness to relate the past to the present. Instead, they set out simply to ascertain the extent of women's work. Soon after *Die Frauenfrage* first appeared, several major studies confirmed its finding that women in late medieval cities of northern Europe practiced skilled crafts, belonged to guilds, and dealt in long-distance commerce.[21] The century of research since Bücher first published has undeniably produced a wealth of data about women's work in cities of the late medieval North; it has, however, led to very little refinement of Bücher's thesis or efforts to construct new arguments.[22] Valuable monographs such as Margret Wensky's *Die Stellung der Frau in der stadtkölnischen Wirtschaft im Spätmittelalter* (1984), which lays out the archival evidence regarding women's work in late medieval Cologne, overtly refuses even to speculate about causality. Jenneke Quast's 1980 essays on women's work in The Netherlands parallel Wensky's method: archival files are read, data is accumulated, summaries are written. To be sure, Quast is not uninterested in some of the theoretical issues of concern in Britain and America, such as the argument of Alice Clark, whose *The Working Life of Women in the 17th Century* (1919) remains the best-known statement of the case that women's work changed in the transition from "traditional" medieval society to early modern capitalist society. But she simply comments on how her data seem to support Clark without assessing the thesis itself.[23]

The few scholars in Germany who have begun to question Bücher today have done so out of the entirely traditional academic concern with sources. Kurt Wesoly has, for example, used such methods to attack the body of scholarship that builds upon Bücher. In an analysis of Wachendorf's *Die wirtschaftliche Stellung der Frau in den deutschen Städten des Spätmittelalters,* one of the most important successors to Bücher's study, Wesoly argued that the author had simply misread his sources. The word *wib* appearing in a late fourteenth-century ordinance from Frankfurt am Main's textile crafts, which Wachendorf had read to mean "woman," usually, Wesoly pointed out, is read as "wife" or "widow." Other women mentioned in the same ordinance were not skilled workers, as Wachendorf had described them, but were doing ancillary work. The confusions made Wesoly skeptical about the thesis as a whole: "That women took part in the weaver's guild in Frankfurt as 'full members' . . . while not entirely out the question, seems to me in no way fully assured." He even more directly challenged Bücher's statement that women were regular members of crafts: "Whether it was really the rule for girls in the thirteenth century to learn a craft and whether, [quoting Bücher] in the cities of the high Middle Ages women were generally excluded from no industry for which their strength was adequate is out and out speculation. The evidence does not suffice for real proof."[24]

Others in the academy have recently expressed similar skepticism. Edith Ennen, for example, has long reserved judgment on the validity of Bücher's claim that women outnumbered men in most cities, and in a recent article Michael Mitterauer has persuasively argued that to the extent such imbalances existed, they were caused, not by higher death rates for men, but by differentials in immigration ratios.[25]

The interest of scholars like Mitterauer, a social scientist, and the renewed interest in women's history among traditional medievalists may presage a full-scale re-examination of Bücher's thesis in Germany and, with it, of the lives of medieval women. The body of literature produced since Bücher first published is testimony to the availability of sources for the investigation; as we have seen, it is supplemented by an even richer vein already dug by the legal and constitutional historians of the late Middle Ages.

The traditional interests of German medieval historians, especially when prompted by the speculations of Bücher, led many of them to examine women's place in other aspects of medieval life as well, at least as life could be studied through the documents left by medieval institutions. Arguably the most important of these investigations treat women's roles in religious institutions and in spiritual life in general. Much of the literature is biographical: the lives of important abbesses, mystics, and intellectuals constitute a significant subset of the genre. Hroswitha of Gandersheim, the well-known tenth-century poet and intellectual, has been recently translated; Herrad von Landsperg and Hildegard of Bingen, both twelfth-century women of intellectual accomplishment and institutional power, have received their share of scholarly attention as well.[26]

The importance of the mystical tradition in Germany in the high and late Middle Ages has long been recognized by German historians, and they have also long acknowledged the role of women in this tradition. Elizabeth of Schonau's works were edited by F. W. E. Roth in 1886; and in 1884 her biography was published as *Die Visionen der hl. Elisabeth*.[27] Both Protestant and Catholic historians in Germany have given us biographies of the nuns of Helfta, one of the most important convents in the history of women's mysticism in the thirteenth century. It remained, however, for an American scholar, Caroline Bynum, to explore the significance of their religiosity.[28] Margaretha Ebner has been given better treatment in Germany; a 1914 scholarly study placed her life as a mystic in the context of the political, ecclesiastical, and religious upheavals that wracked Germany during the six decades of her life, 1291–1351.[29]

The work on female mystics has sometimes been tied with another issue concerning religious women of the medieval past: the extent and significance of the expansion of female religious orders and of female religious activity in the late Middle Ages. The Praemonstratensians have received attention as the first male order to accept women. Although founded in the middle of the twelfth as an order of double monasteries, it reversed its policy later in the same century. When the Lateran Council of 1215 forbade the formation of new orders, women had no recourse but to attach themselves to the existing male orders. Many did, and the half century between 1200 and 1250 saw the foundation of 150 female monasteries allied with the Cistercians; yet only the Pope's intervention prevented this order from following the precedent set by the Praemonstratensians and forbidding new female monasteries. The Dominicans and Franciscans proved consistently more attractive and hospitable to women: of the fifty-eight Dominican cloisters for women in 1288, forty were in Germany, and the Franciscans counted forty as well.[30]

The Béguines, lay religious orders made up of financially and institutionally independent women, which were almost unique to Germany and the Low Countries, constitute an important, related thread of this history. Originally secular retreats for aristocratic women who wanted to pursue a contemplative life, beguinages later admitted women from the artisanal classes who supported themselves by skilled work in crafts (textiles were of greatest importance) or who were active in teaching, charity, and nursing. Most houses were founded between 1250 and 1350. Frankfurt am Main had fifty-seven houses, and Strasbourg had sixty; other cities had fewer, but it was the rare west German or Netherlandish city that did not host a beguinage.

Germans have documented the histories of these institutions rather well. E. H. Schäfer's *Die Kanonissenstifter im deutschen Mittelalter* (Stuttgart, 1907) is an early representative of the institutional histories available to us, but it as been largely replaced by Herbert Grundmann's *Religiöse Bewegungen im Mittelalter,* now in its third edition (Darmstadt, 1970). More than a traditional institutional history, Grundmann's study explores both the social context within which religious movements took place and the spiritual needs that gave rise to them. Taking another approach, Matthaus Bernards has sought to understand the piety of cloistered women in the late Middle Ages by examining their devotional literature. His observations about women's spiritual capacities may strike many as implausible, but his method merits our consideration.[31]

The Béguines have been especially well served by local studies such as J. Asen's "Die Beginen in Köln," *Annalen des historischen Vereins für den Niederrhein insbesondere die alte Erzdiozese Köln* 111 (1927), 112 (1928), and 113 (1928); E. G. Neumann's *Rheinische Beginen- und Begardenwesen* (Meisenheim am Glan, 1960); and Florence W. J. Koorn's *Begijnhoven in Holland en Zeeland gedurende de middeleeuwen* (Assen, 1981). A more general perspective is provided by L. J. M. Phillippen, *De Begijnhoven. Oorsprung, Geschiedenis, Inrichtung,* (Antwerp, 1918); J. Grevens, *Die Anfange der Beginen. Ein Beitrag zur Geschichte der Volksfrommigkeit und des Ordenwesens im Hochmittelalter* (Münster, 1912); H. Grundmann, "Zur Geschichte der Beginen im 13. Jahrhundert," *Archiv für Kulturgeschichte* 21 (1931); and A. Mens, *Oorsprong en Betekenis van de Nederlandse Begijnen- en Begardenbeweging* (Louvain, 1947) or idem, "Les béguines et les bégards dans le cadre de la culture mediévale," *Le moyen âge* 64 (4th series, vol. 13, 1958).

While most are simply descriptions of institutions based on close reading of charters and testaments, some of these studies have addressed the key question of why so many new female orders were founded at this moment in European, especially German, history. Bücher's argument has wide currency in this literature, and a certain plausibility as well, for the growth of female religious does seem to correspond with the oversupply of women Bücher thought he documented. Grundmann, for one, however, has emphatically attacked this interpretation: "The often expressed opinion that the feminine religious movements of the thirteenth century can be explained by the economic and social needs of women in the under, the poorer, classes, and were to a large extent begun by such women . . . not only contradicts the evidence from sources but misunderstands religious sensibility." Later, he noted that it was not the poor, but the rich, with their ideal of voluntary poverty, who began these movements.[32]

Bücher's thesis has not, however, been entirely abandoned, for most scholars have agreed that the number of women who desired a religious life in the period greatly exceeded the number of places in monastic foundations available for them. Beyond that assessment, alas, historians have not come a long way, and the essential question remains unanswered: what about religion or about women's needs and opportunities changed in this age to produce the sharp rise in women's visible religious activity?

A similar question attends the study of heresy itself. The movement best studied is the Cathar heresy, for which the standard work is Arno Borst's *Die Katharen* (Stuttgart, 1953). It proposed that the sect's dualism led to a "radikaler Frauenhass." Ernest Werner responded in 1961 that women and men obtained spiritual equality in Cathar religion, but that in the Church itself "patriarchal feudal structures" denied women authority.[33] Gottfried Koch followed with an argument that built on the notion of a *Frauenfrage*.[34] The excess women from each class, he contended, used Catharism to address their individual social, economic, and personal problems: artisanal women found economic security and a way to express class interests; urban patrician women found refuge from the burdens of a declining socioeconomic status; noble women found autonomy and prestige. Although Koch has been attacked for an approach that seems to some rigidly Marxist, his work has stimulated discussion and, with its argument that women lost power in the movement as it gained institutional power, his book has provided a useful structure for analyzing women's roles in medieval religious movements.[35]

Traditional German scholarship has also documented the witchcraft persecutions of the late medieval and early modern period. From 1843, when W. G. Soldan published his *Geschichte der Hexenprozesse* and J. G. T. Grasse, his *Bibliotheca Magica et Pneumatica,* German historians played a leading role in collecting, editing, and publishing sources, as well as in providing narrative histories. In recent years, however, British and American historians, along with French scholars of the Annales school, have surpassed the Germans in the number and quality of witchcraft studies, and in fact some of the best of the new case studies and interpretations of witchcraft prosecutions in Germany itself have been done abroad.[36]

So broad and so deep have been the traditional interests of German historians in their medieval past that they have also provided studies and published sources about areas undoubtedly of peripheral interest to them but of great interest to contemporary feminist historians: prostitution and gynecology. Early general studies of prostitution include Max Bauer, *Liebesleben in deutschen Vergangenheit* (Berlin, 1924); Iwan Bloch, *Die Prostitution,* 2 vols. Berlin, 1912 and 1925); and W. Rudeck, *Geschichte der öffentliche Sittlichkeit in Deutschland* (Jena, 1897); Karl Obser "Zur Geschichte des Frauenhauses in Überlingen," *Zeitschrift für Geschichte des Oberrheins* 70 (1916); Dr. von Posern-Klett, "Frauenhäuser und freie Frauen in Sachsen," *Archiv für die sächische Geschichte* 12 (1874); Gustav Schönfeldt, *Beiträge zur Geschichte des Pauperismus und der Prostitution in Hamburg* (Weimar, 1897); Josef Schrank, *Die Prostitution in Wien* (Vienna, 1886); and Gustav Wustmann, "Frauenhäuser und freie Frauen in Leipzig im Mittelalter," *Archiv für Kulturgeschichte* (1907) exemplify the range of local studies available.

As the titles indicate, two separate impulses seem to have motivated these studies, in addition to the general interest in women's issues that characterized the period when they were published. One is an interest in folklore, an active field of research in Germany, at least since the Grimm brothers. While their field was downgraded as history writing was professionalized under Ranke, folklorists did not abandon their work but continued to produce a steady stream of often interesting and reliable descriptions of customs and culture of the Middle Ages, which were by and large ignored by the academy. The second source of studies on prostitution emerged in the academy itself, out of an interest in urban institutional history. For these historians, prostitution demanded attention either because brothels were publicly regulated or because prostitution was part of the history of poverty and the institutions that dealt with it.

These beginnings have not been pursued actively in recent years in Germany. The original impulses that fueled them lost power after the First World War and died out entirely with the Nazis. In the conservative and cautious medieval academy of post–World War II Germany, such nontraditional subjects found few chroniclers. Hence, what we find in this genre of German historical literature, as in so many others, is a reliable body of monograph literature and a guide to source collections, which allow us only to begin to ask the questions of the past that now seem important.

With the historiography of gynecology, our assessment must be even more qualified. We have a wealth of studies from medieval and intellectual historians that tells us about gynecological science as it was taught to the university-trained and that gives us increasingly reliable histories of disease, but we know far too little about how gynecological medicine was practiced or what part women took in it. Nevertheless, as a recent study from the Low Countries shows (Anna Delva's *Vrouwengeneeskunde in Vlaanderen,* Bruges, 1983), sources do exist for making these judgments, and the past scholarly work provides an indispensable tool for beginning this inquiry.[37]

The Present and the Possible Future of Germanic Historiography on Medieval Women

Historians of medieval women today owe a great deal to the rich traditions of German historiography. We could not ask the questions we are now asking and could not begin to answer them without the monographs and sources these scholars have left us. Yet, despite its traditional strengths (and maybe because of them), German historiography on medieval women remained until very recently disappointingly isolated. Marxist theory has informed only the occasional medieval monograph; the influence of the Annales school, while profound in Belgium, is barely perceptible in Germany. Surely most disheartening for American historians of medieval women is the German medievalist's refusal to take account of the work being done outside Germany. The result is a women's history that often seems arid and purposeless, one that clings to old sources and old questions, seeking simply to fit women into a world traditional medievalists have already defined.

Even outside the medieval academy, where tradition is not so firmly entrenched, Germany historians have been slow to explore the potential of the new social history. While England's *Past and Present* was begun in 1952, while France's *Annales* was established at the sixth section of the Ecole Pratique des Hautes Etudes in 1946 (now the Ecole des Hautes Etudes en Sciences Sociales), and while the United States' *Comparative Studies in Society and History* was founded in 1958, it was not until 1975 that *Geschichte und Gesellschaft,* Germany's social history journal, began publication.

Both the strengths and weaknesses of German scholarship on medieval women as it exists today can be illustrated by *Frauen im Mittelalter,* Edith Ennen's 1984 synthesis of past work (most of it German) on medieval women (principally German women). The corpus of scholarly literature attributable to Ennen is impressive; her own research and theorizing on urban origins and institutions in medieval Germany and her ability to synthesize the complex historiography on these issues for academic nonspecialists have rightfully earned her respect in scholarly circles in and well beyond Germany. Ennen has also long been interested in medieval women's history. In two useful articles from 1980 and 1981, she adroitly summarized women's roles and status in cities and in late medieval society at large and, as the first-class scientific historian she is, showed how the sources permitted the generalizations she made. Ennen has also encouraged new research on women: Wensky's monograph on Cologne's women was done at the University of Bonn under her supervision.[38]

Ennen's own book on medieval women extends these inquiries. Drawing upon her unparalleled knowledge of the German monograph literature and the sources on medieval women, she systematically summarizes the information now available concerning women from all walks of life during the three epochs of the Middle Ages: the early, the high and the late Middle Ages. Her survey is surely *the* indispensible guide to the German-language literature on medieval women.

Its weaknesses are, however, equally apparent. Ennen begins with an astute and learned critique of the theory and scholarship underlying Shulamith Shahar's *Die Frau im Mittelalter,* a book not without empirical value, but one that is inferior to Ennen's. Shahar not only misreads the occasional source, Ennen argues, but she shows an incomplete understanding of medieval society, tending to confuse social boundaries and to minimize temporal distinctions as she looks for commonalities in the lives of all women. Medieval women, Ennen rightly insists, were separated by material conditions, by spiritual opportunities, as well as by political and legal realities, which makes it impossible to consider them a "fourth estate," as Shahar would have it.[39] Apt as her critique may be, Ennen does not provide a better interpretation. Instead, she contents herself with a dry summary of literature, arranged by topic in a rather pedestrian way, sometimes simply summarizing the biographies of famous women published by others. Only when Ennen is dealing with her own material, on urban legal systems for example, does she offer fresh insights or make a serious effort to explain the patterns she sketches.

Yet, promising new stirrings exist in the German academy. Haltingly but surely, medieval scholars are not only building on past work done in their own land but, with the help of theory drawn from related academic disciplines, they are beginning to raise new questions. Intellectual history (*Geitesgeschichte*) has now become a major component of traditional political and constitutional history. The pioneering work of Percy Ernst Schramm (1894–1970) on political symbolism and ritual was instrumental in establishing this link. Today his medievalist successors in Germany are following his lead with comparative studies of how political concepts shaped, and were shaped by, the actual exercise of public authority in medieval Europe.

While this new scholarship has so far affected the historical literature concerning medieval women in only a few works, Thilo Vogelsang's *Die Frau als Herrscherin* among them, another new development in medieval German historiography had had greater influence. Since the 1950s, German medieval history has been acquiring a distinctly sociopolitical cast (what is called *Strukturgeschichte*), and that tendency has slowly begun to produce a history of the medieval family and, tangentially, of medieval women. Otto Hinze's efforts in the 1920s to introduce typologies into historical studies and to employ social science concepts in historical studies received new attention once the war ended and German historical scholarship could begin again. Otto Brunner's *Land und Herrschaft* of 1939 and his insistence that a state's constitution and its political institutions are rooted in its social structure, has provided an important theoretical impetus as well. Since the war Theodor von Mayer II has developed these ideas into a concrete research program centered on an "Arbeitsgruppe" in Constance that is undertaking close regional studies (*Landesgeschichte*) of sociopolitical structures, essentially constitutional systems, in a comparative context. In the 1960s the Max Planck Institute for History inaugurated a broad comparative study of corporative (*ständisch*) institutions in Europe of the Old Regime.

Although not addressing the history of family and women as such, the "German" form of social history has led to such interests and has undoubtedly helped open the medieval academy to social history as practiced elsewhere. Erich Maschke, one of Germany's best-known students of medieval social structures, has for example recently turned to the history of the family, self-consciously drawing from work by historical sociologists and practitioners of demographic history associated with the Cambridge Group for the History of Population and Social Structures.[40] Legal and constitutional history relating to medieval women's history continues as well, and scholars are still producing solidly researched reports on women's work based on traditional models.[41] Wensky's work on the women of medieval Cologne is only one of several recent studies on women and family in the period: B. Handler-Lachman's, "Die Berufstätigkeit der Frau in den deutschen Städten des Spätmittelalters und der beginnenden Neuzeit," of 1980 and

H. Loose's "Erwerbstätigkeit der Frau im Speigel Lübecker und Hamburger Testamente des 14. Jh." of the same year also count among the many new additions to archival research on urban women's economic roles.

The new *Haus und Familie* from the Institute for Comparative Urban History in Münster, where many of these separate interests seem to converge, suggests how contemporary historiography on medieval women might develop in Germany in the next years. In addition to an article on the family economy by Michael Mitterauer, who writes historical sociology, and Köbler's already mentioned piece on family law, it contains essays, for example, on canon law as related to marriage, on daily life in the medieval city, on marriage and the family as portrayed in contemporary poetry, and on women's work as family members. Let us hope this is the beginning of more interdisciplinary work that could break down the boundaries German medievalists seem to have built for themselves.

We surely are justified in hoping for more adventuresome research such as that towards which the volume from Münster points, and it is understandable as well why we might deplore German medievalists' traditional reluctance to engage scholarship on women from other countries, from other periods, and from other disciplines. Yet, we owe Germanic medievalists too much to complain too loudly: from them we can learn the critical skills so necessary for interpreting the obscure documents of a remote past, and we can turn to their past publications for a wealth of information about medieval women. Women are a documented presence in the medieval histories produced by Germanic scholars, and we owe their presence to the craftsmanship that distinguishes these histories.

Notes

1. This essay owes a great deal to a preliminary draft begun by Suzanne Wemple of Barnard College. Although she was unable to complete the essay, Professor Wemple generously allowed me to use her work, and I have relied heavily on her expertise in several sections, above all in the discussions pertaining to women's legal status in the early and high Middle Ages and to marriage practices during these periods.

2. Two journals in The Netherlands are devoted to women's studies: *Tijdschrift voor vrouwen studies,* now in its eighth year of publication, and the somewhat newer *Jaarboek voor vrouwengeschiedenis.*

3. Humanists like Hartman Schedel (d. 1514) and the Fuggers amassed col-

lections of medieval annals. Eager to promote research on his Hapsburg ancestors, Emperor Maximilian supported the library at the University of Vienna.

4. As early as 1693, Gottfried Wilhelm von Leibniz (d. 1716) published the *Codex juris gentium diplomaticus,* following it with the *Scriptores rerum Brunsvicensium* (1701–11) and an annal covering the years 768 to 1005. His aide, Johann G. Eckhardt, subsequently compiled and edited the *Corpus historicum medii aevi* (1723).

5. Quoted in Ernst Breisach, *Historiography: Ancient, Medieval, and Modern* (Chicago and London, 1983), p. 209. Part of the discussion in my historiographical essay closely follows Breisach's narrative. Also see Konrad Jarausch, "Illiberalism and Beyond: German History in Search of a Paradigm," *Journal of Modern History,* 55 (1983), 268–84; Hans-Ulrich Wehler, "Historiography in Germany Today," in Jürgen Habermas, ed., *Observations on the Spiritual Situation of the Age* (Cambridge, MA and London, 1984); G. G. Iggers, *New Directions in European Historiography* (Middletown, CT, 1975); and idem, *The German Conception of History* (Middletown, CT, 1968).

6. Edith Ennen, *Frauen im Mittelalter* (Munich, 1984); Margret Wensky, *Die Stellung der Frau in der stadtkölnischen Wirtschaft im Spätmittelalter* (Cologne and Vienna, 1980).

7. J. Grimm, *Deutsche Rechtsalterthümer* (Göttingen, 1828), pp. 417–54.

8. Lothar Dargun, "Mutterrecht und Raubehe, und ihre Reste im germanischen Recht und Leben," *Untersuchungen zur deutschen Staats- und Rechtsgeschichte,* 16 (1883), 13–76.

The Morgan thesis did not survive much scrutiny. For a discussion of its weaknesses, see Marianne Weber, *Ehefrau und Mutter in der Rechtsentwicklung* (Tübingen, 1907).

9. Julius Ficker, *Untersuchungen zur Erbenfolge der ostgermanischen Rechts,* 4 vols. (Innsbruck, 1891–96).

10. Elsbet Kaiser, *Frauendienst im mittelhochdeutschen Volksepos* (Breslau, 1921), p. 328. Lulu von Strauss und Torney, *Deutsches Frauenleben in der Zeit der Sachsenkaiser und Hohenstaufen* (Jena, 1927).

11. Gerda von Merschberger, *Die Rechtstellung der germanischen frau* (Leipzig, 1937) and R. Köstler, "Raub-, Kauf- und Friedelehe bei den Germanen," *Zeitschrift der Savigny-Stiftung für Rechtsgeschichte,* Germ. Abt., 63 (1943), 92–136.

12. Noel Senn, *Le contrat de vente de la femme en droit matrimonial germanique* (Porrentruy, 1946) and Karl August Eckhardt, *Germanisches Recht,* 2 vols., 4th ed. Grundriss der germanischen Philologie 5, no. 1–2 (Berlin, 1967).

13. Among those employing the concept was Karl Ferdinand Werner, "Bedeutende Adelsfamilien im Reich Karls des Grossen," *Karl der Grosse: Lebenswerk und Nachleben,* vol. 1, ed. Helmut Baumann (Dusseldorf, 1967), 83–142. For the opposing interpretation, see S. Kalifa, "Singularités matrimoniales chez des anciens germains: le rapt et le droit de la femme à disposer d'elle-meme," *Revue historique de droit française et étranger,* 48 (1970), 199–225.

14. Suzanne F. Wemple, *Women in Frankish Society* (Philadelphia, 1981).

15. There is some debate about this history. In addition to R. Schröder, *Geschichte des ehelichen Güterrechts in Deutschland,* 2 parts, 4 vols. (Stettin, Danzig, and Elbing, 1863–74) and Wemple (see note 13), see Diane Owen Hughes, "From Brideprice to Dowry in Medieval Europe," *Journal of Family History,* 3, no. 3 (Fall 1978), 262–98 and Jack Goody, *The Development of the Family and Marriage in Europe* (Cambridge, 1983).

German scholars have also made important contributions to the history of noble lineages and the role of maternal kin, especially during the Saxon period. The work of Karl Schmid and Karl Leyser on this subject is fundamental. For a useful review of this literature, see John B. Freed, "Reflections on the Medieval German Nobility," *The American Historical Review,* 91, no. 3 (June, 1986), 553–75.

16. Max Kirschner, *Die deutschen Kaiserinnen in der Zeit von Konrad I. bis zum Tode Lothars von Supplinburg,* Historische Studien 79 (Berlin, 1910).

17. Thilo von Vogelsang, *Die Frau als Herrscherin im hohen Mittelalter* (Göttingen, 1954).

18. Gerhard Köbler, "Das Familienrecht in der spämittelalterlichen Stadt," in *Haus und Familie,* ed. A. Haverkamp (Göttingen, 1983).

19. Karl Bücher, *Die Entstehung der Volkswirtschaft* (Tübingen: 1898) and *Die Bevôlkerung von Frankfurt am Main im xiv und xv Jahrhundert* (Tübingen, 1886).

20. In addition to *Die Frauenfrage im Mittelalter* (1882, rev. ed., Tübingen, 1910), see his *Die Berufe der Stadt Frankfurt am Main im Mittelalter,* Abhandlungen der Sächischen Academie der Wissenschaften, Phil.-Hist., Classe 30–3 (Leipzig, 1914). The quotations in the text are from pp. 19, 68, 75, and 72 respectively.

21. The three most important were Wilhelm Behaghel, *Die gewerbliche Stellung der Frau im mittelalterlichen Köln.* Abhandlungen zur mittleren und neueren Geschichte, 23 (1970); Julius Hartwig, "Die Frauenfrage im mittelalterlichen Lübeck," *Hansische Geschichtsblätter,* 14 (1908), 35–94; and Gustav Schmoller, *Die Strassburger Tucher- und Weberzunft. Urkunden und Darstellung* (Strassburg, 1897).

22. Helmut Wachendorf, *Die wrtschaftliche Stellung der Frau in den deutschen Städten des späteren Mittelalters* (Quakenbrück, 1934); Bruno Kuske, "Die Frau im mittelalterlichen Wirtschaftsleben," *Zeitschrift für handelswissenschaftliche Forschung,* 11 (1959), 148–56; Rudolf Wissel, *Des alten Handwerks Recht und Gewohnheit* (Berlin, 1929); L. Hess, *Die deutschen Frauenberufe des Mittelalters.* Beiträge zur Volkstumsforschung, 6 (Munich, 1940); Gertrud Schmidt, *Die Berufstätigkeit der Frau in der Reichsstadt Nürnberg bis zum Ende des 16. Jahrhundert,* Beitrag zur Wirtschaftsgeschichte Nürnbergs (Erlangen, 1950); Rudolf Endres, "Zur Lage der Nürnberger Handwerkerschaft zur Zeit von Hans Sach," *Jahrbuch für Frankische Landesforschung,* 37 (1977) 107–123; B. Kroemer, "Über Rechtsstellung, Handlungsspielraume und Tätigkeitsberieche von Frauen in spätmittelalterlichen Städten," in *Staat und Gesellschaft in Mittelalter und früher Neuzeit,* Gedenkschrift für J. Leuschner (Göttingen, 1983). For a fuller list, see the Bibliography.

Economic and industrial histories of the period also regularly commented on the role of women: see, for example, G. des Marez, *L'organisation du travail à Bruxelles au xvme siècle* (Brussels, 1904) and N. Posthumus, *De Geschiedenis van de Leidsche Lakenindustrie,* vol. 1 (The Hague, 1908).

23. Jenneke Quast, "Vrouwenarbeid omstreeks 1500 in enkele nederlandse steden," *Jaarboek voor vrouwengeschiedenis* (Nijmegen, 1980), 46–64 and "Vrouwen in gilden in Den Bosch, Utrecht en Leiden van de 14e tot en met de 16e eeuw," *Fragmenten vrouwengeschiedenis,* ed. Wantje Fritschy, vol. 1 (The Hague, 1980).

24. Kurt Wesoly, "Der weibliche Bevölkerungsanteil im spätmittelalterlichen und frühneuzeitlichen Städten und die Betätigung von Frauen im zunftigen Handwerk (insbesondere am Mittel- und Oberrhein)," *Zeitschrift für die Geschichte des Oberrheins* 128, new ser. 89, (1980), 102 and 89, respectively.

25. Edith Ennen, "Die Frau in der mittelalterlichen Stadtgesellschaft Mitteleuropas," *Hansische Geschichtsblätter* 98 (1980), 1–22; Michael Mitterauer, "Familie und Arbeitsorganisation in städtischen Gesellschaften des späten Mittelalters und der frühen Neuzeit," in *Haus und Familie,* ed. A. Haverkamp (Göttingen, 1983).

26. H. Homeyer, *Hrostvithae opera* (Munich, Paderborn, and Vienna, 1970). See also his translation of her works, *Hrostvitha von Gandersheim: Werke in deutscher Übertragung* (Munich, Paderborn, Vienna, 1970); Bert Nagel, *Hrostvit von Gandersheim. Samtliche Dichtungen* (Munich, 1966). For Herrad von Landsperg, see Gérard Cames, *Allégories et symboles dans l'Hortus deliciarum* (Leiden, 1971). For Hildegard of Bingen, see *Wisse der Wege: Scivias,* trans. Maura Bockler 1928; rprt. Salzburg, 1963); Joseph Schomer, *Die Illustrationen zu den Visionen der hl. Hildegard als künstlerische Neuschöpfung* (Bonn, 1937).

27. F. W. E. Roth, *Das Gebetbuch der hl. Elisabeth von Schonau* (Augsburg, 1886).

28. Caroline Bynum, *Jesus as Mother: Studies in the Spirituality of the High Middle Ages* (Berkeley and London, 1982).

29. Ludwig Zoepf, *Die Mystikerin Margaretha Ebner (c. 1291–1351), Beiträge zur Kulturgeschichte des Mittelalters und der Reanaissance,* ed. W. Goetz, no. 16 (Leipzig and Berlin, 1914).

30. Herbert Grundmann, *Religiöse Bewegungen im Mittelalter,* 3rd. ed. (Darmstadt, 1970).

31. Matthaus Bernards, *Speculum virginum: Geistigkeit und Seelenleben der Frau im Hochmittelalter* (Cologne and Graz, 1955); Eleanor Simmons Greenhill, *Die geistigen Voraussetzungen der Bilderreihe des Speculum virginum. Versuch einer Deutung,* Beiträge zur Geschichte der Philosophie und Theologie des Mittelalters no. 39–2 (Münster, Westfalen, 1962).

32. Grundmann, p. 192 and passim (1935 edition).

33. Ernest Werner, "Zur Frauenfrage und zum Frauenkult im Mittelalter," in *Forschungen und Fortschritte,* 29 (1955), 269–76.

34. Gottfried Koch, *Frauenfrage und Ketzertum im Mittelalter* (Berlin, 1962).

35. See, for example, the papers from the colloquium on medieval and early

modern heresy: *Hérésies et sociétés dans l'Europe pre-industrielle, 11e–18e siècles,* ed. Jacques LeGoff (Paris and The Hague, 1968).

36. See, for example, H. C. Erik Middelfort, *Witch Hunting in Southwestern Germany* (Stanford, 1972). German scholarship includes the work of folklorists such as I. Hoffmann-Krajer, "Lüzerner Akten zum Hexen- und Zauberwesen," *Schweizerisch Archiv für Volkskunde,* 111 (1899); Fritz Byloff, *Volkskundliches aus Staatsprozessen der österreichischen Alpenlander mit besonderer Berucksichtigung der Zauberei- und Hexenprozesse 1455–1850* (Berlin, 1929) as well as more purely historical treatments such as Joseph Hansen's *Zauberwahn, Inquisition und Hexenprozess im Mittelalter* (Munich, 1900) and *Quellen und Untersuchungen zur Geschichte des Hexenwahns und der Hexenverfolgung im Mitterlalter* (Bonn, 1901).

37. For modern compilations and new research in this vein, see H. Fasbender, *Geschichte der Geburtshilfe* (2nd ed., Hildesheim, 1964); P. Diepgens, *Frau und Frauheilkunde im Kultur des Mittelalters* (Mainz, 1963); M. Dumont and P. Morel, *Histoire de l'obstétrique et de gynecologie* (Villefranche, 1968); E. Fischer-Hanberger, *Krankheit Frau, und andere Arbeiten zur Medizingeschichte der Frau* (Bern, Stuttgart, and Vienna, 1979).

38. Ennen's work is best approached through her *Geschichte der europäischen Stadt,* 3rd. ed. (Bonn, 1981) and *Die europäische Stadt des Mittelalters,* 3rd. ed. (Göttingen, 1979); the latter exists in an English translation.

39. Shulamith Shahar, *Die Frau im Mittelalter* (Köningstein/Ts.: 1981); in English as *The Fourth Estate.*

40. Erich Maschke, *Die Familie in der deutschen Stadt des späten Mittelalters,* Sitzungsberichte der Heidelberger Akademie der Wissenschaften, Phil.-Hist. Klasse (Heidelberg, 1980).

41. See Ennen's *Frauen im Mittelalter* (Munich, 1984) and the bibliography she cites: H. H. Kaminsky, "Die Frau in Recht und Gesellschaft des Mittelalters," in A. Kuhn and G. Schneider, eds., *Frauen in der Geschichte,* vol. 1 (Düsseldorf, 1979). For additional citations to material on women's legal position, see the bibliographies in the *Haus und Familie* volume, ed. by A. Haverkamp, as in the Bibliography.

BIBLIOGRAPHY

England

SURVEYS

Abram, Annie. *English Life and Manners in the Later Middle Ages*. London, 1913.
———. *Social Life in England in the Fifteenth Century*. London, 1909.
Baker, Derek, ed. *Medieval Women*. Oxford, 1978.
Barraclough, Geoffrey, ed. *Social Life in Early England*. London, 1960.
Browne, George Forrest. *The Importance of Women in Anglo-Saxon Times*. New York, 1919.
Bullough, Vern L. *The Subordinate Sex; A History of Attitudes Toward Women*. Urbana, 1973.
Coulton, George Gordon. *Life in the Middle Ages*. Cambridge, 1967.
———. *Medieval Panorama: The English Scene from Conquest to Reformation*. Cambridge, 1970.
———. *Social Life in Britain from the Conquest to the Reformation*. New York, 1968.
DuBoulay, F. R. H. *An Age of Ambition*. London, 1970.
Fell, Christine. *Women in Anglo-Saxon England and the Impact of 1066*. Bloomington, IN, 1984.
Gies, Frances and Gies, Joseph. *Women in the Middle Ages*. New York, 1971.
Herm, Gerhard. *The Celts: The People Who Came out of Darkness*. New York, 1975.
Hill, Georgiana. *Women in English Life from Medieval to Modern Times*, 2 vols. London, 1896.
Hodgetts, J. Frederick. *The English in the Middle Ages*. London, 1885.
Hume, David. *The History of England*. London, 1840.
Kanner, Barbara, ed. *The Women of England from Anglo-Saxon Times to the Present*. Hamden, CT, 1979.

Kendall, Paul Murray. *The Yorkist Age: Daily Life during the War of the Roses.* New York, 1962.
Lester, G. A. *The Anglo-Saxons: How They Lived and Worked.* London, 1976.
Macaulay, Catherine. *The History of England from the Accession of James I to That of the Brunswick Line.* London, 1763.
———. *Letters on Education.* London, 1790.
Markale, Jean. *Women of the Celts,* trans. A. Mygind, C. Hauch, and P. Henry. London, 1980.
Mill, John Stuart. *The Subjection of Women.* London, 1869.
Morewedge, Rosmarie Thee, ed. *The Role of Women in the Middle Ages.* Binghamton, NY, 1975.
Page, R. I. *Life in Anglo-Saxon England.* London, 1970.
Polydore Vergil's English History from an Early Translation, ed. Henry Ellis. Camden Society 36. London, 1864.
Polydore Vergil. *Three Books of Polydore Vergil's English History, Henry VI, Edward IV, and Richard III,* ed. Henry Ellis. Camden Society 29. London, 1844.
Power, Eileen. *Medieval Women,* ed. M. M. Postan. New York, 1975.
———. "The Position of Women." In *Legacy of the Middle Ages,* ed. G. C. Crump and E. F. Jacob, pp. 401–33. Oxford, 1926.
Salzman, Louis Francis. *English Life in the Middle Ages.* London, 1927.
Snell, F. J. *The Customs of Old England.* London, 1911.
Stenton, Doris M. *The English Women in History.* London, 1957.
Stuard, Susan Mosher, ed. *Women in Medieval Society.* Philadelphia, 1976.
Stuart, Dorothy Margaret. *Men and Women of Plantagenet England.* London, 1932.
Thrupp, John. *The Anglo-Saxon Home: A History of the Domestic Institutions and Customs of England from the Fifth to the Eleventh Century.* London, 1862.
Trevelyan, George M. *England in the Age of Wycliffe.* London, 1899.
Wollstonecraft, Mary. *A Vindication of the Rights of Women.* 3rd. ed. London, 1796.
Woolf, Virginia. *A Room of One's Own.* New York, 1929.
Wright, Thomas. *A History of Domestic Manners and Sentiments in England during the Middle Ages.* London, 1862.
———. *Womenkind in Western Europe: From the Earliest Times to the Seventeenth Century.* London, 1869.

POLITICS AND LAW

Cleveland, Arthur Rackham. *Women under the English Law.* London, 1896.
Given, James B. *Society and Homicide in Thirteenth-Century England.* Palo Alto, CA, 1977.
Griffiths, R. A. "Queen Katherine of Valois and a Missing Statute of the Realm." *Law Quarterly Review,* 93 (1977), 248–258.
Hanawalt, Barbara A. "Community Conflict and Social Control: Crime in the Ramsey Abbey Villages." *Mediaeval Studies,* 39 (1977), 402–423.

———. *Crime and Conflict in English Communities, 1300–1348*. Cambridge, MA, 1979.
———. "The Female Felon in Fourteenth-Century England." *Viator*, 5 (1974), 253–268. Reprinted in *Women in Medieval Society*, ed. Susan Mosher Stuard, pp. 125–40. Philadelphia, 1976.
———. "The Peasant Family and Crime in Fourteenth-Century England." *Journal of British Studies*, 13 (1974), 1–18.
———. "Violent Death in Fourteenth and Fifteenth Century England." *Comparative Studies in Society and History*, 18 (1976), 297–320.
Hand, Geoffrey. "The King's Widow and the King's Widows." *Law Quarterly Review*, 93 (1977), 507–607.
Helmholz, Richard H. "Bastardy Litigation in Medieval England." *American Journal of Legal History*, 13 (1969), 360–83.
———. "Infanticide in the Province of Canterbury during the Fifteenth Century." *History of Childhood Quarterly*, 2 (1974–75), 282–390.
———. *Marriage Litigation in Medieval England*. Cambridge, 1975.
Hyams, Paul. *King, Lords, and Peasants in Medieval England*. Oxford, 1980.
Kellum, Barbara A. "Infanticide in England in the Later Middle Ages." *History of Childhood Quarterly*, 1 (1973–74), 367–388.
Lander, J. R. "Marriage and Politics in the Fifteenth Century: the Nevilles and Wydevilles." In *Crown and Nobility 1450–1509, Collected Essays of J. R. Lander*, pp. 94–126. London, 1976.
Pike, Luke Owen. *History of Crime in England*. 2 vols. London, 1873.
Pollock, Frederick and Maitland, F. W. *History of English Law Before the Time of Edward I*. London, 1923.
Ross, Charles, ed. *Patronage, Pedigree, and Power in Later Medieval England*. Gloucester, 1979.
Stephen, J. F. *A History of Criminal Law in England*. 3 vols. London, 1883.
Walker, Sue Sheridan. "Widow and Ward: The Feudal Law of Child Custody in Medieval England." *Feminist Studies*, 3 (1976), 104–16. Also in *Women in Medieval Society*, ed. Susan Mosher Stuard, pp. 156–72. Philadelphia, 1976.
———. "Feudal Constraint and Free Consent in the Making of Marriages in Medieval England: Widows of the King's Gift." *Canadian Historical Association: Historical Papers* (1978), 97–110.
———. "Violence and the Exercise of Feudal Guardianship: The Action of '*Ejectio Custodia*'." *American Journal of Legal History*, 16 (1969), 320–33.

ECONOMIC LIFE

Abraham, Annie. "Women Traders in Medieval London." *Economic Journal*, 26 (1916), 276–85.

Ault, Warren O. "By-Laws of Gleaning and the Problems of Harvest." *Economic History Review,* 2nd ser. 14 (1961), 210–17.
———. *Open-Field Farming in Medieval England.* London, 1972.
———. *Open-Field Husbandry and the Village Community: A Study of Agrarian By-Laws in Medieval England.* Transactions of the American Philosophical Society, new ser. 55. Philadelphia, 1965.
Beveridge, William. "Wages in the Winchester Manors." *Economic History Review,* 7 (1936), 22–43.
———. "Westminister Wages in the Manorial Era," *Economic History Review,* 2nd ser. 8 (1955), 18–35.
Bolton, J. L. *The Medieval English Economy, 1150–1500.* London, 1980.
Boserup, Ester. *Women's Role in Economic Development.* London, 1970.
Bridbury, A. R. *Economic Growth: England in the Later Middle Ages.* London, 1962.
Charles, Lindsey and Duffin, Lorna, eds. *Women and Work in Pre-Industrial England.* London, 1985.
Clark, Alice. *Working Life of Women in the Seventeenth Century.* London, 1919.
Fowler, G. H. "A Household Expense Roll, 1328." *English Historical Review,* 55 (1940), 630–32.
Hanawalt, Barbara A., ed. *Women and Work in Preindustrial Europe.* Bloomington, IN, 1986.
Mate, Mavis. "Profit and Productivity on the Estates of Isabella de Forz (1260–92)." *Economic History Review,* 33 (1980), 326–34.
Miller, E. and Hatcher, J. *Medieval England: Rural Society and Economic Change, 1086–1348.* London, 1978.
Scott, Joan W. and Tilly, Louise A. "Women's Work and the Family in Nineteenth-Century Europe." *Comparative Studies in Society and History,* 17 (1975), 336–64.

SOCIAL LIFE

Altschul, Michael. *A Baronial Family in Medieval England: The Clares, 1217–1314.* Baltimore, 1965.
Amundsen, Darrel and Dreis, Carol Jean. "The Age of Menarche in Medieval England." *Human Biology,* 45 (1973), 363–68.
Ashley, William. *Bread of Our Forefathers.* Oxford, 1928.
Baker, A. R. H. "Open Fields and Partible Inheritance on a Kent Manor." *Economic History Review,* 2nd ser. 17 (1964), 1–23.
Baldwin, Frances Elizabeth. *Sumptuary Legislation and Personal Regulation in England.* John Hopkins University Studies in Historical and Political Science, 44. Baltimore, 1926.
Bennett, H. S. *Life on the English Manor.* Cambridge, 1937.
———. *The Pastons and Their England: Studies in an Age of Transition.* Cambridge, 1970.

Bennett, Judith. "Medieval Peasant Marriage: An Examination of Marriage Licence Fines in the *Liber Gersumarum*." In *Pathways to Medieval Peasants*, ed. J. A. Raftis, pp. 193–246. Toronto, 1981.

———. "The Tie that Binds: Peasant Marriages and Peasant Families in Late Medieval England." *Journal of Interdisciplinary History*, 15 (1984), 111–29.

———. "Village Ale Wives." In *Women and Work in Preindustrial Europe*, ed. Barbara A. Hanawalt. Bloomington, IN, 1986.

Bennett, Michael. "Spiritual Kinship and the Baptismal Name in Traditional European Society." In *Principalities, Powers and Estates: Studies in Medieval and Early Modern Government and Society*, pp. 1–12, ed. L. O. Frappell. Adelaide, SA, 1979.

Berkner, Lutz K. "Recent Research on the History of the Family in Western Europe." *Journal of Marriage and the Family*, 35 (1973), 395–405.

Biller, P. P. A. "Birth Control in the West in the Thirteenth- and Early Fourteenth-Centuries." *Past and Present*, 94 (1982), 3–26.

Bossy, John. "Blood and Baptism: Kinship, Community and Christianity in Western Europe from the Fourteenth to the Seventeenth Centuries." In *Sanctity and Society: The Church and the World*, ed. Derek Baker, pp. 129–44. Oxford, 1973.

Brand, Paul A. and Hyams, Paul R. "Debate: Seigneurial Control of Women's Marriage." *Past and Present*, 99 (1983), 123–33.

Britton, Edward. *The Community of the Vill: A Study in the History of the Family and Village Life in Fourteenth-Century England*. Toronto, 1977.

Brothwell, Don. "Palaeodemography and Earlier British Populations." *World Archaeology*, 4 (1972), 75–87.

Bullough, D. A. "Early Medieval Social Groupings: The Terminology of Kinship." *Past and Present*, 45 (1969), 3–18.

Chibnall, A. C. *Sherington: Fiefs and Fields of a Buckinghamshire Village*. Cambridge, 1965.

Clark, Cecily. "Women's Names in Post-Conquest England: Observations and Speculations." *Speculum*, 53 (1978), 223–51.

Clark, Elaine. "Debt Litigation in a Late Medieval English Vill." In *Pathways to Medieval Peasants*, ed. J. Ambrose Raftis, pp. 247–79. Toronto, 1981.

———. "Some Aspects of Social Security in Medieval England." *Journal of Family History*, 7 (1982), 307–20.

Clay, Rotha M. *The Medieval Hospitals of England*. London, 1909.

Contamine, Philippe. *La Vie quotidienne pendant la guerre de Cent Ans: France et Angleterre, xiv siècle*. Paris, 1976.

Davenport, Frances G. "The Decay of Villeinage in East Anglia." In *Essays in Economic History*, vol. 2, pp. 112–24, ed. E. M. Carus-Wilson. London, 1962.

DeWindt, Anne. "A Peasant Land Market and Its Participants: King's Ripton, 1280–1400." *Midland History*, 4 (1978), 142–58.

———. "Peasant Power Structures in Fourteenth-Century King's Ripton." *Mediaeval Studies*, 38 (1976), 236–67.

DeWindt, Edwin B. *Land and People in Holywell-Cum-Needingworth*. Toronto, 1972.

Dodghson, Robert A. "The Landholding Foundations of the Open-Field System." *Past and Present,* 67 (1975), 3–29.

Dodwell, Barbara. "Holdings and Inheritance in Medieval East Anglia." *Economic History Review,* 2nd ser. 20 (1967), 53–66.

Dyer, Christopher. *Lords and Peasants in a Changing Society: The Estates of the Bishopric of Worcester, 680–1540*. Cambridge, 1980.

English, Barbara. *A Study in Feudal Society; The Lords of Holderness, 1086–1260*. Oxford, 1979.

Faith, Rosamond J. "Debate: Seigneurial Control of Women's Marriage." *Past and Present,* 99 (1983), 133–48.

———. "Peasant Families and Inheritance Customs in Medieval England." *Agricultural History Review,* 14 (1966), 77–95.

Firth, Catherine B. "Village Gilds of Norfolk in the 15th Century." *Norfolk Archaeology,* 18 (1914), 161–203.

Fussell, G. E. "Countrywomen in Old England." *Agricultural History,* 50 (1976), 175–78.

Gottfried, Robert S. *Epidemic Disease in Fifteenth-Century England: The Medical Response and the Demographic Consequences*. New Brunswick, 1978.

Gransden, Antonio. "Childhood and Youth in Medieval England." *Nottingham Medieval Studies,* 16 (1972), 3–19.

Hair, P. E. H. "Bridal Pregnancy in Rural England in Earlier Centuries." *Population Studies,* 20 (1966–67), 233–43.

———. "Bridal Pregnancy in Earlier Rural England, Further Examined." *Population Studies,* 24 (1970), 59–70.

Hajnal, J. "European Marriage Patterns in Perspective." In *Population in History, Essays in Historical Demography,* ed. D. V. Glass and D. E. C. Eversley, pp. 101–43. Chicago, 1965.

Hallam, H. E. "Population Density in Medieval Fenland." *Economic History Review,* 2nd ser. 14 (1961), 71–81.

———. "Some Thirteenth-Century Censuses." *Economic History Review,* 2nd ser. 10 (1958), 340–61.

Hanawalt, Barbara A. "Childrearing Among the Lower Classes of Late Medieval England." *Journal of Interdisciplinary History,* 8 (1977), 1–22.

———. "Conception Through Infancy in Medieval English Historical and Folklore Sources." *Folklore Forum,* 13 (1980), 127–57.

———. "Introduction." In *Women and Work in Preindustrial Europe*. Bloomington, IN, 1986.

———. "Keepers of the Lights: Later Medieval English Parish Gilds." *Journal of Medieval and Renaissance Studies,* 14 (1984), 21–37.

———. *The Ties That Bound: Peasant Families in Medieval England*. New York, 1986.

Haskell, Ann S. "The Paston Women on Marriage in Fifteenth-Century England." *Viator,* 4 (1973), 459–71.

Hassall, W. O. *How They Lived: An Anthology of Original Accounts Written before 1485*. New York, 1962.

Hatcher, John. *Plague, Population, and the English Economy, 1348–1530*. London, 1977.

———. *Rural Economy and Society in the Duchy of Cornwall, 1300–1500*. Cambridge, 1970.

Hilton, R. H. *The English Peasantry in the Later Middle Ages; The Ford Lectures for 1973 and Related Studies*. Oxford, 1975.

———. *A Medieval Society: The West Midlands at the End of the Thirteenth Century*. London, 1966.

Hilton, R. H. and Rahtz, P. A. “Upton, Gloucestershire, 1359–64.” *Transactions of the Bristol and Gloucestershire Archaeological Society,* 85 (1966), 70–146.

Hollingsworth, T. H. “A Demographic Study of the British Ducal Families.” *Population Studies,* 11 (1957–58), 4–26.

———. *Historical Demography*. Ithaca, NY, 1969.

Homans, George C. *English Villagers of the Thirteenth Century*. Cambridge, MA, 1941.

———. “The Frisians in East Anglia.” *Economic History Review,* 2nd ser. 10 (1957), 189–206.

———. “The Rural Sociology of Medieval England,” *Past and Present,* 4 (1953), 32–43.

Hoskins, W. G. *The Midland Peasant: The Economic and Social History of a Leicestershire Village*. London, 1957.

———. “Murder and Sudden Death in Medieval Wigston.” *Transactions of the Leicestershire Archaeological Society,* 21 (1940–41), 176–86.

Howell, Cicely. “Peasant Inheritance Customs in the Midlands, 1280–1700.” In *Family and Inheritance: Rural Society in Western Europe,* ed. J. Goody, J. Thirsk, and E. P. Thompson, pp. 112–55. Cambridge, 1976.

Kelly, Henry A. *Love and Marriage in the Age of Chaucer.* Ithaca, NY, 1975.

Krause, J. “The Medieval Household: Large or Small?” *Economic History Review,* 2nd ser. 9 (1975), 420–32.

LeBarge, Margaret Wade. *A Baronial Household of the Thirteenth Century*. New York, 1965.

Lancaster, Lorraine. “Kinship in Anglo-Saxon Society.” *British Journal of Sociology,* 9 (1958), 230–50, 359–77.

Levett, A. E. *Studies in Manorial History,* ed. H. M. Cam, M. Coate, and L. S. Sutherland. Oxford, 1938.

Loyn, H. R. “Kinship in Anglo-Saxon England.” *Anglo-Saxon England,* 3 (1974), 194–210.

McLaughlin, Mary Martin. “Survivors and Surrogates: Children and Parents from the Ninth to the Thirteenth Centuries.” In *The History of Childhood,* ed. Lloyd deMause, pp. 101–81. New York, 1974.

Naughton, K. S. *The Gentry of Bedfordshire in the Thirteenth and Fourteenth Centuries.* Leicester, 1976.

Painter, Sydney. "The Family and the Feudal System in Twelfth-Century England." *Speculum,* 35 (1960), 1–16.

Phillpots, Bertha S. *Kindred and Clan in the Middle Ages and After: A Study in the Sociology of the Teutonic Races.* Cambridge, 1913.

Platt, Colin. *Medieval England: A Social History and Archaeology from the Conquest to 1600 A.D.* New York, 1978.

Raftis, J. Ambrose. *Tenure and Mobility: Studies in the Social History of the Medieval English Village.* Toronto, 1964.

———. *Warboys: Two Hundred Years in the Life of an English Medieval Village.* Toronto, 1974.

Ravensdale, J. R. "Deaths and Entries: The Reliability of the Figures of Mortality in the Black Death in Miss F. M. Page's *Estates of Crowland Abbey,* and Some Implications for Landholding." In *Land, Kinship and Life-Cycle,* ed. Richard Smith. Forthcoming.

———. *Liable to Floods: Village Lands Cope on the Edge of the Fens, A. D. 450–1850.* Cambridge, 1974.

Razi, Zvi. "Family, Land and the Village Community in Later Medieval England." *Past and Present,* 93 (1981), 4–36.

———. *Life, Marriage, and Death in the Medieval Parish: Economy, Society, and Demography in Halesowen, 1270–1400.* Cambridge, 1980.

Rickert, Edith, ed. *Chaucer's World.* New York, 1948.

Ritchie (née Kenyon), Nora. "Labor Conditions in Essex in the Reign of Richard II." In *Essays in Economic History,* ed. E. M. Carus-Wilson, 2, 91–111. London, 1962.

Roden, David. "Fragmentation of Farms and Fields in the Chiltern Hills, Thirteenth Century and Later." *Mediaeval Studies,* 31 (1969), 225–38.

Rogers, James E. Thorold. *Six Centuries of Work and Wages: The History of English Labour.* London, 1884.

Russell, Josiah Cox. *British Medieval Population.* Albuquerque, 1948.

———. "Demographic Limitations of the Spalding Serf Lists." *Economic History Review,* 2nd ser. 15 (1962), 138–44.

Salzman, L. F. *English Industries of the Middle Ages.* New York, 1913.

Schammell, Jean. "Freedom and Marriage in Medieval England." *Economic History Review,* 2nd ser. 27 (1974), 523–37.

———. "Wife-Rents and Merchet." *Economic History Review,* 2nd ser. 29 (1976), 487–90.

Searle, Eleanor. "Freedom and Marriage in Medieval England: An Alternative Hypothesis." *Economic History Review,* 2nd ser. 29 (1976), 482–86.

———. "Seigneurial Control of Women's Marriages: The Antecedents and Function of Merchet in England." *Past and Present,* 82 (1979), 3–43.

———. "A Rejoinder." *Past and Present,* 99 (1983), 149–60.

Sheehan, Michael M. "The Formation and Stability of Marriage in Fourteenth-Century England: Evidence of an Ely Register." *Mediaeval Studies,* 33 (1971), 228–63.

———. "The Influence of Canon Law on the Property Rights of Married Women in England." *Mediaeval Studies,* 25 (1963), 109–24.

Smith, Richard M. "Kin and Neighbors in a Thirteenth-Century Suffolk Community." *Journal of Family History,* 4 (1979), 89–115.

———. "Hypothèses sur la nuptialité en Angleterre au XIIe–XIVe siècles." *Annales E.S.C.,* 38 (1983), 107–36.

Stenton, F. M. "The Place of Women in Anglo-Saxon Society." *Transactions of the Royal Historical Society,* 4th ser. 25 (1943), 1–13.

Stevenson, Kenneth. *Nuptial Blessing: A Study of Christian Marriage Rites.* New York, 1983.

Thirsk, Joan. "The Family." *Past and Present,* 27 (1964), 116–22.

Thrupp, Sylvia. *The Merchant Class of Medieval London.* Chicago, 1948.

———. "The Problem of Replacement Rates in Late Medieval English Population." *Economic History Review,* 2nd ser. 18 (1965), 101–19.

Titow, J. Z. *English Rural Society, 1200–1350.* New York, 1969.

———. "Some Evidence of the Thirteenth-Century Population Increase." *Economic History Review,* 2nd ser. 14 (1961), 218–24.

———. "Some Differences between Manors and the Effects on the Condition of the Peasant in the Thirteenth Century." *Agricultural History Review,* 10 (1962), 1–13.

Walker, Sue Sheridan. "Proof of Age of Feudal Heirs in Medieval England." *Mediaeval Studies,* 35 (1973), 306–23.

Weissman, Hope Phyllis. "Why Chaucer's Wife Is from Bath." *The Chaucer Review,* 15 (1980–81), 12–35.

RELIGION

Aston, M. "Lollard Women Priests?" *Journal of Ecclesiastical History,* 31 (1980), 441–61.

Atkinson, Clarissa W. *Mystic and Pilgrim: The Book and the World of Margery Kempe,* Ithaca, NY, 1983.

Bateson, Mary. "The Origins and Early History of Double Monasteries," *Transactions of the Royal Historical Society,* new ser. 12 (1899), 137–98.

Bourdillon, A. F. C. *The Order of Minoresses in England.* Manchester, 1926.

Burton, E. *The Yorkshire Nunneries in the Twelfth and Thirteenth Centuries.* New York, 1979.

Byrne, Mary. *The Tradition of the Nun in Medieval England.* Washington, DC, 1932.

Clay, Rotha M. *The Hermits and the Anchorites of England.* London, 1914.

Chambers, Percy Franklin, ed. *Juliana of Norwich: An Introductory Appreciation of an Interpretative Anthology.* New York, 1955.

Cholmeley, Katherine. *Margery Kempe, Genius and Mystic.* London, 1947.

Collis, Louise. *Memoirs of a Medieval Woman: The Life and Times of Margery Kempe.* New York, 1946.

Colledge, Edmund and Walsh, James. "Editing Julian of Norwich's Revelations: A Progress Report." *Mediaeval Studies,* 38 (1976), 404–27.

Dobson, Eric J. *The Origins of Ancrene Wisse.* Oxford, 1976.

Eckenstein, Lina. *Women under Monasticism.* Cambridge, 1896. Repr. 1955.

Graham, Rose. *St. Gilbert of Sempringham and the Gilbertines: A History of the Only English Monastic Order.* London, 1901.

Goodman, Anthony. "The Piety of John Brunham's Daughter, of Lynn." In *Medieval Women: Dedicated and Presented to Professor Rosalind M. T. Hill,* ed. Derek Baker, pp. 347–58. Oxford, 1978.

Graves, Coburn V. "English Cistercian Nuns in Lincolnshire." *Speculum,* 54 (1979), 492–99.

Meyer, M. A. "Women and the Tenth Century English Monastic Reform." *Revue benedictine,* 87 (1977), 34–61.

Molinari, P. *Julian of Norwich, the Teachings of a Fourteenth-Century Mystic.* London, 1958.

Power, Eileen. *Medieval English Nunneries, 1275–1535.* Cambridge, 1922.

Russell, Jeffrey Burton. *Witchcraft in the Middle Ages.* Ithaca, NY, 1972.

Talbot, C. H., ed. and trans. *The Life of Christina of Markyate: A Twelfth Century Recluse.* New York, 1959.

Warren, Ann K. *Anchorites and Their Patrons in Medieval England.* Berkeley, CA, 1985.

Windeatt, B. A. "Julian of Norwich and Her Audience." *Review of English Studies,* new ser. 28 (1977), 1–17.

Zettersten, A. ed. *English Text of the Ancrene Riwle.* Oxford, 1976.

CULTURE

Aveling, James. *English Midwives: Their History and Prospects.* London, 1872.

Bendel, Betty. "The English Chronicler's Attitude Toward Women." *Journal of the History of Ideas,* 16 (1955), 113–18.

Gardiner, Dorothy Kempe. *A Study of Women's Education Through Twelve Centuries.* London, 1929.

Harris, Adelaide E. *Heroines of the Middle English Romances.* Folcroft, PA, 1929.

Leach, Arthur F. "The Medieval Education of Women in England." *Journal of Education,* 42 (1910), 838–41.

Rowland, Beryl. *Medieval Woman's Guide to Health, the First English Gynecological Handbook.* Kent, OH, 1981.

BIOGRAPHY

Abbott, Jacob. *History of Margaret of Anjou, Queen of Henry VI of England.* New York, 1861.

Bagley, John J. *Margaret of Anjou, Queen of England*. London, 1948.
Bennett, Henry Stanley. *Six Medieval Men and Women*. New York, 1962.
Cutler, Kenneth E. "Edith, Queen of England, 1045–1066." *Mediaeval Studies*, 35 (1973), 222–31.
Erlanger, Philippe. *Margaret of Anjou, Queen of England*. Coral Gables, FL, 1971.
Green, Mary. *Lives of the Princesses of England from the Norman Conquest*. London, 1850.
Hardy, Blanche Christable. *Philippa of Hainault and Her Times*. London, 1910.
Hookham, Mary Ann. *The Life and Times of Margaret of Anjou, Queen of England and France*. London, 1872.
Key, Frederick George. *Lady of the Sun: The Life and Times of Alice Perrers*. New York, 1966.
Kelly, Amy. *Eleanor of Aquitaine and the Four Kings*. Cambridge, MA, 1950.
Kempe-Welch, A. *Of Six Medieval Women*. London, 1913.
Meade, Marion. *Eleanor of Aquitaine: A Biography*. London, 1978.
Pain, Nesta. *Empress Matilda: Uncrowned Queen of England*. London, 1978.
Parsons, John Carmi, ed. *The Court and Household of Eleanor of Castille in 1290*. Toronto, 1977.
Power, Eileen. *Medieval People*. New York, 1966.
Putnam, Emily J. *The Lady: Studies of Certain Significant Phases of Her History*. New York, 1910.
Strickland, Agnes. *Lives of the Queens of England from the Norman Conquest*. 5 vols. New York, 1843.
Tease, Geoffrey. *The Seven Queens of England*. London, 1953.
Thornton-Cook, Elsie. *Her Majesty: The Romance of the Queens of England, 1066–1910*. New York, 1926.

Italy

SURVEYS

Braggio, C. "Vita privata dei genovesi. La donna del secolo XV nella storia," *Giornale ligustico di archaeologia, storia e letteratura*, 12 (1855).
Chojnacki, Stanley. "Patrician women in early Renaissance Venice." *Studies in the Renaissance*, 21 (1974), 176–203.

Chiapelli, L. *La donna pistoiese del tempo antico.* Pistoia, 1914.

De Filipis, Felice. "Dame napoletane del Rinascimento," in *Cronache e profili napoletani,* Naples, 1968.

Del Lungo, Isidoro. "La donna fiorentina nel Rinascimento e negli ultime tempi della libertà," in *La vita italiana nel Rinascimento,* pp. 99–146. Milan, 1910.

De Matteis, Maria Consiglia, ed. *Idee sulla donna nel Medioevo: fonti e aspetti giuridici, antropologici, religiosi, sociali e letterari della condizione femminile.* Bologna, 1981.

Frati, L. *La donna italiana secondo i più ricenti studi,* 2nd ed. Turin, 1928.

Rodocanachi, Emmanuel Pierre. *La Femme italienne avant, pendant et après la renaissance: sa vie privée et mondaine, son influence sociale.* Paris, 1922.

Savi-Lopez, Maria. *La donna italiana del Trecento.* Naples, 1891.

POLITICAL LIFE

Bellomo, Manlio. *La condizione giuridica della donna in Italia. Vicende antiche e moderne.* Turin, 1970.

Camobreco, Fortunato. "Il matrimonio del Duca d'Atene con Beatrice principesse di Taranto," in *Nozze Federle De Fabritiis,* pp. 303–307. Naples, 1908.

Columbo, Alessandro. "Il 'Grido di dolore' di Isabella d'Aragona duchessa di Milano," in *Studi di storia napoletana in memoria de Michelangelo Schipa,* pp. 331–46. Naples, 1926.

Fasola, Livia. "Una famiglia di sostenetori milanesi di Federico I. Per la storia con le forze sociali e politiche della Lombardia." *Quellen und Forschungen aus italienischen Archiven und Bibliotheken,* 48 (1968), 64–79 and 52 (1972), 116–218.

Giardina, Camillo. "Sul mundoaldo della donna." *Rivista di storia del diritto italiano,* 35 (1962), 41–51.

Kent, Frances William. "A Proposal by Savonarola for the Self-Reform of Florentine Woman (March 1496)." *Memorie Domenicane,* new ser., 14 (1983).

Marin-Muracciole, Madeleine-Rose. *L'honneur des femmes en Corse, du XIIIe siècle à nos jours.* Paris, 1964.

Mor, Carlo Guido. "Intorno ad una lettera di Berta di Toscana al Calliffo di Bagdad." *Archivio storico italiano,* 112 (1954), 299–312.

Odegaard, Charles E. "The Empress Engelberge." *Speculum,* 26 (1951), 77–103.

Rossi, Guido. *Le Statut juridique de la femme dans l'histoire du droit italien. Epoque médiévale et moderne.* Milan, 1958.

Salvioli, G. "La condizione giuridica delle donne a Genova nel secolo XI," *Rivista di storia e filosofia del diritto,* 1 (1897), 198–206.

Schwarzmaier, Hans Martin. "Zur Familie-Viktor IV in der Sabina." *Quellen und Forschungen aus italienischen Archiven und Bibliotheken,* 48 (1958), 64–79.

Staley, Edgcumbe. *The Dogaressas of Venice.* London, 1910.

ECONOMIC LIFE

Biagi, G. *Due corredi nuziali fiorentini 1320–1493*. Florence, 1899.
Bistort, G. *Il magistrato alle pompe nella Repubblica di Venezia*. Venice, 1912.
Bonardi, Antonio. *Il lusso di altri tempi in Padova*. Venice, 1910.
Bonds, William N. "Genoese Noble Women and Gold Thread Manufacturing." *Medievalia et Humanistica,* 17 (1966), 79–81.
Briganti, Antonio. *La donna e il diritto statutario in Perugia. La donna commerciante (secoli XII e XIV)*. Perugia, 1911.
Brown, Judith C. "A Woman's Place Was in the Home: Women's Work in Renaissance Tuscany," in *Rewriting the Renaissance: the Discourses of Sexual Difference in Early Modern Europe*. ed. Margaret Ferguson, Maureen Quilligan and Nancy Vickers, pp. 206–24. Chicago, 1984.
Brown, Judith C. and Goodman, Jordan. "Women and Industry in Florence." *Journal of Economic History,* 40 (1980), 73–80.
Dallari, Umberto and Gandini, Luigi Alberto. "Lo statuto suntuario bolognese del 1401 e il registro delle vesti bollate." *Atti e memorie della R. Deputazione di Storia Patria per le Provincie di Romagna,* 3rd ser., 7 (1889), 8–22.
D'Ancona, P. *Le vesti delle donne fiorentine nel secolo XIV*. Perugia, 1906.
Fabretti, Ariodante. *Statuti e ordinamenti suntuarii intorno al vestire degli uomini e delle donne in Perugia dall'anno 1266 al 1536*. Memorie della R. Accademia delle Scienze di Torino, 2nd ser., 38. Turin, 1886.
Herlihy, David. "Land, Family and Women in Continental Europe, 701–1200." *Traditio,* 18 (1962), 89–120.
Jehel, Georges. "Le rôle des femmes et du milieu familial à Gênes dans les activités commerciales au cours de la première moitié du XIIIe siècle." *Revue d'histoire économique et sociale,* 53 (1975), 193–215.
Krueger, Hilmar C. "Genoese Merchants, Their Partnerships and Investments, 1155 to 1164," in *Studi in onore di Armando Sapori,* 2 vols., I, 257–72. Milan, 1957.
———. "Genoese Merchants, Their Associations and Investments, 1150 to 1230," in *Studi in onore di Amintore Fanfani,* 6 vols., I, 413–26. Milan, 1962.
Lopez, Robert. "Le origini dell'arte della lana," in his *Studi sull'economia genovese nel Medio Evo*. Milan, 1936.
Pistarino, G. "La donna di affari a Genova nel secolo XIII," in *Miscellanea di storia italiana e mediterranea per Nino Lamboglia,* Collana storica di fonti e studi, 23 pp. 155–69. Genoa, 1978.
Riemer, Eleanor Sabina. *Woman in the Medieval City: Sources and Uses of Wealth by Sienese Women in the Thirteenth Century,* Ph.D. Dissertation, New York University, 1975.
———. "Women, Dowries, and Capital Investment in Thirteenth-Century Siena," in *The Marriage Bargain,* ed. Marion A. Kaplan, pp. 59–79. N.p., 1985.
Segre, Marcello. "Jewish Female Doctors in the Middle Ages." *Pagina de storia della Medicina,* 14 (1970), 98–106.

RELIGION

Bell, Rudolph M. *Holy Anorexia.* Chicago, 1985.

Benvenuti Papi, Anna. "Le forme comunitarie della penitenza femminile francescana. Schede per un censimento toscano," in *Prime manifestazioni di vita comunitaria maschile e femminile nel movimento francescano della penitenza,* ed. R. Pazzelli and L. Temperini, pp. 389–450. Rome, 1982.

———. "Il modello familiare nell'agriografia fiorentina tra Duecento e Quattrocento. Sviluppo di una negazione (da Umilina dei Cerchi a Villana delle Botti)." *Nuova DFW,* 16 (1981), 80–107.

———. "'Velut in sepulchro': cellane e recluse nella tradizione agriografica italiana," in *Culto dei santi, istituzioni e classi sociali in età preindustriale,* ed. Sofia Boesch Gajano and Lucia Sebastiani, pp. 365–456. Aquila, 1984.

Boyd, Catherine. *A Cistercian Nunnery in Medieval Italy: The Story of Rifreddo in Saluzzo, 1220–1300.* Cambridge, MA, 1943.

Brown, Judith C. *Immodest Acts. The Life of a Lesbian Nun in Renaissance Italy.* New York, 1986.

Casagrande, Carla, ed. *Prediche alle donne del secolo XIII.* Milan, 1978.

Ciammitti, Luisa. "Una santa di meno. Storia di Angela Mellini, cucitrice bolognese." *Quaderni storici,* 41 (1979), 603–43.

Colagiovanni, E. *Le religiose italiàne. Ricerche sociografiche.* Rome, 1976.

Craveri, Marcello. *Sante e streghe: biografie e documenti dal XIV al XVII secolo.* Milan, 1980.

De Luca, Paolo. "Una Giuliana del monastero benedittino femminile del SS. Salvatore di San Marco d'Alunzo." *Benedictina,* 25 (1978), 365–407.

Esch, Arnold. "Tre sante ed il loro ambiente sociale a Roma: S. Francesca Romana, S. Brigida di Svevia e S. Caterina da Siena," in *Atti del simposio internazionale cateriniano-bernardiniano: Siena, 17–20 aprile 1980,* ed. Domenico Maffei and Paolo Nardi, pp. 89–120. Siena, 1982.

Esposito, Anna. "S. Francesca e le comunità religiose femminili a Roma nel secolo XV," in *Culto dei santi, istituzioni e classi sociali in età preindustriale,* ed. Sofia Boesch Gajano and Lucia Sebastiani, pp. 537–62. Aquila, 1984.

Gloria, A. "Un fondo archivistico inesplorato concernente monache cisterciensi." *Bollettino storico bibliografico subalpino,* 57 (1959).

Gozzi, Romano. "Monastero (ora Organatrofio) di S. Chiara. Via delle Organe. Secc. XV–XVIII." *Archivio storico lodigiano,* 15 (1959).

Hamilton, B. "The House of Theophylact and the Promotion of Religious Life Among Women in Tenth Century Rome." *Studia monastica,* 12 (1970), 195–218.

Lodolo, Gabriella. "Pomo dei Visconti da Goito e il monastero di S. Giovanni Evangelista di Mantova." *Aevum,* 48 (1974), 514–25.

Mantese, Giovanni. "Fratres et sorores de poenitentia di San Francesco in Vicenza dal XII al XV secolo," in *Miscellanea Gille Gérard Meersseman,* 2 vols. 2, 695–714. Padua, 1970.

Martin, John. "Out of the Shadow: Heretical and Catholic Women in Renaissance Venice." *Journal of Family History.* 10 (1985), 21–33.

Novelli, L. "Due documenti inediti relativi alle monache benedettine dette 'santuccie'." *Benedictina,* 12 (1975), 189–253.

Pazzelli, R. and Sensi, M., eds. *La beata Angelina da Montegiovre e il movimento del Terz'Ordine Regolare Francescano femminile.* Rome, 1984.

Paschini, Pio. "I monasteri femminili in Italia nel 500," in *Problemi di vita religiosa in Italia nel Cinquecento,* Atti di Convegno di storia della chiesa in Italia, Bologna 2–6 sett. 1958, pp. 31–60. Padua, 1960.

Petroff, Elizabeth. *The Consolation of the Blessed: Women Saints in Medieval Tuscany.* New York, 1980.

———, "The Paradox of Sanctity: Lives of Italian Women Saints 1200–1400." *Occasional Papers of the International Society for the Comparative Study of Civilization,* 1 (1977), 4–24.

Ranza, G. *Delle monache di S. Eusebio.* Vercelli, 1785.

Rocca, E. Nasalli. "I monasteri cisterciensi femminili di Piacenza." *Rivista di storia della chiesa in Italia,* 10 (1956), 271–74.

Sallmann, Jean-Michel. "La sainteté mystique feminine à Naples au tournant des xvie et xviie siècles," in *Culto dei santi, istituzioni e classi sociali in età preindustriale,* ed. Sofia Boesch Gajano and Lucia Sebastiane, pp. 681–702. Aquila, 1984.

Samaritini, A. "Ailisia de Baldo e le correnti riformatrici femminili di Ferrara nella prima metà del sec. XV." *Atti e memorie della Deputazione Provinciale Ferrarese di Storia Patria,* 3rd ser., 13 (1973), 91–156.

Schulte van Kessel, Elisja. "Gender and Spirit, Pietas et Contemptus Mundi. Matron-patrons in Early Modern Rome," in *Women and Men in Spiritual Culture XIV-XVII Centuries,* ed. Elisja Schulte van Kessel, pp. 47–68. The Hague, 1986.

Sorelli, Fernanda. "Per la storia religiosa di Venezia nella prima metà del Quattrocento: inizi e sviluppi del Terz'Ordine Domenicano," in *Viridarium Floridum,* ed. Maria Chiara Billanovich, Giorgio Cracco and Antonio Rigon, pp. 89–114. Padua, 1984.

Spanò Martinelli, Serena. "La canonizzazione di Caterina Vigri: un problema cittadino nella Bologna del Seicento," in *Culto dei santi, istituzioni e classi sociali in età preindustriale,* ed. Sofia Boesch Gajano and Lucia Sebastiani, pp. 719–34. Aquila, 1984.

Tocco, G. "Guglielma Boema e i Guglielmiti." *Atti della R. Accademia dei Lincei, Memorie,* 5th ser., 8 (1900), 3–20.

Trexler, Richard. "Le célibat à la fin du moyen âge: les religieuses de Florence." *Annales É.S.C.,* 27 (1972), 1329–50.

Vauchez, André. *La sainteté en Occident au derniers siècles du moyen âge.* Rome, 1981. Bibliothèque des Ecoles Françaises d'Athènes et de Rome, 241.

Volpe, G. *Movimenti religiosi e sette ereticali nella società medievale italiana.* Florence, 1922.

Wessley, Stephen. "The Thirteenth-century Guglielmites: Salvation Through Women," in *Medieval Women,* ed. Derek Baker, pp. 289–303. Oxford, 1978.

Zarn, Gabriella. "I monasteri femminili di Bologna." *Atti e memorie della R. Deputazione di Storia Patria per le Provincie di Romagna,* new ser. 24 (1973), 145ff.

Zarri, Gabriella. "L'altra Cecilia: Elena Duglioli Dall'Olio (1472–1520)," in *Culto dei santi, istituzioni e classi sociali in età preindustriale,* ed. Sofia Boesch Gajano and Lucia Sebastiani, pp. 573–614. Aquila, 1984.

———. "Le sante vive. Per una tipologia della santità femminile nel primo Cinquecento." *Annali dell'Istituto Storico Italo-germanico in Trento,* 6 (1980), 371–445.

SOCIAL LIFE

Bartoli, Marie-Claude. "La femme à Bonifacio à la fin du Moyen Âge." *Etudes Corses* 4 (1975), 310–22.

Belgrano, L. T. *Della vita privata dei genovesi* 2nd ed. Genoa, 1875.

Bellomo, Manlio. *Profili della famiglia italiana nell'età dei communi.* Catania, 1966.

———. *Richerche sui rapporti patrimoniali fra coniugi. Contributo alla storia della famiglia medievale.* Milan, 1961.

Besta, Enrico. "Gli antichi usi nuziali del Veneto e gli statuti di Chioggia." *Rivista italiana per le scienze giuridiche,* 26 (1899), 205–19.

———. *La famiglia nella storia del diritto italiano.* Milan, 1962.

Bizzari, Dina. "Il diritto privato nelle fonti senesi del sec. XIII." *Bullettino senese di storia patria,* 33–34 (1926–27).

Bongi, Salvatore. "Le schiave orientali in Italia." *Nuova antologia.* (1866), 215–46.

Brandileone, Francesco. "Contributo alla storia della comunione dei beni matrimoniali in Sicilia," in his *Scritti di storia del diritto privato italiano,* I, 321–42. Bologna, 1931.

———. "Studi preliminari sullo svoglimento storico dei rapporti patrimoniali fra coniugi in Italia," in ibid., I, 229–319.

———. "Sulla storia e la natura della 'donatio propter nuptias'," in ibid., I, 117–214.

Brucker, Gene. *Giovanni and Lusanna: Marriage in Renaissance Florence.* Berkeley, 1986.

Casanova, E. "La donna senese del Quattrocento nella vita privata." *Bullettino senese di storia patria,* 8 (1901), 3–93.

Cecchetti, Bartolomeo. "La donna nel medioevo a Venezia." *Archivio veneto,* 31 (1866), 33–69, 307–49.

———. *La vita dei veneziani nel 1300.* Venice, 1885–86.

Chiapelli, L. *I nomi di donna in Pistoia dall'alto medio evo al secolo XIII.* Pistoia, 1920.

Chojnacki, Stanley. "Dowries and Kinsmen in Early Renaissance Venice," in *Women in Medieval Society,* ed. S. M. Stuard, pp. 173–98. Philadelphia, 1976.

———. "Kinship Ties and Young Patricians in Fifteenth-Century Venice." *Renaissance Quarterly,* 39 (1985), 240–70.

———. "Patrician Women in Early Renaissance Venice." *Studies in the Renaissance,* 21 (1974), 176–203.

Cohen, Sherill. "Convertite e Malmaritate. Donne 'irregolari' e ordini religiosi nella Firenze rinascimentale." *Memoria,* 5 (1982), 46–63.

Colafemmina, Cesare. "Donne, ebrei e cristiani," *Quaderni medievali,* 8 (1979), 117–25.

Cozza-Luzi, G. "Gemma Colona e l'instrumento dotale pel suo matrimonio." *Studi e documenti di storia e diritto,* 24 (1902), 187–204.

Davidsohn, Robert. *Storia di Firenze,* trans. by G. B. Klein, 6 vols. Florence, 1956–65, vol. 6.

Di Prampero, Antonio. *Dismontaduris et morgengabium, documenti friulani.* Udine, 1884. Nozze Schiavi-Bressanutti.

Dorini, U. "Un nuovo documento concernente Gemma Donati," *Bullettino della Società Dantesca Italiana* new ser., 9 (1902), 181–84.

Ercole, Francesco. "Vicende storiche della dote romana nella practica medievale dell'Italia superiore, *Archivio giuridico,* 80 (1908), 393–490; 81 (1908), 34–148.

———. "L'istituto dotale nella practica e nella legislazione statutaria dell'Italia superiore." *Rivista italiana per le scienze giuridiche,* 45 (1908), 191–302; 46 (1910), 167–257.

Fabretti, Ariodante. *Documenti inediti sulla prostituzione in Perugia nei secoli XIX e XV.* Turin, 1885.

Ferrara, Mario. "Linguaggio di schiave nel Quattrocento." *Studi di filologia italiana. Bullettino dell'Accademia della Crusca,* 8 (1950), 320–28.

Forchieri, Giovanni. "I rapporti matrimonali fra coniugi a Genova nel secolo XII." *Bollettino ligustico per la storia e la cultura regionale,* 22 (1970), 3–20.

Fornera, Cesare. *Lis dismontaduris, uso nuziale friulano.* Udine, 1885. Nozze Folchi-Trivellato.

Frati, Ludovico. *La vita privata in Bologna dal secolo XIII al XVII.* 2nd ed. Bologna, 1928.

Garufi, Carlo A. "Ricerche sugli usi nuziali nel Medio Evo in Sicilia." *Archivio storio siciliano,* new ser., 21 (1896), 211–307.

Guillou, André. "Il matrimonio nell'Italia bizantina nei secoli X et XI," in *Matrimonio nella società alto-medievale* 2, 869–86. Spoleto, 1977.

Gioffrè, Domenico. *Il mercato degli schiavi a Genova nel secolo XV.* Genoa, 1971.

Grohmann, Alberto. *Città e territorio tra medioevo ed età moderna, (Perugia, secc. XIII–XVI)* 2 vols. Perugia, 1981.

Heers, Jacques. *Esclaves et domestiques au moyen âge dans le monde mediterranéen.* Paris, 1981.

Herlihy, David. "Mapping Households in Medieval Italy," *Catholic Historical Review,* 598 (1982), 1–24.

———. "Marriage at Pistoia in the Fifteenth Century," *Bollettino storico pistoiese,* (1972), 3–21.

———. "The Population of Verona in the First Century of Venetian Rule," in *Renaissance Venice,* ed. John Hale, pp. 91–120. London, 1973.

———. "The Tuscan Town in the Quattrocento, a Demographic Profile." *Medievalia et Humanistica,* new ser., 1 (1970), 68–81.

Herlihy, David and Klapisch-Zuber, Christiane. *Les Toscans et leurs familles.* Paris, 1978, abridged English translation *The Tuscans and Their Families.* New Haven, 1985.

Hughes, Diane Owen. "Distinguishing Signs: Ear-rings, Jews and Franciscan Rhetoric in the Italian Renaissance City." *Past and Present,* 112 (1986), 3–59.

———. "Domestic Ideals and Social Behavior: Evidence from Medieval Genoa," in *The Family in History,* ed. Charles Rosenberg, pp. 115–43. Philadelphia, 1975.

———. "From Brideprice to Dowry in Mediterranean Europe." *Journal of Family History,* 3 (1978), 263–96.

———. "Kinsmen and Neighbors in Medieval Genoa," in *The Medieval City,* ed. H. Miskimin, D. Herlihy, and A. Udovich, pp. 95–111. New Haven, 1977.

———. "Representing the Family: Portraits and Purposes in Early Modern Italy." *Journal of Interdisciplinary History,* 17 (1986), 7–38.

———. "Struttura familiare e sistemi di successione ereditaria nei testamenti dell'Europa medievale." *Quaderni storici,* 33 (1976), 929–52.

———. "Sumptuary Law and Social Relations in Renaissance Italy," in *Disputes and Settlements,* ed. John Bossy, pp. 69–99. Cambridge, 1984.

———. "Urban Growth and Family Structure in Medieval Genoa." *Past and Present,* 66 (1975), 3–28.

Inchiostro, Ugo. *Il matrimonio o comunione di beni nei' documenti e negli statuti istriani del Medioevo.* Trieste, 1909.

Jacobsen-Schutte, Anne. "Trionfo delle donne': tematiche di rovesciamento dei ruoli nella Firenze rinascimentale." *Quaderni storici,* 44 (1980), 474–96.

Kirshner, Julius. "Pursuing Honor While Avoiding Sin: the 'Monte delle doti' of Florence," *Quaderni dei Studi Senesi,* 87. Siena, 1977.

Kirshner, Julius and Molho, Anthony. "The Dowry Fund and the Marriage Market in Early Quattrocento Florence." *Journal of Modern History,* 50 (1978), 403–38.

Kirshner, Julius and Pluss, Jacques. "Two Fourteenth-Century Opinions on Dowry, Paraphernalia and Non-Dotal Goods." *Bulletin of Medieval Canon Law,* new ser., 9 (1979), 65–77.

Klapisch-Zuber, Christiane. *Women, Family, and Ritual in Renaissance Italy,* trans. Lydia G. Cochrane. Chicago, 1985.

———, "Le 'zane' della sposa. La fiorentina e il suo corredo nel Rinascimento." *Memoria,* 11–12 (1984), 12–23.

Kuehn, Thomas. "*Cum consensu mundualdi*: Legal Guardianship of Women in Quattrocento Florence." *Viator,* 13 (1982), 309–33.

———. "Women, Marriage and *Patria Potestas* in Late Medieval Florence." *Tijdschrift voor Rechtsgeschiedenis,* 49 (1981), 127–47.

Larivault, P. *La vie quotidienne des courtisanes en Italie au temps de la Renaissance (Rome et Venise, XVe et XVIe siècles)* Paris, 1975.

Lenardi, Francesco. "Regime patrimoniale fra coniugi nel diritto friuliano." *Studi goriziani,* 17 (1955), 19–55; 18 (1955), 7–38.

Lopez, Robert. "Familiari, procatori e dipendenti di Benedetto Zaccaria," in *Miscellanea di storia ligure in onore di Giorgio Falco,* pp. 211–49. Milan, 1944.

Mistruzzi de Frisinga, Charles. "La succession nobiliare feminine en Italie dans le droit et dans l'histoire." Appendix to Ida Auda-Gioanet, *Une randonnée à travers l'histoire d'Orient: les Comnenes et les Anges.* Rome, 1953.

Molmenti, Pompeo. *La storia di Venezia nella vita privata dalle origini alla caduta della Repubblica,* 7th ed., 3 vols. Bergamo, 1927–29, reprint, Trieste, 1973.

Origo, Iris. "The Domestic Enemy: Eastern Slaves in Tuscany in the Fourteenth and Fifteenth Centuries," *Speculum,* 30 (1955), 32–66.

———. *The Merchant of Prato.* London, 1960.

Ortalli, Gherardo. "La famille à Bologne au XIIIe siècle, entre la realité des groupes inférieurs et la mentalité des classes dominantes," in *Famille et parenté dans l'Occident mediéval,* ed. Georges Duby and Jacques le Goff, Collections de l'Ecole Française de Rome, 30, pp. 205–23. Rome, 1977.

Pandiani, E. "Vita privata dei genovesi del Rinascimento." *Atti della Società Ligure di Storia Patria,* 23 (1941).

Pandimiglio, L. "Giovanni di Pagolo Morelli e le strutture familiari." *Archivio storico italiano,* 136 (1978), 3–88.

Pavan, Elizabeth. "Police des moeurs, sociétéet politique à Venise à la fin du Moyen Âge." *Revue historique,* 536 (1980), 241–88.

Piacentino, Maria. "La vita aquilana nel Trecento." *Bulletino della Deputazione Abruzzese di Storia Patria* (1947–49), 5–89.

Pistarino, G. "Tra libere e schiave a Genova nel Quattrocento." *Anuario de Estudios medievales,* 1 (1964), 353–74.

Puncuh, Dina. "La vita savonese agli inizi del Duecento," in *Miscellanea di Storia Ligure in onore di Giorgio Falco,* pp. 127–51. Milan, 1962.

Rezasco, Giulio. "Segno delle meretrici," *Giornale ligustico di archaeologia, storia e letteratura,* 17 (1890), 161–220.

Rossi, Giovanni. *Il matrimonio medioevale. Esegesi comparata delle consuetudini dotali in Puglia.* Bari, 1910.

Rossetti, Gabriella. "Il matrimonio del clero nella società alto medievale," in *Il matrimonio nella società alto medievale* 1, pp. 473–576. Spoleto, 1977.

Ruggiero, Guido. *The Boundaries of Eros.* New York, 1985.
———. "Sexual Criminality in the Early Renaissance: Venice, 1338–1358." *Journal of Social History,* 8 (1974–5), 18–37.
Salmone-Martino, Salvatore. *Le reputatrici in Sicilia nell'età de mezzo e moderna.* Palermo, 1886.
Sanfillipo, Mario. "Spoleto: il matrimonio nella società altomedievale." *Quaderni medievali,* 2 (1976), 212–18.
Tabacco, Giovanni. "Il tema della famiglia e del suo funzionamento nella società medievale." *Quaderni storici,* 33 (1976), 892–928.
Tamassia, Nino. *La famiglia italiana nei secoli decimoquinto e decimosesto.* Milan, Palermo, Naples, 1911.
Taylor, Michael D. "Gentile da Fabriano, St. Nicholas, and an Iconography of Shame." *Journal of Family History,* 7 (1982), 321–32.
Trexler, Richard C. "The Foundlings of Florence (1395–1455)." *History of Childhood Quarterly,* 1 (1973), 259–84.
———. "La prostitution florentine au XVe siècle." *Annales É.S.C.,* 36 (1981), 983–1015.
———. "A Widow's Asylum of the Renaissance: The Orbatello of Florence," in *Old Age in Pre-Industrial Society,* ed. Peter Stearns, pp. 119–49. New York, 1982.
Tria L. "La schiavitù in Liguria (ricerche e documenti)." *Atti della Società Ligure di Storia Patria,* 70 (1947).
Vacca, Nicole. "Le consuetudini nuziali nei Salento," in *Nuptiae Sallentinae* pp. 5–23. Lecce, 1955.
Vacca, Pietro. *Il regime della comunione dei beni nel matrimonio rispetto all'Italia.* Pavia, 1908.
Vaccari, Pietro. "Aspecti singolari dell'istituto del matrimonio nell'Italia meridionale." *Archivio storico pugliese,* 6 (1953), 43–49.
Vismara, Giuilio. "I rapporti patrimoniali tra coniugi nell'alto medioevo." In *Il matrimonio nella società altomedievale,* 2, pp. 633–700. Spoleto, 1977.
Witthoft, Brucia. "Marriage Rituals." *Artibus et Historiae,* 5 (1982), 43–59.
Zdekauer, Lodovico. *La vita privata dei senesi nel Dugento.* Siena, 1896–7; reprint, Forni.

CULTURAL LIFE

Abati Olivieri Giordani, A. Degli. *Notizie di Battista Montefeltro moglie di Galeazzo Malatesta signore di Pesaro.* Pesaro, 1782.
Bornstein, Diane. *Distaves and Dames: Renaissance Treatises For and About Women.* Delmar, NY, 1978.
———. *The Feminist Controversy of the Renaissance.* Delmar, NY, 1980.
———. *The Lady in the Tower: Medieval Courtesy Literature for Women.* Hamden, CT, 1983.

Brown, Malcolm C. "Le insaciabile desiderio nostro de cose antiche: New Documents on Isabella d'Este's Collection of Antiquities," in *Cultural Aspects of the Italian Renaissance,* ed. Cecil H. Clough, pp. 324–53. Manchester, 1976.

Cavassana, C. "Cassandra Fedele: erudita veneziana del Rinascimento." *Ateneo veneto,* 29 (1906), vol. 2, 73–91, 249–75, 361–97.

Cereta, Laura. *Laurae Ceretai Epistolae.* Ed. J. F. Tomasini. Padua, 1640.

Cropper, Elizabeth. "The Beauty of Women: Problems in the Rhetoric of Renaissance Portraiture," in *Rewriting the Renaissance: the Discourses of Sexual Difference in Early Modern Europe,* ed. Margaret Ferguson, Maureen Quilligan, and Nancy Vickers, pp. 206–24. Chicago, 1984.

Dal Pino, A. M. *Iconografia mariana da secolo VI al XIII.* Rome, 1963.

De Blasti, Jolanda. *Antologia delle scrittrici italiane dalle origini al 1800.* Florence, 1930.

———, *Le scrittrici italiane dalle origini al 1800.* Florence, 1930.

Fahy, C. "Three Early Renaissance Treatises on Women," *Italian Studies,* 11 (1956), 30–55.

Fedele, Cassandra. *Cassandrae Fidelis Venetae: epistolae et orationes,* ed. J. F. Tomasini. Padua, 1636.

Franceschini, G. "Battista Montefeltre Malatesta, signora di Pesaro." *Studia oliveriana,* 6 (1958), 7–43.

Frugoni, Chiara. "L'iconographie de la femme au cours des Xe-XIIe siècles." *Cahiers de civilisation médiévale,* 20 (1977), 177–88.

Gripkey, Mary. *The Blessed Virgin Mary as Mediatrix.* New York, 1938.

Harris, Ann Sutherland and Nochlin, Linda. *Women Artists, 1550–1950.* New York, 1976.

King, Margaret L. "Book-Lined Cells: Women and Humanism in the Early Italian Renaissance," in *Beyond Their Sex: Learned Women of the European Past,* ed. P. H. Labalme, pp. 66–90. New York, 1980.

———. "Goddess and Captive: Antonio Loschi's Poetic Tribute to Maddalena Scrovegni (1389). Study and Text." *Medievalia et Humanistica,* new ser., 10 (1980), 103–27.

———. "The Religious Retreat of Isotta Nogarola (1418–1466): Sexism and its Consequences in the Fifteenth Century." *Signs,* 3 (1978), 807–22.

———. "Thwarted Ambitions: Six Learned Women of the Italian Renaissance." *Soundings,* 59 (1976), 280–304.

Kristeller, P. O. "Learned Women of Early Modern Italy: Humanists and University Scholars," in *Beyond Their Sex: Learned Women of the European Past,* ed. P. H. Labalme, pp. 91–116. New York, 1980.

Luzio, Alessandro and Renier, Ridolfo. "La coltura e le relazioni letterarie di Isabella d'Este Gonzaga." *Giornale storico della letteratura italiana,* 33 (1899), 1–62.

Luzio, A. and Renier, R. *Mantova e Urbino.* Turin, 1893.

Nogarola, Isotta. *Isotae Nogarolae Veronesis opera quae supersunt omnia,* ed. by E. Abel, 2 vols. Vienna and Budapest, 1886.

Parducci, A. "La ystoria della devota Susanna di Lucrezia Tornabuoni," *Annali delle Università Toscane,* new ser. 10 (1925), 177–201.

Pesente, G. "Alessandra Scalla, una figurina della Rinascenza fiorentina." *Giornale storico della letteratura italiana,* 85 (1925), 241–67.

Rabil, A. (Jr.). *Laura Cereta: Quattrocento Humanist.* Binghamton, 1981.

Segarizzi, A. "Niccolo Barbo patrizio veneziano del secolo XV e le accuse contro Isotta Nogarola." *Giornale storico della letteratura italiana,* 43 (1904), 39–54.

Macinghi negli Strozzi, Alessandra. *Lettere di una gentildonna fiorentina del secolo XV ai figliuoli esuli,* ed. C. Guasti. Florence, 1877.

Torraca, Francesco. "Donne italiane e trovatori provenzali." *Studi Medievali,* new ser., 1 (1928), 487–91.

Volpe, G., ed. *Le laudi di Lucrezia de' Medici.* Pistoia, 1900.

Walker, John. "Ginevra de' Benci by Leonardo da Vinci," *National Gallery of Art, Report and Studies in the History of Art,* 1967, pp. 1–38. Washington, DC.

BIOGRAPHY

Angela of Foligno

Andreoli, Sergio. "La beata Angela da Foligno contempla Gesu Cristo." *L'Italia francescana,* 55 (1980), 35–55.

Blasucci, Antonio. "Il cristocentrismo spirituale e la vocazione alla mistica in una grande beata francescana." *Vita cristiana,* 13 (1941), 44–71.

Colosio, Innocenzo. "La beata Angela da Foligno." *Rivista di ascetica e mistica,* 9, no. 6 (1964), 3–28.

Ferré, M. J. "Les principales dates de la vie d'Angèle de Foligno." *Revue d'histoire franciscaine,* 2 (1925), 21–34.

———. *La spiritualité de Sainte Angèle de Foligno.* Paris, 1927.

Faloci Pulignani, Michele, ed. *L'autobiografia e gli scritti della beata Angela da Foligno pubblicati e annotati da un codice sublacense.* Città di Castello, 1932.

———. *Saggio bibliografico sulla vita e sugli opuscoli della beata Angela da Foligno,* 2nd ed. Foligno, 1889.

Valugani, Pasquale. *L'esperienza mistica della beata Angela da Foligno nel racconto di Frate Arnaldo.* Milan, 1964.

Beatrice d'Este

Antonio Rigon. "La santa nobile: Beatrice d'Este (d1226) e il suo primo biografo," in *Viridarium Floridum,* ed. Maria Chiara Billanovich, Giorgio Cracco and Antonio Rigon, pp. 61–86. Padua, 1984.

Benvenuta Bojani

Anonymous. *Vita della beata Benvenuta Bojani del Terz' Ordine di San Domenico coll' aggiunta di alcune note tratte dal Padre de Rubeis.* Udine, 1848.
Rubeis, Bernardus Maria de. *Vita Beatae Bojanae de Civitate Austria in Provincia Forijulii, Quae nunc primum latine, ex originali codice ms. in lucem prodit cum praefatione, et annotationibus.* Venice, 1757.

Catherine Fieschi Adorni

Bonzi da Genova, Umile. *S. Caterina Fieschi Adorni,* 2 vols. Turin, 1961–62.
Genoa, St. Catherine of. *Treatise on Purgatory and the Dialogue,* trans. Charles Balfour and Helen D. Irvine. London, 1946.

Catherine of Siena

Bizzicari, Alvaro. "Stile e personalità di S. Caterina da Siena." *Italica,* 43 (1966), 43–56.
Capelcelatro, A. *Storia di Santa Caterina da Siena e del papato del suo tempo.* Siena, 1878.
Cardini, Franco. "Santa Caterina da Siena nella vita del Trecento," *Bullettino senese di storia patria,* 88 (1981), 7–20.
Catherine of Siena. *Le lettere di S. Caterina da Siena ridotte a nuova lezione e in ordine nuovo disposte con note di Niccolo Tommaseo,* ed. by Piero Misciatelli, 6 vols. Siena, 1913–21; repr. Florence, 1939–40.
Centi, Timeo M., ed. *S. Caterina fra i dottori della chiesa.* Florence, 1970.
Chiminelli, Piero. *S. Caterina da Siena 1347–1380.* Rome, 1941.
Curtayne, Alice. *Saint Caterina of Siena.* New York, 1929.
Dupré Theseider, Eugenio. "La duplice esperienza di S. Caterina da Siena." *Rivista storica italiana,* 62 (1950), 533–74.
Falassi, Alessandro. *La santa dell'oca: vita, morte e miracoli di Caterina da Siena.* Milan, 1980.
Fawtier, Robert. *Sainte Catherine de Sienne. Essai de critique de sources:* I. *Sources hagiographiques,* Rome, 1921; II. *Les oeuvres de Sainte Catherine de Sienne,* Paris, 1930.
———. *La double expérience de Catherine Benincasa (Sainte Catherine de Sienne).* Paris, 1948.
Gardner, E. G. *Saint Catherine of Siena.* London and New York, 1907.
Moria, G. F., ed. *Caterina da Siena: Una donna per tutte le stagioni.* Atti del seminario cateriniano Circolo Tincari, Bologna 1979–80. Aquila, 1981.
Taurisano, Innocenzo M. *Santa Caterina da Siena: patrona d'Italia.* Rome, 1948.
Valli, Francesco. *L'adolescenza e la puerizia di santa Caterina da Siena: esame critico delle fonti.* Siena, 1934.
Volpato, Antonio. "Between Prophetesses and Doctor Saints: Catherine of Siena,"

in *Women and Men in Spiritual Culture, XIV–XVII Centuries*, ed. Elisja Schulte van Kessel, pp. 149–61. The Hague, 1986.

Zanini, Lina. *Bibliografia analitica di S. Caterina da Siena, 1901–1950*. Rome, 1971.

Claire of Assisi

Brooke, Rosalind B. and Brooke, Christopher N. L. "St. Claire," in *Medieval Women*, ed. Derek Baker, pp. 275–87. Oxford, 1978.

Cresi, Domenico. "Cronologia di S. Chiara," *Studi francescani*, 50 (1953), 260–67.

De Robeck, Nesta. *St. Clare of Assisi*. Milwaukee, 1951.

Fassbinder, Maria. "Untersuchen über die Quellen zum Leben der hl. Klara von Assisi," *Franziskanische Studien*, 23 (1936), 296–335.

Fortini, A. "Santa Chiara," in his *Nova vita di Assisi*, 4 vols. 1 (i), pp. 409–53. Assisi, 1959.

———. "La famiglia di Santa Chiara," in ibid., 2, pp. 315–49.

———. "Luoghi e persone che si ritrovano nella vita di Santa Chiara," in ibid., 2, pp. 384–426.

Franceschini, Ezio. "Biografie di S. Chiara." *Aevum*, 27 (1953), 455–64.

———. "Storia e leggenda nella vita di S. Chiara." *Vita e pensiero*, 36 (1953), 394–404.

Gilliat-Smith, Ernest. *Saint Claire of Assisi: her Life and Legislation*. New York, 1914.

Oliger, L. "De origine regularum ordinis sanctae Clarae." *Archivum Franciscanum Historicum*, 5 (1912), 181–209, 413–47.

Pratese, R. Riccardo. "Letteratura occasione VII Centenarii a transitis S. Clarae (1253-1953) edita." *Archivum Franciscanum Historicum*, 47 (1954), 208–16.

Thomas of Celano. *The Life of Saint Clare*, trans. and ed. Fr. Paschal Robinson. Philadelphia, 1910.

Vian, Nello, ed. *Il processo di Santa Chiara d'Assisi*. Milan, 1962.

Claire of Montefalco

Herzmer, Volker. "Donatellos Madonna vom Paduaner Hochaltar—eine 'Schwarze Madonna'?" *Mittelungen des Kunsthistorischen Institutes in Florenz*, 16 (1972), 142–52.

Leonardi, Claudio and Menestò, Francesco, eds. *S. Chiara da Montefalco e il suo tempo*. Perugia-Florence. 1985.

Rotili, Marcello. "I processi per la canonizzazione di Chiara da Montefalco. A proposito della documentazione trecentesca ritrovata." *Studi medievali*, 3rd ser., 23 (1982), 971–1031.

Columba of Rieti

Astur, Baleonus. *Columba da Rieti: la seconda Caterina da Siena 1467–1501.* Rome, 1967.
Ricci, Ettore. *Storia della b. Columba da Rieti.* Perugia, 1901.

Eleanor of Aragon

Gundersheimer, Werner. "Women, Learning and Power: Eleanora of Aragon and the Court of Ferrara," in *Beyond Their Sex, Learned Women of the European Past,* ed. Patricia H. Labalme, pp. 43–65. New York, 1980.
Chiappini, Luciano. *Eleonora d'Aragona.* Rovigo, 1956.
Olivi, L. "Delle nozze di Ercole I con Eleonora d'Aragona," *Memorie della R. Accademia di Scienze, Lettere ed Arti di Modena,* 2nd ser., 5 (1887), 34ff.
Olivi, L. and Corvisieri, C. "Il trionfo romano di Eleonora d'Aragona nel giugno del 1473," *Archivo della Società Romana di Storia Patria,* 1 (1876), 475–91.

Eustochia of Messina

Terrizzi, Francesco, ed. *Il "Libro della Passione" scritto dalla b. Eustochia Calafato, clarissa messinese (1434–1485).* Messina, 1975.
Vaccari, Geronima and Ansalano, Cecilia de. *La leggenda della beata Eustochia da Messina. Testo volgare del sec. XV restituito all'originaria lezione,* 2nd ed., ed. Michele Catalano. Messina, 1950.

Francesca Bussa dei Ponziani

Armellini, Mariano, ed. *Vita di S. Francesca Romana scritta nell'idioma volgare di Roma del secolo XV (1469).* Rome, 1882.
Berthem-Bontoux (pseud. for Berthe M. Bontoux), *Sainte Françoise Romaine et son temps (1384–1440).* Paris, 1931.
Esch, Arnold. "Die Zeugenaussagen im Heiligsprechungverfahren für S. Francesca Romana als Quelle zur Sozialgeschichte Roms im frühen Quattrocento." *Quellen und Forschungen aus italienischen Archiven und Bibliotheken,* 53 (1973), 93–151.
Lugano, Placido Tommaso, ed. *I processi inediti per Francesca Bussa dei Ponziani (Santa Francesca Romana) 1440–1453.* Biblioteca Apostolica Vaticana, Studi e Testi, 120. Vatican City, 1945.
———. "I processi del 1440 e del 1451." *Rivista storica benedettina,* 3 (1908), 42–110.

Joan of Orvieto

Passarini, Luigi, ed. *Leggenda della beata Giovanna (detta Vanna) d'Orvieto*. Rome, 1879.

Joanna I

Crivelli, Domenico. *Della prima e della seconda Giovanna, regina di Napoli*. Padua, 1832.
De Feo, Italo. *Giovanna d'Angiò regina di Napoli*. Naples, 1968.
De Frede, B. Carlo. 'L'umanista Tristano Caracciola e la sua 'Vita di Giovanna I,'" *Archivio storico italiano*, 105 (1947), 50–64.
Scarpetta, Domenico. *Giovanna I di Napoli*. Naples, 1903.

Margaret of Cortona

Benvenuti Papi, Anna. "Margherita filia Jerusalem. Santa Margherita da Cortona ed il superamento mistico della crociata," in *Toscana e Terrasanta nel Medioevo*, pp. 117–37. Florence, 1982.
Cuthbert, R. P. *A Tuscan Penitent. The Life and Legend of St. Margaret of Cortona*. London, 1907.
Marchese, Francesco. *Vita di Santa Margarita di Cortona*. Venice, 1757.
Mariani, Eliodoro. *Leggenda della vita e dei miracoli di Santa Margherita da Cortona*. Vicenza, 1978.
Montenovesi, Ottorino. "I fioretti di Santa Margherita da Cortona." *Miscellanea francescana*, 46 (1946), 253–93.

Matilda of Tuscany

Briey, Renaud Marie Charles Eugene de. *Mathilde, duchesse de Toscane*. Genbloux, 1934.
Da Mantova, P. D. Benedetto Luccino. *Cronica della vera origine et attioni della contessa Matilda et de'suoi antecessori et discendenti*. Mantua, 1592.
Duff, Nora. *Matilda of Tuscany*. New York, 1910.
Gills, Florance M. "Matilda, Countess of Tuscany." *Catholic Historical Review*, 10 (1924): 234–45.
Grimaldi, Natale. *La Contessa Matilde e la sua stirpe feudale*. Florence, 1928.
Mansi, Gian Domenico. *Memorie della gran contessa Matilda restituita alla patria lucchese da Francesco Maria Fiorentini*, 2nd ed. Lucca, 1756.
Mellini, Domenico. *Dell origine dei fatti, costumi e lodi di Matelda la Gran Contessa d'Italia*, 2nd ed., Florence, 1609.
Mor, G. C. "Il vicariato italico di Matilde," in *Studi Matildici*, Atti e memorie del II

Convegno de Studi Matildici, Modena-Reggio-Emilia, 1-2-3 maggio 1970, Deputazione di Storia Patria per le antiche Provincie Modenesi, Biblioteca, new ser., pp. 67–80. Modena, 1971.
Ori, Pier Damiano and Perich, Giovanni. *Matilde di Canossa.* Milan, 1980.
Overmann, Alfred. *Gräfin Mathilde von Tuscien.* Innsbruck, 1895.
Pannenborg, A. *Studien zur Geschichte der Herzogin Matilde von Canosa.* Göttingen, 1872.
Santini, Giovanni. "La contessa Matilde, lo 'studium' e Bolgana 'città aperta' del XI secolo," in *Studi Matildici,* pp. 409–27. Modena, 1971.
Schenetti, Matteo. "La vittoria di Matilde di Canossa su Arrigo IV," in *Studi Matildici,* Atti del II Convegno di Studi Matildici, Reggio-Emilia, 7-8-9 ottobre 1977, Deputazione di Storia Patria per le antiche Provincie Modenesi, Biblioteca, new ser., pp. 235–42. Modena, 1978.
Simeoni, Luigi. "Il contributo della contessa Matilde al papato nella lotta per le investiture." *Studi Gregoriani,* 1 (1947), 353–72.
Tondelli, Leone. *Matilde di Canossa.* Bizzocchi, 1926.
Tosti, L. *La contessa Matilde e i romani pontifici.* Florence, 1859.

Rose of Viterbo

Abate, G. *S. Rosa di Viterbo, terziana francescana. Fonti storiche della vita e loro revisione critica.* Rome, 1952.

Serafina of San Gimignano

Di Coppo, F. Giovanni. *Leggenda di Santa Fina da Sangiminiano.* Imola, 1879.
Malenotti, Ignazio. *Vita di Santa Fina de S. Giminiano.* Colle, 1818.
Medici, P. M. de. *Ragguaglio istorico della vita, miracoli e culto immemoriale della Gloriosa Vergine Santa Fina de S. Giminiano.* Florence, 1750.

Umiliana dei Cerchi

Battelli, Guido, ed. *La leggenda della beata Umiliana de' Cerchi.* Florence, 1932.
Benvenuti Papi, Adriana. "Umiliana dei Cerchi. Nascità di un culto nella Firenze del Dugento." *Studi francesani,* 77 (1980), 87–117.
Cionacci, Francesco. *Vita della beata Umiliana de' Cerchi vedova fiorentina del Terz' Ordine di San Francesco.* Florence, 1682.
Franco, R. *La beata Umiliana de' Cerchi francescana del Terz' Ordine in Firenze.* Rome, 1977.

France

SURVEYS

Abensour, Léon. *La femme et le féminisme en France avant la révolution*. Paris, 1923. On the early modern era with some reference to the Middle Ages.

Bardeche, Maurice. *L'histoire des femmes*. 2 vols. Paris, 1968.

Butler, Pierce. *Women in All Ages and in All Countries*. Vol. 5, *Women of Medieval France*. 1908, rprt. New York, 1975.

Duby, Georges. *Le chevalier, la femme et le prêtre*. Paris, 1981; trans. Barbara Bray. *The Knight, the Lady and the Priest*. New York, 1983.

———. *La societé aux XIe et XIIe siècles dans la région mâconnaise* Paris, 1953; trans. Cynthia Postan. *The Chivalrous Society*. Berkeley, 1977.

Evans, Joan. *Life in Medieval France*. London, 1925.

Fauré, Christine. "L'absente." *Temps modernes* 410 (1980), 502–13; trans. in *Signs* 7 (1981), 125–35.

Lacroix, Paul. *France in the Middle Ages: Customs, Classes and Conditions*. New York, 1963.

Lehman, André. *Le rôle de la femme dans l'histoire de France au moyen âge*. Paris, 1952.

Le Tourneau, Charles-Jean-Marie. *La condition de la femme dans les diverses et civilisations. Bibliotheque sociologique internationale,* Vol. 26. Paris, 1903.

Michelet, Jules. *La femme*. Paris, 1860; trans. J. Palmer, *Woman*. New York, 1873.

———. *Le peuple*. Paris, 1846; trans. John P. McKay. *The People*. Urbana, IL, 1973.

———. *Du prêtre, de la femme et de la famille*. Paris, 1845; trans. in *Women, the Family and Freedom: The Debate in Documents, 1750–1950,* ed. Susan Groag Bell and Karen Offen, 2 vols. Stanford, 1983.

Mongellaz, Fanny de. *L'influence des femmes sur les moeurs et les destinées des nations*. Paris, 1828.

Pernoud, Régine. *La femme au temps des cathédrales*. Paris, 1980.

Pierre, Alexandre Joseph, Vicomte de Ségur. *Les femmes, leur condition et leur influence dans l'ordre social chez differens peuples anciens et modernes,* 3 vols. Paris, 1803.

Piettre, Monique. *La condition féminine à travers les âges*. Brussels, 1974.

Ribbe, Charles de. *La famille et la société en Durance avant la révolution d'après des documents originaux*. Paris, 1873.

Rose, Mary Beth, ed. *Women in the Middle Ages and the Renaissance*. Syracuse, 1986.

Shahar, Shulamith. *The Fourth Estate: A History of Women in the Middle Ages*. New York, 1983.

Société Jean Bodin pour l'histoire comparative des institutions, Recueil XII: La Femme. Brussels, 1962. Covers many European countries.

Thierry, Augustin. *Récits des temps mérovingiens précédés de considérations sur l'his-*

toire de France. Paris, 1840; trans. M. Jenkins. *Tales of the Early Franks, Episodes from Merovingian History*. University City, AL, 1977.

Thomas, Antoine Léonard. *Essai sur le caractère, les moeurs et l'esprit des femmes dans les différents siècles*. Paris, 1772; trans. *Essays on the Character, Manners and Genius of Women in Different Ages, enlarged on from the French of M. Thomas by Mr. Russel*, 2 vols. Philadelphia, 1774.

Verdon, Jean. "Les Sources de l'histoire de la femme en Occident aux Xe–XIIIe siècles." *Cahiers de civilisation médiévale*, 20 (1977), 219–51.

Wemple, Suzanne. *Women in Frankish Society*. Philadelphia, 1981.

Wemple, Suzanne and Julius Kirshner, eds. *Women of the Medieval World*. New York, 1985.

Witt, Henriette Guizot de. *Les femmes dans l'histoire*. Paris, 1889.

POLITICAL LIFE

Abensour, Léon. "Un mouvement féministe au XIIIe siècle." *Nouvelle Revue*, 3 (1911), 211–46.

Albistur, Maite and Daniel Armogathe, eds. *Le grief des femmes. Anthologie des textes féministes de moyen âge à la séconde république*, Vol. 1. Paris, 1978.

———. *Histoire du féminisme francais*. Paris, 1977.

Ascoli, Georges. "Essai sur l'histoire des idées féministes en France du XVIe siècle à la Révolution." *Revue de synthèse historique*, 13 (1906), 25–57, 161–84.

Barry, Françoise. *La Reine de France*. Paris, 1964.

Brown, Elizabeth. "Royal Marriage, Royal Property, and the Patrimony of the Crown: Inalienability and the Prerogative in Fourteenth Century France." *Humanities Working Paper 70*. Division of the Humanities and Social Sciences, California Institute of Technology, Pasadena, January, 1982.

Destefanis, Abel. *Louis XII et Jeanne de France*. Avignon, 1975.

Dhondt, Jean. "Sept femmes et un trio de rois." *Contributions à l'histoire économique et sociale*, 3 (1964–65), 37–70.

Facinger, Marion. "A Study of Medieval Queenship: Capetian France, 987–1237." *Studies in Medieval and Renaissance History*, 5 (1968), 1–47.

Faquet, E. *Le féminisme*. Paris, 1910.

Frager, Marcel. *Marie d'Anjou, femme de Charles VII*. Paris, 1948.

Ganshof, François. "Le statut de la femme dans la monarchie franque." *Recueils de la Société Jean Bodin*, 12 (1962), 5–58.

———. "Note sur quelques textes invoqués en faveur de l'existence d'une tutelle de la femme en droit franc." In *Etudes d'histoire du droit privé offertes à Pierre Petot*, ed. Pierre-Clement Timbali. Paris, 1959.

Griffiths, Ralph. "Queen Katherine of Valois and a missing statute of the Realm." *Law Quarterly Review*, 93 (1977), 248–58.

Guilhiermoz, Paul. "Le droit de renonciation de la femme noble, lors de la dissolution de la communauté, dans l'anncienne coutume de Paris." *Bibliothèque de l'école des chartes,* 44 (1883), 489–500.

Joran, Theodore. *Les féministes avant le féminisme.* Paris, 1935.

Laboulaye, Edouard de. *Recherches sur la condition civile et politique des femmes.* Paris, 1843.

Lacarra, J. M., and Anton Gonzales. "Les testaments de la reine Marie de Montpellier." *Annales du Midi,* 90 (1978), 105–20.

Levis-Mirepoix, Antoine. *Philippe Auguste et ses trois femmes.* Paris, 1957.

Lefebvre, Charles. "Interferences de la jurisprudence matrimoniale et de l'anthropologie au cours de l'histoire." *Revue de droit canonique,* 27 (1977), 4–102.

Lepointe, Gabriel. *Droit romaine et ancien droit français. Régimes matrimoniaux, liberalités, successions.* Paris, 1958.

Lightman, Harriet. "Sons and Mothers: Queens and Minor Kings in French Constitutional Law." Ph.D. diss. Bryn Mawr College, 1981.

Maude le Clavière, R. *Jeanne de France, duchesse d'Orleans.* Paris, 1883.

Robert, Louise Keralio. *Les Crimes des reines de France.* Paris, 1791.

Stafford, Paula. *Queens, Concubines and Dowagers. The King's Wife in the Early Middle Ages.* Athens, GA, 1983.

ECONOMIC LIFE

Boileau, Etienne. *Livre des métiers,* ed. G. B. Depping. Paris, 1837.

Bornstein, Diane. "Women at Work in the Fifteenth Century." *Fifteenth Century Studies,* 6 (1983), 33–40.

Burgues, Jean. *Les garanties de restitution de la dot en Languedoc, des invasion barbares à la fin de l'Ancien Régime.* Paris, 1937.

Comet, Georges. "Quelques remarques sur la dot et les droits de l'épouse dans la région d'Arles au XIIe et XIIIe siècles." *Mélanges offerts à René Crozet . . . ,* ed. Pierre Fallais and Yves-Jean Riou, Vol. 2. pp. 1031–34. Poitiers, 1966.

Cornuey, Louis-Maurice-Andre. "Le régime de la 'dos' aux époques mérovingienne et carolingienne." Ph.D. diss., Université d'Alger, 1929.

Dixon, E. "Craftswomen in *Livre des métiers.*" *Economic Journal,* 5 (1895), 209–28.

Fagniez, Gustave. *Etudes sur l'industrie et la classe industrielle à Paris, au XIIe siècle.* Bibliothèque de l'école hautes études. Sciences philologiques et historiques, no. 33. Paris, 1877.

Franklin, Alfred. *Les corporations ouvrières de Paris, du XIIe au XVIIIe siècle, histoire, statuts, armoires, d'après des documents originaux ou inédits.* Paris, 1884.

Gay, Jean. *Les effets pécuniaires au mariage en Nivernais du XIVe au XVIIIe siècle.* Paris, 1953.

Genicot, Leopold. *L'économie rurale namuroise au bas Moyen Âge (1199–1429).* vol. 2, *Les hommes. La noblesse.* Louvain, 1960.

Gonon, Marguerite. "Les dot en Forez au XVe siècle, d'après les testaments enregistres en la chancellerie de Forez." *Mélanges Pierre Tisset: Recueil de mémoires et trauvaux publiés par la Société d'histoire du droit et des institutions des anciens pays de droit ecrit,* 7 (1970), 247–65.
Gouron, Andre. "Pour une géographie de l'augment de dot." *Le droit de gens mariés (Mémoires de la Société pour l'histoire du droit et des institutions des anciens pays bourguignons, comtois, et romands)* 27 (1966), 113–31.
Geremek, Bronislav. *Le salariat dans l'artisanat parisien du XIIIeme au XVeme siècle. Etude sur le marché de la main-d'oeuvre au moyen âge.* Paris, 1968.
Hauser, Henri. *Les ouvriers du temps passé.* 1st ed. Paris, 1899.
Hilaire, Jean. *Le régime des biens entre époux dans la région Montpellier du début du XIIIe siècle à la fin du XVIe siècle.* Montpellier, 1957.
Jordan, William. "Jews on Top: Women and the Availability of Consumption Loans in Northern France in the Mid-Thirteenth Century." *Journal of Jewish Studies,* 29 (1978), 39–56.
Le Ménagier de Paris, traité de morale et d'économie domestique composé vers 1393, par un bourgeois parisien. Paris, 1846.
Maillet, Jean. "De l'exclusion coutumière des filles dotées à la renonciation à succession future dans les coutumes de Toulouse et Bordeaux." *Revue historique de droit français et étranger,* 4th ser. 30 (1952), 514–44.
Myers, A. R. "The Captivity of a Royal Witch: The Household Accounts of Queen Joan of Navarre, 1419–1421." *Bulletin of the John Rylands Library,* 24 (1940), 263–84.
Weinberger, Stephen. "Peasant Households in Provence: ca. 800–1100." *Speculum* 47 (1973), 247–57.
Wolff, Philippe. *Commerces et marchands de Toulouse (vers 1359–vers 1450).* Paris, 1954.
Yver, Jean. *Egalité entre héritiers et exclusion des enfants dotés: essai de géographie coutumière.* Paris, 1966.
———. "Note sur quelques textes coutumiers relatifs à l'exclusion successorale des filles dotées." *Etudes historiques à la mémoire de Noël Didier,* pp. 351–61. Paris, 1960.
———. "Sur deux jugements du Maître-Echevin de Metz (1361 et 1376) concernant le partage successoral entre enfants de plusieurs lits." *Mélanges offerts au Professeur Louis Falletti: annales de la faculté de droit et des sciences économiques de Lyon,* pp. 591–600. Lyon, 1971.

RELIGION

Abels, Richard and Harrison, Ellen. "The Participation of Women in Languedocian Catharism." *Medieval Studies,* 41 (1979), 215–51.
Auriol, A. "Sainte Cécile et la cathédrale d'Albi." In *Mélanges de littérature et d'his-*

toire religieuse publiés à l'occasion du jubilé épiscopal de mgr. Cabrières, pp. 329–42. Paris, 1899.

Barber, M. C. "Women and Catharism." *Reading Medieval Studies* 3 (1977), 45–62.

Bynum, Caroline. *Jesus as Mother: Studies in the Spirituality of the High Middle Ages*. Berkeley, 1982.

Corbin, Solange. "Miracula Beatae Mariae Semper Virginis." *Cahiers de civilisation médiévale* 10 (1967), 409–33.

Daudet, Pierre. *L'établissement de la compétence de l'église en matière de divorce et consanguinité*. Paris, 1941.

———. *Les origines carolingiennes de la compétence exclusive de l'église (France et Germanie). Études sur l'histoire de la jurisdiction matrimoniale*. Paris, 1933.

Esmein, A. *Le mariage en droit canonique*. 2 vols. 1891; rprt. New York, 1968.

Farmer, Sharon. "Persuasive Voices: Clerical Images of Medieval Wives." *Speculum,* 61 (1986), 517–43.

Geary, Patrick. "Saint Helen of Athyra and the Cathedral of Troyes in the 13th Century." *Journal of Medieval and Renaissance Studies,* 7 (1977), 149–68.

Huyhebaert, Nicolas-Norbert. "Les femmes laïques dans la vue religieuse des XIe et XIIe siècles dans la province ecclésiastique de Reims." In *I laici nella "Societas christiana" dei secoli XIe–XIIe,* pp. 346–89. Milan, 1968.

Laurent, Theis. "'Saint sans Famille.' Quelques remarques sur la famille dans le monde franc à travers les sources hagiographiques." *Revue historique,* 255 (1976), 3–20.

Laurentin, Rene. "Bulletin sur la Vierge Marie." *Revue des sciences philosophiques et théologiques,* 56 (1972), 433–91.

Lefebvre-Teillard, Anne. "Ad matrionium contrahere compellitur." *Revue de droit canonique,* 28 (1978), 210–17.

Leclercq, Jean. *Monks and Love in Twelfth-Century France*. New York, 1979.

LeGoff, Jacques. "Melusine maternelle et défricheuse." *Annales E.S.C.* 26 (1971), 587–603.

Lorcin, Marie-Thérèse. "Retraite des veuves et filles au couvent: quelques aspects de la condition féminine à la fin du Moyen Age." *Annales de demographie historique* (1975), 187–204.

McNamara, Jo Ann and Wemple, Suzanne. "The Power of Women Through the Family in Medieval Europe." *Feminist Studies,* 1 (1973), 126–41.

Metz, Renee. "Le Statut de la femme endroit canonique médiéval." *Recueils de la Société Jean Bodin,* 12 (1962), 59–113.

Mundy, John. *The Repression of Catharism at Toulouse*. Toronto, 1985.

Roisin, Simone. "L'efflorescence cistercienne et le courant féminin de piété au XIII siècle." *Revue d'histoire ecclésiastique,* 39 (1943), 342–78.

Saxer, Victor. *Le culte de Marie-Madeleine en Occident, des origines à la fin du moyen âge*. 2 vols. Paris, 1959.

Schulenberg, Jane. "Strict Enclosure and its Effects on the Female Monastic Experience." In *Distant Echoes: Medieval Religious Women,* ed. John Nichols and Lilliam Tshank, pp. 51–86. Kalamazoo, 1984.

Verdon, Jean. "Les moniales dans la France de l'Ouest aux XIe et XIIe siècle. Etude d'histoire sociale." *Cahiers de civilisation médiévale,* 19 (1976), 247–64.

———. "Notes sur le rôle économique des monastères féminins en France dans la seconde moitié du IXe et au debut du Xe siècle." *Revue Mabillon,* 58 (1975), 329–43.

———. "Recherches sur les monastères féminins dans la France du Sud aux IXe–XIe siècles." *Annales du Midi,* 88 (1976), 117–38.

SOCIAL LIFE

Aries, Philippe. "Sur les origines de la contraception en France." *Population,* 8 (1953), 465–72.

Aries, Philippe, and Begin, André, eds. *Western Sexuality,* trans. Anthony Forster. Oxford, 1985.

Biraben, Edouard. "La Population de Toulouse au XIVe et au XVe siècles." *Journal des Savants* (1964), 284–300.

Bonnecorse de Lubières, Gabriel de. *La Condition des gens mariés en Provence aux XIVe et XVIe siècles.* Paris, 1929.

Bouchard, Constance. "The Structure of a Twelfth-Century French Family: The Lords of Seignelay." *Viator,* 10 (1979), 39–56.

Camerlynck, Eliane. "Féminité et sorcellerie chez les théoriciens de la démonologie à la fin du Moyen Age." *Etude du Malleus Maleficanum. Renaissance Reformation,* 7, 1 (1983), 13–25.

Chamberlin, R. *Life in Medieval France.* London, 1967.

Cherel, Albert. *La Famille française. Pages choisies de nos bons écrivains de 825 à 1924. I: Le moyen âge et le XVIe siècle.* Paris, 1925.

Coleman, Emily. "Medieval Marriage Characteristics." In *The Family in History,* ed. T. Rabb and R. Rotberg, pp. 1–15. New York, 1973.

Defourneaux, Marcelin. *La vie quotidienne au temps de Jeanne d'Arc.* Paris, 1952.

Donahue, Charles. "The Canon Law on the Formation of Marriage and Social Practice in the Later Middle Ages." *Journal of Family History,* 8 (1983), 144–58.

Duby, Georges. *Hommes et structures au Moyen Age.* Paris, 1973.

———. *La Société aux XIe et XIIe siècles dans la région Mâconnaise.* Paris, 1971.

———. *Medieval Marriage, Two Models from Twelfth-Century France.* Baltimore, 1978.

Duval, Paul-Marie. *La vie quotidienne en Gaule pendant la paix romaine.* Paris, 1953.

Fedou, Rene. "Une famille aux XIVe et XVe siècles: les Jossard de Lyon." *Annales E.S.C.,* 9 (1954), 461–80.

Flandrin, J. L. "Marriage tardif et vie sexuelle: Discussion et hypothèse de recherche." *Annales E.S.C.,* 27 (1972), 1351–78.

———. *Les amours paysannes.* Paris, 1975.

———. *Le sexe et l'occident.* Paris, 1981.

Franklin, Alfred. *La Vie privée au temps des premiers Capetiens.* Paris, 1911.

Genestal, R. "La femme mariée dans l'ancien droit normand." *Revue historique de droit français et étranger,* 4th ser. 9 (1930), 472–505.

Gonthier, N. "Delinquants ou victimes, les femmes dans la société lyonnaise du XVe siècle." *Revue historique,* 271 (1984), 25–46.

Gottlieb, Beatrice. "The Meaning of Clandestine Marriage." In *Family and Sexuality in French History,* ed. R. Wheaton and T. Hareven, pp. 49–83. Philadelphia, 1980.

Hajdu, Robert. "The Position of Noble Women in the Pays des Coutumes, 1100–1300." *Journal of Family History,* 5 (1980), 22–44.

Hilaire, Jean. *Le régime des biens entre époux dans la région de Montpellier du début du XIIIe siècle à la fin du XVIe siècle.* Montpellier, 1957.

———. "Vie en commun, famille et esprit communautaire dans le Midi de la France." *Revue historique de droit française et étranger* 4th ser., 51 (1973), 8–53.

Lebande, Edmonde-Rene. "Conclusions of the Colloquium 'La Femme dans les civilisations des Xe–XIIIe siècles'." *Cahiers de civilisation médiévale,* 20 (1977), 253–60.

Laribière, Geneviève. "Le Mariage à Toulouse aux XIVe et XVe siècles." *Annales du Midi,* 79 (1967), 335–61.

Lefebvre, Charles. *La coutume française du mariage au temps de Saint Louis.* Paris, 1901.

Lelong, Charles. *La Vie en France au moyen âge à l'époque mérovingienne.* Paris, 1963.

LeRoy Ladurie, Emmanuel. *Montaillou: village occitan de 1294–1324.* Paris, 1972; trans. Barbara Bray, *Montaillou, The Promised Land of Error.* New York, 1978.

Molin, Jean Baptiste and Mutembe, Protais. *Le rituel du mariage en France du XIIe du XVIe siècle.* Paris, 1974.

Petot, Pierre. "Le mariage des vassales." *Revue historique de droit française et étranger,* 56 (1978), 29–47.

Petot, Pierre and Vandenbossche, A. "Le statut de la femme dans les pays coutoumiers francais du XIIIe au XVIIe siècle." *La Femme. Recueils de la société Jean Bodin,* 12 (1962), 243–54.

Pounds, Norman. "Overpopulation in France and the Low Countries in the Later Middle Ages." *Journal of Social History,* 3 (1970), 225–47.

———. "Population and Settlement in the Low Countries and Northern France in the Latter Middle Ages." *Revue belge de philologie et d'histoire,* 49 (1971), 403–81; 1119–74.

Ribbe, Charles de. *Les fiancailles et les mariages en Provence à la fin du moyen âge.* Montpellier, 1896.

Riche, Pierre. *La vie quotidienne dans l'empire carolingien.* Paris, 1973; trans. Jo Ann McNamara. *Daily Life in the Time of Charlemagne.* Philadelphia, 1978.

Sullerot, Evelyne. *Le Fait feminin.* Paris, 1978.

Prostitution

Billot, Claudine. "Les enfants abandonnés à Chartres à la fin du Moyen Age." *Annales de démographie historique* (1975), 284–300.

Le Croix, Paul. *Histoire de la prostitution chez tous les peuples du monde.* Paris, 1851–53.

Otis, Leah Lydia. *Prostitution in Medieval Society.* Chicago, 1984.

Parent-Duchatelet, A. J. B. *De la prostitution dans la ville de Paris.* Paris, 1836.

Rabutaux, A. P. E. *De la prostitution en Europe depuis l'antiquité jusqu'à la fin du 16e siècle.* Paris, 1851.

Rossiaud, Jacques. "Prostitution, jeunesse et société dans les villes du sud-est au XVe siècle." *Annales E.S.C.* 31 (1976), 289–325; trans. in *Deviants and the Abandoned in French Society,* ed. Robert Forster and Orest Ranum, pp. 1–31. Baltimore, 1978.

Solé, Jacques. "Passion charnelle et société urbaine d'Ancien Regime: amour vénal, amour libre et amour fou à Grenoble au milieu du regne du Louis XIV." *Villes de l'Europe méditerranéenne et de l'Europe occidentale du Moyen Age,* pp. 211–32. Nice, 1969.

CULTURE

Atkinson, W. "'Precious Balsam in a Fragile Glass': The Ideology of Virginity in the Later Middle Ages." *Journal of Family History,* 8 (1983), 131–43.

Beauvais, Vincent de. *De Eruditione Filiorum Nobilium,* ed. Arpad Steiner. Cambridge, MA, 1938.

Bell, Susan Groag. "Christine de Pizan (1364–1430): Humanism and the Problem of a Studious Woman." *Feminist Studies,* 3 (1976), 173–84.

Benton, John. "The Court of Champagne as a Literary Center." *Speculum,* 36 (1961), 551–91.

———. "Clio and Venus: An Historical View of Medieval Love." In F. X. Newman, ed. *The Meaning of Courtly Love.* pp. 19–42. Albany, 1968.

Bogin, Meg. *Women Troubadors.* New York, 1979.

Bornstein, Dianne. *The Lady in the Tower: Medieval Courtesy Literature for Women.* Hamden, CT, 1983.

———. *Ideals for Women in the Work of Christine de Pizan.* Detroit, 1982.

Borodine, Myrrha. *La Femme et l'amour au XIIe siècle, d'après les poèmes de Chrétien de Troyes.* Paris, 1909.

Davenson, Henri. *Les Troubadours.* Paris, 1961.

Davis, Judith. "Christine de Pisan and Chauvinist Diplomacy." *Female Studies,* 6 (1972), 116–22.

Ferrante, Joan. *The Woman as Image in Medieval Literature.* New York, 1975.

Frugoni, Chiara. "L'iconographie de la femme au cours des Xe–XIIIe siècles." *Cahiers de civilisation médiévale,* 20 (1977), 177–88.

Guadier, M. "De l'education des femmes au XIVe siècle, étude historique." *Annales de l'academie de Mâcon,* 9 (1870), 30–42.

Hoepffner, Ernest. *Les troubadours dans leurs vies et dans leurs oeuvres.* Paris, 1955.

Jonin, Pierre. "Les types féminins dans les chansons de toile." *Romania,* 91 (1970), 433–66.

Jourdain, Charles. "Mémoire sur l'éducation des femmes au moyen âge." *Mémoires de l'académie des inscriptions et belles-lettres,* 2nd ser. 28 (1874), 79–133.

Kay, Sarah. "Love in a Mirror: As Aspect of the Imagery of Bernart de Ventadorn." *Medium Aevum,* 52 (no. 2, 1983), 272–85.

Kelly, Joan. "Early Feminist Theory and the Querrelle des Femmes, 1400–1789." *Signs,* 8 (1982), 4–28.

———. *Women, History and Theory: The Essays of Joan Kelly.* Chicago, 1984.

Lefay-Toury, Marie Noelle. "Roman breton et mythes courtois: L'évolution du personnage féminin dans les romans de Chrétien de Troyes." *Cahiers de civilisation médiévale,* 15 (1972), 193–204, 283–93.

Marie de France. *French Medieval Romances from the Lays of Marie de France,* trans. Eugene Mason. Paris, 1924; rprt. New York, 1975.

MacMillan, Ann. "Men's Weapons, Women's War: The Nine Female Worthies, 1400–1600." *Medievalia,* 5 (1979), 113–39.

McLaughlin, Mary Martin. "Peter Abelard and the Dignity of Women." In *Pierre Abelard, Pierre le Vénérable: Colloques internationaux du Centre de la recherche scientifique,* Abbaye de Cluny, 2–9 juillet, 1972. pp. 287–334. Paris, 1975.

McLeod, Enid. *The Order of the Rose, the Life and Ideas of Christine de Pizan.* Totowa, NJ, 1976.

Mickal, Emmanuel. *Marie de France.* Boston, 1974.

Noble, Peter. "The Character of Guyinevere in the Arthurian Romances of Chrétien de Troyes." *The Modern Language Review,* 67 (1972), 524–35.

Pernoud, Régine. *Héloise et Abelard.* Paris, 1980.

Petit, Aimé. "Le traitement courtois du thème des Amazones d'après trois romans antiques: Enéas, Troie et Alexandre." *Moyen Age,* 89, 1 (1983), 63–84.

Pizan, Christine de. *A City of Ladies,* trans. E. R. Jeffries. New York, 1983.

Romantisme. Revue de la Société des Etudes romantiques (issue speciale). Paris, 13, 14, 15, *or* 16, 1976.

Solente, Suzanne. *Christine de Pisan.* Paris, 1969.

Stevens, John. "The *granz biens* of Marie de France." In *Patterns of Love and Courtesy,* ed. John Lawlord, pp. 1–25. Evanston, 1965.

Thieboux, Marcelle, trans. *The Writings of Medieval Women.* New York, 1984.

Waddell, Helen. *Abelard and Eloise.* London, 1950.

Willard, Charity Cannon. "A Fifteenth-Century View of Women's Role in Medieval Society: Christine de Pizan's *Livre des Trois Vertus.*" In *Role of Women in the Middle Ages,* ed. Rosemarie Morewedge, pp. 90–120. Albany, 1975.

———. *Christine de Pizan, Her Life and Works.* New York, 1984.

BIOGRAPHY

Blanche of Castile

Berger, Elie. *Histoire de Blanche de Castille, reine de France* 1895; rprt. Geneva, 1975–76.

Bertrand, René. *La France de Blanche de Castille*. Paris, 1977.

Brion, Marcel. *Blanche de Castile, femme de Louis VIII, mere de Saint Louis*. Paris, 1939.

Gonzalez Ruiz, Nicolas. *Blanca de Castilla: Maria de Molina*. Barcelona, 1954.

Germiny, Maxine de. "Blanche de Castille, reine de France." *Revue des questions historiques,* 59 (1896), 506–11.

Orliac, Jehanne d'. *Blanche de Castille, mère de Saint Louis et de Sainte Isabelle*. Paris, 1861.

Pernoud, Régine. *Blanche de Castile;* trans. *Blanche of Castile*. New York, 1975.

Eleanor of Aquitaine

Brown, Elizabeth. A. R. "Eleanor of Aquitaine: Parent, Queen and Duchess." In *Eleanor of Aquitaine, Patron and Politician,* ed. William W. Kibler, pp. 9–34. Austin, TX, 1976.

Chambers, Frank. "Some Legends Concerning Eleanor of Aquitaine." *Speculum,* 16 (1941), 459–68.

Chapman, Robert. "Notes on the Demon Queen Eleanor." *Modern Language Notes,* 70 (1955), 393–96.

Greenhill, Eleanor. "Eleanor, Abbot Suger, and Saint-Denis." In *Eleanor of Aquitaine, Patron and Politican,* ed. William W. Kibler, pp. 81–113. Austin, TX, 1976.

Kelly, Amy. "Eleanor of Aquitaine and Her Courts of Love." *Speculum,* 12 (1937), 3–19.

———. *Eleanor of Aquitaine and the Four Kings*. Cambridge, MA, 1950.

Lejeune, Rita. "Rôle littéraire de la famille d'Aliénor d'Aquitain." *Cahiers de civilisation médiévale,* 1 (1958), 319–37.

McCash, June Hall Martin. "Marie de Champagne and Eleanor of Aquitaine." *Speculum* 54 (1979), 698–711.

Markale, Jean. *Aliénor d'Aquitaine, reine de France*. Paris, 1979.

Meade, Marion. *Eleanor of Aquitaine: A Biography*. New York, 1977.

Pernoud, Régine. *Aliénor d'Aquitain*. Paris, 1965; trans. P. Wiles. *Eleanor of Aquitaine*. New York, 1968.

Richardson, Henry. "The Letters and Charters of Eleonor of Aquitaine." *English Historical Review,* 74 (1959), 193–213.

Rosenberg, Melrich. *Eleanor of Aquitaine: Queen of the Troubadours and of the Courts of Love*. Boston, 1937.

Seward, Desmond. *Eleanor of Aquitaine*. New York, 1979.
Spens, Willy de. *Eleonore d'Aquitaine et ses troubadours*. Paris, 1957.
Walker, Curtis. *Eleanor of Aquitain*. Chapel Hill, NC, 1950.
———. "Eleanor of Aquitaine and the Disaster at Cadmos Mountain on the Second Crusade." *American Historical Review,* 55 (1949–50), 857–61.

Ste. Geneviève

Jullian, Camille. "Sainte Geneviève à Nanterre," in *Mélanges offerts à M. Gustave Schlumberger*. 2, 373–75. Paris, 1924.
Kohler, Charles. *Étude critique . . . sur Geneviève*. Paris, 1881.
Lesêstre, H. *Sainte Geneviève*. Paris, 1900.
Sertillanges, A. O. *Sainte Geneviève*. Paris, 1917.

Joan of Arc

Bourassin, Emmanuel. *Jeanne d'Arc*. Paris, 1977.
Champion, Pierre. "Notes sur Jeanne d'Arc." *Le Moyen Age* 20 (1907), 193–201; 22 (1909), 370–77; 23 (1910), 175–97.
Cordier, Jacques. *Jeanne d'Arc: sa personnalité, son rôle*. Paris, 1948.
Desama, Claude. "Jeanne d'Arc et Charles VII. L'entrevue du signe (Mars–Avril 1429)." *Revue de l'histoire des religions* 170 (1966), 29–46.
Duby, Andrée and Duby, Georges. *Les Procès de Jeanne d'Arc*. Paris, 1975.
Enklaar, Diederik and Post, R. R. *La fille au grand coeur: Étude sur Jeanne d'Arc*. Groningen, 1955.
Febvre, Lucien. *Jeanne d'Arc*. 1947, rprt. Paris, 1977.
Gérard, André-Marie. *Jeanne la mal jugée*. Paris, 1964.
Grandeau, Yann. *Jeanne insultée: Procès en diffamation*. Preface by Regine Pernoud. Paris, 1973.
Grayeff, Felix. *Joan of Arc: Legends and Truth*. London, 1978.
Hartemann, Jean. *Une Jeanne d'Arc possible*. Paris, 1978.
Joly, Henri. "La Psychologie de Jeanne d'Arc." *Etudes,* 119 (1909), 158–83.
LaMartinière, Jules de. "Frère Richard et Jeanne d'Arc à Orleans, Mars-Juillet 1430." *Le Moyen Age,* 44 (1934), 184–98.
Leroy, Oliver. *Sainte Jeanne d'Arc*. Paris, 1958.
Lightbody, Charles. *The Judgements of Joan: Joan of Arc, A Study in Cultural History*. Cambridge, MA, 1961.
Luce, Simeon. *Jeanne d'Arc à Domremy. Recherches critiques sur les origines de la mission de la Pucelle, acompagnées de pièces justificatives*. 1866; rprt. Geneva, 1975–76.
Lynn, Therèse. "The *Ditie de Jeanne d'Arc:* Its political, feminist and aesthetic significance." *15th Century Studies,* 1 (1978), 149–56.
Lyonne, René. *Jeanne d'Arc, légende et histoire*. Nancy, 1973.

Michelet, Jules. *Jeanne d'Arc*. Paris, 1840; trans. Albert Guerard. *Joan of Arc*. Ann Arbor, MI, 1967.
Paine, Albert. *Joan of Arc, Maid of France*. New York, 1961.
Pernoud, Régine. *Jeanne d'Arc*. Paris, 1959; trans. Jeanne Unger Duell. *Joan of Arc*. New York, 1961.
Quicherat, Jules. *Le Procès de Jeanne d'Arc*. 5 vols. Paris, 1854.
Scott, Walter Sidney. *Jeanne d'Arc: Her Life, Her Death and the Myth*. New York, 1974.
Sermoise, Pierre de. *Joan of Arc and Her Secret Missions*. Trans. Jennifer Taylor. London, 1973.
Smith, John Hollard. *Joan of Arc*. New York, 1973.
Steinbach, Hartmut. *Jeanne d'Arc*. Gottingen, 1973.
Thomas, Edith. *Jeanne d'Arc*. Paris, 1947.
Tisset, Pierre. *Procès de condamnation de Jeanne d'Arc*. Vol. II, *Traduction et Notes*. Paris, 1970.
Waldman, Milton. *Joan of Arc*. New York, 1935.
Warner, Marina. *Joan of Arc*. London, 1980.
Xerrie, Jean-Francois. *Jeanne d'Arc n'a pas existé*. Paris, 1973.

Germanic

SURVEYS

Ennen, Edith. *Frauen im Mittelalter*. Munich, 1984.
Finke, Heinrich. *Die Frau im Mittelalter* Sammlung Kösel, vol. 62 Kempten, 1913.
Portmann, Marie-Louise. *Die Darstellung der Frau in der Geschichtsschreibung des früheren Mittelalters*. Basler Beiträge zur Geschichtswissenschaft, no. 69. Basel, 1958.
Harksen, S. *Die Frau im Mittelalter*. Leipzig, 1974.
Haverkamp, Alfred, ed. *Haus und Familie in der spätmittelalterlichen Stadt*. Cologne and Vienna, 1984.
Shahar, Shulamith. *The Fourth Estate*, trans. Chay Galai. London and New York, 1983.
Weinhold, K. *Die deutschen Frauen in dem Mittelalter*, 2 vols. Vienna, 1897, rprt. 1968.

POLITICS AND LAW

Bechstein, Susanne. "Die Frauen in Hohenlohe im mittelalterlichen Vormundschaftsrecht." *Württembergisch Franken,* 50 (1966), 268–75.

Bohne, G. "Zur Stellung der Frau im Prozess- und Strarecht der italienischen Statuten." In *Gendenkschrift für L. Mitteis.* Leipzig, 1926.

Bosch, Jan Willem. "Le statut de la femme dans les Anciens Pays-Bas séptonrionaux." In *La Femme.* vol. 2. Récueils de la Société Jean Bodin pour l'histoire comparative des institutions, vols. 11–12. Brussels, 1959–62.

Bovet, S. "Die Stellung der Frau im deutschen und in langobardischen Lehnsrecht." *Jahrbuch der Basler Juristenfakultät,* 5–7 (1926–28).

Brants, M. "De vrouw in 't Germaansch en in 't oud Vlaamsch recht." *Tss. van het Willems-Fonds,* 5 (1900).

Brauneder, Wilhelm. *Die Entwicklung des Ehegüterrechts in Österreich.* Salzburg, 1973.

Brunner, Heinrich. "Die frankisch-romanische dos." *Abhandlungen zur Rechtsgeschichte,* ed. Karl Rauch. 2. Weimar, 1931.

———. "Das Geburt eines lebenden Kindes und das eheliche Vermögensrecht," in ibid.

———. "Kritische Bemerkungen zur Geschichte des germanischen Weiberbrechts," in ibid.

———. "Die uneheliche Vaterschaft in den alteren germanischen Rechten," in ibid.

Dargun, Lothar. "Mutterrecht und Raubehe, und ihre Reste im germanischen Recht und Leben." *Untersuchungen zur deutschen Staats- und Rechtsgeschichte,* 16 (1883), 13–76.

Demelius, Henrich. *Eheliches Gütterrecht im spätmitteralterlichen Wien.* Vienna, 1970.

Eckhardt, Karl August. *Germanisches Recht,* 4th ed. Grundriss der germanischen Philologie, 5, nos. 1 and 2. Berlin, 1967.

Eisenmann, Hartmut. *Konstanzer Institutionen des Familien- und Erbrechts von 1370–1521.* Constance, 1964.

Ennen, Edith. "Die Frau im Mittelalter." *Kurtrierisches Jahrbuch,* 21 (1981).

———. "Die Frau in der mittelalterlichen Stadtgesellschaft Mitteleuropeas." *Hansische Geschichtsblätter,* 98 (1980).

Espinas, Georges. "La femme au moyen âge dans les villes allemands." *Annales d'Histoire Économique et Sociale,* 8 (1936), 390–93.

Fahrner, Ignatz. *Geschichte der Ehescheidung im kanonischen Recht.* vol. I, *Geschichte des Unauflösingkeitsprinzips under der vollkommenen Scheidung.* Freiburg, 1903.

Fehr, H. *Die Rechtsstellung der Frau und der Kinder in den Weistümern.* Jena, 1912, rprt. 1971.

Ficker, Julius. *Untersuchungen zur Erben folge der ostgermanischen Rechte.* vols. 1–4. Innsbruck, 1891–96.

Flossmann, U. "Die Gleichberechtigung der Geschlechter in der Privatrechtsgeschichte." In *Rechtsgeschichte under Rechtsdogmatik,* Festschrift H. Eichler zum 70. Geburtstag, ed. U. Flossmann. Vienna and New York, 1977.

Frölich, Karl. "Die Eheschliessung des deutschen Frühmittelalters im Lichte Forschung." *Hessische Blätter für Volkskunde,* 27 (1928), 144–94.

Ganshof, F. L. "Le statut de la femme dans la monarchie franque." In *La Femme,* vol. 2. Récueils de la Société Jean Bodin pour l'histoire comparative des institutions. vols. 11–12. Brussels, 1959–62.

Gellinek, Christian. "Marriage by Consent in Literary Sources of Medieval Germany." *Studia Gratiana,* 12 (1967), 555–79.

Grafe, R. *Das Eherecht in den Coutumiers des 13. Jahrhunderts. Eine rechtsvergleichende Darstellung des französischen Ehepersonen- und Ehegüterrechts im Mittelalter.* Göttingen, Zürich, and Frankfurt am Main, 1972.

Gilissen, J. "Le statut de la femme dans l'ancien droit belge." In *La Femme,* vol. 2. Récueils de la Société Jean Bodin pour l'histoire comparative des institutions, vols. 11–12. Brussels, 1959–62.

Grimm, J. *Deutsche Rechtsalterthümer.* Göttingen, 1828.

Herzog, H. U. *Beiträge zur Geschichte des eherechtlichen Güterrechts der Stadt Zürich.* Züricher Beiträge zur Rechtswissenschaft, new ser. no. 92. Aarau, 1942.

Hörger, K. "Die reichsrechtliche Stellung der Fürstabtissen." In *Archiv für Urkundenforschung,* 9 (1926).

Kaiser, Elsbet. *Frauendienst im mittelhochdeutschen Volksepos.* Breslau, 1921.

Kalifa, Simon. "Singularités matrimoniales chez les anciens Germains: le rapt et le droit de la femme à disposer d'elle-meme." *Revue historique de droit français et étranger,* 4th ser. 48 (1970), 199–225.

Koebner, Richard. "Die Eheauffassung des ausgehenden deutschen Mittelalters." *Archiv für Kulturgeschichte,* 9 (1911), 136–98 and 279–318.

Köstler, Rudolf. "Raub-, Kauf-, und Freidelehe bei den Germanen." *Zeitschrift der Savigny-Stiftung für Rechtsgeschichte.* German. Abt., 63 (1943), 92–136.

Krauz, Eberhard. *Die Vormundschaft im mittelalterlichen Lübeck.* Kiel, 1967.

Kroemer, B. "Über Rechtsstellung, Handlungsspielräume und Tätigkeitsbereiche von Frauen in spätmittelalterlichen Städten." In *Staat und Gesellschaft in Mittelalter und früher Neuzeit,* Gedenkschrift für J. Leuschner. Göttingen, 1983.

Kroeschell, Karl. *Haus und Herrschaft im frühen deutschen Recht.* Göttingen, 1968.

———. "Söhne und Töchter im germanischen Erbrecht." In G. Landwehr, ed. *Studien zu den germanischen Volksrechten.* Gedächtnisschrift für W. Ebel. Frankfurt am Main, 1982.

Leineweber, A. *Die rechtliche Beziehung des nichtehelichen Kindes zu seinem Erzeuger in der Geschichte des Privatrechts.* Beiträge zur Neueren Privatrechtsgeschichte 7. Königstein/Ts., 1978.

May, G. "Zu der Frage der Weihefähigkeit der Frau." *Zeitschrift der Savigny-Stiftung für Rechtsgeschichte.* Kanon. Abt. 60 (1974).

Mayer-Maly, Theo. "Die Morgengage im Wiener Privatrecht des Spätmittelalters." *Festschrift Hans Lentze,* ed. Nikolaus Grass und Werner Ogis. Innsbruck, 1969.

Melicher, Th. *Die germanischen Formen der Eheschliessung im westgotisch-spanischen Recht.* Vienna, 1940.

Merschberger, Gerda. *Die Rechtsstellung der germanischen Frau.* Leipzig, 1937.

Meyer, Herbert. "Friedelehe und Mutterrecht." *Zeitschrift der Savigny-Stiftung für Rechtsgeschichte.* Germanistische Abteilung, 47 (1927), 198–286.

———. "Ehe und Eheauffaussung der Germanen." In *Festschrift E. Heymann zum 70. Geburtstag,* vol. 1. Weimar, 1940.

Mikat, P. *Dotierte Ehe—rechte Ehe. Zur Entwicklung des Eheschliessungsrechts in fränkischer Zeit.* Opladen, 1978.

———. *Religionsrechtsliche Schriften. Abhandlungen zum Staatskirchenrechts und Eherecht,* 2 vols. Berlin, 1974.

Neckel, Gustav. *Liebe und Ehe bei den vorchristlichen Germanen.* Leipzig, 1934.

Neubecker, Friedrich Karl. *Die Mitgift in rechtsvergleichender Darstellung.* Leipzig, 1909.

Overvoorde, J. C. *De ontwikkeling van den rechtstoestand der vrouw volgens het oud-Germaansche en het oud-Nederlandsche recht.* Rotterdam, 1891.

Pappe, H. *Methodische Stromungen in der eherechtsgeschichtlichen Forschung (bis zur Epoche der germanischen Christianisierung).* Würzburg, 1934.

Pfaff, V. "Das kirchliche Eherecht am Ende des 12. Jahrhunderts." *Zeitschrift der Savigny-Stiftung für Rechtsgeschichte.* Kanon. Abteilung 63 (1977).

Schmelzeisen, G. K. *Die Rechtsstellung der Frau in der deutschen Stadtwirtschaft.* Arbeiten zur deutschen Rechts- und Verfassungsgeschichte 10. Stuttgart, 1935.

Schröder, R. *Geschichte des ehelichen Güterrechts in Deutschland,* 2 parts, 4 vols. Stettin, Danzig, and Elbing, 1871–74.

Senn, Noel. *Le contrat de vente de la femme en droit matrimonial germanique.* Porrentry, 1946.

Stammler, Rudolf. *Über die Stellung der Frauen im alten deutschen Recht.* Berlin, 1877.

Strätz, H. W. *Der Verlobungskuss und seine Folgen, rechtsgeschichtlich besehen.* Constance, 1979.

von Strauss und Torney, Lulu. *Deutsches Frauenleben in der Zeit der Sachsenkeiser und Hohenstaufen.* Jena, 1927.

Thieme, Hans. "Die Rechtsstellung der Frau in Deutschland," in *La Femme,* 2 vols. Récueils de la Société Jean Bodin pour l'histoire comparative des institutions, vols. 11–12. Brussels, 1959–62.

Verhulst, A. "La divérsite du régime domanial entre Loire et Rhin a l'époque carolingienne. Bilan de quinze années de récherches." In W. Jannssen and D. Lohrmann, eds. *Villa-Curtis-Grangia.* Munich, 1983.

Weber, Marianne. *Ehefrau und Mutter in der Rechtsentwicklung.* Tübingen, 1907.

Weigand, Rudolf. "Die Rechtsprechung des Regensburger Gerichts in Ehesachen unter besonderer Berücksichtigung der bedingten Eheschliessung nach Gerichtsbüchern aus dem Ende des 15. Jahrhunderts." *Archiv für katholisches Kirchenrecht,* 137 (1968), 403–63.

Weinhold, Karl. *Die deutschen Frauen in dem Mittelalter,* 2 vols. Vienna, 1897.

Wemple, Suzanne. *Women in Frankish Society.* Philadelphia, 1981.

Wührer, K. "Zum altschwedischen Eherecht," *Zeitschrift der Savigny-Stiftung für Rechtsgeschichte,* Germanische Abteilung, 74 (1957), 231–33.

Political Roles

von Boehn, O. "Anna von Nassau, Herzogin von Braunschweig-Lüneburg." *Niedersächsisches Jahrbuch für Landesgeschichte,* 29 (1957), 24–120.

Disselnkötter, H. *Gräfin Loretta von Spanheim geborene von Salm.* Bonn, 1940.

Düffel, J. "Gräfin Adela von Hamaland und ihr Kampf um das Stift Hochelten." In *Gedenkbuch für J. Düffel.* Emmereich, 1978.

Kirschner, Max. *Die deutschen Kaiserinnen in der Zeit von Konrad I. bis zum Tode Lothars von Supplinburg.* Historische Studien 79. Berlin, 1910.

Klewitz, Hans-Walter. "Die Abstammung der Kaiserin Beatrix." *Deutsches Archiv für Erforschung des Mittelalters,* 7 (1944), 204–12.

Konechy, Silvia. "Eherecht und Ehepolitik unter Ludwig der Frommen." *Mitteilungen des Instituts für österreichische Geschichtsforschung,* 85 (1977), 1–21.

———. *Die Frauen des karolingishcen Königshauses. Die politische Bedeutung der Ehe und die Stellung der Frau in der fränkischen Herrscherfamilies vom 7. bis zum 10. Jahrhundert.* Vienna, 1976.

Leyser, K. "The German Aristocracy from the Ninth to the Early Twelfth Century: A Historical and Cultural Sketch." *Past and Present,* 41 (1968).

———. "Maternal Kin in Early Medieval Germany: A Reply." *Past and Present,* 49 (1970).

Lintzel, Martin. "Die Mathilden-Viten und das Wahrheitsproblem in der Überlieferung der Ottonen-Zeit." *Archiv für Kulturgeschichte,* 38 (1956), 152–66.

Scheidgen, H. *Die Französische Thronfolge (987–1500). Der Ausschluss der Frauen und das Salische Gesetz.* Stuttgart, 1976.

Schmidt, Karl. "Heirat, Familienfolge, geschecterbewusstsein." In *Il matrimonio nella società altomedioevale* Settimane di Studio del centro italiano di studi sull'alto medioevo 24. Spoleto, 1977, 103–37.

Schreiner, Klaus. "'Hildegardis regina.' Wirklichkeit und Legende einer karolingischen Herrscherin." *Archiv für Kulturgeschichte,* 57 (1975), 1–70.

Vogelsang, Thilo. *Die Frau als Herrscherin im hohen Mittelalter* Göttingen Bausteine zur Geschichtswissenschaft, 7. Göttingen, Frankfurt am Main, and Berlin, 1954.

Werner, Karl Ferdinand. "Bedeutende Adelsfamilien im Reich Karls des Grossen." In Helmut Baumann, ed. *Lebenswerk und Nachleben.* vol. 1. Düsseldorf, 1967.

ECONOMIC LIFE

Barchewitz, J. *Beiträge zur Wirtschaftstätigkeit der Frau. Untersuchungen von der vorgeschichtlichen Zeit bis in das Hochmittelalter auf dem Boden des Karolingerreiches*. Breslau, 1937.

Bastian, F. "Das Manual des Regensburger Kaufhauses Runtiger und die mittelalterliche Frauenfrage." *Jahrbuch für Nationalokonomie und Statistik* 155, 3rd series 60 (1920), 385–442.

Behaghel, Wilhelm. *Die gewerbliche Stellung der Frau im mittelalterlichen Köln*. Berlin, 1910.

Braun, Lily. *Die Frauenfrage, ihre geschichtliche Entwicklung und wintschaftliche Seite*. Leipzig, 1901.

———. *Die Frauenfrage im Mittelalter*, rev. ed. Tübingen, 1910.

Brodmeir, B. *Die Frau im Handwerk in historischer und moderner Sicht*. Forschungsberichte aus dem Handwerk, 9 (Münster i.W., 1963).

Bücher, Karl. *Die Berufe der Stadt Frankfurt am Main im Mittelalter*. Abhandlungen der Sächsischen Akademie des Wissenschaften, Phil.-Histor. Klasse 30, no. 3. Leipzig, 1914.

Coornaert, Emile. *Un centre industriel d'autrefois. La draperie-sagetterie d'Hondeschoote (xive–xviie siècles)*. Paris, 1930.

Endres, Rudolf. "Zur Lage der Nürnberger Handwerkerschaft zur Zeit von Hans Sach." *Jahrbuch für Frankische Landesforschung*, 37 (1977), 107–23.

Espinas, Georges. *La vie urbaine de Douai au moyen âge*, 2 vols. Paris, 1913.

Handler-Lachmann. "Die Berufstätigkeit der Frau in den deutschen Städten des Spätmittelalters und der beginnenden Neuzeit." *Hessissches Jahrbuch für Landesgeschichte*, 30 (1980).

Hartwig. "Die Frauenfrage im mittelalterlichen Lübeck." *Hansische Geschichtsblätter*, 14 (1908), 35–94.

Hess, Luisa. *Die deutschen Frauenberufe des Mittelalters*. Munich, 1940.

Höppner, Martin. *Die Frauenarbeit in Paris im Mittelalter*. Braunschweig, 1921.

Kriedte, Peter, Medick, Hans, and Schlumbohm, Jürgen. *Industrialisierung vor der Industrialisierung*. Göttingen, 1978.

Kroemer, B. "Über Rechtstellung, Handlungsspielraüme und Tätigkeitsbereiche von Frauen in spätmittelalterlichen Städten." In *Staat und Gesellschaft in Mittelalter und früher Neuzeit*. Gedenkschrift für J. Leuschner. Göttingen, 1983.

Kuske, B. "Die Frau im mittelalterlichen deutschen Wirtschaftsleben." In *Zeitschrift für handeswissenschaftliche Forschung*, new ser. 11 (1959), 148–157.

Loose, H. D. "Erwerbstätigkeit der Frau im Spiegel Lübecker und Hamburger Testamente des 14. Jahrhunderts." *Zeitschrift des Vereins für Lübeckische Geschichte und Altertumskunde*, 60 (1980).

des Marez, G. *L'organisation du travail à Bruxelles au xve siècle*. Mémoire de l'academie royal de Belgique, 65. Brussels, 1904.

Medick, Hans. "The Proto-industrial Family Economy: The Structural Function of Household and Family during the Transition from Peasant Society to Industrial Capitalism." *Social History* 3 (1976), 291–315.

Mummenhoff. "Frauenarbeit und Arbeitsvermittlung." *Vierteljahrschrift für Sozial- und Wirtschaftsgeschichte* 19 (1926), 157–65.

Posthumus, N. *Die Geschiedenis van de Leidsche Lakenindustrie,* vol. 1. The Hague, 1908.

Quast, Jenneke. "Vrouwen in gilden in Den Bosch, Utrecht en Leiden van de 14e tot en met de 16e eeuw." In Wantje Fritschy, ed. *Fragmenten vrouwengeschiedenis,* vol. 1. The Hague, 1980, 26–37.

———. "Vrouwenarbeid omstreeks 1500 in enkele nederlandse steden." *Jaarboek voor Vrouwengeschiedenis* (1980), 46–64.

Schmidt, Gertrud. *Die Berufstätigkeit der Frau in der Reichsstadt Nürnberg bis zum Ende des 16. Jahrhundert.* Beitrag zur Wirtschaftsgeschichte Nürnbergs. Erlangen, 1950.

Schmoller, Gustav. *Die Strassburger Tucher- und Weberzunft. Urkunden und Darstellung.* Strassbourg, 1879.

Schuster, Dora. *Die Stellung der Frau in der Zunftverfassung. Quellenhefte zum Frauenleben in der Geschichte,* ed. Emmy Beckmann and Irma Stoss, vol. 2. Berlin, 1927.

Till, R. "Die berufstätige Frau im mittelalterlichen Wien." *Wiener Geschichtsblätter,* 25 (1970), 115–18.

Verbeemen, J. "De Werking van economische factoren op de steadelijke demografie der XVIIe en der XVIIIe eeuw in de zuidelijke Nederlanden," *Revue Belge de philologie et d'histoire,* 34 (1956), 680–1055.

Wachendorf, H. *Die wirtschaftliche Stellung der Frau in den deutschen Städten des späteren Mittelalters.* Quakenbrück, 1934.

Wensky, Margret. *Die Stellung der Frau in der stadtkölnischen Wirtschaft im Spätmittelalter.* Cologne and Vienna, 1980.

———. "Women's Guilds in Cologne in the Later Middle Ages." *The Journal of European Economic History,* 11:3 (1982), 631–50.

Wesoly, K. "Der weibliche Bevölkerungsanteil in spätmittelalterlichen und frühneuzeitlichen Städten und die Betätigung von Frauen im zünftigen Handwerk (insbesondere am Mittel- and Oberrhein)." *Zeitschrift für die Geschichte des Oberrheins* 128, new ser. 89 (1980), 69–117.

Wissel, Rudolf. *Des alten Handwerks Recht und Gewohnheit,* 2 vols. Berlin, 1929.

RELIGION

Religious Experience

Ancelet-Hustache, Jeanne. "Ascétique et mystique féminine du haut moyen âge." *Études germanique,* 15 (1960), 152–60.

———. *Mechtilde de Magedebourg 1207–1282.* Paris, 1926.

Bernards, M. "Die Frau in der Welt und die Kirche während des 11. Jahrhunderts." *Sacri Erudiri,* 20 (1971).

———. *Speculum Virginum. Geistigkeit und Seelenleben der Frau im Hochmittelalter.* Forschungen zur Volkskunde 36–38. Cologne and Graz, 1955; 2nd ed., 1982.

Bihlmeyer, Karl. "Die schwäbische Mystikerin Elsbeth Achler von Reute (d. 1420) und die Überlieferung ihrer Vita." In *Festgabe Philipp Strauch zum 80. Geburtstag.* Halle, 1932, 88–109.

Bynum, Caroline. *Jesus as Mother: Studies in the Spirituality of the High Middle Ages.* Berkeley, 1982.

Dietz, Josef. "St. Helena in der rheinischen Überlieferung." In *Festschrift Matthais Zender: Studien zu Volkskultur, Sprache und Landesgeschichte,* ed. Edith Ennen, Günter Wiegelmann, et al., vol. 1. Bonn, 1972, 356–83.

Emminghaus, Johann. *Ursula.* Heilige in Bild und Legende, no. 26. Recklinghausen, 1967.

Greenhill, Eleanor Simmons. *Die geistigen Voraussetzungen der Bildereihe des Speculum Virginum. Versuch einer Deutung.* Beiträge zur Geschichte der Philosophie und Theologie des Mittelalters, 39, no. 2. Münster, Westfalen, 1962.

Grundmann, H. "Die Frauen und die Literatur im Mittelalter. Ein Beitrag zur Frage nach die Entstehung des Schriftstum in der Volksprache." *Archiv für Kulturgeschichte,* 26 (1936), 129–61.

———. *Religiöse Bewegungen im Mittelalter,* 3rd ed. Darmstadt, 1970.

Haas, R. *Devotio moderna in der Stadt Köln im 15. und 16. Jahrhundert.* Veröffentlichungen des Kölnischen Geschichtsvereins 25. Cologne, 1960.

Kern, Peter. *Trinität, Maria, Inkarnation. Studien zur Thematik der deutschen Dichtung des späteren Mittelalters.* Philologische Studien und Quellen, no. 55. Berlin, 1971.

Klauser, Renate. *Der Heinrichs- und Kunigundenkult im mittelalterlichen Bistum Bamberg.* Bamberg, 1957.

Koch, G. *Frauenfrage und Ketzertum im Mittelalter.* Forschungen zur mittelalterlichen Geschichte, 9. Berlin, 1962.

Krebs, Engelvert. "Die Mystik in Adelhausen. Eine vergleichende Studie über die Chronik des Anna von Munzingon und disthaumatographische Literatur des 13. und 14. Jahrhunderts als Beitrag zur Geschichte der Mystik in Predigerorden." In *Festgabe Heinrich Finke.* Münster, 1904, 43–105.

Krogmann, Willy. "Die heilige Ursula auf Helgoland." *Classica et Medieaevalia,* 19 (1958).

Kurth, G. *Sainte Clothilde.* Paris, 1897.

Meier, Eugen A. *Marienverehrung und Mariengebete im mittelalterlichen Basel.* Basel, 1967.

Raming, I. *Der Ausschluss der Frau vom priesterlichen Amt. Gottgewollte Tradition oder Diskriminierung? Eine rechtshistorisch-dogmatische Untersuchung der Grund-*

lagen von Kanon 968 $ 1 des Codex iuris canonici. Cologne and Vienna, 1973.

Scheffczyk, Leo. *Das Mariengeheimnis in Frommigkeit und Lehre der Karolingerzeit.* Leipzig, 1959.

Werner, Ernest. "Zur Frauenfrage und zum Frauenkult im Mittelalter." *Forschungen und Fortschritte,* 29 (1955).

Zoepf, Ludwig. *Die Mystikerin Margaretha Ebner (c. 1291–1351). Beiträge zur Kulturgeschichte des Mittelalters und der Renaissance,* ed. W. Goetz, no. 16. Leipzig and Berlin, 1914.

Religious Institutions

Asen, J. "Die Beginen in Köln." *Annalen des Historischen Vereins für den Niederrhein,* 111 (1927), 81–180; 112 (1928), 71–148; 113 (1928), 13–96.

———. "Die Klausen in Köln." In *Annalen des Historischen Vereins für den Niederrhein,* 110 (1926).

Bernards, M. "Zur Seelsorge in den Frauenklöstern des Hochmittelalters." In *Revue benedictine,* 66 (1956).

Blessing, E. "Frauenklöster nach der Regel des Hl. Benedikts in Baden-Würtemberg (735–1981)." *Zeitschrift für württembergische Landesgeschichte,* 41 (1982), 4.

Brückner, Albert. "Weiblicher Schreibtätigkeit im schweizerischen Spätmittelalter." In *Festschrift Bernhard Bischoff zu seinem 65. Geburtstag.* Stuttgart, 1971.

Degler-Spengler. "Zisterzienserorden und Frauenklöster. Anmerkungen zur Forschungsproblematik." In *Die Zisterzienser. Erganzungsbd.*, ed. v. K. Elm, P. Joerissen. Cologne, 1982.

van Eeghen, I. H. *Vrouwenkloosters en Begijnhof in Amsterdam van de 14e tot het eind der 16e eeuw.* Amsterdam, 1941.

Elm, K. "Ordensleben und Frommigkeit in deutschen Frauenklostern des 14. Jahrhunderts." *Atti del xx convegno Sotirco Internazionale, sul tema: Temi e Problemi nella mistica femminile trecentesca.* Todi, 1979.

———. "Die Stellung des Zisterzienserordens in der Geschichte des Ordenslebens." In *Die Zisterzienser. Ordensleben zwischen Ideal und Wirklichkeit.* Bonn, 1980.

Grevens, J. *Die Anfange der Beginen. Ein Beitrag zur Geschichte der Volksfrommigkeit unter des Ordenwesens im Hochmittelalter.* Münster, 1912.

Grundmann, H. *Religiöse Bewegungen im Mittelalter.* 3rd ed. Darmstadt, 1970.

Grundmann, H. "Zur Geschichte der Beginen im 13. Jahrhundert." *Archiv für Kulturgeschichte,* 21 (1931), 296–320.

Haupt, H. "Zwei Traktäte gegen Beginen und Begharden." *Zeitschrift für Kirchengeschichte,* 12 (1891).

Hlawitschka, E. "Zu den klösterlichen Anfängen in St. Maria im Kapitol zu Köln." *Rheinische Vierteljahrsblätter,* 31 (1966–67), 1–16.

———. "Beobachtungen und Überlegungen zur Konventsstärke im Nonnenkloster Remiremont während des 7.–9. Jahrhunderts." In *Secondum regulam vivere*. Festschrift für P. N. Backmund O. Praem. Windberg, 1978.

Hofmeister, Philipp. "Von den Nonnenklostern." *Archiv für katholoisches Kirchenrecht,* 114 (1934), 1–96 and 353–437.

Koorn, Florence W. J. *Begijnhoven in Holland en Zeeland gedurende de middeleeuwen*. Assen, 1981.

Kuhn-Rehfus, M. "Zisterzienserinnen in Deutschland." In *Die Zisterzienser. Ordensleben zwischen Ideal und Wirklichkeit,* ed. K. Elm. Bonn, 1980.

———. "Die soziale Zusammensetzung der Konvente in den oberschwäbischen Frauenzisterzen." *Zeitschrift für württemberg. Landesgeschichte,* 41 (1982).

Lipphardt. W. "Die liturgische Funktion deutscher Kirchenlieder in den Klostern niedersächsischer Zisterzienserinnen des Mittelalters." *Zeitschrift für katholische Theologie,* 94 (1972), 158–98.

Lobbedey, Uwe. "Zur archaeologischen Erforschung westfalischer Frauenkloster des 9. Jahrhunderts (Freckenhorst, Vreden, Meschede, Herford)." *Frühmittelalterliche Studien,* 4 (1970), 158–98.

Mens, A. *Oorsprong en betekenis van de Nederlandse begijnen- en begardenbeweging*. Antwerpen, 1947.

———. "Les béguines et les bégards dans le cadre de la culture medievale." *Le moyen âge,* 64 (4th series, vol. 13), 1958.

Neumann, E. G. *Rheinisches Beginen- und Begardenwesen*. Mainzer Abhandlungen zur mittleren und neueren Geschichte 4. Meisenheim am Glan, 1960.

Nübel, Otto. *Mittelalterliche Beginen- und Sozialsiedlungen in den Niederlanden. Ein Beitrag zur Vorgeschichte der Fuggerei*. Tübingen, 1907.

Perst, O. "Die Kaisertochter Sophie, Äbtissin von Gandersheim und Essen (975–1039)." *Braunschweigisches Jahrbuch,* 38 (1957), 5–46.

Peters, G. "Norddeutsches Beginen- und Begardenwesen im Mittelalter." *Niedersächsh. Jahrbuch für Landesgeschichte,* 41–42 (1969–70).

Phillippen, L. J. M. *De Begijnhoven. Oorsprong, Geschiedenis, Inrichting*. Antwerp, 1918.

Schäfer, E. H. *Die Kanonissenstifter im deutschen Mittelalter. Ihre Entwicklung und innere Einrichtung*. Kirchenrechtliche Abhandlung, vols. 43–44, ed. Ulrich Stutz. Stuttgart, 1907.

Scheibelreiter, G. "Königstöchter im Kloster, Radegund (d.587) und der Nonnenaufstand von Poitiers (589)." *Mitteilungen des Institutus für osterreichische Geschichtsforschung,* 87 (1979).

Toepfer, M. "Die Konversen der Zisterzienserinnen von Himmelspforten bei Würzberg. Von der Gründung des Klosters bis zum Ende des 14. Jahrhunderts." In *Ordensstudien I. Beiträge zur Geschichte der Konversen im Mittelalter,* ed. K. Elm. Berlin, 1980.

Wemter, Ernst M. "Die Beginen im mittelalterlichen Preussenlande," *Zeitschrift für die Geschichte und Altertumskunde Ermlands,* 33 (1969), 41–52.

Zuhorn, K. "Die Beginen in Münster." *Westfälische Zeitschrift,* 91 (1935).

Witchcraft

Byloff, Fritz. *Volkskundliches aus Staatsprozessen der Österreichischen Alpenländer mit besonderer Berücksichtigung der Zauberei- und Hexenprozesse 1455–1850.* Berlin, 1929.
Grasse, J. G. T. *Bibliotheca Magica et Pneumatica.* 1843.
Hansen, Joseph. *Zauberwahn, Inquisition und Hexenprozess im Mittelalter.* Munich, 1900.
———. *Quellen und Untersuchungen zur Geschichte des Hexenwahns und der Hexenverfolgung im Mittelalter.* Bonn, 1901.
Hoffmann-Krajer, I. "Lüzerner Akten zum Hexen- und Zauberwesen." *Schweizerisch Archiv für Volkskunde,* 111 (1899).
Kunstmann, Harmut. *Zauberwahn und Hexenprozess in der Reichsstadt Nürnberg.* Nuremberg, 1970.
Merzbacher, Friedrich. *Die Hexenprozesse in Franken.* Munich, 1970.
Middelfort, H. C. Erik. *Witch Hunting in Southwestern Germany.* Stanford, CA, 1972.
Soldan, W. G. *Geschichte der Hexenprozesse.* 1843.
Ziegler, Wolfgang. *Möglichkeiten der Kritik am Hexen- und Zauberwesen im ausgehenden Mittelalter. Zeitgenössische Stimmen und ihre soziale Zugehörigkeit.* Cologne, 1973.

SOCIAL LIFE

Bauer, Max. *Liebesleben in deutschen Vergangenheit.* Berlin, 1924.
Bloch, Iwan. *Die Prostitution.* 2 vols. Berlin, 1912 and 1925.
Bücher, Karl. *Die Frauenfrage im Mittelalter.* Tübingen, rev. ed. 1910.
Buschan, Georg Hermann Theodor. *Leben und Treiben der deutschen Frau in der Urzeit.* 1893; rprt. New Haven, 1975.
Deeters, W. "Zur Heiratsurkunde der Kaiserin Theophanu." *Braunschweigisches Jahrbuch,* 54 (1973).
Delva, Anna. *Vrouwengeneeskunde in Vlaanderen.* Bruges, 1983.
Diepgens, P. *Frau und Frauheilkunde im Kultur des Mittelalters.* Mainz, 1963.
Dumont, M. and Morel, P. *Histoire de l'obstretique et de gynecologie.* Villefranche, 1968.
Eisenbart, L. C. *Kleiderordnungen der deutschen Städte zwischen 1350 und 1700.* Göttingen, 1962.
Fasbender, H. *Geschichte der Geburtshilfe,* 2nd ed. Hildesheim, 1964.
Fischer-Hanberger. *Krankheit Frau, und andere Arbeiten zur Medizingeschichte der Frau.* Bern, 1979.
Jung, Gustav. *Die Geschlechtsmoral des deutschen Weibes im Mittelalter.* Leipzig, 1921.
Kroemer, B. "Über Rechtsstellung, Handlungspeilraume und Tätigkeitsbereiche von Frauen in spätmittelalterlichen Städten." In *Staat und Gesellschaft in*

Mittelalter und früher Neuzeit, Gedenkschrift für J. Leuschner. Göttingen, 1983.
Loerzer, Eckart. *Eheschliessung und Werbung in der "Kundrun".* Munich, 1971.
Lorenzen-Schmidt, K. J. "Zur Stellung der Frauen in der frühneuzeitlichen Städtegesellschaft Schleswigs und Holsteins." *Archiv für Kulturgeschichte,* 61 (1979).
Maschke, E. *Die Familie in der deutschen Stadt des späten Mittelalters.* Sitzungsberichte der Heidelberger Akademie des Wissenschaften, Phil.-hist. K1., vol. 1980, 4th appendix. Heidelberg, 1980.
Mühlberger, J. *Lebensweg und Schicksale der staufischen Frauen.* 2nd ed. Esslingen, 1977.
Neckel, Gustav. *Liebe und Ehe bei den vorchristlichen Germanen.* Leipzig, 1934.
Obser, Karl. "Zur Geschichte des Frauenhauses in Überlingen." *Zeitschrift für Geschichte des Oberrheins,* 70 (1916).
Posern-Klett, Dr. von. "Frauenhäuser und freie Frauen in Sachsen." *Archiv für die sächische Geschichte,* 12 (1874).
Rudeck, W. *Geschichte der öffentlichen Sittlichkeit in Deutschland.* Jena, 1897.
Schönfeldt, Gustav. *Beiträge zur Geschichte des Pauperismus und der Prostitution in Hamburg.* Weimar, 1897.
Schrank, Josef. *Die Prostitution in Wien.* Vienna, 1886.
Weiler, A. G. "Einege aspeckten van de man/vrouw-verhouding in de middeleeuwen." *Jeugd en Samenleveing,* 5 (March–April, 1975).
Weinhold, Karl. *Die deutschen Frauen in dem Mittelalter. Ein Beitrag zu den Haushalterthumern der Germanen.* 2 vols. 1882, rprt. Englewood Cliffs, NJ, 1968.
Wesoly, K. "Der weibliche Bevölkerungsanteil in spätmittelalterlichen und frühneuzeitlichen Städten und die Betätigung von Frauen im zünftigen Handwerk (insbesondere am Mittel- und Oberrhein)." *Zeitschrift für die Geschichte des Oberrheins* 128, new ser. 89 (1980), 69–117.
Winter, A. "Studien zur sozialen Situation der Frauen in der Stadt Trier nach der Steuerliste von 1364." *Kurtrierisches Jahrbuch,* 15 (1975), 20–45.
Wustmann, Gustav. "Frauenhäuser und freie Frauen in Leipzig im Mittelalter." *Archiv für Kulturgeschichte,* 5 (1907), 469–82.
Zallinger, Otto. *Die Eheschliessung im Nibelungenleid und in der Gudrun.* Vienna, 1923.
———. *Heirat ohne Trauung im Nibelungenlied und in der Gudrun.* Innsbruck, 1928.

CULTURE

Bindschedler, Maria. "Gedanken zur Marienlyrick des Mittelalters und der Romantik." In *Geschichte, Deutung, Kritik, Literaturwissenschaftliche Beiträge dargebracht zum 65. Geburtstag Werner Kohlschmidts,* ed. Maria Bindschedler and Paul Zinsli. Bern, 1969.

———. "Weiblich Leitbilder in der alten Literatur." *Reformatio,* 18 (1969), 102–13.

Brietzmann, Franz. *Die böse Frau in der deutschen Literature des Mittelalters.* 1912, rprt. New York, 1967.

Engelen, Ulrich. "Die Edelsteine im rheinischen Marienlob." *Frühmittelalterliche Studien,* 7 (1973), 353–76.

Heise, Ursula. "Frauengestalten im 'Parzival' Wolframs von Eschenbach," *Deutschunterricht,* 9 (1957), 37–62.

Kern, Peter. *Trinität, Maria, Inkarnation. Studien Zur Thematik der deutschen Dichtung des späteren Mittelalters.* Philologische Studien und Quellen, no. 55. Berlin, 1971.

Mohr, Wolfgang. "Die 'Vrouwe' Walters von der Vogelweide." *Zeitschrift für deutsche Philologie,* 86 (1967), 1–10.

Portmann, M. L. *Die Darstellung der Frau in der Geschichtsschreibung des frühen Mittelalters.* Basler Beiträge zur Geschichtswissenschaft 69. Basel and Stuttgart, 1958.

Schneider, Annerose. "Zum Bild von der Frau in der Chronistik des frühen Mittelalters." *Forschungen und Fortschritte,* 35 (1961), 112–14.

Wenzel, Horst. *Frauendienst und Gottesdienst. Studien zur Minneideologie.* Philologische Studien und Quellen, no. 74. Berlin, 1974.

BIOGRAPHY

Adelheid

Bäumer, Bertrud. *Adelheid, Mutter der Konigreiche.* Tübingen, 1949.

———. *Otto I und Adelheid.* Tübingen, 1951.

Paulhart, Herbert, ed. *Die Lebensbeschreibung der Kaiserin Adelheid von Abt Odile von Cluny.* Cologne, 1962.

———. "Zur Heligsprechung der Kaiserin Adelheid." *Mitteilungen des Instituts für österreichische Geschichtsforschung,* 64 (1956), 65–67.

Uhlirz. "Die rechtliche Stellung der Kaiserinwitwe Adelheid im Deutschen und im Italischen Reich." *Zeitschrift der Savigny-Stiftung für Rechtsgeschichte.* Germanistische Abteilung, 74 (1957), 85–87.

Wollasch, Joachim. "Das Grabkloster der kaiserin Adelheid in Selz am Rhein." *Frühmittelalterliche Studien,* 2 (1968), 135–43.

Saint Elizabeth of Hungary

Justi, Karl Wilhelm. *Elisabeth die heilige Landgräfin von Thürigen.* Marburg, 1835.

Maresch, Marix. *Elisabeth Landgräfin v. Thüringen.* Bonn, 1931.

Nigg, Walter. *Elisabeth von Thüringen,* trans. Otto Krage. Dusseldorf, 1963.
Sankt Elisabeth. Fürstin-Dienerin-Heilige. Aufsätze. Dokumentation. Katalog. Ausstellung zum 750. Todestag der hl. Elisabeth, Marburg, Landgrafenschloss und Elisabethkirche. Sigmaringen, 1981.

Hildegard von Bingen

Bernhardt, Joseph. "Hildegard von Bingen." *Archiv für Kulturgeschichte,* 20 (1930), 249–60.
Brück, A. P., ed. *Hildegard von Bingen 1179–1979.* Mainz, 1979.
zu Eltz, Monika. *Hildegard.* Freiburg, 1963.
Fischer, Hermann. *Die heilige Hildegarde von Bingen, die erste deutsche Naturforscherin und Ärztin, ihr Leben und Werk.* Münchener Beiträge zur Geschichte und Literatur der Naturwissenschaften und Medizin 7–8. Munich, 1927.
Führkötter, Adelgundis. *Hildegard von Bingen.* Salzburg, 1972.
———. "Hildegard von Bingen 1098–1179." *Die grossen Deutschen,* 5 (1957).
Haverkamp, A. "Tenxwind von Andernach und Hildegard von Bingen. Zwei 'Weltanschauungen' in der Mitte des 12. Jahrhunderts." In *Institutionen, Kultur und Gesellschaft im Mittelalter. Festschrift für J. Fleckenstein.* Sigmaringen, 1984.
Koch, Josef. "Der heutige Stand der Hildegard-Forschung." *Historische Zeitschrift,* 186 (1958), 558–72.
Lampen, W. *Hildgard von Bingen (1098–1179).* Utrecht, 1956.
Liebeschutz, Hans. *Das allegorische Weltbild der heiligen Hildegard von Bingen.* Leipzig, 1930.
Schipperges, H., ed. *Hildegard von Bingen "Heilkunde": das Buch von dem Grund und Wesen und der Heilung der Krankheiten.* Salzburg, 1957.
Schmelzeis, John. *Das Leben und Wirken der Heiligen Hildegardis.* Freiburg, 1879.
Strubing, E. "Nährung und Ernährung bei Hildegard von Bingen, Aebtissen, Aerztin und Naturforscherin (1098–1179)." *Centaurus,* 9 (1963), 73–124.

Hroswitha of Gandersheim

Aschbach, Joseph von. "Roswitha und Conrad Celtis." *Kaiserlichen Akademie der Wissenschaften.* Sitzungsberichte, 56 (1867).
Klose-Greger, H. *Roswith von Gandershem.* Berlin, 1961.
Kronenberg, K. *Roswitha von Gandersham. Leben und Werk.* Aus Gendersheims grosser Vergangenheit, no. 4. Bad Gandersheim, 1962.
Nagel, Bert. *Hrotsvit von Gandersheim.* Stuttgart, 1965.
Neumann, Friedrich. "Der Denkstil Hrotsvits von Gandersheim," in *Festschrift für Hermann Heimpel zum 70. Geburtstag,* vol. 3. Göttingen, 1971–72, 37–60.
Trumper, Bernarda. *Hrosvithas Frauengestalten.* Münster, 1908.

INDEX OF SUBJECTS

INDEX OF PROPER NAMES

CONTRIBUTORS

BARBARA A. HANAWALT is Professor of History at Indiana University. She is the author of two books, *Crime and Conflict in Medieval England,* and *The Ties That Bound: Peasant Families in Medieval England.* She has written articles on the history of crime, medieval women, and the medieval family.

MARTHA C. HOWELL is an Associate Professor of History at Rutgers University. She is the author of a book on women's work in late medieval Europe, *Women, Production, and Patriarchy in Late Medieval Cities.* She has written articles on late medieval urban economics, urban family structures in the era, and women's work.

DIANE OWEN HUGHES teaches at the University of Michigan. She has written extensively on the social and urban history of medieval Italy. A forthcoming book, *The Death of Mourning,* investigates the process of repression of female ritual alluded to in her essay.

DENISE KAISER received her B.A. and M.A. in medieval studies from Barnard College and the University of Toronto respectively, and her Ph.D. in history from Columbia University. Her dissertation was entitled "Sin and the Vices in *Sermones di Dominicis* by Berthold of Regensburg."

SUSAN MOSHER STUARD is a medieval historian concerned with social and economic questions. Her interest in women may be seen in twin volumes from the University of Pennsylvania Press, *Women in Medieval Society* (1976) and the present volume. She is currently Visiting Associate Professor of History at Haverford College.

SUZANNE FOLEY WEMPLE is Professor of History at Barnard College, Columbia University, and holds a Ph.D. from Columbia University. Her specialization is the social and intellectual history of the early Middle Ages. She is the author of *Women in Frankish Society: Marriage and the Cloister,* and co-editor of *Women in the Medieval World.* She has written numerous articles on medieval women's history, and is presently working on a study of women in Italy, France, and Germany from 850-1050.

University of Pennsylvania Press
Middle Ages Series
EDWARD PETERS, *General Editor*

Edward Peters, ed. *Christian Society and the Crusades, 1198–1229*. Sources in Translation, including The Capture of Damietta by Oliver of Paderborn. 1971
Edward Peters, ed. *The First Crusade: The Chronicle of Fulcher of Chartres and Other Source Materials*. 1971
Katherine Fischer Drew, trans. *The Burgundian Code: The Book of Constitutions or Law of Gundobad and Additional Enactments*. 1972
G. G. Coulton. *From St. Francis to Dante: Translations from the Chronicle of the Franciscan Salimbene (1221–1288)*. 1972
Alan C. Kors and Edward Peters, eds. *Witchcraft in Europe, 1110–1700: A Documentary History*. 1972
Richard C. Dales. *The Scientific Achievement of the Middle Ages*. 1973
Katherine Fischer Drew, trans. *The Lombard Laws*. 1973
Henry Charles Lea. *The Ordeal*. Part III of Superstition and Force. 1973
Henry Charles Lea. *Torture*. Part IV of Superstition and Force. 1973
Henry Charles Lea (Edward Peters, ed.). *The Duel and the Oath*. Parts I and II of Superstition and Force. 1974
Edward Peters, ed. *Monks, Bishops, and Pagans: Christian Culture in Gaul and Italy, 500–700*. 1975
Jeanne Krochalis and Edward Peters, ed. and trans. *The World of Piers Plowman*. 1975
Julius Goebel, Jr. *Felony and Misdemeanor: A Study in the History of Criminal Law*. 1976
Susan Mosher Stuard, ed. *Women in Medieval Society*. 1976
James Muldoon, ed. *The Expansion of Europe: The First Phase*. 1977
Clifford Peterson. *Saint Erkenwald*. 1977
Robert Somerville and Kenneth Pennington, eds. *Law, Church, and Society: Essays in Honor of Stephan Kuttner*. 1977
Donald E. Queller. *The Fourth Crusade: The Conquest of Constantinople, 1201–1204*. 1977
Pierre Riché (Jo Ann McNamara, trans.). *Daily Life in the World of Charlemagne*. 1978

Charles R. Young. *The Royal Forests of Medieval England.* 1979
Edward Peters, ed. *Heresy and Authority in Medieval Europe.* 1980
Suzanne Fonay Wemple. *Women in Frankish Society: Marriage and the Cloister, 500–900.* 1981
R. G. Davies and J. H. Denton, eds. *The English Parliament in the Middle Ages.* 1981
Edward Peters. *The Magician, the Witch, and the Law.* 1982
Barbara H. Rosenwein. *Rhinoceros Bound: Cluny in the Tenth Century.* 1982
Steven D. Sargent, ed. and trans. *On the Threshold of Exact Science: Selected Writings of Anneliese Maier on Late Medieval Natural Philosophy.* 1982
Benedicta Ward. *Miracles and the Medieval Mind: Theory, Record, and Event, 1000–1215.* 1982
Harry Turtledove, trans. *The Chronicle of Theophanes: An English Translation of* anni mundi *6095–6305 (A.D. 602–813).* 1982
Leonard Cantor, ed. *The English Medieval Landscape.* 1982
Charles T. Davis. *Dante's Italy and Other Essays.* 1984
George T. Dennis, trans. *Maurice's Strategikon: Handbook of Byzantine Military Strategy.* 1984
Thomas F. X. Noble. *The Republic of St. Peter: The Birth of the Papal State, 680–825.* 1984
Kenneth Pennington. *Pope and Bishops: The Papal Monarchy in the Twelfth and Thirteenth Centuries.* 1984
Patrick J. Geary. *Aristocracy in Provence: The Rhône Basin at the Dawn of the Carolingian Age.* 1985
C. Stephen Jaeger. *The Origins of Courtliness: Civilizing Trends and the Formation of Courtly Ideals, 939–1210.* 1985
J. N. Hillgarth, ed. *Christianity and Paganism, 350–750: The Conversion of Western Europe.* 1986
William Chester Jordan. *From Servitude to Freedom: Manumission in the Sénonais in the Thirteenth Century.* 1986
James William Brodman. *Ransoming Captives in Crusader Spain: The Order of Merced on the Christian-Islamic Frontier.* 1986
Frank Tobin. *Meister Eckhart: Thought and Language.* 1986
Daniel Bornstein, trans. *Dino Compagni's Chronicle of Florence.* 1986
James M. Powell. *Anatomy of a Crusade, 1213–1221.* 1986
Jonathan Riley-Smith. *The First Crusade and the Idea of Crusading.* 1986
Susan Mosher Stuard, ed. *Women in Medieval History and Historiography.* 1987
Avril Henry, ed. *The Mirour of Mans Saluacioune.* 1987
María Menocal. *The Arabic Role in Medieval Literary History.* 1987
Margaret J. Ehrhart. *The Judgment of the Trojan Prince Paris in Medieval Literature.* 1987
Betsy Bowden. *Chaucer Aloud: The Varieties of Textual Interpretation.* 1987